BEYOND
ATLANTIS

BEYOND ATLANTIS

AN EPIC OF THE ANCIENT AMERICAS

LUCIUS BEAUCHAMP

First published in Australia in 2011

Revised 2015, 2020

National Library of Australia
Cataloguing-in-Publication entry:

Beauchamp, Lucius.
Beyond Atlantis / Lucius Beauchamp.
2nd ed.

ISBN: 978-0-6488929-0-8
A823.4

The characters in the book are fictitious and any resemblance to real persons,
living or dead, is purely coincidental.

Editor: Trevor Douglass
Design and Typeset: Flametree Creative
Cover design: Alistair Mclean, Flametree Creative

BEYOND ATLANTIS:
AN EPIC OF THE ANCIENT AMERICAS MAP

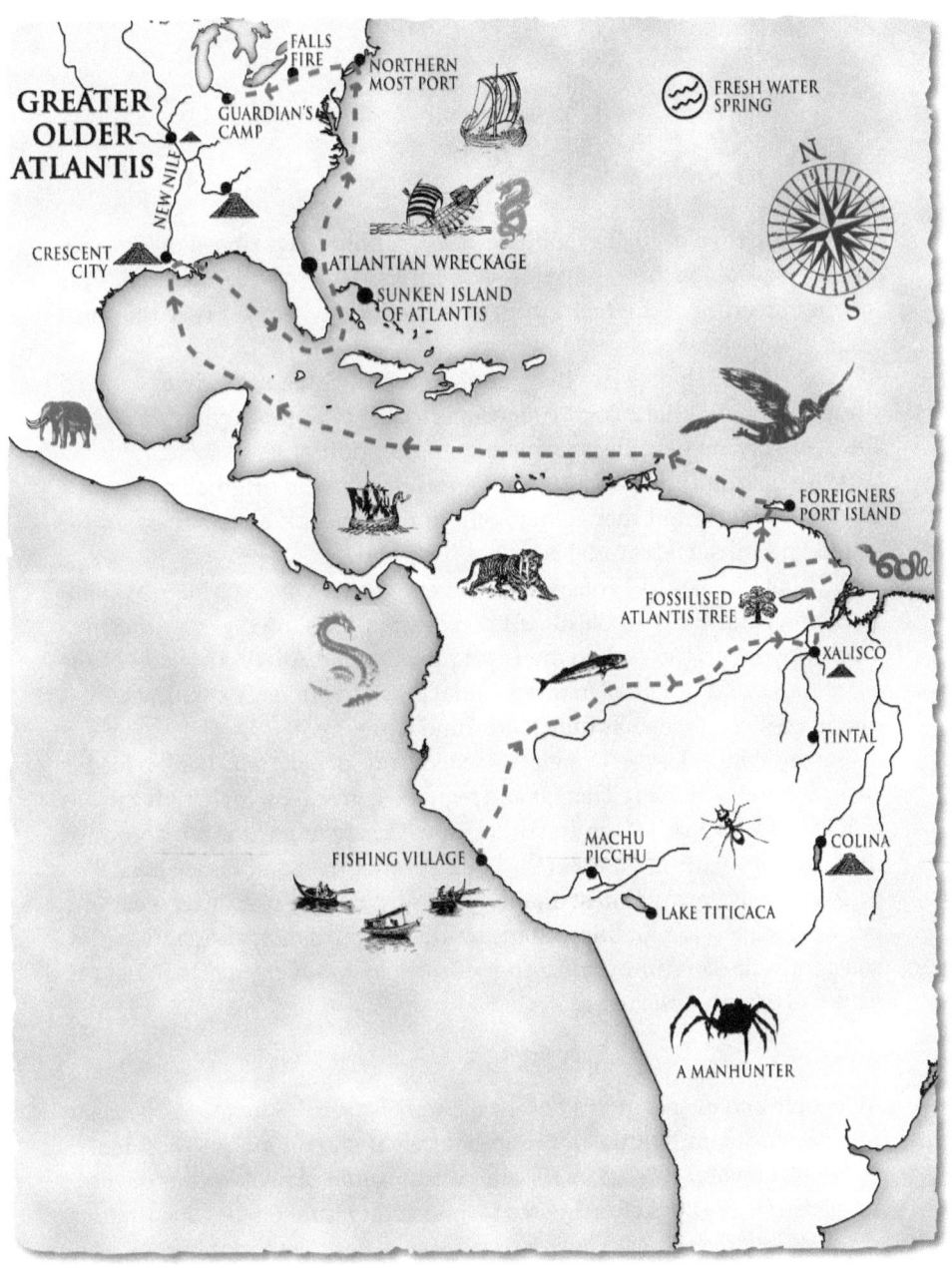

Acknowledgements

With great thanks to the National Geographic magazine. For decades its issues, old and new, have provided invaluable source material. Plus splendid reading. I still feel a thrill of excitement whenever I see the latest issue in my mailbox.

Also, with thanks to the Encyclopaedia Britannica. I've trawled through our 1961 hard copy collection, from A to Z, throughout my adult life ever gaining new and fascinating information.

With heartfelt thanks to author Dave Luckett who originally critiqued Beyond Atlantis and then generously tutored me, on a weekly basis, for several months. His tutorial style was inspired.

Further thanks to Professor Van Iken, who I was fortunate enough to have critique my book after I'd redrafted it following my intensive workshops with Dave. Van then critiqued Beyond Atlantis a second time for me, once I'd finished an almost final draft. Even Van's smallest pieces of advice were as sage as they were almost prescient.

To my editor Trevor Douglass I extend my deeply felt thanks, for his superlative attention to all details and required corrections, for his advice plus also for his patience. It was Trevor's astute concept to include a map, which then became an integral part of the book's Front Cover and Back Cover.

And lastly, my greatest thanks to my partner. Year after year my partner listened to plot lines, character descriptions dialogues and scenes; constantly making improving suggestions. Without my partner I could never have accomplished this.

chapter 1

'Heritage-caller,' said the woman placing Zithia's hands on her bulging belly, 'whisper again to my baby, to call upon its Atlantian birthright. You've the knack.' Both women smiled at the violet eyed, peaches-and-cream toddler beside Zithia. 'Mama swears Agatha will reach a full six feet.'

Zithia spread her fingers wide. 'Darling, sweetest darling, listen. Let Atlantis live anew through you. Call to your great grandparents, to their parents and so back. Beg them to pick from their Atlantian traits for you, that your very features will do them honour.' As she intoned, three times, Zithia's hands grew hot.

'Be it thus.' prayed the woman, throwing her sister-in-law a large strawberry pearl. 'For your collection. I'd rather give you something of value.'

Zithia shook her head, saying 'It's a good mist-fall today.'

She headed up to the family market garden, her thick layered burgundy hair curling to well below her waist. Once on the hill, she savoured the mist-covered valley. Thick white layers dissolved, revealing her home by degrees. No rain in seven months, yet the valley was still lush. Each tree and plant had its own diamond-windowed net, placed seaward like a sail to capture the mist's precious water. Without the nets the daily fog would roll tantalisingly in from the sea, but not even leave dew.

Like many others, every morning Zithia turned seaweed compost in the fields. She was taller than most, being five feet seven inches. Her laughing vivid eyes, blue, skimmed the family's water-nets, now dripping with moisture. Swallows, enjoying the short-lived fog, swooped around busy farmers.

Duties mostly done, amid a swallow squadron, Zithia lay flat on the slope facing the sea and the village's walking trail. Few people came up this late. Zithia half dozed, when suddenly she was in a sitting position and glaring at a wizened woman standing twenty feet away. Zithia had been stung by insult, 'Reader!' seeming to have been spat at her. The woman, caught by Zithia's unblinking stare, instantly erupted with laughter. 'But I didn't say anything.' More laughter, hysterical in edge, 'I was only thinking it.' The mirth, the protests became shrill.

'Come along, aunty.' A middle aged man tried, not very successfully, to drag the woman away.

Stop, start. Giggling, aunty kept looking back to Zithia and murmuring. A younger woman, following the others, just reached the top of the hill. 'You mustn't mind the great aunt, Zithia. She hasn't been the same since that pair of leather-wing birds plucked her husband off his fishing boat.'

'True and all.' Zithia stood, frowning, 'Still, that's no reason to be nasty.' And went back to her gardening.

Two hours before noon, Zithia descended to her home, where she checked the just-smouldering black earth, ever being made at low burn from plants and refuse. The resultant charcoal, enriched with condensed smoke, produced magic soil when mixed with dirt. Making black earth was as important as water conservation.

Zithia cut a third off a grey barrel, two-feet in diameter, which was a cactus fruit. Then taking a slither, she hung the purple circle up on the pergola for her tiny golden lizard and family. Covering the rest, she was soon in the village proper, carrying the end-slab of fruit on one shoulder, to exchange for bread.

Arriving earlier than expected, Zithia observed the bronze Meztli moving with care, while she held tight to a forked pole edging the family's raised patio. Delivering the slab, Zithia lounged against the hut's wall and peeled a grapefruit-sized hard-boiled egg.

Meztli brushed pale blue powder from very high cheekbones. 'You could help!'

'With my dirty feet?' Zithia's brow wrinkled. 'Besides, you know I'm no good with bread.'

Poking her tongue out at Zithia, Meztli popped shapely chocolate toes into a nearby flour bag. Extra blue corn-flour was gathered in a heap then added to the mix. Toned feet pulled the dough, kneading it for the day's last baking.

After lunch Zithia took an obsidian razor to Meztli's glossy black hair. While they were laughing over village gossip, Zithia abruptly felt a tingling elation. Intensifying moment by moment. Rushing her task, Zithia climbed the patio's pergola. Searching for… something… that was in the air. All around, a sense of...

'What're you doing?' demanded Meztli.

But Zithia simply gazed seaward. Dazzling light reflected on the ocean, the gong began to chime. Sails, glowing heaven's molten-yellow, dotted the horizon and grew larger.

A very old vision broke, as vibrant and enticing as that one time she'd dreamed it. She was there, caught within it, within its utter warmth again.

According to heaven they'd been married for decades, or was it forever? He came to her one day, stating 'I'm going back.'

'Not without me.'

'I thought you'd say that. So I persuaded them to let me glimpse the book of your future, in the Hall of Records.' She bit her lip while he continued. 'You're coming back, too,' shadow seemed to cross his face, 'just a few years.'

'No!'

'Time will flash past up here.' He put a finger on her lips. 'Shhh. I promise you, we'll be together again.'

'What if life gets in the way?' Her brow wrinkled. 'You've told me that it often does.'

'How could it, when you have my heart!'

Her smile was tremulous. 'I love you in heaven; I'll love you on earth.' She clung to him tightly, unable to let go, whispering, 'Find me quickly! Then teach me about the world.'

She was still hugging him when his solid image became mere streams of light and disappeared. She shouted to the glistening ether: 'My heart pines until we meet again.'

In just a blink of time she and a guide were deciding her new body's features. That is, those features she was allowed to pick. Different looks appeared before her, at speed. Genetic codes from her future parents, plus their ancestors, provided the choice. First decision, burgundy hair...and blue eyes the exact shade of his... Then heaven's final gift. Forgetfulness.

Zithia was fully in the present once more, 'Meztli, I've got to go home.' She reached the ground, her face beaming. Then, in an afterthought, 'Dearest, lend me your new top. The one that goes with my feast-day skirt.'

'But it's my seventh-day best!'

'Please? I'll do the same for you.'

Meztli fetched the garment, covered by delicately woven motifs. 'Why?!'

'Because my future is coming.' Zithia took the prize and ran home.

Just over an hour yet before the vessels arrived. The white, plastered hut was deserted. Everyone was farming. Taking two entire buckets of water to the little room she shared with an aunt, Zithia stripped to bathe. There'd be hell to pay about this luxury tonight.

While drying herself she poked her head out the door. The ocean-going canoes were close now. Tall sails, wider at the top than the bottom, billowed. Canary coloured, flecked with actual gold. Men rowed, furiously. *"Yes,"* she thought and said, 'He has come.'

Quickly Zithia donned her finest skirt, decorated by herself, then Meztli's blouse. Under the vine-covered pergola on the earthen terrace, Zithia slipped on her only sandals, cactus fibre, while checking the convoy's progress. Ready! Although in a desperate hurry, Zithia watered her father's gourd tree. Given all excess household water, its fruit hung like fat pumpkins from the branches.

Fingering through her long tresses, Zithia raced down the path meandering round thick-walled huts. A gaggle of dodos, taking dust baths, flapped tiny wings in fright, growling. From a raised dais, llamas stared. The gong's cathedral resonance grew louder until Zithia strode past a fat rock pillar, on a stone base, which the gong ringer pounded with a boulder. The deep voice was spoilt by tiny random pings.

One boy throwing pebbles at the gong rock, suddenly yelped. 'You'll put the bell man off his timing,' a matron chastised, still pinching his ear.

In the crowd Zithia walked on air, her ever-ready smile blossoming. She easily saw above the assembled village, most of them didn't top five feet. Except for the headman's extended family. The thirty-foot long reed canoes, with stabilising outriggers, were racing within the harbour now. The temple's emblem at the prows read "Xalisco".

All at once Zithia sensed him, her future, on the lead boat. She breathed in deeply and heard, felt, the echo of his breathing. But his turned ragged. Joy seemed to lift her off the ground. His emotions were less clear, a fact she hardly noticed. The order was given to stop rowing; the anchor hastily dropped on the first canoe. A balsawood dinghy fled the stationary ship. Sailors leaped onto the other passing canoes, many dived, swimming furiously till they beached themselves in front of startled villagers.

A nobleman disembarked the dinghy at undignified speed, followed by two priests carrying kegs of tequila. All of Atlantian heritage, you could tell by their height. None was less than six feet tall. The handsome aristocrat called, 'Friends, peace. Peace. Yonder magician priest of Xalisco,' he pointed at the anchored vessel, 'bade us hurry to drink a libation to the one God with you.'

The tequila, pale silver blue, was usually reserved for high clergy. Generous shots were being poured, people dashed for mugs.

From the anchored ship, a cultured voice projected to them all, the words clipped. 'Good people, today we toast God's marvels. Drink well.' The fiery alcohol slid down their throats, the priests replenished their cups. 'I stay upon the ocean throughout the coming miracle, for we are all under the one God's protection. A toast.' The mugs were emptied again. 'Now all who wish to keep their sight bow your heads in prayer.'

The mystic lead a prayer and then the sun went out. Screams, fainting followed.

But Zithia was drawn to the voice, to his figure, as he stood beneath the canopy erected over the vessel's central decking. Zithia longed to see his eyes. In the melee she struggled down onto her own tiny boat. She was untying the rope when…her father hauled her back onto the quay.

'Are you mad, daughter?' She struggled with him. 'Going onto the sea during an eclipse.' Then, instead of spitting, he exclaimed, 'T, T, T…Will you bring more bad luck upon yourself?'

The noble strode to them, offering his own gold mug to Zithia. 'You look shaken.' Putting the cup to her lips until she drank, while he shaded her eyes.

Zithia trembled, her face turning again to the ship. From the mists of the prayer the mystic's eyes snapped onto hers and Zithia felt complete, whole, for the first time. He, too, knew her; experienced their last moments together before his birth. Zithia had always believed they'd find each other. And they had! No, he'd found her. Her mind declared: *"Here I am."*

The mystic's prayer faded and stopped. Surprised, the priest on the beach continued the psalm.

The stranger-not-stranger emerged from under the silken cover. In the dark she felt his eyes bore into her and she drew breath sharply through parted lips. Then, stunningly, freed of body, her soul flew to him through the ether. Contact. Above the water their spirits danced entwined. They melted together. *"Ecstasy!"* :whispered Zithia's heart, surrendering to him. This moment lasted till the sun started to reappear.

With supreme effort the mystic pulled the hood of his cloak up to hide his face, and their connection ebbed. The golden vision bleached before the priest's blue eyes and other memories filled them.

His parents dedicating him to the temple as a boy... his uncle teaching him to draw on his impressive talents... years of training, becoming decades... the upper priesthood, being the youngest deacon in memory. Could he forget all he had accomplished? All he'd sacrificed? Could he? The deacon searched his soul for the answer.

On the quay, Zithia could almost feel his arms around her. Observing him give an order, she waited for him to come to her. Therefore she was puzzled when he didn't move from the canoe's side, but simply watched her. A blast on a horn recalled the other ships and men.

"No!"

"Not yet." Floated back; almost an appeal: *"Not now."*

"How can you go?" she sent, her hand reaching for him.

There was no answer and the scene of two over-manned ships going seaward swam before her eyes.

The mystic and Zithia watched each other while the lead canoe turned; he couldn't stop himself from walking down the length of the canoe to keep her in sight. The crowd quickly dissolved without the protection of the priests.

Tears welled into Zithia's eyes, dripping down her cheeks. *"Damn you!"* she sent, and his shoulders crumpled as though hit.

*

With the village disappearing, the mystic felt something inside him tear. 'I'll get over this.' He straightened his back. 'Duty requires it.' And he believed both.

Then the nobleman was beside him, smirking. 'You should've come ashore cousin. There was a girl there who made me think I was in Atlantis still. And throughout the eclipse her eyes never left this ship. Definitely a worthy dalliance.'

The magician priest turned and clasped the other's hand. His clear eyes pierced the aristocrat, seeing what his cousin had seen. Zithia's image burned into the priest's mind. His grip tightened and pain shot through the noble's fingers.

'Galen! I didn't mean it.' The pain intensified. 'I'd never, not again!' Sweat beaded his forehead. 'I've agreed to marry the woman.'

Zithia's image disintegrating, Galen recollected himself. 'Only after I tracked you down, dear cousin. My very dear cousin.'

'Galen,' the nobleman whined, 'my parents can always afford the money.'

Galen suddenly increased and then released his grip. The blood rushing afresh through crushed white fingers, was a new pain. 'You're already married... I was your proxy. And your child will bear your name.'

chapter 2

Lord Galen sat in a curtained sedan chair, borne on the shoulders of temple servants. Filmy drapes were drawn back, affording him a view above the throng. The carriers stopped. He emerged, six feet four inches, dark hair cut short in temple style in direct contrast to local custom. Raising his strong, clean-shaven chin, he found the market already wearied him. The riot of colours and patterns; the crush. Golden trays hung on the outer wall reflecting, unnoticed, Galen's handsome face. As he looked down upon the tops of the heads of many of the crowd, a quiet circle of space appeared around him.

At a distance, Galen saw an image suddenly disappear, then reappear. It was a man. Looking straight at him, Galen watched the 'there' figure fade until transparent. Galen signalled for his bearer to wait and approached a nearby stallholder. 'Who is that?'

'Where?' The vendor, in whose family some 'sight' ran, looked directly into the transparent face. 'Oh… Hayanil.' He looked puzzled. 'For a moment I… forgot… him.' Frowning, 'It's a sad case. His employer keeps him working on promises alone. No money. Not for a month.'

Galen moved to Hayanil, 'Friend, why are you here?' He looked deep, deep into the suddenly solid eyes.

Hayanil spoke, but seemingly from far away. 'I farmed a riverside plot until a rich man stole it. Because he could. For a holiday villa. We came here for work, now my family's thinned to the bone and…'

'Enough.' Galen gently guided Hayanil, by the arm, back to the bearer. Hayanil put up no resistance. 'Ezhad will take you to the old library. Your family will join you; there's work plus rooms enough for you all. And your back wages will be sent to you.'

Galen watched them go. Hayanil was still somewhat dazed. He'd been going to kill himself very soon. His soul had been detaching itself from life for weeks now. Galen said softly, 'A rich man is about to lose his villa.'

Taking his ceremonial staff from the litter, Galen allowed another bearer to drape a long high priest's cape on his shoulders. He was one of eight. The circle of space around him doubled. Cynically the priesthood named this enclosed bazaar the people's temple, for it was always full. No complaints. It paid a healthy tithe to the clergy.

As the masses automatically cleared a path before him, Galen reflected. He was a direct descendant of the refugees fleeing long dead Atlantis, the first and seventh tribes. His family traced its forebears back to the very first ship that had brought culture and learning to this land. Unlike many direct Atlantian descendants he didn't have a name traditional to his tribe.

A woman with milk-white skin minced purposefully into his path, a flower-shaped emerald adorning her navel. *"Unmarried!"* Galen thought, looking through her smile. The crowd was a clatter with jewellery that often overwhelmed vibrant, yet minimal, clothing. Maybe that was what grated on him, or maybe he was picking up the static from a thousand minds. Had he closed his senses before he'd left the temple? Galen spent so much time developing his senses. Walking on, he caught his thumbs within his fists, emphatically thinking: *"Close!"* Instantly the world became more pleasant.

At the carver's alcove, he approved the plans for a ten-foot tall stele and decided the colours for the intricate stonework. This curved-topped edifice would pair with another already in situ, at the furthest end of the Avenue of the Dead.

The task completed, the high priest made his way to a friend's stall deep in the market. Galen passed a body painter removing a latex sheath from a woman's almost black, long legs. Swirling blue designs drew Galen's glance from ankle to high up one thigh. Between midnight ringlets, the customer's black eyes sparkled with promise. The high priest's gaze turned neutral.

Finally Galen reached his goal at the T-junction of a busy thoroughfare facing the seers. The small old stallholder beamed.

'Lord Galen.' Bowing, Chuan touched his open left hand to the right side of his chest. 'My lowly stall is privileged to receive you.'

No one else knew herbs, rocks and minerals the way Chuan did. He clapped his slightly yellow hands together and an extra stool appeared for the high priest. Short for his tribe, Chuan's being the eighth tribe, he stood five feet eight inches tall. His shop was an unusual choice for one of his lineage, as the eighth tribe was the guardian of the old technologies.

Chuan was the province's only Dragon-Land herbal practitioner. Standing in front of six hundred and fifty substantial labelled wooden drawers, each containing an essential herb or seed or mineral, Chuan's son lay out seven heaps of ingredients for a new patient. He parcelled up each heap, giving directions for the boiling time. The patient, rubbing his arthritic hands, listened eagerly to the instructions which would result in a vile tasting liquid concentrate. One of many such horrid elixirs that changed lives.

Disregarding Galen's protests, Chuan's willowy daughter waited on him personally, bringing select crystals for his perusal. Since the high priest had officiated at the woman's wedding, to a groom brought from the Dragon-Land, nothing was too much trouble. The eighth tribe often married those from the Dragon-Land, where silk and paper was even now being made.

Galen bought the iodised salt which Chuan dictated was a must, as it prevented certain adult diseases plus abnormality in new-borns. Then the high priest gave an incantation to fulfil Chuan's daughter's hopes for her future baby. Bowing, she presented Galen with a tub of ointment, direct from the Dragon-Land, that wasn't just medicine for burns; it was an antidote. Chuan quietly explained that when the ointment was placed on a fresh burn the injury ceased to exist. Boiling water had no power over this treasure. Thanking the daughter profusely, Galen left.

The high priest took a few steps. Just a few, before he was hit by a wave of warmth. It engulfed him. Hurriedly, he used his eyes and instincts to search the crowd around him. Nothing unusual there.

With the warmth lessening, Galen scanned those moving away. The mob parted, revealing a woman who stopped abruptly and was turning as if she'd heard her name called. Galen cloaked his mind. Finding no one she recognized, the woman turned back to her partner.

Zithia tossed her head, cascading burgundy curls down her back, around and past her slim waist. Even in village clothes, men stared. Galen turned to a stall and beckoned an apprentice. With little difficulty, the youth followed Zithia while Galen trailed at a discreet distance.

She was in his domain. His heart thumped despite himself, despite his training while he reassured himself, 'She's only a woman.'

Through an incense haze, rare luminous green quexatl feathers caused Zithia to pause. A short man ahead of her uttered a command and walked more slowly, expecting the woman to catch up. But she was trying on blue ostrich-like plumes. Scowling, the man stamped back to her.

Zithia forestalled his complaints by pointing out the charms written along each blue feathered quill. Absently she put a hand upon her flat stomach. 'I think, perhaps, we could use a temple charm.' He bit back the reply that he made his own luck.

'They're so small,' Ilt twisted his face, 'so badly dyed.'

The stallholder snorted, 'I coloured them myself, with best blue from over the oceans! You're lucky they're this cheap.' The reference to 'the far world' easily tipped the scales.

While the money was changing hands, a middle-aged man rushed up to the stallholder, interrupting. 'I must have a white eagle's feather.'

Vendor, 'A potent antidote.'

'The priest assured me that one, inscribed so,' he showed a written spell, 'would stop two deaths I've had from troubling me.'

'Violent deaths were they?' Then corrected himself, 'Well, obviously they were.'

The customer shuddered, 'I wish I could remember the good times in my past lives.'

Seller, 'I'd have a scribe do the calligraphy. Now the feather must be a natural white, rare, yet worth every bean for what it'll do.'

Finally with the charm in Zithia's hand, the couple moved further along admiring chinchilla furs and ginger vicuna wool. Zithia ran the woollen cloth along an arm, closing her eyes momentarily, and when she opened them, her vision was hazy. Then the couple was at a prayer booth. While the priest uttered Ilt's chosen prayer, he was irked by Zithia's lack of attention. They'd paid good money for those words. He thought: *"I can't fathom her. First she must have those charms. Now it's as if the prayer doesn't matter. And today of all days."*

'Zithia!' The name rang out like she was a child. Her gaze left the rainbow parrot fluttering in the rafters. She lowered her eyes in an apparently passive gesture.

Had he been able to look into her mind he'd have been angered indeed: *"Common little prayer."* She mused. Then a thought stuck her: *"God might think Ilt's prayer is mine also."* After this, she prayed in earnest.

At the fortune-tellers, Ilt left Zithia while he sought the most reputable seer. Galen was guided to a column, a little away from Zithia. Spotting the wedding ring on her longest finger, Galen turned ashen. Still watching Zithia, Galen took off his signet ring and sent the youth to obtain the section organiser's presence.

Running to the seers' manager the adolescent clamoured for attention. The man continued talking to his large audience, in particular to Ilt. Caot stated conditions, bouncing his fingertips together. Moving between the two men, the youth made the gold ring dance before Caot's eyes. The seers' master instantly held up a hand for silence and bent to the youth.

'I have important business to attend to. Remain in the queue.' Alabaster ear flares wobbling, Caot bustled after the youth.

Having withdrawn behind the pillar, Galen addressed Caot. 'Tell your fat peasant-of-a-client that in half an hour he'll see a reliable fortune-teller.'

'But... my lord, I must apologize. My best fortune-teller is away visiting a nobleman.'

Galen looked at the man, 'I didn't say the best, I said reliable.' He paused, 'I want someone who is aware how much it's appreciated when an artist cooperates with the priesthood. Further, I require privacy.'

Caot bowed Galen into an empty seer's room, before hurrying off to Ilt.

'Exactly how much will a fortune-teller cost? And no novice, mind you.'

After appraising Ilt, 'Six cacao beans, but only if you're here in half an hour. I've had a cancellation and I'll not see my workers idle.' It was a good price.

'Four.'

'Five, and only because I've no one else to take the timeslot.' Caot ignored a woman muttering that she'd be glad to see a soothsayer at any time. After the seers' master watched Ilt walk off, his hands flapped absently at the now vociferous crowd, 'My nephew will take care of you.'

From his seclusion, Galen regarded Ilt: *"How could she have been paired with that... dullard? That fool?"* And his very displeasure unsettled the high priest.

Zithia, from the moment of her soul mate's desertion, had cared for nothing. Only able to weep when sailing her boat. Her father Pacal had recognized the symptoms, but none had died. One dusk Zithia's family shared a square green pineapple on the patio.

Pacal had tentatively said 'Ilt made a second offer of marriage for you today.'

Jeering was heard from Zithia's brothers, who'd been privy to Zithia's witticisms when the first proposal had been made. In a monotone, Zithia slowly announced, 'One husband is as good as another to me papa. Choose whomever you please.'

In the hush, Pacal choked on a red pineapple segment. 'Then Ilt is my choice.'

After all no local man would court Zithia. Pacal blamed himself. Thinking: *"Before she changes her mind…"* he swiftly went to where Ilt was staying the night. The joyous announcement had been made.

The son of a trader named Quetzl, Ilt increased his father's profits by sailing around the villages hawking Quetzl's wares. Widowed seven months, Ilt needed a wife. Zithia's Atlantian beauty meant Quetzl had had to offer a much larger dowry than he'd wanted.

At the bridal feast, Ilt's eyes had often drifted to where the bride price was displayed. Scanning the many cacao beans, the bridegroom's bottom lip was automatically pushed out. Then his look became crafty: *"It could've been worse,"* Ilt thought, *"And my sons will be almost pure Atlantian."* Leering, he licked his lips.

*

In the bazaar Ilt returned to Zithia, who was listening to a seer's comments as he scanned a client's aura. 'Yes, I can see that you were born in the wrong body. When descending to earth, your spirit's stream has crossed with another stream. Fortunately, both to be born female. Still, it's a mix-up and no denying it.'

Ilt, 'Our appointment is in a half an hour. With a reputable seer, not an apprentice. I stood firm about that.' He was nodding fast, 'My negotiations alone produced this quick service.'Come back tomorrow,' he'd said until I insisted.' Not believing a word, Zithia stopped listening. Long minutes later Ilt ended, 'You see, wife, the proper way to deal with merchants.'

Shuddering, his use of 'wife' implied chattel, Zithia spied a huge piece of jewellery. 'You know Ilt, this lip ornament might suit you.'

The heavy flat golden eagle would hang from his lower lip, with a supporting bar hooked over that lip. 'Very distinguished,' Ilt stroked his chin, 'though it'd be hard to talk, with it on.' Suddenly Ilt's head jerked back; he looked for Zithia.

Ahead, a jaguar-hide kilted proprietor eyed Zithia ardently. He threw her an egg-like object, light as cork. 'It's chunu.' He beamed. 'In the Alps potatoes freeze at night. Next morning, villagers tread the moisture out, then sun-dry the potatoes.'

After watching Ilt and Zithia disappear, the seer's manager made arrangements for the august high priest's presence. He went to a stall sandwiched between the two large seer's rooms. Caot cuffed the little boy who guarded the goods, shouting, 'Move everything to the perfumers.'

Shoving crystals and herb-filled snakeskin pouches onto a mat, the child hastened off. Meanwhile the overlord brushed aside the stall's cloth backdrop, lifted a latch and slid into a watcher's gallery. A room with a secret observation post. It was handy for effects, not to mention spying. Looking around, Caot detached a fulsome padded fold of material from his ample loincloth, and dusted a little table. Then he replaced a rough stool with one that had armrests and alpaca hide, positioning it to face one wall. Sweating now, he removed an almost invisible paper bark square from the wall.

Light shone through holes in an intricate wooden relief mounted on the other side of the wall. Above and between a pair of huge eyes was a third eye, the traditional seer's motif. Within the three large eye-outlines were carved numerous tiny eyes.

On being shown into the spy hole Galen nodded his approval. No, the high priest didn't want any white tea, not even cold white tea. Caot backed out of his presence. Galen settled himself and was introduced to the seer in the connecting room. By the overlord's humble tone, the fortune-teller gathered that her temporary employer was exalted indeed. Caot's words suggested the priesthood. Therefore a deacon.

Galen commanded. 'Question your next clients and have them return this afternoon.'

Little more was said, and then Galen cloaked his presence once more, as he heard the section overlord loudly directing Ilt to this cubicle.

Tashi acknowledged the couple and took her place on a cushion, gesturing them to do the same. They were grouped around a low table built into the baked clay floor.

The table ensured participants always faced the elaborate wall carving.

Tension filled the air. Obviously, the woman was the object of interest to her employer. Blue eyes, heart shaped face and pale skin. The seer knew it must've cost Zithia's parents dear to obtain a true heritage-caller's services, rather than a provincial charlatan. Otherwise Zithia's features couldn't have thrown back, so completely, to her Atlantian ancestry.

Tashi calculated: *"Dramatics,"* and ignited crystals on the table producing purple smoke. 'Spirits, be my bridge across the veil. Use my body to speak the future.' Twitching, Tashi's eyes rolled back until only the whites showed. From a long way away the high keening voice demanded, 'You've journeyed long...from the other side of our land to seek me. Why come so far?' This information was from Galen.

'This temple's seers are legendary.'

Galen's eyes twinkled with amusement. So that's how she got him to come.

Usually, Tashi would have now warned her clients' about the ability of individuals to change their destiny, regardless of what was revealed here. Not this time. 'Your names?'

'Ilt and Zithia.'

'Why have you sought a teller?'

Ilt began, while Zithia had the presence of mind to look modestly at the floor. She hated it when Ilt spoke for them both, yet now wasn't the time to flout convention and get this woman offside.

'Seer, I was a widower with three daughters. I took another bride, yet in four years there's been no sign of a baby.' Voice high, he continued rapidly. 'There was nothing in my wife's family to make me suspect... Why doesn't God smile upon my wife?' From his vantage point Galen raised his chin high, nose wrinkling.

'I long for sons.' Tashi could well understand why. 'My father is anxious for his Atlantian grandchildren. What must we do?'

During this recitation, Zithia smothered a small yawn. When she couldn't look at the floor a moment longer she fixed her eyes on her husband's profile, glazing over a little. Ilt reiterated all he'd already said.

Galen found that even without the feeling of familiarity that occurred in Zithia's presence, he'd have wanted to meet her. Watching her, the years slid away before the high priest's eyes. Again, Galen calculated the precise start of the sun's eclipse. Once more his ships sped beachward at an undistinguished harbour. Then Zithia's spirit had called its greeting and his soul had flown with hers.

As a deacon with expectations, Zithia was far beneath him. Yet only on returning to Xalisco had Galen managed to subdue her ghost. His vulnerability to Zithia had appalled him. So, Galen had perfected this cloaking technique. While he visualized an invisible barrier around him,

Zithia couldn't guess that her soul mate was in the city, let alone within earshot.

At last, Ilt finished his discourse.

Creating a voice small with tragedy, Zithia spoke. 'Great seer, although it distresses me more than I can say,' her voice quivered, 'if we can't have children; I'm prepared to be renounced for my husband's sake.'

When Galen heard her voice for the first time, his heart reached out to her unbidden. She shivered.

Ilt took her hand, 'That'd be a last resort.' Zithia rocked a little to comfort herself.

Tashi thought: *"Not bad, I almost believe you sincere."* She looked at Ilt: *"He certainly does."*

Raising her hands high, Tashi's strange voice wailed, 'My connection... my link is fading.' The fortune-teller went limp. 'It's gone.' She spoke in normal tones. 'But, my spirit guide is always strongest in the afternoon. Return then.' Ilt grumbled. 'No extra charge.' Brightening, Ilt led the way out.

In the next room the high priest didn't move from the padded stool. He reflected quietly on the predicament. He'd become high priest a year after he'd last seen Zithia. If anything, the danger she represented to his position, and his ambitions, had escalated, not decreased. Nevertheless! Then he was momentarily back in heaven, remembering as though there. He'd pledged himself to this woman in that world, and she to him. Of course, things were much simpler there.

Outside, in the thoroughfare Zithia searched herself. 'My new plumes, they must be in the seer's room. I'll get them.'

The high priest was still musing, his strong chin resting on the ball of his hand, when he heard Zithia's returning footsteps. Entering, she knelt before the seer and retrieved the feathers from where she'd managed to drop them. When she raised her eyes to Tashi's, the future-teller observed a new quality in Zithia. As did Galen. There was nothing demure about this person.

Zithia's tone was beguiling. 'Wise one, I seek your guidance,' she flashed a winning smile, 'your understanding, as a woman.' Breathing deeply, 'I find myself untrue...to my soul. I'd be in temple service now, except for...my marriage.'

At this speech, Galen leaned forward grinning. Silently he laughed, his mental camouflage diminishing a fraction. Zithia raised her head sharply in Tashi's direction, hearing the phantom mirth. The woman was expressionless. Galen thought: *"I'll have to be careful."*

'Ahh,' Tashi chanted 'your husband can't live without sons and you may not be able to give them to him.'

Zithia's intensity betrayed for her. 'He must have sons.' Simultaneously she laid a heavy gold necklace on the table. 'And I must have freedom to devote myself to God.'

It was a traditional gift given to a bride on her first wedding anniversary. *"It will suit my new daughter-in-law,"* Tashi thought. Not that it meant she'd give the wanted answer. Zithia ignored the necklace: *"That was given up rather easily. The deacon won't mind my testing this woman's resolve."*
'I can't guarantee an outcome. The future falls as it may. The one God frowns upon a seer who misuses her gifts.'

Zithia's hand went protectively to her bodice. She thought of having to stay with Ilt. Slowly Zithia retrieved a shining brooch from her cleavage. Putting it on the edge of the table, Zithia traced its design with her fingertip. She prayed this sacrifice wouldn't be in vain. Inherited from her mama, the antique brooch contained a gem. Tashi was well pleased.

'August seer, a woman who can't bear children is often blamed in a divorce.' The fingers on the brooch trembled as she thought about her village. 'It's a burden...my family couldn't face.' Zithia bowed her head low.

"A pity; nothing else to offer." Tashi's face was blank. 'The fates can sometimes be interpreted in several ways.' This was all the hope she offered Zithia.

In his gallery, Galen was uncomfortable at seeing Zithia abase herself before this trickster. His eyes darted between the two women.

Rising, Zithia re-joined her husband before Ilt could come blundering back.

Galen had grinned more broadly with Zithia's every sentence. To turn from her now, in her time of need, was impossible. Galen and the seer didn't move again, until the bazaar swamped the last steps. A shadow, whose existence Galen had always denied, was gone from his life.

Zithia's bribes remained where she had placed them, Tashi knowing better than to touch them. Standing on his side of the multi-eyed screen, Galen slowly spread his fingers toward the two pieces. Feeling. Only the brooch had Zithia's impressions upon it. 'You may keep the necklace.' Without touching the brooch, Tashi wrapped it in a layer of new cloth. Going to the base of the latticework, she pulled out a hidden drawer. Into this niche, she placed Galen's prize. Taking the parcel, Galen gave instructions.

Even though lunch was the day's main meal, Zithia had no appetite and Ilt only ordered duck's feet soup. Then Ilt leaned his back against the restaurant's wall in an hour's doze, beckoning Zithia sharply to sit beside him. She didn't move from the cafe's low wall. Glancing sideways at her husband, Zithia's stomach knotted.

Well before the appointed time, Galen took his hidden position again. Hearing Ilt's voice, the high priest couldn't suppress a smile. The couple sat. Solemnly the fortune-teller faced them. 'By the powers of the one God, prepare for good news,' she paused 'you will have sons.' Horrified, Zithia held her breath lest her emotions betray her. Ilt grasped her hand with pleasure. 'However, you'll not achieve sons together.'

Ilt spluttered. 'But you said…'

'Yes, I've seen healthy sons for you.' She added, 'From a wide hipped woman.' None could describe Zithia in these terms. The teller watched the lines disappear from Zithia face. 'You will also have children, but only girls.'

Ilt cleared his tight throat, the sound becoming a question, to which Tashi answered, 'Eight sons. That most lucky of numbers; continuance guaranteed.'

'Sons!' Zithia sobbed on cue, piercing him with the word.

Tashi, 'Healthy son.'

He repeated. 'Eight.' And Zithia watched him crumble under their weight. He let go her hand, thinking: *"No woman is worth the loss of eight boys."*

'Ilt, knowing you will have sons, even by another, is joy enough for me.' Zithia's eyes were teary. 'I've never been able to deny you anything. I can't deny you this.'

Galen grinned lopsidedly.

The seer commended, 'To keep a wife who will never bear you children is a great piety.' Adding in an afterthought, 'Such… courage.'

Three weak girls would hardly support the elderly Ilt. It was too much for him. Eight sons! 'Zithia.' He capitulated. 'I'm sorry. I'll name my youngest boy after your father.'

'No don't do that.' Zithia protested hastily. Ilt's eyebrows shot violently up into his hair, Zithia sped on, 'It wouldn't be right, to your children's mother.' He ceased goggling. Immediately Zithia looked away from Ilt, her face shining. 'A divorce, I …understand.' She faltered, but Galen could see her face !

Tashi took charge. 'Zithia, after the divorce, to be purified a year's temple service is necessary.' She brushed the side of her nose, 'Ilt, as a man, complete immersion in the sea is all the purification required.' She handed a note to Ilt. 'Take this to the bazaar priest. I've included the wording of the divorce that will guarantee you your next family.'

After the couple had gone, Zithia's golden frippery burned in Galen's pocket. Tashi heard Galen drop a weighty purse into the secret drawer. Her eyes lit up. The high priest believed in being generous to those who accommodated his wishes.

Tashi was opening the drawer when, suddenly, Galen's voice was loud in her ears. 'Unquestionably seer, my largess never happened. I was never here.' Tashi's hand halted mid-air. Her eyes went to the screen, but she saw only shadows. 'And,' Galen's presence grew icy, 'in future, when you're being creative in your readings, kindly refrain from even mentioning the one God.' She blanched. 'Or should I take your blasphemy up with the seer's council?'

'No! My gracious lord,' rasped Tashi, falling to the floor with her hands flat on the ground before her. Entering a moment later, Caot frowned at the teller's prone state.

'Take your price and leave us.' Alone, Caot waited. 'I wish to know more about this man Ilt. I assume you can arrange such a thing?'

'Definitely, august lord.'

'Your temple patronage, Caot, is it adequate?'

'Only half my seers currently have attained the temple seal, great lord.'

'Then perhaps it's time to have your seers re-tested.' Caot looked pleased, then his face fell somewhat. 'I could arrange extra tuition before the tests.'

Caot grinned broadly. 'Lord Galen, my own brother, will follow the couple.'

Ilt hurried Zithia to the priest. To dissolve the union Ilt simply had to renounce Zithia in public, before a reputable witness. The priest read aloud Tashi's prescription for the couple's happiness.

Beginning the divorce, the priest intoned to Ilt. 'Recite after me. Without blame attaching to myself or my wife, I find this union isn't sanctified by heaven.'

Ilt hesitated, scowling. Tashi hadn't told them about the divorce's terms. He had expected Zithia to be blamed, wives always were. What would his father say? Quetzl had been happy knowing that a divorce would retrieve their entire dowry. And they'd take it in livestock and crops, not cacao seeds. Now only two-fifths of the bride price could be recovered.

Seeing Ilt waver Zithia said, as though hopefully, 'My husband, you're reconsidering? I am blessed.'

Ilt began reciting at once, finishing with, 'Therefore, I dissolve our marriage. I divorce you. I divorce you. I divorce you.'

It was Zithia who asked the priest for three copies of the divorce decree.

Hours ago, Galen had handed Caot the divorce saying casually, 'An unblemished history is my gift to this woman.'

The seer's master had been surprised. He'd assumed the high priest would want the fault to be Zithia's: "It'd make future events easier for Lord Galen... mind you a high priest wouldn't wish to be linked long with damaged goods."

After Caot had left, to pass on half the bride to the decree priest, Galen had added, 'Besides, that dolt should pay for his time with Zithia.'

chapter 3

With two copies of the divorce in her hand, Zithia saw the world in new colours. The chatter sounded friendly now, not merely frenetic. Looking back towards the seers' hallway, she noticed Caot strutting to join a huddle of all the other seer's masters. The group were conversing heatedly and glancing occasionally at a tall man, of the Irish tribe. Some shook a finger in the man's direction. Finally the huddle broke and the bazaar manager stepped from their midst. Approaching the man, the manager put his fists on his hips, looked up into the man's eyes and exploded, 'Ya banned!'

'But,'

'So far four out of the five seers you've seen have lost their calling.'

'But…'

'Or can't cope anymore.'

'You're not counting today's, surely.'

'No! But she's the fifth. The fact that she was semi-hysterical after the last customer dared question her reading hasn't helped. You just finished her off. We've had to sedate her.'

The Irish-triber frowned.

The bazaar manager became more fatherly, 'Now, loooook, listen; why don't you buy a priest's set of shells and driftwood to scatter for yourself.' Walking the young man away towards where Zithia stood, the manager leaned up and put a friendly arm around the other's shoulder. 'The way your chi upsets seers, you'll pick it up easy. A set of small pieces is best. With a little blue feather.'

'Pale blue?'

'What else? Now, run along, there's a good fellow, I think I see your father hailing to you.'

'My father's dead.'

In a monotone drawl, 'As I said.'

The manager waved genially at thin air further down the gallery, while giving the young man a little push between the shoulder blades.

Simultaneously the manager turned on his heel, back to his raised chair in the middle of the passageway, above the crowd.

Moving off, Zithia and Ilt neared a tiny stall, wherein floated gossamer cloth. Ceiba silk, reserved for royalty. Plus silk imported by Dragon-Land traders. Zithia spied an ebony warrior-knight from the elite jaguar house. Helmeted by tight black curls, the knight's eyes examined a huge half-circle breastplate. A pectoral. Its minuscule turquoise beads hugged the woman seller's full breasts. The beauty wore no top. Another knight, a woman, chided the first warrior for being so easily distracted.

Leaving the bazaar, Zithia noticed that the sky was slightly hazy from fires serving two hundred thousand citizens. She thought: *"I'm home."* Buying a hand-held parasol, on the broad steps surrounding the bazaar Zithia gazed at the distant top section of the Pyramid of the Sun.

Zithia knew that the entire city was arranged for astronomical importance. Buildings, avenues, ceremonial skylights were all oriented to heavenly bodies. Even the river's course had been diverted to mimic the river in ancient Atlantis.

In one direction Zithia observed the main open-air market, with its myriad coloured canopies. Far off in the opposite direction were the religious apartments, multi-storied dwellings, growing smaller with each level. The balconies had sheer drops and elaborate potted gardens. Across a vast square lay the Knowledge Citadel holding a library, the priest-schools plus a hospital. Pyramids in many sizes arose within the city bounds.

With so much to see, even Ilt's nagging couldn't annoy Zithia. Tens of miles of broad paved avenues extended from the main pyramid cluster to a near mountain. The streets were scrupulously clean, for collecting rain against the dry season. Moving to the dappled shade of the footpath, Ilt bumped into a potter carrying bowls wedged into bamboo racks slung on his back. Twice the couple was forced to hurry out of the path of ornate private litters. Llamas plodded along, bearing over-sized jars or cotton bales. Slapping a llama in his way, Ilt had to duck the bright green spittle that was its protest.

Beside a communal bathhouse the elderly lay in shade covered by mud. At a public school, the blast of bouncing-rocks greeted them. Surrounded by boys, a vendor was popping rainbow-coloured corn in a huge flame-hardened gourd.

Ilt counted the street numbers, which were combinations of animals and other objects. Among the guesthouses, each with a thin second story balcony, a cactus with long silky hair distinguished their inn. Squatting outside, men smoking bee-shaped cigars challenged each other with maths puzzles. A national pastime, unlike reading.

Now the marriage was over, Ilt was eager to be gone from the city. Especially after he'd learnt that all rents skyrocketed for a holyday, the day after tomorrow. Entering the inn, he prattled on about the future.

'It's inconvenient; still the girls will soon manage your household work.' His lips puckered, 'You did teach them to weave the patterns I like?'

Zithia's mouth snapped open. 'If only the divorce had been declared this morning, I could've left the city already and saved the cost of an extra room.'

True. Now they weren't married they must have separate accommodation, as far from each other as possible for decency's sake. Considering Ilt had chosen the cheapest room, Zithia was confident in engaging a comfortable front room for herself that night.

'After I've written to my brother about our divorce, I'll deliver the letter to you.'

Ilt looked quickly to see if the innkeeper had heard Zithia's unwomanly statement that she could write and, therefore, read. He made a sign to protect him against any ill luck. It was the first time he'd done this in her presence. Zithia turned icy.

'My brother will return two fifths of your dowry. In cacao beans.'

'Livestock will do.'

Smiling sweetly, Zithia glared. 'A dowry is always returned as it was given, unless there's a problem.' The smile vanished. 'Is there a problem Ilt?' Hiding his hands, her ex-husband averted his eyes.

'Ilt, to obtain the predicted result, we'll both need to be scrupulously correct in this transaction.'

'Yes.' Shaking his head.

'And of course you wouldn't shame me by leaving me here without some money.'

'But you're going on a spiritual journey in the temple, you won't need any.'

She eyed him levelly. 'You will forward me ten cacao beans and I'll inform my brother to add this to the dowry we owe.'

By habit Ilt touched the quipii at his waist. A string hung with a fringe of coloured threads, for calculations. 'Ten cacao beans? Next you'll want to open a bean and drink it as chocolate.' He gulped. 'No. Five.' Fingers working overtime.

'Ten, plus the rent for my room tonight.' Ilt sucked his cheeks in compulsively. Zithia added a sweetener. 'I'll have my brother reimburse you my expenses for the entire trip.'

An unforeseen bargain. Ilt handed over ten beans. 'The total is thirty two.' Zithia nodded, surprised, that was about right. 'I'll pay the hotel bill as I leave.'

'What; and wake the owner up so long before dawn?' She struck a tiny copper gong.

The proprietress appeared, carrying a small hairless dog. She explained, 'Mama gets bad rheumatism. A living hot water bottle is the only thing that brings her relief.'

She set the dog before an aged matron, who carefully placed her bare feet on it. The hotelier adding archly, 'Mind you, we don't have any spare for guests!' She gave her mama a new washed potato. 'It's fresh from the garden… don't forget to put it near your feet in the bed tonight, or you'll get cramps again.'

'Ilt will settle our bill now.' While moving away, Zithia cautioned Ilt. 'Remember my room.'

Immediately the innkeeper, who was between husbands, was all attention. 'Two rooms?' She lilted. No information was forthcoming, 'Two rooms! I have one next to yours, will that do?' Knowing the few circumstances in which it wouldn't.

Scarlet, Ilt stammered. 'No, no, one of your front rooms. Zithia deserves the best.'

The proprietor took the proffered money, smiling widely. 'When you're ready, my dear, I'll show you to your new chamber.'

The lady of the house disappeared again, but not far. Zithia returned to Ilt.

Zithia, thinking she should say something gentle now she had her divorce scroll in her pocket started, 'Ilt thank goodness…' She bit back the next words on her lips: *"it's over,"* finishing '…you'll have sons.'

He went to put a hand on her bare forearm. She stepped back, body stiffening. 'Good life.' And was gone. He farewelled an empty space.

Moving into the corridor, Zithia bumped into the innkeeper who was dusting madly. The woman's face was alive with speculation. On the way to Zithia's room, 'If you're staying for the festival we could go to Lake Quetomem together.' Showing Zithia around her room, 'Half your lineage must be from my own tribe…' The proprietress waited for confidences. None came. '…although your parents should've requested greater height.'

*

Dangling her legs over the unrailed balcony outside her room, Zithia wrote to her eldest brother: *"Tomce, I'm now honourably divorced. No fault attaches to me and therefore none to our family. Here is the exact wording of the proclamation. I'll send an official copy next week.*

"Beloved Tomce, I well remember the cacao beans you've been saving up all these years. As you love me, I beg you sacrifice them to pay Ilt the sum of thirty-two cacao beans plus the usual two fifths of the bride price. I go to the temple for a year."

She finished knowing Ilt would read the letter despite its wax seals.

Taking the letter downstairs Zithia ran into the innkeeper. 'Now don't you worry, my dear, you'll be in each other's arms again soon. At your age making-up is half the fun of marriage.'

Zithia's eyes opened wide at that image. 'It's somewhat difficult to make-up, after a divorce!'

'Divorced.' The other woman comprehended Zithia's carefree attitude. 'A blameless divorce.'

Zithia's eyes twinkled. Moving off she waved the sealed scroll, 'A letter for my family, my ex-husband will deliver it.'

Horror overtook the proprietress' face. Was it horror? The expression was a little too amused for that. 'But you weren't thinking of taking it to him yourself? A single woman! Most improper. To spare both our blushes, let me deliver it for you. The least I can do.'

Back on her balcony Zithia watched the mammoth-leg palm tree silhouettes. For a moment her father was with her there. So strong a feeling was it, that it was as if he'd never died. As if all the mourning had been an illusion. All she had to do was turn her head to see him. Zithia's breath caught a little and she continued to look ahead, instead going over the steps that had begun her journey here.

Perhaps being the only girl in the family had made her different. After quickly bearing four boys, Zithia's blue-eyed mama, Lilis, fell pregnant again. When her nails and hair started to break Lilis knew she was bearing a girl. Despite Pacal calling it extravagance, Lilis had cajoled him into buying the services of a top heritage-caller, his cousin's teacher, thus maximising Zithia's chance of inheriting any Atlantian breeding from her forebears.

Zithia's farmer papa read well and he taught his sons. Quick with words, Zithia had implored Pacal for months to join her brothers at lessons, to no avail. Lilis had finally won her husband over. Thus, Zithia became the only female in the valley, in the region, to read. And a grand scandal it was. Later, Pacal admitted to himself the unwisdom of teaching her. He never shared this with his wife, who'd later died in childbirth, leaving Zithia to mama and harangue eight brothers.

Then, a well-remembered day. The signing of the nuptial contract. Zithia had observed Ilt's father, Quetzl, smirking and rubbing his hands together often at the family's new acquisition. Atlantian grandsons! Occasionally a well-wisher gave him a look he didn't understand. *"Envy, "* he'd thought, for all the men in his family ran to affluent fat, including the groom. No one in Zithia's community had shared with Ilt the knowledge that Zithia could read. It was considered a great joke on him. Besides, Zithia was a dutiful daughter; they didn't really want to blight the girl's reputation.

In five months of wedded bliss Zithia hadn't fallen pregnant, despite Ilt's self-absorbed attentions. Each month Ilt harassed her for this information then instantly broadcast her failure to his kin. His first wife had become pregnant on her honeymoon; he'd expected similar success.

One afternoon everything changed. Hidden among branches in a tree, Zithia read a letter from her brother. Hearing Ilt and his papa approach, Zithia hid her little scroll in a tree hollow. Quetzl, with a jade cylinder hanging beneath his nose, was speaking with large, sudden arm gestures. They didn't look up.

'Your bride has opinions,' Quetzl spat out. 'She's a vixen.'

Ilt grunted his assent, 'And she's still not with child! It's not as though I'm...'

'Yes, yes! I'm sure you are.' Quetzl leered, slapping his son on the back. He narrowed his close-set stare. 'At least she cost a lot less than her family thinks.' And laughed.

Ilt, always eager to mimic Quetzl, joined in. 'You always liked a bargain, father.'

'It's as well!'

Still talking, the pair moved off. Zithia's cheeks glowed with mortification and concern for her family. Their ugly laughter. What had it meant?

Days later Zithia allowed herself to be discovered reading a goods list Quetzl had made for the next bartering trip. The ensuing row involved Ilt's whole family. A woman who could read. Quetzl wondered how to keep it secret. Her face expressionless, Zithia said, 'But it's common knowledge. I assumed you knew, especially as Ilt offered his proposal twice.' The old man glowered at his son's lust. 'I was so very grateful.'

Quetzl glowered from Zithia to his son, who looked at his feet. No wonder she'd been available, with such a blasphemy in her. After this, Ilt avoided his wife. When he sailed off on a bartering sojourn, Zithia raised the sail of her little reed boat for home.

There they examined the dowry. One-third was suspect, having a different feel to the real cacao beans. Finally, Zithia's father cut one cacao bean open. Mud. The bean skin had been packed with mud. Skilful city fraud!

Pacal's face had new lines. 'I'll tell Mochcouoh.' Half Zithia's bride price was earmarked to pay his marriage contract.

Zithia knelt before her father, 'Is there no other way?'

Pacal shook his head. 'None. The money can't be recovered. We accepted the bride price as is, and the bargain has been irrevocably sealed.' Zithia went pink. 'We'll not speak of this again.' Pacal patted Zithia on the shoulder, 'Destroy the frauds.' Leaning on his second son for support, Pacal left the room.

Sitting on a reed mat Zithia opposite her eldest brother Tomce, Zithia pondered clenching and unclenching one hand. When the others were gone Tomce said, 'I'll hide the fakes in case we can return them to Quetzl one day. If we get that chance, I'll put a pinprick in each counterfeit bean, making them useless.'

'Put these toward the price for Mochcouoh's bride.' Zithia unhooked her gold earrings, Ilt's wedding gift to her. 'What a pity they were washed overboard on the journey back to my honourable family-in-law.' Betrayed, Zithia's loyalty remained with her father. Her voice was a rock. 'A man shouldn't have what he hasn't paid for.'

'No, he shouldn't!'

'Ilt paid for children, Atlantian children.' Her eyes glittered, 'Then buy me some picqu pichana powder.' His face took on a dark smile. If Zithia took this powder at a certain time each month, there'd be no babies. It was the only justice available to the family.

The seasons flew by. One winter Zithia's father grew ill of a wasting malady. On his final night he lay on a cot under the pergola, where passion fruit was flowering yellow; Zithia would now loathe their scent forever. The favourite meal they'd cooked for Pacal remained untouched. Pacal's hand dropped to near his best friend, a Pekinese, Alinson, whose eyes never left Pacal's face. 'Whoever would've believed that I'd have a Dragon-Land dog,' he whispered more than said.

Then, to Zithia, more in his usual voice, 'I wish I'd seen your children.' Zithia stifled a gasp as it was about to escape, and then smiled shakily.

Looking at Zithia's hair, Pacal knew she'd cut it all off to mourn him. Hoarsely he whispered, 'Darling child, can you promise me to learn to hold your tongue?'

She'd have pledged anything she could deliver. Tears filled Zithia's eyes.

He sighed, 'I knew it.' She went to talk but he silenced her. 'Then promise me you'll never cut your hair, not even in grief.' He took a rattling gasp. 'A woman's hair is her glory. And with your sharp tongue,' he grinned feebly, 'you'll need a waterfall of such beauty.' The Pekinese shared the joke and Pacal smiled at his best friend.

Zithia nodded. Then closed her eyes tight, skin crinkled hard at the corners in pain. Slowly she bent her head forward to hide the emotion, lest he look up before she had control.

'Good, now leave me awhile.' He'd already sent everyone else off.

Once out of her father's sight, Zithia ran through the small dry paddock to a rickety gazebo. There she fished out one of her father's small cigars and lit it from a piece of fire she's brought within a firestone. Breathing out a voluminous pall of smoke she smiled a little.

Then she squatted down, saying 'You sure get around.' The Pekinese lay on a cushion, tethered by a long lead. 'If you didn't insist on intermittently baying at the moon each night, you could be with papa in body, as well as in spirit.'

Zithia had half-finished the cigar when Alinson awoke and began to bay. But not at the night. Stubbing out the cigar, Zithia let Alinson off his lead, upon which he was pulling fit to choke himself. Arriving back, Zithia stood, her soul quivering within a shaking body. Alinson hadn't gone to the body but stopped, seemingly, next to nothing. Looking up at Pacal's spirit.

A brilliant tunnel of blue, white light appeared. With it, the shade of Pacal's wife. Pacal moved to her, taking her hand, without looking back.

They both entered the light and were gone.

Zithia's aunt, who'd lived with them a decade, put an arm around Zithia's waist. 'You mustn't mind, my dear.' She tried to smile, 'People often slip away when loved ones leave for a little. It's their last gift.'

Before the stars resumed their usual glow for her, Zithia had grieved for over a year. With seasons passing, she began to be able to set her pain aside, when she felt it clawing at her. She could participate in the little pleasures of life. A few months later Zithia accepted her marriage's failure and that she must leave her home. Visiting her brothers, Zithia watched the shadows from the loufa vine above the family dais. Leaning backwards she held taut the material on a backlap loom. Her eldest brother was moving two rhea birds on leads. Plump, flightless and tall enough to look Zithia in the eyes.

Flying the scuttle through her threads, Zithia tamped the new row of weaving. 'Would you prefer me divorced or a publicly acclaimed shrew?'

'How public?' and knew the answer.

Thus to Xalisco. Quetzl had vetoed the journey automatically. So the next time a trader visited, Zithia offered to read a scroll. 'Always making jokes daughter-in-law,' said Quetzl, adding in an undertone, 'Alright. Xalisco! On one condition.'

Zithia whispered sweetly, 'On my return, I pledge never even to speak about reading again.' She'd already planned to go into temple service, this being the only respectable way for a woman to disappear from her community.

The next morning Zithia told the proprietress that she planned to stay two extra nights. She was about to go adventuring in the city when the innkeeper called loudly, 'Stay out of alleys, I don't want you knocked on the head.' She added in a mutter, 'before you pay for your two nights' rent.'

Crossing the hostel's threshold Zithia went immediately to the temple area, with a note stating:

"I've decided to delay entering temple service until the day after the festival. Zithia, daughter of Pacal."

While leaving the precinct, she couldn't stop her head turning to the title written above it. 'Flyers.' There were no flyers in her home village and she'd always promised herself a trip. Her dress was already sticking to her back. She thought: *"I'll never see the city in this humidity."* Stopping, Zithia bought a flight. 'Two adventures at once.'

'This flyer has studied for five years,' stated the priest, giving Zithia a herb to loosen the body's hold on the soul. 'Watch with open eyes, breathe evenly and don't move.'

In a darkened room the flyer sat cross-legged. Sitting beside him, Zithia placed her hand on his. After a few heartbeats the cloud-hung sky shimmered above her. The vision winked into being and then ceiling closed her in. Zithia relaxed her breathing. The flyer mentally collected her again and the city came in view. So very far below. The tidy grid lines of the streets, the scattered reservoirs and the sparkling lake at one side. The vision settled into clarity. *"Have I died?"* But she felt her guide's warm hand beneath hers.

Astral travelling! A suburb appeared, where every set of houses had its own steam bath with a tiny entrance hole. At one such doorway, a little girl pulled with all her might on fat-bangled hands. The exit was jammed with a yelling, sweating woman. Gaping Zithia thought: *"Sometimes, wealthy girth can be a disadvantage."*

Turkeys scrabbled for food. Their gold, blue and green patched feathers were so solid that Zithia felt she could stroke them. Next they watched the arch priestess's guards practise an Atlantian self-defence discipline on a wide stone parade ground. Most had Atlantian features. Finally they were gliding along the Avenue of the Dead and rushed to the top of the pyramid at the avenue's end. A woman with features termed Egyptian, standing on this summit, looked straight through her as Zithia passed overhead.

Back in her body, Zithia scrabbled in her money pouch. Her face fell; she couldn't afford another trip. Looking hungrily at the flyer, Zithia sighed: *"Five years training."*

chapter 4

An underling handed Ixchup, deaconess of women, Zithia's note. 'How dare this peasant play truant?' Narrowing her eyes, she planned how to make Zithia pay.

A visitor interrupted the deaconess's reverie. She'd met him in the upper clergies' dining hall. Xiao Chen, the truth-sayer deacon of the arch priestess's tribe.

Looking around him, Xiao Chen winced inwardly. During the decade he and Galen had worked together, Xiao Chen had prided himself that he'd never needed to call upon Ixchup. Indeed all other priests associated with the high priests had. Yet Xiao Chen was connected to, and guide to, a mystic high priest. Only mystic high priests were attended by deacons. And such mystic status shouldn't lead here; mind you, Xiao Chen knew better than to believe in any generalisation. His forehead creased slightly, he should've made Galen come himself. Only friendship had got him here.

Xiao Chen nodded to the deaconess. 'The high priest Galen is interested in a woman arriving today.' Ixchup smiled encouragement. 'Zithia, daughter of Pacal!'

'Zithia?' Ixchup folded the note, *"I'll sacrifice Dragon-Land incense to the one God today, for this opportunity to have Lord Galen under obligation to me. The alabaster high priest, no less!"*

Xiao Chen's tone was dry: 'Lord Galen has seen this woman.'

'Which is more than I have.'

'And feels he'd one-day like to be introduced to her.'

'They haven't met?' It sometimes happened like that, but Lord Galen … Her mouth curled with amusement.

'Galen will decide when they'll meet.' He announced dryly.

The deaconess rasped, 'Is our august lord inclined to interfere in my realm?'

'A high priest may show an interest in any section, whenever he chooses.'

Tight-lipped, 'I assume Lord Galen means to encourage my hopes that my cousin will finally be ordained.'

Xiao Chen thought: *"So all her brothers and sisters have already been settled."* He knew the cousin. Not an Atlantian bone his body, his name a byword for laziness. 'Galen has spoken about a post available on the Western coast.'

'I'm sure high priest Augustus has someone in mind to retire there.'

'Recently I had the privilege,' Xiao Chen's visage was stony, 'of hearing your cousin lead a service.'

Ixchup's back shrank. High Atlantian pronunciation wasn't her cousin's forte. 'Perhaps a position at a minor temple would suit him.'

Xiao Chen considered, 'A small observatory temple is expanding. They'll need another priest.'

'My cousin could shine in such a place.' Handing Xiao Chen Zithia's note, with a bow.

'Absolutely, Ixchup.'

The deaconess reflected: *"I like this new arrival more and more."* 'I thought... light tasks for this Zithia!'

*

Placing the note before Galen, Xiao Chen sat opposite him. 'What are you doing?'

Being a close associate to a high priest meant it was the place of the said deacon to keep the high priest in line. Throughout the decade long partnership, Xiao Chen and Galen had both assisted each other in work and career decisions. And if ever Xiao Chen had seen a career decision, it was Zithia.

Galen put the report from Caot away. *"Having followed the man Ilt to his inn I engaged him in conversation, buying him maize beer till he was drunk."* There followed a summation of Ilt's character, life and marriage.

'I don't know.' Galen muttered beneath his breath; and then said in an audible voice, 'You always say I should relax a little.'

The truth-sayer tapped a gold cylinder slowly, repetitively on the desktop.

'That can be very annoying.'

'Mmmmmm.'

Galen read Zithia's note, 'What does she mean, she's arriving tomorrow? She had instructions.'

Xiao Chen kept tapping, until Galen relented. 'She's someone I promised to meet one day.'

'Cryptic'.

'Accurate.'

'As long as this isn't anything trivial.' He inspected his hands as though they were soiled. 'It wasn't a pleasure dealing with Ixchup.'

'My friend, would I involve Ixchup if it were trivial?'

Xiao Chen saw an unusual confusion on Galen's face. Concerned, the truth-sayer resumed the tapping.

Galen took the cylinder from him. 'Don't worry Xiao Chen, remember my reputation for always being in control.'

*

It was First Day already. As pledged, the innkeeper roused Zithia in time to robe herself before the crowded twilight walk to Lake Quetomem. A lake fed by the city's river, plus channels beneath the avenues and plazas.

Purple-dye trees grew either side of the festive path. They passed a vendor grilling a green seven-foot long, huge-headed fish. Black paving stones led onto a border of sacred reeds and water. A flock of leggy, pink winged birds scooped fish into horizontal platter-bills.

They reached a rise. Before Zithia floated over two thousand tiny farm islands, called chinampas. A great patchwork quilt, with thin blue liquid borders separating the squares. For this festival, gilded half-moon bridges linked the ceremonial island with surrounding chinampas where flowers were liberally interspersed among crops. Wide planks bridged many chinampas for the day.

Two hours after dawn and the arch priestess, Yin-Hsin, appeared, attended by fifteen priests. Each displayed the distinctive attributes of an Atlantian tribe. She was perfection, from slanting brown eyes and petite nose. Five feet eleven inches. Though old, her still-beautiful face was highlighted by long straight, black hair.

Yin-Hsin, a name from the eighth tribe, announced, 'Today we celebrate the arrival of culture from Atlantis and its spread throughout our entire continent. We're privileged to have with us many guests, including the great magician priest, Davot.' Everyone could recite ballads about Davot's exploits and a muted whisper broke out. Smiling, Yin-Hsin floated gracefully to one side.

The ancient mystic came forward. Looking skyward, he banged his staff to the ground. A treble rainbow appeared. Davot beamed, 'Let the pantomime begin.'

Adolescents, masked as the first Atlantian leaders, emerged from smoke. In cloaks and robes that priests now wore, they moved among coffee hued people. One Atlantian bore a calendar plus a multi-dimensional sextant for shooting the stars. The second focused the sun through a lens, creating fire. A pale, blue-eyed man tipped a pouch of soil onto the earth, mixing it in. Lastly, a woman with a crinkly red corncob hairstyle offered the people maize.

Davot's snowfall of blue flashes signalled the crowd to disperse over the chinampas. Everyone dressed up for First Day celebration. Those with observable Atlantian breeding merely applied cosmetics to accentuate their features; others wore elaborate masks. This was the perfect day on which the unmarried could exhibit, and prove they were worth the asking dowry.

Wandering, Zithia came to an island dominated by a thirty-foot tall avocado tree. Orchids with bunches of small pink tiger-face flowers, the mouths and eyes drawn in white, grew shaded between willows which edged the chinampa. Crossing lush grass, she looked over open water.

The noise of the crowds in the patchwork plantation had reduced to a buzz. Taking off her shoes, Zithia felt a branch beneath her feet, one of many used to stabilise the chinampas, sandwiched between dirt dredged from the lake. In the water several metallic gold-armoured fish, dazzling as the sun, shimmered around begging for fruit.

Alone. From a pouch, Zithia withdrew a ring and flung it across the rippling water. 'I'm free!' From behind her came a deep cough. She froze.

'There's no need to worry, child.' Stated a rich enchantment of a voice.

Zithia rounded the tree's girth. An intensely masculine man leaned against the trunk. Finishing the paragraph he was reading, he lowered an irregularly shaped magnifying glass. Palm sized, gold framed. The man tenderly wrapped the glass up before placing it into a slim padded box. After becoming long-sighted, he'd found this treasure among the temple antiquities.

He queried, of no one in particular, 'Off this continent, but to the north, and east of here?' Closing his book with inked fingers, he turned magnetic brown eyes on Zithia. 'So you're free, are you? There are many definitions of freedom. Now, is yours a spiritual freedom or have you escaped a prison?'

It was decided; she liked him. 'You could say both.' She took the book. 'It's a sort of scroll, isn't it?' Opening it, her finger traced down several vertical lines of letters before, looking puzzled, 'I don't understand the writing.'

'Sorry, that's halfway between Atlantian and the Dragon-Land language. Some mystics use it. They say it's the language used on the astral plane; to write the scrolls of life, in the Hall of Records. I gained admittance to that hall once, and it's true. Only they use silk scrolls and because each scroll covers an entire life, one follows important events within small squares of vertical writing. Tiny horizontal lines separate events, experiences,' He closed his eyes. His hands and eyes, beneath his lids, moved as though he still re-examined his book of life. 'Yes, that's right, and growths. Other thicker, vertical lines divide the rolling years and decades. The silk; such a comforting warm pale yellow.'

Zithia, all interest, 'Do you remember any of your future?'

'Of course not. I was allowed to slake an old academic's curiosity only. You don't think they'd have given me entrance if I wanted to read the thing, do you?'

Then Torim tilted his head to one side and handed Zithia a silk scroll. 'Perhaps this one will be better.'

Hesitantly she began to read aloud, her finger again slowly tracking the letters in their vertical progress down the page. The text was ancient with the 'T' written as 'S'. The man corrected her pronunciation of each archaic version of familiar words.

"And so it came to pass that it was through the thirteenth tribe's desire to be gods that sweet Atlantis came to grief. Morally bankrupt, the thirteenth made war on the other tribes for the power sources they needed to conquer the world. Capturing one power source, it escaped its stone confines within the bowels of a dormant volcano. The volcanic range erupted and within twenty-four hours beloved Atlantis was swallowed by the sea. Thus the Island Atlantis joined the cities of First Atlantis in the Atlantis Ocean."

To Zithia's relief, the man finally held up his hand, 'Good enough, good enough. Though you obviously haven't been practising. My name's Torim.'

'Zithia.'

Minutes flew in conversation, while people encroached on nearer chinampas. Zithia's eyes flitted from group to group.

'Run along, girl. Mingle and be flattered. I'm content alone.'

'Alone? With your features?' She flashed her eyes. 'Women will be enticing you into improving their children's birthright.'

He searched for the twin sisters he'd barely been able to discourage. 'I'm a priest, my dear. Far too wise for that sort of folly.'

Abruptly, in the crowd Torim recognized Galen. 'Though I'm surprised to see others aren't.' He frowned: *"Now what is a high priest doing dressed as a lowly deacon's assistant?"*

Following Torim's gaze, Zithia spotted a walnut hued man with black curls and a flared nose. A flock of women circled him, reaching up to the child on his wide shoulders.

'He's certainly enjoying himself.' Torim looked at Zithia sharply. 'The boy is exactly like him, proving strong Atlantian ancestry.'

Torim saw the tableau intriguing Zithia, then looked again for Galen. The high priest was gone.

Zithia tapped Torim, above the wrist. 'Your strange scroll...'

'My book!'

'It's more of the legend?'

On First Day, Torim always read the earliest record regarding the Atlantians' coming. He began to recite as they walked from one chinampa to the next.

"And those fleeing Atlantis, having survived spewing volcanic lava and tsunamis, paused on their sister continent. When the skies cleared of ash, Atlantis lay on the ocean's bottom. The shattered remains from Atlantis had been dashed onto nearby land. One of man's loveliest dreams had been laid waste.

"Now came the wrath against the ones who called themselves the superior tribe. They were exiled forever, to an unpopulated region devoid of mineral deposits. In a damaged ship, the thirteenth tribe was transported over half a world away. To ensure the thirteenth tribe's cooperation, a fully armed escort ship accompanied it."

Thirteen, being an unlucky number, was replaced everywhere by the number twelve plus the symbol against evil. An eye. On First Day, householders burned any flawed replacement thirteens. This was the sole remembrance of the outcast tribe. Walking towards a bonfire Zithia quoted a village rendition:

"The criminals were deprived of technology. Once delivered to their harsh wilderness, they were left to sink into barbarism." Triumphantly, she tossed

a damaged quipii into the flames. *"Their description, though recorded, was never recalled again. Their name gladly gone."*

'How do you think the Atlantians truly travelled? The stories are…'

'Incredible?… Yes!'

'Ships without paddles or sails. Vessels that didn't voyage through the water?'

'Believe them.'

Moving through chinampas they bought strawberries and hairy orange tomatoes with green flesh. The lakeside carnival was visible again. Whole tapirs, similar to miniature hippopotamuses, roasted on spits.

Zithia remembered her dry village. 'Is it true they made deserts flourish by turning sea water into drinking water?'

'It wasn't even a miracle to them.'

They mounted yet another, very steep, gilded half-moon bridge. 'And they lived to two hundred?'

'With youthful vigour, going by the sources.' Leaning on the rail at the top, they threw strawberries to a silver-plated school of fish.

Torim pointed to a half-moon bridge opposite and its reflection. 'There hides the secret of Atlantian technology. The first-ones designed these bridges, as a joke I suspect.' Tracing the heavy edge of the bridge and its watery image, 'You see, it makes a wheel. My research shows that the wheel was the basis of their technology. Yet, in their wisdom, the Atlantians decided not to give us the secret of this power.' Torim laughed. 'But here it is, all around us, just waiting to be recognised.'

Crossing onto the lake shore they came to a barbecue of lines of small, skewered fish.

'Piranha; very sweet.' Torim bought several. 'Caught far up-river and hauled overland while comatose.'

On a nearby knoll they ate. 'Now where was I? Ah…'

"Only weeks later the sixteen remaining tribes departed for their various new homes, taking with them relics washed up from Atlantis. Marble, stone and even soil."

Zithia bit into a drumstick of purple moorhen, 'Why didn't they stay in the northern part of this great land, up past the New Nile? Legend says they loved those cooler lands well.'

'Too well. They had kept it for themselves, their personal reserve. Though asked by many, the Atlantians had never given permission for anyone to settle there. When faced with Atlantis' destruction, the survivors had to go where there were already large populations. So they lost both Atlantis and her sister-land. A double curse, for the mystics say that to walk upon the northern shores is to see Atlantis arisen.'

chapter 5

The high priest came to the limestone building, wherein lay a minor library, and memories. Galen strode the familiar high vaulted arched passageway leading through the building to an immense courtyard enclosed by rough stone walls.

It was the oldest garden in the city. Slowly descending a few stairs, Galen's smile was contented reviewing the rainforest. Since his last visit, ruffled ribbons had traced delicate secrets upon the three-storeyed walls, with twelve-inch leaves creating commas. He recalled climbing the three ancient mahogany trees that towered over the buildings, to plant vanilla orchids. Beneath the first giant's canopy was a pyramid shaped tree, leaves obscured by flowers.

A building-block vine, named by the Atlantians, climbed the first mahogany. Its two huge interlocking stems spiralled ever upward. The seemingly endless vine was believed to link man to his mythical beginning. Galen touched a plant he'd once pruned; now all peach blossoms and heart leaves. The other mahoganies ruled in their own domains extending to the far wall.

The high priest hadn't been here for years. Frowning, he remembered why. Creamy stones meandered round the natural spring to the only internal stairs, which led to the second floor library. With this stairwell in view, hugging the wall, Galen experienced a sense of loss. What was happening to him? Where were all these unnecessary emotions coming from? In the sun-flooded area, running the entire length of the stairway swayed a deep uneven pool of aquinoa grain. Galen followed the paving through waist high clumps of purple seed bubbles.

Halfway up the wide stairs, on a square balcony, Galen observed Torim sitting on a crate, a scroll in his lap. Two steps below the librarian, Galen stopped and looked at the arched library doorway with its one eye above.

He said to Torim's bent head, 'I remember this library being on the opposite side of the building.'

Torim replied without looking up. 'It was, until the scribe deacon was persuaded of the advantages in moving.'

Galen gave Torim a half smile, his eyes alight. 'The main advantage being that you now possess the only internal entrance into the garden.' The high priest would've come to the same arrangement.

Torim's brown eyes returned Galen's mischievous twinkle, 'Exactly brother.' Then the librarian's gaze became piercing.

'The vanilla orchids now bear you a tidy sum.'

'It's as we planned. They're such a useful bargaining item.'

Torim smiled, 'Hayanil no longer wants to die and his wife cooks so well she's a menace to my girth.' He'd softened toward Galen because the high priest had saved Hayanil.

They grew silent. All at once Galen was fascinated by his surroundings, avoiding Torim's scrutiny. He had expected this visit, yet... not so soon. After all, the librarian had only stepped over his threshold an hour ago.

'And to what do I owe the pleasure of a visit from the court's favourite high priest?'

The civilities over, there was a pause. 'It's a shame to see a man of your brilliance relegated to these mundane tasks.'

'I didn't hear you speak for me when the decision was made.'

Galen walked around. 'It would've done no good.' He picked up a jar of red pigment Torim used to touch up wounded scrolls, 'Have you forgotten who helped you keep this garden?'

Torim's face drained white. The high priest had committed a grievous sin by reminding his one-time mentor of the favour Torim owed him. And such a costly debt. The high priest flushed.

'But I bring good news. I'm now in a position to offer you a place in the main library again.'

The main library. Torim's library. He'd been forbidden access to this resource since a judgment had come against him.

A scene from seven years before replayed itself in their minds. They'd sat side by side at the main entrance of the garden, Galen saying, 'Torim, that was some insult!'

Torim rubbed the side and back of his neck, 'Well, I never thought the prince would actually understand what I was saying.' A rueful smile appeared, 'And those around him were definitely too feeble minded to comprehend it.'

'It did take two full days for the meaning of your words to register.'

'That little amount of time! Then the prince is brighter than I thought.'

All at once Galen snapped, 'Why go to the banquet at all?'

'I was invited by a princess, with a rather exquisite mind, who thinks I'm amusing.'

'Not his sister!'

'It's very obvious they have different mothers.'

His hand ruffled his hair. 'I agree I should've been… a little more subtle.' The librarian shrugged. 'In my defence, I was under the influence of a gargantuan meal and a pair of extremely lovely eyes.'

Galen took up his staff and paced. Facing the librarian, his pupils narrowed, 'A deacon shouldn't be flattered into being discreet.'

'And a mystic priest should know better than to become embroiled in politics.'

Galen leaned his staff at a sword angle, and raised his chin. 'Be that as it may, Torim, you appear to be suicidal. I'm not.' With that, Galen had left his old friend.

Seven years on, the offer hung in the silence like the answer to a prayer.

'You could cease your midnight rambling.' The librarian currently visited his beloved haunt in the witching hours, when the most interesting reading was locked away. 'We both like to read at odd hours.'

Torim's whole manner lightened. Still, one concern existed. Gripping a trowel, the librarian looked at a distant buttress tree. It badly needed fertilizer. 'And if I refuse your generosity?'

'I'd never stop you reading. Who do you think leaves out the oldest texts?'

Relaxing his grip on the trowel, Torim smiled anew. He didn't really want Galen's blood on his hands. Suddenly he recalled the first book he'd found accidentally left out. 'I suppose the "Treatise on the Consequences of Arrogance" was an attempt at humour?'

'My friend, it could all be yours again.'

Torim considered. To once again borrow ancient manuscripts from other temples, to debate the meaning found in Egyptian texts and to enjoy the few remaining works from Atlantis!

'Friend.' The librarian repeated, mulling the word over like he was examining a suspect mushroom. His eyes were amused, 'Well friend, in return for what?'

Galen opened his drying mouth, and then closed it again. He frowned over Torim's head. 'A high priest stuck for words. How you do surprise me, Galen.'

Galen's arms folded themselves. Despite having rehearsed this visit, he hadn't been able to find the right opening line.

Torim broke into a grin. 'Or can't you ask me? Is it so disreputable; this boon?'

Galen's cloak ties seemed tight at his neck. Feverishly his mind sought a dignified angle to begin this topic.

Torim, 'I did see you today at the chinampas.'

'I, I need… an intermediary regarding a new arrival.'

'An intermediary!' Torim gave a derisive snort. 'My dear boy, the more appropriate term is a procurer.'

Galen's countenance darkened. 'I resent that.'

'So do I!' The librarian raised, and then lowered his eyebrow. 'I'm unused to high politics; and procuring.'

'This woman has importance to me.'

'Obviously, brother. For a mere sexual encounter, you'd never have broken your silence. Still, you petition me to act less than heroically.' He drew back. 'You really should've worn a mask, then we need never have had this meeting.' Torim's eyes blazed. 'Will the high priest return in an hour for my decision?'

Silent, Galen turned to leave.

'Wait!' Torim's eyes suddenly narrowed. He glowered. 'Exactly when did you meet this woman?' He demanded.

'I thought I told you, we haven't met.'

'Then, when did you first not meet?'

'That's another story.'

'Is it?' Torim paused. 'So, you've not met before! Then when did you not meet recently?'

'I'd just bought some iodised salt at Chuan's shop. Oh, I thought you'd like some.' Almost absently Galen produced a heavy pouch from a satchel, at his waist, the same colour as his robe. Torim nodded at the gift, he knew the shop's location. 'Shortly after, I felt her.' Galen's expression grew hazy. 'And I followed her to the seers.'

'Ah.' Torim was relieved, saving Hayanil hadn't simply been a means of gaining entree into Torim's good graces. His conversation quickened, 'Followed her like a puppy eh? Well, well!'

Galen reddened deeply, which stupefied Torim. He began pottering with a herb. 'Go' He really did need to process what was happening. 'One hour.'

During the wait Galen was drawn to the sand-covered plaza where the arch priestess's bodyguards practised Atlantian self-defence. Disrobing down to a kilt, Galen lost each of his three matches. In the last bout he flinched at recalling Torim's disdain and thought: *"How did I come to this… merely by seeing her?"* His opponent slammed Galen back to his immediate situation. Another bruise.

*

On returning, Galen found Torim among the aquinoa plants. He added purple millet-like pearls to a salver containing blue, pink and red bubbles.

Torim smiled briefly, 'Let me see if I understand you correctly. I help you with this woman and, once more, I'm a priest of the great library.' Galen nodded. 'I hardly think that's reward enough for demeaning myself so.' He watched the high priest recoil. His voice came flat as a tax demand. 'I want my name cleared.'

Galen let out a breath; 'It can't be done!'

'You excel at expediency, Galen. Persuade the council.'

'The prince you insulted has massive influence. He'd never permit it.' Galen locked eyes with Torim. 'What else would satisfy you?'

Torim had suspected as much. 'To be a senior librarian again would be something. Perhaps in Yucatan province?'

Galen stared at the wall. Leafy lassos of rope-vine, symbolic umbilical cords between man and heaven, strangled it.

'Well, high priest?'

Galen felt an empathy with that wall. Turning on his heel, he departed.

On the way to his underground study, Galen's mind raced: *"If I choose to do this… Which debts to cash in? There was the favour done for the deaconess whose, much loved, companion had a roving eye. Then there was the exorcism no one else was able to achieve. And then… No! They're for the next archpriest election."* He thumped a fist onto innocent stone.

"Besides, I know why he wants the Yucatan. He plans to find the crystal library where our ancestors hid their knowledge… Why can't he wait a few lifetimes before he looks… What if he actually finds it?… He knows all the signposts to the vault…"

chapter 6

Zithia assembled with the other female temple newcomers in a cavernous hall. Several priestesses were already there. The deaconess, Ixchup, entered with a storm and a timid priestess following hard. In presence, Ixchup's exceedingly receding chin was her great frustration.

Scouring her charges with a practised eye, she stopped at Zithia's magnificent locks. *"It's that mane."* Ixchup decided. *"That's the net that has caught the high priest."* Ixchup tutted. If only she'd known Lord Galen's preferences before; Ixchup could've presented several girls to him over the years… *"Mind you, this one's hardly a girl."*

She lectured; 'All of you coming into service will be housed and kept by the temple Xalisco for the period of your stay. The benefit to you will be great.

First lesson, there is only one God. And regardless of your village superstitions, it's not the sun.' The deaconess stared at them all in turn, daring anyone to disagree. 'I'll be conducting on-the-spot quizzes regarding progress in religious instruction. Don't disappoint me.'

'This temple's priesthood numbers four thousand: novitiates, priests, deacons, high priests and the arch priestess. Deacons number thirty and high priests eight. All answer to the arch priestess.' She stared fixedly at the assembly. 'You will be respectful and obedient. My assistant has your duty allocations. Any questions?'

Zithia stepped forward. 'Deaconess, we have an afternoon free a week?'

Ixchup opened her eyes in incomprehension at this newcomer's lack of dedication. Crooking a finger, she beckoned Zithia to her. Each priestess stood motionless, waiting for the reverberating slap that would follow.

Ixchup's high-pitched snarl rose. 'Why?'

The newcomer's reply couldn't be heard. To everyone's shock Ixchup merely inclined her head and left, palm itching.

In the chapel of the Sun, deaconess Minuet directed minions.

The silver panelled walls were polished weekly. When chants and incense filled the mirror chapel, it was mesmeric. Minuet twisted out a smile. On certain nights, she hung the entire room with black veils, changing the vibration from the mirrors dramatically.

Immediately after the newcomer formalities, one of Ixchup's attendants raced to Minuet. Further inquiries were made. At mid-afternoon deacon Minuet strode through the torch lit corridors, toward her mistress's apartment. Meeting the high priestess Eten not far from the apartment door, Minuet gave her news.

'And no one knows who the interested party is?' Asked the attractive woman, her clear grey-gold eyes rapt.

'Ixchup refuses to comment, my lady.' Minuet opened the apartment door and waited.

'It must be someone royal, for such secrecy.' Eten, of superb Atlantian height, passed her attendant, 'My compliments to the high priest Augustus. Would he join me when he can.'

Entering her refuge, she lit a black incense ball. High-backed chairs, with patterned margrave fur, were scattered around. Square pillars bloomed with ferns and massive clusters of green-white hanging orchids. Eten inhaled their lemon scent while admiring her alpaca wall rug, on which indentations created a herd of line-drawn llamas. She relived seeing these very line-drawings while flying over the Alps.

In a mellow mood Eten went into her bedroom. There was a slimy cane toad on her bed, a bird in its mouth. The eyes beneath the toad's bony ridges stared at the high priestess. Eten grimaced, 'Disgusting!'

And she made to grab the warty amphibian. Dropping the rainbow parrot, it leaped onto the bed head. Carefully Eten looked at the bird, then turned side-on to the bed…growling. 'How many times do I have to tell you?' She speared the wing of the bird with two of her dagger-long claws, 'Not on the bed!' Eten flung the parrot high off her nails and through the air, with the cane toad in pursuit. 'Keep disobeying me, Venus, and I'll remove your poison glands myself!' Eten flexed her blood red claws, glaring at the enlarged glands on Venus' shoulders. His prize in his maw, Venus jumped into the highest orchids.

There was a knock on the door. Blowing parrot fluff off her hand, Eten raised her eyes quickly skywards, then down. 'I suppose I owe that idiot next door another bird.'

Minuet unlocked the door as usual. But it wasn't the neighbour. A balding man stood there, with a lovely companion on each arm. And it wasn't only his status that they came for; it was his eyes. Those knowing, luring eyes. The high priest lingered to watch their departure.

Entering, he kissed Eten's shapely hand. 'You called, my lady?' He gazed, all attention, into her striking face. One couldn't call it beautiful, but it wasn't handsome either. Eten's features were somewhere in between.

'Augustus.' The word warmly caressed.

For years they had had a quiet understanding. He liked his ladies young and Eten liked power.

'You dragged me away from arms practice.'

'Yes', she drawled, 'I heard them giggling.'

'I didn't say which arm I was practising.'

Inviting him to sit near the terrace window Eten walked past the hidden Venus who burrrrrred apologies at his mistress.

Augustus noted the coolness between the two. 'Had a quarrel?'

'Ignore him, he's in disgrace.' She drummed her nails on a side table. 'Now, have any of your noble friends been bragging about a new arrival?'

The high priest's expression lost its haze. His perfect recall of conversations that transpired when he was in his cups had frequently astonished. 'Absolutely not.' He leaned toward Eten.

'One of the new women has a patron who is determined to remain anonymous.' Calling a number, she threw a pair of llama-kid knucklebone dices. Her numbers came up. 'It must be a royal patron. I wonder. Perhaps Francis?'

Stating a figure, the high priest threw the dice. 'I'm dining out tonight. I'll send you word at morning prayers.'

'Meanwhile I'll tell Ixchup that there's another potential benefactor.' Eten spoke a number and won again.

'No using your powers.' Augustus threw. 'The arch priestess made Galen the keeper of the temple cacao farm today. As if he'll make any real use of the position.'

'I expect that's why Yin-Hsin chose him.' Eten looked at Augustus from the corner of her eyes. 'If you were archpriest you could keep that position for yourself.'

'And thereafter would follow many poor crops.' He smiled dreamily.

Augustus remembered their conversation months earlier. Eten had announced, 'My dear, how'd you like to be archpriest?'

'I wouldn't! I'm not enamoured of study, nor fasting. Do you realize how early that sort of zealot gets up each day?'

'Being that sort of zealot, I do.'

Only after much convincing had Augustus had finally decided: *"No woman could resist me; the temple treasury... mine to discretely plunder."* He'd look superb in the archpriest's jewels, while Eten wielded the power.

In truth Eten lusted after more than power... she wanted to prevent Galen from becoming archpriest. Galen and Eten were at the top of their field, magic, and Eten worried about her rival's future achievements.

*

Curiosity took Eten to the top of a small pyramid at the jungle's edge, seeking out Zithia. This pyramid, like all formal structures and pathways through the land had steps to suit an Atlantian's stride. Long steps that proved hard-going for anyone of lesser height.

Eten had heard no news, other than the reply from Zithia's patron: 'Tell him... to look elsewhere!'

The high priestess's black hair didn't stir despite the breeze. Treading up the steep pyramid Eten knew she was symbolically rising to the heavens; and was unmoved. Below, to the left was a silversmith's enclave, to the right a huge covered stone reservoir.

Snowy egrets, sleeping on the upper steps, hastily took flight. Weeding the pyramid, Zithia scanned the rush of wings and observed the high priestess's presence. Head bowed, Zithia fell to her knees at the altar room's entrance. Eten swept past Zithia into the stone hut, placing an ivory incense ball on the altar. From the corner of her eyes Zithia saw the copal ball self-ignite. Goosebumps crowded Zithia's arms.

Finished, the high priestess turned to Zithia, 'And you're?'

'No one, august lady... merely a new arrival.' Abruptly the air sizzled, which made Zithia add hastily, 'Zithia, daughter of Pacal, son of Woodrow, my lady.'

'You've entered temple service. You're a daughter of the temple now.'

Zithia bowed her head lower. The high priestess walked outside, gesturing Zithia to rise. 'Well, new arrival, what think you of all this?' In one motion Eten captured the entire city of Xalisco.

'It makes me breathless, my lady.'

'It looks impressive. Yet with every generation we lose another piece of knowledge from Atlantis.'

'I didn't know.'

'Only the higher priesthood does. The people don't pay attention to the fact that they can do less than their grandparents could.' Eten tilted her head and looked down her nose at the city. 'Our Atlantian forebears gave us the world, and it drifts through our fingers like sand.'

'But we still know how to fly.' Zithia brandished the scroll she'd already borrowed on the subject. The high priestess heard the desire in Zithia's voice.

'That's one glory we've retained.' Her tone gentled, 'You have an interest in flying?'

'Oh yes great lady. Since I experienced waking astral travel, through a guide, I think I'd sell my soul to be able to fly at will.'

'Call me... Eten!' The high priestess smiled at Zithia. 'You know the only way to true power is through the priesthood. Still it'll take you years to learn to fly, even if you have a natural aptitude.' The high priestess walked behind Zithia, around her. Lilting, 'I know a way where it could take only months, instead of years.'

"Months! only months..." thought Zithia, elated. *"To see the Sphinx, The Yellow River's cities!"*

Eten spread her web. 'There's an easier way, a more interesting path to your goal. I could teach you... help you... with your' Eten flashed her eyebrows, 'inhibitions.'

"To be wherever I want at any time... to enjoy the guided tours of the Old Nile museum..." Zithia's hungry eyes met the high priestess's.

Eten's eyes locked, her pupils boring into Zithia's soul. Deeper. Eyes widening with alarm, Zithia couldn't tear her gaze away. Deeper! Reaching Zithia's core, Eten was triumphant and so exposed a glimpse of her own spirit. Zithia's skin crawled from the vision, her body staggered hard. The contact broke. She fled the high priestess.

Eten remained motionless, gleaning the last information from their connection. Her top lip curled, she spat on the step. For Zithia was a person given to light; and dark despises light. 'And she's one I can't turn.'

*

On a plaza facing the dying sun, hundreds of priests were gathered. Eten went to the front row but before she began praying she glanced at Minuet, some rows behind. The assistant came hurrying. It was now imperative that Eten find out with whom Zithia was to be aligned in future.

After a few words, Minuet slipped quietly towards the back half of those praying. Finding Ixchup, Minuet moved to her side. 'High priestess Eten wishes someone to take a gift to Prince Francis.' The hairs running down Ixchup's spine stood on end. 'The woman Zithia.'

Ixchup goggled and then gulped, 'I've already allocated duties to her.'

'Nevertheless, this new arrival will take my lady's gift to the prince.'

'But Minuet,' Ixchup wrung her hands 'we all know that Francis never sees a lovely flower he doesn't want. It's safest to send a man.'

'Zithia. Lady Eten is sending the prince a golden corncob, with silver threads escaping the opening silver leaves.'

Sweat beaded Ixchup's brow at the thought of Zithia delivering a fertility symbol to an ever-hungry royal: *"What will Lord Galen do when he finds his flower already plucked?"*

'Unless there's some particular reason this woman shouldn't be sent?'

Ixchup's mind reeled: *"I'll end up scrapping cochineal insects off cacti, my skin permanently stained scarlet."* No one was to know, let alone Eten. She scanned the throng. 'He must never know,' one eye developed a nervous tick 'never even suspect!'

Minuet smiled at the dancing twitch. 'On my honour.' Ixchup moved her lips, but couldn't force her vocal cords to respond. Minuet squinted: *"Who could make Ixchup so… tactful, besides my own mistress?"* 'The high priestess Eten swears your protection.' Minuet reflected: *"Not that I'll bother my lady with this detail."*

Ixchup closed her eyes. 'Lord Galen.'

Minuet couldn't believe her ears. Neither could Eten.

*

Having watched Zithia's induction from a nearby dark passage, Galen returned to the old library's courtyard. Torim stood at a second storey window, pointing. A blue heron, who had lost his way, flew off. 'Veer to the left my friend, the left.' The bird changed direction.

Galen sighed. 'Which temple? As if I didn't know.'

'La Ventixa, unless your research on the crystal library suggests another city.'

'But what if you find it?'

'I don't want to rule the world, Galen.'

'Then I'll have your holy word that you will carry any La Ventixa secrets to your grave.'

'Given! In return, you'll have six months of my life."

*

The room was spacious. Sitting on the bed Zithia sank into four layers of reed matting, instead of the usual one. The water jug, for cold white tea, had been freshly filled. None in the temple drank unboiled water. A window overlooked the rare-fruit orchard, a communal retreat especially in the evenings. On each side of Zithia's terrace a Dragon-Land orange tree spread its branches, while orchid-butterflies seemingly hovered at the trees' bases. On this patio was a charcoal burner with a pottery kettle ready for the making of tea. If only Zithia had known that this favour wasn't usually achieved until one was a priest.

Galen had specified a garden view for Zithia. Albeit it had meant moving Ixchup's most attentive sycophant, who's resultant sulking looked to be permanent.

Then there were Zithia's duties. She assisted in preparation of the upper priests' dining hall for meals. Not for her the constant refilling of the great water urns or toting flasks of brewed water around the temple. Though she was being allowed to learn the art of making teas, from cakes of tea and from leaves. Uncommonly, she found she always had some free time around dusk, while each morning she helped set up the living mushroom centerpieces in the upper hall. Today's display was of cotton fluff on thin stems, plus shrimp mushrooms, all attached to a log.

Laying the high priests' table with golden plates, goblets and cutlery was hardly an onerous task for Zithia, though it was weighty. Minuet had dictated this duty, for it pleased Eten to think about Galen's secret being employed so close to him.

Days later, waiting for word from Torim proved too much for Galen. Zithia... she walked across his dreams. And when she laughed, its wraith echoed through the city to him.

Torim returned from the markets to find Galen seated at his

workbench, reading a scroll the librarian was mid-writing. An obsidian sheet, backing a fat candle, doubled the light. 'Your style lacks elegance. Far too wordy.' The high priest stabbed a line. 'I don't see where this is taking us.'

Torim went to a ladder hooked onto a heavy stand full of scrolls. He gave Galen a wide-eyed, innocent look. 'Ahh. Brother, have you really come to discuss my fiction?' He ascended the ladder, resuming cataloguing works where he'd left off earlier.

'It's been five days. I expected word within one!'

'May I remind you, Galen, that you're not speaking to a lackey now?' He tutted, 'You sound emotional dear boy. I have a herb growing outside...'

Galen stiffened. 'When do I meet her?'

'Why this unseemly impatience, my fledgling archpriest? You can't be experiencing adolescence this late in life, surely.'

The librarian's attention became diverted, as glowing fireflies sauntered in through one window and out through another.

'When?'

Torim gave his companion an amused look. 'Right now, if you stay where you are.' Galen was puzzled for a second and then he, too, heard Zithia's tread on the stones outside. 'Your robes, are they quite in keeping with the image you wish to convey?'

Galen moved in silence behind two tall scroll laden racks, mentally cloaking himself.

Torim turned to the doorway.'Zithia.' Galen closed his eyes, breathing deeply. For him, the very air was intoxicated by her presence.

Zithia opened a palm leaf, to reveal apricot coral that was a mushroom. 'From the high priests' table.'

'Obviously.'

Zithia looked into the garden below, where myriad firefly glows had created a fairyland. Tantalisingly Torim waved a papyrus concertina scroll, tied with blue ribbon. 'Poems from Atlantis.' She came to him, but he held the paper bark beyond her reach. 'Its words deserve a better surrounding than this.' Zithia's eyes lit up. 'I've forgotten the last time I fished on Lake Quetomem.' Behind the shelves Galen frowned. 'Be here an hour after dawn.'

Zithia nodded. 'I have to run. The deaconess is giving yet another of her interminable lectures.' Zithia grimaced. 'Yesterday Ixchup gave me an on-the-spot quiz, testing me on the morning's lessons. Next time I'll be able to describe all the animals it's acceptable to eat, if drained of blood.'

The second Zithia was out of earshot, Galen emerged. 'You didn't mention me.'

'You, my august lord, are going to be a surprise. Satisfied?'

'And what is she doing in the upper dining hall?'

'When you have her duties reallocated, I know she'd enjoy working in the mushroomeries.'

chapter 7

When Galen arrived at Torim's domesticated forest, in the dawn, the high priest found Torim engrossed in conversation. With his cat. A feline whose forebears had known Atlantis. Indeed the Atlantians had adored cats, almost to reverence. In atlantis, cats stood equal to the first dogs, the Dragon-Land dogs. The cat, *"… old friend; an eternal spring."*

'You're early.' The librarian threw testily at Galen; very testily.

Galen looked intently at the cat. Frowning, the cat drummed some claws.

'No.' Galen nodded at the cat, 'He's late; in every way.' Addressing the cat. 'Why are you here?'

The cat, a silver bell under his chin, thought, *"Tact! Galen, have you ever come across the word? And yes I am; in every way."* Turning to Torim, *"I'd better be off."* And while melting away, *"Remember Torim, life has been an eternal spring."*

The librarian half-smiled, then sighed heavily. 'I thought he'd always be here; looking after me.'

Galen, 'Death does tend to separate people.' Then, more heartily, 'Besides he's still checking on you.'

Galen then walked a few brisk paces, before abruptly asking, 'Do you miss being a deacon?'

Torim's gaze became focused. 'At first. Now I miss the mushrooms they serve in your dining hall.' He locked onto the simple priest's robes Galen wore. 'Suitable. Anonymous. Now peel off your costume, we're going to plant this zintli.'

Obligingly Galen dropped his outer garments on the stairs. The eight-foot mint was a revered healing plant. Galen broke the dark earth with a spade. 'I use a cherry wood shovel.'

'Greenheart wood has better psychic energy for growth.'

Galen found a disgruntled earthworm a new home. Reciting a growing chant the priests arranged the zintli in its earth.

Stretching, Galen was aware of movement. Zithia was framed in the archway. She took one long look at him, from his large eyes to his well-built chest. Torim called out, 'My dear, right on time. Ah, this is Carn, back from touring the far Alp temples.' His tone was leisurely. 'Seeing he was here, I've invited Carn to join us today. I trust you don't mind.'

Zithia's eyes widened for a millisecond, taking in Galen's washboard stomach. She thought: *"Mind, what's there to mind?"* They accompanied Torim to his fishing basket. Sitting on the handles was a sleepy cormorant, wings primly folded.

'I like to fish the old way.' With care, the cormorant attached herself to his outstretched arm.

To Zithia's surprise they walked to the city's market section. Rounding a squat warehouse across from a small pyramid, a waterway came into view, filled with canoes. This wide canal ferried merchandise into the city's heart. Torim hailed a farmer who, having delivered his produce, was returning to his chinampas. Galen arranged the return fare, drawing his cowl full over his head from habit.

Stepping aboard, his face shadowed, the high priest turned to assist Zithia into the craft. Hand halfway to his, Zithia stopped. Her heart skipped a beat while a memory tried to surface. Galen realised his mistake instantly and drew the hood from his head, revealing his face. She relaxed, taking his hand easily. The feeling in the air was gone.

Red-purple orchids with yellow patches grew in overhanging trees, their coconut scent wafted down to the canoe. Gliding through the thinning built-up areas, they came to the tree-edged lake with its far off mist-clad chinampas. Near the vast canopy of a purple-dye tree capybaras waded, eating sacred reeds. With short ears, these were hairless guinea pigs. One hundred pound web-toed guinea pigs.

Landing the canoe, the farmer promised to return before the mosquitoes. Through glass-clear water darted tiny glowing blue fish. Wading on a sunken bank out to a rock, Torim put a long lead on the cormorant. The bird perched on the stone, stretching her long neck the better to view the water.

After a few minutes the cormorant dove, submerged briefly, then exploded into flight again with a fish disappearing down her gullet. Clucking approval, Torim attached a loose neck ring. The next time the bird struck she came up with fish still in her beak, but turned her head away from Torim's hand. He cleared his throat; the bird spat the fish neatly into a basket suspended in the water. Zithia clapped her hands, but was stilled by a hard warning look from both the librarian and the cormorant.

Galen said quietly, 'You'll scare the fish.'

Soon Torim removed the neck ring and the cormorant then fed contentedly. Meanwhile Zithia was juggling with fruit and drink from a hamper. Watching her, Galen spread his hands over gathered firewood. A cheerful blaze burst forth. Zithia looked up, 'That was quick.' Galen smiled.

Burping discreetly, the cormorant stepped onto Torim's arm, dragging it down. The librarian called to Galen, 'You can carry the bird home.'

He tethered the bird on a near branch rising from the lake, where she fanned her wings wide. Bringing in the fish bag, Torim tripped. Instantly the cormorant swooped, reclaiming the librarian's prize then returned to her perch. The fish wriggled in the bird's beak. Aghast, Zithia watched tiny feet attaching themselves to the outer beak. The thing tickled the bird's chin, the cormorant bellowed a laugh and the quarry dropped. Zithia watched the feet disappear in the distance. 'What was that?'

'Lunch.' Answered Torim. 'Axolotls, a delicacy.'

'Obviously an acquired taste.' Zithia frowned. 'Where I come from, fish don't have legs!'

'What a strange place you lived in.'

'Strange or not, we're not eating those.' Taking the fish-bag to deeper water she loosed all but three fish.

'Really, Zithia, you're so fussy' Torim smiled impishly, 'anyone would think you were a high priest.' Galen glared. Axolotls were banned to the upper clergy.

Galen lay on his side during lunch, almost opposite Zithia. While they picnicked Torim recited Atlantian history from memory.

"When the Atlantians came to this land they found primitive and warring tribes, who worshipped idols. Speeding across the skies, the newcomers ended the barbarians' wars, then offered great learning to the peoples."

Not to be outdone, Galen interrupted.

"One tribe, on meeting the Atlantians chose to honour them by stabbing a youth in the heart. Thus our ancestors were introduced to human sacrifice, which they immediately forbade for the glory of the one and merciful God."

'Now that our Atlantian links are weakening there are those who want a return to that native ceremonial killing. To satisfy some barbarian bloodlust,' Torim added.

Then to clear the air, the librarian brought out his poetry scroll. 'The original of this volume is in the library of the Old Nile. It's part of the Atlantian knowledge hidden in Egypt and the Yucatan. The Sphinx sits atop our ancestors' Egyptian vault.'

Galen's look pierced Torim. 'Legend has it that in some future millennia, mankind will again be wise enough for these libraries to be revealed.'

While Torim read aloud, Zithia caught Galen gazing at her. Not twice, but several times. On the last occasion his eyes held hers for a little too long, a slow smile appearing.

Around mid-afternoon, in dappled sun, Torim dozed off. Suggesting a walk, Galen offered his hand to Zithia to aid her rising. His strong grasp enclosed her hand.

'Carn...' her hand touched the hair at her own temple. 'you have a leaf... here.' His eyes followed her pale inner wrist down to the exposed elbow. The leaf gone, Zithia unconsciously fluttered her eyelashes, and then walked on.

The high priest carefully held branches back for Zithia along the way. They avoided each other's gaze, daring only sidelong glances. Coming across macaws eating from the lake's bank, Galen came close to Zithia. 'Daily these birds consume mud to enable them to devour toxic seeds without being poisoned.'

Facing him squarely, Zithia's lips formed an 'Oh.' Their faces were only inches apart.

Not wanting her to move, he watched her pupils continue to enlarge. 'Villagers in the far Alps do the same when eating wild potatoes.'

In the silence she could hear him breathe and didn't know how to stop listening. Finally she purred, 'I didn't know that.'

Torim's dulcet voice remarked behind them, 'Not many people do.' Galen and Zithia moved apart far too quickly. 'But Carn always has that much more to offer than other people.'

*

Weeks passed. Suggesting a trip to a bottomless cenote, Galen arranged for a picnic to await them there. Torim, Zithia and Galen had a routine now. As unusual, Zithia and Galen fell well behind the librarian without really noticing. Torim was intent upon some goal, the exact nature of which he hadn't mentioned. The greenery was vibrant and fat pink orchids with small yellow lips were prolific.

Galen said, 'Did you know that many Atlantians were able to converse telepathically over short distances?'

Zithia gasped. 'But the lack of privacy! What about the extravagant wife, who wishes to pass her new dress off as purchased for half the price?'

'She'd have to think very carefully,' Galen paused, 'which indeed she should've done, before she made her purchase.'

Zithia was so engrossed in Galen that she didn't notice the jungle changing. Overhead the trees met and the lush green included grey patches. The high priest picked a long seedpod, resembling a machete, and handed it to Zithia. 'It's our source of toothpaste.' Her eyes sparkled at his showing off.

Hanging moss drifted in the eddies created by their passing. These thick grey shawls grew more dominant. Zithia stopped, peering all round. Dense grey in both directions. Zithia called out to Torim, far ahead. 'Amazing moss.'

Torim unfolded a cloth and pointed upwards with his staff. 'It's even thicker up there. But it isn't moss.'

'Then, what is it?' Zithia put her hand out to a misty drift. Fine strong strands tightened on her fingers.

'Spider web.'

Her own brain had come to the same conclusion. Flinching, her eyes dragged themselves away from the lace sticking her fingers together. Scrubbing the web off onto the machete pod, she looked at Torim. He was pulling down a dense mat of web with his staff. The hairs on the back of her neck stood on end. When she detected actual spiders, her brain clamoured: *"Thousands!"* And seized up.

Torim prattled on.

'Carn!' Seeing Zithia's quick, shallow panting, Galen instantly cut off her view. But she didn't raise her face to his; spiders and webs etched themselves upon her retinas.

'Zithia.' No response. He shook her hard. 'Zithia, look at me!' Slowly her eyes met his. 'That's better,' he supported her with an arm around her small waist. 'We're leaving!'

As she tottered on, he fanned his spread fingers before her eyes and an image appeared. A river; a jaguar sitting on the river bank. The great cat flicked his tail across still water. Again and again, till a fish leapt after his line, to be caught on claws. The scene continued.

Finally Galen turned Zithia's chin and she beheld vivid green. 'Nothing here except trees.' Seating her on a fallen log, Galen rubbed warmth back into her icy hands.

'Was that telepathy?'

'A lesser form of it.'

Torim sauntered up to them. 'What happened to you two?'

Galen's face hardened. 'Old friend, before taking someone into a web tunnel, first inquire if they happen to like spiders.'

'Zithia, my dear! How very…' his brow wrinkled, 'awkward of you. It'll take us twice as long to get to the cenote now.'

Galen insisted Zithia lean against him until they reached the waterhole. Discovering the picnic basket near the fifteen-foot wide cenote opening, the high priest settled Zithia on a rug. Her gaze fell modestly, then irrepressibly, down to Galen's thighs, then far down to the cenote's sun-shafted aquamarine water. Zithia's eyes glistened when Galen proffered some high tequila. Torim put his hand out expecting a cup to come his way. Galen didn't see him. The librarian raised his eyebrows, before helping himself.

During lunch Zithia blushed when Galen caught her glancing quickly at him. Looking away, she fetched a fungus-risen damper from the shade.

Contemplating her, Torim volunteered, 'Zithia told me a very bitter story about being deserted by her soul mate.' The high priest picked up a golden pear-shaped fruit Torim had brought. 'My dear Carn, I neglected my trees this year. Beware you don't bite, to find a wasp within.' Galen inhaled the fruit's scent, then savoured the flavour.

Returning, Zithia was sufficiently recovered to be playful. Cutting the heavy loaf, peppered with gamey mushrooms, she handed a piece to Galen. Their hands touched. Electricity! 'Speaking of gossip,' Zithia's words rushed out, 'I hear we'll see a new archpriest in the nearer future.'

Torim smiled at Galen. 'And what is said about the contenders for the post, the very honourable high priests?'

Zithia grinned. 'Oh, they're set up as examples of all the virtues. Though several are only as Atlantian as they need to be. Then there's Lord Galen and…', shuddering, 'the Lady Eten! They're reputed to be carved stone, though I'm sure they'd prefer to be considered carved emeralds!' Galen changed the subject.

After having delivered Zithia back to the rare fruit orchard, Galen and

Torim walked together. The high priest stated, 'She hears too much.'

'What do you expect. The temple seethes with gossip.' The librarian pointed to a scroll in their hamper. It was the subject of high temple protocol. 'And you can't expect her to be disinterested when you give her this rubbish to read. That's the third scroll on protocol. One could suspect you to be grooming Zithia for greater things, brother.' Torim smiled at his own jest, expecting Galen to icily refute the suggestion. When no response was forthcoming, Torim stared hard and long at the high priest.

*

Xiao Chen hung a golden hairpin on an inverted silver-wire basket. The latticework tracked the heavenly bodies across this year's sky. Looking up from blue-moon
computations, Galen examined the delicate ornament. A golden sunrise, with an emerald eye suspended beneath it and petite green quexatl feathers dangling from the emerald.

'One pays for an original design.' The truth-sayer poured himself a drink. 'How long is it since you gave jewellery?'

'I really don't remember.' Galen admired the elegant workmanship.

Xiao Chen's voice was monotone. 'You're neglecting your duties.'

'Only minor ones.'

This was true. 'What about your mystic development?' He'd hit the mark. Disdain flickered, 'For a woman!'

Galen's nostrils flared, 'Not just a woman; she's the partner of my life.'

Xiao Chen sat down hard. And after time, 'What are you going to do?'

'Whatever I have to.'

*

Ixchup had sent Zithia to the lower markets. To one side of the bazaar a line of hooded priests walked single-file, wearing long beige capes. A man avoided the advancing line. A voice at Zithia's shoulder said, 'They've been fasting,' Zithia jumped, 'to reach a higher spiritual plane. It's forbidden to touch them, for that pulls them down to the world.'

'Carn, what are you doing here?'

'On my way to a temple duty. You?'

'A fool's errand. Ixchup wants a two-headed snake, and from this market.' She added dryly, 'She must be watching temple money.'

'Well then, let's see what we can find.'

They smiled warmly, walking slowly, passing two women who were examining reed mats. A thin matron declared, 'The nerve of the man. An exorcist! In my house.' She jabbed her finger at the air, 'I told him, over my dead body.' She riffled through a pole of garish dried leaf saucer-hats. 'He insisted his mama live with us, when alive.' She tried on a yellow saucer, her face a question mark. Her friend grimaced, the matron swept it off. 'Well, I want her living us now she's dead.' Moving on, she picked up and handed some small pearls to a vendor. 'We get on so much better since she died.' Receiving them back crushed, the matron rubbed her stomach, 'For my indigestion.'

Zithia had also stopped in front of the pearls, but there wasn't one that made her heart flutter. Putting a hand on Zithia's elbow, Galen steered her toward a leaves-seller. No fear of recognition here, in a place he hadn't known existed a day ago.

Obnil, a short man, sat on a herb-filled sack. On a mat and in rough baskets were dried and powdered goods. 'Hair tonic just received from the Dragon-Land,' he called. Only recently had inches of thick hair circled the base of the merchant's skull. This personal miracle had trebled his clientele of aging males, who eagerly purchased the flowery liquid responsible. 'Newly arrived,' he repeated. As usual, men's servants came bustling.

Smiling, Obnil handed catuaba to a customer. Mentally reciting: *"Before fifty a man's child is his own, after that any baby is catuaba's."*

Hanging from a rod were various snake-skins. Obnil held aloft one with vibrant blue, green and yellow scales. He hailed all, 'A more potent cure-all I've never seen. Only look at the colours!'

The merchant cocked an eye at Galen. And soon he was presenting Zithia with... 'a two-headed serpent. Its large tail markings are like the head of a dangerous snake. When threatened, it hides its own head while raising its tail menacingly.'

'Really.' Zithia's voice echoed tinkling bells.

Moving through the stalls Zithia noted that the feathers were dyed. Touching cloth she wrinkled her nose, the fabric was stiff with cactus fiber. Even the pectorals were gold plate with copper beads.

Galen handed Zithia an agave-fiber bundle. Beaming, she unwrapped the sixteen golden hairclips. Her mouth half-open, she reached to stroke them, but then drew her hand away.

'Carn, I'll not accept such an expensive gift.'

Galen picked one up; her gaze followed the beautiful clip. 'They must be better copies than I thought.' He slid a comb into her curls. 'Remember, here much isn't what it seems.' Zithia's eyes spoke her thanks, 'I'm on my way to the temple cocoa farm. Come with me.'

Zithia wasn't expected back until nightfall. She held Galen's gaze, 'Maybe Torim would like to join us?'

'Do you need a chaperone?' A slight smile in his eyes. 'Besides, Torim has no interest in money.'

The high priest hailed a pair of public chairs to take them to the city's limits. There, stopping before two stele, they alighted.

While Galen paid the bearer, Zithia read aloud the title on one great stone tablet. 'The archpriest Shao-Sheng.' The skin a faint yellow hue, a long silver beard framed his flattish face. She turned to the almost-complete, second stele. Here the features were a male version of Yin-Hsin. 'When I entered the city this stone was a blank. It's marvelous.'

'I'll pass on your compliments.' Galen's voice was deadpan.

Zithia whirled around, playfully bowing her head, 'Please do.' Thus she missed the foreman, who having seen Galen, clapped his right hand to over his heart. It was due to Galen's own rigorous timetable that the artisans were working unexpectedly late.

'It's well done.' Galen stated in a carrying voice, slightly inclining his head to the foreman. 'I'm sure a bonus is in order if it's finished on time.' The sounds of hammer strokes trebled.

Galen led Zithia on. 'The location of the cacao orchid is secret.' He unfurled a blindfold and covered Zithia's eyes.

'And pray tell me why you don't need a blindfold.'

He whispered in her ear, 'Because I'm a very important person.' He helped her up a step into a high priest's chair. A gilded conveyance, intricately carved, with silk cushions. Galen took up a shortened, gold staff of office.

Being carried at shoulder height, Galen leaned over and plucked blossoms from passing branches. On their arrival the bearers immediately withdrew with the chair, while Galen purposely fumbled with Zithia's blindfold. When Zithia opened her eyes, Galen's arms circled her waist with a rope of purple, yellow-flecked winding orchids. Her eyes dazzling, they walked toward the head gardener.

Seeing them approach, this guardian muttered to another, 'Lord

Galen's note stated to treat him as any common priest.' The headman waited for them to reach him, 'So we won't leave the high priest alone for a moment. With each cacao fruit holding fifty beans, weeks of wages, he'd expect no less.'

Galen bowed his head to the gardener. 'I was told a tour of the farm has been arranged.'

'My lord...'

'Carn.' Galen offered this guardian a jar of waterfly eggs. Caviar. He was overwhelmed to have been thought of. Galen introduced Zithia.

They were in a clearing where peanuts grew and the local partridges foraged. Beyond these, in a gully, was a stand of chocolate trees shaded by wild-sewn hardwoods. On each money-tree, red cantaloupes grew from the tree-trunks. Going around the plantation, the guardian found a ripe fruit. His knife followed a dark rib from top to bottom, revealing tight clusters of white beans, each covered in a thick creamy butter layer, sheltered within the orange flesh. Zithia had rarely enjoyed an outing more. To see money growing, the chance meeting with Carn, and that rapt attention the priest gave her. Her smile came to her all afternoon. It was only when they were being carried homeward, she realised that she'd been happy. Quite happy, all afternoon. She'd forgotten.

*

A light was on when the high priest returned to his apartment. Xiao Chen was reading.

'And did you seduce this one with Atlantian endearments?' Galen fell into a chair. 'Was it entirely appropriate to take this woman on your first official visit to the cacao farm?'

'The occasion promised to be a pleasant one for her, and it was.' Xiao Chen let his scroll roll shut, with a snap. 'Thank you for arranging full witnesses rather than novices to carry my chair today.'

'Well, we can't have anyone revealing...the cacao farm, now can we?' Truth-sayers, being trained in silence as well as witnessing, were often called upon to be bearers.

chapter 8

The season had definitely changed. Zithia awoke one crisp morning for the treat she had promised herself, remembering Torim's words, 'It's an ancient Atlantian steam bath, beyond our technology. So fond were they of cleanliness, it was the first thing they built.' She followed deep rough-cut steps down to the small entrance of the cave. At the opening runnels of cooling water ran over sloping ground to distant greenery. A vine crawled across a tree thick with salmon, trumpet flowers. Between the flowers the vine's deer-eye seeds peered soulfully at the world.

Zithia looked about for the bath attendant, who was absent. Zithia noted the upside-down cup on the door's right, indicating a man was already in the bath. She flipped a cacao bean into a slot in the rock, as payment. Then she turned a cup on the left wrong-way up. Pushing aside the heavy curtain, Zithia entered an antechamber with changing stalls.

Barefoot and sarong clad she opened another barrier into the steam room. Through the haze she could barely make out the roof high above. Low marble benches ran around the room's perimeter. A shallow water-trench ran parallel between the bench and the wall. The Atlantian architects had funneled the heat from large fires into a man-made cavity behind these walls. Relaxing, Zithia sat.

At the far end of the gallery the other occupant had recently thrown water on the wall, for a dense fog was developing. Neither could see the other. The man was aware of Zithia's form, nothing more. He was about to say the bath was shut to the public that morning. Then he changed his mind. More water splashed into mist. Taking off his sarong, a short kilt was now his only garment.

At the movement Zithia looked towards her companion for the first time. The man's shape dissolved into the steam. Then, without warning, she sensed him.

Effervescence, golden tumult, as on that day back at the harbour five years before. She swayed, dizzy, 'I'm imagining things.' It came again, a knowing of her soul mate. A weeping, wordless joy lifted her. In a micro-flash the scene of parting, before they were born, possessed her.

'What about Carn?' Her mind clamoured protests. 'No, no attachment can compete with the other half of my heartbeat.'

Pure love surged forth from Zithia, snapping the man's eyes open. He threw another jar of water on the wall, before Zithia's love took his breath away. Galen lay back, 'What's done is done.'

Slowly she came on, a tremulous bride. 'I'd given you up.'

His telepathic answer came clearly. *"Lately I've been near you all the time."*

Her mounting joy took him heavenward. With astral memories spinning before him, Galen's spirit responded in kind. Their auras glowed golden. He telepathed: *"By the one God, how you touch me."*

Barely one step apart, their physical bodies were still only blurs. Zithia knelt on one leg beside Galen, unable to utter a word.

The mists were dissipating. She looked into Galen's familiar face, 'Oh Carn, it's you!' Tears spilled, 'I've come to have feelings for you.' Blushing at her own perceived infidelity. 'I didn't know why.' She traced his jaw-line.

Galen's smile faded as he watched the inevitable happen. Her eyes lost that love-light and became a stare. She sat back on her heels, 'Carn?' She stood up, 'Carn!!' Why didn't I know you?'

Sitting up, he mentally cloaked himself. 'I was afraid.'

And he was simply Carn once more, not her soul mate. Zithia gaped at him, thinking: *"Hidden. He hid from me. Me!"* Images escaped Galen's memory and flickered between them. *"Galen leading his first ritual atop a pyramid... the Magi Davot with him when he doused a fire using an ancient chant... being introduced by Yin-Hsin to two visiting eminences..."* Zithia shook.

Rapidly Galen uncloaked his inner self again. Anew they were connected, yet she was stony, 'Afraid for your career?' She remembered Galen's reaction on his temple barge so long ago, 'I suppose you always were.' She tried to take a breath. Nothing happened and her eyes widened in panic. Galen placed a hand upon her chest, instantly she was able to draw in air. He removed his hand.

Galen's voice was husky base, 'Listen, please!' She half turned from him.

'You left me.'

'I was a deacon.'

'You were my soul mate.' She turned to him.

'And you were married before I had even returned to Xalisco!'

'What?' Her look was contemptuous, 'You were about to sail back to me? Oh my gracious lord, if only I had known.'

The report on Ilt was still fresh in Galen's mind. 'Your husband, a childhood sweetheart was he?'

She recoiled, then glowered, 'Did you think I'd stay virgin all my life, simply because you rejected me?'

'No, but I expected you to show some taste in the choosing of a mate.'

She gasped: "*Torim*." Yet stated, 'I was born to be with you and you betrayed me.' Zithia's arm swung in an arc, landing Galen a stinging blow to the face. 'You promised we'd be together.' Another slap, a backhander.

Regal, remote, Galen he stood. His knuckles touched one stinging cheek. 'That day at the harbour, it was a peasant's soul that sang to me. Did you really expect me to be pleased?'

She was sprung tight to pounce. Then suddenly she thundered away from him. 'Zithia!' The word a searing plea.

Wheeling round, 'Priest, we met here by accident. Hide yourself again; I vow I'll not find you.' She was gone. Groaning, Galen lay down again... falling into darkness.

*

It was twilight and Torim was riffling through numerous small scrolls for a botanical description he was eager to re-read. A pale Galen stalked in from the second-storey verandah fronting the building. Torim continued scanning the rattlesnake pleides star system while the high priest asked, 'What did she say?'

'My dear boy, no woman likes to find that she comes second, especially to ambition.'

'I told her the truth.'

Putting the drawing aside. 'In this case the truth may have been better left unsaid.'

'How can the truth ever be better unsaid.'

Torim eyed him, 'Phantom, cease your possession of the fledgling archpriest.'

'Possession indeed! The very air glows with her presence.' Galen rubbed throbbing temples. 'What now?'

'Nothing.'

'Nothing?'

Torim shrugged, 'She rather blames you for her first husband.'

'I didn't even know her then.'

'Exactly her point, brother.'

Galen paced the line between a corridor of fig bark scrolls. Various parchments tossed themselves into the air in his wake. Concertinaed scrolls broke their bonds violently, becoming jack-in-a-boxes on their shelves. A paint jar spontaneously combusted; Torim smothered the flame. 'Now that's enough! I'll not have my beloved library incinerated just because you can't control yourself, high priest.'

Galen stared out the window.

'Forget about her.'

'I can't!'

'She won't see you and there's an end to it.'

Galen's world became desolate. Closing his eyes, they moved rapidly back and forth until... 'She'll see me.' He opened tranquil eyes on Torim. 'The flight festival is held soon, up on Cochilat mountain. You'll invite Zithia to accompany you.'

Expressionless, Torim exhaled deeply. 'That's your last command of me, high priest.'

*

On the festival morning thousands walked in stars' light, adorned in their best feathers from headdresses, to loincloths to sandals. Torches ten-foot tall lit the way until second-light. Torim and Zithia arrived at a deep, wide ravine with white water below. There were two bridges for crossing, but neither was yet finished. Waiting, watching the work, Zithia suddenly began to grin. Then to grin more widely. For the sun held no taint of sorrow for her father, and memories came softly as smiling friends. Now all that was left of mourning was love remembered.

Zithia stayed quiet, wrapped in sweet contentment, while Torim was eager to chat on about irrelevancies. 'It's an annual competition among the mountain range's villages. The first one to complete their rope overpass is declared the keeper of the region's bridges. Yesterday, ropes were pulled across the gap.' He pointed at stone anchors. 'Once cables were secured, the building began in mid-air.' Harried men laid golden reed floors, and then wove close knit half-walls.

A stall sat between the two U-shaped bridges. Metallic chrysalid colours flashed, the vendor shouting, 'Scarabs, all the way from the cloud forests, ready to take your messages to heaven.'

Torim walked to the tree on which hung tiny reed cages of iridescent jeweled beetles. 'I'll buy you one.' He chose a glistening ruby red specimen and Zithia a silver beetle with blue markings. A man buying a golden scarab, the most expensive of beetles, slapped Torim on the back. 'Xing.' Torim smiled broadly. 'Zithia, this is an old friend.' Creases fractured Torim's brow, 'And Xing, this is the daughter I never asked for, Zithia.'

Xing, 'Tomorrow I'll return your book.'

'I've a scroll in Atlantian, on silk as the Atlantians preferred, that you haven't read in this lifetime.'

'The work feels familiar?'

'Like a jasmine scented breeze.'

Xing, all smiles, to Zithia, 'We've been swapping written material for a thousand years. Once it was crystals, always silk.' He wagged a finger at Torim, 'See you tomorrow.'

Black smoke exploded high in the sky, announcing that the competition had been won elsewhere. Soon, walking in single file, Torim and Zithia began crossing their golden bridge. They were relatively alone.

'Zithia, I wasn't always a simple priest.' Watching golden threads strain beneath her feet, Zithia clutched her parasol of curling pipe feathers more tightly. 'No, once I was a lordly deacon.'

'A deacon!?' Her eyes grew round, but her hand insisted on gripping the rail. 'Which section?'

'The great library was mine. I had everything. There's even a book in the Old Nile Library donated in my name.'

'Who could want more?'

'No one. Yet, my reputation for a subtle, caustic wit was a point of pride. Often I indulged myself using this talent. In so doing I lost it all.' Torim dropped a feather flower into the void. 'Now, I can't enter the great library.' She grasped his hand. 'I no longer debate works from Atlantis. No future scholars call me mentor. All lost to arrogance!' Zithia's expression matched his sorrow.

'A lifetime ban?' The lines on his face deepened visibly. 'Oh, that's too harsh. Can't you have the decision softened?'

'In seven years I've been offered only one opportunity to change my situation.' She looked him a query, but he was silent. *"Well,"* he thought: *"I've now done all I can to preserve our friendship."*

Arriving at their destination, they ascended a steep slope. She took in other mountains and dozens of golden bridges crossing ravines. Their own peak rose behind and above them, while the vast grassy festival area ended in a sheer drop. Lengthy ribbons flapped a vibrant warning near the edge. The crowd was a prattling migration of rainbow birds.

Flyers were selling trips. Well beyond the gusting wind, a more dangerous form of flying took place. A hundred-foot pole rose, topped by a square frame where a man stood beating a drum. Four brightly dressed flyers, ropes attached to their legs and the drummer's frame, circled the pole to the ground, performing aerial ballet.

At the jungle, children freed butterflies and adults whispered to scarab beetles. Wordlessly Torim pulled a string. His tiny cage collapsed outwards, startling his living ruby into flight. Nor did Zithia whisper, though her eyes followed her jewel with longing.

Torim presented the flyers' drink, raw eggs and grated imported carrot. 'May you see both in dark and light.' He toasted Zithia with the watcher's wish.

Several high priests were lunching with the rich, whose wealth was displayed in the intricate designs of their feather capes and dresses. Peregrine, Eten and Augustus dripped with blue quexatl feathers. Eten commented to the merchant host, 'Yin-Hsin looked a little peaked this week.' They scanned the crowd.

The man approached Peregrine. 'Our arch priestess isn't here today. Pressures of state?'

Poker-faced, Peregrine thought: *"As if I'd admit to you that she felt too weak to make the journey."*

The emerald-mine owner signaled; a drift of butterflies was released. 'I still can't believe my finest gems are at the bottom of the sea.'

Peregrine remembered: *"The contract signed, delivery accepted, but not yet paid for… my entire fortune and then some."* His smile faded over-fast, 'I've convinced Yin-Hsin to reconsider her decision about increasing the tax on emerald mining.' *"That should hold my creditors."*

'My lord; always the champion.'

A cloth-of-gold marquee demanded attention, with flowers strewn from the entrance to the cliff's face. Pan pipes began a haunting lilt and the crowd settled. Stringed instruments, made by Dragon-Land masters, chimed in causing the spirits to rise ever higher. Masked, a high priest left the tent, a falcon on his arm. The ritual mask of jade oblongs and gold completely hid his face.

Zithia shaded her eyes. 'Which high priest is it?'

'The great Lord Galen himself.'

'Oh! I haven't seen him yet.'

Absent-mindedly Torim commented, 'Are you sure?'

Watching the high priest's progress, Zithia leaned her hand on her cheek. Deja vu?

He trod the flowered path to the very edge of the cliff, paused and then...strode beyond. A murmur broke out. The falcon was being loosed. Facing his audience, the high priest slammed his long golden staff onto a rock for silence. Projecting his voice he intoned, 'We thank the one God for good flights this last year. No travellers were lost to lightning, no evil spirits followed watchers back to their bodies.' He opened his arms wide. The breeze gusted. 'We pray to the one who sees all, that he'll continue to bless flyers in the coming year.'

All assented devoutly.

"Now who does he remind me of?" Zithia wondered.

Feeling the wind behind him reach its full-strength, the high priest beckoned to the sky. 'We beseech you, oh God; show us that you hear our plea.'

Zithia let out a gasp. A huge purple serpent's head had violently shot up... above the high priest. Its green body, with a crimson belly, then roared into view. Simultaneously gongs and drums blasted. She smothered a giggle; the monster wasn't real.

'Kites!' She laughed. 'You could've warned me.' Previously she'd only seen death kites, flown at important people's funerals. The rippling serpent was twelve linked, silk kites with tiny yellow scattered wings.

The serpent's bearded head descended to within inches of the high priest. 'People of Xalisco, our great ancestors flew even as the feathered serpent flies. They travelled in ships as well as in their minds. Though we can't physically cross the skies, astral flight continues to allow us to share knowledge. Therefore we celebrate this blessed gift.'

Zithia dragged her eyes from the dragon to the high priest. She did know his voice. The high priest was staring fixedly at her. He bowed and then slowly lowered his mask. Zithia's eyes clouded briefly, and then she was seeing stars. To general applause Galen returned to the marquee.

Zithia began to follow him as in a dream. Unaware of near misses between herself and the preoccupied party-goers. Thinking: "Carn... What a ridiculous coincidence. No... it's not!... Torim!" Three steps on, she twirled around sharply and marched back to Torim, stabbing an index finger at him. 'You!'

'Could have warned you?' He look was mild, 'Yes.'

'You... Later!'

Unnoticed beneath the merchant's canopy, Eten saw Zithia's rigid stride. Gathering Augustus's eyes, Eten moved her head in Zithia's direction. 'I like her look today,' smiled the high priestess, observing Zithia's clenching unclenching fists.

A corner of Augustus's mouth curved upward. 'I thought Galen was wooing this one incognito.'

'Obviously without his status,' Eten's eyelids hooded her eyes, 'his charms failed to produce the required result.'

Zithia passed the guards at the tent's opening. Galen stood waiting with his spirit cloaked. Thus he was both Galen and Carn, resplendent in headdress and costume. The staff of office rested against a throne of a chair, an unnecessary golden frippery Xiao Chen had sent. Zithia's mind spun: *"This can't be... Carn, the alabaster high priest!... How good he looks... Carn!... What arrogance... The temple's favourite son..."*

'You wanted to see me,' Her eyes were unblinking, 'Lord Galen!' He gave a courtly bow. 'And yet, you cloak yourself.' The whites beneath her glaring eyes increased.

'It gives you the chance to be objective.'

'I'll not speak with the high priest, I'll speak with my soul mate.'

'I fear the two are inextricably intertwined. Nevertheless...' He uncloaked his soul. It took her breath away. 'Zithia, in the time before birth you said, "life can get in the way." It did.'

He offered her orange flavoured tea. She gave one shake of her head. Galen added simply, 'One day I'll be archpriest!'

Glaring, 'And where does that leave me?'

Unconsciously he raised a closed hand, turned it over and spread his fingers.

Zithia winced, eyes liquid with unshed tears. 'As you wish, high priest.'

Instantly he knew he'd never see her again. He should've been pleased. Instead Galen cut off her exit. 'Live with me.' A deep need of her, devotion, burdened his face. 'Share my status, my life!'

A smile lit her countenance. Outrage replaced it, for he'd made no reference to matrimony. 'Be your concubine?'

'I've never honoured another with this proposal.'

'And neither do you honour me by it.'

'But I'm a high priest, I can offer no more!' Frowning, 'And as high priest, even without marriage, a soul mate is … inconvenient.'

'Inconvenient?' Keeping eye contact, she raised her chin high. 'As it was in heaven, let it be thus again.' He shook his head. 'Marry me.' Zithia's pupils became pinpricks. 'Personally, I'm stunned I still want you.'

'Not such a surprise lady. After all, I'm a high priest. No… I cannot marry.

'And I can't not!'

'Zithia, have you forgotten that the word wife means "one who is the owner of a man?" An archpriest may only be owned by the mysteries.'

'Then don't be archpriest.'

His head reared back, the suggestion was beyond belief. Yet he wanted her. 'Even a high priest would have a difficult time explaining a wife.' She clenched her teeth. 'Perhaps a compromise?' She leaned toward him, though her look was sceptical. 'We could become friends, dear friends.'

'Friends? Soul mates; just friends?!' She was horrified: *"My God, I'm considering it."* He cupped her face in his hands and kissed her lips. Pure euphoria.

'Platonic friends, with only a kiss between us.'

Zithia protested softly, 'My Lord,' But his lips were, once more, a lingering persuasion. When he finally released her, they were both gasping. Her only remaining thought was: *"I live to love him."*

Galen's now smoky eyes enveloped her. 'Friendship is the best we can do…at the moment.'

Zithia trembled against his chest, their golden spirits entwining, until the thought of disengaging was a mortal wound. *"How I've pined for this"* she thought.

'If I could do more at present, my lady, I would.'

Her breasts heaved, 'At present?'

For a third time his lips closed on hers. He caressed her neck, she longed for more. *"Perhaps…"* she wondered, needing their physical closeness. Instantly her mind reeled: *"To be disgraced… and by my soul mate."* Therein lay madness. *"But to leave... to free them both..."* Their spiritual joining had been too complete; she must have him in her life somehow. 'Friends then.'

He smiled enigmatically. With his handsome features and status as good as a prince, no woman he'd wanted had ever denied him long. 'Now that's settled, I can't have you living where you are.'

'It was good enough before.'

'It's not good enough for the friend of a high priest. I'll arrange an apartment on my own floor.'

'But everyone will think we're...' She blushed.

'No.' He brushed at a stray tendril of hair. 'Concubines never live in the high priests' building. Their quarters are in the complex opposite.'

Her mouth fell open: *"Did he understand what she'd agreed to?"* She pushed him away, feeling an almost physical pain as their bodies parted. 'Carn... I mean, Galen...'

'You'll love the view.'

'Lord Galen, I fear you've mistaken my meaning.'

A young priest entered the tent, for every two steps forward he shuffled on-the-spot. 'My Lord Galen?... the concluding formalities?... The novice flyers await your blessing!'

Galen, his eyes locked with Zithia's, waved a hand in the priest's direction. He fled.

Zithia's smile was hard, 'I've named my terms, Galen, I'll keep to them. '

'What classes do you wish?'

'Flying.'

Galen put on his headdress, 'Not flying,' He walked to the entrance, 'you're not ready.' And he was gone.

Eten and Augustus observed the confidence radiating from Galen when he left. Shortly, the tent opened again to reveal Zithia in a daze, eyes unfocused. Augustus smirked, 'How interesting.'

'Our dear brother Galen appears to be... in danger.' Eten's face lit up, 'Yes, great danger.'

chapter 9

The next day a priest showed Zithia to her new quarters, a novice carrying her possessions. Leaving Zithia in the corridor outside Galen's apartment, the priest went to Xiao Chen. 'Deacon truth-sayer, the Lady Zithia is here.'

Xiao Chen thought: *"Lady indeed."* He examined a sitting llama ornament, 'Thank you.' He sat down, 'Send in the little girl and her family whose appointment was set a week ago.'

'But my lord, the lady is waiting... and the child's issue will take time...'

Calmly Xiao Chen inspected his fingernails. 'Bring them in.'

A four year old entered, with parents, having passed Zithia in the hallway. With great command the freckled girl announced, 'My name's master Randolph.'

Mama, 'Deacon Xiao Chen, she's been like this for weeks. She refuses to be called by her name. Such a nice name too, Julia.'

'But it isn't my name Deacon.'

'Really?' Xiao Chen asked, and lowered his head to the girl's, looking deep into her eyes.

Xiao Chen watched just outside the child's outline, both sides and above. Seeing the aura grow in size, then shrink down again, he asked, 'Show me the ribbons of your past.'

The aura doubled in size, then trebled, things being revealed and then folded away again. 'You have remarkable control. A control not usually seen without training.'

'I told you, I'm master Randolph.'

'Yes, and I see the problem.' He smiled, a deep conspiratorial smile which enveloped the girl. 'Now... if you could choose any name you liked, other than Randolph, what would it be?'

Without delay the girl replied, 'Ariadne.'

Her mother gasped, 'But... that's the other name we were considering calling her.'

Father, 'And we never told her that name.'

"Xiao Chen, 'Ariadne it is. Your parents will officially change your name.'

The attendant who'd accompanied Zithia and had been standing near the closed door, plainly showed his relief at the interview's conclusion. Catching his eye, Xiao Chen continued slowly, 'Not a difficult problem. Now the one I saw,' the attendant's face was frozen dismay, 'the other day... A seven year old at an antiquities exhibition suddenly reverted back a thousand years. And still demands to taken home to Atlantis. Nothing can be done. He must've touched several objects that meant a lot to him in that life. Not, of course, that they were his in that life.'

As time had expanded, Zithia had paced a little, hand on hip. Then she'd paced a lot. Finally the truth-sayer appeared from Galen's doorway. 'Welcome Zithia.' His eyes looked at a spot behind her.

'Ah, deacon Xiao Chen.' Her eyes lasered, 'Leader among witnesses. You grace me with your presence.'

Xiao Chen inclined his head and he walked on. 'This way. All is prepared for you.' They passed a doorway, well-nigh opposite Galen's. 'My apartment.'

He stopped at the next portal. Looking at the three entrances, Zithia's cheeks reddened. The cedar door opened, revealing a gorgeous woman.

'This is Esontair, your attendant.'

Zithia smiled at Esontair's come-hither mouth, with its full top-lip an inviting bow.

'I chose a truth-sayer for the position. A witness's word will still any gossip.'

'So long as the truth is credible.' Zithia smiled, 'Which it is.'

Xiao Chen went to the balcony, followed by the chamberlain, Madison. Zithia adjusted a silver wall-mirror and rearranged the silk cushions padding a built-in lounge shelf. Watching her, Xiao Chen noticed she looked prettier than before. Even Esontair looked better, a thing incomprehensible given the perfection of the proportions of her face. Narrowing his eyes, the witness thought: *"It's the reflection from the pink ceiling that's doing it. It'll be painted avocado green tomorrow."* Quietly he gave Madison instructions.

Zithia joined him; they both looked at Esontair. 'Do I threaten you that much, master-witness?'

His eyes registered scorn. 'We share the same balcony.'

Brightly, 'Then a line of trees will prove the perfect addition.' She gestured to their common boundary. 'There!'

Madison looked to Xiao Chen for direction. 'Yes, a line of trees would look well. Dragon-Land magnolias.'

Zithia, nibbled part of her bottom lip, 'A double row would be better for feng-shui.'

Madison hadn't taken his eyes off Xiao Chen, who nodded once.

Zithia breathed in the reaching view. Blue ribbons divided parks, tiny fields and residential compounds. Immediately Xiao Chen walked back to the doorway, all round which grew a white flowered rope vine. 'If you have questions, simply ask Esontair. Good day, Galen is meeting me for lunch.'

Xiao Chen spoke to Esontair, also at the doorway. 'Tell the treasury to send up jewellery to match each new gown.'

'That won't be necessary, Esontair. Having Lord Galen's friendship, I need no further splendour.'

Much later, Galen entered the apartment. Zithia and her attendant were considering gown designs. Taking in Esontair, the high priest was mindful his glance fell only down to her neck. He thought: *"Xiao Chen my old friend, I asked for company for Zithia not a comparison to her."*

Zithia watched Galen's reaction. 'We'll finish tomorrow, Esontair. You may retire.' The attendant bowed low to the high priest, passing close by him. Zithia flashed her eyebrows. 'She's a truth-sayer … quite remarkable, don't you think?'

'I don't know her reputation as a witness.' He gave Zithia a hungry look. 'Her eyes will never have your lustre.'

Zithia's head moved down and away, lashes resting on her cheeks. *"Highly inappropriate"* she thought, wishing Xiao Chen had been within earshot. 'Friends!' *"Friends."* She clung to that. *"It must be possible."*

'Come.' He smiled. 'I've wanted to show you something for weeks.' Taking a deep breath, Zithia put her thoughts aside.

They were in a library within the great library. Scrolls, worn from handling, abounded. Zithia commented dryly, 'The inner sanctum.' Deacons, plus a high priest were perched on tall stools reading intently from tomes on individual chest-high bookstands. 'They didn't let me in, last time I was here.'

At one stand Galen opened a two-foot long edition. 'A scroll of quotes, including a few on Atlantis. This one is of real interest.' He translated,

"When Atlantis was at its finest, it was a grand, broad continent. Then the bones of the earth moved and broke the entire eastern edge off our land, First Atlantis. Thereafter, only one city remained. On a large island surrounded by sea where, days before, meadows had abounded. That precious land closest to the island now called Atlantis, was once First Atlantis, Atlantis prime. Therefore, it's beloved of all Atlantians and we keep it for our sole use always."

Then he recited in the original Atlantian. There was romance in every word, every nuance.

'When can I read such books?'

'The sanctum is at your disposal, once you learn Atlantian.' He switched to Atlantian. 'Dearest friend.' Again translating. She glowed.

'I start today.'

Going to a grand stairwell at the hall's end, they descended several levels. Librarians and novices puffed past them, both ways, carrying scrolls or salt blocks.

They exited where the air vibrated to the roar of a waterfall. 'These tunnels open onto the river.' A chiseled three-storey esplanade appeared. 'Carved out, to provide building blocks for the pyramids.'

In a cavern where the rushing crystal waterfall formed one wall, Galen guided them behind the thick sheet to a gilded canoe. The crew rowed, while a servant used a paper fan to shelter Zithia from water spray.

'Shall we surprise Torim?' Galen tested.

'Definitely not!'

He signalled the boat's direction. 'Don't blame him.'

'I don't, he was bargaining for his library.' She looked away from Galen.

He laughed, without humour. 'Whereas I was bargaining for something much more important.'

The high priest uncovered a half-pectoral lying on a cushion. 'My great, great grandmother's.'

Superbly carved blue jade. Rarest of jades. Draping the heavy gems upon her, he murmured, 'As in death, so in life. Slowly, let us spin ever closer together; and when we can tear our eyes from each other, then we'll observe the world.'

A barely audible gasp escaped Zithia.

*

Crossing a main plaza Xiao Chen was beckoned by the arch priestess. 'A moment deacon truth-sayer.'

He bowed low, 'At your service, your eminence.'

'Galen and this Zithia grow into a happy familiarity.' Her face was composed. 'And she lives in the upper priests' block.'

'Galen is even more obsessed with his duties than usual.'

'Which circumvents most criticism, except from Eten. Mind you, the comments don't come from Eten's mouth, but they're hers nonetheless. Eten's jealousy of Galen grows in proportion to his abilities.'

'Galen and Zithia are merely friends, eminence.'

'Constant friends.' Yin-Hsin's pause went on. Eventually, 'I make it a policy never to interfere with the domestic arrangements of my high priests.'

'The woman's attendant is also a witness.'

'Yes! Thank you Xiao Chen.' She walked on.

.*

One early dusk, Xiao Chen knocked on Zithia's door. 'Deacon Xiao Chen, how unusual.' They rarely interacted, although Xiao Chen knew her every move. For instance, when alone, Zithia often wore Galen's heirloom pectoral. She wore it now. Xiao Chen rubbed the edge of his eye.

'High priest Galen commands the lady to attend him.' He disregarded her glare. 'A temple chair is ready for you.'

In a leafy district, Galen waited by a forty-foot stone obelisk. 'I planned somewhere special for dinner.'

They strolled along a wide breezy ridge past palaces, the vast surrounding grounds and guards. Zithia was unusually quiet... for far too long, Galen realised. 'Happy with your tutors?'

She snarled, 'Xiao Chen is very protective of you.'

Galen's head tilted to the right, his eyes following. 'Perhaps he feels he has reason to be.'

'Really?' Her cleavage swelled.

A jaguar roamed toward them until a brittle command recalled him. A regal lady, leaves in one hand, dipped a long gold spatula into a jade pot of ground lime. Her pupils were full moons. Galen commented, 'We're now surrounded by the cream of society.' He pointed out a particular mansion, 'There lives a great trader who looks at the world through a hand-sized slice of emerald. He insists this filter soothes his unexpectedly sensitive nerves.' Zithia smiled and Galen slid his thumb down her finger.

'And there lives a great lady addicted to staying young. Wherefore she mixes powdered jade in her drinks and dusts her desserts with gold.' Galen worked his fingers slowly, fluidly, between hers.

Red-breasted macaws played tag with green parrots across their path. Zithia's hand slipped away. 'Deer herds seem popular among the wealthy this year.'

'It was lakes last year, I wonder where they all went?'

Galen and Zithia began to climb the marble steps up to a small plaza. By the third step Galen stopped; he was aware of violence. Death. Only, not yet. Looking pensive, he said, 'Go on up and enjoy the symbols on the terrace. They're quite intricately carved. I'll be with you shortly.'

Alone he opened his senses and felt. Yes, there it was. Someone who passed here regularly, by foot or chair, saw this as a good murder place. He, yes, he'd wait one day for a victim. Weeks… or months from now.

There was a city gardener tending the green slope. Calling him over, Galen wrote a signed note with instructions for the deacon-in-charge. The gardener left at once to carry out a task he was told was imperative. Galen waited several minutes, then scanned again. Ah, that was better.

He'd ordered the stairs removed, and replaced by thorny cacti. The murder would, now, not occur here. Galen felt a wider area of the ether and thus the solid world. Not only here; as it was to be a killing of convenience, it wouldn't occur at all.

The high priest was smiling as he reached the top of the stairway. Pale blue-veined pillars rose to different heights, indicating where to locate stars on the horizon. On a raised dais a gold filigree stand held a mysterious instrument. Zithia had left the ornate carvings to stare at the unusual thing, as yet unable to decipher its purpose. 'I borrowed it from the astronomers.'

The four-foot long leather telescope bent its eye heavenwards. Two lenses, both from Atlantis, magnified the skies. A national treasure, Galen's request for it had sent tremors through the astronomy sector. The shadowy figure of the head astronomer retired to a nearby garden. His vigil would only end when he could reclaim his prize. With him waited his noble host, Laed, plus a truth-sayer patronised by the prince.

Pink-faced warblers sang, while Galen and Zithia watched the brightest star in the sky set after its brother, the Sun. A burnt-sugar scent reached them from twelve-foot long asparagus. Zithia tipped her head back while ice-cream fruit pulp melted in her mouth. 'Earthly paradise.' Opening her lips wide, she languidly engulfed another spoonful.

Helping Zithia to her feet, together they examined the rabbit on the moon through the telescope. Hair touching. After several minutes thus, Galen let his cheek brush Zithia's. 'To be a high priest's concubine is a coveted position.'

Zithia thought: *"Without marriage, I'm a toy... Would be..."* she corrected herself, then looked at the ground: *"After all these months, he still thinks of that."*

She closed her eyes, a mistake that intensified the sensation of his touch. 'To be his wife is more so.' She went back to the safety of the rug. 'Women crave commitment as men crave power.'

Knowing her daily increasing need for distance, he sat close. 'Considering that to attain commitment is power, the sexes have a lot in common.'

'Marriage!' Sipping from her cup, Zithia ignored his fingers that traced her jaw-line.

His lips, fuller now, were a rakish smile. 'We shall see.'

She drew back sharply. 'Your contempt won't be borne, high priest.' And threw her drink in his face.

Astonished, Galen grabbed her wrist. His touch was explosive. 'I burn for you.'

'Are you speaking of your heart, or your loins.'

'That's unworthy of you.'

'Next time, you use that line' she pulled her wrist free, 'the answer is "My soul, tis my very soul which burns so."' She shook her head. Across an unbridgeable gap, they glared at each other: *"And yet... can I part from him? Could I bear it?"*

Thrice during the evening Laed's witness had silently approached the picnickers, to ascertain that the telescope was secure. On the last occasion he had overheard that most interesting word, 'marriage'.

*

Finally Torim prepared to leave his little library. The farmer and family, who'd been tending the garden were also on a journey, back to their riverside farm. The oldest son had decided to stay on permanently. Torim climbed the wall beside the portals leading into the garden and called to

79

the empty corridor, 'Pass me that mirror, will you?'

Xiao Chen stepped away from a column where he'd been quietly contemplating on Torim and events. The deacon handed Torim a silver-backed concave crystal. Praying, Torim fixed it within the stone third eye above the archway. It'd intensify negative thoughts and intentions, throwing them back onto their owners. He'd placed several protective mirrors around the building.

On the ground again, 'Brother, you came.'

The truth-sayer's nostrils flared. 'Your protege will ruin Galen.'

Torim said under his breath. 'This is going to be as hard as I thought.' Then aloud,

'She's not my protege. And it's my considered opinion that Galen has ruined himself already. Temple politics indeed!'

'He's bewitched.'

'They've enchanted each other.' He gave a mischievous smile. 'She's his soul mate.'

'A poor jest.'

'Ah yes, it's exactly the thing I'd bring up for a laugh.' The librarian's eyes moved heavenward momentarily. 'Would our fledgling archpriest compromise his ambitions for anything less?'

Xiao Chen touched his earlobe. 'It's a lie. Galen would've told me.'

'What, and risk losing your good opinion of him?'

The witness thought: *"That at least has the ring of truth."*

'Know this, Xiao Chen, as soul mates their first duty is to each other.'

Xiao Chen's pressed his lips tight together. 'What of Galen's goals?'

'If he's prepared to endanger his ambitions, you should be prepared to let him.'

'Without distractions Galen could be a great magician...'

Torim sighed. 'They need your guidance, brother. Both of them.' So saying, the librarian went into his garden to fetch his llama.

*

Torim had wanted to say all his goodbyes in the city, but Zithia insisted on seeing him off in the jungle. Arriving at their rendezvous, Zithia put a lemon-scented orchid, with large yellow blossoms hanging low, on top of a pack, next to a gourd Torim had grown into a cube, with a fabulous picture on each side. The intricately carved bamboo frame he'd set around the growing fruit was an original from the Dragon-Land. The llama wriggled his disapproval at having to wait.

Galen, 'Where's your cat?'

Torim, 'Listen.' They all heard the silver bell the cat had always worn. 'He can't manifest visibly anymore. He's too far into heaven's ways.' They looked at each other, both aware that even this would cease very soon. 'I expect to see him everywhere. And so, I go.'

Galen, 'You always wanted to.'

'True.' Torim then immediately headed off into a gully, declaring in a deep base, 'Yes. Relics of Atlantis call me.' He beckoned Zithia and Galen to follow him, 'The fungal flowers are out.' He disappeared into the greenery. Galen, having taken only a step, with a wave of the hand opted to wait by the llama.

On joining Torim at the bottom of the gully, a scent hit Zithia and she clamped her fingers tight over her nose. Oblivious to the smell of rotting meat, Torim stood near several spongy flowers. Each was an arm-length and reddish with huge yellow dots. The librarian said 'That they're open is…'

'Repulsive!' Immediately coughing because she'd inhaled the noxious perfume. She could even taste it.

'I admit the odour is a tad intense.' Beaming, he leaned over a flower, 'but they're very rare.'

She pulled a face, 'I wonder why?' Removing herself hurriedly to fresher air, she found Galen smirking.

Having gathered the fungal spores, Torim put them in a saddlebag on the llama. The brown animal blew hard onto Torim's neck.

While Zithia hugged Torim goodbye, she got a whiff of his clothes. 'Thanks for the final memory.'

'You wanted to come. Wouldn't listen.' He nodded a farewell to Galen. 'And here's something else neither of you will listen to. You both think you can change each other,' he turned away, 'and you're wrong!'

*

At her apartment, over a week later, Zithia found Xiao Chen giving instructions to a stranger. The woman was a middle-aged truth-sayer. 'Lady Zithia, this is Malinali.' Xiao Chen's tone virtually warm. A first. 'I've had Esontair replaced. Her talents were needed elsewhere. I trust you've no objections.'

Zithia rocked on her heels and immediately her words flooded out. 'That charming girl? So watchful, such pretty lips, what shall I do without her?' Her tone lowered, 'No objections.'

'Of course Malinali will report to me, as Esontair did.'

'Obviously, deacon truth-sayer.'

Scanning the roof Xiao Chen frowned, 'The ceilings in this apartment are an appalling colour. I'll have them painted. Apricot.'

Puzzled, Zithia peeped at the truth-sayer from the corner of her eyes.

*

Ixchup was waiting outside Galen's subterranean office, there by command. She was in the long passage leading to, and only to, Galen's sanctum. Careful not to stand on the Atlantian symbol directly before the door, Ixchup meditated on Zithia: *"Denying a high priest! Who does she think she's? An aphrodisiac slipped into her food would…"*

Without warning, Galen was behind her. 'The ritual kept me longer than expected deaconess.' Ixchup jumped and spun round, bowing.

He walked into the study, a large room, well lit. The high priest sat behind a smoky quartz table, closing the lid of a rare glass jar. Ixchup observed the shelves of potions plus herb bundles, the alpaca rug before the desk. She wasn't invited to sit.

'I believe congratulations are in order, Ixchup. On your sister's bearing another daughter.'

The deaconess thought: *"That news spread fast."* She tightened facial muscles, 'Another blessing from the one God.'

Galen held a finger in front of his lips, 'Having delivered six girls by a nobleman of his uncertain temper must be… distressing.'

Ixchup snorted, 'He blackened her eye immediately after the birth, while threatening divorce.' She rung her hands, remembering how she'd unsuccessfully petitioned Augustus's intervention.

Looking sympathetic, Galen came around the table. 'Please be seated, Ixchup.' The deaconess sat on the edge of a chair. 'Now to another matter; your advice would be invaluable.' Galen leaned against the desk, 'I wonder if you've noticed how quickly Zithia learns the mysteries?'

'Her powers are interesting.' Galen stared hard; she hurried on. '… having observed her devotion to priestly studies.'

Blinking, Galen's pupils grew to their normal size. 'Ixchup, by chance

I'm seeing your sister's noble husband today. I'd like to tell him I have the honour of being your new niece's spiritual guardian.' He leaned back, 'A tonic for him.'

"His companion a priest?... my sister's future will be secure... the family honour intact." Hidden, one thumb and finger rubbed together quickly, "How best to phrase this?" Her face cleared, 'Lord Galen, may I make a suggestion that temerity has previously forbidden?'

'I've always valued your honesty, Ixchup.'

Her eyes lit up. 'My lord, I feel that with her unique gifts Zithia needs more scope. After much consideration I wish to put Zithia's name forward as a novice priest.'

Galen gave a ghost of a smile. 'I bow to your excellent judgment Ixchup.'

*

The arch priestess's abode was the highest in the city, at the furthest end of the upper priests' block. Surrounded on three sides by a hanging garden, two wind-bent pines had long ago draped themselves over the one corner, anchored in soil and the cliff face.

Yin-Hsin sat in front of a freestanding matt filigreed marble slab, working on a wall picture. Thin clay bodies adorned the wall, most with clothes already layered on. Galen put a tray of baked clay weapons, fans and jewellery on a side-table, after flicking off violet-blue petals. These had dropped from a tall, gnarled wisteria. More shade-tree than creeper, supported almost invisibly. Bowing, Galen left, passing Peregrine who had entered a natural opening in the rock wall that marked the entrance to the garden. Peregrine merely stretched his lips at Galen, by way of a smile.

Peregrine stalked an exquisitely winding path of river-stones, edged by shortish grasses, past a juniper tree towards Yin-Hsin. Soon he gazed upon a pond, which ended only feet from the precipice's edge. Walking a few paces, he was at a vantage point allowing observation of the progress of a truly natural waterfall to its base three hundred feet below. Yin-Hsin had come to meet him and Peregrine looked up. They continued a leisurely progress, arm in arm. Not really sensing the fragrance from an oversized peony tree, the high priest reminisced: "Two more years before Yin-Hsin retires. Even with creating every advantage, *it's barely enough time to recoup my losses after the emerald blunder."*

'I saw Galen leaving.' He hesitated, then 'What of this woman of his?'

'She has been in training to be a priest these many months…'

Peregrine snorted. 'Yes! Now no-one can accuse Galen of having an interest outside the temple.'

'I have it on unquestionable authority that they are only friends. He's still the same devoted son of the temple he always has been.' She patted her confidant's arm. 'There really is no one to match Galen in Xalisco.'

'Except for you.'

Yin-Hsin guided them over a small curved bridge to a hillock island, part-shaded by a cherry tree. The arch priestess touched the tree, buds appeared then burst into full bloom. 'I know I shouldn't… still… an old woman has so few pleasures.'

'You're never old.'

Yin-Hsin moved aching bones carefully. 'Dear friend, for months now I've had chest pains after evening prayers.'

She looked beyond the island and its surrounding irregularly shaped pond, to a boulder. It had been river-carved into a mountain. Yin-Hsin loved to vision herself, small as a beetle, upon that mountain. 'Two more years in office will kill me, Peregrine. I must retire.' She nodded to herself, she'd take the rock with her.

'But your duty; the temple's needs!' His eyes became watery: *"She can't do this to me."*

'A dead arch priestess is no good to anyone.' Yin-Hsin drifted over the bridge again, to the mural. She put a clay skull in the mural's sky. The symbol for the bright evening star, Venus.

"I'll be ruined." He reflected, white-faced, and handed Yin-Hsin a clay triumphal headdress.

Cementing the piece in the scene, 'In three weeks' time I'll announce my retirement and an election, plus my support of Galen.' Peregrine's face fell. With Yin-Hsin's support Galen was a certainty to be next archpriest. Yin-Hsin adjusted the headdress, 'I'll tell no one until then.' She worked away, 'And I'll advise Galen to rely on your counsel, as I've done.'

Peregrine rolled his eyes whispering, 'As if that'll help?'

Yin-Hsin stood and moved to the other side of the filigree marble, inspecting an ink-wash landscape created by a master on the other side of the wall. A plain dominated the foreground, with a lone pine in the middle ground and two small people near it. Blue-green rocky mountains, with mist around the peaks, covered a third of the background. Yin-Hsin admired it, 'This makes my mural look… primitive.'

'I shall live in the observatory city by the ocean...' She continued talking about her retirement.

"The ocean." :His mind went back several years. A wealthy noble, he'd always been true to the temple. If he liked luxury, so what? Then there'd been one rather heavy investment, in this world's finest emeralds. Gobbled up by the sea; shipwreck. He groaned silently. If he never saw the ocean again, it'd be too soon.

Thus, on the wrong side of middle age he'd found himself seriously without money. *"Was it really so wrong to buy off the creditors by using my influence with Yin-Hsin?"*

'My dear, promise you'll be a regular visitor. Then when you retire …'

'Oh yes, yes; absolutely.'

That night, in his apartment Peregrine came to a decision. Covering his face with a cage of fingers, the high priest's narrowed eyes darted around as he worked out his tactics.

*

On her wide terrace, the arch priestess arose from a glazed stool. She'd been meditating on a silk veil, suspended on a frame under eight emerald green tiles. By religious custom the fluttering gossamer ended eight inches short of the ground. Only the Dragon-Land could make either the tiles or the silk or that particular colour. That luminescent, yellow-gold seen in high rays of sunset and on some sunset cloud-tips. Echoing the very highest astral plane. The colour of God.

Feeling hazy, fuzzy after her meditation, Yin-Hsin walked into her living area where a large bronze cauldron sat on three decorative feet. A steaming glazed red ceramic pot drew Yin-Hsin to it. Pouring a cup of lemon scented tea, Yin-Hsin sat content. She preferred this even to orange flavoured tea. On a lacquered table a half-completed pectoral hung from a square frame. Pink jade and gold beads lay beside the funerary necklace.

Yin-Hsin ignored it, looking instead at her latest acquisition, bought from a prince of her tribe the week after she'd first experienced chest pains. She wasn't sure she had time to wait for one to be sent from the Dragon-Land. It stood upon a low square table. The arch priestess patted the wooden contraption, full of connecting toothed-wheels. Topped by a statue that always pointed in the same direction, no matter which way the base turned. It was a fascination and she'd always wanted one. A little carved horse, on wheels, pulled the thing in any direction.

Moving the horse, Yin-Hsin clicked her tongue at yet another tear in her thin skin. Lighting candles, she fanned her hands, seeing liver spots and bony fingers. These hands had once been graceful as flying swallows. 'Definitely time to abdicate.' She patted an oversized mat black jar. It sat at an angle, on a stand with divinely carved dragons. Untying the net at its mouth, she inspected the grey web within. What better way to close her never-ending wounds than with spider web and a whisper of magic?

Yin-Hsin swept a hand into the jar, but harvested very little grey lace on her splayed fingers. 'Have you all lain off spinning?' Delving up to her elbow this time, she brushed the bottom. Sticky film now coated her hand. Sitting on a nearby stool, she applied it to her ragged tear. Something shimmered, at the edge of her vision, but Yin-Hsin was intent on pulling a cloud-wisp cashmere shawl around her shoulders. It, like most of her possessions, had been brought from the Dragon-Land. A small movement drew Yin-Hsin's eyes back to the jar's mouth.

The spider, filling the opening, was shivering off its hairy outer skin. Her face blanched. 'Beloved God!'

Instinctively Yin-Hsin flung up her hands, but the thorny spider had already launched itself at her throat. Tens of barbs pierced her neck. Writhing in pain, 'God,' Yin-Hsin's hands closed over the glistening pink manhunter.' we come to thee…'

A shot of blue power lit the spider's body, it tried to spring away but it couldn't escape Yin-Hsin's embrace. The blue jolted it hard again. Its legs went rigid, stiffening into a choker around the arch priestess's neck. Yin-Hsin croaked her death prayer. 'I've lived but to attain the joy of thy divine presence.' Her face contorted. 'I pray thee, see my faults and still do not hide thy glory from…' Body convulsing savagely, her heart gave out.

"…Your daughter." Yin-Hsin's spirit finished where her physical form had left off, while standing up out of her body. Then, after rearranging her skirt, Yin-Hsin was forty years younger.

Simultaneously, the manhunter had rolled out of its corpse, on the other side of Yin-Hsin's prone form. Rubbing between its eyes, the spider said, "That blue flash really hurt. What are you? A magician?"

"Yes." Frowning. "Well, I was."

"I won't make that mistake another time." It jumped back from its shell. *"Hey, is that my body? Damn, I'm dead. Again!"*

Small tumultuous patches of darkness were gathering near the spider. Half-closing one eye, *"I don't like the looks of them… at all."* The manhunter scurried in agitation over Yin-Hsin's corpse.

"Show some respect." Yin-Hsin said with irony.

But the manhunter was too intent on ducking behind Yin-Hsin's phantom skirts. She took two steps to one side, *"Surely you don't expect help from me?"*

"Uh, look… uh, I'm really sorry…" it was swooped upon by the patches and dragged through the floor.

Yin-Hsin was spotlighted by a white-blue tunnel of light. Love wrapped its warmth around her. A joy so complete she could barely think. Ancestors of hers appeared within the far end of the light, smiling welcome.

When the arch priestess's body was found, they had to prize the dead manhunter from her hands.

*

The high priests accompanied Yin-Hsin's body to a frigid cavern. In shifts they kept company with Yin-Hsin until the funeral, praying constantly. Chanting, the high priestesses washed and dressed Yin-Hsin's husk, placing carved jade in her mouth and on her eyes.

Into his friend's hand Peregrine put an intricate obsidian knife, its blade edges chipped into human profiles. True to Yin-Hsin's request there was no mask. Someone had completed her funerary pectoral. Finally the corpse was wrapped in silk, with crimson shells and emeralds between the layers.

Simultaneously a hurried investigation ensued. Other archpriests around the continent were kept informed via astral travellers. When an archpriest spoke in his own city, a flyer instantly took the message to the meeting place. There, a master-flyer repeated the words at cross-temple meetings. The flyer representing each archpriest stood before that temple's banners. At the final one the Magi Davot mused, 'A manhunter, that night killer attracted to the warmth of a human body. Always lethal. I'd hoped we had eradicated them.'

'Someone was taking no chances.' An archpriest said.

The chairwoman stated, 'Publicising the truth about Yin-Hsin's end won't help public morale. We'll announce only that a massive chest seizure has taken our dear sister home.' Soon the communications flyers registered the other archpriests' agreement. 'The investigation will continue; quietly.'

*

People had gathered early at a low pyramid, eager to begin painting the wide-fronted edifice white as was tradition at a great death. Due to Yin-Hsin's popularity, the job was completed within a day. On a terrace step, Galen and Zithia coated one of the large carvings that decorated either side of the central walkway.

Meanwhile teams made the death kites. Silks, framed by balsa wood. Normally the silk was created as vivid stained glass pictures with mystic messages. In deference to Yin-Hsin's tribe the kites were matt white, with glossy white writing upon them. When finished each kite was a shallow dome, five-feet in diameter. Despite their thirty-eight pounds, they flew well.

Two hundred thousand attended the body at the Death Pyramid. Galen and the other high priests carried Yin-Hsin's bier around the vast plaza. White flowers rained on the procession until a mound of snow hid the corpse and brightened the paving.

Beneath the Death Pyramid, Yin-Hsin's body was laid in a vaulted, rock-hewn crypt with three stone orange trees, in fruit, as the pillars. Foliage and fruit had been carved into the ceiling. Eten placed alabaster bowls of a lost-herb around the body, Galen adding ears of corn and copal incense. Soon the lost-herb and the incense would interact together, quickly disintegrating flesh and bones. Temple culture insisted upon the law: 'We came from dust and we return to dust'.

Peregrine sprinkled jade tears over the flowered shroud. Then priests walled up the tomb. When the final stone alone remained to be placed, Galen looked into the hole concentrating for a second, and the incense balls began to burn. The final stone quickly sealed all.

Outside, the populace sipped lime-juice then ate honeycomb, a reminder that death's bitterness could also hold great sweetness. Rubber soled pauper's sandals were worn, symbolising loss, and not one golden flash was seen. It was bad luck to wear such finery to a funeral.

Drizzle started causing a rapid desertion of building tops. Influential people clustered at the center of the main plaza. Above the Death Pyramid three massive death kites rose in the air, carrying messages to the dead. From a hidden door a young man stepped out. Ming Ue, of the eighth tribe. A rubber umbrella immediately sheltered him, held by a brawny assistant. He wore a latex cape, sandals and a wide upturned bowl of a hat that fell to below his nose. He looked through a viewing panel in the rubberised straw, at the top of the pyramid, the kites and the sky.

On this level, ropes and gold wire anchored two kites, fourteen strides apart. One level up, the other two kites flew closer together. Wire lay on the ground between each pair. Ming Ue discarded his cape and hat. He wore a ceiba silk kilt. Twice that morning the small man had gathered clouds and now the dark sky above him was becoming a growling animal. It began to sprinkle.

In the plaza the archpriest Jerome called out, 'In death we are lighter than a bird's feather. Yet even so we are weighed. All are shown what we could have been, and dread the seeing. Now Yin-Hsin's life is in the balance. May the one God bless her crossing over.'

Groups of pan pipes sang in concert with myriad Dragon-Land stringed instruments. With shamisens leading, the combination made the spine tingle. The strings, particularly, tugging at the very soul. With the back of his long fingers Ming Ue touched a kite string. Lightning that was forking across the sky halted in its path to descend. A bolt hit the rope and followed it down to the man. Mere seconds before the white flash reached him, Ming Ue danced sideways beyond the power's reach. Then drawing lightning continuously he glided, leapt, even somersaulted from one flying picture to the next. Zithia was round-eyed in the gasping crowd; Galen never once looked her way.

Inflamed by the lightning-summoner's presence, the sky above howled for blood. For the finale Ming Ue flipped two handles. The wire joining each pair of kites leapt to a height of five feet. A hush came over the audience. Looking up, Ming Ue touched one horizontal line. A great ridge of lightning appeared directly above these two kites and, confused, the jagged teeth hung temporarily suspended. He was already stepping to the next golden bar, laying the back of his hand on it. *"Wait,"* he thought: *"1...2...3. Break contact."* He crouched, throwing his cape over him. The four kites lit up together, with a dazzling power comb standing between each pair.

Seconds later archpriest Jerome announced, 'The kites still fly. The one God is pleased to welcome his child home. A favourite daughter.' Cheering resounded and became competition for the thunder. Unknown except to the high priests, the lines securing the airborne pictures changed one foot from the kites. At that point the rope was rubber coated.

Adjourning to a joyous mourning feast. Zithia found Galen alone. 'How?' she said to Galen's back. He stood next to a corner that hid Ming Ue. Both turned to her. A little breathless, Zithia bowed. 'Please excuse me, Grandmaster Ming Ue, Lord Galen.'

'Grandmaster Ming Ue, this is Zithia of Xalisco, in training to be a priest.'

Watching Galen and his woman, Ming Ue deigned to address Zithia. 'Lady, very rarely a child is born who attracts lightning. If the child is still alive by the time his destiny is understood, he's lucky indeed.'

Galen added, 'At present we have only five lightning-summoners.' Zithia couldn't take her eyes off this living treasure. 'And Grandmaster Ming Ue's bravery makes every exhibition a potential farewell performance.'

Zithia put her open right hand on her heart, 'A privilege, grandmaster.' And backed away. Galen took Ming Ue to the officiating archpriest.

During the afternoon, sets of line-dancers celebrated life. Her fingers beating time, Zithia joined the woman's dances, moving with pent-up fire.

Archpriest Jerome observed Zithia, as he had all during the mourning feast. Almost ebony, with a warrior's build, his tribe was the fifteenth. Watching Zithia's progress among the tables, Jerome's nostrils suddenly flared. He beckoned deacon Rupert to him.

A few minutes later Rupert went to a man, of mid-twenties, in the room. Rupert spoke quietly, po-faced. 'Archpriest Jerome sends this exact message. You will go... now! And never again be in the same city as he.' The man glanced quickly in Jerome's direction, and then ducked he head. 'The archpriest knows you.' Rupert paused, 'He knows you haven't changed. Even after death... and rebirth.' The man scurried away.

Jerome was there to inaugurate the next archpriest, but first it was required he gather information from the high priests. Finally he spoke to Eten; the high priestess had managed it thus.

'What was my revered sister's preference regarding her successor?'

'Our brother Galen, without a doubt, though is he somewhat young for the position?' No one else had been so forthright.

'I was around his age when I was elected.'

'But, eminence, Galen can't be compared to you!'

The archpriest watched Zithia, 'His companion isn't the partner a sober-minded mystic usually chooses.'

'Never companion, eminence.'

'Ahh, that pretence... She's more than I expected.' He pursed full lips. 'Her dancing; a little too intense.'

'Her solo performances are even more fascinating.' Eten looked into Jerome's dark eyes. 'She wishes to marry.'

'And she's still in Galen's life?' Small worry lines appeared. 'You've a truth-sayer who will verify this?'

'One was guarding the temple's telescope when Galen dined with his lady under the stars. That witness was privy to a conversation between them.'

'Yin-Hsin can't have known of Galen's divided loyalties!'

'Perhaps she suspected.' Eten beckoned the truth-sayer forward from the throng. 'After all, her choice was never announced.'

At the appointed time Jerome banged his staff on the hall floor. 'One archpriest is dead, another must be found. An election will be held in three days.' His staff thundered again. 'The archpriest's council supports high priest Peregrine in that election.' Some slapped Peregrine's back, others produced quick smiles that disappeared as suddenly. Eten and Galen traded looks.

As Jerome left the banquet he passed Galen. 'Walk with me my son.'

They went onto the terrace. It rained lightly. Jerome passed a hand through the air above his head. The drizzle stopped. They walked on.

'A delicate situation has been brought to my attention.' He searched Galen's face. 'I'm concerned about your lady's expectations, Lord Galen.' Galen paled, blinking slowly. 'A woman determined on marriage isn't a suitable friend for a high priest.' His eminence measured his words, 'Let alone a future archpriest.'

Galen's expression didn't change. *"Eten"* he thought. Jerome's voice softened, 'My son, Yin-Hsin had such great hopes for you. Consider your priorities!'

The high priest bowed, 'Yes, eminence.'

'Out of respect for Yin-Hsin's memory, this matter will remain between us two.' As if as an after-thought, Jerome finished, 'I shall speak to those who told me of the lady.' He dismissed Galen.

After the archpriest, left Galen's head went back, his eyes closing. Finally he expelled a deep breath and straightened up. His face was set.

*

The day after the funeral, Eten was on her way to her apartment. When farewelling a visitor, the high priestess had been given a baby-stingray spine, for special occasions. She ran her tongue along her top teeth.

Eten lived two doors from Peregrine and a wing from Galen. Passing Peregrine's chamber, Eten's fingers caressed the wall: *"Once my mentor's, it should be mine!"* The high priestess saw her cane toad squatting outside her own door. Saliva dripped from Venus's maw, and from the black thing gripped there.

'A gift for me?' He spewed his prize out at her feet. 'Thank you.' A large spider, its first skin half shed and hanging from it. Pride filled Eten's face. 'A manhunter.' She stroked the amphibian's chin. 'And where did Venus find my lovely present?'

Screeching, Venus leapt to Peregrine's apartment where he landed with a screech. Eten clapped her hands together. 'Mustn't forget my present,' she cooed skewering the spider with her two-inch nails.

The door was locked, but Eten soon walked unhindered into her old mentor's lair. Her nose wrinkled at the peasant art. Bright pottery figurine jugs. Boisterous, complicated woven patterns. Eten shuddered, 'To cleanse the place...' In particular she loathed the main rug. A gift to her, Peregrine had been in raptures when she'd passed it on to him.

The high priestess put Venus's trophy on a table next to some nuts, 'Well, well. Two manhunters in the upper priests' quarters in the same week. What a coincidence.'

Looking around she screwed up her eyes, 'Now where'd I conceal a secret?' She proceeded to check her teacher's hiding places. Then throwing a rug back from a concealed floor compartment Eten heard a creature throwing itself against the lid. 'Eager, isn't it?' She said to Venus, who watched her intently.

While reciting a spell, her finger outlined the edges of the lid. Ice sprouted along the lines, immediately digging into the box. The assaults against the lid stopped. Eten knocked on the compartment. No reaction. 'Wonderful.' She opened it, her face lighting up. Peregrine had kept a reserve in case something happened to his first courier.

Pulling out a reed cage Eten collected Venus's gift. It had escaped when the spider for Yin-Hsin was removed. 'I wonder why it didn't kill Peregrine?' She deposited it with its dead mate. 'Sluggish from cold or... simply professional courtesy?'

Drumming her fingernails on the cage, the high priestess tried to remember her mentor's most secret niche. Once, long years ago, she'd entered unexpectedly...a blood cup was being put away... but where?! In the study, Eten stood on a chair and felt the ceiling above the window. She tapped the stone in the sequence her tutor had used, memory aided by the punch on the face she'd received for not knocking. The trap door popped out into Eten's hands, a blood splattered feather floating down. This cache was still safe; unknown. The high priestess inserted the cage. Back in her room she kissed Venus's warty head. 'Now, to blackmail.'

*

Eten hunted Peregrine to his favourite lair, the extensive tequila fermentation halls. Overseeing the high tequila production was Peregrine's specialty. Called the water-of-life, this alcohol was so pure that it left no hangover.

Seven-foot deep processing vats were sunk into the ground. In one such pond, a thick layer of agave pulp covered fermenting liquid. Herbs and the gelatinous clumps gave this vintage drink a unique zest. Further along, a curling silver pipe dripped clear liquid into a tub.

Once the election date had been announced Peregrine had come here. At this time of year he spent many happy hours doing extra distillations to perfect his tequila.

Observing they were alone, Eten cleared her throat.

'Eten, the high priests' jars aren't ready yet.'

'I haven't come about tequila. I came to talk about spiders.' She quickly raised then lowered her upper eyelids.

'Well you won't find any in my brews, this place is pristine.'

Eten's slow smile was a drawn dagger. 'And you won't find any in your apartment.'

Sucking in his breath, Peregrine's eyes darted up and to the right. 'I moved your package.' His feet shuffled of their own accord. Eten soothed,

'You've been very clever Peregrine, don't stop now.' Sweat beaded his forehead. 'After your election we will achieve much.'

*

All the rich colours fought with each other on the floor. Peregrine was wrecking his apartment attempting to find his manhunters. He knew the spiders were there somewhere, otherwise Eten had no hold over him. *"If I can only find them."* He thought and shredded the rug Eten had given him.

In the corridor, listening to the sounds, the high priestess hummed a tune.

When he was inaugurated, the new archpriest kept his old quarters as a private study. Sentimental reasons. Weeks later, Eten invited herself to afternoon tea with archpriest Peregrine. She stroked his ego, flattering his decisions. From then on, they met weekly. Eten so consummately blurred the edges between friendship and threat that he often forgot her true reason for being there. Only rarely did she ask a favour.

After many productive months, Eten arrived late for their afternoon tete-a-tete in the archpriest's garden. Peregrine had already poured cashew juice with guarana.

'Greetings, Peregrine,' Eten sat at the table set before the freestanding stonework. 'This black bamboo is an excellent idea.' Her hand snaked out, tracing a supple leaf. Only one clay magician's headdress was still visible from Yin-Hsin's unfinished mural.

Looking sharply at Eten's fingers, Peregrine began to quiver. Her ring was a large elegant spider. She suggested one of her tribe be given a certain post. Goggling, Peregrine gave in.

After she left, he smashed a plate against the archway, snarling: 'Will I never be allowed to forget?'

Immediately, Peregrine summoned a man highly regarded for his ability to trail people. 'I don't care how long it takes.'

Every time he saw Eten's emerald ring, Peregrine went over the investigator's reports. Finally he saw a pattern developing in Eten's movements. After the next three reports, he recognised her routine as a blasphemy. A cardinal blasphemy.

chapter 10

Nine initiates had fasted for three days, drinking water and their choice of mushrooms after dark. They had had no physical contact since the fast began. Select priests attended the ceremony that welcomed initiates into the fold. Arriving, they found the novices standing barefoot in the Cave of Crystals. The sand was raked into flowing mystic designs, each whirl in blue, green, mauve, black and deepest pink. The coloured sand had been brought from far, far north by old-world traders at marvelous expense. Elevating incense seemed to follow the patterns. The ancient cavern was high roofed. The initiates faced a wide wall dotted with different crystals inserted in the rock face, which glowed from inner fires. This was an illusion, for a corridor ran behind the crystal wall, hung with lighted torches.

The archpriest appeared. Each novice faced Peregrine in turn, declaring his oath. Soon it was Zithia's turn. 'I dedicate myself to the one God and his mysteries. I'll put God above temple, and temple above all worldly concerns.'

Then she walked to a crystal, gazing hard at it until a vision directed her next studies. Herbs. Damn, not flying. Then a priest's robe and short cape was placed over her shift.

At the following banquet, all the upper clergy had gathered to welcome the new priests. Zithia sat with the others at the high table, with the archpriest and high priests. She radiated happiness. Peregrine stood and banged his staff down. 'Let the revels begin.'

It was an Atlantian night, from food to dancing. Novices brought in roasted venison, geese and turkeys. Still euphoric from the ceremony, Zithia looked at Galen, not far from her. The high priest didn't return her smile. It was five months since Yin-Hsin's death.

Dancing began. Batting her eyes, Zithia rose and Galen led her to the dance floor. Standing opposite her, he held his right arm up, the palm facing her. She stepped forward and entwined her own arm so that the backs of their hands pressed together.

Zithia, still affected by fasting, 'You've been different since Yin-Hsin's funeral, even distant.'

'His eminence Jerome gave me a lot to think about.' He remembered to smile.

In prescribed measures they floated through the routine, their bodies drawing closer and closer. The high priest felt her shiver at the contact and the intensity in their eyes matched.

"Tonight must be the night," Galen thought. 'Tonight...'

'Just ask me.' Her voice was husky; she blushed. Galen looked relieved. They danced a step. 'Who will sanctify our union?'

'Sanctify?'

'Marry! Who will marry us?'

His eyes cooled. 'I thought you'd forgotten that nonsense.'

'Nonsense? But you encouraged me to become a priest, so we could marry.' Her nostrils flared. 'Didn't you?'

Galen swung her around the floor, his manner aloof. 'Have you forgotten your vows already?'

Her eyes were deadly. 'You planned this, so I couldn't ask for marriage.' Zithia tried to release her hand from his, but he held it firm.

'I put God, not your ambition, before everything.' Curtsying to Galen as the routine required, she added through gritted teeth, 'Galen, I want children.'

'Nothing easier.'

'Never without marriage.'

Galen wanted her more today than he had in those first weeks. Realisation hit, he needed her. The depth of his feelings terrified him. 'Torim was right, we can't change each other.' He memorised every part of her face. 'I'm sending you to another temple.' With the dance's end, he bowed.

She didn't curtsy. 'If it must be, my lord.' Her upper lip trembled. 'But know, truly, how I love thee.'

Quickly summoning power, Zithia touched him on the forehead where his third eye was and opened the well of her love for him. Her connection literally took his breath away. Technique perfect, Zithia reached the depths of his being. Too late Galen raised a barrier against her intrusion. Her desire to be one with him tore at the high priest, triggering a flame in his soul.

Galen backed away from her, his own love becoming a raging torrent. Softly, Zithia sentenced him, 'And feel pain, as I do.'

He escaped the banquet room, entered a secret tunnel outside the hall and was in the crystal cavern. Feelings Galen had kept hidden, especially from himself, were fire in his veins.

The sand continued to swirl mysticism, the air was still incense dense. Zithia's touch glowed on his forehead. Stumbling, Galen tried again to close the floodgates she'd opened. 'No!' He groaned, then his voice resonating with power. 'I'll be archpriest.'

An earthquake promptly cracked the cavern. Thunder filled the room and Galen's mind, while the ground beneath him tilted. Table-sized rocks fell from the roof, bits of walls shattered to burst into Galen's sanctuary. He ducked a jagged column then, hands on the sand, Galen realised that the patterns remained intact.

Standing erect he closed his eyes and became detached. The cacophony stopped. Opening his eyes, he now stood upon on a cloud facing east, watching far over the ocean.

A ripple started in the distant horizon, an invisible wave of air distorting the water it passed over. It gained speed on reaching land and with it came a rushing noise. The wave morphed all in its wake. Then the ripple reached him, hurling him backwards, into reality.

'I live in interesting times,' the high priest reflected, 'Perhaps I can be archpriest and keep my soul mate.'

*

Well after daylight, Xiao Chen found Galen in the library vault. For the first time Galen researched the records for high priest's marrying. That there were as many as three examples shocked him.

The oldest instance had required a terrible price, the death of the first son. A relieved postscript added that the high priest conceived only female children during his marriage.

The other married high priests had had the price amended, to giving the first son to the temple at an early age and never laying eyes him again. Galen's needed precedents were established. Though no married high priests had gone on to the greatest office, 'With the coming changes, anything's possible.' A hushed thought followed: *"And divorce would instantly make me eligible for election again."*

Galen looked for Zithia who, Malinali reported, had earlier been washing her hair. The high priest walked up a small pyramid overlooking lush forest. This pyramid had a sheer drop on the side facing the jungle, and atop it was a stone offering hut. The high priest circumnavigated this flat-roofed room.

Zithia's burgundy hair bubbled over the end of the roof, floating against the wall. Strolling around the back, Galen breathed in the forest. Saying dryly, 'You're committing sacrilege.' He watched her lying full-length along the roof.

'Name me a better place for drying my hair.'

Turning over to face him, Zithia leaned her head upon her hand. Simultaneously, her full skirt fanned down the stone. 'And how do you fare today my lord?'

He rubbed his chin, 'Remind me not to drop my guard around you again.' Her loving attack could never have been successful had he been prepared, and they both knew it.

She flashed her eyebrows at him. 'Where am I banished to?'

'What if I were to say this temple?'

'I'd say you were proposing to me.'

'I am.' Galen's voice pitched even deeper and lower. 'Do you trust me?'

'With my life.' She rolled quickly off the roof. Galen caught her in his arms and they both looked over the sheer drop.

'You must learn to take real risks.' He carried Zithia to the front of the pyramid. Putting her down, the high priest said, 'Let me show you.' And he passed a hand over her face.

The winds of change tumbled around, till hollows showed beneath her eyes. When it finished, elongated seconds later, he smiled, 'Within three months, we marry.' She kissed him with all the passion she usually kept battened down.

From that day Zithia sat next to Galen at the high priest's table and rigorously extended her studies in self-defence. Busy ruling with Peregrine, Eten contentedly observed her brother high priest dashing headlong toward a precipice. Then invaders landed and sacked a northern temple. A hush fell over the cities, for no one had attacked the descendants of Atlantis before.

*

It seemed but a moment later that Zithia, blurry eyed, called on Galen for an early breakfast. With an elusive pain draining her head, mind and body Zithia slumped into a chair. Images flashed at her, shadowy and too fast for recognition.

'Sensing the imminent future is often painful.' Galen added powders to a drink. 'Especially when it's violent.' He handed her the cup. 'This will help.' The pain receded; the images became dim feelings.

They read, on the terrace, all morning. At lunchtime the atmosphere in the city below them changed, the usual frenzy replaced by furtive crowds wandering aimlessly. Galen kissed the exposed nape of Zithia's neck, 'The future is upon us.'

*

The refugees made a slow progress through the city. In the great plaza, enclosed by the religious citadel, the battered herd was received by the archpriest. Peregrine scanned the audience; many were making the sign against the evil eye. 'Children and pregnant women will leave.'

After a time, 'What have you seen?' A spokesman, sagging after a week's trek, talked with haunted eyes.

'Barbarians taking their ease before bonfires, whereon whole families burned.' He took a ragged breath. 'Hounds, tearing babies from their mama's arms... and bellies.' Groaning, he covered his face with a shawl.

Fear scented the air. 'Where are these demons now?'

'Coming.' Dragging the linen from his face, 'On the backs of monsters.'

Peregrine announced to the city fathers. 'The temple precinct is sanctuary for our poor brothers. Thinking: *"Their talking only to the priests will slow panic."*

'An archpriests' council is being arranged and our flyers are airborne. Any news will come to you directly.'

Peregrine and the high priests adjourned to a chamber, taking the spokesman with them. 'What are the features of those calling themselves the pure race?'

'They're tall and all muscle, including the women.' Peregrine leaned forward. Puzzled, the man continued. 'Fair skinned, hair white... blonde.'

'Go on.'

'Square jaws, straight noses.' He started shaking. 'Mad blue eyes.'

'Rest now, my son.' The refugee left.

'The thirteenth tribe.' Peregrine's face was grey dough. 'Say nothing!'
He went to the archpriest's meeting.

*

The air was thick with flight masters. Several dialogue flyers faced
Peregrine, reporting the other archpriests comments. Peregrine agreed to
send a thousand men from Xalisco to help an endangered temple, leaving
in three days. Another contingent would depart as soon as possible.

Galen came forward 'Eminence, I pledge myself to go with the initial
force.'

Sitting on an alpaca rug on Galen's balcony, Zithia waited. Approaching
her, Galen's face was drawn.

'What have you done?'

'The thirteenth tribe has returned.'

'Even in my worst nightmares, I never saw the thirteenth tribe.'

'So; you understand. I do what I must do.'

She put a hand on his cheek. 'If you die, how shall I survive my grief?'

'Self-centered as usual.'

She clung to him, slipping into an everlasting kiss. Their souls spun
together, with infinite promise. Galen slowly disengaged himself and half
reclined on the rug. Stroking her inner ankle, he looked up at her. Zithia
was transfixed. Galen remained where he was, pupils dilating.

'Beloved,' she moved one step, 'even now, not without a wedding.'

*

The next morning, Galen was due to receive Peregrine's blessing. Coming
into the audience hall where his eminence and the high priests awaited him,
Galen gracefully sank to his knees, head bent. This wasn't on the program.
Peregrine demanded testily, 'Why this excessive humility Lord Galen?'

'Eminence, I confess… myself unworthy for this campaign. My
energies are divided at a profound level.'

Peregrine signalled him to rise.

Galen looked around. 'One of my esteemed brothers or sisters must
have the privilege of leadership.' The silence deafened. 'Now I beg leave
to retire, that you may discuss who is to be distinguished in the coming
battles.'

Galen withdrew. Stupefied, the high priests avoided each other's glances. No volunteers. Long minutes of immobility. Peregrine glared hard at them, waiting further. Finally, exasperated, he clicked his fingers and high priest Francoise scurried after Galen. The mystic priest was halfway across the plaza.

'Lord Galen.' Francoise's voice broke, in concern for his own neck. Galen continued walking with Francoise jogging after, calling his name.

Turning, Galen's face was neutral. 'Brother?'

'Brother.' Francoise plucked at Galen's sleeve. 'Come, you are needed.'

Galen returned to the chamber. Even Eten had been horrified by the turn of events, for all acknowledged that she was equal to Galen in magic. He went to Eten, 'I knew, sister, you'd chose to sacrifice yourself in God's cause.'

Involuntarily she looked away.

Galen looked around him. 'Then, who…?'

Peregrine cleared his throat, 'My son.' his eyes darted upwards, swinging from side to side. Abruptly, he focused. 'My son, as your spiritual father I must know the exact basis of your unworthiness.'

'The matter is supremely delicate, eminence.' Peregrine's whole body nodded. 'There is a priestess of this temple.'

'Zithia.' Peregrine thought: *"And…"*

'We are twin souls;' he paused, 'linked before we were born.'

Peregrine threw himself back into his chair. 'Soul mates!' Everyone else goggled, except Eten, whose mask was now contemptuous. The terrible attraction between such souls was well known. None would've dreamed that Galen was so afflicted. 'Soul mates.' His eminence screwed up his eyes. 'You?'

'Other than priestly service, my soul mate has only one wish.' Galen stopped. 'Marriage.'

The audience was entranced. A stage whisper was heard, 'But high priests cannot marry.'

'You see my dilemma, eminence. I can't lead others with my energies thus torn between temple and soul mate.'

Calculating that Galen had a solution, Eten said mildly, 'Regardless of the campaign, a mystic of Galen's talents mustn't be diminished by inner conflict. Surely there are alternatives.' Her voice became sugary, 'Brother, any precedents?'

The texts were sent for. Until their arrival Eten's eyes followed Galen from beneath lowered lashes: *"His soul mate, that creature of light!"* Eten's lips compressed into a granite line. *"While they stand united, he'll never turn to the dark path."*

Quietly Peregrine conferred with the others, over the scrolls. At last he stated, 'Galen my son... we are content for you to marry, if you will but pay the price.'

'I'm prepared to give up my first born son to the temple.'

'To never see or hear of him again.'

'Agreed.'

Eten recalled one precedent, which wouldn't suit her at all. 'Obviously, you'll vow that your firstborn will be male and that you'll not prevent conception.'

Galen bowed his head; controlling the sex at conception was easy.

'Then I proclaim, as archpriest, you may marry.' It was final.

Eten observed, 'It'd be a kindness to Zithia to take the bride-price when he's a day old.'

High priestess Rachael countered, 'The last bride-price was left with his parents for five years!'

Ainsley, 'Well the bride-price won't be a mystic,' everyone nodded, such talents always missed the next generation, 'therefore I believe he'll need the comfort of his family for longer. I say six years old.'

'That's all very well, Rachael, Ainsley,' to Peregrine's eyes alone the spider on Eten's ring awoke and crawled across her knuckles, 'but I agree with Eten. It's kinder.'

The contract was written, and all signed. Frowning over the age of removal, Galen appended his name last.

Peregrine added, half his mind on looking compassionate, 'To further minimise Zithia's pain, all here now take a vow of silence about this bargain. Galen will tell his soul mate in his own time.'

The idea that Zithia might refuse the bargain wasn't contemplated. This campaign had to have a mystic priest.

Eten folded the parchment, 'How shall you tell Zithia?'

But Galen planned that Zithia never know of this agreement. The oath gave him needed time to have the price amended.

Augustus looked up from studying the precedents. 'I see that a high priest can only marry between night and day, midnight, between one moon and the next. Tonight!'

Eten, 'How auspicious, brother, that your crisis of faith occurred now.'

Leaving the council, Galen promptly forgot the price he'd pay in the future. He came across Zithia in a corridor near their two apartments. His shining eyes lightened her step. He grasped her by the waist and swung her high in an exultant circle. Aloft she asked breathlessly 'When?'

'Tonight, midnight.'

'But how?' Their bodies slid together in tantalising promise, while he lowered her.

'I'll tell you later.' Blithely she ran off. 'Much later.'

*

Xiao Chen then went straight to Galen, who was with Madison making plans to welcome his bride. As the scope of these changes was in direct proportion to Galen's sense of guilt, Madison found it necessary to direct a troop of assistants. Furniture was unearthed from storage, Galen's family treasures and decades of gifts. Each piece was exquisitely sculpted metal. When everything was in place, including the new full-size mirror for the living area, Xiao Chen was invited to inspect. The sun hit the apartment at that moment, and the deacon was obliged to raise his hand to his eyes against the glare. 'All this grandeur could be… overpowering.'

Galen's gesture was dismissive. 'The place needed a little colour.'

'Madison, have that gold disc removed,' Xiao Chen instructed. The disc was huge and reflecting the sun painfully. Madison went to obey the deacon. When Madison was gone, Xiao Chen said, 'The price for this marriage was high then?'

Galen rubbed between his eyebrows. 'Our first son is temple property.'

Xiao Chen looked away from Galen, waiting.

'And no, Zithia doesn't know.' There was an awkward pause. 'Old friend, she'll have marriage…'

Xiao Chen bowed ever so slightly. 'Excuse me high priest, I've duties to attend to.'

chapter 11

Torches flickered in the moonless sky and on a herb-strewn platform on the lake. The stars seemed in touching distance. Galen and Zithia arrived in separate canoes for the midnight service. Zithia wore a long shimmering grey garment, luminous with quexatl filaments. A thin gold chain attached a Seeing crystal to her forehead.

A truth-sayer, witnessing the ceremony, assisted her from the canoe. Waiting for Galen's vessel, Zithia felt his love travelling on the breeze, gathering around her. Then he was beside her. While Peregrine solemnised their union, their golden auras expanded until the light became one blazing twenty-foot tall star.

Galen placed a rippled gold band on Zithia's index finger. 'With this ring, brought from Atlantis by my forebears I, Galen, mystic high priest of Xalisco take thee, Zithia, priestess of this temple, to wife.'

The archpriest placed a gold-foil cup on the ground. 'Now, in remembrance of Atlantis we crush this cup, as Atlantis was crushed.' Galen's heel came down firmly. 'You are priest and wife.'

Kissing Zithia, Galen whispered. 'We're married again, as in heaven.'

Upon their landing on the shore, a local farmer approached grinning and presented Zithia with a gift, a knobbly, pitted, black potato, impossible to peel. The high priest thanked the laughing man. 'It's a wedding jest. It's called the potato that makes a young bride weep.'

Zithia radiated joy, 'Well, I'm one bride who won't weep.' And threw it into the lake.

Unable to resist witnessing Galen commit political suicide, Eten and Augustus had observed the wedding from the shadowy shore. They'd heard Zithia's last comment. Watching the newlyweds climb into a litter, Augustus asked, 'Speaking of tears. Was there any special reason you wanted to take her firstborn so young? Or was it merely for your pleasure?'

'She gapes at the sunset clouds like a lover, seeking...' Eten growled, her superbly painted mask rippling, 'seeking to spy the colour of God.'

Augustus shivered. Both he and Eten avoided sunsets, not wanting to be reminded of the one God. The one God's ultimate power.

Eten watched the litter depart. 'Dark loathes light, it has always been the way. Who am I to break with tradition.'

She reflected: *"Perhaps a plague rat brought down from the Alps..."* Curling her lips back from all her teeth. 'Until Zithia appeared, I had thought to convert Galen to darkness someday.' They walked on a little. 'Still, she has her uses; Galen's career now lies in ruins.'

A green-eyed vixen joined them and Augustus languidly took in her voluptuous form. 'Augustus, my half-sister Jasmine, come to join me from distant Chol-ula temple. Her new name is Roxanne, from...'

'...My home temple. Enchanted.' He took her hand, twirling Roxanne round. 'A formidable weapon Eten. A temptation even Galen may fall to, at the right time.'

Eten eyed Roxanne speculatively, as coldly as a mother assessing a neighbour's daughter's chance on the eternal market. 'Perhaps... when Zithia is heavy with a child.'

Roxanne pursed her lips at the idea that Eten thought her powers limited.

'Ahh, fate smiles upon me Roxanne, by allowing you time to tempt a connoisseur.' Augustus gave Roxanne's hand a playful bite. 'Believe me, I'm worthy practice.' Her eyes which were ever so slightly, so appealingly, cross-eyed, sparkled.

Roxanne looked over her shoulder, her smile atremble.

'Oh very well,' Eten let out a breath, 'you may play with him.'

Augustus announced, 'She'll be my protege; a second cousin.' The tip of Roxanne's tongue showed between lush lips.

*

Coming up the terraces, Galen and Zithia were talking softly when they almost walked past an elegant wedding feast. With a start, Zithia looked at the grove of trees in huge ceramic pots. From each tree dangled fragrant, foot-long trumpets. Intricate urns of snowy flowered mint added a delicate touch. Galen examined the garden in one glance. 'I always suspected my chamberlain, Madison, had a green thumb.' He offered Zithia a drink in a slender flute, not wanting to admit that most of the changes to his apartment had been chosen by himself, including the garden. It was he who'd watched the servants placing each piece, then asking them to change the arrangements. Quite driving them crazy, over several days. *"Maybe,"* he thought, *"too many trees."*

Zithia sipped, then took the lid off a golden dish, revealing a quail-egg omelete, garnished with mushroom slithers. Arching her back, she drew her fingers through the hair at one of her temples. One hand smoothed the dress at her thigh. 'I'm too excited to eat.'

'Then come explore your new domain.' Galen gestured toward the apartment.

Scattered beeswax candles lit the apartment. Glittering stands supported gleaming lily-leafed pots of orchids, whose long spikes were crammed with cream flowers, their lips yellow-ridged. Zithia made a bell chime, from the Dragon-Land, and was transfixed. It was their most perfect bell, with a tone so clear and of such a pitch which brought heaven to mind. Hearing it, one felt that if one but turned round one would find the astral at the door. And the door to be right next to you.

A hand mirror awaited Zithia on a slender table against a wall. In sequence, Galen touched five squares in the table. A draw opened to reveal hairbrushes, combs and a miniature dustpan. Galen closed the draw, took Zithia's hand in his and repeated the combination. She stroked Galen's clean brush. 'Who is to say I won't use your hair in a spell?'

He wound one of her thick curls round a finger, inhaling its scent. 'Why would you resort to clumsy spells, when you've already enchanted me?'

Passing a low scrolled table, Zithia read the book on an antique stand. Then she gasped at a half-wall of mirror. In its golden reflection, candle flame glinted off every surface. Gold, the furniture was gold. 'You didn't have to go to all this trouble.'

'I felt I should.' And basked in her delight. He moved through to the bedroom, drawing back a silk sheet.

In the darkling before dawn, Galen awoke Zithia, 'A surprise.'

She sat up, fluffing pillows up behind herself. Galen put a crystal in her hand and sat beside her. Showing her a crystal in one hand, he took her empty hand in his. Instantly, gloriously, they were in the real world where dawn was breaking. Zithia could almost feel the breeze raising flurries on the sand dunes. Feeling her tense, Galen thought: *"Relax. Breathe evenly."*

"We're honeymooning in a desert?"

"Shhhh." And he slowly floated them high up into the sky.

Water. The dunes were riddled with pools of transparent crystal green water, linked far away to a river.

Then they were flying down and down fast; Zithia put an astral hand up before her face as they dove into one of the long irregular pools without a splash. She felt the atmosphere around her become more dense. Different to astralling through air. Side by side they flew past water lilies above, past schools of fish diving for insects well below. For hundreds of feet; then they'd race through the sky and dive again. A full half-hour of magic.

*

Galen's calendars had, this moment, been delivered back to Zithia after having their dots and bars repainted. Still dressed for class with the martial arts' deacon, Zithia examined the three notched, wooden rings. The largest ring represented the ordinary year. Moving along the outside of this, a smaller wheel gave the sacred round, and within this was a tiny mystic wheel. Laying the calendars on the mahogany desk, Zithia moved a witchcraft cure-all plant closer, fluffing its purplish white flowers.

Xiao Chen entered. They ate together around this time everyday.

Zithia said, 'There were only half the usual number of men at my class this morning.' The master truth-sayer nodded.

'I'm pleased with the calendars. Do you think I should have them gilded as a surprise?'

Xiao Chen's face crinkled a little. 'There's no need to be vicious.'

'Perhaps I could have Madison paint Galen's vision-wall a new white, with just the merest hint of blue. I'm told the Mystic Davot's wall for visioning and meditation is always that colour.'

'It'd require a priest specialised in such walls, to do the job. And they're fully occupied with other matters at present.'

'Oh.'

Xiao Chen then continued in Atlantian, 'Galen is always impressed by well-spoken Atlantian. Your tutor reported to chamberlain Madison that your pronunciation was off these two weeks.' He placed a scroll on the desk. 'So I've brought you a more interesting text to practise on.'

The Atlantian title was, *"Flying through the Ages."* Zithia's hand was already tracing the words. Xiao Chen looked at her squarely, 'Remember, your flying lessons aren't to interfere with learning the mystic language.'

Then he turned and gestured to someone on the terrace. The flyer bowed to the high priest's wife and Xiao Chen.

'Lord Galen sends his greetings, my lady. He's with magi Davot's circle. The barbarian warlocks are puny beside the great sorcerer. Yet...' the flyer's head drooped, his attention on Xiao Chen.

'Continue. The rest will be public knowledge by midday.'

'We're losing every battle. The invaders speed along our highways stealing or destroying whatever they find. Their swords are an unknown metal that slash shields and shatter daggers.'

Zithia said, 'Some women follow the fourth contingent leaving tonight. Tell my husband I'll join him.'

Xiao Chen cleared his throat, and then addressed the flyer. 'I don't think the lady Zithia is quite serious.'

Zithia stared at him unblinking, and then smiled tightly at the flyer. 'I'd appreciate an answer before lunch.'

An absolute negative was Galen's reply.

A week later she was still brooding over it when she attended a dance class. The teacher was in a heap, weeping. Women murmured in a huddle. 'Her sister went with the fourth column. Two days' journey from safety, the invaders set a cavalry ambush, separating the followers from their protectors. All were captured.' A girl, her face blue-tinged, whispered, 'They died after nightmare abuses, screaming. A flyer witnessed only their last minutes and upon returning fainted.' No more women joined their warriors near the battleground.

After this incident the temple censored the news and princes hired their own flyers. The season changed. Refugees dribbled into the city, but never stayed. Fear drove them south, away from the blond monsters. Then a great city fell. The army was providing support for the fleeing inhabitants, but the flight masters weren't hopeful that the panicked tens of thousands could be saved.

*

Early the next morning Zithia was in the market, examining the marvelous detail of a green ceramic jug shaped like a huge-headed fish. Holding it up against the blue sky, she noticed that the cigar merchant's stall was missing. 'Don't the wealthy want their snuff and smoke today from old prince Yum-Kaax?'

Knowing the nobleman's devotion to profit, the potter replied, 'He must be near dying...' then flung out an arm, 'in which case, there's a plague among the princely.' Looking around, Zithia's spine tingled. The market was half-empty and not one wealthy woman squabbled over a price.

Forgetting the jug, Zithia hired a bamboo chair and went through the suburb where she had picnicked at the observatory. Most of the palaces were disgorging their superior occupants. Litters, over-laden, tottered away. Hundreds of llamas, festive in crimson head halters and tassels, meandered into the distance. It was an unusual way out of the city, being the most concealed route.

A woman, make-up askew, stood in front of Zithia's litter. When it stopped, the cobwebbed matron came to the side and put a dusty hand upon the armrest. 'Bearers, I'm Princess Norgay. This is your payment to take me to the southern fortified temple of Tepeque.' She presented a dusty gold funerary mask with emerald eyes, her late father's.

Glaring, Zithia rearranged a wave of her hair. A signet ring Galen had given Zithia sparkled on her finger. 'Highness, my husband fights in the north this day. Do you really want my chair? ' The other woman lurched backwards.

Shortly after, a startled white deer bounded over a reef of copper. Similar reefs were this year's must-have novelty. Zithia pointed to the mansion's entrance path. In the grounds, a man lay on an elaborate silken hammock strung between two stelae. Zithia watched the scarlet-edged llamas. 'So they flee.'

The man dipped a lengthy golden teaspoon into a black-fruit pudding. Commoner's chocolate. Zithia detected little white flecks where the spoon neatly cut the dessert. 'A hired flyer described a city burning. The nobles there, who'd tried to make a deal with the barbarians, are taking days to die.'

'Yet you're still here.'

He chuckled, 'I'm only a poor relation. It was a toss up between the pet ocelot and me.'

Zithia raced back to the temple. It was about lunchtime. Dressed in her priest's clothes, she pulled now-wet hair back into a rope. When another priest left the flyers' dining room, Zithia picked up a platter of raw eggs and slipped into the private banquet. On the table was a golden bowl, with lush carrot tops growing in water. Not due back on duty for six hours, the flyers slumped in their chairs, some holding tiny gold cups.

Eyes downcast, Zithia offered eggs to each flyer in turn. One picked up a black carrot. 'What I'd give for a yellow carrot.'

A man spilled more tequila than he poured into his cup. His companion flyer frowned. 'That's your third.' They spoke high Atlantian, for secrecy.

The drinker's eyes glazed. 'Why torture...' He steadied his cup with two hands, till he downed the alcohol. 'I can't go back today.'

The companion put a hand on his shoulder, 'Davot's power circle may save them.'

chapter 12

In her apartment Zithia absently moved Galen's calendar wheels round. How often she'd seen him bent over this instrument. Or sitting before his mystic's wall, that blank mat cream space, in front of which deep meditation and prayer were easily achieved. She wore the exquisite necklace and bracelets Galen had managed to send her.

All at once she felt Galen's presence and her day lit up. Wistfully, he seemed to be looking at her over his shoulder. Love filled her, soothed, comforted her. Sad-eyed, his face faded. Zithia heard a rising cry of pain. It was hers.

In Galen's vigil cloak, Zithia arrived at a little chapel. She bowed low to its occupant. 'Lady Becor, master flyer, you know that today is a day of great battle.' Becor nodded. Zithia drew herself up tall. 'I'll have your aid to reach my husband this day, that my strength may be his... should he need it.'

Becor blinked several times. 'Lady Zithia, the danger! You'd be severely weakened by such a journey. I also.'

'Then I'll be greatly in your debt.' She removed her necklace, a double string of gold peanuts whose indentations were outlined in black. 'The symbol of our bond.'

Becor's face was totally blank. Zithia reflected: *"So it's that hazardous."* 'Lady Becor, I'll repay this grand obligation in equal magnitude... at any time.'

Taking off the matching bracelets, she put all into the flyer's hands. 'Think about my children, yet to be born.'

Becor glanced at the intricate jewelry. 'I'm a sentimental fool.' She eyed Zithia levelly. 'If too much of your energy is being lost, I'll break the connection. Lord Galen won't thank me for your death.'

Becor brought out a few necessary items. While Zithia lay on Galen's cloak, Becor covered Zithia with a cloud of a vicuna blanket. 'You'll get very cold at this day's work.'

'Will you see what I see?'

'No, I'll see only your aura.'

The master flyer placed a polished antique crystal disc on Zithia's forehead and one on top of her head. Taking out a small vial, 'You've had flying dew before?'

'No.'

"Becor tutted. Black lily dew was gathered during a blue moon, was dramatic in freeing the spirit from the body's bonds. Zithia imagined a starlit night. Then visioned falling up into that endless ocean, until she was no longer even aware that she breathed.

'Ignore the shudders when they come. Go with each swing of the spirit and don't look at your body when you're out of it.' Becor placed a single drop of dew on Zithia's lips. 'Now think of where you want to be. See Lord Galen's face.'

Sitting cross-legged at Zithia's head, Becor watched her. Zithia skipped Galen's name across the still pond that was her mind. Visualising his face, a fluttering began. It increased until her spirit rocked like a boat in a storm. A second drop of dew.

Without warning, she was high up in the air watching a city in flames. Zithia fixed upon Galen's face and the inferno abruptly vanished, to be replaced by a large dim room. She stood to one side of eight figures, the power circle, and they gazed past her. She found herself pulled to her husband. He was pale. Indeed they all were. A seasoned team, they'd already been working for hours to stall the invaders.

Zithia floated to almost behind Galen. Battle sounds erupted from a rough circle that was the wall opposite. The edges of the scene melted into rock. Men lurched towards them in full battle kit. A horse snorted and raised a spray of dust. The smell of dry turf came to Zithia. An arrow on the battlefield burst from the wall to disintegrate a meter into the room.

The Magi Davot looked smaller than on First Day, his dark wavy hair streaked with grey now. 'My friends, we may save fifty thousand lives. Such an achievement is worth sacrifice.'

Zithia saw another ethereal traveller appear as Davot intoned a spell. Galen's lips moved in unison. While the repetition rose in volume, Zithia felt the power build-up in the room. They were in the eye of a storm.

And mist appeared from nowhere, covering the space between the invaders and the fleeing city dwellers. Soon after the warriors entered the fog, thunder cracked in a series. The invaders cringed, looking skyward, fearing the Lightning God. High-pitched shouts took the place of battle cries as the mist and the thunder swelled.

A witch took a sip from a horn tumbler before giving it to the warlock. About to drink, he poured a libation on the ground to the God whose thunder was now a continuous reprimand. Then, he felt the mist warriors. Standing on a hillock above the mist, Hans the Dreaded leered. His reputation was so formidable that he worked alone, without the support of a coven.

Throwing his hand to heaven, the thunder halved. Hans spoke an unmaking at the fog; clear patches appeared. The fog thinned, yet expanded, despite Hans's efforts. As he cursed his drinking and womanising, Hans grabbed the nearby witch by her shoulders. She contorted; Hans's eyes glowed red.

A bolt of ruby light appeared from the vision, seeking Davot, and kept coming. Two magician priests stepped one pace forward. Raising their hands, a blue luminescence formed around the power circle. The fireball exploded on contact with the shell. More balls hurtled through the vision, disintegrating in sparks. One large shot penetrated the shield, and a second flew through the opening. The woman in its line of fire dropped.

White vapor leaked into the room from the battle site. The bones of the mystics' faces stood out jaggedly. Other travellers were already adding their weight to the fight. Zithia let part of her energy course into Galen. His eyes gained lustre, instantly he straightened.

Within the mist, cringing men slashed at anything that touched them. Reinforcements milled around outside the fog, trembling. At renewed lightning, many groveled low, praying, others ran.

Davot's charcoal eyes blazed. 'We hold till dusk! Another hour.'

The refugees would be away by then and the barbarians wouldn't be eager to encounter the darkness that night. Zithia kept a thick line of light flowing to Galen. A priestess collapsed. The rest quivered under the increased burden, then held firm. Shortly after a traveller shimmered and disappeared. Another man fell to his knees. The travellers became opaque behind the magicians.

Davot began letting out his core energy, the energy that spoke the length of his life. His circle did the same. Tears trickled down Zithia's face as she watched how much life-force Galen was releasing. Already gaunt from the loss of her normal energy, she drew on her own core energy, throwing six years into the fray. Galen's face lost its lines. Glowing, Zithia released another ten years.

Becor, intent on Zithia's aura, hadn't dreamed that she'd relinquish the second lot of life. The flight master swore. Four of the ten years remained with Zithia, when she felt cool liquid on her lips. Her mind protested: *"Not yet."*

Zithia slapped the master flyer hard across the face. The grounding elixir went everywhere. 'I knew what I was doing; women live longer than men.'

The older woman pushed her lips forward. 'And high priests outlive other men.'

Zithia drew in a rapid breath, and then her gaze steadied. 'What of that?'

Despite the blanket Zithia began to shiver violently. Becor shouted for a novice. 'Carry Lady Zithia to her apartment, she's ill.'

Days later, a servant had finished brushing Zithia's mane. Examining the brush, Xiao Chen tossed the gleanings into the fire. So doing, he saw Zithia's eyes flutter and quickly announced. 'Galen lives. The city's people were saved.' Thus far, he'd spoken these words five times.

Zithia was a plume trembling in the wind, then dry-retching into a gold basin. Malinali strewed more orchids on the floor, gifts from well-wishers. Green butterflies, with red dots and yellow lips, topped the orchid carpet. On a table sat Peregrine's gold lattice platter of star-fruit.

*

The invading commander-in-chief, Rhaim, passed the witch's body, as it rolled down the hill. Her entire life-force had been stolen to combat the mist; only then had Hans accessed his own energy. Fortunately, Rhaim found the warlock still on his feet. Rhaim alone helped Hans, skin now shrunken tight onto his bones, back into his tent.

'Never put your trust in a warlock,' Rhaim sneered to the captain on guard outside, 'they always let you down. Regardless of reputation. No one enters.' The commander stayed till dawn, apparently drinking with Hans.

Several visits later, Rhaim ordered a reviving bath for the warlock. When Hans was fully in the bath, Rhaim took hold Hans's feet and pulled them gently up to chest height, watching Hans's comatose head sink beneath the bath water. 'There's an end to your three percent of the campaign's gold.'

Drowned while drunk, the report already read. If Hans had died due to battle, the Guild of Warlocks would've claimed his share.

*

Two weeks after mist-night, Galen arrived back at Xalisco. Flowers were thrown before him as he stood in a gilded litter, carried on the bearers' shoulders. His hair lapped the golden edges of a headdress presented to him at the city's outskirts. Long blue feathers glistened down his back in a V. In the hollow beside Galen's right eye, fourteen lines were emphasised in black and gold. Fourteen years he'd given to the mist.

Zithia stood on the elevated official dais with Peregrine. Joining them, Galen faced the masses. He placed his right hand on his heart, denoting him as their servant. The populace went wild.

'I, Galen, a son of Xalisco, was privileged to join the legendary mystic Davot in mist making. Our efforts were rewarded... at a cost.' He held out his hand to Zithia. 'My own wife, the Lady Zithia, flew that night and willingly sacrificed twelve years life-force to the battle.' Zithia's scars were on her left temple. 'All those who fought that day are listed in the scrolls of record.' He read the names.

During the banquet that followed, Peregrine privately congratulated Galen. 'Eminence, my wife and I were glad to shorten our lives in the service of our temple.'

Peregrine half bowed. 'A dreadful night. Yet the bonds you forged with the great power circle...'

'Indeed, we're now family!' He paused, 'Eminence, the mist-circle was surprised that the price of my wedding will be paid so soon after his birth.' Galen gave Peregrine a sealed sheet.

"Archpriest Peregrine, it's the recommendation of Davot the mystic and the mist-circle, that the bride-price for Lord Galen's marriage not be exacted until the boy reaches a proper age of six. Definitely six is the best age."

Frowning at the words, Peregrine smiled bitingly. The archpriest's glittering eyes slid to Galen's face, his head following. 'You can't imagine my feelings on receiving the great Davot's... request.' He tapped the letter against his arm. 'It gives me the opportunity to rescind a decision I always thought harsh. It will be as the mist-circle suggests.'

115

'With the vow of silence extending till my son's fifth birthday.'

*

Augustus's second cousin, Roxanne, was quite a success and, equally, a scandal. Since her arrival the sisters had only passed in halls, seemingly without recognition.

A few nights after Galen's victory procession, Roxanne's soft tread was heard on Eten's terrace. The new date for taking the bride price had been known among the high priests during the banquet. Davot's interference was revealed to very few. Within the general babble, Roxanne had watched her sister's anger from afar knowing better than to offer immediate sympathy. The green eyed siren still bore a faded scar from the day she had tried to comfort a sixteen year old, pre-menstrual, Eten.

The dark gauze at the balcony windows shivered, and then Roxanne stood before an inner doorway, barred by heavier drapes.

'Come in, Roxanne.' From childhood, Eten could always feel when Roxanne was sneaking around. Roxanne moved the curtain. A chink of yellow showed a tray of strawberries. Walking through, she picked it up. Observing Eten, Roxanne hastily shut the curtains behind her.

Eten sat on a chair with her foot upon a stool. From a cut in her ankle, blood dripped into a golden bowl. Engraved skulls danced around the inside. Eten offered her cheek, 'My dear…'

Roxanne planted a kiss, their cheeks brushing. Then she watched the dripping red, eating the while.

'I've been worried over you.' Roxanne smiled lightly, not referring to the bride price or Davot. 'And now I find there's no need, for you're obviously in fine spirits.'

She licked a strawberry, 'Did you use a stingray spine to open your wound?'

'A temple healer opened the flesh without instruments. Stingray spines are only for exceptional occasions.' Roxanne sank gracefully to the floor at Eten's feet. The hole was very neat. 'He'll close the wound without a mark.' Eten purred. 'No one suspects I'm bloodletting to increase my powers.'

The high priestess's eyes hardened. 'Darling, you shouldn't have come. What if we're seen together?'

Roxanne, 'That's why I'm here so late.'

Eten stroked Roxanne's hair, 'My love, you're very popular. Now, for which conquest do you feel tenderness?'

Roxanne ate a strawberry whole. 'None!'

Eten rang a fingernail hard along Roxanne's dusky cheekbone. 'And, dearest… which would you use?'

Now Roxanne responded in Augustus's accents. 'Which do you want me to use?'

'Ahh, mama's blood runs strong in your veins.'

'I follow our blood and the dark path.' Roxanne flicked her hair. 'My spells are getting ever so potent, Eten.'

Eten patted her sister on the top of her ebony head. 'Of course they are darling …' Handing Roxanne the bowl of blood, Eten waved her into a shadowy alcove.

The healer answered the ring of a gong. *"Do I still believe that a seer recommended her being bled for health, specifying the dead of night?"* He wondered, then concentrated on her vein. It sealed. A cane toad appeared from nowhere and the healer closed the skin in puckers.

Acidly, Eten addressed him, 'Fix that, or I'll make a scar of my own.'

Sweating, he reopened the skin. This time the mend was invisible.

After his departure, Roxanne reappeared, 'What're you up to tonight?' She held out the bowl. 'Convulsions? A sudden extreme allergy to cashew fruit? I know… the bleeding death.'

The precious blood was locked away in a wall cache, without Roxanne being enlightened. She oohed over Eten's unblemished ankle and sat down again, one foot wriggled rhythmically. 'Next time I want to do it, too. I also have important spells requiring blood.'

'Little sister, your natural magic is the one I want you to hone.' Eten closed her teeth with a snap. 'I see you've been ignoring the temple women.'

Roxanne twitched her small nose, nervously, and moved beyond Eten's reach. 'They're no use to me.'

'Silly child.' Eten knew why her sister had moved. 'Waste not, want not. Some are useful to me!'

Roxanne's face puckered, 'Alright; I'll charm them. Just tell me which.' At the periphery of her vision, Roxanne spotted Venus sitting on an alpaca cushion, watching them. Roxanne picked out the largest strawberry. 'I'll be off then.'

'Better had. Or the blood will spoil before I do my incantation.'

Roxanne threw the strawberry at the cane toad, hitting Venus between the eyes. His poison glands bulged. 'No, Venus, no!' Eten shook her index finger at him. 'Honestly, Roxanne, must you always be jealous of my darling?' Roxanne made a pouting mew of her full lips.

Despite the danger of being seen, Eten walked onto the terrace to see Roxanne off, though she did lighten her physical impression to the world by quashing down her thoughts and personality, before crossing her threshold. There, on the broad walkway, Eten and Roxanne brushed finger-tips in adieu. Watching her sister prance away, Eten heard wings only inches above her head. A yellow swan flew over, passed Roxanne and gracefully turned… to fly through an apartment's wall.

Roxanne was now near that apartment's wide, open terrace door. The high priestess gazed at her sister who danced, unknowing, through streams of misty colours winding out from the rooms. Roxanne waved at Eten between snatches of memories. Eten murmured, 'I had no idea Abagail was so near death.' More brightly, 'Perhaps I can get her calligraphy set.'

*

Late the next morning the Magi Davot, unable to trek far at one time, still journeyed home by litter. Materialising from camouflaged hides, the barbarians rode at Davot's entourage from two sides.

The barbarian captain hadn't had any quarry for days. Before bed, he'd stabbed a captive in the stomach, but interpreting the pattern made by the writhing man's blood had proved illusive. In a dream this ambush came to him.

Davot's two hundred attendants and warriors surrounded his litter, fighting hard. Throughout the battle Davot lay drained, seemingly impassive, yet sending threads of strength to his companions. The prisoners were taken to a large barbarian encampment.

The leader, Celal, was ecstatic. A squadron of soldiers to guard one sick, old man.

'Who are you?' No answer. 'Who's he?' Silence. Celal tightened an arm around the chest of Davot's young apprentice, saying something that produced catcalls from the gathered army.

The magi stood, speaking Phoenician, 'I'm Davot, mystic of the north.'

'No, a sorcerer. A mist maker!' Celal examined the haggard face. 'The mist maker.' He roared. 'We have rare entertainment… the lead mist warlock… revenge!' There were men here who had been caught in that mist.

The army howled, while horses were brought forward. A frantic prisoner was tied to four steeds by his hands and feet. Seconds before the general gave the order to slap the horses on the rumps, Celal sneered, 'Save him.'

With muscles and sinews tearing, the screams began. But before the bones popped from sockets, the captive stopped shrieking. Then he was in bits. Sundered arms and legs were thrown to the horde, which fought over them. Another attendant was delivered to the stallions, then another. Both times the shrieking died well before the skin split. Between killings, the general's hounds snapped jagged bits from the ground. A single high-pitched whistle returned them to either side of Celal's chair.

Tunnels of light appeared, which only Davot observed. Both victims were gathered, smiling, into the warm embrace of the light, and were gone.

When the third victim, a woman, died soundless, realisation dawned on Celal. He head butted Davot. Shoulders massive, Celal pounded toward Davot, but stopped. 'Let the men have the rest.' Smirking, 'Which one will you help?'

Thirty men and women, previously untouched, were dragged into the mob. Saliva dripped from some of the barbarians' maws. The hounds begged Celal, who clicked his fingers. They joined the fun. But before the clawing and hacking could start, all the victims dropped. Their spleens pierced by a single thought. Davot quivered with exertion. Motionless for a second, the throng mangled the corpses into raw meat. Lapping blood, the dogs remained forgotten at the carnival.

A plethora of tunnels of light appeared in such a cluster as to give the scene above the crowd a blue-white radiance. One woman, as she began gliding upwards in her light, turned in mid-space to Davot and blew him a kiss.

The executioner, Hanzan, hadn't been having a good day. As he was about to enjoy the bloodshed, a minor officer had arrived, 'Sharpen your axe. I'm executing my woman, after all. No, use the sword; I once found her ravishable.'

Hanzan delivered a curse with every turn of the sharpening stone. All the while the mob roared, not many feet away. The general called for him.

The executioner's jowls beamed and in his haste to attend the carnage he took the sword with him. Passing a friend, Hanzan laid a heavy hand on him and the assistant fell in behind the executioner without a word.

Celal gulped wine. 'Cut off this accursed sorcerer's head.' He threw himself onto his campaign chair, a few steps from Davot.

Bowing to Celal, Hanzan pushed Davot to his knees. Expressionless, Davot looked at the general, who sat legs apart. Hanzan faced Davot, beginning his swing. Terror in a victim's eyes was better than mating to him. Now he saw none. Hanzan paused, deliberated on the flaming brazier which had been set up on the dais. Grinning, eyes on Davot's face, Hanzan passed the sword through the flames.

Watching the simmering blade, Davot sent all his strength, all his magic, down through his body. Then Hanzan began his stroke anew, this time completing the swing. The sword sliced through Davot's throat and spine. Blood spattered; some veins new-cut smoldered shut. Leaning on the sword, Hanzan took the severed head from where it rolled and swung it in a wide arc. Tumultuous cheering.

The executioner teased the crowd by almost throwing the prize. But Davot's brain wasn't yet finished with life, for sentience remains after beheading … just awhile. His eyes watched a small stream of the blood sprinkle eager, clutching, barbarians. Suddenly Davot's world went silent; yet he saw the whites of thousands of eyes. Jaws dropping, the pack was no longer intent on the magician's head. A corner of Davot's mouth twitched into a smile.

Moments before, behind the swordsman, Davot's legs had pushed his corpse to its feet. It walked, with purpose, the distance to the frozen general. The mystic's hands fastened themselves to the blonde's throat, thumbs pressing into the tender hollow at the neck's base. Celal screamed, unable to take his gaze from the gory stump at his eye level.

No one intervened; none had the will. The dead hands increased their pressure, jetting blood convulsively from severed arteries. Celal's blue face matched his eyes and then his jerking legs ceased. Davot's torso toppled into its enemy's arms.

Many were trampled deserting the scene. While they ran, shadow patches appeared in an almost solid cloud and fell upon the gawping ghost of Celal. His phantom eyes were still locked upon his death scene as his spirit was dragged off and under. Meantime, Davot's soul was almost at the top end of his tunnel of light, basking in the warmth of pure love and with the golden light of God drawing him even further up through the astral, to that highest of planes.

Regrouping, the battalions didn't rest till they'd joined other camps.

The barbarians spread their horror. Over the next months, the mere sight of a high priest saved many refugees. Beheadings were forbidden and the men demanded warlocks, a full coven.

The temple cities mourned Davot with ballads and feasts. On publicly hearing the news Eten was grief-stricken. When alone, she smiled until her facial muscles ached. She'd definitely chosen the right path, when her blood-spell could influence the great Davot's destiny.

chapter 13

In great excitement Zithia arose late one morning so as to avoid Galen, who had gone to early prayers. She made her way to an area across a main city river. Not taking the half-oval stone bridge, but deciding to use the tall rickety wooden bridge that was only ever meant to be temporary. So temporary was it, that it had no handrails. Bulging cargo canal boats trekked the waterway, stacked high with freight. Zithia dashed the zigzag of the slat walkway high above the shouting congestion resulting from boats going both ways.

On finally reaching the herbarium, Zithia sought out a gaunt deaconess. The woman addressed Zithia with speculation, 'So my lady, you're two weeks late?'

The woman felt Zithia's belly and looked into her pupils, before requesting Zithia's first water of the day. Adding rainwater to the specimen, the deaconess went to some newly planted aquinoa seeds. 'A female flyer saw this done in the land of the Sphinx.'

The deaconess poured the mixture over the seeds. 'In nine days the aquinoa will sprout or not. Then, we'll know.'

On the prescribed day Zithia again dashed across the rickety wooden bridge, too eager for news to take the long way. A woman walking directly behind Zithia looked longingly at Zithia's progress and thought: *"Surely once won't hurt."* She continued to watch Zithia, somewhat wistfully. *"Can it?"*

Violet turned, only turned towards the bridge. A shiver went through her. Taking one step; another shiver. She wasn't as good at keeping her balance as most people. Then, unbidden, Violet felt... sensed... semi, almost-saw it again. At some time. A heavy barge would bump against one of the bridge's struts. And where others would be fine, she was falling. Then lying across the barge's crates. Alive, yet so very broken.

As Violet continued on to the stone bridge, a mystic watched her from that stone oval. He thought to her: *"You're decision is correct, as is your sight."*

On her way back to the temple, Zithia was ecstatic. Her feet barely touching the ground, she caught up with her husband while crossing a side-canal bridge. No more short cuts for Zithia. Galen's smile grew very, very slowly and he took her into a tender hug. 'I assumed we were too weak to conceive.' His eyes grew moist; Galen sensed the unborn baby. Lines appeared between his brows. *"So, I'm to have a son."* The high priest thought. Without even trying, he'd kept his side of the bride-price bargain.

That dusk, Galen reserved the high priests pool. 'You asked for something for morning sickness.' Galen flourished an intricately carved golden basin, from which he poured exotically scented leaves into the pool.

'What do they do?'

'Nothing.' And presented her with the empty basin. 'There's no draught to stop morning sickness.' When they finished laughing, 'I'll be the heritage-caller.'

With Galen helping their baby call upon its Atlantian heritage, Zithia's joy was complete.

Finally, Zithia entered their bedroom, which was ablaze with candles. A fine dust gilded everything. Standing on the threshold, Galen blew gently and all the shining particles lifted off, floating midair. Twirling slowly around, Zithia set the golden snow dancing. Glittered, she lay on the vicuna rug, in front of the fireplace, and stretched out her arms to her soul mate.

Much later Galen whispered, 'Let me name the child.'

*

The nursery was ready. A jade alphabet mobile hung over a silk-sheeted crib. On top of papyrus paper lay coloured crayons with golden holders. A bird-shaped flute awaited playing. Galen pulled a wooden alpaca, on wheels, across the room by its lead.

'Aren't we over-doing it?' Xiao Chen set a jumping bean to prance and examined the baby quipii, 'If you had chosen the jeweled quipii, Zithia would definitely suspect you of hiding something.'

'I'm simply a doting father-to-be.' Galen looked at a rainbow frog, seated on jade in its gold-wire atrium. He juggled three bouncing stones.

Xiao Chen tilted his head forward. 'When will you tell her?'

The stones leapt at speed to walls and ceiling, ricocheting madly around the room. Xiao Chen looked steadily at Galen, who sidestepped a rock whizzing at him from behind. The master-witness caught it. 'If you don't want to talk…'

*

When Zithia was heavy with child she found the heat unbearable. Hence, Galen reproduced their apartment in a lower cave. An ancient cavern with its own natural light, like the temple mushroomeries. The Atlantians had tunnelled to the surface, using slabs of magnifying crystal to bring in the sun. If Galen finished his duties late, he slept in their usual apartment, to avoid disturbing Zithia.

Around this period Galen commenced attending banquets alone and Roxanne was always seated near him. Often she'd ask after Zithia, leaning towards Galen and flicking the top edge of her billowing bodice. Or she was at the table opposite, green eyes smoldering while one pretty foot slowly thrust in and out of a sandal.

Following a very late ceremony celebrating the full moon, Galen arrived at his bedroom to find it already occupied. Roxanne wore an emerald sheath. Without saying a word she lowered it slowly down her body revealing a fine, net-covered underdress. Straining in all the right places. With hands caressing the curve that was her waist, she tossed her head.

Looking long, the high priest undid his cloak fastening. Roxanne slipped onto the bed, with a grace born of practice. 'Can you compare Zithia to me?'

Xiao Chen chose this moment to come in for a nightcap. They both gave Roxanne a look that was far from appreciative. She stiffened.

'Something has crawled into my lady's bed, Xiao Chen. Will you favour me by having Madison…?' With that, Galen turned his back on Roxanne, getting the drinks.

Xiao Chen bowed very, very slightly and rang a bell. An angry red flushed Roxanne's face, extending down to her cleavage. Grabbing up her gown, Roxanne's gilded high heels rang out staccato shots as Madison arrived.

*

Galen brought purple cherry juice and a trance to numb the pain. In her husband's arms, Zithia rocked on a low bench until it was time to use the birthing chair. This was a high-backed affair carved all over with big-bellied women in warrior garb. Labour was considered to be a battle fought against unseen enemies.

Crouching among cushions, Galen caught the baby when the boy decided to arrive. After the high priest cut the umbilical cord, he handed his son up to Zithia. Tears filled Galen's eyes. An hour later he presented his son, dressed in ceiba silk, to the archpriest. In the name of the temple Peregrine accepted the boy, before formally requesting Galen to care for the child until his sixth birthday.

When Galen held the eight-day old baby for his circumcision, Zithia stood next to the long-legged gold chair on which her husband sat. Circumcision was a requirement of the one God. For once the one God had even given a reason; circumcision greatly reduced diseases, even potential killers, especially when one lived in warm or wet climates. White-knuckled, Zithia watched the physician, who could circumcise while drawing only a single drop of blood. He lived up to his reputation.

The baby was then named. Ti-Kylyn-Coatl. A word, created by his father, whispering presence and charm when spoken. It was Galen's best gift to his son. At home they called him Kylyn or, like all parents, darling.

*

One year had passed since Davot's death, his martyrdom remembered in epic terms. In her garden Eten scratched Venus's chin. 'How time flies, my lovely. Yet, Galen's brat is two weeks old and still with his parents.' Screwing her mouth up, she pinched the cane toad. He jumped some distance from her. 'To go against the mist knights' decree would be disastrous. I'll have to find another way.'

There was a deacon's woman called Tahey. Though she conceived many times, Tahey never managed to carry a baby to term. After her last miscarriage, a burning light gleamed eternal in Tahey's fair eyes. During Kylyn's third month, Tahey visited Eten.

'High priestess, I was honoured by the flower drops you sent me... for my depression. Three times now.'

Eten smiled.

'I didn't think you'd noticed... I mean... I'm only a concubine...' She trailed off. Then she started again, brightly, 'And they work, the drops that is. My goodness, the relief after only a week. Obviously, I am still taking the physician's draughts.'

'Oh, unquestionably. And seeing the counsellor priest.'

'Yes.' Tahey blushed.

'I feel for your pain, my dear.' Eten, having spoken to the counselor, was interested to hear that, after the depression, Tahey still suffered from deep anger. Useful. Eten had required Tahey to be free of depression; the high priestess needed a person who could act. And who'd act under instruction.

Eten sighed heavily, looking away. 'For you to be blessed as Zithia has been would've come as a fair gift from the one God. I wonder if the high priest's wife appreciates her good fortune.'

Rage threatened to engulf Tahey, causing her to gag on a rush of invectives.

'There, there...' Soothed Eten. When Tahey had recovered herself, Eten spoke softly,

'What say you, gentle sister, if I could promise you a well-born son?' Tahey's eyelashes dipped. Instantly she fell to her knees, kissing the hem of Eten's skirt. And crying.

They were still conversing when the medicine-leaves seller, Obnil, was announced. Tahey needed more of the herb catubua. And if Obnil didn't have any, then turnerup would do as well. She'd been spiking her partner's drinks to encourage success in bed. 'One could almost call this an omen,' Eten announced.

Obnil entered and bowed, revealing a bald patch on the top of his skull. Eten bought fresh herbs. 'We start today.'

*

On the first day that the new mother could be officially visited, a gaggle of women came to Zithia, bringing gifts. Ensconced within the party were Tahey and Roxanne. A miniature pectoral of tiny feathers and beads was much admired. While the others were in the lounge cooing over the infant, Tahey insisted on hanging a dream catcher above the baby's cradle.

Rejoining the group, Tahey held Kylyn for a long time and sang to him.

The next morning, Zithia was in the living area reading an ancient manuscript, using a latex teething rod for a pointer. A whisper occurred, echoed, and out of the corner of her eye Zithia thought she saw movement. Turning her head; nothing. Not long after, she had the merest impression of something silvery by the hall door. Drawing her eyebrows together, Zithia stood, opening her senses. But an hysterical wail from Kylyn drove everything else from her mind.

When the baby was finally settled that evening, and the nurse had retired, Zithia remembered the whisper. She walked onto the terrace where, Galen was walking up the slopes of a miniature mountain. A peak made from bamboo root, the whole only a few inches high. His body sat in a chair in front of the perfect miniature. Zithia addressed the paths on the mountain, where a few finely placed trees stood. 'Beloved, have you been bringing your work home with you?'

From the chair, 'Why?'

She turned to face Galen's body. 'Today I thought I felt something in this room.' Her fingers tingled. 'You are careful, aren't you?' Kylyn began to wail.

'I'm a high priest.' Then, his eyes narrowed. Feeling for psychic energy, he found nothing suspicious. He shook his head.

Relaxing, Zithia frowned at the diminutive peak. 'You never take me mountaining.'

'Every man likes to have one space to call his own.'

Kylyn began to wail. He cried all night.

*

Presently Tahey was delighted to confirm herself pregnant and it felt a healthy, full-term pregnancy. 'I didn't think it'd happen this fast.' She grinned at Eten, without another thought.

'The whole transition has to be much quicker than normal, because it's Galen's child.'

Tahey patted her stomach, 'Soon, very soon my darling, you'll be all mine.'

*

Kylyn broke his heart in tears, weakening by the day. The physicians were at a loss. Nine days later there came a dreadful evening when Galen looked in his son's cradle to find Kylyn motionless, silent. The high priest lifted his son in his arms. 'Kylyn!'

The baby opened his eyes. Galen dropped him, and then caught him again. Kylyn's eyes were silver. A rare sign of a soul-snatcher at work. Yet, none of the other signs were there.

'Zithia, get Xiao Chen.' Galen stripped Kylyn, dropping the clothes on the nursery floor. They both appeared. 'Magic!' Galen spat out, and then enveloped Kylyn with a green healing light.

Zithia rang a gong for the serving priestesses. Xiao Chen instructed, 'We'll need fires to cleanse the place, lots of water and an Atlantian gold basin for bathing Kylyn.' Gold was known to have beneficial properties; Atlantian gold more so.

Xiao Chen said to the wet-nurse, 'Get emeralds from the treasury.'

Galen took Kylyn onto the terrace. Passing a pot plant, he pulled off some leaves to help combat the spell. Much more rapidly than they thought possible, the gold basin was full of water and Xiao Chen added the emeralds plus crushed leaves. Galen gave the baby to Zithia, who lowered Kylyn into the liquid.

'Repeat.' Galen said to Zithia. She took over a charm he'd been saying. Xiao Chen followed the high priest.

Fires, pungent with myrrh, now glowed in ceramic bowls. The water was renewed frequently.

Galen and Xiao Chen examined the nursery, tapping the walls for hidden cavities. Floor, ceiling. They had to find the magic affecting Kylyn. To cure this spell, Galen needed to know exactly what it was. It must be in the nursery. Systematically, they tore everything in the room apart. A potted black orchid was smashed on the balcony. The frog, re-housed in a tree outside. Blocks of painting pigments were crushed beneath Xiao Chen's foot. Dismembering the dream catcher, Galen found several gold coloured strips woven into it.

Pulling on a piece, Galen could feel the extra weight. 'Lead! For hiding witchcraft. Lead neutralises the feel from a spell.' Xiao Chen witnessed what was found and where, then the broken dream catcher was cast into a fire.

'Tahey gave the dream catcher.' Zithia was ashen faced. 'She hung it herself.'

Without its shield, Galen could almost smell the hidden evil. He went at once to the remains of the cot. The dark wood lay in a jumble. Galen observed that there was one more slat than he expected in the base of the tiny bed. This extra piece, at Kylyn's heart level, wasn't wood. While Xiao Chen witnessed, Galen peeled the counterfeit.

Three hairs. One his wife's, one his son's and a gold blond strand. A dozen tiny grey metal balls rolled out. Platinum to magnify the spell. The packet itself had the four symbols to call a soul snatcher, delicately written in blood.

They looked again at the golden hair. 'Tahey!' Zithia thought she'd faint.

'This is well beyond Tahey,' stated Xiao Chen. 'And how did they get the hairs?'

'A bird... a blackbird dove at me one day.' She sobbed, 'Been brushing Kylyn's hair and hadn't yet tidied up.'

Xiao Chen, 'I wonder who that blackbird was?' Then, specifically to Zithia, 'Galen should've warned you. Always be watchful of interested blackbirds; never say a word in front of one.'

Galen, 'Hairs are light enough even for a spirit-bird to carry off.' He looked grim. 'It's a death spell.' Galen's whole body felt heavy. 'The reversal may kill Kylyn.'

The high priest crumpled half the tainted slat. Mixing it with the platinum and a rare extract, he spoke a command. A spectre appeared. At once, snarling, it tensed to pounce.

Galen's voice rang with magic, 'Know me! Know my power!'

He held up his staff. Lightning crackled around the crystal topping it. A blue-ish line lashed out at the soul-snatcher. The wraith backed away, curling into itself. Then, observing the crystal grow calmer, the soul-snatcher began to jabber while making tearing and breaking movements with its elongated fingers.

Throwing some salt and crushed crystal over its head, Galen watched smoking holes appear where the mixture landed. It keened at the lacework effect.

'Retrieve the soul of Ti-Kylyn-Coatl, from whence that precious spark was taken.'

The snatcher's transparent claws spasmed. Fading, it became a mere whisper. A moving whisper.

Galen accompanied it. Passing a few people along the way, the snatcher was quiet. Yet, alone with Galen, it rumbled continuously. Galen thought: *"If Kylyn dies... Zithia can't lose two children... He's as light as a husk... The spell caster is Kylyn's only hope."*

Nearing a common room, the beast stopped. A small fire burned and Eten was steeping a mescalin mushroom in water. Tahey sat sewing feathers onto a baby's naming dress.

Galen strode across the threshold. Glancing at Tahey's work, he drawled, 'Somewhat premature, surely?'

Recoiling, Tahey covered her belly with her hands. The flames of the fire went black as the soul-snatcher entered. When it realised Eten was present it gave her a wide berth, while emitting a high-pitched gibbering.

The wraith floated toward her, opening its elongated fingers wide. Kylyn's soul drifted gently from Tahey's womb. The soul-snatcher swooshed away. Immediately Tahey began to haemorrhage, spilling bright red onto the floor.

Galen looked from Tahey to Eten, his top lip drawn back. 'So you can transform.'

'You could too.'

'The dark path,' Galen looked bored. 'I'm not interested in parlour tricks, Eten.' The high priestess narrowed stony eyes. 'Now, how safe will the other high priests feel when they hear that you've used hair to cast?'

'I have the blood spell and Xiao Chen's testament. They'll blind you. Then, bind your powers.' Muscles in Eten's face altered minutely, her shoulders raised themselves half an inch.

'Still, it needn't come to such unpleasantness, if my son lives!' Tahey groaned, they ignored her. 'I promise you my evidence and my amnesia.'

Tahey stood up. The high priest and priestess looked at the ruby pool at Tahey's feet. Galen's face hardened. 'Decide, Eten.' He turned on his heel.

Once he was gone Tahey beckoned the high priestess for help. Motionless, the high priestess contemplated the expanding blood, as though seeking inspiration. 'My dear; you're indisposed?' Eten brushed imaginary fluff from her dress, 'We must continue our chat another time.'

*

Hearing a slithering whisper, Zithia held the baby closer. The snatcher floated up to her, carrying a small bright spark within its claws. Xiao Chen took Kylyn and the spectre replaced Kylyn's soul within its mortal shell again. Immediately the baby's eyes changed from silver to deep blue. The wraith cringed near the door.

Entering, Galen commanded, 'Be gone!' And the snatcher fled back to its own world.

*

The news next day was appalling. Tahey hadn't haemorrhaged to death. Eten roared at Minuet, 'Get me a bunch of orchids.' Venus promptly hid among Eten's ornate collection of dry ink-cakes.

At the hospital, Tahey was propped up in bed. The high priestess gasped. 'Little sister.' she lowered her face close to Tahey's. The other woman pressed herself back into her pillows. 'Tell me you're recovered.'

Eten grasped a posy of yellow orchids tightly. 'My dear, forgive me for yesterday. Galen's impertinence entirely… distracted me. I'm quite vexed with myself,' Eten batted her eyelids, and then slowly raised her eyebrows. A hopefully sympathetic gesture. 'for leaving you so soon… I didn't realise…' The high priestess tried not to think too loud: *"you'd survive."*

Unlocking stiff fingers, Eten laid the flowers on Tahey's lap. Tahey breathed in the sweet perfume of the semi-open blossoms. The scent contained something extra. *"I adore these."* She thought, breathing deeply a potion which diminished judgment. She breathed in again.

Watching Tahey's facial muscles relax, Eten continued, 'The evil in that man; destroying your chance of happiness.'

Tahey's feverish mind forgot the acid comment she'd been about to make. Twisting sour lips, Tahey thought: *"Yes… it's Lord Galen's fault."*

'You may yet need this.' Eten proffered Tahey the unfinished baby's dress.

Tahey's trembling hands stroked the cloth.

'I've found another pregnancy to steal, a day's travel from here.' Eten sighed, 'Though perhaps it's too soon… in your weakened state.'

'What about Lord Galen?'

Eten gave a soft laugh. 'You don't have to worry about him.' Her smile became fixed. 'Remember, he'll do nothing if his son survives, and I can guarantee that.'

Eten called the physician. 'The Lady Tahey wishes to make a small pilgrimage, to take her mind off this latest unhappiness.'

*

They'd been on the road for about four hours when Eten called a break. The bearers went off to swim, while the ladies stretched their legs. They wandered down a natural walkway where huge snake-vines flourished on one side. Masses of tubular flowers brightened the path.

'I threw the flower seeds here. Actually, I'm responsible for all these vines.' She gestured down the green carelessly, her scarf playing with the breeze. 'Now, the new baby will be a boy, of course. In a good body. It's a fine healthy soul, flamboyant.'

The breeze increased and suddenly took the scarf, sending it flying down to a nearby tree where it tangled among the flowers.

'Flamboyance is good. Mind you, I'd even take an old soul...'

When the high priestess made no move to retrieve her scarf, Tahey took the hint and after a dozen steps moved off the path. '...though, what we'd have in common, I don't know.' She reached up among the foliage and petals, to pull it free. Stretching behind the scarf so as not to tear the silk.

She became aware that her arm was caught on thorns. Pushing upwards to escape the barbs, she was hooked on higher thorns up the vine. There was a second type of vine behind the blossoms.

Looking closely, Tahey's mouth went dry. Therefore, it was with difficulty that she shrilled with a parched tongue, 'Eten, I'm caught on skull thorns.'

These thorns each had three prongs, maws with the lower teeth curving upwards and back toward the vine. There was no escape through struggling; the effort only impaled the victim more firmly on yet higher hooks. From the path, Eten peered intensely at Tahey's arm now suspended like a puppet. 'Hmm, I believe you're right.'

The high priestess reached a helping hand toward the perspiring woman. At the last minute, she slammed Tahey on the tip of the nose, while simultaneously saying, 'They have grown well, haven't they?' Lurching back, Tahey became impaled on a wall of hooks. Before she could scream, Eten made a cutting motion over Tahey's throat. 'Haven't I told you before, don't whine!' There was no sound to Tahey's cry.

The high priestess picked blossoms from around the bewildered Tahey. 'Remember the spell I caste, to fix Kylyn's soul in your womb? Linking you both.' Eten gave a small shrug. 'The link won't be severed till one of you is dead.'

The information sank in. 'See, you didn't have to worry about Galen.' Deftly, by a few magic words, Eten called her scarf to her. 'Roxanne was fond of you; I may need to lie to her about your death.' Tucking a posy into Tahey's belt, 'Then again, probably not.'

Almost at the top of the walkway, Eten heard a sound. Startled, she crouched down and, instantly, she was a blackbird. She stayed a blackbird until the panther had passed her and sighted Tahey.

When the men returned from swimming, Eten ordered their silence. 'The Lady Tahey is sleeping.' With little psychic effort, she increased the litter's weight to match what it had been during the morning. As dusk drew close, they stopped to brew tea and Tahey supposedly went off to answer a call of nature.

*

Where Eten returned to Xalisco, she found the city jubilant. Word had come from flyers around the country. The enemy's campaign was at an end. A small troop of horseman had galloped down the highways to the barbarian's main camp. In fever country. Where malaria is prince and his cousin, dengue fever is king !

Within two hours of the cavalry's arrival, the army had begun a forced march back to the coast. A third of the soldiers, who were deathly ill with fevers, remained. Throats slit. The commander-in-chief, Rhaim, was eager for a speedy journey.

A fleet awaited them at Tulum. Hastily stowing their loot, the army sailed at the next tide. On the convoy's lead ship, Rhaim read again the letter calling them home. *"The high king is dead. Each of his nine sons vies to lead. You and your officers are needed in the fatherland to guarantee the correct succession. Bring your army to secure your rightful places within the new order."*

*

Neither the council of archpriests nor the general population could understand why the barbarians had left. The people were merely grateful. Celebrations broke out, though restrained because there had been no victory. Still, the party lasted three days. Meanwhile the archpriests made preparations, treating this peace as but a lull between storms.

Months earlier, a mystic of the Dragon-Land tribe, an ancient soul, had

133

meditated upon the problem of the barbarians for three days. Thereafter, Feng sought the Plane of Pure Prayer. And reached it.

High up in the ether, where the round world was somehow translucently visible below. That sight being a vision not a solid reality, against a midnight background. Lit, here and there, with thin mist lines of pure astral colours. Those lines pulsing constantly in change. On the plane of pure prayer impartial darkness surrounded him. Standing, it seemed, upon a dome of crystal transparency, Feng banged an astral staff on the clear ground. A deep crash of sound resulted. 'Brothers, sisters, hear me.'

The staff cracked twice more upon the veining dome. Seams of light spread from beneath the staff. They'd hardly overtaken the dome's horizons, visible and sensed by Feng, before the world below was all attention. Souls both asleep and awake. He projected his quest regarding the barbarian king. Those interested stayed with him. Then, summoning his energy, Feng began a sending. Others joined in the prayer. Thousands and thousands lent their energy, focusing on one thought towards one man. Sent their prayer upon the mystic's leading. For a time.

Everything, that day, was just right! They all got lucky.

A wind tore through the ether, returning all the evil the barbarian king had done, and caused, back to him. That was all... and enough. Karma, in its truest sense. No one knew what he saw, before he ran for the palace entrance, vaulting, his eyes popping, onto a horse and galloped away. Riding as though banshees nipped at his heels. Every hair on his body turning white as he raced on.

All of his own making. None knew what filled his ears. What caused every hair on his body to turn white as he raced on. Or what caused him, when crossing a bridge, to throw himself off his mount and into the river's icy white-water.

The king's startled shade made it to the top of the waves, before the shadow patches were all around it. Eager shadows latched hard onto the dear departed, determined to be part of this judgement-time. Seeing into the depths of these black patches, the dead king emitted a continuous bloodcurdling scream.

*

Kylyn had been well for a fortnight. A blast of hate reverberated down the hallway in which Zithia walked. Eten appeared out of the gloom, Zithia's countenance froze.

'Felicitations on your baby's renewed health.' Zithia began to move off. 'I rejoice!' Pleasure lit Eten's eyes. 'Now Kylyn will live to be given to the temple, as arranged.'

Eten spread the fingers of one hand across her open mouth. 'No, don't tell me, I've spoilt Galen's surprise.' Zithia turned to stone. 'Your first son is the bride-price for Galen's marriage.' The high priestess's laughter echoed in her ears long after Eten had left. Only then did Zithia seem able to breathe. She had been on her way to Galen's private sanctuary.

*

She'd rarely been to his private sanctuary. Finally, Zithia reached the underground passage to his den. As she strode along she remembered how Galen always avoided making decisions about Kylyn's future. The thick door was ajar. A fire had been lit to negate the tomb-like cold, so he wasn't far.

With swift steps Zithia moved to where Galen hung his rare herbs. Jerkily she gathered them all and fed the blaze. Turning, Zithia swept her arm along a shelf of decorative jars. The smashing noises were totally satisfactory, the spill of precious powders and liquids, gratifying. Tipping over a side-table, the imported glass bottles were extinct. Part of the fire crackled out of the hearth.

Delighted, Zithia spied Galen's staff and hurled it out the door. She frowned, not hearing it clatter onto the stone. Galen appeared, the staff in his hand. He'd caught the sceptre mid-flight. Perfumed smoke was beginning to swirl around the room, giving off strange aromas. Zithia coughed a little.

He picked up a jagged section from a once-lovely bottle; 'I was attached to these.'

'And I'm attached to my son.'

Lines appeared on his brow. He sighed. 'He'll be given a good home, education and status.'

'How could you agree to this?' He was silent. Zithia coughed some more, 'Eten told me.' Swaying, she glared anew, 'She taunted me with it.'

Galen dropped the jagged glass. 'I'll have to find a suitable way to thank Eten.' Without haste he moved toward the door.

'Where are you going?'

'Outside. The Seeing herbs you set ablaze have unusual effects. You won't enjoy the sensations.' A few feet from the open study door he waited for her. 'A high priest's marriage always requires a tithe.'

Her hair flew as she moved. 'Not my child.' Smoke began drifting around their ankles. 'When?'

Galen's fingers adjusted his sleeve. 'Not until he's six.' He added, reasonably he thought, 'We've years with him yet.'

'And a lifetime without him.' She looked this way and that. 'Six... he'll still be a baby.'

'Only if you keep him a baby.'

The smoke was billowing down the long hallway by then. She rocked on the balls of her feet. 'And when, may I ask, was I to know?' Her hands were fists. 'The day before you delivered him up, perhaps?'

'You insisted on marriage. I planned to tell you after our next child, a son, was born.'

A new thought struck her. She searched his face, 'Did you... can you purposely conceive a son?'

He looked away from her. 'I wanted to give you a girl first... to soften the coming blow... the bargain demanded a son first.'

Numb, her eyelids reddened. 'You even sold the child of my comfort away.'

'Next time I'll give you twins, identical twins.'

Zithia's mouth opened and closed of its own accord. 'Well, you can forget any more children for a start.' She spat out, 'I'm dismissing the wet nurse, I'll breast feed Kylyn myself.' Temple custom dictated that a nursing mother couldn't make love.

'By all means dismiss the wet nurse, but I won't have my son contaminated. He'll be weaned.' Zithia inhaled sharply through her mouth. 'And as for your body...' He raised an eyebrow, 'I'm offered better at every festival.'

A moment later Galen was watching her retreating back. He was po-faced, flat voiced, 'That went well.'

She was two-thirds of the way down the corridor when Xiao Chen appeared, coincidentally. Xiao Chen made his way through a smoke snake winding along. Galen greeted him. 'Zithia dropped one or two things in the study.'

The truth-sayer looked past Galen, into the ruined room. 'I see you finally found the right time to tell her.'

*

On his return to their apartment that evening, Galen thought: *"She'll get used to it."*

Shortly after, Zithia came out of their bedroom. Glaring at Galen, she threw a pillow on the sofa. Hands on hips, she stood there. Galen said 'Have a good night.' And walked into their bedroom, shutting the door behind him. The pillow hit the door.

Over the next few days, Galen often surprised Zithia doing nothing, just gazing into the middle distance, tiny wrinkles working her brow. Eventually he sat opposite her. 'Zithia we must to talk.'

She gripped her hands together, fingers intertwined, near her face. 'No. We must act... do something.'

'Beloved, we can't keep Kylyn. I made a bargain, and to have any hope of ever becoming archpriest I must keep my word.'

Her eyes narrowed. 'You dare to sit there contemplating your career when we're going to lose a son.' To his surprise Zithia caressed his cheek, whispering huskily, 'Beloved, run away with me.'

He laughed. 'Run away? Without a place in temple. Without gold, cacao beans?'

'We'd all be together.'

Galen snorted. 'It's asking too much.' He went to his private study.

The outer corners of her eyes turned down. 'I suppose it is, for you.'

Later, she walked into the nursery. She couldn't understand Galen. Rocking Kylyn, she whispered, 'He does love us darling.' Thinking: *"But he loves ambition more."* She put her son in his cot: *"Better had I been Galen's sister. Then, I could've supported his ambitions... loved him, regardless... helped choose his main mistress... he'd have approved my husband."*
Settling on a chair beside her son, 'How Galen pulls at my heart.' Zithia blinked back tears: *"I can't simply stop loving him."* Her hand gripped her throat. 'But I can stop liking him.'

Awaking in the chair, she discovered she'd made two resolutions. Immediately she told Kylyn, 'You, my darling, shan't be a baby at six. Plus I've a lot of botany and fauna study to catch up on; just in case.' She balanced Kylyn on her hip. 'For, if papa won't help us, darling, we'll have to help ourselves.'

Retrieving the pillow from the sofa, Zithia noticed that her breasts were plumping up and firming nicely since she'd stopped breastfeeding. A potion had helped her to regain this most potent of weapons in a woman's arsenal.

'Of course, I need to have papa's trust, before I can use it.' Plus, she admitted very softly to herself, she'd sorely missed Galen's presence at night.

chapter 14

Kylyn was lately six months old. Galen was packing. 'A mist maker's council has been called. To make the rendezvous I have to leave immediately.'

Judging each step precisely, Zithia moved around the room. 'Why?'

He looked pensive, his eyes flicking back and forth. 'Xiao Chen has been summoned, also.'

When the high priest was gone Zithia dropped a powder in cashew juice. She'd be able to breastfeed tomorrow. Removing a cube beside the lounge room fireplace, Zithia took cacao beans plus a golden baton.

It was early morning. She ordered a luxurious picnic hamper, telling the nurse, 'Having assisted the mist makers during the making, I've decided to join my husband.' Four sturdy bearers were engaged for the journey.

Alighting from the litter near an agave cacti plantation, Zithia walked a little distance. Labourers were sucking the liquid from the plants through tall bulbous, latex tubes. She stood motionless awhile, and then returned to the bearers. 'My husband, Lord Galen the mist maker, has sent his thoughts to me. I'm commanded to meet him at a village, in that direction.' Using Galen's short ceremonial staff, Zithia pointed down a road among the fields.

The bearers padded along the new road, ignoring the harvesters who brushed insects off nopal cactus leaves, thick with the bugs. Dried and then pulverised, these produced cochineal for scarlet dye and pink food colouring.

Hours later, a one-ton armadillo blocked their path. While it burrowed for ants at the road's edge, the party lunched. A surfeit of barbecued duck, plus a little tequila, put the bearers in a good mood. Eventually arriving at the designated village, they looked in vain for the high priest's entourage. Their disappointment was obvious. To meet a real mist maker in the flesh. And who was to pay for their day's work?

Zithia returned with ale from the miniature tavern. 'My husband and men are fasting till midnight at a jungle shrine.' The bearers were distinctly worried until Zithia opened her hands, revealing an extravagant number of cacao beans. 'My Lord left money.' Her voice became small and a little tremulous, 'I expect it's all for you...'
Grinning, the head bearer quickly took the beans.

One of the men made for the tavern, while Zithia opened the hamper. 'A wasted effort, Lord Galen has already ordered a feast.' Fat corn loaves jostled with smoked venison and a huge hard-boiled rhea's egg. Ignoring the tequila, Zithia pulled out the mushrooms. A square red pineapple fell into the vacated space. 'Please, take the hamper.' The head bearer picked up cigars that had escaped onto the road. Five minutes later the men and chair had disappeared.

*

Zithia resumed her journey at dawn in a new litter. They went fast through gullies, amid nests of sharp peaks, rotating carriers every hour. Rounding a bend Zithia looked up onto a mountainside village sprawling between clumps of giant bamboo and six springs. The houses staggered around the obstacles of plants and water, each room on a different level. Flimsy bridges crossed the laughing brooks and, in spots, small waterfalls dropped.

Tintal. Entering the bamboo village, the litter climbed to an open area. The hostel behind this was dwarfed by hundred-foot bamboo whose culms were as wide as a man's thigh. Vanilla orchids waved aerial roots from these stands, and quexatl sound was everywhere.

Passing a pregnant woman making a feather parasol, Zithia entered the hostel. Behind the desk there hung a complicated woven quilt, in patterns shining with quexatl filaments. Zithia admired, 'Exquisite.'

The woman blew dust off a patch of luminous yellow. 'It took my mother and aunts months to weave it for my wedding day.'

'Have I missed the quexatl harvest?'

The proprietor was organising Zithia's room. 'Only two days. You'll be able to join the village tomorrow on the rest of the annual gathering. You'll see birds snared, a few tail feathers taken and their health checked before they're released.' She cooed at a fledgling in its pen. 'This little darling fell out of his nest. Needs four-hourly feeding.'

*

At Xalisco, Mairead the permanent concubine to high priest Able personally stopped at Galen's apartment. She had an invitation for Zithia, to a high luncheon. The other guests would also be long-term companions. On being told that the Lady Zithia had gone to join Lord Galen, she mentioned this to Able.

Suspicious, the high priest had a flyer communicate with the mist-circle. The flyer interrupted Galen in council, whispering, 'Lord Able sends his regards. Mist maker, your lady wife left Xalisco two days ago, to join you.'

In his mind, Galen instantly threw Zithia's name, as a spear, through the ether.

*

In Tintal, Zithia was breast-feeding Kylyn. Kylyn pawed crossly at the talisman around his neck. Zithia pulled the silver pendant over his head. Its mate was around Zithia's throat. The net-like container was full of platinum balls and salt crystals. Tracing the pendant's spell, all at once her name filled the room, echoing off the walls. Zithia dropped the talisman. Hastily picking it up, she clicked a knob and swung the silver cage in full slow circles. After a time she stopped, having blocked his sight. 'But how much does he know?'

Dressed in brine-washed clothes, Zithia waited for the bird-gatherers to leave. First she mentally built up a circle of golden light, like the salt circles, around Kylyn and herself; for protection from Galen when he was searching the ether. Then, she strode off in the direction already harvested.

*

Walking, Zithia pondered a vague notion about going to Nascas. She could get lost in that most remote mud-brick city. Though it'd take months to get there.

Her mind thus engaged she padded over moist river sand, on a beach set adrift in the jungle. A hundred bright green leaves quivered in the breeze at her approach. Suddenly they took panic and floated away, being butterflies after all. Putting Kylyn on some grass, Zithia scooped water into her cupped palms. Kylyn reached for a vivid blue frog on a nearby philodendron. It jumped beyond his grasp into the undergrowth.

Trekking again, Zithia pointed out objects of interest along the way. 'A greenwood tree, snapping turtles, writing in the sand, a toucan.' Her mind made a question mark and she repeated the list, looking for the odd one out. 'A greenwood tree, snapping turtles, writing in the sand.' She corrected herself, 'Atlantian writing in the sand.'

Before her was a deep sketched word. *"Welcome."* Zithia's eyes lit up. From behind her a long thin stick appeared and wrote, *"Hello."* She swiveled to greet one of the old people, about whom Galen had often spoken.

Her legs reacted before her mind caught up. She was dashing away backwards, Kylyn clutched tight. Two large, longhaired black apes stood upright, right behind her. Howler monkeys. One had raised his arms above his head with a stick held high, a habit he had when not writing. Never having met a human before, the stick waved excitedly. The second howler took the stick away. So the first tried a smile. Unpractised in this expression, he succeeded only in baring his teeth. Still retreating, Zithia reached the jungle's edge. Stumbling, she landed in a seated position.

About to jump over a fallen log, she noted that the monkeys weren't pursuing her. Hurriedly they wrote. With her head held well back, Zithia watched a hairy paw beckon her. The howlers retreated. Tentatively she retraced her steps and read. *"Don't be afraid. This is why we're called the sacred ones, gods of writing."*

The woman looked from the words to the monkeys and back. She had heard the howlers called thus. Voice aquiver, Zithia called in Atlantian, 'Come back.' They returned on all fours.

They wrote, and she talked. *"It's a long time since we've heard our mother tongue,"* Colrav wrote.

Common courtesy meant they didn't ask what she was doing here, though they accompanied her when she walked on. Late in the afternoon Nefer wrote, *"You must be heading home. The jungle is dangerous at night, especially for humans."*

She looked at the sky, 'I can't go home.' Nefer raised her eyebrows. 'I've good reason!'

Zithia looked miserable. The two howlers talked to each other, and then Colrav sped up a tree. Nefer, *"Zuivsat will ask the leader if you may stay the night."* After some time Zuivsat appeared halfway down a different canopy, signalling Zithia to ascend.

Nefer took Kylyn and immediately began to climb. After a seventy-foot hardwood, they transferred to a much taller tropical fig adorned by mistletoe. Eating a fig, Zithia watched dewy clouds brush the trees on distant mountains.

Zithia sat in a nest made in a dimple in a branch. Nefer brought rough, homemade paper, which said, *"Sleep."*

'Should I pay respects to your elder?' Nefer shook her head and tied vine securely around the waists of the two guests then around the tree.

*

The entire troop was on the sunlit ground. Only two guards sat high on branches, checking the forest for danger signs. Youngsters preened each other. Zithia half-dozed on a warm rock. Mothers brought out palm-leaf parcels and children loped up for the treat. Dashing to a quiet part of the river, the little ones bobbed their coloured potatoes in the water, rubbing the dirt off. Nefer, *"Presents for the sacred ones."*

A potato escaped and a youngster swam to recover the prize in his mouth. An elderly aunt moaned to Zithia, *"The gifters forgot my salt again."*

Sitting with Zithia and Kylyn, Nefer scrawled in the silt, *"Our ancestors lost faith in man after the destruction of Atlantis. So, shortly after reaching this continent, they parted with the human tribes. But we still keep the Atlantian language alive."*

Lying on her side, Zithia ate corn cakes. She became aware that she was being observed by a group of older howlers, who sat separately from the rest. Before two of these were placed cleaned potatoes. Nefer pointed out the grey-flecked female. *"Apet, our wise woman; she has the sight."*

The leader barked a command, and everyone started to return to the trees, except Zithia. Apet came over at a dignified pace. Her lady-in-waiting handed Apet rough paper and pen. *"What is your husband?"*

Zithia's eyes skidded downward, to the right. 'Just a man.'

Apet snorted noisily. *"Yet you speak fluent Atlantian."*

Zithia looked into Apet's enormous black eyes. 'I'm a priest.'

"That's no answer." She sensed the air. *"Your husband is a high priest. He's very near."* Zithia became a startled deer. *"We won't detain you for him. We don't interfere between husband and wife."* Zithia said nothing. *"You run... he chases... Is he such a bad husband?"*

'The high priest accepted a bride price in both our names. He promised our son to the temple.' There was much excited talking in the branches. 'I begged Galen to leave the temple for the sake of our son. He'll not. So, I trade my marriage for my son.'

"What he does is against family. Family comes before everything."

Zithia gave a brief nod, and then bowed, placing two hard cakes before Apet. The ancient looked pointedly away from the gifts. All shoulders, the troop's leader shambled up to Apet and jutted out his huge jaw. Xander had recently lost his youngest son to the river. He bit into one of the biscuits, looking at Apet. Apet took the second cake, to a pleased clamour.

Zithia put on a fistful of heavy jade rings. 'And now… and now we go on.'

Apet lowered her head closer to Zithia. *"Because we're strong."*

A note fell from Colrav. *"I'm going to visit my cousin in the next valley."*

Consequently he began to move off. Zithia followed on the ground. Swinging down from a branch, Nefer touched fingers with Zithia and handed her a foot-long spiral fruit. Zithia bit into the sweet white pulp.

*

When the mist maker's rendezvous concluded, on the night Able's message came, there was consensus. The chairman said, 'Three visions have warned against revealing the identity of the barbarians. As the dreams have guided, thence we go. The archpriests will let the invaders reveal that they're the thirteenth tribe.' He paused. 'To prepare our people, we will remind them that our ancestors defeated the thirteenth tribe. Cast them off and shipwrecked them for their crimes.'

Talking afterwards, Galen said casually, 'My wife sends her regards.' There was gracious inclination of heads. 'She's attending a quetzal harvest. I join her now.'

Not commenting on Galen's statement, Xiao Chen went back to Xalisco alone.

*

It was the third day that Zithia had been missing and Galen's senses had brought him to Tintal. Alighting from his litter, Galen stood in the clearing before the inn. His face was set in hard lines; the static in the air doubled.

The innkeeper murmured under his breath, 'What now?' He could only think of one thing. Through smiling teeth, he added to his wife, 'Get the headman.'

He hastened out to give salutations to this grand visitor. A mere flicker of Galen's eyelids acknowledged these.

'My lord, my name is Joel and I can assure you that no birds have been harmed during the gathering.' Killing a quexatl was a stoning offence.

'I believe you've mistaken me,' he took up his staff of office, 'for someone else.'

Joel paled, 'My august lord high priest, I beg your pardon.' He bowed very low.

'No harm done, though I find it interesting that you assumed a harvest inspector had been sent to your village.' Galen looked around the square. 'Have you been expecting trouble?'

The headman arrived. 'Only from the surrounding villages, my lord. They find our success with the quexatls a trial.' Coming toward Galen, he beamed a smile of delight. 'I'm Liam of the ninth tribe. Seventh son of a seventh son, of a seventh son, all the way back to Atlantis.' He extended his arm and Galen grasped it. He'd already noted the lines in the hollow beside Galen's left eye. 'Headman of this insignificant village. Now, which mist maker have I the privilege of welcoming?'

'Galen of Xalisco, cousin. There is the blood of the ninth tribe in my lineage also.' He lied blithely.

Their smiles were warm and familiar, as if they'd met before in complete harmony. 'Now aren't we the lucky ones. And what could bring a mist maker here?'

'My wife is in your village for the harvest festival. I've come to join her.'

The innkeeper said hastily, 'The only lady staying here, august lord, has already left.'

'Then I'll join her in the gathering party.'

Liam hadn't seen a high priest's wife, either leaving the hostel or in any of the harvesting parties. He scanned Galen's face closely. The high priest's entire body was controlled.

Joel stammered, 'My lord misunderstands me. The inn guest has left the village.' At Galen's frown, Joel went on quickly, 'But she couldn't be your wife, my august lord. She didn't announce herself and she was somewhat… unconventional.'

Liam gazed from Galen's worried look to his relaxed hands. 'She must've gone off with one of the smaller groups.'

'I'd have preferred her to go gathering in a large party, cousin… in her condition.' The last words hung suspended.

Liam tilted his head slightly. 'Galen, there's some very good cigars in my house. Join me?'

Sitting on the headman's verandah, Liam and Galen rustled their cigars. Liam was poised to light his, when the end ignited spontaneously.

'Thank you.' He inhaled deeply. 'And is it time yet, to tell me what's going on?'

Galen sighed, an intensity within his eyes shot through Liam. 'Cousin, my wife had a miscarriage a week ago.' He looked into a bamboo stand. 'She wasn't yet three months pregnant.' By tradition, a pregnancy of less than three months duration was never announced. Nor could its loss be publicly mourned. 'Zithia has had growing distraction ever since. She must've wandered off, in search of birds, alone.'

Liam smoked. 'Disoriented…' He reflected: *"Joel mentioned the request for a bag of salt late at night… her clothes smelling of brine when she left. That sounded purposeful, not disoriented."* He tapped ash off his cigar. 'Don't worry Galen, today's gathering groups will become searching parties.'

An emotion flitted too momentarily behind Galen's eyes. 'Liam, my wife is already confused. If she hears her name echoing through the forest, she might think the little people are calling her.' The little people were seen at times in the cloud forests and in swaying cornfields.

'True, and that'd frighten anyone.' Liam took another draught of smoke. 'My great aunt disappeared as a child. When the little people returned her to us twenty years later, the girl hadn't aged a day.' The high priest followed Liam's gaze. He was looking at a wild-eyed adolescent, with vanilla orchid pods in her hair. She was eating specially dried corn kernels, a sweet treat given to children.

'Has anyone attempted to stop her nightmares?'

'Yes, but… Serindin is skittish and won't leave the village.'

Galen went over to the girl and spoke soothingly. After a few minutes Serindin took two of the pods from her hair.

'When we find my wife I shall take her to famous physicians at Colina temple.' Galen's tone deepened. 'Your great aunt will be well enough to travel by then.'

Soon Liam, a guide and Galen alternately jogged and fast marched through the jungle. At a river bordered by the cornfield, Galen stripped off his priestly garb. In front of the first cornrow was an offering to the little people, set out on a stone. Corn; pink. Crossing from the corn, a tapir with a striped baby wandered into view, then disappeared into the river. Drinking a sensitising tea, he quieted his mind.

Hours later Galen heard Nefer call. Alone, the high priest went into an area of huge mossy tree trunks, lying like tumbled sticks. A fifteen-foot wide posy of black orchids corsaged one tree. In the centre were boulders and a small stream wound round the rocks. Shafts of light showed the water to be a rich blue, due to reflection from its blue jade bed.

Apet made her presence known to him from atop a tree trunk. Sweating from jogging, Galen inclined his head. 'Ancient one, has your tribe seen my wife?'

Apet expelled a sharp breath noisily through her mouth. Paper drifted down to him. *"Where are your manners, high priest, no female likes to be called ancient?"*

He gave a sweeping bow. 'Forgive me, serene lady. Sleeplessness has robbed me of a courtier's ways.' He began again, 'My wife…'

"Isn't here." Apet held up her hand, another note landed. *"Lord high priest, it's not our way to interfere between husband and wife."*

Galen looked all-round the amphitheatre. 'May I speak to the leader of the tribe?' The world went silent. The old male growled. Xander crumpled paper into a ball and hit Galen with it.

"Your insolence is noted, high priest. In our world, children are worth sacrifices."

Another ball hit Galen. *"You may withdraw."* The high priest put his hand to his shoulder and withdrew.

Back at the river he paced: *"Where is she?"*

He heard a sound in his mind and he extended his left arm out in front of his body, fingers splayed. Slowly he turned in a circle, feeling for her. Her thoughts were ghostly half whispers in his ears. Then he saw a vision. Zithia was tiptoeing past a golden longhaired anteater, while the giant dreamed on a mound.

Feeling his anger ignite, she cried aloud, 'No.' She was hours away.

Leaving the track, Zithia dove into trees of begonias and lacy fern pergolas. Yard-wide leaves were her stepping stones. Resting again, Zithia put Kylyn's cradle on her back. Tying the sling securely to her shoulders and waist she brushed a low branch. She saw a flicker. A movement, an inch from her eyes. She stifled a brief scream, but her mind became a brief signal beacon. Zithia shied away from a snake, small for a snake, yet with a large head and glittering eyes. She began to run.

Galen ran too. Half an hour later he was in front of the snake. Crouching, Galen laughed when he saw it. Zithia's serpent now crawled along its tree limb, tiny sucker feet now visible. Seeing a new danger in Galen, the caterpillar inflated its head again and the snake reappeared. Liam and the guide caught up. Galen said, 'Wait here, I'll bring her back. I don't want to panic her.'

Liam smiled dryly. 'I can see that.'

Galen had hardly left his companions when he felt a new horror beacon from Zithia, followed by a dropping sensation. Then the high priest couldn't feel either of them, and his life turned black before him. Running at breakneck speed, Galen followed, and at a plant shrouded cliff-face he came to a dead stop. A scrap of cloth hung there.

His mind swam. Then he heard the baby crying. Zithia had gone over the precipice and landed on a shelf six feet down. This ledge ran parallel to the river, taking Zithia to a series of rocks crossing the divide. Water thudded into that jigsaw puzzle of stones. Zithia was crouched upon a sixty-foot tree trunk, between rocks, behind a sapling growing there.

Standing tall, he grinned, 'That's my wife.'

Zithia sprinted forward, sharing the route with a line of green butterflies. When they didn't take flight, she danced over the convoy of leaf-cutter ants. Thousands of tiny adventurers sailed their bucking, bright-green windsurfers to the far side of the river.

Peppered by spray, she was near the middle of a river. On a rock platform, Galen called lightly, 'Zithia, be sensible.'

Swiveling, she threw a stone at him. 'Sweetheart...' He ducked it, although her aim was good. 'Do we have to do this?'

She undid her golden belt, with its two solid balls on each end. Swinging the bola above her head, the balls stopped their musical jangle. With a small sigh, Galen backed off. 'I guess we do.'

At the last minute Zithia let go of the middle of the chain, grabbed it by one end and spun the other toward Galen. It wrapped around his arm momentarily and Zithia punched at him with her jade covered fist. His feinted away, so that she landed only a glancing blow. He in return hit the space where she had been. Galen's arm tingled badly.

Drenched by spray, Zithia struck Galen on the jaw. He rubbed his chin and spat out blood. 'I see we're not talking.'

Galen caught the bola, dragging it sideways and delivered a hit to Zithia's chest. Winded, she went down, striking out at groin level, only to miss by a fraction. He raised his eyebrows. She glared, 'I wouldn't care if I gelded you.'

The cloth tying Kylyn to his mother's waist had snapped and the harness hung by the shoulder straps alone.

'Good, we're talking again.' He smiled, rolling away from a kick while he landed a blow to her ribs.

The bola slipped in her fingers, merely burning his shoulders when it flew passed him, to clatter over rocks and into the river.

Galen advanced. Each drew ragged breaths. 'You know I'll win.'

She forgot her stance, 'Because you're a man?'

The words were still on her lips when Galen lunged at her and folded her into a vice-like bear hug. Kylyn hung beyond Galen's arms. 'No; because I don't allow myself to be distracted.'

Zithia slumped onto the ground, drawing oxygen painfully back into crushed lungs while Galen gently laid Kylyn on the rock. She was still gasping when he took out a vial and poured it between her lips, clamping her mouth shut until she swallowed. He threw the vial over the falls. Running both hands through his hair, he stretched then winced.

'Zithia,' he examined the welts on his arm, 'you know I hate it when we fight.'

She began to see colours move. 'Time to go.' Taking his son, Galen walked ahead of her.

Stumbling after him, Zithia was in a semi-daze. Re-entering the jungle, everything went blurry. Nearing Liam and the guide, Galen arranged the baby's wrappings to hide his blotched arm. 'Quickly Liam, my lady is ill.'

Liam picked Zithia up, and carried her to a rug. Handing his son to the guide, Galen drew on his robe. Going to Zithia, he touched her clammy forehead. 'Be wise, or never see Kylyn again.'

Galen's jaw was beginning to darken into a blue-black bruise. Moving his lips, Galen massaged the skin. The bruise dissipated. 'You see, nothing you do can mark me.'

He handed her a bottle. The scent was pungent. Within minutes, distorted colours were surging into each other.

Canoeing into the village after dark, Zithia was delirious. 'I've lost him; I've lost my baby,' she sporadically cried out to the shadows.

Galen carried her to Liam's house. Like all dwellings here, it traversed several levels down and around obstacles. Thin water-reed blinds enclosed verandas, keeping insects at bay. The guestrooms were at the bottom. Liam's wife had taken Kylyn to a room next to the mayor's.

Depositing Zithia on the bed, the high priest looked at an inkblot developing on his wife's shoulder. He needed his powers for Liam's aunt.

Liam's brother called Galen to join his host for refreshments. The headman was examining feathers when Galen arrived. He gave Galen an aromatic juice. 'The blues are superb this year.'

Sipping the nectar, Galen took in the sheer volume of feathers. 'I can see why your neighbouring villages may dislike Tintal.'

'We care for our birds, cosseting their most beloved trees. Plus we prevent flooding of nesting hollows, by drilling drainage holes. More fledglings reach maturity here than anywhere else.'

'You'll get an excellent price.'

Liam's eyebrows crashed down. 'Not when our local feather merchant has a monopoly in this region.' He offered his guest a cheroot. 'How is your lady wife, cousin?'

Galen exhaled smoke at eye level. 'When the temple finds out her condition, I fear she'll get much worse. The gossip, on top of a grief which can't be discussed…' He sighed. 'Plus being missing for three days.'

'But what three days are those, cousin?' Liam's gaze at Galen was penetrating. 'The Lady Zithia has been in my brother's harvesting party since she arrived. We've all grown very fond of the lady.' He stirred the fire.

'Liam, when I leave for Colina, I wonder if you'd accompany me, with your great aunt Serindin. She'll receive excellent care in Colina.' Once more, Galen perused the plumage on the table. 'And it will give me the pleasure of introducing you to their deacon of stores. He's always looking for reliable sources of quexatl feathers.'

On his way to treat Serindin, Galen heard a horn announce a village meeting. The little town spilled, murmuring, into the tavern. When Liam explained the bargain, muffled cheering was hurriedly reduced to grins.

When they left, there was much winking. 'Temple prices.' Said one, rubbing his hands together.

Another added, 'Let the other valleys try to accuse us, when we have a temple banner of patronage.' Torches burned all night.

The next morning, the innkeeper invited Galen to check the account Zithia had run up. Taking Kylyn, Galen joined Liam's party for the last day of harvesting. They returned early. Galen saw Zithia reclining on the verandah. 'You look better, beloved.' Her brain still fuzzy, Zithia didn't answer him.

Liam grinned. 'It's a relief to find you so well, lady. I'll see you at the feast tonight.'

He smiled at Galen, 'And there's no need for you to worry over the meat, Galen. I made the kills today, at first blow, of healthy whole animals. They were drained of blood till noon, then salted and washed twice. Not a whit of spirit in that meat.'

"Galen was flattered; salt wasn't cheap. And it had been a long couple of days.

Liam's wife bustled over, holding a dress. 'Zithia, my dear, here's your gown for the banquet tonight. I do like the little orchids, such a good idea of yours.' Muzzily, Zithia knew there was something wrong with that sentence, yet couldn't quite place it.

Miniature quexatl feathers, sewn into orchid designs, dotted the purple dress. The headman's wife flourished a pair of high-heeled slippers, covered with a rainbow of quexatl filaments. Slipping the shoes on, Zithia found them a perfect fit. She frowned. Liam's wife said, 'That was worth the four days it takes to make them.'

'What do you,' the woman had gone, 'mean…?'

The shoemaker and his sons had been working on these sandals since the village meeting. They had only put in the last stitches as Liam's wife appeared to collect the slippers.

Zithia came to the feast from the bamboo-lined track connecting her room to the village square. Lanterns of glowing fireflies illuminated the night, making the delicate blue veins now apparent beneath Zithia's skin more prominent.

Standing to greet her, Galen straightened his belt and offered his hand. As the high priest's lips touched her soft cheek, she whispered, 'My one consolation is that my debacle must injure your ambitions.'

He seated her. 'Debacle? You really are confused.' She looked hard at him while he took a place further up the table, beside their host.

Instantly a matron bustled up. 'Zithia sweetheart, we missed you at the gathering today. Still, I found a grand orchid plant for you. Like the ones you're wearing.' She smiled coyly into Zithia's blank face. 'You did so admire its cinnamon scent.'

The villager placed a jumble of feather flowers, a dream-catcher, plus a quexatl nest on the table. 'And here are the things you asked me to mind for you, while we were harvesting.'

Zithia's head snapped up to find Galen looking at her, a soft smile on his lips. Liam passed him, saying something. Eyes on Zithia, the high priest laughed.

Zithia drawled in a honeyed voice, 'But, my dear, you forgot that lovely woven quilt, the image of the one hanging in the inn.'

The woman drew in a sharp breath. Liam sauntered nearby and the matron joined him, hissing at him. Liam appraised Zithia, 'Now... you know she's not herself.'

Glaring at Zithia, the matron huffed. 'At least the high priest has a sense of gratitude.'

Drinking tequila from a tiny bamboo box, Liam approached Zithia. 'I thought you'd changed your mind about the quilt.'

'I suppose my husband gave you that impression.'

The food then arrived in state. A great roasted bird, quite big enough to feed the table, was delivered. Zithia dined lightly on bamboo shoots and young pachira flowers.

After the banquet, Galen escorted Zithia to their hut. 'Did I enjoy my five days here?'

'Immensely.' He flicked a mischievous smile, and then kissed her on the lips.

To her own surprise her lips responded somewhat. 'Galen, I'm so much in your fiction that I'd invite you in, except...'

'I might say yes?' They laughed deeply, at times sensually. Each aware of the other's awareness of their own entanglement. 'We're not that much in the narrative.'

Still smiling, Galen walked around the balcony, which leaned out over a cascade, to a hammock.

Alone, Zithia's lips ceased their pleasant curve and trembled: "*So this is hell!... Close enough to touch my soul mate, only to know that he'll do anything for his ambition … instead of for me."* She turned her face into her pillow, muffling sobs.

*

It was a little after dawn and they'd been Colina bound for hours. Two litters, plus eighteen men and the harvest; journeying fast. Awaking, Zithia was aware of an increasing buzz of wings. 'The little people.' In a half-dream she watched glistening purples and apricots through the litter's curtains.

Liam called a halt, while the jeweled scarabs surrounded the party; iridescent beetles playing in the growing light. In wonder, Zithia left her litter. Galen was beside the quivering Serindin, passing his hand across her face. Serindin's breathing deepened, quietened. A zephyr eventually moved the jeweled beetles on. Galen lowered his hand. 'We must reach Colina as soon as possible.' Liam nodded.

One team of bearers after another was hired. At length Zithia felt better and sat with her litter curtains open. Liam and Galen were attending Serindin once more. Feeling Zithia's penetrating stare, the high priest turned to her. Leaning forward, she slowly pulled the curtain closed, thinking: *"I'll escape you."*

He strode to the litter and threw the veil open. 'What did you say?'

Zithia emptied her mind. 'Did you have to drug me?'

'You must be seen to be ill, you've had a relapse.' Zithia hugged a cushion tight.

Sooner than she anticipated, they drew near Colina. Kylyn was beside his mother at a rest break. Galen appeared, tousled his son's hair and leaned across him. The high priest ostentatiously took a sip from a cup, before handing it to a parched Zithia. After watching Galen narrowly for an entire minute, Zithia downed the nectar. And then she picked Kylyn up and placed him on the other side of her. Golden slices of fruit were demolished while Zithia whispered happily to her son.

Galen pushed open all the litter's curtains onto a fog-laden jungle. 'Colina in two hours. The views are spectacular.' He took Kylyn.

'I've always wanted to see them.'

'Pity.' Galen tipped her empty cup upside-down.

'Not again!' Her eyes fluttering closed Zithia's head fell back into a pillow. After straightening his wife's body, Galen reached to a hook above

Zithia, on which he hung the cup. 'I didn't think you'd be that cruel.' He stepped away from Zithia, looking down at her. 'And to think I believed you.' The top half of Zithia's astral body was sitting up while her physical form slept on.

'Enjoy, sweetheart,' said Galen, pulling all the curtains wide, his face momentarily wistful, thinking: *"There must've been some mugwort, maybe a speck of mescalin, left in the cup."*

Soon, Galen walked with his son through a misty pass to a clear day. The mountains formed a decided crown of peaks around the wide expanse of blue. Each snow-capped summit was bejeweled by a gigantic gilded disc, carved into stone near the top of its pinnacle. Broad pyramids rose from the lake itself, the blue water cut by dusty ribbons joining the buildings. Atop every floating pyramid was a pair of huge flashing gold discs, matching those on the mountains. These picture-discs leaned into each other at their apex. Thus supported, their dazzling message was visible from either shore.

Ten thousand people lived on the farther side of the lake, where a plain ended in a low cliff. Two gold-disked Alps backed this. Their disks, being the furthest away, were larger than the others. The closest foothill was cut by myriad oblong openings, thin at the top and wide at the bottom, trapezoid windows. Mesa-like stores were scattered on the plain, between conical mud-brick villages of windowless beehives.

A sweeping zigzag of road led down to the lake. While descending, belled calls rang from shorn, orange vicuna on the slopes. Newly released from temporary corrals, they sorted themselves into wild herds. Unable to survive in captivity, vicunas roamed the highlands under the same protection as the quexatl.

*

The view through the two floor-to-ceiling trapezoid windows was of a small pyramid. A pair of stone disks was being gilded in situ. Cotton veiling provided privacy. When Galen entered the room, cape flying, Zithia was already lying half-conscious on the bed. He had been kept from Zithia by the rambling welcome of the hospital deacon. A dark woman, with full black lips, leaned over her. 'Lady Zithia, let me help you change clothes.'

'Physician Shianti, I'm high priest Galen of Xalisco, mist maker.'

'And the lady's husband.' Shianti's voice was soft, 'Call me Shianti.' She started to undo Zithia's sash.

Galen smiled. 'Shianti,' he removed the sash himself. 'Shianti, only the priesthood' he paused, 'best understands the needs of a high priest…' Shianti took off Zithia's shoe 'and a high priest's wife.' The physician's eyebrows crashed together at Zithia's scratched feet. 'For instance, the Lady Zithia is a very private person.'

Deaconess Shianti replied, blank faced. 'Yet she dances, shall we say, magnetically.' A slight smile formed.

'Yes, well… dancing!' Galen's hand traced Zithia's shoulder, 'Other than that my wife is obsessively modest. I'll ready her for bed.'

Shianti tilted her head slightly sideways. 'Certainly, mist maker.' The physician went to the door. 'When you wish to discuss the Lady Zithia's symptoms, call for me.'

*

Zithia awoke. A priestess by her side offered Zithia fruit sorbet, made with shaved mountain ice. Galen sat by a fire, reading. While the priestess went for Shianti, Galen volunteered, 'I undressed you myself. Your bruises…'

Shianti entered. 'Ahh, Lady Zithia.' All the while that Zithia murmured suitable answers to Shianti's questions, her foot kicked the air sharply in Galen's direction.

Eventually the physician addressed Galen. 'My lord, was a second pregnancy wise when your first child is only six month old?'

Zithia gripped her hands tight. 'Even high priests make mistakes, Shianti.'

When the physician described the therapies for Zithia's recovery, Galen paid particular attention to the drugs Shianti prescribed.

Going to his own room, he requested a communicator flyer. Soon the high priest was talking to Peregrine. 'Eminence, Zithia fell ill while we were at the quexatl harvest in Tintal, necessitating a trip to Colina. Physician Shianti has great success with those suffering miscarriages.'

The reply was immediate. 'Our sympathy on Zithia's malady, my son.' Nearly without pause, 'I hear that Colina is doing its seven-yearly vicuna shearing. We'll exchange pumice stone for their pyramid facades in return for fleeces. A pelt would also be welcome.' After the flyer left, Galen sat down and clasped his hands behind his head.

In a room lit with oil lamps, stood a golden, phoenix-shaped bath. The Atlantians had placed it in the original complex built at Colina. Those buildings now lay at the bottom of the lake.

Resting on its tummy, feet folded beneath it, with wings spread high, the bath was over three-feet tall and three inches thick. The tail feathers were raised decoratively. Its therapeutic benefits were legendary.

Twice a day Zithia was carried to this underground room. After the second day she walked there, leaning on a nurse. Thereafter she went alone. On the first occasion, when she stepped from the gold shower recess, her tears began to flow. This was the one place she was alone. Eyelids already swollen, she mounted the bath steps and added an extra jug of flower essences, drops of dew taken off flowers in the dawn, to the full bath.

Wiping the tears away with the back of her hand, Zithia laid her head on a pillow sculpted into the rim of the bath. She stared into space. How could it all turn out this wrong? *"Do I love him too much, or too little?"* She wondered. *"Do I love him at all?"*
She sobbed. 'So much for soul mates.'

But she did love him and if he offered to run away with her tomorrow, she'd forgive him everything. 'I'm weak!' Zithia poured a jug of water over her head. 'And so is he.'

Leaving the golden bath on the fourth day, Zithia traversed the corridors back to her lake view. Stopping for breath, she wondered for the first time, what exactly was the matter with her? Shaking her head, Zithia's world seemed off-balance. As she was herself.

Resting her cheek against the wall's cooling surface, Zithia watched a man without his body step briskly out of a doorway. 'No, grandpapa. My children will be fine without me.'

In his thirties, he half-flew down the passage towards a blue tunnel of light which was appearing towards the other end of the hallway.

A boy of nine followed him, 'What about your wife? You know she depends upon you.'

'She'll cope.' And he ducked around the boy, who'd flown in front of him. 'She's always been a fighter.'

'And your calligraphy? You haven't yet reached your full talent.'

He paused a moment; Beatrice got nearer to him. 'Nice try, gramps.'

The boy blew air noisily out of his nostrils; scowling, glaring. He'd always loathed being called gramps.

The man was off again, gaining on the light. 'No, I'm going home. Now, I'm not saying that this experience isn't a little earlier than I expected.' His grandfather gained on him again. 'Still, I want to go... all that love... it feels better than...'

'It's not your time.'

'My dead body says otherwise.'

'That was an accident.'

'Of course it was an accident.'

'No, I mean you weren't supposed to...' The boy finally reached him; reached out and tipped his spirit off balance.

'Noooo...' The man cried as his life-stream pulled him back toward his nearby body. 'I'll never forgive you aunty, for as long as I live.' His last unconscious grumble rushed out of him, 'And to think I thought you loved me.'

Zithia made her way slowly back to her room.

During her convalescence, Zithia's memories were out of sequence, sometimes blurred; then she was gradually allowed to get better. Galen changed his own potions to match the Shianti's expectations. Meanwhile Shianti and Zithia spoke often, about grief and love, especially when Galen was praying in the chapel.

*

It was the sixth day at Colina. Twenty rowers propelled a ceremonial barge around the lake. At the back, Galen sat on one of two gilded benches, fishing for catfish. Kylyn sat on his lap. On the other bench Zithia watched the view, having crossed her legs away from Galen. Even in the distance, the villagers' multi-patterned clothes were vibrant. Seen in a group, the effect was more than impressive, especially to a feverish mind.

An hour later, Zithia's gaze swept the lake yet again, to discover a tiny island. Galen followed her gaze, 'Our destination. I particularly wanted you to see this.'

The vessel made its way to a sandy coloured terrain. Soon they tied up to a stand of reeds and a wide plank was extended to dry land. A crewmember alighted, pulling the prow onto the shore.

Carrying his son, the high priest handed his wife onto dry land. It was spongy beneath Zithia's feet. A simple bulbous hut sat alone on the island, with foot-thick walls and roof. Zithia eyed the earth and building. 'It's the same colour.'

Her husband picked up some straw and put it into her hand. 'Totora reed. Everything here is reed, including the ground.'

Drying totora sheaths leaned into a cone reaching for a ghost moon. Laying down straw bundles had created the island, till they were six-foot deep. Randomly, along the island's edges self-germinated totora grew.

The sole occupant of the place had brought out his handicrafts for sale. Zithia walked around while Galen admired gourd bowls, with elaborate designs etched into them in silver. Giving Kylyn a tiny straw boat, Galen handed his son to a priest following several steps behind.

A crewman threw two dead geese at the islander's feet. The islander remained with downcast eyes. Other staples were tossed in a pile. Galen stepped very close to Zithia. His face and voice were neutral. 'Ah, my surprise.' He held his hand up as though giving a blessing. 'Behold; a prison.'

Zithia blanched, her jaw dropping. 'For crimes against the priesthood.'

'My dear, if the temple ever finds out that you absconded with the bride-price, you'll end up on your own island.' Shivering, she walked away.

The warders returned to the barge with Kylyn. Selecting a jug, Galen dropped thrice the required gold into the prisoner's hand. When Zithia was on the gangplank, the high priest leaned out to give her the pretty gourd. 'Something to remember this day by.'

She had been reaching to take its silver handle. Instead, Zithia recoiled as from a jar of leeches. The jug splashed into the water, disturbing several lake seahorses as it descended through the warm depths. 'I see you won't need any further lessons.'

*

Galen was making his way to Zithia, when he crossed a balcony near her room. A bed there was totally surrounded by two separate barriers of heavy red veiling, from roof to floor. Indeed the red spilled over the ground for an extra yard. A nurse was delivering new red sheets, a red nightgown and an unlit lamp shaded totally in red cloth on a frame. The high priest started violently, looking up the corridor to Zithia's room. Shianti met him there, saying 'Don't worry, it isn't smallpox. Only a man covered in violent skin eruptions. The total red, as you know, will prevent any pockmarks.'

Galen plainly looked relieved.

Shianti, 'I'm sorry to have called you from your prayers, mist maker.' Galen waited. 'The Lady Zithia's recovery has been spectacular. She's now quite well.'

'Excellent news.'

Galen didn't quite smile and his pupils contracted for only a second. The physician began to frown, then wiped her face clean of expression.

Shianti's voice had flattened out. 'Indeed… I put your wife's recovery down to you my lord.' Galen's eyes changed the merest fraction. 'Your actions made all the difference…' his pupils contracted a little, 'your prayers, mist maker… were heard.'

On an angle, Galen inclined his head. 'You're too kind.' He opened Zithia's door.

Watching him go, 'Yes, I think perhaps I am.'

Closing Zithia's door, Galen observed the room in an obsidian cube. Each side of the cube had been polished into a mirror. A girl was brushing Zithia's hair. The high priest gathered the girl's eyes and then looked at the door. Without a word, she put down the golden brush. Galen replaced her at the task.

Zithia watched the discs on top of the pyramid. The last wafers of gold were being smoothed over the intricate stone engravings. After a minute she picked up a hand-mirror and saw her husband. She sprang violently out of her chair, to the window.

Galen advanced, brushing the burgundy curls spilling over her breasts and down to her waist. 'Congratulations my lady, the physician has pronounced you well.' She sneered.

The brush rippled through the tresses at her temple. Galen followed its progress. 'If you had cost me my allotted time with my son, I'd have gladly set you adrift on the lake.'

Zithia stayed his hand. 'When do you announce that you've turned to the dark path?'

*

Zithia found a new bed in their room at Xalisco. A corn shuck mattress, yes. Requiring eight women for its daily turning and fluffing. Together, husband and wife slept alone.

chapter 15

Months flew by. Alone, in a hall, Zithia was practising. Bare arms were positioned exactly so and her spine was perfectly straight. This exercise should connect her with the universe's energy source. Moving one leg forward, she slipped into the link and then straight out again, unable to get her body quite right. Somewhere behind her, a piece of the wall opened up. Galen appeared.

'Hello, husband.'

'My dear.'

Zithia kept changing her position.

The high priest was next to her. 'Hold your arms like this.' So saying, he swept his arms beneath hers, bending them to the correct angle. 'Breathe.' Over her shoulder he watched the rise and fall of her breasts. No problem there. He wondered: *"What scent is she wearing… manaca… plus?"*

Bending one knee, Galen followed Zithia's own bodylines. He tapped one foot with his own. 'Change your position.'

She moved and felt pure energy pour into her. Oneness, chi. Her eyes closed while the chi flooded her being from the astral. Connection; to her higher self. Power, clarity. Then, his chi matched hers. Galen was as connected as she. Standing so close, it was like being joined; their energies more than doubled. Together they were more than the sum of their parts. Both were lost awhile, within this understanding.

After some moments, Galen exhaled. His warm breath burned Zithia's shoulder, bare because her top had fallen back. He spoke Atlantian, 'Part of me still breathes in, when you breathe out.' Instantly she was in the solid world, pulled away from what might be. Gently Galen kissed the spot already tingling from his breath. Galen continued in Atlantian, 'Change your position.'

Her body whispered: *"Forgive him and be complete once more."* Her strength was ebbing away. 'No, change yours.' Then she staggered beyond his reach and began her exercises once more.

Galen swayed. Clearing his throat, 'I've arranged that when Kylyn's time comes, he'll be settled on the western coast. In the safest region.'

Zithia put both hands over her heart and breathed. Turning, the hall was empty.

While mingling at a banquet a week later, Roxanne sat down beside Zithia to talk to the person opposite. Finally Roxanne smiled at Zithia, with her lips alone. She nodded in Esontair's direction. 'Your rival's mouth is… so sensuous!' Zithia went white. Roxanne leaned nearer. 'Finally, someone to crumple the centre of the sheets on that huge bed of yours.'

Zithia's eyes were flint. A smile painted on her face, she gazed at Esontair. Roxanne went on, 'Of course the moment Galen divorces you, he can run for archpriest again.'

Coquettishly, Esontair raised her eyes, to find that it wasn't a man who examined her. The truth-sayer darted a look towards Galen.

'Did you think your attractions could outweigh his ambition forever?'

Eten had been seated at high table well in time to observe all, with that particular smile which always gave those who saw it the shivers. Servitors brought in high-stemmed gold filigree bowls of fruit, quinces being the flourish of the creations. For high table alone.

Eten didn't know why she disliked quinces, yet she did. Something from a past life, and… Again Eten searched, again the answer didn't come. Had it been poison in a quince? Or a quince not poisoned enough? No, she could never get closer, so she let it go.

Eten said to a server, 'Take the cenrtrepieces away.'

'But archpriest Peregrine specifically asked for them.'

Eten smiled that smile again, with an edge. 'Remove them, I'll speak to the archpriest.'

*

It had been a busy night in the distillery caverns. A young priest called Antony was tapping a cask of the finest tequila when the archpriest unlocked the heavy main door. Diving for shelter, about twenty feet from Peregrine, Antony listened. Wearing an old robe, his eminence added a herb plus more cactus heartleaves to his special brew. These floated on the surface, while Peregrine stirred the liquid with a paddle.

Eten stalked in, banging the door shut. Publicly, and with sarcasm, Peregrine had gone against her wishes in a council yesterday.

'I wondered when you'd seek me out.' Peregrine smiled.

'Peregrine, what's happened to our bargain?'

He took a scroll from his belt, and brandished it high. 'This.' He gave it to her to read. 'I've had you followed for years.'

Peregrine turned back to his work. 'It shows the ancient places you've disturbed in your treasure hunt.' The list was comprehensive. Peregrine pushed his mixer through the vat. 'Cardinal blasphemy; disturbing the relics of Atlantis for personal gain.'

The archpriest smiled unpleasantly and gave Eten another scroll. In it she found her transfer orders to a very minor temple. 'I'll want my spiders back before you leave.'

Again he poled away from the high priestess. A red mist slowly descended before Eten's eyes. Her claws tightened around the scrolls, crushing them. The red deepened, while Peregrine leaned at an angle over the full container. She sprang at him as the archpriest moved the stirrer. 'Watch out, or I'll fall.'

Then he was in the vat and the pole was on the brink, trying to join him. Eten snatched the rod before it disappeared, holding it toward Peregrine. But each time he stretched for it, the pole twisted beyond his reach. Treading tequila, the archpriest finally registered Eten's expression and he grabbed madly for the side of the vat.

She lifted the paddle. Her full force landed on Peregrine's shoulder, pushing him inexorably down. "*Yes!*" Eten thought, when only his flailing arms were visible. Her tongue met her top lip. A violent expulsion of air bubbles surfaced. Motionless, Eten groaned.

She was still applying pressure when she saw, off to one side, something dive at her. The shade of Peregrine had clambered out of the vat, unseen, and then threw itself at Eten. Watching his spirit sprawl around ground level, Eten said, 'What was that supposed to do?' Pointing at the vat, she let the body rise to the surface. 'Tell me, is drowning as peaceful as they say?'

'I don't know; I choked to death on the heartleaves and herbs.'

Eten shrugged one shoulder. Then hastily stepped back several paces, as shadow patches appeared and latched onto Peregrine's dumbfounded soul. He was telling them that they had the wrong person; vowing they'd made a mistake; he was a high priest damn it, which only made the shadows laugh. Eten thought it was laughter. She couldn't tell as they pulled Peregrine's, still insistent, psyche away and down through the floor. The high priestess made a potent sign against bad luck, and promised to sacrifice three snakes to the dark ones that very day.

Her exaltation had truly passed. Frowning now, Eten's mind recited the rule she'd learned at her mama's knee: *"Kill in cold blood, never hot. Such a death is bad begot."*

'You'd think you were a novice.' Eten chided softly. 'Could this be an accident?' She hung the paddle on the vat's edge. 'No.' It had been too spontaneous, there were bound to be flaws. The high priestess picked up the damaged scrolls. 'Still, why waste a good murder?'

Eten pressed one of Zithia's unique hair ornaments into the damp ground, beside the vat. Since Roxanne had brought it to her, Eten had carried it constantly. Be prepared, was a personal motto.

Looking around, Eten brushed her fingers together, then removed her shoes. She switched her mind off; blank. So her soul merely watched the world. Its concerns, vibrations, colours flowed right through her. It was then that the high priestess's dark shape disappeared.

Antony hadn't heard any movement for five minutes. He had to look. The door moved and Antony saw a flicker of a shape. No more. Disappearing was among the rarest of feats. To be able to move while remaining invisible, even rarer.

Standing with a view of the murdered Peregrine, Antony thought: *"I must know this extraordinary woman."* He'd momentarily seen through ghostly long red fingernails and a flash from a platinum earring. Smooth, therefore antique. Today's rare and beaten platinum was rougher.

Antony left by the backdoor. His simpering lady found him pre-occupied.

*

Back in her inner chamber, Eten rubbed her hands all over the detective's scroll, seeking a face. She stopped, screwing her eyes up tight on the vision: *"Unfortunate man, but a week to live… at most."* Roxanne would assist.

Quickly Eten changed into a hidden outfit. A novice emerged on the stairs leading up to Zithia's apartment.

Zithia half-pranced along the terrace, concentrating on a high kick she'd been learning. Where a lit torch should've been, the novice appeared. There was a hoarse croak. 'My lady, Lord Galen wishes to see you in the distillery.'

"*What on earth does he want?*" She thought, pursing her lips. 'Inform Lord Galen that I'm far too tired for games.'

'Your lord told me to say, "Our son will soon be six."'

Zithia's colour heightened: "*He reminds me.*" Throwing back her head, 'Tell him… I'm his to command.' Saluting her, the novice backed out of sight.

Bursting through the distillery door, Zithia's staccato tones rang out. 'Galen! How dare you give that message to…?' The atmosphere in the distillery was heavy. One torch lit the way. Look as she might, Zithia couldn't see her husband. Wrinkling her nose at the fumes. 'Galen…' At one vat, Zithia scanned it: "*That's supposed to be covered.*"

She peered more closely. There was something in the liquid, amid the leaves and herbs. 'Ugh, a rat.' Her mouth contorted. 'That's the end of this year's vintage.' But her brain discovered another pattern within the tub.

Breath rushed in for the coming scream, then stopped. She was looking at a high priest's cape. Then she was stretched precariously over the edge, her fingertips at the edge of the robe. Pulling.

The hood popped above the liquid. It was indeed a high priest's cowl. 'No!'

Tears mixed with tequila. Zithia hauled at the slippery body. Nearer, nearly. Fumbling, it sloshed down and away once more. Shaking violently, she jumped up, immediately stamping her foot. 'Damn you Galen, how could you die without my feeling it?' Somewhere logic asked: "*Yes, how could he?*"

Seconds later, Zithia's hands were on the corpse's temples, raising the head. She had to see the face. Her teeth locked together, she gripped the corpse's hair and wiped the face clean with one hand. She stared. 'Galen, you didn't leave me.'

Peregrine sank back into his finest vintage.

*

Galen met Roxanne in a corridor. Looking him over, she lingered on his lower body. 'I called on you earlier tonight, hoping to catch you… home alone.' Roxanne's nipples strained against her gown, her sultry voice became its most beautiful. 'I live in hope, Galen.'

Roxanne then looked theatrically crestfallen. 'The whole call was such an anti-climax. Not even Zithia there to greet me.' Her grin was derisive.

'And I was so looking forward to some kind of excitement.'

The alarm drums went. Galen was among the first to arrive at the distillery. It was he who found the Zithia's hairpin. And stood on it. Bending to ascertain the cause of death, Galen retrieved the trinket and smudged the imprint in the dirt.

Hearing footsteps in the living area, Zithia opened the bedroom door. 'What's wrong?'

Galen and Xiao Chen both stood there. There were tiny lines on Galen's neutral face. Zithia gulped: *"He sent me to go to the distillery."*

Galen clutched Zithia's hairpin. 'Peregrine's dead.'

'An accident?' Zithia broke eye contact with Galen.

Galen's look became grave. 'I've been asking myself the same question? Peregrine drowned in a vat.'

He went into the bedroom. 'It's a warm night for a fire.'

She flushed. She always lit a fire when she needed comfort. Smothering the flames, she rose quickly and bumped into him. Sleep came hard, her thoughts ceaseless. In the moonlight, Galen watched his wife toss and turn.

*

A single coat of red paint was rapidly slapped on the Death Pyramid. An archpriest taken before his time. Rumours whispered round. The populace began to question Yin-Hsin's death. At this painting, an elderly priestess predicted, 'With such wickedness going unpunished in the temple, God will allow the barbarians to win next time.'

Her family came from the last region to give up violence, in exchange for Atlantian knowledge. 'Surely the true way to cleanse the temple is the oldest way known in this land. By blood.'

Whisperers slithered among the throng, mostly from Eten's tribe. 'The Lady Zithia wasn't in her apartment when the archpriest died.' These comments spread like lice.

No officials from other temples attended the burial two days later. High priest Lexis officiated. He said little, finishing with the traditional, 'In death we're lighter than a bird's feather. Yet even so, we're weighed. All are shown what we could've been and dread the seeing. Now Peregrine's life is in the balance; may the one God bless his crossing.'

By the time lightning was flashing earthward, the gossip about Zithia had grown to include Roxanne's testimony. When the lightning show was accelerating, Galen turned to his wife. 'You've heard the rumours?' his tone was aloof. 'Well, it's one way to avoid the bride-price.' She looked startled. 'My becoming archpriest, then declaring the price immoral; barbarous.' It hadn't taken him long to find a motive for Zithia killing Peregrine.

'I can't save you.'

Thunder detonated, Zithia rocked on unsteady legs. 'Is that what you planned?'

At first he didn't understand, and then he glowered at her. Galen went to speak and... abruptly Eten was next to them.

One single death kite was soaring into the finale. It drew everyone. The lightning struck the kite. It ignited! Fried! And, a cindered bird, it plummeted onto the pyramid. Peregrine had not passed over well. Immobile, the throng breathed rapid, short breaths. Before the stampede began, Eten held up her arms. 'Good people of Xalisco, I've feared such an omen as this. Feared it and made ready. The one God's wrath is seen. An innocent will show us the way to appease that anger in two days' time. By ancient ritual.' The city roared its approval.

Eten was luminous with triumph. 'Come brother, I haven't yet had a chance to speak to you about this ceremony.'

'Nor to any of us, I suspect.' Walking away with her, 'Tell me...'

'The ritual will take place at the Pyramid of the Moon.'

'Oh, not that.' He smiled sardonically. 'How did you sabotage the death kite?

Did you strip the latex from the rope or simply add some gold wire?'

*

Galen didn't return home that night, or the next day. Every time he thought to go, he recollected icily: *"She accused me."* Meanwhile the temple authority prepared to interrogate Zithia. The far-flung archpriests required quick results.

Zithia arrived at a class next day. All speech, all movement in the room ceased. Eyes shifted like sands, always away from her. No one spoke. After a very few minutes she left and, when she was but three steps outside, Zithia heard an explosion of scornful laughter.

At home she found a guard had joined Kylyn's nurse. One of Kylyn's private tutors was leaving. He had three. One in reading, one in general knowledge and one in self-defence. All the tutors were recommended for their successes with Kylyn's age group. His self-defence tutor took small groups of children on hikes through the temples and Torim's garden. A future priest or deacon required discipline and resilience.

Zithia dredged up some cheeriness. 'My darling, let's play Follow-Me.'

They were both up a balcony tree, when Roxanne came out of the apartment next door.

Seeing her, Kylyn lost his grip and was only saved from falling by Zithia catching hold of his wrist. Roxanne sauntered over and took Kylyn in her arms. 'Ti-Kylyn-Coatl!' She was a fantasy in green, complete with a latticework feather helmet. Exalting in his stupefied face, Roxanne grinned. 'Like father, like son.'

Smirking at Zithia's disheveled hair. 'So this is what it takes to fascinate a mist maker.' Roxanne placed Kylyn on his feet. 'How strange. Speaking of which, the august Lady Eten was asking after you Zithia, something about your innocence...'

'Roxanne.' A high priest pleaded from his apartment.

'Visiting another friend?' Zithia drew her top lip back. 'The night Peregrine died, can you be certain it was my door you knocked at, Roxanne? After all, you knock on so many doors.'

Roxanne's large green eyes glittered. 'I came not to your door, Zithia.' With that she caressed Kylyn's dark curls. 'How is your papa, sweetheart?'

Zithia blushed. 'Kylyn go inside.' He dawdled away, looking back several times. 'Ti-Kylyn-Coatl!' They were alone when Roxanne's host appeared. Rolling her hips with each step, Roxanne went indoors.

*

Zithia stood at the entrance to Eten's terrace garden. Remembering the soul-snatcher, she marveled that she'd come. The high priestess sat there among ferns. Around her, white-lipped orchids with orange backgrounds grew on spreading branches.

At the sight of Eten, Zithia involuntarily looked away, only to spot Venus squatting under a tree, where he gobbled up orchids: *"I must be mad!"*

'Zithia, at least let's look at each other in the eyes.'

Zithia turned her head to the high priestess. 'No matter how much it hurts?'

'Not an insurmountable problem, surely.' She showed her open palms.

'Small talk, Eten?' She shrugged. 'Very well. Many call your toad disgusting, whereas I call him... your soul mate.'

Eten's eyes flashed with darkness. 'And how's your son, the bride-price?'

Zithia's head drew back. 'Enough of courtesy, what do you want?'

Venus curled at Eten's feet, a leather bag with warts. 'Did you know that only an innocent can survive my ritual? Do you qualify?'

Zithia's eyebrows flattened.

'Then here's your one chance to prove you haven't shed blood.' Po-faced, her tone social, 'Unless, of course, you've an alibi?'

'I haven't been formally accused of anything.'

'Zithia... in our complicated world, what is formality?' She paused. 'Especially when it's obvious your own husband believes you guilty.'

'It's not obvious.' Drawing breath in, Zithia gasped. Her eyes raced to and fro. She
gathered up her skirts: *"I must talk to Galen."*

Seeing her hooked fish wriggle free, Eten loosed the only weapon left to her. 'I saw Galen find your hairpin in the distillery.' It was a risk but after tomorrow Zithia would be in no position to tell anyone.

'Impossible.'

'Yet it happened.'

Zithia collapsed in a seat: *"Found my hairpin? Or planted it."*

Eten instantly bent to Zithia, speaking about the ceremony, while Zithia's mind whirled: *"The bond between us... does it mean nothing to him?"* She gave Eten not even half her mind. *"But he hasn't reported it."* Zithia said to herself, 'Why...' she added for Eten, 'me?'

'Because I know you've never shed blood. How many others could I be certain about?'

Zithia looked deep into Eten's eyes. 'I want...' Her lips paused. Her mind cried: *"to go to Galen."*

'...to prove your innocence to Galen.'

Imperceptibly Zithia nodded. The high priestess took Zithia's hand in a firm grasp; a golden cube nestled in her palm. 'Then repeat.' She recited in Atlantian. 'I swear on my son's head, to hold the ritual cup tomorrow noon.'

Zithia echoed the oath. When she said the word 'cup', Eten lowered their joined hands and the cube rolled between their fingers. Zithia felt a curious sensation. Eten gripped her hand ever tighter, till Zithia finished the sentence.

Then the hands parted and the little gold cube fell to the floor. Eten licked one bloody finger. Zithia looked at her stinging finger. Their blood had mingled. Extending beyond two of the cube's edges were razors.

'A blood oath. You're disgusting.' Crushing the golden box beneath her foot.

'And what would Galen say about your bonding blood with me?' Laughter chased Zithia down the terrace.

*

That evening Galen ate in the high priests' hall. Roxanne sat several places from him and watched the high priest. The memory of Galen's son being dazzled by her had filled Roxanne's mind with fresh thoughts of conquest. A friend of Galen's, who had been talking to a flyer in temple Chol-ula, spoke quietly to him.

Galen leaned forward, 'Are you sure?' The woman flashed her eyebrows at him. Galen looked at Roxanne with new interest. At that moment Roxanne, laughing at an inner joke, showed her profile and Galen recognised Eten in her. The same set to the cheekbones; shared mannerisms.

Roxanne looked in Galen's direction. The high priest turned one foot towards her; his gaze descending well past her navel before returning. She came over to him, her mouth slightly open. Standing up, Galen offered her a chair, reflecting: *"Eten's sister!"* Roxanne's eyes drifted momentarily towards Eten: *"What secrets have they shared?"* Pouring high tequila for her.

Examining every angle of her face, 'It's as though I've awakened from a sleep, and only now see you as you truly are.' He caressed the back of her hand. Her long nails, beginning to curve like talons. Eten's were identical. He traced the love line on her hand. 'Many.'

'Not too many. And always satisfied.'

'With your emerald eyes, how could I have chosen Esontair over you?'

Roxanne pushed her mouth into a bow like Esontair's lips, and mimicked her voice. 'I thought my warm and loving heart would sunder apart.'

'She was sex, nothing more.'

Roxanne's eyes narrowed. 'And me?'

Galen looked down quickly and his eyes came to rest on her cleavage. 'Rapture. Romance.' His eyes rested on her low cut bodice. A half-circle of deep pink appeared. 'Yet how could I come to you when Zithia has a harpy's jealousy, reserved only for you?' He dragged his eyes back to hers. 'I was forced to settle for a poor second best. For exercise.'

Without warning Galen looked into snake's eyes. Roxanne hissed, 'And that night in your apartment?'

'Xiao Chen was present. Besides... Zithia can sense a betrayal of the heart!' He smouldered. 'And, don't forget, to be archpriest I needed a well-born bride-price.'

Flushing with pleasure, Roxanne's vast pupils promised the night. 'The vision of your untouchable beauty has taunted me ever since!'

They moved to a bench on the terrace, Galen guiding Roxanne with a hand in the small of her back. The tequila came with them. Eventually he said, 'Dance with me after the ritual tomorrow.'

Thinking about tomorrow's ceremony, Roxanne's recalled that she was still angry with Eten: *"The jewel in Eten's crown and she has denied me, her own blood, a part in her glory. If only I could tell mama."* Her mouth turned down and she drummed the bench with her claws.

Galen leaned his shoulder on hers. 'With your fine looks, your grace, you could be the central figure in any ritual. Private or public.'

'I've told the high priestess Eten that very thing. She simply won't listen to my being in the Cup Ceremony.' Roxanne's hand fluttered over her mouth.

Taking her hand, Galen kissed her wrist, speaking Atlantian endearments. Here, a deacon, who begged Roxanne for in a dance, interrupted them. Galen kept a restraining hand upon her.

'You can watch!' Roxanne tempted.

He released her. 'Unfortunately, my duties call.'

In the banquet hall, Roxanne gave her sister a wolfish grin.

*

The library's inner sanctum was always open to a high priest. Chaperoned by the deacon himself, Galen ran his fingertips down the spines of books on different shelves. His eyes misted over at a history of the Atlantians in this land. In another aisle, he removed a small book from a shelf, took it to the end aisle and patted the volume into its place. His search took time and the deacon was yawning over his book.

Pulling out a huge volume, Galen examined the cover, showing the North Pole without its icy mantle. Leaning it over, a book further along was visible. On its cover was etched a picture of a vast Atlantian continent, from eons ago. Looking at the back, Galen traced a drawing of the island Atlantis, with the line of the coast to its left misted. Years since he browsed in that volume.

Somewhere between these two books, was a dark volume the high priest didn't recognise. Untitled, squat, thick. In various writing, the subjects had been penned haphazardly across the edges of its closed pages. The word 'power' was written across a few pages. Placing the six-inch thick volume on an angled bench, Galen leafed his way through until he found the Cup Ritual.

Engrossed, Galen didn't wonder that Eten had banned the ceremony to her sister. He took some notes.

*

In an airy cavern, which opened up onto shallow pools and numerous waterfalls-cum-showers, Zithia lay on a stone table. A novice dried her hair. The mane was bathed in light, brought down from the surface by shafts and Atlantian magnifying crystals.

Eten had been right. Zithia couldn't face her husband after taking a blood oath. Blushing, she shuddered at the idea of her blood mixing with Eten's. 'Galen need never know.'

Then, out of the blue, a thought struck: *"The novice. Galen is always served by priests."* Even Kylyn's wet-nurse was an ordained priest. Soundlessly, her lips moved: *"Someone else sent the messenger... yet, Galen has my hairpin... But he hasn't used it..."* She gasped. 'He really thinks I killed...' Zithia arose from the cool stone. 'I have to see Galen.'

Pulling on her shift, she threw a vicuna sheet around her shoulders. It had been hanging over an ornate screen, left on display by a high priest's companion. Zithia felt for her husband. 'He's in his study.'

Racing to him, she seemed to grow years younger. Eight small wall torches lit the dim corridor leading to Galen's sanctum. The door at the end was open. She dashed across the Atlantian symbols in the floor.

He felt the tumult that was her coming and remained at his desk. Now he shaved ribbons off the shaft of a springy feather, giving it a quarter turn between incisions. The pieces he deposited near Zithia's hairpin. *"It's too late for you to confide in me."* he sent to her sharply. And the door slammed shut with a resounding crash.

'No!'

He tested the nib and shaved another piece off, but her slowed-down image invaded his mind. The washed-blue sheet tumbling, drifting around Zithia with each step. Galen picked up the hairpin. She thudded into the door. 'You must listen.'

Zithia could bear almost anything rather than his thinking her a murderer. Peregrine's death had shown Zithia how much she still cared for Galen. 'Galen! I live without your love; don't make me lose your respect as well.' Galen laid the pen down.

She laid her cheek against the wood that separated them. 'A novice said you wanted me in the distillery.' She hit the door. 'Peregrine was dead when I got there.' She pounded on it, in time with her next words, 'I thought you killed him.'

The great door opened so quickly that she fell into his arms. 'I sent for you?' Zithia nodded. Galen held up Zithia's hairpin. 'What about this?'

'I don't know how it got there.'

'How did you know I have it?'

Zithia was puzzled. 'Eten watched you pick it up, after Peregrine's body was found.'

'Zithia, she wasn't there.'

The truth dawned on them both. Still taking the information in, 'Then why does Eten want to help me?'

'Does she?' he raised his eyebrows.

'Yes. I'm in her ceremony today. To prove my innocence, to everyone.'

Galen's tone was deadly, 'I'll take your regrets to Eten personally.'

She put her hand to her throat. 'Galen, I have to attend.'

'Have to?'

She looked away from him, gulping. 'I've sworn a blood oath.'

Lightning seemed to flash in his narrowed eyes. 'Tell me; exactly!'

Later he glowered at Zithia. 'You fool.' But something in his voice was pure relief. He dragged Zithia to her feet. 'You should've come to me.' And Galen kissed her. 'Then we'd not be in this predicament.'

'We?'

Writing a note with his new pen, Galen took up the thin obsidian blade. He pierced his thumb and gently took her hand. After pricking her thumb, he pressed blood to blood reciting, 'I, high priest, mist maker, take this oath from my wife. If debt there be… I alone owe it.'

She looked at him, incredulous. 'I can't let you do it.'

Galen walked to the door. 'You can hardly stop me,' swinging the door closed behind him. It locked, while the torch above the door was abruptly extinguished.

Marching along the hallway, Galen passed the first torch there. It also died, its life snuffed out, blackening the path behind him. Each light in turn withered as he reached it, leaving in his wake dark impenetrable night.

Reaching ground level, a priestess crossed his path. 'Deliver this to the Lady Roxanne without delay.'

*

In his apartment Galen found a blood red dress on the bed, from Eten. A mask and headdress had also been arranged on the enormous surface. Galen polished his game plan until he heard a knock on the door, not five minutes later. Briefly passing before a mirror, he frowned. His eyes were wrong. Moving back to the reflection, Galen smiled roguishly at himself, pouring pleasure into his brilliant orbs.

Then opening the door, he strafed Roxanne's figure. 'Let me look at you.'

Her whole body became more taut and trim. Pheromones oozed, making her perfume a symphony. She grinned, thinking: *"The celibate always fall hard."*

Roughly Galen pulled her inside, against him. 'Since last night I can't get you out of my mind.'

This was partially true. In his mind's eye he'd recalled Roxanne and Tahey standing with their arms around each other's waists, giggling secretly at each other. The day the soul-snatcher had come.

Roxanne's eyes were smoky. 'Your message implied a delightful urgency.'

Taking her by her tiny waist, Galen drew Roxanne into that very room from which he'd once had her ejected. Over his shoulder, Roxanne saw the gown and mask Zithia was to wear. From habit she became coquettish. 'What of Zithia?'

'The lady is no true wife to me.'

'So I've heard.' Gripping his hair tight, Roxanne kissed him hungrily.

Yet Roxanne couldn't close her eyes on the ritual garment. Galen fell back on the bed with her in his arms, near the ensemble. Shortly she stretched an arm over his head, reaching for the headdress. Galen admired the view. Then, she stood up.

'Roxanne, that night you came to me...' His eyes seemed to undress her, devour her. 'How can I forgive myself,' sitting up, Galen made a grab for her, 'or make it up to you?' For a second he looked vulnerable, and there wasn't much acting in the look. Everything he wanted spun upon Roxanne's belief in her own ability to attract.

Licking her lips with her pointed tongue, Roxanne slowly thrust her pelvis forward. 'I'll be everything to you, Galen, if I'm in Zithia's place today.'

Galen caught her between his spread legs. Seeming to misunderstand, he slipped the dress off Roxanne's shoulders. 'You are.'

Roxanne tapped her toes, until she observed confusion on his face. 'Galen, I long to be in your arms. You know I do.' Gently she pushed off his embrace. 'Only, I want to be in the ritual, too, and it starts in half an hour.'

'Forget the ritual.' He picked up the gown and headdress, ringing for a servant. 'I'll make you the centre of a dozen ceremonies. Let Zithia have this one, while you have me.'

Careful not to crush the dress, she put an arm around him, 'My lord, what're you used to? There's insufficient time for all my pleasuring, before you have to join the other high priests.' She went to kiss him, instead biting his lip then backing away. 'Far too little time.'

'Have you really set your heart on it? The high priestess Eten won't like your taking Zithia's place. And she's not at all a forgiving woman.'

Quickly Roxanne opened her mouth and almost replied, 'Oh, I can cope with Eten.' Stopping herself she pulled her lips into a kiss instead, the mask in a tight grip. Roxanne then showered Galen with her brightest smile. She possessed the gown.

'Shall I help you dress?'

'No!' The sex appeal exuding from her was abruptly turned off, the tap snapped shut. Even her scent dissipated. She pushed him from the room. 'You must keep your wife from attending the ceremony.'

Galen's smiled enigmatically. 'Consider it done.'

The bedroom door closed behind him and the attendant Madison entered from the balcony. Galen handed him a key and sandals. 'I left the Lady Zithia in my study. Invite her to join me on the high priest's viewing platform. Take some priest's garments with you.'

Re-entering the master bedroom, Galen found Roxanne tying herself into the outfit. He tucked the bows under the joining seams. Attaching the headdress, they fitted the mask over Roxanne's face. Now, from the front, she could easily be mistaken for Zithia.

Roxanne looked at Galen from over her raised shoulder, and clasped one of Zithia's armlets to her wrists. When Galen smiled wryly, Roxanne thought: *"He's mine."*

*

Well before noon, the pyramids were terraced fields covered with bright swaying flowers. The reflection from jewelry and plumage competed with the sun itself. A masked woman appeared on the main walkway.

Eten's voice reverberated, 'Today, this woman's purity will be tested. Only one who has never shed blood can survive the ritual.' A flurry of excitement ran through the masses.

Roxanne's step faltered, and then she recalled: *"I've never personally delivered a killing blow."* Eten had only ever let her watch.

When Roxanne reached the side of the pyramid, Zithia mounted the high priests platform. Head held high, she walked to Galen's side. He raised his right hand a fraction, in which he held his staff. Zithia took the cue and placed her hand on his. To her right were three high priests, to her left, four. Whispering began.

Listening to the buzz, doubt gnawed Zithia: *"What if Galen is wrong?... If I've given up my only chance to prove my innocence..."*

Roxanne took long minutes to swagger up the steps to Eten. Tossing her head, she soaked up every second. This multitude was here for her! How she hoped Zithia was watching. Halfway up the pyramid, smiling she reached her sister. The high priestess drew Roxanne's mask off with a flourish. And froze, the visor held high. Simultaneously the city heard a voice rang out, 'Behold Roxanne, sister to the high priestess Eten!' You could've heard a tear drop.

Zithia flinched, jealousy re-igniting: *"Roxanne has bewitched Galen. It should be me on that pyramid."*

She heard Galen say very softly. 'Wait.' But Zithia bridled further.

Eten, the mask still held in mid-air, came to life again. At her grim face, Roxanne stammered 'D... don't be angry, darling.'

Looking into those jade irises, Eten's smile was all memories. 'Close your eyes.'

While she instructed Roxanne on what to do, Eten directed a single laser glare past Roxanne to where Galen stood. Her heart pumping venom, on sighting Zithia.

The high priest stepped back from Roxanne, and intoned the Cup ritual's phrases in purest high Atlantian, the mystics tongue. All felt raw strength gathering... becoming more potent with each word. Then Eten broke into the common language. 'Do you come freely to this ritual?'

Roxanne opened starry eyes, exultant. 'Yes!' She sauntered to the top of the pyramid.

'Powers that be. If this supplicant is innocent of blood, take her purity and let her descend to us again. Be she guilty, take her body and extinguish her soul for all time.'

The hundred thousand strained the better to see. Some wondered why the high priestess suspected her own sister of murder. Others wondered why Zithia wasn't ascending the heights. Unawares, Roxanne was in bliss.

At the pyramid's summit there was a stone pillar, on which sat a large crystal goblet. Standing beside the pillar, Roxanne took the empty cup by its stem, raising it slowly to the sun. Again, she made her salute.

Simultaneously, Eten spoke a cryptic rune in high Atlantian. The words themselves sizzled. The third time Roxanne raised the shining crystal to the sky. Her arm remained extended. Abruptly Eten's chant ceased.

A second later, the challis left Roxanne's hand to float beyond her reach. The multitude gasped.

Eten rang out, 'Accept.'

And Roxanne... simply... disappeared! While the cup began to fill with bubbling red liquid.

Transfixed, the people couldn't even blink. Then, glowing and transparent, everyone saw Roxanne's wraith still standing beneath the floating goblet. She too watched the blood filling the vessel, unaware that it was her own. That her body was gone. That only her spectre remained.

When the crystal cup was full, it demanded more. The very air turned upon Roxanne's host, drawing the threads of her wraith up into the goblet. Then, at the speed of light, the goblet rejected that within, scattering it to the four winds, each darkling dot of spirit. That instant, Roxanne's soul simply ceased to exist. Finally, the glowing challis exploded in a ruby starburst and was gone.

Barely in time had Galen's announcer remembered his lines. 'Guilt has been paid for, by execution of the body and annihilation of the soul.'

There was a deafening, relieved roar from the multitudes. Sweat seeped down people's backs, their hair disarranged by strands trying to stand on end. Eten, feeling her reward for conducting the ceremony almost on her, stepped into the privacy of an empty maintenance tunnel.

There, the force she'd conjured up released Roxanne's soul-energy to Eten. White flame enwrapped the high priestess. She could taste blood, but her psychic powers increased a mere two notches. Only an older soul, possessed of innocence, gave great power.

Meanwhile temple dancers, with belladonna eyes, had stepped onto the broad avenue and music raced at heartbeat tempo. At intervals along the way, jars of cactus beer were struck open. The high priests remained above the celebration, while Zithia made polite conversation with those who had shunned her an hour ago. The gossip now was about Roxanne and Eten.

When Eten joined her colleagues, all felt a new intensity within her presence. Those immediately around her fell back. Here was a woman who had executed her own sister. Galen advanced, smiling a welcome. 'Thank you for proving my wife's innocence.'

Teeth gritted, 'Brother, you've stolen from me.' A burst of anger roared toward him. Only to hit an invisible wall that Galen had carefully built, then to be absorbed by that shield. The literature on the Cup Ceremony had recommended this defence.

'What? Did your sister's destruction not give you the power you were hoping for?'

Eten looked longingly at Zithia. 'Your wife's obliteration would've given me more.'

'True, Roxanne never had much soul.' Unconsciously Eten's hands flexed. Blue energy flamed and leapt from her palms, crackling, reaching in Galen's direction. The high priest's monotone continued, 'I suppose we'll never know who killed Peregrine now.' He finished with a wisp of a smile.

Eten threw a pure darkness at him, a new talent. Galen felt it pierce the shield, connect, then hit his second shield and slide off. Eten pushed a little harder; looked a query, and knew. 'You've always read too much.'

Galen, 'Be prepared. Isn't that the priesthood's motto?'

Smiling blackly, Eten nodded. Then, of a sudden, her eyes flamed with a startling hunger. 'What a team we'd make, Galen.' Her voice dropped, taking on its deepest base tone. 'Can't you overlook this little incident?' Eten drew a husky breath. 'I know I could… in time; despite Roxanne.'

Galen's visage was stony. Eten took a sip from a goblet. 'Brother, you might yet be one of the greatest magicians,' she offered him her cup, 'using my path.'

He didn't take it. Eten's pupils became tiny. 'Then, to the dark path.' And drained the chalice.

chapter 16

The day after the Cup Ceremony, the archpriest's council met with Xalisco's high priests through a communication-flyer. 'After much grave reflection, we've chosen Xalisco's next archpriest. Franklin, previously archpriest of Zuivan until its destruction. Descended from the first tribe, he's known for his integrity.'

When the new archpriest arrived, his hair was ashen and his complexion befitted old age, though he was only thirty-nine. Franklin leaned heavily on a staff. 'Today a stranger leads you. Know me, a survivor of Zuivan.'

'The day our barbarian captors learned about the mist making, Zuivan's priests were thrown into a huge pit. When the hole was two-thirds full of broken people, the barbarians added wood. Mercifully, by the time lit jugs of oil were thrown, many of my friends had suffocated. The pure race laughed through our screams. All, all the city was made to watch and hear, until the flames turned to ashes.

'A day later, the invaders departed for a far battlefield. Immediately, those people left dug into the pyre with their bare hands. We six lived, out of seven hundred. Of these, two died in my arms from shock.'

He took a ragged breath. 'They say our survival was a miracle. If so, the purpose of that miracle is that I know the enemy. I promise you that this city will be prepared for the barbarians.' People wrung their hands. Why this talk of invaders? They were long gone.

'Flyers have reported that the pure tribe is at Tulum as we speak.' Someone banged a staff on the floor for silence. 'Our armies didn't stop them last time. So we shall fight in new ways. The Great Council has decided to take the war into the jungle.'

*

At the inauguration banquet, Galen and Zithia glanced often at each other. They hadn't been alone since the Cup Ceremony. Zithia's expression was soft, dewy. She was alight with vitality, renewed zest. He had saved her.

Retiring to their apartment, their bodies brushed when Zithia slowly passed Galen in the bedroom doorway. Tingling! Prolonged. Next, they were tearing off each other's clothes. They slept entwined.

*

Shortly after Galen and Zithia left the banquet, Eten introduced herself to Franklin. 'Eminence, the bride-price for Lord Galen's marriage is now three and a half.'

Franklin knew the history of this bride-price. 'Six more months. The Great Council is still considering which temple would best suit him.'

Eten looked concerned. 'I fear for the child, eminence.' Franklin faced her squarely. 'The boy needs independence. Yet, he's seldom out of his mama's sight.' She paused. 'It seems unkind, when she'll shortly disappear from his life forever.'

Before prayers the next afternoon, Galen was called to the archpriest's garden. Franklin arose from meditation. 'My son, time draws near for the bride-price. For his sake and your wife's, Ti-Kylyn-Coatl will sleep in the temple nursery from now on.'

*

Galen stormed into Torim's garden. Years ago, Galen had enlarged the natural spring there. It now meandered throughout, attended by ponds. Kylyn dived onto Zithia hidden behind a bush. Their game was 'Hide and Seek'. Daily, earnestly, they played this and 'Follow Me'.

Galen heard Zithia say, 'You're not a baby any more, my darling. You're a big boy. Almost five and a half.'

'Nearly six.' He bragged. Zithia's face clouded.

Over the boy's head his parents exchanged a strained glance. Smiling at Kylyn, Galen said, 'Give this bread to the heron.'

Kylyn went off to throw bits to a green bird. The heron took one piece to a large pond, placed it in the water and waited. Small fish gathered around the crumb; then the heron struck. Dinner. Removing the bread, the bird strode to the next pond and put the piece in the water again.

'Kylyn leaves us tonight.'

'No!' Zithia fell to her knees and clasped her arms around his calves, sobbing silently.

Galen's nostrils flared. 'Franklin thinks it will be better for Kylyn to live in the temple nursery.'

Releasing her grasp, Zithia fell back. 'I thought you meant...' She looked bewildered, 'Galen, where's your kindness?'

'I've offered to conceive a comfort for you on numerous occasions, and you've refused.' Raising his hand over Zithia's belly, Galen sensed then scowled, 'Even last night's efforts were wasted.'

Zithia's tears dried up; she stood. 'I want my son, not a replacement!'

'And I told you I wanted all my allotted six years with Kylyn. Remember the island of straw. Your clutching self-indulgence has lost me eight precious months.' His look withered. 'After my son leaves, you'll move into the nursery.' She shuddered at the thought of sleeping among Kylyn's toys.

Xiao Chen appeared, and sat down heavily on a rock. 'Another contingent of barbarians has landed in the far south.' The south had been thought safe, and many nobles had deposited their valuables there.

'But then, where will they send my son?'

Galen assured. 'It's agreed Kylyn will go to the west.'

Kylyn returned from the ponds. Galen dangled a bracelet of faceted stones, alternately green and mauve, before Kylyn's eyes. 'Gems from the Far World.' Holding the bracelet up to the setting sun, the stones changed. The mauve to blue and the green to red. The boy clapped his hands with glee. 'You'll be able to watch this magic every dawn and dusk.' A distraction for when Kylyn awoke in the temple nursery tomorrow.

*

Eten's image materialised, then dematerialised. Her invisibility kept slipping as she gulped up the blue wave of energy, which flooded from an unconscious psychic's third eye into her own three eyes. The high priestess had taken to visiting the hospital in the witching hours. Despite the energy she'd had from Roxanne's soul, Galen was still often a step ahead of her. This was her answer.

Seeing another patient ripe for draining, Eten glided along the two rows of beds. She was one bed from the next victim when a stool sailed through the air in front of her and landed on an empty bed. Still invisible,

Eten turned to face the gaunt man.

He yelled, 'Go away!'

Eten stepped back, unsure; it wasn't possible. But he wasn't looking at her. Turning her head well to the right, she saw a gold-lit spirit standing there, saying, 'It's time.'

'No.' bawled the patient.

'I'm afraid it is.'

'Come back tomorrow.' He flung a cup at the spirit.

Almost simultaneously, Eten thought: *"It's really getting far too like visiting hour."* She dropped back, silently.

The spirit, 'Same time tomorrow then.' And evaporated.

In her apartment, after her vampire's feast, the high priestess opened her jewellery box. It was the first anniversary of the death of Eten's mama. 'Thank the darkness, mama's no longer in that time when communication with the newly dead is easiest.'

Eten reminisced. On the solstice following the total annihilation of Roxanne, she'd visited the Pyramid of the Moon. There, she'd cracked a jade necklace into fragments then dropped it down a shaft. A sacrifice to propitiate her mama, before the solstice doorway between this world and the next opened.

Eten's mama might've understood Roxanne's death, but the obliteration of her baby daughter's soul?

Tonight, Eten's antique platinum anklet, too, would tumble down a shaft. Gently untangling Roxanne's most loved necklace, a vengeful light ignited in Eten's eyes. 'Daryus,' she announced to herself. Handsome Daryus, with an unfailing charm combined with more than a hint of the beautiful. As reconciliation was an almost palpable force in the city at the moment, and with that most romantic of festivals looming, Eten laid ink to paper. *"My friend, come onto my stage for the equinox festival. Here, rare entertainment is yours for the taking."*

This year, preparations for the equinox festival and the invasion went hand in hand. Equinox activities, normally lasting three weeks, were condensed into one. Always away at war, Galen had returned from his battalion for the celebration of a new Knight-house. The Monarch knights, his guerillas, were being officially named after the butterflies of Atlantis.

Zithia, like everyone else, was caught up in the storm of preparations for fun and fleeing. Distributing her wardrobe among the refugees, she had but five superb dresses for the week. Every day for months now,

Zithia had covered herself in layers of gold and jade. 'Rather a heavy comfort,' some commented.

True to his threat, Galen and Zithia slept in different rooms now. Rarely did they meet, and on those occasions each spoke with such a formal civility as to ice a summer's breeze.

Trying on a new gown, made completely from feathers and net, Zithia reflected: *"War. With war comes opportunity."*

The seamstress declared, 'Bending will be a problem Lady Zithia.'

Zithia whirled in a circle. 'Then, I simply won't bend.' The dress's train settled beside her. Frowning, she gave it a sharp kick and it fell in behind her.

*

Daryus arrived with a cavalcade. Alighting smoothly from the litter, his blue-black hair was perfect. Right now, the nobleman wanted a bath and several women watching him would've been glad to assist. Thick lashes framed bright blue eyes. He was of the tribe known, over the oceans, as Persian.

Daryus didn't attend the dawn ceremony of spring equinox; it was altogether too early. The Pyramid of the Sun was a jumble of people facing east. Each wanted the first rays of the day on their faces, gaining the greatest power from the sun until next spring. Having received this blessing, elaborate breakfasts were consumed and the ball courts took the focus.

These fields were flat stone corridors. On either side of the flat surface was a raised area, sloping up to a wall. Atop two parallel walls, the wealthy audience sat shaded by intricate parasols.

Zithia, dressed in her tight feather creation, joined Galen on one court wall. Because the game symbolised the battle between death and rebirth, the high priests blessed the playing fields. After the prayer, Galen threw the ball high above the two teams. *"He looks wonderful."* She thought. He'd put on more muscle. Holding Kylyn, she whispered, 'I miss him.'

Galen came home irregularly and then mainly to visit Kylyn. Her breasts swelled, 'He does his duty well.'

Then the solid rubber globe was whizzing off walls and padded players. Finally it thunked through a vertical stone circle, set somewhat beneath Galen. After a breathless fifteen minutes, an intermission was necessary. Sweating players were towelled down and fresh deerskin cushioning placed over collarbones and loins. Comparing notes, bookies reassessed the odds on the thirty-six teams. To guarantee spring's success, everyone participated in the games. Mostly by betting.

Clasping his betting tabs, Daryus watched Zithia hungrily watch her husband. His smile twitched higher on one side: *"Interesting."* Immediately, he found out their names. The high priest was no less interesting to Daryus than was Zithia.

All over the city, reconciliation was in the air. Galen took Kylyn from Zithia's arms. Her husband, tanned, athletic. Zithia looked away quickly. The high priest noticed. She looked back, presenting Galen with Kylyn's successful gambling token.

*

Sitting before a full-length mirror, Daryus leaned back. One finger on his lower lip, he turned his face this way and that. A servant handed him cologne. 'No, no. A more rugged scent. Something musky with a touch of dirt.'

He clicked his fingers, then removed the blusher from his cheeks and wiped his lips. Feeling the stubble on his jaw, he grinned. The shadow gave him a dangerous air that appealed to married women.

'Only the sapphire thumb ring.' He took off seven pieces of jewellery. Dressed in a simpler robe, he was ready.

Twenty minutes before sunset, people again gathered, facing a tall, thin pyramid. The spring and autumn miracle began, with a shadow snake appearing at the top of the pyramid's northern face. The feathered serpent descended along the side of the steep steps, to disappear into an underground chamber.

All over the city, families ceased their bickering and united. Pan pipes and Dragon-Land stringed instruments played the crowds into their banquets. In the Great Hall, Eten seated next to Augustus scrutinised the scene intently, not wanting to miss the beginning of her command performance. For the occasion Eten wore the platinum earrings, which she'd not worn since Peregrine's murder.

Zithia had removed a panel from her feather dress. The now backless gown revealed a curve of delicate skin, just above her buttocks. Feeling unaccountably, or was it justifiably nervous that night, she sank a shot of high tequila. Then Galen entered the hall. Casually Zithia turned away from him, her hair swinging over one shoulder. His eyes dropped down her naked back to the crease, was it the crease… at the top of her buttocks. A dignitary walked in front of Galen, addressing him.

Dancing with a lovely girl, Daryus deigned to turn on the laser of his attention. For a few moments, she was the focus of his universe. Before the beauty realised it, she had told him every fact and rumour. His looks always suspended good judgement. Soon Daryus stood in Zithia's way, conversing with a deaconess, his fingers caressing a golden goblet.

Zithia silently willed Galen to look up. At the precise moment Galen did look in his wife's direction, so did Daryus. Two pairs of piercing eyes sparkled. Zithia smiled a question at her husband, only to have a knight ask her for the next dance. Barely sighing, she took her place. As the dance was finishing, Galen excused himself from a covey of royals, moving towards Zithia, but Franklin's assistant beckoned him.

Looking after her husband, Zithia was again caught by Daryus's admiration. And he came to her, all grace and glory. Bowing, 'Lord Daryus.'

'My,' She drawled, 'I wish I were as attractive as you.'

He hesitated, and then the whites beneath his eyes showed. 'Lady you are!'

Her laughter peeled. 'Pretty lie though it is, we both know better.' All the females within sight shared an unseemly interest in their interlude. 'Come, let me introduce you to our more dazzling flowers.'

'The one before me is sufficient.'

'Ah, to drown within your eyes… No my lord, I'd not waste your time.'

His eyes became smoky. Zithia frowned. 'Do you know to whom I'm married?'

'Indeed lady, it was my first inquiry.' His eyes caressed her now-open mouth.

She closed her teeth with an audible snap. 'Then Lord Daryus, you know that I'm very married.'

'Not quite the report I had.'

She moved off without a word. An avalanche of admirers instantly swallowed Daryus.

*

In the darkness of the early hours Daryus knocked quietly at Eten's balcony windows. She was waiting for him, resting semi-recumbent on a chaise reading a scroll. He inclined his head, looking at Eten's earbobs. 'Those bring back memories.'

Taking a cushion, he lay down on a large rug and clasped his hands behind his head.

'How sensible of you to come unannounced.'

Daryus smiled at the ceiling. 'Well, no friend of Zithia's would've asked me here.'

Eten put down her scroll. 'You were right, I'll enjoy this hunt. Vivacious, that hair... she could be playful.'

'And in love with her husband.'

He moistened his lips. 'Marriage is never a problem.'

Eten was intent on inspiring Daryus to exert himself more than normal. 'They're soul mates.'

'Really? I've never had someone's soul mate.' That did give the game a rare thrill. He rolled over. 'I'm curious, what has she done to earn your hatred?'

'She has Galen. I wanted him for our path.' Exposing her teeth, Eten wrinkled her nose. 'Besides, you see only her body, I've seen her essence.'

Minutes after Daryus left, there was another knock at Eten's terrace. 'Do come in. What have you...' the priest Antony stood before Eten, with a bunch of green orchids, 'there?' Antony presented his gift. 'How nice, let me put them somewhere safe.' Her hand plunged through a curtain and let the bouquet drop to the floor.

'Now, how long have you been outside?' She smiled.

'I've scarcely arrived, august lady.' He went down on one knee. 'Allow me to tell you of my esteem.'

"Could be useful." Eten gestured for him to rise, handing him a shot-cup of tequila. 'Enjoy, I doubt we'll see this quality again. Peregrine really was a brilliant brewer. I had the last jar reserved for me.'

Antony laughed, at which Eten's facade froze momentarily. 'I was privileged to witness your own brilliance in the distillery.' His eyes were lustrous. 'I'd given up hope of finding you.'

She thought darkly: "My earrings."

'Since that night I've looked for your earbobs everywhere.' He prattled on.

Eten mirrored his crinkled eyes and her hands even followed his: "He knows it all."

'I wish to learn at a sage's feet.' He touched the toe of her shoe.

She smiled the more sweetly. 'You'll be my apprentice.' Eten traced his eyebrow with one talon. 'Now what should I teach you first?'

'How to kill; like you. Secretly.'

She put her hand to her heart. 'You read my mind.' Rising, her claws curled around his arm. 'You'll join my party for Picnic Morning, will you not? We leave this instant.' She rang a gong for Minuet. 'Remember, not a word.'

'I'd rather die than put you at risk, my lady.'

Eten tilted her head to one side. 'A comforting sentiment.' A tiny smile appeared, her voice all warmth, 'I'll hold you to that.'

*

On the far edge of the mist shrouded chinampas was a hilly island, its slopes outlined by the sun's first glow. Waking from the trip, the picnic party arose from their vessels among the chinampas to discover a maze had been set up. Not all the chinampas were joined to each other or the island. The island was the objective. With much laughter they all eventually found their way, through thinning fog, across to land. Except for one perfectly, blissfully handsome young man. Bewildered, he dashed from one dead end to another.

Princess Penelope waved a headdress, 'Would someone go and help him.' The courtier returned with the youth. Penelope's liver-spotted hand tapped her paramour under the chin. 'Don't worry, my dear, I've a game you're good at.'

Then she flipped a gem into the clear water. He retrieved it expertly. Penelope cast more jewels into the lake, and many of the party dove in.

'He's a lovely boy, Eten.' The princess touched her wrinkled neck. 'Yet there are days when I feel like throwing jade until he simply doesn't come up again.' Penelope yawned into her headdress. 'Eten, when you made him love me, couldn't you have made him smarter?'

Inspecting the concubine, the high priestess slowly shook her head. 'There isn't a spell in the world that powerful.'

They moved on to the three-course breakfast, complete with gold dining ware. 'Not my best set,' Penelope apologised, 'That's hidden,' while looking at her reflection in a plate.

'We'll all simply have to make do today. There're no servants, so we can have some well-earned privacy.'

After lunch, the princess declared, 'A treasure hunt.'

Once most of the precious trinkets had been found, couples drifted off to luxuriously appointed nooks. Penelope and her lover went off. Stopping, the princess recovered a jade dangling from a branch, which the youth had failed to find. He blushed, then took his shirt off and put his arm around Penelope's large waist.

When all were gone, Eten gave her attention to Antony. 'Now to your first lesson.'

They walked silently for twenty minutes. Though unable to make them invisible, the high priestess could diminish other people's awareness of them.

She picked up two philodendron leaves. 'I've something to amuse us both. Wild honey. The flower isle is known for its honey.'

They came to an isolated hill, which was in part cliff. A deeply overhanging wave topped the cliff. Taking Antony's hand, Eten moved under the thick-ridged frozen crest. They went closer to this steep face. There was an increasing buzzing. Antony looked up, way up. A huge hive hung above him, with uncountable honeycomb hexagons. Three hundred pounds in each hive. Other hives lower down were much smaller. A swarm totally surrounded them, but not one bee landed or stung. Eten said, 'I was born a bee charmer.'

'You're full of surprises.'

Releasing his hand, Eten purred, 'More than you can imagine.' Her smile grew and around her attractive eyes crow's feet appeared.

Antony's visage became uncertain, 'My lady, this is no test.'

He took several light steps away from Eten. The bees continued to ignore him. She joined him at the cliff's base. Antony took a leaf. 'Allow me.'

He jumped up to the hive and put a small dagger into the midst of the honeycomb. A dripping segment came away.

Eten passed him the second leaf, woven into a small basket. 'The best honey is higher up.'

He climbed, and then gazed at Eten who gestured to climb further up the cliff. Ledges formed stepping stones most of the way up. Becoming intoxicated by his own daring, he went further still; sweating. And never a bee came near him. Close-up, the hives were amazing. Here, even the honeycomb cells were remarkable in size. Finally, balancing on the highest ledge, Antony plunged his dagger into the honeycomb which was clear of bees. Liquid gold gushed out from the broken wax into the leaf basket.

On turning to drop it into Eten's hands, he found himself looking into two huge black eyes. Hovering there was the largest bee he'd ever seen. Wing to wing it spanned three feet. The leaf fell. A frenzied drum of buzzing started. Antony jerked, and the buzz thundered.

'Eten...' No response. From the corner of his eye, he saw the high priestess metres from the cliff. 'My lady?' He cried quietly.

One of the bee's antennae touched Antony. Shouting, he threw his dagger. The bee hovered up and the blade glanced off the toy-like body. Fluffing itself larger, the insect presented its sting and darted at Antony. Going rigid, Antony lost his footing and fell twelve feet onto his back.

From his prone position, the priest watched three giant bees crawl from the hive above him. His mouth hung open. A normal bee flew near his lips and he shut them. Another giant appeared from the jungle, loaded with pollen.

A black sword was descending at speed. Screaming, he rolled to one side. It pierced his ear. Blood flooded; Antony put a hand to his maimed flesh and whimpered. The priest staggered to his feet. Again, the sword darted at him, embedding itself in the earth. Meanwhile the others hovered, buzzing at ever more loudly.

He pushed the grabbing feet of the earthed bee away and broke into a jog. A second bee dived and its sting sliced a path right through his arm. Thrown onto his back once more, Antony found the sword alone attached to him. Nearby, the bee lay dying. Another sting lightninged down and sheathed itself in the priest's belly. Watching his stomach and chest balloon, Antony saw no more.

Eten, 'He said he'd rather die.'

On reaching full jungle she became invisible till she reached a distant chinampa. There, a couple came upon her gathering herbs. It was only when the canoes arrived, an hour to noon, that Antony's absence was noticed. Penelope was tired. 'I see no cause for missing the afternoon's dancing, simply because he's got himself lost. The servants will find him.'

They did. But they didn't dare approach the bloated corpse until the head beekeeper arrived for his evening visit. Three of his darlings lay dead. With tears running down his face, he petted each fluffy ball in turn while the hive keened. Little was thought about the young priest's death.

*

It was the Avenue of the Dead. Music commenced and double lines of twirling ribbons, thirty-foot long, floated from atop all buildings. Young women moved the ribbons to the melody. Below, friends and new families-in-law cheered. Picnic Morning had seen an unprecedented number of engagements. Marriage prices, usually haggled over for months, had been settled. Portable wealth was popular this year, and well before noon, there had been a run on priests to perform marriage ceremonies.

When the strains faded, another song rang out. From ten performance areas, solo dancers appeared. Zithia stepped out to her audience. Her loose silk top and skirt were peasant fashion. She was any woman in the fields, totally clothed from elbow to ankle for sun and modesty.

Dressed in expensive purple, her right hand fanned beneath her eyes. A corsage of flat gilded orchids was entwined around her fingers, hand and arm. Maidens wore such corsages in their first season on the marriage market. Zithia curved her hands and arms enticingly as she wrapped herself in the changing pulse. The dance built, she leapt high in the quickening music.

A spark ignited the performance. Every step, every movement, was pure joy. Not quite abandoned, somehow chaste. Somehow, only for her chosen one. Her chi, welling and expanding within her, Zithia glimmered with energy. Gathering it. Gathered. Suddenly she leapt up onto a three-foot water-clear crystal cube and, spreading her arms wide, instantly let the called-up energy blaze from her in all directions. Almost a second it lasted. Seeming to float before the audience, during the half second after that loving blast Zithia began to twirl.

Pivoting thus, in several fast circles, she seemed to scatter the echoes of that bliss like a faceted crystal reflecting rainbows among the crowd. All were hushed, men stood mesmerised. They wanted her.

The energy spent, Zithia abruptly folded herself into a crouch before hesitantly stepping on tiptoes to the ground. With the music now a slowing refrain, Zithia's hips rolled while her hair veiled and unveiled her body. Balancing on her toes again, she arched her back until the burgundy waterfall kissed the ground. Her hands, a poem curling and uncurling high in the air, her eyes only aware of her hands, Zithia lowered herself so very slowly down to the ground.

With the final note, she collapsed on the ground. The only movement, her heaving breasts. Petals rained on her prone body, a gemstone landing on her flat stomach. Zithia opened her eyes and saw her husband, offering her his hand.

Galen pulled her up with a force that sent her reeling against his chest. Then, interlocking fingers with Zithia, Galen held her arm high. The maiden's corsage had fallen to the ground. The audience went wild, the men smiling indulgently at Galen. Who among them wouldn't have taken Zithia to wife, if she'd refused other terms? Today, for the first time, they'd been told the courtship story of the mist maker and his lady. It had been disseminated throughout the crowds; Archpriest Franklin had seen to that.

Then, smiling radiantly, Zithia, 'You helped with my chi burst.'

'It was important to you.'

'How much?'

'Fifty-fifty. Remember, you've been training for that moment for months.'

'Galen,' Zithia's voice was melting, 'you always know just what my heart desires.'

She caught his hand in hers again; the high priest led his wife over to mingle with the privileged few.

*

At a late lunch, an ornate chair with a high back indicated Galen's place. There were similar chairs strewn around the hall for the other high priests. Galen personally seated Zithia next to him, lingering on her naked back. Still hoping for results from her backless feather gown, she wore it once more. Galen had just taken his seat, when Franklin required his presence.

Daryus appeared and strafed Zithia's figure. A spark passed between them. Daryus was especially good at sparks. Zithia, 'Do you do that to many women?' She arched an eyebrow, 'It must be wearing.'

Slightly taken aback, Daryus picked a jade ring from the trophy bowl before her. 'Their appreciation was less than you deserved.'

She made no answer, watching Galen in the distance. Then the nobleman filled her view. Daryus undid the heavy golden belt on his hips. He draped it over Zithia's hand, 'This is more worthy of your exhibition.'

The room stopped and held its breath. Zithia straightened. Without even one look at the belt, she turned to an attendant. 'Distribute my trophies among the refugees.'

The belt slid into the attendant's miraculously-waiting hands.

Daryus sat in Galen's place. He took up Zithia's fan and casually fanned himself. Hastily she looked away, only to see her husband leaving the hall. Zithia sat down, her mind on Galen. Daryus twisted the fan so as to cool them both, but Zithia continued to look abstracted.

'Can it be possible that I'm boring you?'

She leaned forward and her hair uncovered the length of her back. He moved the fan to his other hand, and the feathers stroked from the nape of her neck, downward. Embers flared. The hunger, always awakened by her dancing, began to ignite within her once more. 'How could I be bored, when you've made me the centre of attention?'

'You look hot. Let's go onto the balcony where we can catch a breeze.' The fan brushed her spine.

The busy mouths of the gathering made the hall hum. 'Why not, my lord, I'm already judged.'

Making their way through the melee, Zithia discovered she actually needed fresh air by this time. They mounted several steps to a wide doorway. In a pool of space, Daryus swung round to her. With a single graceful movement, his arm was around Zithia's waist. Before she could react, he dipped her backwards dramatically, while his lips found hers. Tenderly Daryus's mouth consumed her. Zithia was intoxicated by his scent, his taste.

Parting, Zithia's eyes were wild: *"My God, the scandal!"* The audience was motionless, hushed. *"What is, is."* Zithia reflected, casting an icy look over her them all. Offering Daryus a glittering smile, Zithia kicked the train of her gown behind her and exited the banquet.

Outside, she reeled on him. 'Are you mad?'

Daryus was dismissive. 'I was trying to give you courage.'

Her bejewelled hand swung to slap him, but he stepped back. 'Not my face.'

'As you like.' And kneed him in the groin.

*

Having returned to the hall, from the archpriest's study, Galen too had seen the display. Nearby tittering ceased on seeing him. Other than a quick narrowing of the eyes, Galen's face remained expressionless, if a little stony. Galen had stayed at the feast, discussing the guerilla's requisitions, for another full hour.

A heap of leaves lay on the apartment floor, and Zithia was arranging the last clothes in a bag when Galen strode up the corridor. He heard Zithia's voice across to Xiao Chen's apartment. 'I'm taking our litters to storage in an hour. Have yours already gone?'

Galen passed the deacon in the hallway as Xiao Chen was placing a full net bag onto his pallet. Xiao Chen raised his eyebrows at Galen's drawn, white face.

Virtually empty, the apartment echoed strangely. Everything they owned was on the litters now cluttering up the terrace. The servants had gone. Zithia had packed all of Kylyn's and her own possessions herself. She had been insistent.

Sitting on an upturned box, Zithia's back was to the half-wall of mirror. Avoiding Galen's eye, she absently scrunched a handful of curls. 'Zithia,' his voice was loaded with disdain, 'it'd be wise to mind your reputation, more than your appearance.'

'But I thought the whole temple was about appearance.' Her tone was very flat. 'I appear to be married, I appear to have a son, and you appear to be faithful.'

'I'm always discreet.'

'I suppose that's all that matters.'

He went whiter. 'It's better than becoming a public exhibition.'

She bit her lower lip. 'I had no idea he was going to kiss me. I've only just met Daryus.'

'Imagine the damage you could do, to my position, if you actually knew this man.'

Zithia flushed deepest red and he flung something at the mirror. Quivering, Zithia ducked the golden object. She heard it scratch the mirror before clattering, over-loud, to the floor. Simultaneously Galen sneered, 'I should've left you in the market place, where you belonged!' He marched out.

She didn't understand. Then she saw her own heirloom brooch winking at her from the floor. Given long ago to the fortuneteller. Recalling the unaccountable laughter in the seer's room, she was mortified: *"Where had he been hiding?"* Framing the brooch between finger and thumb, Zithia gazed at it through red and puffy eyes. Zithia's little finger caressed the stone at its heart. Bought a hundred years ago in a village market, her mama had loved that gem.

She sobbed: *"Not now... I can't think on it now."* Shakily, Zithia pinned the brooch to the inside her bodice, over her heart.

In a daze she resumed packing, starting with a bag that contained Galen's treasures. Looking at the horizon, she dropped it on the terrace beside the goods pallet. It tinkled agreeably. Inside again, Zithia kicked a glass jar. Immediately she was hopping around, seeing stars. Puff stars to be exact. Dried flowers had escaped, in a cloud, from the shattered glass.

Zithia accompanied the litters to the refugee centre, where one pallet was to be distributed. Arriving at the plaza, Zithia looked into the sea of haunted eyes. All six litters to be unloaded.

*

That night Zithia slept alone in the apartment, on a thin reed oblong. Awaking in the dead hours, she pulled on forty thick, gold bands. Each bore a bearded serpent's head, with little wings protruded from the edges. She wished she could keep them.

She went to a fireplace, which flashed dozens of gold glints. Bending, Zithia gathered the hefty stack of jewellery she'd worn to recent functions. Until the evacuation, the treasury was open at all hours. Pushing her way along the crowded tunnels, Zithia passed a team of priests sealing up the oldest mushroom cave. Its entrance was becoming undetectable.

The treasury priests were ants in a disturbed nest. After waiting in line, Zithia handed over her cloth parcel. Pushing back the loose sleeve of her priest's robes, she revealed the bracelets. 'I'm keeping these a little longer.'

The priest's pen recorded, *'Fifty bracelets still in Lord Galen's possession.'*

While he marked off the other items returned, Zithia wandered through the treasury. The attendants hardly noticed her. After all, she'd often been in and out during the last months. Leaving, Zithia approached the bursars.

Just then a treasury deacon touched a large, antique gold and jade ornament. Recoiling, a pulse throbbing at his temple, Beregrind threw it into the burning brazier nearby. He looked at his mottling palms, stunned by the evil which had been exuded in solid mass from the ornament. Beregrind was one who was a sensitive in this area. Someone poured salt onto his palms. Then Beregrind was washing in a stream for water poured by another. Salt again. Immediately, the fallen salt and the water were thrown out.

'By the one God, where did that come from?' He was told. 'Write: the inherent malevolence within the artifact required its instant destruction.'

No compensation would be given for loss under these circumstances. 'I'm done for the day. Deborah can take over.'

Zithia renewed her smile, she glowed at the guards. 'Do you wish to search me?'

The guards dashed forward, only to hear a bursar state, 'It's not necessary to search the wife of a high priest. And someone fetch Deborah.'

*

The next day, almost alone, Zithia and Kylyn raced hand in hand the length of the stone roof over a colonnade. Below, having marched from the Avenue of the Dead, a parade of knights marched in formation. Zithia and Kylyn tossed flower petals down to the warriors, a third of whom were women. The confetti whirled in a playful breeze. Roars of cheers were heard from the buildings and under the colonnade.

To the pulse of carved drums jaguar knights led the parade, spectacular in jaguar pelts. Each warrior, painted with protection symbols and ritual make-up, wore a posy at his or her waist. The eagle knights followed, rich in feather accessories, flourishing knives, red oil dripping from the blades. For battle, an anti-coagulant was mixed with the oil in its sheath.

In crocodile leathers, the Cayman knights, raised golden ceremonial shields in a salute. At the end of the roof, Zithia and Kylyn scanned the square that was filling with ranks of fighting men and women. Kylyn pointed to the newly-made Monarch knights, in flowing butterfly-painted capes. Galen was among them.

The massed forces faced the eastern horizon from which the bright war star had risen. Cheering Venus, the planet of fighting, they threw their bouquets high while the archpriest blessed them.

It was late afternoon in the high priests' hall. Two fair maidens, back to back, oohed and ahhed in sweet terror while Monarchs juggled knives over their heads.

Flanking this display was a mock battle between jaguar and Cayman warriors. The instant the winner was declared, spears were flung from the heart of the room toward the far walls. The missiles hit several high targets spilling, flowers.

In unison, female Eagle knights were then catapulted up to the spears, and climbed to the ceiling. Unraveling bright headbands, the slings they created loosed rocks at suspended pinyatas. Treats exploded over the crowd.

Perceiving Daryus in the crowd, she veered away. Instantly catching the smirks begin, Zithia resumed her course. The wave of his desire was palpable, thundering towards her, and then crashing over Zithia and washing all around her. Most watching felt its power; the smirking stopped. Daryus and Zithia met. Yet her smile was a thing of lips alone. 'How's your face?'

His smouldering stopped mid-step, and then she was again his universe. 'Red for happiness? Or for courage?' He purred, admiring the miniature orchids at her breast and picked one. Zithia's head reared back. 'Someone's token?' he enquired, seeing Zithia's heirloom brooch entangled within the flowers.

Zithia flushed, 'A memento of deceit.'

'Ah, the gift of husbands.'

'Surely, the gift of all men.' Zithia retorted, while passing on.

Franklin opened the revelry with a solemn toast. 'To our freedom, to the tribes of Atlantis.' He took a long drink. 'Today we defend our blessed heritage. We may be driven from Xalisco but our spirit will survive. May the one God grant us success.'

Spring fever took hold of the city. With it came behaviour that many, wisely, didn't see. Plush cushions had been artistically arranged all over the floor. Very low tables, holding fruit, were dispersed among cushion circles. Atlantian dancing began in the plaza, to the melody of stringed instruments and bells.

A Jaguar knight advanced to Zithia and held up his hand, palm facing her. Her own palm travelled lightly up over his. Palms touching, they took their places for an elegant reel. Returning to her place, Zithia found Daryus reclining on a cushion near her.

*

'Sit,' Zithia purred, patting the cushion next to her. Every move Daryus made was gobbled up by the room. 'Come, make the whole hall jealous,' Daryus scanned his large audience. Zithia added, 'of me.'

Daryus's eyes flashed, temper flaring. 'Exciting? To feel a man hold you once more?' Zithia's breath left her. 'Atlantian reels are so intimate.' He sat over-close to her. 'Dance?'

She went to fan herself, but he was watching the tips of the feathers.

Hastily she folded the fan away. 'Far too dangerous.'

He took a cherry-tomato from a bowl. 'Where is your august husband, Zithia? I haven't seen the next archpriest all day.'

'It appears Lord Galen is leaving me to the wolves.'

'When your lips taste so of honey, I wonder that he dares?'

Zithia's hand brushed her heirloom brooch. Abstractedly, she whispered, 'I don't know how he dared!' The prey being abstracted hadn't occurred to Daryus before. It stung yet added zest to his appetite. Zithia thought: *"What to do?"* Daryus was perfectly still, recognising a pivotal moment; smouldering. Zithia's eyes seemed drawn down Daryus's washboard chest, *"What..."* then back up. *"Whatever I want."*

Daryus presented her with a tall alabaster tumbler. The drink's sweetness belied its power. After a refill, Daryus suggested fresh air, adding, 'Oh, but we've done that.' From beneath heavy eyelids. 'And what would your husband say?'

Resplendent she arose, 'Nothing he hasn't already said.'

*

Xiao Chen arrived at a third storey council room; on the walls were life sized murals of warriors. Galen nodded to him, before continuing to those assembled. 'Publish orders that if those fleeing overload themselves with gold, it's to be thrown into the nearest cenote.'

'Many will be safely away using the roads alone, if they leave in time.' A priestess said.

Someone added, 'We've guides on the main jungle tracks.'

Xiao Chen, 'The horisons are constantly watched by flyers.' He let a scroll roll up of its own accord.

Galen rubbed the lines etched across his forehead. 'Enough for now. We meet in three hours.'

Shortly, only the high priest and Xiao Chen remained in the room. The chamberlain, Madison, had come to him a few minutes before, with information. Xiao Chen said evenly, 'Your wife's up late tonight.'

'Aren't we all?' Galen played with a half full oblong pouch, gold dust rolling back and forth within.

'The night sky must be refreshing.' Xiao Chen looked hard out a window, at the next pyramid. 'You did return her mother's brooch.'

'Is Zithia alone?'

The truth-sayer gave him a wry look, and left.

Galen paled. He sensed for Zithia and felt her beating fast, faster and the table Galen leaned upon shook itself free of the floor. 'Control!' He demanded of himself. But two quill pens took flight, embedding themselves deep into a mural-warrior's clay kilt, which fragmented and crumbled revealing a well speared loincloth beneath.

When the dark mist dissipated from his mind, Galen found himself walking towards Zithia and Daryus's rendezvous. Clouds drifted across the star emblazoned midnight. Without knowing it, Galen still held the gold pouch in his hand.

Inaudibly he approached. Legs astride a cornerstone, Zithia dangled one shoe off her toes while drinking in the view. Daryus examined her, calculating. They'd lapsed into silence. Tendrils of Zithia's hair were caught by the breeze and swaying to the wind's rhythm Zithia watched them float.

A hand drew her to her feet, simultaneously spinning her around. 'My shoe,' she complained faintly, losing the second one. Then, astonished, 'Galen!' She hardly tried to pull away, her hands against his chest.

'Lady wife, you were expecting someone else?' he smiled, but his mouth had a bitter twist.

Zithia looked back to where Daryus had been sitting. He was now lying prone on that step. Unconscious. While passing Daryus by, Galen had hit him on the side of the head with the gold cosh. He'd dropped without knowing he'd been hit.

'Daryus.'

'Let him sleep.'

'What've you done?' She strove to free herself in earnest, causing the brooch to scratch him. Galen tore it from her fragile bodice, rending the material.

He laughed softly. Zithia growled, 'You manipulated me, from the very first.'

'As you manipulated me.'

'Never!' She ceased her struggles.

'You took my clarity, my focus! Before you, all I wanted was to be archpriest. Now look at me.'

Her voice was gravelly, 'High priest, I beg you to retire. I've an affair to begin.'

'You mean... continue.'

Zithia tried to fetch him a slap across his face, unsuccessfully, so turned her eyes upon Daryus, her expression hungry for...

'Take your vengeance some other way,' Galen spat, flinging Zithia's brooch high. Both listened to it splash into a distant reservoir.

Twisting from his grasp, Zithia moved toward Daryus.

'Not part of the bargain, my love.' Eyes ablaze, Galen caught one of her wrists.

Swinging back to him, Zithia threw herself at him. Body against body, they were at once still. A single alabaster figurine. Out of nowhere, she kissed him. Her hands went up behind his neck, pulling him even closer. 'You've ruined my life.' She declared between ferocious embraces.

Galen picked Zithia up. 'And you mine.'

He walked passed Daryus. With one foot Galen pushed the nobleman over the pyramid's edge. The dark shape tumbled down coming to rest ten long drops below, on a broad plateau. Galen had hardly broken his stride.

At ground level, he put her down but continued to hold tight, tighter. Their lips touched, exploding rapture in senses and souls. After a dazzling time, breathless, they surfaced on a delicious, growing tide. 'Galen, what are we doing?'

'Making a mistake.' His tone then went to deepest base. 'We're drinking to eternal love.'

Drifting among sensations, 'Why can't I not love you?' Breathing hard, 'I try to.'

'Don't we both.' He nibbled her earlobe. 'It's war. Let's have our night without the world.'

Shuddering luxuriously. 'We can always fight tomorrow.'

The stars revolved somewhat through the sky. Zithia moved away from Galen's arms, straightening her clothes. In the warm afterglow she felt playful. Batting her eyelids slowly, Zithia placed a bare foot on his chest and pushed, then darted off. Instantly Galen was after her. Zithia managed to stay beyond his reach, letting out little high-pitched squeals when nearly caught. Dashing this way, feinting that way, and then rounding a corner, Zithia nearly ran into a deacon.

Following Zithia, Galen glared at the man. The deacon found sudden interest in a well-known constellation. 'My lord, the archpriest has called for all high priests.'

Galen, 'The enemy is two days from here.'

'Flyers have sighted a second fleet, lord.'

*

Within the hour the city was being evacuated. Daryus's party begged leave to have a word with the archpriest. Franklin and his high priests poured over final lists in a room where three broad steps put them above the guests. Refusing offers of help, Franklin distractedly farewelled the guest high priest.

Galen accompanied the party to the corridor, hailing Daryus as the entourage moved off. They walked side by side.

'A pity I didn't have the opportunity to show you the old labyrinth.' Galen stopped and faced Daryus. 'It's really not the danger people say.' The high priest bared his top lip fleetingly. 'Perhaps, next time?' Daryus knees buckled momentarily.

*

On the avenue, face still drawn, Daryus walked soberly to his litter, when Zithia happened to cross his path. She experienced a slight sinking feeling. The nobleman flicked an insect off him with a tight movement. 'Forget something last night?' Then recognising her afterglow. 'Ah, a reconciliation.'

Today, finding Daryus's very scent nauseating, despite cologne, Zithia's nose wrinkled as she stepped back apace. Daryus flushed red beneath his natural hue.

Zithia, 'You succeeded in inspiring commitment after all.'

Looking down, Daryus tilted his head on one side, and then slowly raised his eyes. 'Give Eten my love.' No smile. 'Tell her, I couldn't maintain… interest… in the quarry.'

Zithia rocked minutely, then. 'There I have the advantage of you Dar…' his name had so obviously flown from her memory. Frowning, Daryus glowered, '…being so little touched by your… magnetism that I didn't even notice your exit last night. And as for interest,' she drawled on, 'your only real interest for me was in your ability to arouse Galen's jealousy.'

chapter 17

The day was organised chaos. The roads had been filling since sundown yesterday. Yet many had hoped the invaders might turn aside from city and had remained until the last minute. Now the highways and jungle tracks were overwhelmed. Eten and Augustus walked with a Cayman knight guard, set to rendezvous with the other high priests that night. Eten jabbed people on the heels with her stick of office when their pace held her up. The hood of her cloak lay on her shoulders and Venus nestled comfortably within its folds, snapping his tongue out at children in their mamas' arms. The women hustled away. A deaconess slowed to speak to an elderly man. 'You're still here? I thought you'd have gone by now.'

'I thought I should stay.'

'But... you were expected home a year ago. I see the lines of your life.'

He shrugged and stopped. 'It was my shop. Too much to do. I couldn't leave the apothecary.'

For a brief part-second, the shop was all around them. Polished woodwork, marble floor. 'Ah, well,' She said, looking around at every sweet detail, 'we all get caught up.'

'You know, I think I'll sit a while,' he said, sighing so deeply it seemed to go on forever.

The deaconess touched his shoulder lightly. The old man's heart attack was massive when it came; he was alive one minute and dead thirty seconds later.

The temple was a hive of activity. The bakery continued to make hard corn bread for the refugees as long as possible. When each batch slid from the ovens on over wide wooden spatulas, another batch took its place. Flour made powder clouds everywhere in the unbearable heat.

Though the fires still burned, they closed the chimneys, scattering the remaining flour. The air became super-saturated with yellow white-dust. The head baker was worried about all that heat because of an incident he'd once read about. About to open the chimneys, he was ordered to leave. In his rush, he simply shut the door behind him.

About the time the bakery closed, Xiao Chen gave Zithia a message from Galen. He'd be at the temple nursery within half an hour. Zithia went to the priests' showers, with its dozen waterfalls and almost interlocking, natural pools of different temperatures. Wading to a distant waterfall, Zithia held her breath and stood within is foot-deep curtain. She bent to the rocks immediately beneath it, using a knife to prise a medium stone from its place. After taking a breath on the hidden side of the waterfall, she pushed the rock well away and retrieved a parcel.

In a changing stall, she took two heavy necklaces from the bundle. Stripping to one layer Zithia secured the necklace to a padded belt. Thick golden oblongs in an elaborate triangle now covered her rump. A similar pectoral, in emeralds, hung from the front. She pulled on two fine, black shifts. Finally, donning her priest's garb, she took a short cut to the nursery, praying she wouldn't bump into Galen. The serpent bracelets jangled all the way.

On her arrival Zithia found the temple nurse, Marian, sitting with a migraine and Kylyn. Calling out, 'Galen, have you been waiting long?' Zithia simultaneously gave a decisive flip of a hip against the door, slamming it shut.

Swiftly she perused the room, 'But where's my husband?' She picked up her son. 'Never mind,' Zithia threw Kylyn's pack at the nurse, 'we'll meet Galen on the way.' And went briskly out the back door, narrowly missing Xiao Chen.

They strode through the multitude, only halting in a stele's shadow to catch their breath. Zithia gave Kylyn to Marion. Taking a cloak from Kylyn's bag, she turned her back to the crowd and took off all the serpent bracelets. 'It feels unsafe to wear these.'

The nurse couldn't agree more. With Kylyn on her hip Zithia dove into the seething masses, with the nurse close behind.

Soon, Zithia marched up a flight of stone to a platform, from which more steps ran in two directions. Turning hurriedly to the nurse, Zithia pushed the bracelet filled cloth at her. 'Take care of these for me.'

As she handed them over, Zithia pulled open the loose bow tying the parcel. Instantly she flipped it upward. The bracelets spilled in a twinkling arc through the air, catching the light. Zithia stretched a hand after them, crying loudly, 'My gold!'

Like the crowds, the nurse watched the golden stream. She dropped

Kylyn's clothes and Zithia promptly kicked the bag into the throng before moving away. The nurse strove to recover the jewellery, but the crowd had risen in a wave to break over her. The leaf seller, Obnil, caught a circle on its downward journey. His thick hair fell into his eyes as he bit it, and then grinned. Hitching his backpack up, he happily trudged on. Zithia pulled her hood over her head and rounded a corner.

The melee here was more crushed, more panicked than those in the throng just yards away and a corner away. After taking just a few rushing steps, Zithia stumbled; both she and Kylyn, in her arms, were going down. A hand caught her hard by the elbow, righting her balance. Sweet relief filled her. And then, beginning to shake, Zithia turned grey. Galen or Xiao Chen must've found them. After all she'd purposely not followed the escape route planned, mainly, for temple people. Thanks and despair filled her.

'I thought it was you,' A beaming matron declared, grinning.

Recognition warmed them both. Zithia clasped the sturdy arm in a tender grasp. Smiling, both were radiant with smiles. Then each took a step on, in a different direction. Moving forward, Zithia thought: *"That's nice. After... how many lives?"*

*

Xiao Chen arrived to find an empty nursery. Zithia and Kylyn's energies were already muffled. Still, Galen had an idea of the direction Zithia took. In the now deserted priest's quarters Zithia came to rest in a clothes alcove. Settled, she completely masked their presence, she was now adept at this. The high priest and Xiao Chen searched for hours.

'Xiao Chen, go.' But another half-hour passed before he could convince the truth-sayer to leave. The high priest slapped Xiao Chen on the back. 'Don't worry, I'll trace them once she's on the move again.'

Galen wandered near the bakery, entering a trapdoor there. Looking at the sky he said grimly, 'Full moon tonight. The pure tribe will be more mad than ever.'

In the cunningly hidden store, the high priest sat on a stack of golden platters. A crack of light seeped through from the balcony floor above. He kept the door ajar. The seconds trickled away like hours. After a year, the hours passed. The quiet was palpable.

"Will you never move?" He thought and heard the slam of marching feet

on stone. The barbarians were early. Galen gently pulled the door to. The shouting came closer. A few minutes later Galen felt Zithia, unaware of the invaders, stir. 'Damn your timing.'

*

It was one of the great tunnels. A triumphal procession could traverse this underground passage in glory. Forgotten torches lit the way for Zithia and her son. Sounds, in front of her. Sweat trickled freely down her back. Grabbing Kylyn she ran back the way she'd come.

A huge steed cantered down the passage, a man astride its back. The stallion was in full red battle leathers, silver studs flying. Zithia froze, her mouth flung wide to scream. Galen saw what she saw and, before her fear gushed forth, he thought to her: *"The sands."* She didn't react, even though she'd heard him. He trebled his volume: *"The sands. Move."*

Like a flung spear she was racing: *"The horse!"*

Galen materialised right in front of the galloping horse. A vision with blazing eyes and an upraised staff. The black stallion stopped dead and reared, pawing the air frantically. Its rider spurred it on, but with Galen's vision moving towards it, the horse backed away. There was a heavy thud. Then the stallion, eyes white-rimmed and flanks prickling with fear, was off.

Two tunnels later, Zithia heard hooves thudding behind her again. At that sound, she ran faster than she thought possible. The stallion caught up to her, ignored her and passed her. The horse took one fork in the tunnel and Zithia the other. In the distance a troop of soldiers briefly saw both Zithia and the horse. The leader shouted to one man to retrieve the steed, before it harmed itself, while he and the others ran Zithia to ground.

*

Galen burst from his hiding place. It was late dusk and his eyes focused too slowly. A stench assailed him. 'What's that?' He rubbed his eyes to clear them. A second had passed, no more. The odour trebled and the high priest gagged. Then the electricity in every muscle demanded action and, following the advice, Galen dropped to the floor. A javelin whistled past him. The enemy had been six feet behind him when Galen had crashed from his bolt hole. She leered at Galen, tossing her greasy hair.

They both ran and, even as they did so, the night was visibly darkening around them. Having outdistanced his noisome follower Galen passed the distillery. Rounding a corner, he went to the bakery door, opening it a fraction before slipping into a shadow. Placing his hand on the hot wall, Galen withdrew it sharply and stood not quite touching the wall. Heat waves distorted his view.

The barbarian skidded round the corner and stopped. She tilted her head, and swung it wide. Then she lit the torch she carried for setting fires. 'Come out pretty.' she called in Galen's tongue. 'Pretty, come out.' The bakery door creaked. She strode to it, pulling it wide. Blackness confronted her; her torso recoiled even as she drew her double serrated long-dagger. 'Pretty.'

A 'knowing' came to Galen, from somewhere astral stating, *"She must throw the torch."* The barbarian was moving back from the doorway when Galen whispered to her soul, 'Stay… put to flame!' And each word had power. He repeated this twice more.

She stopped, hesitating. Then she pitched the torch into the room and leapt over the threshold, spluttering from the flour-filled air. Gasping violently for breath, she withdrew a step and Galen's cloak fluttered to her left. Their eyes met. The barbarian's yellow-coated tongue slithered well out of her mouth and across her upper lip. The high priest pushed himself away from the wall, sprinting.

Then the world became thunder; the bakery a spewing volcano. Still drawing in a breath to yell at Galen, the barbarian swallowed a burst of flame. Instantly driven pottery shards pounded into the barbarian's body, spearing so deep that the skin closed over them again. Nearing unconsciousness, her burned lungs couldn't howl when the second volley struck her.

Meanwhile, Galen had been picked up by the blast, and propelled high through the air. He was flying over the windows when the second blast occurred. Splintered needles from the shutters impaled the opposite stone wall. Orange and yellow octopus tentacles groped Galen. The broken spices store, next to the bakery, caught suddenly ablaze, breathing purple, green, even blue flames high and wide. They licked out at the flying high priest.

His robe alight, Galen curled into a ball and hit the ground rolling, speeding through a startling rose pink fireball. The flames on his back extinguished themselves. Slowing, Galen finally balanced on his haunches and, coming to rest, he vigorously hit the smoking material on his shoulders.

The broiling, simmering bakery, which had been super saturated with fine flour, had only needed a flame to carry it to ignition point.

*

Breathing hard, Galen ran down a large stairwell. Nearing the bottom, he leaned against the wall, bent almost double, hands on his thighs. The high priest's eyes darted around as he placed his spread fingers on the wall each side of him. One thumb touched an indentation, a jaguar's profile. A four-foot tall stone pivoted at its centreline and the platform on which Galen stood spun round. Bright green luminous jellyfish swam up the walls, lighting the tunnel. Mushrooms. Straightening up, he stepped off the platform and the trap door resumed its usual position.

Galen traversed this passage, known only to a few, while feeling for Zithia and Kylyn. Minutes after he broke into a jog, he knocked a stack of torches that shouldn't have been there. Two barbarians heard and shambled over to a wall. One hushed the other; too late. 'Never let a woman hook you,' Galen muttered to himself.

The white haired men pressed their ears to rock. Letting a stone fall, Galen walked on, with the invaders following the wall parallel to Galen's tunnel. Soon the ferrets entered the crystal chamber. Galen lit torches, ducking down below each crystal window that studded the wall. One fighter placed an eye to the sparkling portal. The other did the same.

Galen reached the end of the crystal corridor, doused his own flame and noiselessly doubled back to near the centre. Stepping back, the high priest observed an eye distorted in the window closest to him. This particular pink quartz was thin. Galen hit a lever.

Recognising movement, the barbarian's throat began to rumble triumph. A wood pike, set with four obsidian blades went through his eye, then his brain. It came to rest several inches on the other side of the skull, glistening with bone fragments. Grey hung from the point, trying to drop.

The remaining invader vaulted backwards, seemingly without moving, then fitted arrow to bow. Galen tossed an unlit torch far down the tunnel. Crouching, the barbarian passed under the remaining portals. Galen slid open a door, face to face with the new-made cadaver…

…The ghost of which was also looking at the body, talking to himself: *"And I knew looking into that crystal was a bad idea."* He was still shaking his head when two growly dark patches appeared above the sand he stood on, caught hold of his ankles and began pulling him rapidly downwards. Galen didn't stop or give a sideways glance, as he headed toward the sand cave.

*

Yellow sand spilled out of the echoing cavern. Immediately after entering, a gentle radiance threw twilight over the scene. In the greyish-yellow gloom Zithia stuck close to the wall, making for an exit directly opposite the mouth. Adrenalin raging through her veins, her hands were in constant contact with the wall.

Having seen Zithia and Kylyn disappear into the cave, the troop bellowed hunting cries. Racing in, their torches cast four malformed shadows on the sand. Zithia was only two-thirds of the way to her escape when they spotted her. Remembering the fates of prisoners, Zithia set her jaw, her unblinking gaze steady. 'Not me, or mine!' Her leg muscles tensed to spring forward if necessary. Kylyn clung to his mama's neck, and she pulled her hair over him.

The pack came swiftly on. Zithia held an arm in front of her face, fingers splayed. A single monster now, the barbarians increased their race to be the first to strike a blow.

Ready to leap, Zithia watched. All at once the bottom fell from beneath one man and he was up to his thighs in wet coarse powder. A comrade, eyes still on Zithia, jumped over him and landed waist-deep in sucking sand. All were now on shifting ground. One female tripped, her arms and legs stuck fast. Her head reared, she shrieked in disbelief.

Zithia's face was emotionless, behind her protective arms. Realising Kylyn's hands were over his ears, Zithia began to sing him a nursery song as she moved off, knowing she could never sing it to him again. The barbarians' torches flickered and were gone by the time Zithia reached the exit. A lone wail echoed back from the unsympathetic cavern. Once through the opening, Zithia immediately ducked behind the rocks as more invaders entered the cave. They'd heard something. Observing only rock and sand, they left.

Zithia was now in a cave that opened onto the water's edge, about twenty-five feet further on. She made for a smaller aperture, beyond which were jungle scents. Kylyn gripped her tight and suddenly black stars pranced before her eyes. Touching the lip of the rock hole, "Only a little further." she assured herself.

With Kylyn on her back, she climbed down the rope ladder to another ledge that was overlapped and hidden by the higher rocky outcrop. Hooking the rope onto a stone, Zithia watched the swirling water fifteen feet below and began to sway. Kylyn whimpered and Zithia staggered back from the edge. Releasing Kylyn, she pulled him close to her. 'Darling, hide-and-seek. No noise.'

This sanctuary had been prepared over months. They were both shivering violently and Zithia hugged Kylyn closer still, rubbing his arms to warm him. Yanking a dark cloak from its hiding place, she draped it over them. A bag and an obsidian-toothed machete were now visible. Calming her mind, Zithia concentrated, and their images totally faded from the airwaves again.

Footsteps. She closed her eyes. Then the rhythm of the stride became familiar. Zithia steeled herself. Galen called with his mind twice; Zithia refused to hear the concern in his thoughts. Galen saw her tracks in a patch of moist earth, at the same moment that he heard dogs baying. He looked for long seconds toward the sound. Then he ripped at his robe, which disintegrated along the back. Dropping the cloth to the ground, Galen walked swiftly backwards, dragging it over Zithia's footprints. The imprints, deeply carved at the toes, required a second smudging to disappear. Then standing upright, his muscles rippled as he ran towards the cave's mouth, where night beckoned.

Zithia, too, caught the sounds of war and thought: *"Escape!"* The word was all passion and dread.

He was racing now, the robe forgotten. Dogs and soldiers followed hard on his heels. Three creatures slavered; the hounds bayed. The only way out was to dive. Barely breaking his run, at the last second Galen paused on the brink to change the angle of his descent. A mastiff snapped at the high priest's heels as he left the ledge.

The barbarians saw him go, but not his direction. Nor did they see him twist his body savagely, to push himself to the right. The dark jade water embraced him like the old friend it was. At the rock's edge the dog bayed insults. A barbarian followed Galen, but dove straight out from the cave and smashed onto a submerged rock plateau.

Galen didn't hear the injured barbarian's screams, not even when the man's comrades used him for target practice and deliberately missed vital organs. Other arrows were aimed at the submerged swimmer.

Zithia could sense him, undamaged, swimming hard. She reflected: *"I thought I was finally immune to my knight… must I love him forever?"*

Suddenly there was a void where he had been. She could no longer feel Galen's life-force. Reeling, she extended her mind. *"Galen, Galen!"* Nothing. *"Beloved…"*

"It can't be." slowly, Zithia's head bent down to her chest, eyes closing on the way.

Time passed. A small voice called, 'Mama,' and was scarcely noticed by Zithia's mourning soul. Kylyn shook her.

"Galen's son." Zithia smothered Kylyn in kisses. Then, once more: *"Galen!"*

*

Zithia's plea hit its target and the high priest lost both footholds on his ascent up a fern covered cliff. He hung on by hands alone: *"Zithia. Are you trying to kill me?"* His own name, Galen, came back to him as a sob, so warm and golden that his concentration completely vanished. He grabbed a shrub and it slowly began to come away in his hand. Watching it, his mind was fuzzy from wave upon wave of her love flowing through him. He released the fern and grabbed solid rock itself. *"Sweetheart… I'm half way up a cliff."* The connection broke.

*

The barbarians ravaged the city. While Zithia armoured her breasts and back with two large gold pectorals tied together, Kylyn touched the broad band of glowing emeralds on Zithia's biceps. 'Your inheritance, my darling!' The total burden was heavy but she was used to it. She split the sides of her skirts.

In the reflected light of the warehouses burning, Zithia harnessed Kylyn to her back. She kicked a rope ladder over the edge and, wearing egg-hunters shoes, Zithia lowered herself into the water. Only reaching her knees, the liquid dragged at her, despite the spiked shoes which stuck firmly to the mossy rocks. She traversed the shallows for a time, till a nameless fear came over her, emanating from the dark water. Fairly flying, she dashed way up the riverbank. Behind, she heard a cayman's jaws snap where she had been.

*

The jungle was one green blur with occasional flashes of colour. Around mid-afternoon, hot and tired, Zithia removed her long robe. She listened to her bones complain. 'You should've stolen more emeralds and less gold. And as for the treasures from your youth, those three pouches of perfect pearls…' Finding an overgrown track was a relief.

'Mama, where is home now?'

'Perhaps the sculpture rock-forest of Makawatsi. It's said that happiness seeps through the stones and into those who live there.' She frowned, threw a stick down the track and then waited. Nothing moved. 'Mind you, it's walking all the way and all, all, uphill.' She tossed another stick, lengthways and high this time. A dozen six inch snakes dropped from the trees. Poisonous. 'Or the tabooed coast, north of the New Nile.' She'd just had a feeling about that track; maybe because it was too overgrown, maybe because no sound came from the track. 'It's only really forbidden to those without Atlantian heritage.' Taking Kylyn's hand, she sought another way. 'As we're true descendants of Atlantis, we might go there and even wait for the other Atlantians to return. As the legend says they will.'

In time they found a trail well-tramped, yet not too wide. It was like a picnic-walk, not having to fight through the green. An hour later, they heard someone laugh down the track. It was an ugly sound. Zithia pulled Kylyn into the green behind a fallen tree, whispering, 'We'll be rocks, unmoving and silent. We'll think of nothing at all.'

A troop mopping up refugees grew closer. Drunk with alcohol and blood, they staggered past Zithia and Kylyn. Zithia watched from beneath the fallen log, where a small yellow frog also hid. The leader of the party turned and boomed out a name, raising his arm impatiently. Green-gilled, Kylyn snuffled. A barbarian, following a little behind his party, had heard. The colour drained from Zithia's face and she pushed her son deep among plant leaves. The barbarian yelled something back to his commander, while grasping his groin. Receding laughter ensued.

Deftly Zithia removed the pack. Unclipping her hair, she spread its glory with a practised hand, to the sounds of liquid tinkling on foliage.

Then she pinched her cheeks for blusher and bit her lips. Hastily she took a leaf and picked up the canary coloured frog by the shoulders, not pleasing it. In response, the frog exuded clear liquid from its spotted hide. With her right hand Zithia scooped the liquid onto the back of the two longer fingernails, of her first two fingers. She replaced the frog and faced Kylyn's hiding place. Holding her fingers near her lips, nails outward, she mouthed, 'Shush.'

The soldier was back on the track, adjusting his clothes. He snorted the air for their scent and moved toward the spot the noise had come from. Thinking of the danger to Kylyn, Zithia's unblinking eyes became all pupils. Zithia slowly stood, her eyes moved up his frame, as she did so. She remembered to blink regularly. With an open-mouthed smile, she stepped up to the log and sat there astride. Unmoving, he stared. Gradually her bare legs embraced the log, muscles taut. Then she swung over to face him and alighted. Her hair seeming to float all about her.

The soldier grunted through his cropped blond beard. *"An officer's toy."* He thought, darting a look up the path.

When he looked back, Zithia was much closer to him and holding two fingers before her mouth, 'Shhh.' His eyes went to the log; he'd find what she'd left there when he was done. During that look, Zithia had darted around him. Now she was sashaying into calf-deep foliage on the other side of the track. At every step she'd faced him. Now Zithia arched her back, while taking a deep breath.

Eyes on her cleavage, he snorted: *"Hoping for mercy. Well, she's in luck; I'll have to kill her quick."* He followed her.

When she was close enough to touch him, she kissed her fingers raising them to his mouth. He went to pull her closer but instead she withdrew. Then she was back, touching his dirty beard, her fingertips caressing her mouth. He snapped at her fingers and on a second attempt took the tips into his maw, sucking them. At the same time he pulled her into a painful clinch. A vicious glint in his eyes, he opened his mouth and lowered sharp teeth to her shoulder. He couldn't keep her, but nothing would stop him breaking her skin with an ownership mark.

Zithia freed one hand and pushed his jaw desperately, forcing his bullhead away from her. *"Stronger than she looks."* Yet gradually, inexorably, he was succeeding in bringing her shoulder to his teeth. Suddenly the barbarian clutched at his mouth, releasing Zithia. Seconds later, he toppled over sideways, eyes staring dully, though still a little alive. Zithia wiped her fingernails on the carcass's shirt.

Carefully, she wrapped her poisoned fingers in cloth. Zithia raised her eyes to heaven. 'Beloved God, deadly frogs... superb idea.' Grinning, she dipped her head in thanks.

Just two strokes of the machete hastily covered the body. Putting the knife away, Zithia turned. And faced a pair of dobermans. Silently they bared their teeth, low growls growing. Hackles raised upon their backs as they slowly advanced.

Then, beyond Zithia, the dogs saw the barbarian's ghost flung ten feet up into the air by several very determined shadow patches. Each darkness wanted to be the one to deliver the barbarian to the afterworld. Each had a very firm grasp on a part of the whimpering barbarian. They started to pull, and argue, in harsh static sounds.

Frozen, Zithia watched the dogs. The dogs remained transfixed upon the ghost. He began to scream when the shadows' tug-of-war grew ugly. Bits were taken through to the underworld. The shadow with the part from which the shrieking head lolled, seemed the most gratified.

Whining, low to the ground, the dogs fled. Zithia collected Kylyn and marched smartly into the bushes. The rigid-faced boy clung very tight. Having his mama returned to him, Kylyn had resolved not to disobey her again.

*

Next day the jungle had thickened. Progress was slow. Holding her walking stick directly below its wide nob, Zithia set it and watched where it disappeared into the undergrowth. Her eyes were making their fiftieth weary journey back to head level when she felt something brush the fingers gripping the wood. She focused on her hand. A large hairy spider balanced on the knob, having fallen from a plant above them. Its eight legs, seeking better purchase on the wood, touched her flesh.

Zithia and the spider stood looking at each other. Her arm stiffening, Zithia's eyes opened wide. The spider's eyes did the same. All at once Zithia relaxed. 'I don't have time for this.' She raised the stick. 'Get off!' It waved two mandibles in the air. 'I said, get off.'

She flicked the staff, but after wavering the spider clung tighter. 'Here catch.' Zithia threw a biscuit at it. When two feet grabbed the cookie, Zithia moved the stick quickly sideways, then back in the opposite direction.

The shaggy creature tottered a bit, and then flew through the air before fetching up against a sapling with a resounding squeak. The little stem bent like a bow. Dropping the fruit, the spider grabbed frantically for a handhold then was arced into the undergrowth. Zithia heard a thump and a second squeak.

'So much for my fear of spiders.' The creature grumbled off into the distance. 'Well, for now, anyway.'

*

The dappled area was boggy in places. Thinking about snakes, Zithia checked their anklets. These contained a herbal antidote known to neutralise most snake venom. She looked up and, without warning, felt like a chick among weeds. Each tall thick stem arose to a single leaf, ten feet across. She was in a stand of giant rhubarb, the image of its smaller relatives except in scope. Soon the way became open space again. Zithia's eyes were half-closed with weariness, feet trudging forward of their own accord. The twilight sucked colour from the landscape. All at once her brain awoke fully; she was walking on dark ash. *"Invaders?"* she thought, swinging in circles to scan the blackened land.

But, no, the huge rough field had been freshly created, by burning the jungle. Certain prominent trees were left in the gently sloping meadow, so as not to kill the soul of the land. Fast-growing bean tendrils peeked through the dark earth. The farmer was a godly man indeed, to plant for this spring equinox festivity. True, this was done every year, but not by people expecting to be invaded at any moment.

Turning back to the giant rhubarb, Zithia hacked off a stem and dragged it over the charcoal land. Zithia and Kylyn almost fell when the field dropped down twelve inches. 'Must be a shallow irrigation channel.' This distraction happened twice more and the earth within these runnels was pure white.

In time Zithia found what she wanted. A jagged eighteen-foot wide hole left after a tree stump had been burned. Throwing a rock in to see how deep it was, she disturbed a particularly ugly bug. Without thinking she opened her hand and uttered a snatch of a charm.

Gingerly she hunched down and so avoided the small flurry of insects. At once she felt Galen on the airwaves. He'd been waiting for this very mistake to find her. She crouched lower, both in body and mind, listening to the sounds within the wind. Outside the wind. But the spell had lasted only a second, not quite enough time even for Galen. She was queasy with relief, she reprimanded herself, 'Fool.' She'd been lucky. Any further psychic activity would be folly in the extreme.

Waiting for the slower snakes to leave, Zithia macheted the stem from the rhubarb. Throwing the rhubarb leaves into the bottom of the hole, she gestured. 'Our bed.'

Sliding down, with her son at the rear, they were soon asleep. Fragrant datura scent wafted from the jungle, the hanging bells comforted the night.

*

A harpy eagle wheeled in a cobalt sky, looking balefully down on the ashen field. A giant jaguar face, outlined in white, glared red-eyed back. The majestic bird had been perched, a hundred and eighty feet up, in a kapok tree at the far corner of the field. Farmers never destroyed these trees because it brought bad luck. Besides, the kapok fiber from around the seeds was collected for honeymoon mattresses, replacing the usual thin reed mats. It was part of a girl's preparation for coming-of-age to sew these.

The female harpy had heard a two-toed sloth. Fluffing her facial plumage into a flat dish, she located the hairy mammal at the jungle's edge. Setting flight, the eagle extended her talons, as long as a grisly bear's claws. Feeling rather than seeing the harpy's seven feet wingspan above him, the sloth dashed back into jungle. Dense rope vines hid him. Circling high to spot a new prey, not wishing to waste the calories already expended, the harpy saw a flutter of a movement in the jaguar-face glyph. Something moved within one dusty feline eye, perhaps a red howler monkey.

The great bird folded her wings tight, starting rapid descent. Half-awake, Zithia lay with her back to Kylyn. She was covered with a layer of fine red dust. Slowly Zithia rolled over toward her son, whose skin was likewise tinted. Snuggling him good morning, she touched noses.

The eagle wasn't high above them when Zithia sat up stretching and dusting herself off. Within a microsecond the bird flattened her wings, lifting her head and chest to come out of the dive. In a rising swoop she managed to clear the nearest trees, frightening rainbow macaws and trumpeters to flight. Snapping her beak in distaste the harpy totally ignored the macaws; they always left such a muddy after-taste. Smiling broadly, Zithia waved to the great bird, who soared in a momentarily baby blue sky with puffy candy pink clouds.

Climbing a hill that had been under cultivation within the last year, Kylyn tugged at her skirt. Over-tired, Zithia swung round impatiently and saw the line drawing opposite. Its glorious snarling jaguar face, with a serpent tongue, defied the world. Crafted from white outlines against the charcoal backdrop, tree-holes partly filled with ochre produced the red glaring eyes.

*

Days later, Zithia and Kylyn observed the first stone orb. Within minutes there was a plethora of balls, standing from four to nine feet tall. She smiled broadly. The Valley of Spheres. She had no doubt that this precious vale had escaped the invaders. Traditionally, in times of trouble the villagers simply decamped into the forests.

Beginning the fairy-tale to her son Zithia recited. *"When the world was new God played a game in heaven, rolling marbles across the skies. Some fell to earth, landing here in the valley of his spheres."*

'Your papa and I made a pilgrimage to this valley to pray for a blessing.'

These fields produced better crops than anywhere in the land. 'That year papa outbid other temples and obtained the valley's first corn for Xalisco.'

Zithia recollected that a new priest had been appointed to the village not two years ago. Youngish he was, still proving himself. Ambitious.

Looking forward to a night spent in fireside chat, Zithia called to the villagers. Calling again, she gagged. Meat was spoiling. A pile of robes lay in the dusty street ahead. They stopped in their tracks.

'Please God, not here.' Zithia prayed aloud. Picking Kylyn up, she pulled his bandanna down over his eyes and mouth.

The first body they skirted was the priest's, lying on its side. He'd died clutching at the sword-thrust in his groin. His battle-club and scalp lay nearby, the latter having been dropped by the trophy hunter. The robe had been stripped from the priest's back, and one word carved into his flesh. Zithia retreated.

The priest had led the village in an attack against the enemy. She said to the torso, 'But the stones need no defence.' Then reflecting: *"The idiot expected glory."*

All the victims Zithia came across had had body parts ripped away, more trophies. She dared not look at them closely. Blood lust had gripped the invaders and they'd forgotten to take their pleasures slowly. Zithia's only source of relief was that no children were among the dead; they must've been evacuated very early.

'Why didn't you all go thus?' Zithia asked the air, knowing again the answer... the priest. He'd kept them there with promises from God, until it was too late. 'Damn him.'

Moving along hastily, Zithia stopped to pick up a gourd bowl that had rolled against a nine feet tall ball. In the process of standing, she observed a thin icing sporadically decorated the sphere. Zithia's eyes were drawn to the top. A village woman had watched the priest's downfall from this perch, only to be speared there. The face had been slashed and her right hand was gone.

Eventually, Zithia came to the charred prayer hut, one of whose walls was a huge globe. The defenders had been forced into the sanctuary, after which it had been set alight. An arm rose from the earth, at the base of the corner between wall and sphere. A smoked husk; even the jade thumb-ring was blackened. The man's fingers had contorted in a desperate plea while the rest of him burned.

Zithia's knees gave way and she began to scream soundlessly. Kylyn tightened his grip on his mama, crying. Zithia rocked them both low, back and forth, throwing dirt over her head. The silent dirge continued there, for she knew she hadn't the strength to offer succour to the dead by entering the charnel house. In time, she was able to crawl backwards away from the tomb and the hand.

Making her way to the river, Zithia put Kylyn on a tabletop created by a deep-sunk orb. She pulled the blindfold down from his eyes before she went to a shallow pool, to wash her face and hands. Once done, she caught her raw reflection in the water. She washed again, then again and again until her breathing ceased to be ragged. Her lips were still grey from shock. Kylyn gave her a tiny smile and she ran somewhat jerkily to him, folding him in a bear hug. *"Will I ever sleep well again?"* she thought, dreading the coming nightmares.

Blowing her nose on a handkerchief, Zithia hoisted herself up beside him. Sipping flower-water for trauma, at intervals, Zithia spent a long hour focusing on the area immediately around the river. And its bland normality, while her hands, face and feet gradually lost their iciness in the sunlight.

Near the water's edge were ten-foot tall arrowroot plants. Zithia looked across the rippling liquid to the unchanged, wavy fields beyond. The very orderliness soothed her, slowly drying the stream of her tears. The crops and balls remained untouched; the barbarians hadn't been able to traverse the flow. The view was thick with spheres. Because they were God's own, the land was ploughed around them. Smaller ones lay in greater abundance near the top of the hill. Even the river was pearled by globes, often colossal.

Eventually, Zithia climbed a stone three-foot in diameter, craned her neck to look over a second rock blocking her view. It was peaceful downstream. Turning back towards the village she shuddered, then observed the fruit trees. The prized egg-shaped fruit had all been picked. No crops were left on this side of the river.

A vigorous tree gripped the side of a large globe, its roots having displaced the rock. Given the tree's extensive canopy and that its fruit was grey, Zithia hoped that the pure tribe might've overlooked some fruit. 'Kylyn, darling, stay here and guard these.' She removed her robe then the twin gold pectorals from her shoulders.

The emeralds on her upper arm winked. 'Do you remember the rule about water?'

He nodded. 'Never go near, when you're not here.' She began to climb.

After several minutes' hunting, with no success, there was a rustle in the branches way above and Zithia saw a man's outline. 'Thank goodness you escaped.' She knew it wasn't a barbarian for they'd moved on days ago.

Climbing up to him, he was part hidden by shadow. 'I see you've found some fruit.' His hand was reaching for a grey clutch.

Zithia smiled into his face; an ant walked across one eye. Losing her grip, Zithia fell heavily onto a nest of branches a few feet down. Kylyn cried out in fear for her.

'It's all right, my darling.' She called out cheerfully. 'Mama missed her footing, that's all. You count how many river-birds you can spot.'

It was the leaves that had moved. Not the man. Archers had caught him up the tree and put several arrows in the villager's stomach. He had crawled further along the branches until the arrows became wedged between two branches. She beat her chest, 'God of my heart, does it never end?' and began the prayer for the dead, reserved for a brother.

Shivering, Zithia took the fruit just beyond the man's grasp. She didn't have the strength to look for more. 'Did the demons harvest the tree while he lay dying?' At once she blocked the question out and descended on icy feet. She skidded onto a smaller orb, half in the water, and then finally leapt to the ground.

'Six.'

'Six what, darling?' She'd forgotten his task.

'Six birds. And a tomato bush.' Kylyn pointed to a plant hidden between two small balls.

Kylyn plucked ruffled tomatoes while Zithia gathered their belongings. They moved further along the river where she couldn't see the tree.

Plunging the purple-black tomatoes into the water she saw a submerged rope, pulled tight by the current. Sitting on one sphere, leaning their backs on another one Zithia ate in silence. She had to choke down the fruit. Kylyn prattled on about birds. His mama's eyes never left the water. She could make out the line of the rope. It was taut. Something hidden was at the other end. Devouring a slice of tomato Zithia murmured under her breath, 'I don't know if I can face another corpse.' Biting her lip, 'OK… another mutilated corpse.' Gradually she straightened her back.

'Now, is this piranha country?' She recalled the strings of little fish roasting at the First Day festival: *"And their bodies mostly teeth."* Mother and son watched the water for the carnivores for a very long time. None appeared.

Vultures circled and landed in the village. 'That's not a good sign. Still, they didn't land near our rope.' Nodding, she slapped a hand above her knee.

Remaining cautious about the river, Zithia extended her hands flat over the crystal liquid: *"I'll chance it."* Having lived with little magics for so long, it was hard to give them up all once. A shadow reached her, an echo. Galen, encouraging her, 'Use your talents, Zithia.'

She gulped, 'Not this day Galen.'

Breathing deeply, evenly, she waded in, disturbing the surface as little as possible. At the arrowhead clump Zithia pulled gently on the rope. Whatever it was attached to started to move towards her. Her muscles quivered.

Tugging on the hemp, a flower flashed into view, white with brownish and purple blotches. Far too reminiscent of dried blood for her. The rope snagged on something. Zithia gave one last vigorous wrench and felt the unseen object bob effortlessly toward her. One end rounded a large sphere. Her heart sang: *"A boat."* It was a proud little canoe made from a single tree.

She laughed and faced Kylyn, 'A boat, darling.' All the while she pulled it closer. Then she realised that the water was vibrating from her canoe's passage. Her eyes searched the liquid while she made a grab for its side.

Instantly she recoiled at the touch of a hand beneath hers. A limp hand. Breathing hard she turned to look. A youth lay there, staring at the lovely sky, a knife wound across his throat. He'd staggered here, holding his life within the hands he held tight across the wound.

'Well, it's not really mutilated.' Zithia tried to hard to breathe, 'if I forget his mouth.' The youth's face was all smile, a bird had got his lips. Jerkily throwing her bandana over his mouth, Zithia whispered, 'I'm… alright!'

Kylyn had also seen the body and was losing colour. 'Turn around Kylyn and count the spheres! Aloud.'

The dead youth's head rested on the prow with one hand hanging over the edge, not quite in the water. His awkward position made the small craft unsteady, but she didn't dare dispose of the body so near the shore, for Kylyn's sake.

Taking out her knife, Zithia cut a small bag from his belt. Pocketing his knife, Zithia flung the bag onto the bank.

Standing in water up to her waist, Zithia pushed the corpse. It overbalanced and belly flopped, splashing water on her. Rearing away, Zithia dashed for the shore, still holding the rope. Meanwhile the dead youth drifted in the river, one booted foot alone resting on the bottom.

Sliding off her black shift, Zithia released her belt. 'Don't look yet, darling.' She handed the emerald pectoral and the gold one to him. Clumsily Kylyn put them in the pack. Meantime, Zithia cleaned up the coagulating blood in the canoe. A blade was necessary to dislodge the dried jelly on the prow's edge.

Clothed again, Zithia returned to the river's edge. Unknown to her, the water temperature had changed, as had the current. About to step into the liquid Zithia saw three large fish where the body was submerged. She didn't like the thought of fish hanging around the corpse, not even iridescent blue ones with yellow sides and red bellies. So she threw a rock to scare them off. It landed inches from the corpse. Two of the fish, eighteen-inch dinner platters standing on end, lazed over to investigate.

Zithia put her shod foot into the water and then out again, suddenly remembering to look for tiny carnivores. She was bending down when the third large fish sped over and sprang into the air snapping at nothing. Zithia's back arched away, mesmerised by the razor-studded maw. She screamed, 'Piranha! Don't come near the river.' Malevolent eyes examined her face, considering the tastiest bites to be had there.

Realisation hit her, the First Day piranha were babies. Another thought struck her. Piranha bites were painless. Dry-mouthed, Zithia checked her foot. No blood, she let go a relieved breath.

After pulling the canoe further up the mud, Zithia gathered Kylyn. 'Keep your hands inside the boat.' She loaded her treasure carefully in the skip's centre, before handing him the jewellery.

'At least I won't be drowned if the canoe sinks.' Zithia pushed the boat off the mud, climbing in. 'Eaten possibly; not drowned.'

Riding over the sunken corpse, Zithia polled them into the fast currents. There were arc shaped gashes in the skin. One piranha was hacking at calf meat. The nose was already non-existent and the jaw was down to the bone. Zithia turned away; then they rounded the river bend.

Knees drawn up to her chin, Zithia quivered through the night. Shuddering from each horror-filled doze, she rocked herself long. And one evening didn't wear thin these terrors.

*

Now they travelled while they rested. That day they were lucky, finding an isolated stream and reddish brown fruits, orange sized. Zithia and Kylyn savoured the full flavour and strong aroma. After another day of riding a swifter, green, river they found a few mushrooms for Zithia's dinner.

Well past dawn the following day, Zithia heard barking. Trying to lift her eyelids, she found them stubborn. She commanded them to open and they refused. Reaching for the water gourd, Zithia flushed it over her face. This time her command was obeyed. A yapping, hairless dog pranced before her. She crooked her arm to support her chin. 'How did you get all the way out here?'

She became aware of three small children, giggling. And forty feet behind them, ears of black corn ripened in the sun. 'A village.' Zithia smiled, as Kylyn threw a latex glob back to a girl. 'The canoe must've beached itself while we slept.'

At her voice, the nearest child rose from a sitting position and dashed back to his older brother. There he hid his face, sneaking peeps at Zithia and Kylyn. Zithia sat up, showing her hands palms-up. 'No, don't go.' She wanted to say more...

The children stood on enormous lily leaves. Each up to six-foot wide. Looking at the size of these heavily veined baking trays, Zithia frowned, 'That's not right.'

A larger child sat on her pan-like leaf, with its five-inch sides. Zithia's head pivoted to her right. Lush lily pads, plus huge white, pink and red candle flames, floated into the near distance. All at once the sprites deserted her, half-running, half-skipping across the crinkle-lipped water platters to the cornfields.

The cornfields. Zithia beheld their roots wafting gracefully beneath the plants. 'Oh no, what have I eaten!?' She was sure that she'd mistakenly picked a hallucinogen among last night's mushrooms.

The dog scampered off in the children's wake, only to stop and wag his tail at a leopard catfish, yapping the while. The armour-plated swimmer ignored the hairless creature.

Zithia splashed handfuls of water onto her face and shook her head, then looked again. Everything was as where it had been. A normal sized blue lily winked at her. Groaning, Zithia closed her eyes once more. 'How long is this going to last?'

A voice was at her back, 'Welcome, I'm called Xipe.'

Rapidly drawing in breath, Zithia made a sound like half a hiccup. Then she was laughing. The warm voice moved to beside her, amid muted oar noises. Tentatively, Zithia reached out and touched his arm. He was real. 'Sorry.'

Xipe was short and finely boned, burned a dark chocolate. He stood on a long flat raft, water lapping over the top of it.

'I'm a lake farmer,' grinned Xipe, then stared behind Zithia at the far off jungle. 'We've seen much smoke this season.'

She also looked. A flock of flamingos, white with pink touches, landed in the lake's shallows. Zithia reflected: *"Ten miles, maybe."*

'Any who are found among the lilies are our guests. Come.' He gestured to the corn, now obviously on large rafts.

From his standing position, Xipe, paddled away with the merest swish. Zithia followed with graceless noise, beyond the cornfields, to a village. It was a series of houseboats, each home to an extended family. The community moved slowly around the immense lake, continually taking advantage of virgin water bursting with minerals and nutrients. The lake was mostly deep, yet the vigorous lilies adapted.

The headman welcomed them, and chose a host for the visitors, by lot. A finder never guested a stranger and therefore many more strangers were discovered than would've been. Thus, Chac was privileged to have Zithia and Kylyn on his houseboat.

Reaching the hut, Zithia only managed to grab her emerald laden pack before her host did. Crossing the three-foot walkway that surrounded the dwelling, Zithia felt her cares soothed away by the lapping water. Inside it was one long room. A group of women sat in a circle on the floor, preparing yucca root soup. Zithia dropped the, apparently light, bundle next to a rolled up sleeping mat. No one gave the scruffy pack a second look, including Zithia.

Their hostess, Nhutalu, admired Kylyn's big blue eyes. A bowl of fruit, delightfully sour, was offered to the guests. Nhutalu returned to grinding corn into flour. A daughter of the house, opened a flap in the floor adding a fish to the ones caged there. The fish had been caught that morning. A baby crawled to the raft's edge, watched by a couple of men who smoked pipes. Gurgling, the infant tipped headlong into the depths. Zithia ran over ready to dive in, but the men merely cooed at the tiny one, checking that he came up for breath regularly.

Zithia also sat down, curling her legs under her. Small children floated by on lily pads, dragonflies let their legs dangle into the water then frolicked away. Nhatula came over with a drink for Zithia. Her hostess pointed out a young woman sitting on a large lily pad, thus displaying her delicate weight.

'My oldest daughter.' Nhatula's small bosom expanding. Sitting cross-legged the girl dried and combed her longish, straight black hair. 'She's at courting age.' Several young village men paddled by. 'I've to go to the crop rafts. Join me?'

Both women paddled a semi-submerged float, made from small tree limbs. Kylyn sat between them. They were accompanied by a gaggle of imps. Reaching the rafts, the older children dove in, to examine the roots. Meanwhile, Nhatula gathered potatoes, yucca roots and squashes. 'Three harvests a year.'

A youth jumped the space between this raft and a cornfield. The others soon followed, playing hide-and-seek through the tall plants. At times the raft swayed perilously.

When they got back on the host barge women were already preparing the meal. Eel fish in a hot chili sauce, baked over charcoal. The villagers bartered with shore dwellers for this fuel. During the meal Zithia said to Chac, 'We're making a journey to the coast. Do any rivers flow from here to the sea?'

Chac shook his head. 'But we can show you the shortest route overland.'

Inwardly Zithia lamented: *"Walking again."*

'We hope you will be with us a long time.' Chac gave that most hospitable lie.

Zithia smiled at this courtesy.

*

After sleeping late the next day, Zithia sought out the headman among his family. Waiting to be noticed, Zithia watched a grandfather insert a cactus needle into a blue X, tattooed on his inner ankle. Another man twiddled needles in three short lines on either side of the grandfather's spine. Finally the headman nodded at Zithia. She returned the nod. 'I'm told the corn roots are very strong this planting.'

He uttered a contented sigh. Here the roots of the crops were watched with the same attention given the growing leaves. The lake people even released minuscule fish
amongst the roots, to eat any fungus.

'I'm grateful for the hospitality of your village. Still, as guests, like fish, stink after a short time, I leave tomorrow.' The headman chuckled and popped yet another red-hot chilli into his mouth. His look was euphoric, for the chillies had activated the body's pain-killers.

Some minutes passed in watching the lake-scape. 'Xipe will go with you to the land.'

It was Xipe's duty, having brought her among them, to deliver them from her.

Before dusk, Nhatula took Zithia and Kylyn to the larger lily field. Children floated with them, on miniature rafts. Scattering dragonflies,

224

Nhutalu located large berry-like fruit and tender leaf shoots. Among the lilies, playful squeals filled the air. Zithia joined the swimmers, quickly learning to avoid the soft prickles on the lily pads' undersides.

A girl cut the stem of a lily pad that Kylyn sat on, and spun it so that the boy rotated like a top. The dog raced from one end of the lilies to the other. In the rosy rays of the setting sun, the lilies began to open. Eighteen-inch flowers unfolded their fifty petals, releasing a heady fragrance. Zithia cut a white, pink and red blossom.

When the sleeping mats had been laid out, Nhatula and her daughters were brushing their hair. Lying down, Zithia used her pack for a pillow. 'Nhatula, I leave my boat at the shore tomorrow. Perhaps you can make some use of it.' Her hostess's eyes lit up.

Zithia started to fall asleep, when one of the girls came over. 'Perhaps a few braids in your hair for good luck?' Zithia smiled in assent, Kylyn nestled closer to her, and then it was morning.

On awaking, she tipped her heavy head forward. Numerous tiny random braids, interlaced with coloured corn, curtained her face. Nhatula's daughter beamed at Zithia. Putting her hand near her right ear, Zithia checked that her wooden comb had been put back. Yes, she had brought a comb on this journey. Stowing her things into the canoe, Xipe added a bundle of food. Nhatula slipped rainbow corn necklaces over Zithia's and Kylyn's heads.

They voyaged in silence the eight miles to the land. A mile from shore Xipe pointed to the water. They were paddling over a dozing manatee herd, tubby sea cows floating many feet below the surface, their backs arched and paddle-tails dangling. Others, voraciously culling the water lilies, peered at the humans with mermaid faces.

chapter 18

Twice more the sun rose. To the right, a fine beach lay extended in a graceful curve for fifteen miles. Black sand, created by volcanic eruption, extended left. From eagle height the black bay ended in a pair of ill-matched pincers, endeavouring to meet. Further closing the gap was a permanent sandbank, running partway across the bay.

The obsidian teeth of the machete cut another branch, slipped from Zithia's moist hand and rolled down a steep hill. Her gaze followed it, till she looked down to where white sand met black. There, surging waters threw sand mists through the changing depths. A kaleidoscope of colours mingled. She made the sign against evil, gasping, 'Not Black Bay.'

She couldn't wear gold anywhere near Black Beach. In haste Zithia divested herself of jewellery, plus the three pouches of pearls in a pack she'd had since childhood. Hiding her bundles beneath a tree, she fixed its position in her mind. The water beckoned. Looking at the dazzling white sand, to the right, Zithia took Kylyn's hand. 'We can enjoy Snow Bay.'

With whoops of pleasure they ran down the mountainside, stumbling across white sand to dash into the waves. Between swims, Zithia laid their wet outer clothes on a wind-bent shrub. Bobbing in the cool, they drifted to where the two beaches met to become the centrepieces in the swirling patterns of aquamarines, jades, turquoise and sands.

Retrieving their clothes, Zithia and Kylyn picked the shrub's small, yellow fruit. Sitting on the sand, they slurped the pulp, and then Kylyn's eyes closed to the sound of conversation between the beaches. The dark sands whispering threats, at which the pearly sands laughed.

Shivering, Zithia glanced into Black Bay and tied the torn cape around her shoulders. 'At least I know where there's a port.'

A rose-golden shaft of light appeared high in the late afternoon sky. That particular glow always reminded Zithia of God, and she dipped her head in prayer before blowing a kiss heavenwards.

Muffled noise was heard and, simultaneously, Zithia's arm was grabbed. She was being pulled behind a mounted barbarian, dragged down Snow Beach. The copper haired invader had been grazing his commander's stallion when he'd spied Zithia.

A raiding party sat by a fire, buffing already polished shields. One barbarian wrapped his spearhead in cloth before laying the weapon next to his sleeping hollow. Parallel to the bonfire, the soldier let Zithia go, jumping down beside her. He threw the reins to a companion.

Zithia rolled sideways, bouncing to her feet. Sand liberally daubed her messy braids. Blood oozed where skin had been stripped from a patch of Zithia's right forearm.

Her captor's hand slipped over his beard before he lunged at Zithia. She floated away from him. This time he charged with more purpose. Zithia went down on one knee, so that he sailed over her head. The pattern repeated itself with variations. Grunting, the invader made another pass. There was an audible crunch, causing him to blink. Blood poured from his nose. Broken.

In the gloaming, a tall man emerged from the surf, shaking off water. Unseen by the combatants. He was well built, with white blonde hair, cut very short, clean-shaven. Nethard's sky true eyes twinkled: *"Let the men have their sport."* Making for the fire, he saw Kylyn running by; the boy's eyes riveted on Zithia. The officer stepped forward a pace, clutched the child and threw him in the air like a paper ball. Kylyn stopped crying mid-throw, somersaulted, and then was caught by the smiling man.

On the ground again, Kylyn flew to his mama. She put out a hand for him to take but, instead, he jumped at her attacker, his fingers clawing. Pulling Kylyn back behind her, Zithia clasped his hand in hers. Facing the soldier Kylyn bared his small teeth. Zithia commanded, 'Follow me.'

Kylyn's mouth shut tight and Nethard reflected: *"Might be a recruit."* No. The hair was too dark.

The circling resumed, with Zithia's movements necessarily more clumsy. A blow missed her, but swept Kylyn off his feet. Bending, Zithia picked up a piece of driftwood from the shadows. A few words later, she scythed the air with a sword.

The men around the fire ceased their catcalls. Who had left their sword lying about? Zithia's opponent drew a dagger, advancing towards her.

Watching the entire party, Zithia counter circled. Nethard was patting his stallion's mane when Zithia focused energy. A panther's growl erupted, almost on top of the horses. Nethard jumped back, but his stallion didn't react. Others ran to their steeds; the growl exploded anew. The herd calmly cropped any suitable green.

Sharply, the captain looked back in the woman's direction. She had been watching them go to the horses. In that same instance, Zithia pivoted. 'Feel this…' she struck with the sword. Simultaneously, her mind threw a word across the ether: *"Galen!"*

Falling, her opponent bellowed at the searing in his heart. Zithia gathered Kylyn, calling: *"Where are you, Galen?"* She fled.

Going to Zithia's victim, Nethard took up the sword and found a branch. The prone man observed blood flood his chest, until Nethard prodded him hard with the driftwood. 'Here's the sword that killed you.' An acquisitive smile touched Nethard's lips. 'Sorcery! Magic. No sword, no panther. A witch.' His eyes gleamed. 'Find them.'

Meanwhile, Zithia was kneeling down at a large sand dune, Kylyn safe in front of her. She dug into the dune above them and it partially disintegrated. Twitching the cloak over her head and arms, they were completely covered by the sand and cape. Yet they had space in which to breathe.

Half an hour passed. Nethard drawled, 'Recover the rats or I'll flog one of you until his back shows white with bone.'

Zithia heard the horses in the dunes and then she felt a weighty pressure on her leg. Instinctively she moved a fraction. More weight was applied. A grouse rising, Zithia burst from the sand. A hand reached for her. Locking onto her tormentor's hand, Zithia snapped it back viciously. A second man pulled at her cape, hauling her away. A livid scarlet mark half-ringed her neck. Tearing at her noose, Zithia found a knife in her ribs. The captives were hauled to the fire, with Zithia's arm twisted high up her back, pushing her full breasts forward.

When Zithia's sword victim saw her, he raised his foot to kick her in the stomach. Moving rapidly Nethard off-balanced him with a punch to the eye.

The officer snarled words unintelligible to Zithia. She was released. A barbarian grabbed Kylyn by the neck of his shirt, lifting him off the ground. A blade was buried in the soft flesh under Kylyn's chin.

Zithia screamed, 'No!'

Nethard threw her the stick she'd transformed before. Zithia turned on the illusion, but it became a wraith even as the troop admired it. Without looking at Kylyn, the commander gave an order and blood trickled from the dagger's point. The image returned, but faded to translucence after a few minutes.

After watching the sweat drip from Zithia's face, Nethard signalled. Kylyn was dropped and the boy scrambled to his mama. Nethard stood over Zithia, his bright eyes smug. 'We have the first live magician.'

There was a huge reward for the first native magician. Their own warlocks wanted to test the local capabilities. 'No one touches them.' He didn't want his witch unable to perform because she was damaged.

Searching Zithia himself, the captain kept Kylyn within reach. Binding Zithia's hands, he moved to her feet. Grasping an ankle, he jerked it up and Zithia fell backwards. Looking into Zithia's eyes, Nethard's tongue slid from her inner-ankle upward for several inches. Shuddering, Zithia looked out to sea.

He laughed, they all laughed. Shortening the rope between her hands and feet, Zithia was thus bound. Nethard grabbed Zithia by the hair and cut off a long braid. At the campfire he fondled Zithia's braid. He pivoted his fire-hardened wooden shield, covered by stretched leather. Nethard wound Zithia's hair around a strap on a top corner of the oblong.

At this time, Zithia thought about Galen tracing her through her magic, and wished he would. Indeed, *"where was he?"* her mind demanded of the ether. A blankness came in answer. 'Oh, really,' She muttered, '... can't rely on anything!' Then she paused, and sensed and, just as the fear began, Zithia felt strength ebb into her. From Galen.

"I'm here." His mind whispered, quiet as an echo: *"Till death do us part."*

Zithia: *"No, let's not part. To die on the same day..."*

"The same hour."

"Willingly."

"Willingly."

"We'll be as one, once again."

His mind whisper was fading: *"In ways we still are."*

Zithia closed her eyes briefly, and leaned upon her son.

Their guard maimed his dinner of roasted barracuda. Unconsciously, Kylyn licked his lips and the barbarian held up a square of fish, then threw it into the sand. To avoid the evil eye, the guard faced the ocean.

Zithia began to sing in Atlantian, a jaunty little ballad made popular by the war. She continued, though Kylyn was soon asleep.

"Cut off from his men, a barbarian general came to a hut.

'My lord, rest,' an old woman said, 'I have water-of-life within.'
Drugged, he slept. And against his temple, the lady placed an earring.
Thick gold it was, spiked at one end. And she hammered it home,
With one stroke from a jug, hammered it home and he was dead!"

Long after the camp was quiet, Zithia tapped Kylyn awake with her foot. She sang,

"Darling, get my comb from my hair." While he looked, Zithia continued the song.

Kylyn showed the heavy wooden comb to his mama. *"Now pull on that end."* She pointed with her head. The boy smiled when a little knife came out.

Lying on his stomach, Kylyn watched Zithia work on her bonds. The guard got up to stretch his legs. Instantly Kylyn's head fell quietly into the sand, eyes closed.

Giving the captives a brief look, he sat down again. Nearing dawn, Zithia was free. Breaking the teeth off the comb under cover of the chorus, Zithia slid her fingers through the decorative loops. The guard's head fell toward his chest and he jerked it up again, muttering. Time to pace.

He began to rise. From behind, Zithia struck him on the base of the skull. The barbarian continued to rise, blinking. He received a second hit with the knuckle-duster. Grunting, he descended into a sitting position.

The camp was sprawled between Zithia and her target, Black Bay. Holding Kylyn's hand, they finally rounded the bend, and the sand was ink. The sky was a washed blue with rose streaks by the time they reached the spot Zithia wanted.

Three flat white markers on the kohl canvas pointed the way for her. Zithia's smile was bright. 'Darling, we're going to walk across the bay.'

With a frown, he nodded. If his mama said they would; they would. Standing on the first marker, a gently curving path of stepping-stones was visible, the blocks barely four inches above water. Something about the ocean bothered her. It was too sluggish.

"The horses!" She pivoted towards the herd. She'd forgotten the horses. About then, Zithia heard an insistent slithering. Turning back to the water, her jaw dropped. Rapidly hoisting Kylyn from the ground, Zithia backed off from the waves. Gulping hard, she looked at the stars, 'Beloved God. We have got to talk about your sense of humour.'

The top layer of the ocean was thick with sea snakes. Not very large snakes, to be sure, but that wasn't the point. The current had been wrong and the extended peninsular had caught them like a scoop, interrupting their migratory journey. This happened occasionally each year. Kylyn followed her gaze, shaking slightly. 'Darling, it's all right.' Thinking: *"I'd feel so much better in shoes."*

She dropped her necklace and the knuckle-duster. 'Kylyn, you'll be safe in my arms. Only, we must cross the stones.' Zithia kissed him on the forehead. 'I want you to watch the sunrise.' His nod quivered.

Closing her eyes briefly, Zithia called up power. As her eyes opened, essence of panther was launched at the horses. The steeds felt and heard panther's approach. Hungrily. Immediately, Zithia was walking the stones, gathering speed to skip over them.

Screaming their fear, the horses reared and broke their tether-line. They galloped pell-mell down the white peninsular, until they were tokens on a gameboard; pursued by barbarians, who had roared into wakefulness. Nethard immediately looked to the captives, his dreams of commendation evaporating. He recalled all the men, bar one, from the horse chase.

Rapidly they searched every direction. A man rounded the curve into Black Beach, to see Zithia and Kylyn levitating over the water. The sun was a nearly a half-disc on the horizon, framing mama and child in its blaze. They were a quarter of the way across. The invader bellowed his message.

Zithia's combatant was the first to reach the water. A swim would cut off the witch's retreat. Observing the sea snakes he laughed triumphantly. 'More illusions.'

He plowed into the truth and shrieked when it bit him. For a moment he was frozen there, unable to believe each sear of pain. Then he was tearing the snakes off him. The serpents merely saw an invitation to bite his hands. His veins seemed to be pumping acid. Convulsing, he fell forward under the slithering mass.

The others stopped in their tracks. They, too, had thought the scene an illusion. Undeterred, Nethard was first on the stones, following hesitantly. Their feet pounded the steps.

Although Kylyn had heard the shrieks, his eyes never left the sunrise. Zithia watched the square blocks become random in shape, halfway across. No snakes loitered on top of the rocks yet. Still running lightly, Zithia realised that a stone ahead was missing. Heart racing, she increased her speed and flew across the gap.

The barbarians were gaining, but they kept making the mistake of looking at the strange carpet. One slipped; his hand went into the undulating mess. A dozen bites. Trying to shake off the snakes, he overbalanced into the sea. Having a large weight fall upon them, some very angry vipers bit the man long after he stopped moving.

Another invader one put his foot on a stone while a further man was stepping off. Registering the extra weight, the pillar abruptly disintegrated beneath them. The splash threw a viper flying. An invader, all muscle and proud armour, had crouched over, to see the path better. Landing in his hair, the snake slithered down his neck into his top. There, it bit until its fang ran red. Squirming desperately, the barbarian's antics disturbed his pedestal and it, also, toppled.

Nethard was directly behind Zithia. Four stones separated them. Watching Zithia dance lightly on one stone after another, never quite staying on any of them, Nethard observed that the rocks beneath her feet also tottered. Realisation hit as his sergeant disappeared. Mid-jump, Nethard hurled his helmet. Landing, he drew his sword and threw it in Zithia's direction. It sang over her shoulder. Almost immediately, Nethard's dagger nicked Zithia's hip. Then the captain was racing back to shore. Jumping the gaps, he reached the black sand alone.

Meanwhile, Zithia had crossed from irregular pillars to square rocks and thus was on a solid path again. She slowed down, hardly bothered by the snakes now. Eventually she was on a pale sandbar that joined the stones to the further peninsular. Walking, images came to her from the last time she'd seen Black Bay.

Galen and Zithia's ocean-going canoe had been blown off course. It was festival time and Galen had been asked, in public and with much deference to the temple, to officiate. With an unreadable face the high priest had assented, but he'd made Zithia promise to remain indoors at the village, miles from the bay where the ceremony always took place.

After he'd left, the local headman's wife, Quibock-Nicte, visited. 'I look forward to this festival every year.' Quibock-Nicte looked at the village beach, where people were eagerly paddling off to the ceremonial bay. 'Our region was the last to join the Atlantian Union, and our ancestors kept the right to this one ceremony.' She chuckled. 'Surely you don't intend to miss it?'

When Zithia refused, Quibock-Nicte simply didn't leave. Eventually, sighing heavily, she declared, 'Well, a good hostess doesn't leave a guest in a deserted village.' Another deep sigh. 'I'll stay with you.'

So Zithia found herself watching the spectacle from Quibock-Nicte's boat. 'Today's participant was chosen by lot; the whole region is in the lottery. My own family hasn't been so honoured by such a choosing for decades.'

'That hardly seems fair.'

A vessel was hurrying back and forth among the bright flotilla cluttering the bay. The headman's wife frantically waved the bookie over.

The ceremony began. An exquisitely gowned woman walked the rock path. Loaded with jewellery, her wet eyelashes glittered. She examined each stepping stone before putting a tremulous foot on it. Her looks, well fleshed and tall, were uncharacteristic of the region. A funnelled basket caught jade and gold, thrown from canoes along the way.

Zithia had been watching the lovely face when the stones rumbled, disintegrating. Saw the terror when the water swallowed the woman up. Quibock-Nicte's boat was close enough that they observed the sacrifice's progress to the bottom of the bay. Struggling with the basket, which was chained to her wrists, the woman's eyes had pleaded with those above her. Then fountains of bubbles had gushed to the surface. It was over.

Quibock-Nicte had clapped her hands together, 'I've been lucky today.' The bookie returned with her winnings and she shrugged at him, teeth flashing. 'Four years in a row. I've a knack at picking how long they'll last.'

Half fainting, Zithia had swayed, only to feel Quibock-Nicte's hand steady her. Zithia flinched away. The official barge was beside them and Galen's arm supported her. Galen addressed Quibock-Nicte. 'Lady, I'd like to place a bet on next year's sacrifice.'

'But lord high priest, you can't bet until the sacrifice is chosen, and no one knows who'll be next.'

Galen burned her with his gaze. 'I do.' Quibock-Nicte gulped audibly.

A crazed howl brought Zithia back to the present. Nethard had reached the shore. Zithia threw herself into the jungle, while Nethard began to jog.

*

Hours later, Zithia was still taking the steepest path, fearing horses. Handing Kylyn an emerald-eyed frog, Zithia loaded him into a vine-net backpack. Breaking a branch from a shrub, Zithia swatted insects while she traversed. The soft rain was no longer friendly; it battered, in a steam bath world. She paced an exact number of steps between breaks.

With dusk, Zithia took a leaf from her insect swat and ate it. She'd walk all night, knowing that the barbarian wouldn't risk his horse thus. Fragrant white moonflowers opened. And Zithia felt invulnerable throughout the witching hours. Until the sloth. Tall as a hut, munching scented orchids. Dawn's first light luminesced the algae growing in his long coat. In the slowest-motion, the sloth's claws continued to pick the brown and lavender flowers.

Zithia froze. Minutes went by. Long minutes. Still transfixed. A hand took hers; even before she could flinch, Zithia felt immediate warmth, deep comfort. 'You must keep moving.'

Zithia turned, glowing. His shade was wholly there. *"How are your brothers?"*

'You don't know?' Her transparent father shook his head. 'Then they're doing fine.'

He laughed, *"True."* Excitement entered his voice, *"Child, I'm coming back."*

Zithia stopped, her smile wide, 'Alive again? So soon?'

"I'm almost born." Looking at Kylyn, *"Handsome boy, daughter."*

'Thanks. Where?' Walking on again.

"The Dragon-Land."

Gasping, 'The wonders you'll see. They still have an original Atlantis library. Lit by magic lamps that don't burn fuel. Imagine… Oh papa.' Still walking. 'Papa,' sighing blissfully, 'a good life to you.'

Father, his form fading, *"And you daughter."* Evaporating. Gone.

'Love you, papa.' Zithia said to the air, flying the message after him.

Lazily, of necessity, the sloth's rounded head had turned and turned with Zithia's progress, till the sloth was watching her from over his own back.

Daylight showed Zithia a sleeping dragon of a mountain. She sat rubbing her muscles awhile. The little fly swat was somewhat depleted.

*

Nethard stopped, rubbing his stallion down. His hand brushed against his cheek, fingers touching something new there. Going methodically through the saddlebag, Nethard found the salt crystals. Pouring it onto his hand dry, Nethard applied it to his cheek. He actually felt the leech loosen its grip beneath his skin, before falling off. There were others on his body. The one at the outer edge of his left eye would have to hang like a black tear until it decided to move.

He patted the horse. 'Don't worry, they don't like your beautiful thick skin.' Four leeches came off the hound.

'At least the witch and her spawn will be getting sucked dry, too.'

Nethard rolled himself into a blanket against the drizzle, and slept. Gradually, the sated plump leach released its grip and dropped off.

*

The mastiff had begun to run almost an hour ago. White foam flecked the sides of the stallion. All at once the dog stood and pointed at Zithia's retreating form.

Behind her, Zithia heard the hooves displacing clods of mud. Kylyn looked into Nethard's luminous eyes and clasped his hands tight around Zithia's neck. Already running, she had a further burst of speed.

The sight of Zithia brought the barbarian's sense of malice to the fore. Still mounted, Nethard drew his bow, fitted the arrow. An ineffectual voice within him whispered: *"Remember the reward."* Nethard eased the pressure a notch, and then loosed the barb at Kylyn. 'She may still live. It'll skewer the brat first.'

While the shaft bored down upon Zithia, she stumbled in her race. Nethard held his breath, bloodlust roaring in his ears. An instant later, the witch vanished before his eyes, in a roar emanating from the real world, not Nethard's body. Whizzing passed Zithia, the arrow caught at her flying hair. Shield in hand, Nethard bounded from the steed.

Safe on a rough circle of plants, Zithia surfed down a mudslide. Nethard threw his shield face down in the mud, and then leapt aboard. The mud rushed down a hundred feet, following the curve of the land. Veering right, it flowed up over an outcrop and left the earth for several seconds.

Zithia flew and bumped down. Swivelling to observe Nethard's flight, she saw the scarred face of his shield. Then Nethard's weight crunched down and a window appeared in the hump of soil behind him. A lush green clump of orchids seemed to jack-in-a-box out. Vivid blue, hanging bells swung wildly. Zithia's toes were now on the edge of her diminishing platform.

Nethard felt and heard a rock scrape a long dent in his family shield. He bellowed.

235

The downward path became steeper and the noise increased. Zithia's mouth gaped at a sheer drop coming fast. She contemplated jumping when, from the corner of her eye, she saw a gorilla was swinging from tree to tree beside her. 'I'll catch you, Zithia.' she heard.

A sudden roller-coaster movement left Zithia's stomach behind. 'You?!'

Swinging, the gorilla kept pace. 'There's someone else on this vine?'

She looked ahead at the mud spurting over the edge of the land, with only the distant horizon in view. Images began cascading through her mind. The gorilla mocked, 'You think a lot, for a dead woman.'

Fairly flying, he curled his legs around a vine and was hanging by his feet. He held out his arms. 'Last chance.'

He caught her hands firmly with his great paws. The vine continued to swing like a pendulum, carrying the gorilla, Zithia and Kylyn over the precipice. Looking down, it wasn't the valley fifteen minute's fall beneath which made Zithia grasp the gorilla's hands more tightly. It was the barbarian.

Nethard had watched Zithia's escape, when he himself was cannoned over the edge. Tossed high into the air, he was scrambling after Zithia's ankle, barely inches above him. His fingertips closed on her heel. The gorilla snarled, pulling Zithia beyond the barbarian's reach.

Momentum thrust Nethard after them, lifting him high, and then abandoned him. When he started to fall, still clutching at air, Zithia's party also swung downwards, mimicking his progress. Safe over land, Zithia and Kylyn were dropped into mud.

The ooze had ceased. In the mire, Zithia looked up the grey track.

There was a heavy thud beside Zithia. 'A simple thank you would suffice.'

At once, Zithia began to apologise and to thank, but after a few words the gorilla simply raised the fur ridge running above his eyebrows. 'No need to go overboard.' He looked meaningfully back to the precipice.

'Please tell me you didn't say that,' Zithia groaned.

Kylyn was searching the ape's face. 'But mama, he didn't say it.' Tilting his head to one side, then to the other side, Kylyn said, 'Why don't your lips move when you talk?'

'I'm a ventriloquist.'

Zithia echoed, 'Ventriloquist?'

The gorilla's large dark eyes laughed at her. *"The howler monkeys didn't mention your being simple, Zithia. Telepathy."* He put Kylyn on his shoulders and moved off. *"I'm Xander. Now what's your name, little one?"*

'Oh, the howler monkeys. So that's why you know me.'

Xander pointed to a less dense section of jungle. *"We'll go by this track."*

'Track?' Zithia frowned.

*

After a time they stopped and Xander telepathed, *"We go up."*

Already glowing from the trek, Zithia rested on her haunches. She took in the two hundred-foot tree. 'I can't climb that today.'

"Who mentioned climbing?" A vine appeared with a thin loop.

Zithia put a foot in the vine circle and a gorilla, far above, raised her onto a wide branch. Several of Xander's tribe awaited her. Adolescents scampered about her, despite an adult booming. *"You'll scare the humans."*

They walked the living road, among and below sheltering leaves. The youths soon gambolled around, snuffling the air, engrossed in a game of tag.

Eventually, Zithia could see the foliage thinning ahead. A game of tag circled the adults. Everyone was laughing. The continuous line of trees came to an end. Mossy limbs ventured nervously into open space.

Unexpectedly, the adolescents became more boisterous than ever. Dashing around, before heading straight for the forest's edge. Zithia watched one race, heedless of its peril.

"He's constantly showing off," thought an indulgent aunt. Djau misplaced a hand and was flung upwards into death beyond the trees.

Blinking, Zithia quickened her step. Djau cried out, his face contorted, and spread-eagled himself in the wind. Zithia waited for him to begin his long flailing descent to the ground.

The tragedy never happened. The young gorilla was suspended, an eagle in mid-air, arms spread. Zithia craned her neck forward. Still he didn't fall. Then Djau started to laugh and, curling his body into a ball, rocked backwards and forwards. He rolled thus, three feet above them on… nothing. The other youngsters chorused his amusement.

"Always a prankster," A matron thought. *"Djau get up! You've had your fun."* Simultaneously she stepped off the walkway onto a bridge, five feet wide, with broad steps in varying depths. The colors were a dozen different greens. Yet, even knowing that the bridge was camouflaged

didn't explain the fact that it was those sections Zithia wasn't looking at, faded to ghostly apparitions. Moss and lichen grew on it. Its colours mimicked the jungle, thereby becoming invisible. Someone took Zithia by the hand. *"Careful, it can be hard to keep the steps visible. Keep thinking 'This is rock' and it'll be easier to see."*

They ascended the rock-bridge. Passing Djau, Zithia kicked the side of his leg. Consequentially, Djau's body pivoted round ninety degrees. 'Very funny.'

Laughing all the harder, Djau stood and patted her heavily on the head.

The stone spanned fifty feet, rising dramatically, to reach a mammoth of a tree. Once on the tree, Zithia lay flat to examine the underneath off the bridge. It was sky blue, with clouds. She leaned further over the edge to reach a painted butterfly, and Djau grabbed Zithia by the belt at her waist.

Eyes sparkling, Zithia rested her hand on the tree itself. It had the same ungiving solidness. 'What do you think of the Tree of Life?' came a familiar voice.

'It's fossilised, of course.' Looking up, she saw Torim.

He quoted.

"And when the last tree-of-life outside Atlantis died, the Atlantians petrified it, and then painted it. Finally they convinced the rock bridge, which joins the Atlantis tree to other trees, that it was no longer stone. But air. Thus the bridge ceased to give off rock vibrations and it totally disappeared." She rushed into his arms, clinging there, tears flowing.

'Now what are you doing here?' He straightened his arms, now on her shoulders, to look at her. 'And where is this son of yours?'

*

They sat at a long low slab of wood, the communal table in the crown of the tree.

The crown was a vast hand, with fingers upraised to an azure sky. An eagle nested on the tip of the highest finger. With massed red and white flowers, a vine draped itself over several limbs and managed to look petite. Maidenhair ferns flourished where water gathered. Automatically, Zithia murmured, 'Thank you' to the sky.

Xander, *"Lucky that we've been watching the barbarians and saw you captured."*

'Lucky?' Zithia's eyes, still on the heavens, became quizzical.

Going to a wide, squat ceramic pot, Torim took a fruit from an inner pot. The smaller pot floated in a fine, wet gravel, which kept all vegetables fresh for over a week. Using a jade knife, Torim halved heart-shaped fruit. 'The scout described you and I recognised you.'

"We remembered your name listed among the howler tribe."

Torim went over to a fire enclosed by a mud half-sphere, where a few dried cacao beans were roasting. 'It appears that when you shared food with the howler monkeys, you were accepted into their tribe.' He placed the pods on the table.

Xander, *"Your story has spread throughout the jungles."*

A matron, *"There's really very little to do after dark."*

Instantly, Zithia's beguiled expression changed; to taken aback and then her flattened eyebrows rapidly drew close together creating deep creases between them.

Without registering Zithia's reaction, the matron continued, *"And, luckily for you, males will be gossips."*

Torim tapped Xander. 'Would you mind?' Xander's hairy fist came down on the cacao seeds with unnecessary force, spurting the pulverised contents everywhere. 'Now again, with less feeling.' Torim placed another few seeds on the table.

Torim mixed the cacao powder for several minutes, using mortar and pestle until it became paste, then added elephant-palm molasses for sweetness. 'If you hadn't been a tribal cousin, the gorillas wouldn't have been able to help you.' He scooped chocolate mulch onto the fruit.

Zithia found the dessert exquisite. It left a comforting, rosy-hued sensation. She looked at a bowl full of cacao beans. 'Nice beans.'

'For trade and disaster.' In silence, they contemplated disaster.

*

Two gorillas volunteered to collect Zithia's belongings. After she'd visualised where she had left the pack, they flashed images of the place back to her, until they had the correct tree.

In front of a fire, enclosed by a mud half-sphere, she asked Torim, 'But what brought you here?'

'My love of all things Atlantian.'

He beckoned Zithia and Kylyn to follow him. Going up a level, Kylyn picked a bunch of black grapes from a shrub. Taking the fruit, Torim showed them into a room carved within the tree's trunk. It housed silk scrolls and rice paper books.

Zithia wanted to dive into reading at once. Aghast, the gorilla librarian bared his teeth *"Not until you've cleaned up."*

On one of several upper branches, coveredwith small-leafed shrubs, Zithia was motioned forward. Almost naked Zithia hesitated. 'Bugs?' she asked young Cleopatra.

"No bugs," stated Cleopatra, as Zithia walked into the rain-soaked thicket. *"Well, none that isn't edible."*

Hidden, Zithia sped through the shrubs, being totally showered in the process by warm raindrops. One could tell her progress by the sun-shower dropping from disturbed plants onto petrified branches far below. Handing her a towel, Cleopatra examined Zithia's dripping form, front then back, telepathing, *"See, no bugs."* as she surreptitiously removed a long-legged stick insect from the back of Zithia's hair. While Kylyn followed through, Cleopatra replaced the insect upon a branch. With damp curls glowing, Zithia presented herself and her son to the librarian for inspection.

When she came back, book in hand, Torim gave her a sideways look. 'You did notice the map?'

'Map?'

Zithia dashed back to the library. An hour later he found Zithia there, lying on her back, mesmerised by the roof. Torim lay next to her and traced the edges of three islands contoured in the ceiling. When you looked closely the land was obvious due to its muddy green colour, which contrasted with the ocean's dusty blue. To the left of the islands, a small portion of Greater Atlantis was outlined.

One island was colossal, with two satellites further out in the ocean. Torim said, 'You see the symbol for the north?'

'Beloved Atlantis.' She nodded, putting her head at different angles. 'But exactly where?

When the map was imprinted on her mind, Zithia gazed out of a doorway and didn't even register the colony of large white, coned orchids with green stars there.

Heads on a pillow, Zithia and Kylyn spent the next hours reading beneath the map. Every now and then a tantalising word telepathed from studious gorillas, to drift over the humans like incense. Before dusk, Torim returned. After much cajoling on his part, the librarian allowed Zithia to take a lesser volume out overnight.

With one eye on her silk scroll, Zithia walked down a wide stone branch, waving away several large buzzing insects. 'Zithia,'called Torim, 'here, it's best not to read while you walk.'

Zithia stopped, and was startled to see her path-branch dramatically veering to one side. The buzzing insects also stopped, coming momentarily into focus as minute humming birds.

Torim continued, 'If that scroll plunges to the ground, I'll never hear the end of it.'

The bee-humming birds, losing interest in Zithia dived, twenty feet down to sip nectar. Looking from them to Torim, Zithia tapped her foot. 'It's no good. I'll never read them all before I go.'

'Always ambitious.'

Kylyn and a young gorilla sat on the table. They were eating cashews, with a children's picture book before them. Lifting a foot, preparatory to turning the page, the boy saw Torim stare.

'Some societies consider it bad manners to read at the table.' With a quick flip of his toes Kylyn closed the book.

Torim spoke Atlantian. 'Zithia, about your leaving. Speed is your best chance of escaping Galen.' A baby with a tender tummy ambled over to a maidenhair fern and chewed the antidote. 'Rafting would save time. There's a large sink hole near here and the river in the underground caves runs to the sea.'

'And a boat?'

'Oh, Xander's people will make a boat.'

'Do they know how to build a boat?'

'Indeed they do, the males talk boats constantly.'

'Talk boats?'

'From memory, that river should end near the foreigners' port. I assume you want the foreigners' port.' He leaned back, opening a large book.

Eyes raking the volume, Zithia's brows flattened: *"If we're walking, we have to leave tomorrow."*

'I haven't told you yet about the crystal library at La Ventixa,' Torim put one hand behind his head. 'That vault last seen by the Atlantians.'

'Boating it is then.'

Prizing the emeralds from their setting had been child's play for Xander. They were a problem. Traceable. That morning, loaded with gold fragments, Zithia and Torim descended the Atlantis tree on broad swings. At one stage Zithia's swing began spinning in a pleasant circle. Watching the quickened, turning world she heard someone. *"A real boat, not a model!"*

Zithia tried to identify the thinker. Instead, she discovered a fat reed platform, with growing sides, suspended between branches.

Landing, Zithia approached Torim, 'They've made boats before, huh?' With an innocent expression, she looked up. 'So that'd be why they're building it a hundred feet above the ground.'

'Poetic licence.' Torim dismissed, starting down a track.

A gorilla sat on the vacated swing. He carried a bamboo pole, heavy with gourds, on one shoulder. A friend loomed close. *"I told you we should build it at the cenote."*

The swing jolted upward and the gourds hit the thinker sharply on the chin.

*

Torim built a fire and Zithia heated bits of gold in a small gourd, then tipped it into a brook using a forked stick.

Torim said, 'Do you know, seafarers describe how bubbles from a dragon's breath will lift whole ships,' he raised his upturned hand high, 'only to suck them back down into the dragon's maw.' His hand descended rapidly. 'But no-one has seen the dragon.'

Zithia stabbed the fire repeatedly. 'Now, tell me how your own personal dragon pulled you down.'

'You were wrong. I did get him to change his mind.'

'Obviously; your wedding ring.'

'I'd forgotten…' On roughly trying to remove the ring, she discovered her knuckle had swollen. She sucked her finger, clamping her teeth around metal. Finally Zithia spat the gold out into the fire.

'That's the second wedding ring I've seen you rid yourself of. Marriage doesn't seem to suit you.'

'We were happy, Torim. We had Kylyn. There was a bride-price.' He'd actually heard this in the howler monkey's recital about Zithia. 'He didn't even ask me, nor did he tell me.'

'That was Atlantian gold.'

'Tainted beyond cleansing.'

She watched the flames, 'He'll divorce me, and then I'll know peace.'

'He'll also come after you. A probable archpriest's pride has been hurt.' She leaned her head on Torim's shoulder. 'You were supposed to give in.'

A tear fell, in silence.

'My dear girl, what did you expect?'

'Better from a soul mate.' She sniffed. 'I thought about going north, to the tabooed land.'

'The temple wouldn't expect that. And from there you've the option to cross the oceans.' Zithia chewed her thumbnail. 'You should see the Far World. I doubt even Galen would retrieve you from there.'

'Come with us.'

'Zithia, you know I won't leave this land. I've my library and I may yet find Atlantis.'

With her mind on crossing the oceans, Zithia abruptly developed hiccups. Torim's eyes were kindly. 'You need a fright.' Her shoulders jerked involuntarily. Torim spoke quietly into Zithia's ear, 'To hide properly, reading will be dead to you.' The hiccups dried up in a trice.

*

They stood above the cenote. The boat had already been lowered into the huge rock opening. Vines secured it from above. The cave beneath was only thirty feet high, but four times that wide.

Zithia knew she'd never see Torim again, in this world. Torim put his arm around Zithia's waist. She bent her head to touch his shoulder. 'See you next time round.'

'No next time for me my dear. This is my last life. And it's about time.'

'What?'

'Believe me, I couldn't take even one more civilisation rising and falling, oh... and as for the dark ages... or the apocolypses... don't get me started.'

'But...'

'I'm done with living... thinking of becoming an angel.'

'You?'

He frowned, 'Yes', puckering his lips, 'of the more severe kind.' The air was momentarily heavy. 'Now it's time.'

"Torim's arm was still around her waist. Blinking back tears, Zithia leaned forward, peering right over the opening, 'How do I get down?'

'Like this.' Torim gently overbalanced her.

'Torriiim!' was heard all the way down to the crystalline water. Fish scattered at the cenote's bottom. Fighting her way to the surface, telepathic guffaws filled her ears.

"You should've seen your face."

Zithia took a few strokes through the almost invisible water, her hair spreading into filigree lace. On a wide circuit around the boat Zithia was impressed by the bulbous sides and bottom, the lamps at prow and aft. She straddled the thick reed edge, while Kylyn was lowered into his mama's arms.

Depositing him in the palm-roofed aft, Zithia harnessed him to a supporting pole. These poles were bundles of hollow reeds. The firestone came down next on a slab, then Kylyn's heritage and the bulging satchel from Zithia's home village.

Water from her hair seeped into puffy eyes. 'Exactly how far is it to the sea?'

Torim cut through the anchor vines. 'According to the records, about three hundred miles as the catbird flies.'

'What!!'

Rapidly, the current picked up the raft. 'It'll take three, maybe four, days.'

"And nights."

Zithia lit the torches, protected by obsidian slices on all sides. She thought of a pertinent question, albeit too late. 'Torim, exactly how many times has this trip been done?'

'Twice, at least, in written history.'

'Written history?' Her mouth fell open. Then, 'Twice before now, or twice including now?'

'That's right.' Torim's tone was wistful. 'I wish I were coming with you.'

'Me, too!' The angry words echoed from the tunnel.

*

At first the broad canal strove to be straight, and then snaked through the underworld. Luminous lantern mushrooms spot-lit the rock walls. The little square shelter in the aft gave them a sense of security. Kylyn pulled a loose reed from a pole. Blowing bubbles in the water, he giggled.

Rummaging among the food, Zithia found Torim's parting gift. Under hairy brown fruit balls and quails' eggs, was a small oilskin envelope. Within resided a slim volume. Seeing it, she instantly relaxed. Torim would never have put a book in danger. Awed that he had managed to bribe it from the zealous librarian, Zithia opened the cover and laughed. A poetry book, on stiff silk. The librarian saw little value in romantic verse. Biting into a grainy sweet pear, Zithia read.

Later, drawing water, Zithia observed a glowing yellow school of fish pass under the boat before racing beyond her sight. Zithia drew back, hoping their energy came from youth and not from being chased.

To pass the time, Zithia tied her hair in successive waves across her head, while she piled the waves high. Doing so, she took stock. 'My personal dragon!'

She loved him; hated him yet he was part of her. 'I suppose, we shall have to wait for death to be together.' Zithia glowered, 'Then he'll have a lot of explaining to do.'

*

Late afternoon of the third day they entered a huge sinkhole, radiant with light. Bulbous-leaved plants floated at the cavern's rims and Zithia picked the yellow flowers with blue flashes. The boat gravitated towards the sun.

Moving once more into the semi-haze, Kylyn pointed up. 'A new bird.' His arm followed his discovery, as they moved under it.

'Wonderful darling, how many birds is that so far?'

'Twenty seven!'

'And what is it Kylyn? An owl?' She tipped her head back.

'No, a bat.'

The flowers fell to the deck. 'Don't move Kylyn,' Zithia whispered, 'we don't want to disturb them.'

The boat was directly beneath a bat colony covering half the roof and the tunnel entrance towards which they now drifted. Thousands of sleeping faces hung down. Leather wings rustled a little here, shoved a little there, to get more comfortable.

'Fruit bats.' Kylyn was still pointing.

All at once, two drops of liquid escaped from one of the sleeping sister's mouth. Zithia watched the dark drops land on the back of Kylyn's hand. Hastily she wiped the blood away, before Kylyn saw it. 'Dew.' She explained.

Zithia drew her son under their palm leaf canopy. Miles into the tunnel, she softly told fairytales until Kylyn slept. Moving his head off her lap, Zithia began to shiver. 'Vampires.'

*

By the quipii tally, it was lunchtime on the fourth day. She cut open a leathery fruit and consumed the aromatic white sections. Kylyn alternately sucked a red oblong passionfruit and blew bubbles in the water. Zithia put her precious Atlantian book gently into its oilskin and sealed it, as usual. This was now attached to a sturdy twine round Zithia's waist and popped into a pocket. The aft light went out and Zithia lit one of the remaining torches. Zithia didn't comment on the first speck of daylight, until Kylyn discovered it, when Zithia announced surprised delight. The reassuring sight grew more solid.

There was an aggressive murmuring now around the vessel. Lowering her hand into the water, Zithia felt the current. Faster than ever. Lighting another torch, she went to each side of the boat and then returned to the prow. The cave tunnel had narrowed like a fat woman squeezed into a girdle. She scanned the river. A great rock-tooth reared from the depths and the water foamed white.

'Kylyn, hold on tight.' She tossed the torch overboard.

The boat raced in frothing water, glanced off the first tooth and missed a second rock by a wish. Staggering to Kylyn, Zithia clutched at one of the canopy's poles. She heard it tear. Zithia moved. Where her fingers had grasped tight, the thick reed post had been severed.

Water crashing into the walls, filled the tunnel with thunder. At last she reached Kylyn. Angling a wide paddle into the water behind them, Zithia veered them away from the next rocks. The paddle snapped and the boat leapt down a drop of several feet. They landed with a bone-shaking jar.

Everything went quiet. She stood. The vessel galloped toward another dip, after which there was shadow. Zithia raced to Kylyn, pinning him between her body and the side of the raft. Looking at the broken reeds of the post that Kylyn clung to, Zithia hurriedly blew through several until she found what she wanted. She thrust Kylyn to one reed's end, taking hold of another straw. 'Breath through this. I'll tap you once to hold your breath, then twice to breathe again.'

The prow light was swallowed and they were underwater. Zithia tapped her son once. Darkness, in a fierce current. Seconds later the craft leveled, floating. In the wet night, Zithia took in air, and then indicated Kylyn to do the same. As she had hoped, the water didn't completely fill the next tunnel.

Then there was light, like a fire new lit. A fat eel, sixteen feet long, had been hitching a ride underneath the raft. It was now at their head-height and swimming upstream towards them. The iridescent yellow-green body twitched its tail each time the roof jagged on the top of the tunnel.

More lights filled this new world, for ninety feet down. Two schools of eels, looking tiny in a crazy sideways forest of gigantic scattered quartz columns. Glimmering white in water, virtually air-clear. A warmer, fast current, plus the boat's gourds, were keeping the raft at the top of a bulging cave within the tunnel. While Zithia was bedazzled by the maze of pillars below, the raft's roof connected again with the ceiling of the tunnel. Everything juddered. And Zithia lost her straw.

While she scrambled for air, she saw Kylyn breathing safely. He watched her, wild eyed. The current pushed Zithia further from the air-reeds and too close to the eel. Her lungs ached, and then burned. Zithia reached for a reed, any reed, when the boat was abruptly expelled from the tunnel, one quarter-way up a waterfall.

Landing heavily, the roof groaned and pivoted over the side. However, they were in real dazzling light. Gulping air, Zithia looked ahead, onto the green tongue of river. A smile fled her face. That deep green water was beyond a narrow canyon. There was a white-covered stairway to be survived.

Zithia threw herself toward Kylyn, to anchor him, but the boat was already in mid-flight. Thunder assaulted them. The raft belly-flopped down into another white track of water. Reeds and gourds exploded away.

Kylyn was launched through the spray-filled air. Pushing her knees under the seat in the boat, Zithia grasped the vine around her son's waist. When it snapped, she stretched her body after the end. Kylyn's face and shoulders dipped beneath the surface.

'Oh no you don't.' She shouted at the river, found the vine and yanked hard. 'He's mine!'

Like a hooked fish, Kylyn landed next to her, spluttering. Pain shrieked from Zithia's right arm: *"I've broken it."* But then her arms went around Kylyn.

Hurtling down narrow rock stairs, the prow submerged. A white wave immersed the shell. Anything not tied down flew. The gold and gems jiggled slowly from their place and Zithia stamped firmly on the pack. Two more drops in close succession, landed Zithia and Kylyn on the floor next to the pack. Zithia sat on the bundle, pulling her son onto her lap. Fifteen seconds later, the last step was traversed. Sideways. A granite turtle bit the air behind them, and then the raft collided with its twin and went spinning.

Zithia and Kylyn were dizzy when the remains of the boat slowed. Immediately, a candy-pink dolphin arced out of the water, balancing a gourd upon his nose. Flushing an even more intense pink, the dolphin batted the gourd to them.

Rounding up other balls, the dolphin used his tail to flip them onto the raft. Kylyn threw one back and, with the boat continuing its low turns, they played ball. On a catfish breaking the surface, the dolphin leapt after its dinner, back in his murky fishing area.

*

A few seaside huts lazed before a glistening apricot beach; random palms were bent low over shallow water. A rainbow reef stood several feet above the water and almost completely surrounded the bay. Gentle waves changed from crystal to distant emerald, where a platform climbed from the sea. Dresses, pinafores and kilts fluttered in the breeze. Someone had set up a stall. This was the gateway to an island port.

In a coconut grove, Zithia and Kylyn were in a hut changing into new clothes. Removing a banana-leaf hat from still piled hair, Zithia tied a money corset she'd made at the Atlantis Tree over her ribs. She was now encircled by gold and emeralds. After pulling on a skirt, top, pinafore and deep hood, Zithia opened a window. She tossed their old clothes onto a bonfire.

Outside they sat on a bowed tree trunk and Kylyn traced lines in the pearly, apricot half-moons and quarter moons that was the sand. Zithia adjusted his kilt. 'My darling, we've seen terrible things on our journey.' Kylyn's shoulders came up around his ears. Sitting before him, she helped him with his sandals. 'High priests... papa... says when you feel the angel of death is near, it's time for a new name.' His eyes clouded. 'Kylyn it's time to change our names, before our luck runs out.'

'But how will papa find us?'

Smiling, Zithia swept his hair back. 'My darling, your papa could find us anywhere.' Her smile became fixed and Zithia whispered to herself, 'Almost.'

'I'll be the Lady Melia, and you'll be...' she poked him gently on the chest, 'Lord Olondin.' He beamed at his title. She added, 'Now the seller said you could pick some peanuts.'

He scampered off to a row of dry bushes. Gleefully pulling on the plants' thin tendrils, which grew from the stems from arial roots into a well of soil. Out of the ground burst the attached peanuts.

In celebration, Zithia bought half a foot-long passion fruit. The vendor tossed Zithia's payment into a pouch of melted gold. No one wanted to admit that they were selling heirlooms to survive. Zithia took a bamboo tub from Kylyn's hand. 'Darling, we're not going to need that.' Curare.

Finishing the passionfruit rind, Zithia picked up her pack, then Kylyn, and walked into the water.

She wasn't alone. Wading knee high, Zithia said to a man near her, 'Sharks?' He shook his head as he moved sideways, out of the path of several silver bonefish.

Kylyn was hissing, 'Back mama, back.' She jumped back and a whole school arrowed by.

Simultaneously the man said, 'Don't let those run into you or they'll draw blood.'

Zithia hurried forward again as more bonefish flashed onto a submerged sandbank she was on. Instantly, the school dropped anchor with sleek noses, their tails rippling the surface.

It was a long walk to the high wooden pier where two vessels bumped against the far side. Latecomers jogged through rapidly rising water, back and forth, side to side, carrying out their possessions on their heads.

After hours rowing directly into the ocean, they heard other vessels. Finally the little convoy veered right, to slip between two islands. The furthest out to sea rose steeply from the water. Tucked behind this was an isle of gentle slopes, with beaches and a good harbour. Only then were the rowers called shoreward by bonfires, street torches and lanterns in a moored fleet's rigging. The foreigners' port. That forbidden place where the Far World met this world, in trade.

The large harbour walls and the quay were very grand. Huge rocks had been fitted together, puzzle-like, without mortar. Zithia's people had done much to encourage the traders to return, and to remain on this island. Carved horse-heads were visible at each end of high rounded Phoenician vessels, the single sails towering over the low Viking ships and canoes with outriggers.

Large Dragon-Land junks swayed at the moorings, as they'd for several millennia. Volcanic cement lined the bottoms of their compartmentalised hulls. This, plus their fine rudders and scalloped-edged sails, ribbed like a flying fish, made the junks perfect world travellers.

The dinghies landed at the end of two bustling, well-lit streets, a beach away from the fleet. Disembarking, everyone traversed the road back to the harbour, ignoring the inn up the hill despite its mural of octopuses. Zithia passed a turf-roofed Viking long-house with smoke rising from holes in the center of the green roof. Trellised grapevines and butternuts, brought from the tabooed northern coast, shaded the shop front at one end.

Zithia looked through the windows of a tall Phoenician dwelling to an enclosed courtyard. There, a pomegranate tree grew within a mosaic floor. An old sail ballooned as an awning, with a scarlet runner bean climbing the black and white striped canvas.

Within view of the water, vendors had erected long poles over the street and from these hung bright bargains. A heavily built Viking lounged beneath a tree in the middle of the arcade, protecting the stalls, his leashed, white cayman snapping occasionally in boredom. The Viking picked a dill pickle from a branch and tossed it to Kylyn, who bit into the sweet, egg-yolk pulp.

A fellow refugee bought the necklace of petite flattened glass globs and peacock feathers. One noblewoman was selling her jades to a Dragon-Land trader, who divided the green trinkets into two piles, only buying one. Between the seller's curses, Zithia said to the trader, 'Do you have any emeralds?' As he shook his head, Zithia reflected: *"Good, the stone of love still brings security."*

Whirling around and simultaneously stepping back, Zithia bumped into a young Phoenician. A brick wall! She'd felt a solid wall where the normal tunnel of years should be. He had no future at all. Gulping, Zithia swayed and the Phoenician took hold of her bare arm to steady her. There it was again, a threat so amorphous it was inescapable. His life would end within months. No seer could point a way beyond that wall. Rare, so very rare. Both apologising, Zithia watched his retreating back, and badly needed a drink. *"Too much... too much... to do."* Zithia thought, then steeled her mind, putting this pain away for another time.

Slowly, Zithia looked into a shop where green scarabs lay next to a tiny old-Nile boat. Flattish clay oil lamps and olive oil were on offer. In a gap between two shops a Viking girl stood, selling her bridal gifts. Crockery lay on wedding quilts and alpaca ribbon rugs.

Zithia observed Kylyn stop short in front of another shop. He was gazing, open-mouthed. Out of the corner of her eye Zithia saw a statue of a pale bare-breasted woman. Without breaking her stride Zithia moved up beside Kylyn and simultaneously brushed her palm across his cheek, so turning his head. He now looked at a stuffed two-humped toy camel, and he ran to it, touching the chest-high saddle. When Zithia finally ducked rainbow linens and loops of cotton to reach the harbour, she was clutching the camel.

At the quay Zithia ruefully ignored the magnificent junks, feeling Galen had too many contacts there for comfort. Looking from a Phoenician vessel to a Viking ship that bobbed side by side, Zithia pursed her lips and her nose wrinkled slightly. Due to these features being almost all that could be seen of Zithia's face, one of the Viking crew noticed.

The corn haired man spat neatly. 'Water arrows. The fastest ships in the world.' His chest inflated. 'Born in Atlantis. Hardly any hull, which we paint with hot lanoline so that ships leap through the water.' The sail rotated while Zithia and Kylyn watched. Wider than it was high, two rows of red diamonds swung on long-fibered wool.

Zithia carefully recalled the names of those fourteen captains Galen had recommended over the years. She really wished she could voyage by junk; they'd had Galen's admiration, as well as their captains having had Galen's highest recommendations. Sighing, Zithia called up to a galley, 'I'm seeking passage up the coast. Your price and name, sir?'

"The Phoenician captain called down from his high deck. 'Then, lady, I suggest you try old Hannibal at the end of the pier. He doesn't mind travelling with women.'

Another captain stood with him. The fair skinned man said, 'I heard you carried women on the way out.'

They watched Zithia and Kylyn go to the end of the peer, asking for prices on the way. Zithia holding tight to her son and a bulky peasant satchel.

Matho blew a smoke ring. 'The girl's mother complained all the way. I couldn't get rid of them fast enough. Luckily they disembarked when we hit the coast.'

Matho pulled a string of blue jade beads from his pouch. 'The gift I promised my sister.'

Vethormr took it. 'Don't tell me you've already swapped our cheap greenstone for jade.'

For years, two extended trading families had guarded the secret of this land. The Dragon-Land traders always stood aloof from inter-marriage. Yet this world had been known to those of the Dragon-Land long, long before the secret had been discovered by the Vikings and the Phoenicians. And a secret it was. It had been a prime condition of the archpriests.

The Phoenician, Matho, clasped a papyrus given him by Vethmor. It contained information told by a comely youth, recently escaped from the barbarians. The contents hadn't yet been shared with the host nations:

"*A Phoenician cousin, Elibaal, was voyaging with his wife and caught the attention of a barbarian general. He boarded Elibaal's vessel to claim his flaxen haired, aqua-eyed, wife. Where he found gold.*

"*The square-headed officer caught the woman by the throat. 'My last guest screamed for a week before dying. I'll know where these riches came from. Do my bidding and I'll free you both.'*

"*Elibaal had taken the barbarians to the New World. By the hardest route; straight over the broad ocean. On sighting land, Elibaal was tied hand and foot. 'True to my promise, soon you'll be free.' The general tipped Elibaal overboard.*

"*Before anyone could stop her, Elibaal's wife dived into the water. She was pulling her husband to the surface, when she was speared.*"

Matho expelled smoke downward from his pipe. 'How do you think these mainland cousins will fare in this war?'

Vethormr replied, 'They managed to get all the way here from our world. I set their odds at even.'

On first arriving, the traders had been amazed to find people of their own races living here. Their subsequent contract had agreed to no questions, and total secrecy. The lost parts of the Atlantian legend, and the origins of the tribes, remained unknown to the Phoenicians and the

Vikings. But not to the Dragon-Land people, who still had their own records of the events.

Vethormr watched Matho's crew loading perfumes and dyes. 'I sold all my ostrich feathers, frankincense and myrrh.' He gave Matho a secret smile. 'You've obtained a large quantity of Tyrian purple and saffron.'

'We Phoenicians are ever thankful to the God Melketh for giving us the secret of purple, after his own dog bit into a mollusk and frothed purple.'

All the traders knew that the Phoenicians used brazilwood purple and annatto yellow to counterfeit the royal colors of Tyrian purple and saffron. Intermarriage had been the instant result, plus the Vikings being given first trading claim on emeralds.

'My emerald harvest has been excellent this year.' Vethormr preened his moustache. 'I exchanged that stone legend-tablet for enough tobacco and cocaine leaves to satisfy an entire Egyptian temple.'

Matho watched Zithia's progress down the next pier. 'Much of my olive oil, linen and glass will have to go up north for storage. But I've cochineal for home, plus the Nile scrolls sold well.'

Zithia walked up Matho's gangplank, having been told his name down the quay, and finding it a very good name. Matho wore a plain kilt and a long sleeved top.

'Lady, you must be particularly fussy. Have the others not made you welcome?' His voice deepened. 'If it was the price, I can assure you, you'll be unhappy with my response also.'

'Sir, I'd be unwise to rule out one ship simply because the captain is... reserved!'

'Women are always trouble.' Matho was tall, his black moustache and beard close-trimmed. 'I doubt you'd feel at ease here. We already have passengers sleeping everywhere.'

Zithia stood directly before him, her feet apart, purring very softly. 'How many emeralds would it take... to obtain a cabin?'

Without commenting, the Phoenician took Zithia and Kylyn into his cabin, which was above deck. On closing the door behind them, Matho gave a seed to his talking parrot. The captain sat down. His thumb was on his jaw, while his finger rested at his temple. 'What quality?'

'Turn your back a moment and I'll show you.'

He swiveled his chair around and looked out a window. 'As I said; trouble.'

Zithia undid the tie at her waist. When Matho heard her sit down he turned round again. She released emeralds from a cloth envelope. The Phoenician's expression softened. 'Exactly where do you go?'

'Somewhere north of the New Nile.'

'Then you're buying a berth to the furthest port. No refund if you disembark earlier.'

Matho inspected the flawless gems. 'The last women aboard kept close to their cabin, I expect you to do the same.'

Zithia inclined her head. They had almost done bargaining when alarm drums began furiously. 'I'm afraid the price just doubled.' He smiled wryly. 'In an hour, they'll be paying six times the normal fare.'

She took the only private berth on the vessel. Then like a conjurer's trick, Zithia produced four more parcels and fanned out the contents on his table. The new gems, made those already glittering there look petite. Zithia returned Matho's smile. 'Don't the Vikings own the emerald trade?'

He flicked open a chest sitting stolid next to the table. Gold glowed. 'I won't tell anyone about our bargains, if you won't.'

'Then I'd like to exchange these for gold at journey's end.' At his assent, Zithia placed a fifth parcel in his hand, 'And these for gold now. I need to do some shopping.'

After repacking her corset, Zithia and Matho went on-deck. Eyeing Zithia's waist and midriff, Matho announced, 'You'll be charged for the company of a guard, and my officer, Himilco, whenever you go on land.

On deck the pace was frantic. A horn blew; news. Vethormr yelled to Matho, 'They got Auoolfr's ship, and his brother's arrow only made it by hiding in a mangrove. The temples are taking some ships to their great river until the main threat is over. The barbarians may even be on the western coast.'

Zithia paled; her brothers... their families... Stepping away from Matho, she faced west and her soul asked a wordless question of the very air. It sped across the continent. The ether answered, and Zithia said 'No, the west is safe.' *"And,"* the ether assured looking into time, *"would be safe."*

The captain said to Zithia. 'We depart in two hours.'

On leaving the ship, Zithia saw large bundles of leaves being dropped into the hold, and tried not to hear Himilco's comment, 'We'll need a lot more leaves to cushion the ballast or the ship will roll over in rough seas.'

Making her way straight to a Dragon-Land trader, Zithia asked her guard to wait outside a moment. Just minutes later she called them in. 'Pack it all, including the private quarters.'

The Dragon-Land merchant and his wife were still marvelling over the three heavy pouches of perfectly round largish pearls, as they assisted with the packing and transport back to Matho's ship.

Zithia herself took care of the chess board, checkers and another ancient game. These alone had cost a dozen golden pearls. The black pearls, quails' eggs, had bought the wife's ink-rubbed paper recipe book, plus silk scrolls of poetry and ghost stories. The cook book had originally been produced in batches of fifty. Even the silk scrolls were semi-mass produced.

The merchant's wife, relieved to be going home to civilisation, described a village of such wonder that Zithia would never forget its name or location. As they all left the gutted shop, the good wife grabbed her medium sacks of Catuaba herb and one of Turnerup-Aphrodisia. 'Nothing sells, anywhere, so well as truly effective aphrodisiacs.'

Zithia, 'I'm glad I persuaded you to part with some.'

Wagging a finger, the trader's wife laughed. 'You took advantage of my good nature.'

With the trader's barrow piled high again, they all began their tired way shipwards, when the mother of the Viking bride that Zithia had seen earlier planted herself in their way. The guards instantly tensed, but the mother bared her teeth and pointed to the gap between the shops where her daughter still stood beside her bridal goods. She named one price.

Zithia flushed, 'Lady, you shame me by asking so little. We must agree on treble that amount, else I could never enjoy such fine goods.' Himilco passed Zithia the gold he'd been carrying for her, 'Only, I need your assistance to take the goods to the ship.'

When they were placing everything on the ship's deck, Himilco told the captain about the marriage goods.

The captain appeared as the grinning Viking mother thumped Zithia soundly on the arm with a closed fist.

He watched them leave. 'They look happy.'

Zithia rubbed her arm. 'The price was driven up.'

'Himilco has been depositing a shop in his cabin. That'll cost extra.'

Zithia, 'At the same rates as my own cabin.'

He considered the retreating Viking bride, 'Almost.'

Unfurling canvas, the ships were a ballet of tacking. Below deck, in their cupboard of a room, Zithia and Kylyn listened to the groan of ropes and wood. Kylyn looked out of a tiny window. Zithia wouldn't risk being on deck with the temple canoes in the same water. Nearby, two pair of water arrows used mobile rudders and pivoting sails to fast out-distance their Phoenician cousins.

chapter 19

The evacuation from Xalisco to Machu-Pichu had taken longer than expected. After Galen had caught up with others of the priesthood, the archpriest had asked for him. Galen had addressed Franklin. 'Eminence, my wife…'

But Franklin raised a hand and the high priest fell silent. Children had filed into the tent. 'My son, these little ones and their bloodlines are precious to us. Because they can't keep up with us on the long march, a barge has been arranged to take them to safety. They deserve a champion; you will accompany them.'

Days later, the world around Galen had been dense mist. Relaxed, he'd sat, head slightly bent, his open eyes hazy in the shadows. The barge had been creeping past barbarians for days. Children, hushed, hid under little pinafores with the invader but a breath away. The netting above them seemed to reflect the world. Galen's power had dampened the noise from his children's whispers and minds, after which he'd repeated a mantra for hours before he'd stopped, and then the boat with all its cargo seemed but a stillness upon the water. The mantra had been, *"Let our shadow be fog, our essence be mist, and we only a breath of air."*

Then, Galen had felt Zithia perform her sword trick. If one had been watching his face, the high priest's open eyes would have seemed to open again. Indeed they had, for his physical eyes now flashed wide and so had ended a light sleep. His fingers had itched, yet he'd ignored her. He'd thought not one thought; he'd remained a breath of air. Nor could he have spared even a fragment of energy to trace her. When Zithia's distress call had reached him on the ether, Galen had bent his head in prayer for his wife and son.

*

The host temple was perched like an eagle in its eyrie. Access to the heights was by a dizzying zigzag of steps up the mountain. A few priests and royalty alone lived within the giant jigsaw stone walls. Fruit trees grew in the streets, where only foot traffic was permitted. Water tanks were refilled from a gush on the precipice-side of the mountain. Natural streams on the mount had also been diverted to fill baths, to irrigate corn-filled steps and to feed the myriad cultivated orchids which abounded in Machu Picchu. All possible colours, shapes, sizes and scents of that regal plant were carefully amassed there.

Farmers tilled the lower of a long series of steep, rock-faced terraces. Shining with gold-foil tassels and bells, the kings of alpacas grazed, constantly followed by guards because of coats as soft as cashmere wool.

Galen watched the palm-roofed pergolas of refugees and the military on the plains around the city. Franklin was speaking quietly to the host archpriest. There had been a council of the eminences.

Without warning, Franklin was beside him. 'Galen. Your wife has put you in a very awkward position. My son, you're guiltless. Still, it's remembered that your need to marry has caused this problem.' Franklin paused for breath. 'To be able to stand in any election for archpriest, you must retrieve your family.'

When Franklin left him, Eten drifted alone to Galen, fanning herself with peacock feathers. Like Eten, the fan was all eyes. Galen gazed at the terraces covering the opposite mountain, filled with flowering potato plants.

'Brother, my condolences on your loss of family. And career!'

Gazing at her, Galen's lower lids drew upwards. 'Let your heart not suffer on my account, sister. These are but temporary matters.'

*

Weeks later, the two archpriests were in a general meeting, attended by a large entourage.

Franklin was taking some time out from the interminable discussions, when an old friend moved from his seat to one next to Franklin. Domenic was thirty-ish and high in his tribe. Often, when Franklin caught sight of Domenic unexpectedly, he'd glimpse an elegant black hat upon his head. Of, course it wasn't really there; Domenic hadn't worn such a courtier's hat for lifetimes. Yet, intermittently, Franklin kept seeing it. Black straw with a wide curling brim and a large decorative pearl brooch attached. Franklin had known Domenic when...

Franklin conversationally, 'You should be married.'

'I always choose women who are already married.'

'Then, old friend, make another choice.'

Domenic shrugged.

Narrowing his eyes, Franklin lost his fatherly aspect. 'Your dissembling isn't conducive to progress.' His voice was suddenly icy, 'Get thee a wife.' He went on harshly, 'Lives are too short. And this, the third time unmarried. I'll expect a wedding within the year.'

"The host archpriest came up to Franklin then, and matters of state intruded. After completing the main business, the host archpriest addressed Galen, who had recently settled in a nearby place at the table. 'My son, what news?'

There was only one topic on which the archpriest would trespass without preamble. 'Eminence, my wife is a priest and hides her mind well.'

Someone in the standing audience snorted.

'Perhaps you're too close to the problem, my son. Could someone else try to find your wife?' Galen's nostrils flared.

Augustus coughed delicately. 'High priestess Eten has always had a unique attachment to the Lady Zithia.'

Silently, those from Xalisco agreed. What better conductor was there than hatred? The throng simultaneously opened up, like a datura flower, disclosing Eten. 'I believe my powers are strong enough to assist Lord Galen. If your eminences will allow me this duty.'

*

Immediately after the meeting, Augustus strode into Eten's room and threw down two dice. When they landed, he pursed his lips. 'Eten, it's your fault I've ambitions. I was perfectly happy with women and lethargy.' He grimaced over each new throw of the dice. 'And now even my luck has deserted me.'

The high priestess stroked burring Venus, whom she held in her arms. 'My dear, what has got you into this state?'

'You! Helping Galen to become archpriest.'

'Galen, archpriest? An insufferable idea. How could you think it?'

Augustus fidgeted with the clasp of his new ultra-fine alpaca cloak. 'It's this altitude. I can hardly breathe this high up.'

Eten offered him a tumbler of tea, in which a green-leaf floated. Drinking half, his lips lost their blue tinge and he breathed more easily.

'Meditating also works.' She inhaled deeply.

Augustus drained his second cup. 'But, Eten, what if the stars are with Galen...'

'Luck isn't with Galen.'

Darkly, Augustus tossed the dice again, and then rolled his eyes. 'How can you be so sure?'

She gave him a newly carved pair of skull-shaped dice. 'Because I won't let it be.' Each time Augustus threw the dice, winning numbers came up.

*

Long after all lights had been doused that night, Galen and Eten climbed onto a rock fist, the highest spot in Machu Picchu. Looking directly up to a peak towering above them, Eten said, 'It's agreed then, we'll work from there.'

Alanyou Picchu. Galen, 'Tomorrow night. Leaving here at daybreak, rest in the afternoon...'

Eten rolled her eyes. 'Galen, ever the purist,' she declared, while flinging the contents of a full pouch upwards. Even as the sparkling crystals flew, Eten breathed out deeply. The wind dropped and the crystals moved slowly, in a single mass, to where Eten's mind beckoned. At a word, the specks ignited, releasing a dense purple smoke. Dew gathered there in the smoke, the moisture joining together into drops.

The high priestess was whispering, intensely casting. Fattening drops trebled, then quadrupled. Pausing, Eten flung out her arm, simultaneously giving a command. The drops joined and froze into a shimmering stairway. Eten put a foot onto the first rung.

Galen, following, declared, 'A waste of energy.'

Without a backward look, Eten said, 'And what do you call trudging down one mountain only to climb another?'

'A different kind of energy.'

'Weren't we always taught to practise, practise, practise?'

Galen couldn't argue with that. From the sixth step Eten looked back beyond Galen, 'Besides, I wasn't wasteful.' The first step evaporated.

'I'm glad to see it.'

With each step they took another dissolved.

Debarking at Alanu Pichu's highest platform they stood among the blazing stars, part of them. 'Night air, always better for tracking.' Eten smiled. 'Normally we'd stand... back to back?'

Galen waved an arm. 'After you.'

Flicking a single errant crystal off her shoulder, Eten remained facing Galen. Going into a meditative state, a few feet from each other, they straightened their backs and cast their arms until each achieved a Chi flow. Concentrating further, the connection to the Chi became purer, then a flood. Together they thought: *"Zithia!"* Opening themselves; sensing, gazing from high in the ether, examining any stray energy streams, Zithia's name always on their minds.

An hour went. All at once Galen could feel Zithia asleep in the dark. He was disembodied now, breathing and pulse forgotten. The cabin's transparent outlines flashed before Galen's eyes. Zithia was on a ship, not two days out of harbour. Her nightly protective chant stopped the place from appearing in total reality, the realm was hazy, coming into and out of focus.

"My son," he thought, drawn to where the boy lay in bed. There was a visible ripple across the astral scene. Eten scowled mentally at Galen. The high priest thought himself onto the deck. Noting the rigging, scanning the stars. He turned to Eten... who wasn't there.

A scream. At once Galen was in the cabin, passing a hand over Kylyn: *"Stay asleep."* Zithia was now sitting in bed, her knees drawn up near her chin. Eten floated before her, pulsating jagged red and black. Talons out, advancing.

Before Galen could move between them, one of Eten's claws reached for Zithia's forehead. At that exact moment, Zithia pulled her head sideways. But not quickly enough. Black lightning struck the edge of her forehead. The high priestess had missed piercing Zithia's third eye. A deathblow.

Eten was lunging anew when Galen, energy flaming, tackled her. They both flew over Zithia's head, then through the wall. Disengaging, Eten turned to go back to Zithia, but Galen barred her way.

Drifting above the inky ocean, their energy bubbles around them, which were also them, burned bright. This light grew, instantly expanding to twenty feet in height and ten feet wide. Eten flashed to the other side of the ship. Galen was there. They met again, high up, on either side of the mast. Drifting through the rigging, Galen reached well into her enveloping light, took hold of Eten and flung her far.

Stung, yet Eten reared and flew hard toward the boat, aiming for below deck. Swooping, Galen floated in front of Eten. He banged a staff he'd just visualised, down onto a non-existent ground. Thinking, feeling, demanding: *"Leave!"* A booming sounded, a dazzling light flooded the scene and Eten had vanished, commanded back to her body.

Almost at once, Galen joined her back on the rock. Galen sprang from his place, raging icily to Eten, whose astral form was connected at the waist, only, to the body.

She'd been blasted back with such force that her stunned mind was still trying to gather enough strength to right her spirit within her body, the both being roughly at right angles to each other.

Realising Galen was back, Eten reached her cold physical right hand out, and rested her astral head lopsidedly upon it. She glowered there from among disheveled hair, one dislodged lock almost covering an eye. Galen glowered back. Eten's right astral hand appeared through her physical leg, reached her face and flipped the errant astral lock back into place. Then, pulling on her reserves, Eten shook herself until her soul gave a shimmy and was perfectly alighted within her body. Her mind took a little longer to untangle after Galen's white lightning jolt.

Physically both were perspiring from their exertions.

A smile from the dark side dawned upon Eten's face. 'A world without Zithia; I couldn't resist.'

Galen stood over her now. He spread his fingers above Eten's heart, thinking: *"Slower."* Eten heard the word. After two beats he repeated the thought. His face came close to hers. 'I warned you… not to trouble your heart.' Eten's right arm throbbed violently. He drew the next word out. 'Slower.'

A pain tore at her heart; her maw twisted. Shakily, desperately, her good arm reached up. With a spasm of strength she pulled Galen's face to hers, and kissed him, her claws drawing blood from his jaw.

Flinching backward, the high priest spat, then wiped his mouth with his sleeve. Eten's heart began to drum more regularly. Galen ignited the tops of all Eten's fingernails, and, with them, all his blood. Half her dagger-long claws were gone before she could stop the burning. Scowling at the ruin, Eten listened to the steadied rhythm and declared, 'Of course, Zithia dead would kill your hopes of becoming archpriest.'

Galen's astral form grew and grew until it eclipsed his physical body. Towering over Eten, a flash pulsed from him. Then Galen turned and strode off. He'd flung a power at her again. A different kind; she was encased for the night in an energy prison of light.

Eten's mind laughed, the sound following him until she tried to take two brisk steps forward. And banged into a wall that wasn't there. Rubbing her nose hard, still she whispered, 'Well… I've withered Zithia's life-span by years.' Knowing that now wasn't the time to declare her success. "Yes," she thought, "overall, it's been a good night."

*

On the ship, the Phoenician physician, Himilco, banged on a door. Zithia stayed huddled on the bed, away from Kylyn lest he be included in any further attack from Eten. Finally, 'They've gone.'

She dashed over to Kylyn, still sleeping, not wanting to take her eyes from him.

Box in hand, Himilco thudded on the door more urgently. 'Lady, lady are you ill? In pain? Let me in to help you.' Several of the crew peered from behind him.

Pulling on a cloak, with the hood drawn well over her head Zithia opened the door a crack. Himilco looked into a chalky face. 'Sir, my son. He, he slept through my… cries.'

Himilco went at once to Kylyn. The captain's bark sounded and the men fell away. Zithia bolted the door.

'The boy is fine, my lady, simply asleep.' Zithia's alabaster fingers quivered over her face. 'Are you in pain? My lady, please remove your cloak.'

She drew the garment closer around her, but the hood slipped back into folds on her shoulders. 'I had a nightmare.'

'Only one?' Himilco put his hand upon Zithia's brow. 'You're burning up, lady. Fever has brought on this dream. I'll give you something for a peaceful sleep.'

'For my benefit, or the crews?'

He put a jar of clear alcohol on the bedside cupboard. 'Perhaps a dram of this.'

Seeing the physician to the door, Zithia caught an odd reflection in a polished brass tray that hung on the wall. The whites of her eyes showed suddenly as she looked over her shoulder. Nothing. Himilco watched her. 'Lady?'

'Good night, physician.'

'I'll call on you tomorrow to see how you've slept.'

When Zithia locked the door behind him, she leaned against it, thinking: *"Tomorrow."* She shuddered, but it had taken both Galen and Eten to find her. *"And Galen attacked Eten to protect me."* A light kindled in her eyes. No. There'd be no tomorrow for this nightmare.

Moving across the room, once more she saw a ghostly outline flash by. Wild eyed, she whirled around, and taking in the entire cabin Zithia faced the burnished mirror and gasped. Her hair. Zithia put a hand to her locks. They were now wheat blonde and only wavy. Fear had even taken its curl.

Examining her reflection Zithia shrugged the cape from her shoulders. The blonde hue finished immediately below her shoulder blades. 'It has to come off.' Her knees buckled. 'And tonight.'

Gulping Himilco's fiery alcohol, Zithia's eyes crept back to her reflection. She had another mouthful. With an obsidian dagger Zithia cut through the layers of her glory, sniffing intermittently. Up on the deck, she murmured to herself, 'What a lot of trouble… to go blonde.' Zithia slipped a weighted bundle overboard, into the florescent green trail marking the vessel's wake.

Zithia started awake; someone was staring at her. Kylyn. He leaned over to touch her blonde halo. 'Do you like it? Mama felt like a change.'

Frowning, he went to play on the floor. Occasionally he looked at her out of the corner of his eye. After a time he brought his toys onto the bed. 'It's short.'

'Not really, darling.' Tears threatened. 'But Kylyn, these people think that only bad women change their hair colour.' She hugged him. 'So, I'm sorry, it'll need to be our secret. This new colour. Yours and mine. We keep our secrets, don't we Kylyn?'

His chest expanded. 'Yes, mama.' And smiled.

Later, the physician knocked on the door. Having been assured that all was well, he took Kylyn on deck to meet Matho's nephew.

Alone, Zithia gazed into a hand mirror. 'I feel years older.' There was an unpleasant ring to her words. She looked more intensely. 'No!'

She brushed back the pale waves to the left of her face. The number of lines at her temple had increased. 'Ten more years of my life gone.' Nerveless fingers let the mirror drop.

*

Heads turned on seeing Zithia's blonde hair and lightly tanned face. The captain was in his quarters above deck. Matho stood when she knocked at the open double doors, reflecting coldly: *"She should've remained hooded during the entire journey."*

'Lady, are you feeling better?' He looked pained: *"Did she have Viking blood?"*

'Yes, and no, captain.'

He ignored the no, 'Then may I ask why you're not in your cabin, as we agreed?'

Zithia lit up with a smile. 'But we didn't agree to that, captain. Only that I'd stay close to my quarters.' She looked around the roomy cabin, her head nodding minutely. 'Close, can mean many things.' She smiled hard. 'I forget, you don't know me. My name is Melia. The widow Melia, daughter of Tolen, from the city of Chan Chaun.' She sat. 'Captain I'm come to bargain for a favour.' She looked down, then quickly up. As a woman alone, I find my room is over-close to the men.' She shuddered. 'Then that nightmare... I can't spend another night below decks.'

Matho's eyebrows drew down. 'Lady, there is but one other cabin on the vessel and you're standing in it.'

'Yes, I know.' Zithia tore her gaze from the windows behind him. 'Thus I come to gallantry and gifts.'

His voice had turned colder. 'It'd take a rich gift indeed to even begin to consider such gallantry.'

Zithia tossed a gem high in the air between them, preparing to catch it again. Matho's eyes followed its flashing progress. He caught it mid-flight. Rather large, once the centerpiece of a pectoral. 'Widow Melia,' his eyes danced, 'my chivalry has overcome me.' He weighed the gem on his scales. 'On condition that you remain indoors. Is that plain enough for you?'

'Then I believe I get change from that emerald.'

Matho appeared astounded. 'Lady, a captain's cabin is sacred.'

Zithia's gem disappeared, a mound of gold appeared on the captain's table.

The Phoenician banged his palm upon the table for a sailor to attend him. 'Widow Melia, call me Matho.' The first mate appeared and took in the gold. 'The widow Melia and I are exchanging cabins. Have my things removed.' Matho pulled the gold to him.

The first mate went to the parrot on its ebony stand. 'Widow Melia has offered to keep the bird for me.'

That night Zithia slept in her spacious quarters, with the bank of windows open. It was a very pleasant aft apartment with a section for dining.

In the morning, Zithia opened her wide double doors. A thin curtain hid her from view, though for some reason her silhouette was often visible.

Fishing from her cabin windows, she hummed a tune and, every so often, her husky voice called. 'Could someone take this to the cook, please?'

A fish would appear from behind the cloth, held out delicately by a bare arm. The next day, the crew found more reasons than usual for crossing the terrace behind which Zithia's shadow flitted. Matho said nothing.

The second day was a tantalising repetition of the first. Sweet humming drifted from the cabin. Mid-morning the second mate decided to teach the younger sailors seacraft, setting up a fire where he could observe each flicker of Zithia's shadow. Soon, she was sitting entranced on her side of the world while, over a pot of boiling water, a large sponge filled with liquid from the steam. Squeezing the sponge, the mate passed the cup around for tasting. Blowing on it, they sipped fresh water. Kylyn took some to Zithia, who clapped her delight.

It was late afternoon when Zithia dropped some perfume onto a sunny ledge. A sailor halfway up the mast caught a whiff of the scent and fell into the ocean. While the ship turned to retrieve him, Matho knocked on the cabin's doorframe.

'Widow Melia, you've proved your point. An unseen woman can be more trouble than a visible one. You have the freedom of the vessel.'

At once Zithia drew back the veil, smiling roguishly. 'Captain, will you and Himilco dine with us tonight. We're eager to learn Phoenician.'

Thus began a twice-weekly invitation, at which only Phoenician was spoken.

Continuing to fish daily, Zithia added a rainbow collection for the pot, a gift always welcome. One afternoon, after waiting hours before taking a fine large delicacy, Zithia took the catch to the cook. He was busy with a passenger of Zithia's culture.

Cook, taking the fish absently, 'Baked whole, I reckon.' And then, turning back to the passenger, 'So you were almost trapped, by the barbarians, coming down a river.'

'We only had one chance; go down a tributary known for rapids. If we kept to the quieter side channels, running between shifting sand and white water... By God, it wasn't a favoured choice.'

Kylyn appeared and sat, Zithia paused.

The passenger continued, 'Grey bearded Albert, he had a good belly on him. Yet he'd been a steersman on that river for decades. So, we were twenty minutes from our landing place when he stopped his whispered grumblings. He always grumbled. He took the turns and veered away from the rapids as he'd always done. Albert got us through. It was a hell of a trip. We all left the boat shaking, I can tell you.'

The cook called for a boy to clean the fish.

Taking a ragged breath, his eyes large, the passenger continued, 'Not Albert; he just stayed slumped over the tiller. We called to him, nothing. The landing spot had physicians and one came to Albert. He was dead alright, and quite cold with it. It was declared he'd been dead for twenty minutes. Of course, the physician didn't know what we knew. That Albert had steered, without fault, those last twenty minutes. So a priest was called. Passing his hands over Albert, and without any of our story, the priest also declared Albert dead these twenty minutes. Both were prepared to take their oath on it, that Albert was dead at the time he'd been steering us home.'

chapter 20

The New Nile's broad delta came into view, a river with a fertile basin to rival the Nile itself. At its sprawling mouth, the ship dropped anchor and Kylyn flew his silk kite from the deck. They waved at an outpost, set upon stilts, which guarded the mighty river's entrance. A pilot canoed out to guide the vessel through tributaries, shifting sands and waterlogged prairies of fawn grass.

A farmer held up oysters and kelp geese, signalling prices. Zithia was shaded beneath an awning of camelhair net, whose small holes, remarkably, kept out the light-rain. Grasses gave way to wet meadows edged by white cedar. Here, crowds of orchids raised white stars above pendulous ruby pouches. Rising from the orchids, a blue goose winged low over the water. A flurry of ducks began to follow. Matho loosed an arrow, attached to a line. On hauling it in, he raised the shaft high revealing a duck plus a good sized fish.

Whitewashed villages and monuments, built on higher ground, divided vast plantations. Magnolias lined grid-patterned streets and plazas. Zithia delighted in a field of pink cottonballs surrounding a round-roofed observatory. On the very next farm, red fluff dominated. This, in turn, was dominated by a henge, not stone, but an immense wooden henge carved from giant redwoods. Glowing mud pyramids, painted sandstone yellow, blazed out against blue cotton. Thus was the continuing scene along the New Nile.

Descendants of Atlantis, in canoes, hawked reddish shaggy wolf pelts and coloured cotton, while incessantly gathering news. Buying a yellow fruit, Zithia spread the sweet black pulp onto bread. Sitting on a new magnolia-wood stool, Zithia clutched small purple-fringed orchids with a hundred blossoms per stem.

Close on dusk, the ship anchored between a pyramid and a village. After dining on roasted bison steaks, Zithia and Kylyn walked to a henge. Its colossal tablets glowed ruby in the sun. Below this was a meadow, where creamy-white orchids spiralled up green staffs and sparkled in the sunset.

In the middle distance, they watched bunches of hyacinth flowers fall lightly to the ground beneath a huge tree. Just before another bouquet hit the ground, it suddenly sprouted wings to land in a tangle of feathers and legs. The tree was filled with macaws, slurping fruit. And giggling. A line of birds leaned upon each other, slipped, then hung upside-down for a frozen moment. Finally, squawking indignation, they zigzagged off, occasionally dropping in height as the wind seemed to evaporate beneath their wings. The entire flock was drunk on fermented fruit.

For three nights the air kissed the skin, while tawny panthers exchanged yowls with wetland jaguars. Finally, they saw the Crescent City, so called because the river curled like a crescent moon before it. Rounding a gracious bend in the river the Great Pyramid came into view. Kylyn's mouth dropped open, as his eyes kept going up and up.

'I had no idea.' Zithia beamed, fanning herself against the humidity with a red silk fan. Speaking in broken Phoenician, the only language she and Kylyn used now.

'Taller than the Sphinx, it's a wonder of the world. And all of it mud.' Matho stated. Zithia couldn't take her eyes off the deep gold pyramid. 'And it's served by the largest city in your world or mine. Again mud, but a rammed-earth mud that can last hundreds of years. A Dragon-Land invention.'

He waved Zithia away, 'Hire a chair to the top. You'll see the true scale of the city.'

And then, against a stabbing thought Matho screwed up his eyes. 'I suppose shopping is on your agenda?' Zithia's face glowed enthusiasm. 'Tell your guards when you'll need them.'

Himilco and a muscled young sailor hailed two chairs, beneath a line of pyramid-shaped magnolia trees. These shaded them up to the Grand Avenue. They bought yellow-white blossoms at the base of the Great Pyramid, from a slender woman of the eighth tribe. Handing over the flowers, the woman said, 'See the facing stones of the pyramid? How they glow? My tribe supervised the other tribes in making them. They're very dense clay, mixed with mineral. Aged for a year, once all the moisture has been stamped out of the clay. Gold stones.'

'Thus the pyramid's great beauty.' Agreed Zithia.

Going up the central stairway, Zithia realised the structure was actuality three colossal mounds, each taller than the one before. Reaching the summit, the white city stretched for twenty miles in three directions.

The great river shone more like a crescent moon than ever. Vivid pink, blue and red plantations were rainbow splashes between pyramids, henges and villages. Even the obligatory lake, behind the city, was impressive, with ten thousand chinampas quilting half of it. Live-oaks graced its banks. From a hill, a wood-henge marked sunrises and, in a lush park, a herd of white bison grazed.

At the pyramid's central altar, an elderly man arranged flowers around a transparent lilac gem. Zithia and Kylyn left her guards looking at the city. She added magnolias to the altar. 'Grandfather, are there any buildings left from the time of Atlantis?'

The man scrutinised Zithia's facial bones. 'And what day is today?'

'Nothing. Tomorrow is Guardian Day.'

The man smiled. 'After the great stone cities fell into the Atlantis Ocean, epochs ago, the days of First Atlantis were declared over for a time. Only the city on the island Atlantis remained. So there's nothing left from then, my dear. Even the cats of Atlantis are gone from here.'

'But, didn't the Atlantians build this city?' Zithia's hand swept over the metropolis.

'Oh yes. Still, everything built on First Atlantis, after the east coast disappeared, was made from mud-stone. Eventually it crumbled back to the earth. The humidity takes its toll of even the eighth tribe's rammed-earth stones. Mind you it took six hundred years before the first stones needed replacing.

Our noble forebears kept this northern continent as their personal reserve, after the east coast cities disappeared. He quoted:

"Thereafter, only three small settlements were allowed on First Atlantis, to supervise Atlantian visitors from the island Atlantis. All buildings on the continent, from then on, were made of earth to remind us of the impermanence of man. All was overseen by the Guardian tribes, who were content to watch over the land and its visitors. They alone had the right to live permanently on First Atlantis. Pleasure airships traversed in great numbers this paradise, setting down wherever it took their fancy." He paused for breath. *"After the island Atlantis died, the ranger tribes voted to stay here. The first and the seventh tribes, those blessed tribes that had guarded this land from the time of the first*

tragedy continued their vigil. We remember them still."

The old man moved off. Zithia called to Kylyn. She hugged him to her. 'Darling this is the land of your papa's main tribe. The Guardians.'

*

With sarsaparilla roots in one hand, Himilco paused at a maize-beer stall, but Zithia handed him a tropical apricot instead and kept moving. Thin sheets of silver lured her. Placed behind torches, they doubled the luminescence. Several sheets were packed in tree-moss for her. At a copper ingot, shaped like a miniature ox hide, the young sailor reminded, 'You can get those on the wharf.'

Having bought three bison pelts, Zithia hired a carrier. Then she pounced on an exquisite sewing-bag, covered inside and out with different embroidery stitches. While Zithia caressed the bag, Himilco picked up a tiny spindle and bargained.

Back at the quay, the other passengers were already journeying up the water highway to an inland city. This smaller metropolis was also built on an Atlantian ranger's post. The refugees would remain hidden there until the war was over.

*

Turning left at the coast, the ship made for the Eaten Cape, stopping but once. That day, Zithia and Kylyn were in the dinghy on its first trip to the village. Passing black mangrove trees, Matho's eleven-year-old nephew, Geirroor, snapped off a dark root growing up from the silt to the air. Inserting it into a proffered coconut, he drank. Set back from the open waters, the village was divided by a spring cascading six feet down over rocks. Huts nestled on stilts of varied heights, among the buttresses of water-bound cypress trees. Raised broad-walks zigzagged between houses.

Tying up to a pier, Matho helped Zithia up to where she spied a wall of furs hanging from a roof, mink. An awning of jaguar pelts adorned another hut. The furs fell into deep piles on the verandah. Zithia pushed her fingers through tawny fur, looking up its soft length. A fly tickled her ankle and she brushed the spot. There it was again. Looking down, Zithia saw a pair of huge feline eyes. They blinked. Instantly Zithia was several feet away.

The big cat, three times the usual size, yawned. A woman scratched the panther under the chin. 'You lazy thing.' Purring erupted! 'He's one of the few left… lived with us since he was orphaned as a cub.' The cat stretched prodigiously.

Matho patted the flank; the purr ceased. 'To think of the price he'd fetch in the Far World.' Feline ears flattened and Matho withdrew his hand.

Zithia inspected the resultant scratch. 'He must like you. See, not cut to the bone.'

Breathing in the heady scent of green orchids, they stamped the creaking broad-walks to higher ground. Matho said something too quickly for Zithia to catch and, giggling, a woman invited 'Come, this way.'

There was a bath sitting in the middle of a fen. A hollow tree stump full of warm water, set among long orchid wands. Due to the Phoenician penchant for bathing, every tiny settlement had a tub.

Mink and panther skins had been loaded into a canoe, plus slabs of buoyant yellow corkwood. Dinner, the cook promised, would be a feast of pink palm-fruit jelly, musky sea grapes and venison. The dinghy was halfway to the ship when a Dragon-Land junk appeared, at speed. Raising its rudder, the junk became more maneuverable at this depth. The flying-fish sails were being continuously tweaked for best speed. The junk roared ahead of Matho's vessel and then veered off to the left where, suddenly, a barbarian ship burst out from behind an outcropping of thick mangrove.

Zithia's heart dropped. The blonde monsters were here, where they'd never been seen before. And they were plowing straight for the dinghy, seeing a distraction there. The barbarians were so close, Zithia could smell their sweat upon the air. Grabbing Kylyn, Zithia jumped forward and to the right. There was a thunk in the dinghy's prow, above the waterline. An instant, later Zithia and Kylyn landed. But not in water. They'd landed on fur, on furs in the dinghy they'd just leapt from, and the dinghy was jetting through the water toward the junk. Pulled by thick rope attached to a metal loop on the ship, and so to an anchor which had been thrown overboard. A crossbow's grappling arrow had saved the dinghy.

Then the junk started mechanically firing little lit clay balls, which exploded on impact with the barbarian vessel. The fireworks of black powder and fragments, within the balls, tore through wood and men. Soon the barbarians were all dead in body, and their souls were being set-upon by after-life shadow-gremlins. The frantic shades were pulled, thrashing, down into the depths while their ship, full of holes from crossbow arrow-fists, sank and joined them. Some barbarian souls tried to cling tight to the descending prow or deck, but the midnight collectors plucked them off and drew them screaming away. None alive saw this.

*

Marshland filagreed the Eaten Cape, then the ship headed northwards again. Hitting rough weather, Zithia spent her time hanging out of the cabin's windows. Kylyn recovered from seasickness much more quickly than his mama.

After the weather had settled, they came upon a race of sea between a lagoon and a reef. The mile-long lagoon was filled with yellow lotus plants, captured by sandbanks. Dropping anchor halfway along, canoes paddled out to the ship from a hidden village. A table had been set up on the main deck; Geirroor was already there with barter goods beside him. This was his coming-of-age test. The settlers dropped pearls into a bowl.

Bobbing in the dinghy, reef-side of the ship, Zithia and Himilco floated near green coral saucers, wide as their boat. Living orange pompoms waved their myriad long legs from the coral. Multi-coloured triggerfish felt the dinghy's shadow and clustered together, pretending to be one huge fish.

On board, Kylyn watched different trade items being added and taken away around Geirroor. Zithia was picking lotus, with Himilco watching for alligators, when a fluttering sounded and grew. Everyone looked, except the bargainers. Ten thousand butterflies drifted over the lagoon, going south.

The gold and black monarchs continued their migration. When the party climbed back onto the ship's deck, the end of the butterfly parade was in view.

Without warning, thunder roared from the beach. Zithia instinctively pulled Kylyn down to the deck. Wide eyed, her head pivoted in the direction of another loud thud further up the coast. The monarchs hadn't changed course or formation. At another boom from nowhere, Kylyn jumped. Himilco ruffled Kylyn's hair. 'This close to land, the coastal thunder roars all the way north. The Vikings say it's the Gods' warning not to live here.'

Zithia thought: *"Unless you belong to the Guardian Tribes."* Watching a school of butterfly fish, who'd been scattered by a close half-submerged cannon blast. They took a breath, and their dazzling multicoloured butterfly wings were the main thing Zithia could see from above, their thin orange bodies outshone by their fins.

*

That night everyone, including the boys, celebrated Geirroor's success with crocodile steaks and distilled alcohol. An eight-stringed harp haunted the air with ballads, while Geirroor and Kylyn played knucklebones. Filling his pipe, Matho studied his parchment maps and star charts. Himilco wrote Phoenician labels for the contents of Zithia's Egyptian medicine box, which Zithia attached to the jars. At length the sailors began a song that Himilco could translate for Zithia without reddening. 'It's about a mythical island that lies off our lands.'

Zithia heard the word Atlantis. The more Himilco translated, the more Zithia bit her tongue and looked at her jars. Matho finished, 'Atlantis, the cradle of civilisation, lies somewhere within the very reach of my birthplace.'

Zithia's eyes sparkled dangerously into his. 'Your scholars tell you this?' He nodded. 'Then they're wrong! Our scholars know Atlantis lies off this continent.'

The two men erupted with mirth. Matho's face showed wonder. 'But, woman, we're talking about the world's greatest antiquity.'

Zithia's hard smile cut. 'And?'

Tactfully, the physician joined the sailors and began another song. Matho suppressed a smile. 'How could Atlantis have existed in this isolated, unknown, part of the world? There's no great civilisation here that shows the influence of Atlantis.'

Zithia blushed scarlet. 'Our archpriests call these waters the Atlantis Seas.'

'Proving nothing!'

Swallowing hard, keeping her lips resolutely closed, Zithia opened a backgammon set. But Matho combined his moves with comment set to bait her. Finally, through gritted teeth, she growled. 'Our greatest seer saw

Atlantis in a vision, drowning off this land.' She then made a move that won the game.

'Yours, lady,' Matho bowed his head, 'which is more that can be said of Atlantis.'

Geirroor and Kylyn had gathered around the open charts. Geirroor, showing off, ran his finger along a wide band within the ocean, starting down past the foreigners' port in the south. 'It's the great river within the ocean.' Geirroor said, 'We move at racing speed when in this river, eight to ten miles an hour. This river flows from south to north. Sometimes we're joined by schools of fish and whale pods, all taking the short way home.' The river was marked as existing a few miles off the coast, dipping well into the gulf of the New Nile and almost meeting the land river itself. 'And there's another such ocean-river which brings us here, flowing down our coast, then across the ocean.'

Matho now pointed out where the ocean-river left the coast, far north, and crossed to the next landfall. But Zithia wasn't interested; instead she was following the flow up the long coast ahead of them. Her mouth went dry; she was unable to believe her eyes. Before her lay the location of the ruins of Atlantis, as it had appeared on the map of the library ceiling at the Atlantis Tree. All she had to do was name it.

A hand tapped the map in front of her. 'By the stars and the moon we're here, give or take half a day.' The captain pointed to an area encompassing the island on which Zithia focused. 'In two days we'll be in the Bad Sea again.'

Geirroor whispered a rune, 'May my ancestors protect me, not call me. And if they call me, let it be quickly.'

Zithia traced a pair of small islands, 'Why do they name it thus?'

'Because strange things happen in that sea. All that fly or swim lose their way there. Vessels disappear, in good weather especially. The bad waters extend days out into the ocean.' He looked beyond Zithia's fingers.

Noting when the ship would be closest to dead Atlantis, her mind sang. She was bursting to tell someone her discovery. If only Torim were here.

*

There'd been a storm last night and so Zithia had slept late. Coming on deck she realised that the boat had anchored. The distant coast was visible. What could interest the Phoenicians here? Matho called Kylyn over. Having thrown a gourd into the ocean and retrieved it, Matho handed it to Zithia. Tentatively she sipped. Fresh water.

Matho, 'A spring runs underground from the nearby coast and surfaces here.'

The ship floated within a clear, aqua glass oval. Way, way down, was sand. No fish, no seaweed.

When every water barrel was full, Matho slid off his sandals saying to Zithia, 'The other side of the ship will have a better view for the next hour.'

Some of the crew took off their over-shirts. Hastily Zithia turned round. Himilco appeared, 'Shall I take your son?'

'Thank you.'

Soon she was alone on deck, dabbing perspiration from her cheekbones, listening to boisterous laughter among the splashes.

Pacing the quiet side of the boat, Zithia looked into the shimmering depths as from a hilltop. More splashes erupted; Zithia frowned deeply, and then hopped over the rail into the translucent embrace. She was hanging her wet garments up in the cabin, when there was a cry of triumph and the crew finally clambered aboard. With both hands, a sailor held a grey knobbly lump above his head.

Matho raised his eyebrows at Zithia's dripping hair. 'Ambergris, used in the finest Egyptian perfumes. A good omen.' He gazed at the blue sky. 'And we needed a good omen.' Only then did Zithia remember that they were on the edge of the bad waters.

*

They journeyed fast for days, but dazzling clear skies dampened their spirits. Eyes sliding from horizon to horizon, the crew agreed dourly that it was beautiful weather.

The lookout hailed. All turned in the direction to which he pointed. Cupping hands above their eyes, the sailors tried to identify the two-pronged thing following them. Then the wind changed and the red diamonds on the pale canvas backgrounds were obvious. Vikings. Twin arrows. Brittle laughter burst forth.

On the seaward side, the water arrows were catching upa pace. A Viking checked directions by using the sun's shadow under a wire attached to a wooden plate. Seeing this, Geirroor told Kylyn with pride, 'We use a Dragon-Land compass.' Then was off up the mast, for a better vantage point.

Good-humored insults beat back and forth between the vessels. The sister ships drew abreast of the bulkier Phoenician vessel.

Geirroor cheered from on high and going higher. Looking up the mast, Zithia saw Kylyn climbing after Matho's nephew. Instantly she was scrambling after her son, too frightened to call his name. Ten feet up, Zithia's skirt billowed out.

'All eyes on the water,' snapped Matho, climbing fast.

Zithia reached Kylyn at the top of the mast. Standing behind him, with her arms circling him, her facial muscles relaxed.

'Mama, it's Geirroor's uncle.'

'Really darling?' Following Kylyn's gaze she saw bubbles surrounding the furthest ship. While she watched, the bubbles grew in number and size.

Matho was now beside his nephew, to one side of the mast. 'Geirroor, you should've thought. Olondin is only just six.'

But Geirroor was waving at his uncle.

The water began to boil around the nearest boat. Everyone watched the exploding ocean now, especially those in the water arrows.

"And they only ever see the bubbles," came Torim's words. Zithia laid a vice-like grip upon Matho's arm. 'Turn the ship.' He followed her gaze. 'We see the dragon's breath.' The water fizzed, expanding rapidly. 'Turn the ship or you kill us all!'

Matho bellowed, 'Dragon! Go to port.' Then he shouted to the Vikings, 'The dragon's breath.' Extra sails were already unfurling. He looked at Zithia and the boys. 'Brace yourselves.'

Zithia flattened herself against her son as the vessel listed a hard left; the mast dipped jerkily trying to shake off its occupants. Clinging tight, veins stood out on Zithia's neck like cords. Immediately the deck resumed a normal angle, a battle-speed drumbeat issued forth and the men's backs rippled at the oars.

Meanwhile, the Vikings were also laying oar to water. But to broken water, through which they hardly progressed. A wave of froth then raised the furthest arrow, creaking, above the sea. It rose five feet aloft, and rocked there.

The trapped Vikings flung swords, shields and daggers into the belly of the effervescent fountain. Battle cries and Odin's name were heard. All at once, tiring of its game, the ocean crashed back to its usual level. Then, gripped in an invisible maw, the hull was sucked beneath the waves. Struggling hard, the Vikings also sank. A minute after, only a green pineapple bobbed in the water.

Immediately the twin ship rose. The captain on the second water-arrow, snatched up two torches from a metal fire-bowl. 'Wherefore do I see my kinsmen... ah, tis my death-day upon me...' He set alight the main cargo cache, which was near the sail. 'I sense the shades of my parents...' and passed the torches to his men, who recited while putting flame to the chests beneath their rowing seats. 'their parents... all my ancestors, smiling on me.' The flames carried their goods into the next world. When the lethal bubbles had raised the blazing pyre to its zenith, the Vikings watched the horizon. 'Gladly I cross the divide to be among them. To again be an immortal.' The unseen dragon began to pull once more, pulling the ship down in a rush. The warriors were gone.

Milliseconds later, tunnel upon tunnel upon tunnel of blue-white light appeared and pierced the waters. These lights drew the shades of the newly dead up to the water's surface and then, through the sky, heavenward. Each soul wore an expression of true joy, some waved to those who were beyond living-sight above them.

In his eyrie, Matho saw a dolphin pod fleeing the bubbles towards a glittering patch of yellowish mist, hard to see into, hundreds of feet wide encompassing even the water, down to thirty feet. One dolphin jumped high into the fog and its image became a mirage before Matho's eyes.

Matho now noted a boiling finger of water chasing them. He pointed the way, yelling 'Ramming speed.' The snort of the dragon's breath gained, was very nearly on them. 'Mast and oars to starboard.' The course correction gained them precious seconds while the bubbles, confused, sought to overtake the ship. They hit the mist-patch almost dead centre.

Immediately, sound was dampened. The look-out's voice, telling that dragon's breath hadn't followed them, was swallowed up. There, within the fog, a tunnel appeared and the ship was steering down it. A tingling feeling pervaded all; displacement, each seemingly not quite in his body.

The ship's crew watched the tunnel walls changing; lines of mist started moving anti-clockwise, revealing blue sky beyond and green sea beneath. The hairs rising on every spine and the back of every neck, as the sails went slack. Breathing in the thickened air Matho called, 'Row!' And every back bent to ramming speed, making for the clear blue sky at the tunnel's end.

Shards of yellow mist clung to the ship, like pennants. Ten long minutes later the ship popped, like a cork, out into normal air again. All eyes turned frantically oceanwards; no bubbles lay in wait. And then the horizon took all their breath away. The sun was setting where, ten minutes before, it had sailed high through the mid-afternoon sky.

As the mist evaporated behind them, Matho began his descent, declaring, 'Fortified wine for all. Twice round.'

Back on deck, Zithia looked back at where they'd been; now calm open water. 'That fog, the tunnel. What was it?'

Matho, 'A time in which to hide. A cousin once fled the barbarians by going into a yellow mist. When I saw the dolphins go into it, I saw our only chance.'

An ancient sailor kissed a talisman against monsters. 'I've seen tiny fish caught in a funnel-net of bubbles. Then a whale swam up the bubbles from below, mouth wide, and gulped the fish down.' Muttering bust forth. He drank half his measure of wine. 'If it took a whale's breath to catch tiny fish; how big was the dragon that tried to catch the ship?' The men went quiet.

Matho threw an arm over the ancient's shoulder. 'We're the first to survive the dragon's breath. A ballad must be made, of our luck and the time mist.'

Matho cocked a questioning eye at Zithia. She said, 'A friend told me.'

*

At dinner the next night Zithia, modestly attired in becoming layers, displayed a pink snapper on a cloisonne platter. Matho's favourite fish. A medley of Zithia's dried mushrooms had been cooked, then presented with sprouts she'd been growing on the cabin window ledge. The table was beautifully laid. Matho took in a flowered tree made of jade, with silver wire trunk and branches. Black candy-floss fruit was set out for dessert. The captain was suspicious. 'To what do we owe this feast?'

'Must there be a reason?' Gracefully pouring a cup of wine.

Serving the meal, Zithia listened attentively to Matho's day and told little jokes to make the men laugh. After the second goblet of wine, Himilco played knucklebones with Kylyn and Geirroor. Sectioning chewing-gum plums, Zithia offered some to Matho.

'What month was your eighth child born in?' Slowly, she tilted her head forward. 'I've forgotten.'

'My little princess...' Matho reminisced over the fruit, and halfway through a game of Egyptian Hounds and Jackals. He announced tonelessly, 'I'm playing unusually well tonight.'

'And your eldest son, tell me of the time...'

'You're being obvious.'

Her smile dropped, 'Surely not.'

'What do you want, widow Melia?'

She lowered her eyes, 'Matho, let me choose the place where next we stop for water.' He was silent. Zithia gripped the edge of the table and raised burning eyes. 'Then, when the water-party goes ashore, I wish to join it, with Olondin.'

Matho collected the game-sticks into a bundle and let them fall. 'Why?'

'A whim?' But he only gave Zithia a quizzical look. So, pausing, 'I had a dream.'

Matho grimaced, 'The time-honoured last resort of women,' he continued in a lower tone, 'and priests.'

Zithia's eyes opened fractionally. 'Please, indulge me.'

'Indeed I shall.' Matho moved a man. 'And as you have what you want, you may now play well!'

She turned pink but, after a hard-played game, Zithia managed to lose without Matho being any the wiser.

*

Soon they approached the point closest to Atlantis' ruins. Rummaging through her medicine chest, Zithia found a herb to assist hiding her flight. She could fly alone these days, though not well and not long. On the deck, she looked eastwards, visualising the fabled black roadway leading to Atlantis. Zithia recited:

"With Atlantis to my left; Atlantis to my right.

I pray you, God, give my soul flight."

She began to see micro flashes of vision. Fuzzy. Black and white. Then parts fragmented into colour. Zithia breathed out, slowly. As though cool air had cleared mist, she saw it true.

In a temple, Galen's ritual voice boomed. 'Leave me.' The priests he'd been teaching disappeared, while Galen cloaked his soul.

'I'll see through your eyes and you'll never even know.'

In trance, the high priest closed his eyes. Opening them again, he saw Atlantis and was in seventh heaven.

Zithia moved along on a storm-cleared black roadway. She could almost feel the turquoise liquid touch her skin. Lopsided columns, dotted with coral, lay where they had fallen. On a broken wall, a cracked monarch butterfly flew. Jade letters beneath it proclaimed: *"This emblem of our great culture unites our divided land, by still migrating from Atlantis to Atlantis."*

Zithia floated through the ancient debris. A pyramid, avenues. Reeling with wonder, she gazed up at an ibis, still balanced, atop the corner of a ruined temple. A cat, in tawny marble sat tall among large displaced stones. A leaning archway made from gold-flecked alabaster glowed at her. Passing under it, she tried to touch the elaborate gold panel. There was one on each side of the portal.

Zithia's psychic energy activated a mechanism. A recording told the sea:

" Braeden. Before you lies a maze built from the rubble left after our ancient cities were lost from Greater Atlantis. Enjoy all that's left of our best.

"A thousand years ago, our beloved Atlantis was a far greater continent than now and well populated. When our island was joined to the noble land nearest us, all was Atlantis. With majestic parks, huge farms. The eastern coast held our cities.

"They rose, flourished, and then were gone. They're but memories. We ever mourn the souls lost, when the world shifted and our cities crumbled into the sea. Even now you can hear the echoes of the thunder, the thunder that was heard the day our land was sundered. The coast cries our loss to the world; roars a warning.

"The land that was eons ago Atlantis, is beloved of Atlantians in every way. Only when the world is civilised once more, shall we allow it to be truly repopulated. Not before. Larger Atlantis will then be reborn at its full glory. A phoenix rising from ancient ashes.

"For now, Atlantis in its new shape, an island paradise, goes on. "

Gliding on, Zithia searched for the maze. Only sand remained. Regardless, she'd never felt so high. Heart racing, Zithia's mind fought with her flooding joy.

'Control… control… or I'll be whisked away.'

Juddering, the Phoenician ship changed course, and she was torn away. Also pulled away, Galen cursed Zithia's inability. Back in his body, he didn't move awhile, letting his Atlantis experience wash over him. Then he gave thanks.

*

Back on board the ship Zithia beheld a golden ribbon running through the water. Beginning at sunken Atlantis, the current rushed shoreward. Tracking the ribbon, Zithia sent a message to the captain and the vessel turned. When they neared the shore, she lost the current. But a scarlet flamingo appeared, gliding in a warm shaft of light, across the ship's prow and onwards to an inlet.

Two dinghies were lowered and separated. Rowed by Matho, Zithia and Kylyn rounded some trees. A bevy of radiant flamingos floated, before a small peninsular. Matho rowed between unmoving birds, wading or standing one-legged in the shallows. The captain dragged the skip behind him, the bottom scraping on yellow sand and dark silt. When the water was knee-high, Zithia could wait no longer. Pulling off her decorative red silk slippers, worn especially to honour this occasion, she dropped into the water. Connection was instant. Carrying Kylyn through dreaming scarlet clouds to the shore, she felt herself to be in another land. Another time.

The trees here were thrice the height and girth of those nearby. Looking closely, Zithia saw broken marble columns caught among ancient branches. Younger trees had grown around more stonework. Observing a piece of wall, in black marble, tears flooded Zithia's eyes. Here was the other half of the huge monarch butterfly she'd seen when she'd astral travelled to the ruins of Atlantis. The place was a shrine.

Putting Kylyn down, Zithia kneeled and placed her hand flat against the silt, the sand. And lost herself in communion, at one with the glorious past. She watched the tidal wave, caused by the fall of Atlantis, rushing over the then-old trees, the columns borne like toothpicks on the crest of the wave. To her dismay, the vision faded.

The very earth itself was from dead Atlantis. Without looking at the captain she said, 'Do you know what you see?'

'This is no true proof. These relics could be from any civilisation.'

'They're from Atlantis!' She pressed her hand again to the earth. 'Does anyone live in this area?'

'You could walk for weeks and still be alone.' Wistfully, Zithia looked around, then at Kylyn. Matho added, 'It's no place to bring up a child.'

Zithia sighed deeply and stood. Going to brush her grubby hand, she discovered minute yellow stars clung there among the dark earth. 'Surely...'

'There is no one, and there is war. Would you be caught here alone?'

Zithia was back in the present world. She pressed Kylyn's hand to the sand, and then showed him the galaxy on his own palm. Barefoot, they wandered about touching giant debris in alabaster, marbles, quartz and shining stone.

Eventually they came to rest on an overturned apricot quartz pedestal, made as a base for a colossus of a statue. Lying there attended by somnolent, scarlet decorations, ghostly images echoed around Zithia and Kylyn.

Far too soon, Matho called, 'The water's loaded. We leave.'

Slowly Zithia moved, saying to Kylyn, 'Darling, we'll collect some earth.' Digging a hole beside a root-bound marble cornice, Zithia poured soil from her cupped hand into three oilskin pouches. Tying their drawstrings she told Kylyn, 'One for you, one for me and one for...'

'Papa.'

'Yes; papa would love this place.' The third bag was for Torim.

Walking back to their vessel, Kylyn fell behind Zithia, gathering alabaster pebbles. He ran to his mama with them. Startled, one bird became airborne, which sent the family hovering. In a rippling wave, the scarlet circle slowly rose until the whole flock was surfing the wind.

*

While the next weeks melted into each other, Matho seldom forgot to tease Zithia regarding Atlantis. The ship made good time, only two and a half months had passed. The coastline was a plethora of projections and deep indentations, creating a fringed effect to shoreline. Myriad islands kept the lookout busy on the way to the most northern port.

Long ago, Kylyn's face had lost its sharp lines. Zithia frowned; her skirt and blouse were tight. Fighting PMS, she reflected grouchily: *"With trekking, the weight will soon come off."*

Sitting on deck, Zithia pushed silk thread through a thin quill needle. This was the last needlework stitch to be copied from her much prized sampler-bag. She now had a duplicate bag. Matho joined her, his eyes piercing her. 'Olondin has been telling me about his papa.' The miniature silver sheers, in her lap, fell the ground. Matho retrieved it. 'He's very proud of his father.'

Zithia looked hard at her stitching. 'His father was a hero, a fighter.'

'Was?'

'You'll think me weak. I couldn't bring myself to tell Olondin that his father was dead.' Looking at Matho, she lightly brushed the side of her nose. 'Now that Olondin is used to his papa being gone, it will be easier to break the news.'

'Easier on whom?'

She put a steady hand out for her scissors. 'We soon disembark. What say you of my chosen port?'

'It's not to your taste.'

Gripping the scissors tightly. 'It's quiet, therefore eminently suitable.' She planned to go immediately inland, to a more isolated community.

'When you get bored, consider the Greek peninsula. It's full of weak women, like you.'

Smiling, Zithia's tone deepened considerably. 'I'll never leave the sweet land that guards Atlantis.'

At Matho's wrist were rose marble pebbles he'd drilled and put on leather string. 'Then you must come to the Mediterranean, for there Atlantis lies.'

She blushed. 'What of the evidence we saw among the flamingoes?'

'There was ancient wreckage. As I told you then, from what, I know not!'

'Or won't admit.' Pointing to his bracelet, she rushed on. 'Not only did the island Atlantis lie off this coast, this very land was once ancient Atlantis.' He simply laughed. 'Yet, I stay!' She flushed again, this time at her indiscretion.

'And I say you'll find life dreary here. And hard. So, I'm sending you to a kinsman who'll see you well provisioned for your farmer's life.'

*

Buffeted by wind, the ship rounded an island full of puffins, grapevines and warm-climates trees. The great ocean-river which Matho had been riding in since the trip began, wandered landward here to touch this island with succoring warmth. Matho headed for a port sheltering behind the island. Simultaneously a Viking vessel came from round the north side of the island, piled high with walrus ivory, white furs and ambergris collected from unknown beaches.

Between a pair of pregnant cliffs was broad grassland, intersected by wooden tracks. On the cliffs stood Phoenician dwellings with sails billowing from the rooftops. Tiled mosaics of ocean scenes totally covered the front of each house, and then continued down onto the rock cliff immediately below.

Zithia looked away from a bright swordfish scene, when a geyser erupted on a rocky plateau beside the deep harbour. One after another fountains gushed in a rough zigzag line, progressively taking the eye up onto the pebble beach. Haze also spurted from a dozen holes in the wide velvet-green field. Not haze, fire. As Zithia looked, twenty enormous longhouses de-camouflaged.

In a dry dock, barnacles were being scrubbed from boats, a relatively easy task as the hulls had previously been coated with hot lanolin. Sailors freshened the eyes on their ships, to help them see the way home more clearly. Near the water, compressed cakes of annatto were transformed into saffron yellow. Likewise, vats of purple were being examined for colour, ready for the same moulds used in manufacturing Tyrian purple. A group was laying a thin roadway with lanolined timber. Each street and track was arranged with total randomness.

Matho said, 'Our next landfall is in a curving line from here. Lower Iberia, land of olive groves and grain. The great ocean river flows at ten to twelve knots all the way home. So the pineapples will still be fresh when we reach the Old Nile. '

Possessions already on shore, at Matho's kinsman's longhouse, Kylyn and Zithia walked down the gangplank. Both wore Viking clothes, Zithia's hair still hidden by a straw coloured hood. Above the happy shouts of farewell, Matho gave a parting shot. 'Atlantis is ours.'

With only a backward wave of a hand, Zithia retorted, 'Never, it's ours!'

chapter 21

All became secondary to the war. No love, no ambition, no revenge was allowed to take precedence. Yet another temple was being vacated; the army couldn't hold the barbarians. Galen was among those who helped the small city evacuate. A human tidal wave broke upon the surrounding forests, rivers and plains. The temple was ten miles from the coast and it was decided to take the infirm and elderly to the sea, where canoes awaited them. The weather tore at the refugees. Thunder rolled.

The barbarians had sent a column to cut off those making for the ocean. At a large plain, about a mile from the coast, a flyer suddenly appeared to Galen. Pointing to where the invaders closed on them, the flyer indicated one hour. The high priest looked around: *"We won't make it."*

Here the sea had fought the river and won, for the ground was sand not mud. The water wasn't quite ankle deep. The main party was almost across the wetland, when the barbarians' shrieks were audible.

As usual Grandmaster Ming Ue was enclosed in his rubber-lined litter, his young wife walking beside it. Ming Ue beckoned to Galen, and they conversed briefly. At the conclusion, Galen bowed low to the lightning-summoner. Then Ming Ue handed the high priest one of his twin sons, a child who wore gold trinkets.

Ming Ue's wife looked worn. Fushen was a delicate beauty, with almond shaped eyes and magnificent silk black hair. She was almost six feet tall; only a pure Atlantian was good enough for a lightning-summoner. Ming Ue said, 'I slow you down. You must go ahead with the boys. Galen will provide me with more bearers, so that I can catch up.'

Fushen bowed her head.

Hugging the second boy, Ming Ue checked the child still wore his rubber-soled shoes. Putting a child-sized replica of his own hat upon the toddler's head, Ming Ue gave the child to a bearer. The lightning-summoner kissed Fushen softly on the forehead.

When Fushen had disappeared among the crowd, Ming Ue put on his hat and alighted. He peered through the viewing panel in the latex shell upon his head. Looking at the last of the crowd Ming Ue impassively issued an order. Stunned, the head-bearer went down on one knee, asking for the order to be repeated. The message was unaltered, his master's face determined.

The bearer called to his fellows, while Ming Ue returned to his chair. There were two hollow poles in the litter, lying under the poles used to carry the chair. From these, they took long golden rods and fitted them together, making up eight short poles. And anchored these five feet from each other, with a strand of gold wire joining them at the top. This done he bade the bearers leave. They sprinted away, herding stragglers before them, and galvanising the tired with a renewed sense of urgency.

Once the sodden riverbank was deserted, Ming Ue walked to the glistening antenna straining in the wind above him. Cape over one arm, the lightning-summoner was bare headed. He strode from pole to pole rousing nearby lighting, using his cape as a bullfighter does, to goad the bull and protect the man. Ming Ue's movements between the rods were exact and graceful. The clouds around the riverbank threatened. With each thunderclap Ming Ue twirled his cape up over his head, until the lightning had abated. Seeing the barbarians run across the sand, Ming Ue touched each vibrating rod in turn. His dance stopped where the wire descended from the top of the two middle poles into the water.

The hoard drew close. Here was a madman. The jagged clouds above them were trading electric daggers. An opera was in its final act. Dressed only in his silk kilt, Ming Ue put his bare feet into water. Flinging the cape skywards, Ming Ue faced the mob and quickly circled the wires twice with his hands.

Twelve lightning bolts raced to connect with the antenna. Marveling, the lightning-summoner reflected: *"Never before have I called so much power."* Those bolts that missed the poles shook the ground in angry disappointment. In abrupt shadowless daylight, Ming Ue died.

His body arched, suspended between the wires, and continued to call the white energy. The storm of lightning, in its joy, lashed wildly at Ming Ue and his gold until over a hundred lightning strikes occurred within a forty-foot radius.

With lightning rushing to greet the barbarians, not only sulphur made their guts wrench. That most feared God, the God of lightning, was among them. Sheets of power forked across the ground, felling dozens of the pure race. Repeatedly, the riverbed exploded and sprayed molten sand. Dripping glass sculptures remained and pressure waves threw barbarians into the glowing glass pools. Where some lay stuck, in death or dying.

The false day reached the refugees, the sky pulsing green. From the safety of the hillside they saw it all, with deafening thunder rocking them. Dodging lightning bolts, the barbarians ran when they could, to slide into super-hot streams of glass where their flesh seared so completely that bare bones were exposed among living tissue. There was screaming at newly blackened limbs and sizzling holes within a shoulder or thigh, created by actual lightning strikes. And then more astral screams as the black shadows of the underworld chased and fell upon the freshly dead. Only a handful survived. It was another mist-night.

*

Tancah. Ten ships comprising another fleet had landed. Gold. Mounds of gold were being turned into ingots for shipment to the Far World.

The gangplanks were sunk in the pink sand by the tread of disembarking warriors.

The scarred pyramids were towers with large stone tablets standing on top. Not very wide, with ladder-like stairs, each had an almost sheer drop at the back. Saplings burst forth in unexpected places among the ruins.

The seventh ship to dock was grander than the others. Its occupants always liked to be seventh, from superstition. Rhaim, the commander-in-chief hurried to meet these new arrivals. They were the main reason he'd come back to Tancah. After all he didn't want their leader to take offence. In black clothing with wide purple edging, the thirteen glided down the gangplank. Weary soldiers made hasty signs in the group's direction, while dropping their eyes. Even with a close trimmed moustache, the outlines of the first face were a death mask. Udo, the leader. Tall, white haired and eyes robin's-egg blue. The whole group was from similar moulds.

Not on the land yet, Udo glanced at Tancah. A connoisseur, he breathed deeply of the destruction. Then he put a foot hard on the sand and dogs began to howl. A flock of monarch butterflies, resting on the way to their wintering ground, filled the air. Raising his hand to the sky, Udo cut a swath through the gossamer wings. The lovelies rained down among the pyramids, while the coven roared with laughter.

Invisible to everyone, a watcher hovered over the beach within sight of the ships. As one, the black garbed group turned to look at him, eyes burning. Languidly Udo said, 'Kill.'

Two men vacated their flesh so utterly that their bodies fell to the ground. Their spirits were shadow hounds. Instantly the temple flyer telepathed the sight to his temple, then spirit claws were on him. Dying screams filled the heads of other flyers.

The murdered watcher's body, seated in the temple chamber, spasmed and went limp. A high priest wiped the corpse's brow, 'Where is the other?'

Simultaneously, Udo's face was in the room, hanging in mid-space. Gloating, he disappeared. Then he was back on the beachfront. 'Find the other watcher.'

The two dark hounds pounced forward, but Udo's snarl sent them scurrying into their bodies. He believed in sharing and signalled a fresh pair.

Over her shoulder, the temple watcher saw the two pursuers high in the air. Demon wolves, they plummeted down at her. Too eager, one missed her by a moment. His companion slashed at the watcher's head. The girl's thinking patterns were reduced to phrases. Slithers of her essence hung on the demon's claws, which were licked clean. She flew jerkily, slower, and they sprang on her. Within temple walls her body shuddered, then sighed into death.

*

The warlocks seemed bred to track watchers, snuffling their scent on the ether. Many died that year, even though they now astral travelled in pairs. For the first time in known history, people were afraid to fly.

*

The night Udo arrived, Rhaim joined the lead warlock in his tent. Entering, the Commander-in-Chief said, 'Well met, Lord of warlocks.'

'Great general.' His voice courtly, Udo poured Rhaim a drink. 'It was a pity my coven wasn't with the first fleet a month ago, but my brother attends the new king and required my assistance.'

Rhaim grunted, thinking: *"If the new king wasn't so enamoured of warlocks you wouldn't be here."*

'I find it strange that you didn't tell the old king about mist-night or the beheaded magician.'

'At the time, I didn't think it overly important.' His thoughts whispered: *"Typical of a warlock, interfering from the day he arrives."* 'We took back gold enough.'

'Now that my coven is here, I expect we'll double that.'

'Warlocks tend to make the soldiers overconfident.'

'Don't you mean, confident.'

Their mouths smiled. 'I need you to concentrate on the jungle fighters. They seem invisible.'

'Like the two flyers, spying on your camp, were!'

'In truth,' crows-feet crinkled the corners of Rhaim's eyes, 'I shall sleep easier at night, now you're here.' Udo faced Rhaim. 'The rats we fight call themselves the descendants of Atlantis. And they name several races in our world as Atlantian tribes.'

Udo, 'We, the invincible, what do they have to say of us?'

'Until recently; nothing.'

Udo waited.

Rhaim. 'Then a captive, a scribe, cursed us with a name. The thirteenth tribe.' Rhaim opened a blood-smeared scroll, written in his native tongue. 'A copy of one of their texts.'

The warlock took it, moving his lips while he read silently.

"The thirteenth tribe was well favoured in countenance. Blond to white-haired, with pale skin and piercing blue eyes; they looked upon the world with arrogant disdain. They wished to rule their brother tribes, plus the savage world. This tribe did kill Atlantis. Atlantis! For power. We curse their very name."

His hand rubbing the scroll, Udo could feel the truth of it, in it. 'The features are definitely of our race.' Beneath Udo's closed eyelids, his eyes moved rapidly. 'Our own legends speak about our noble ancestors being usurped from their rightful place. We were leaders in fabled Atlantis!' He glowered at the tent wall. 'Atlantis should've accepted our superiority, their thirteenth tribe's right to power. The world was ours!'

Rhaim just watched the warlock coldly.

Within Udo's heart, loathing sprang. 'And here we fight the descendants of the Atlantians, who robbed us of our heritage. Our supremacy!' He snapped at Rhaim. 'Why haven't you obtained one of their magicians?'

'They take poison before we can interrogate them.'

'Then stop them! And have the next captured librarian brought to me. Until I investigate further, tell no one of this addition to our myths.'

Breathing more easily, Rhaim grinned after he'd turned to leave the tent. Udo now bore sole responsibility for this worrying knowledge.

Alone, Udo stretched his legs out and clasped his hands behind his head. 'We've searched so long for our stolen history. Atlantis!' He reminisced about his last visit to the sacred grove, in his homeland. Going there for advice about the campaign, from the equally sacred white horse. The horse was in direct contact with God, its whinnies interpreted by priests. His message:

"Great truth awaits you. A secret with a double edge."

'Hmm, the double edge must the timing of the release of this knowledge.' His eyes became slits. 'I need a sign. Our Atlantian roots will keep, until I get a sign.'

His face glowed. The army would raise him on their shoulders the day he announced their birthright. 'We'll crush those who stood against us at Atlantis. We'll take our rightful place, over them, once more.'

Meanwhile, to the purity laws. Now knowing his race's Atlantian antecedents, these laws were all the more important. Eager to start, Udo told a warlock, 'Have the officers' concubines attend me.' The man prepared to leave. 'There are also captive children who may conform to our blood rules. Bring them.'

The group assembled outside the warlock's tent was fair-haired and/ or blue-eyed. Walking in front of the women Udo said, 'No.' Several times. The ladies were pulled from the line. Similarly, he took a brown-eyed boy gently by the hand and put him to one side.

In his incense-filled tent, Udo appraised the remaining little ones: *"It's so hard to tell about children."* He set a hanging incense burner swinging slowly. 'Watch.' Minutes later, Udo clicked his fingers. Dreamy eyes were on him. 'Sleep!'

Several children fell unconscious at his feet. Udo brought a handkerchief to his nose, regarding those standing. 'Impure!' He shouted. 'Guards, dispose of the rejects publicly.'

*

A week later a report came that a librarian had been taken. Sitting on a campstool, Udo rubbed his hands together. Two soldiers dragged a man in, holding the captive under the arms. The warlock watched the head loll to one side. Blank faced, he stood and felt the neck for a pulse.

Static sizzled. Advancing far too close to the soldiers for their comfort, the warlock raised his chin which was at an angle. 'What is this?'

Sweating profusely, 'Noble one, the captive you wanted to see.'

The warlock sat down, steepling his fingers. 'Obviously my instructions weren't precise enough.' His voice was a monotone. 'When I said I wanted a librarian, I meant a live one.' Lifting his eyebrows momentarily. 'Or did you expect me to hold a seance?'

chapter 22

Himilco presented Matho's letter to his kinsman. Already bemused by the variety of goods delivered to his home, the Viking read the note, mouthing out the words. *"Ernough, care for this lady as you would a niece of my wife. She'll need sturdy stock, plus all things for an inland life."*

Ernough's orchard was situated within the bounds of three hot-water geysers. That afternoon, beneath lavender clouds, Zithia and Kylyn wandered among stone fruit and citrus trees, munching apples. A striking variety of chickens scrabbled under the trees, all of whose ancestors were from the Dragon-Land. During their stay, Zithia buzzed with horticultural questions, the answers to which became monologues as Ernough spoke on his favourite topic.

Doing the rounds of the village, over the next days, Ernough haggled hard. Many were leaving with the last of the ships, so every day was market day. Accompanying Ernough, Zithia's rich blonde hair played in the light. It was a thousand crinkles, due to voyage-long plaiting.

In the main warehouse, the owner asked, 'Where are you going?'

Zithia had only decided, exactly where, that morning. Not wishing to be specific, she hesitated. Ernough said, 'Inland.'

Zithia, 'Far inland.'

The merchant, 'Far inland? A kinswoman of yours?'

Stung by an innuendo Zithia didn't understand, Ernough nodded, 'A distant kinswoman.' He winked at Zithia, unseen by the merchant. 'Far, yes.' He knew that the merchant had mistaken Zithia's original statement, yet he bridled and let the mistake rest. 'Roaming.'

'Well, then, there are cauldrons and axes, one coated with chromium so it never rusts, from the Dragon-Land. Skins of olive oil. None of these far inland.' He was creating a pile. 'Paper, good for trading...' an expensive bundle. Ernough shot Zithia a pensive look, but she merely smiled. 'Warm cloth, Wei Yi had to go to Iberia by water-arrow.' He put a bamboo container on the counter. 'The south people who ordered these didn't show.'

Ernough, 'Probably had other things on their minds.'

'Like surviving the season, yes, which leaves your kinswoman with cashmere. A large jumper, scarf and wrap.'

The emperor of wools. Zithia stroked a vest tenderly, letting out a rapt sigh. Thereafter, it took hours for Ernough to haggle the price down sufficiently and pay for it with Zithia's gold.

They were on a ridge high above the village, at the lookout for the port. Smiling at the guide for her travelling party and an old woman, named Katerah, Zithia went to the longhouse. A pair of antique mammoth tusks curled from floor to roof, at either side of the door. Kylyn, withdrawn after the news of his father's death, shadowed Zithia.

Inside, browsing, Zithia wanted the polar bear pelt on the wall near the fire opening.

'Lobster?' asked the proprietor, penning blue dye into a carved swirl on a walrus tusk. Zithia shook her head. 'What about you, little man?' Kylyn hid his face in Zithia's skirts. The corn-haired woman smirked.

'This day,' Zithia said, raising her chin. 'my son learned of his papa's death, in battle.'

'He died well?'

'So the prince reported; and quickly.'

The proprietor bent down to Kylyn, 'Little man, be proud! Your papa has been called to his ancestors in glory.' Kylyn drained of colour. 'Even now he smiles down on you.' She slapped his back so heartily that Kylyn skipped forward a pace, then the lady handed him a half-pint of maize beer.

After Kylyn had taken a few sips, Zithia took the mug from him and drank, while Kylyn showed the woman a fine little chipmunk made of reddish wood. Having bought it from the villager with whom they now journeyed, Zithia had slept with it under her pillow until the dreams came. Visions of a happy place, of long springs and short winters. Plus a good people. She and Kylyn could be content there and go unnoticed among them. She had wondered, was Atlantis at their core? 'We go inland to start a new life.'

'Then you're in luck.' The Viking went to a corner and blew dust off the pile there. 'My husband's nieces came out of mourning a year ago.' Inspecting Zithia. 'They're about your size.'

White skirts, blouses, dresses. 'You'll need them all.' The Viking then riffled through another pile, finally grunting as she held up a fistful of large filmy white triangles of cloth, deeply edged with lace. 'And you'll be wanting some of these.' She grimaced, but she was right, the shawls would soften the plain blouses. Outside, Katerah smacked her lips together regretfully after the last piece of lobster and rose to meet Zithia.

Zithia, 'Some of these are for you, too, Katerah.' Holding a white skirt over the new, loose dress Katerah wore. Zithia had outfitted Katerah after they met last night. Accidentally brushing the woman's protruding hipbone, Zithia frowned, 'Cousin dearest, you're all skin and bone.' She handed Katerah a gold coin, 'Buy a beer and more lobster. We need to get some flesh on you.'

Katerah had her copy of a bond agreement at her breast, in an oilskin cover. It stated that after three years of working for Zithia she'd be free. Bought as a slave from a Phoenician, Katerah was now only bonded, with an agreement that she couldn't be sold again. Realising a companion would add to her general background, Zithia had decided to buy Katerah when the seven slaves had passed her in the street. Katerah was chosen because, when Zithia looked out of the corner of her eyes, Katerah's aura seemed all pink bubbles and pastels. Zithia had named them cousins, by marriage, for easier explanation in the life they were entering.

Together, the women packed the clothes onto the pony caravan. Twenty ponies, most owned by the five hired guards, stood with light two-wheeled trolleys attached behind each, to lessen the weight of ponies' loads. Further, Zithia had insisted on four extra ponies, knowing that every single bag or container held a small satchel of gold. Dust, coins, nuggets, exchanged with Matho for her emeralds two days before reaching port.

Finishing his lobster the guide, Norbert, took a drink from his flask. The men, including Ernough, checked the fully laden ponies. Ernough had surprised Zithia this morning with his two ponies, packed with dried fruit. 'If the barbarians get here, I want my ponies safe. They're family. When it's secure again, I'll send for them.' He touched a pack. 'For their board and keep. Fresh oranges, dried apricots, garlic...'

Norbert, 'The sheep and goats may bring wild cats.' To each pony, a sheep or goat was tethered.

Seth positioned the puppies' hutch to where they had a view. 'Do you think you bought sufficient breeding stock for the widow's future husband, Ernough?' In FallsFire only men could own property.

Looking seaward, Zithia observed a single water arrow speed toward the horizon. It carried a message to Matho. No sooner had Zithia arranged to go inland with Norbert than she discovered an obstacle. Her letter read:

"Matho, greetings. Deciding to settle in a small community, I find myself in difficulty. To be accepted, I must have a death certificate for my husband. Unfortunately, due to the war, I'm unable to provide this. Perhaps, when you get to the Far World, you'll see a way to help me. I offer a seal of friendship to your wife."

Zithia had stuck her last two emeralds in thick wax blobs on the parchment, and then sealed the letter in a pouch, sending it with another kinsman of Matho.

The, mostly Viking, port was now a miniature. Blinking against the sun's blaze, Zithia heard the lap of water near her. Startled, her eyes flew open. Before her was ocean. The harbour village was gone, the land no more. Zithia sensed, thinking: *"No catastrophe... the sea simply... rises and rises!"* This future image, dazzlingly clear, deserted her again. She was glad. Before her, the busy port, the hectic settlement. *"Not for a few thousand years."* Zithia shrugged. 'Nothing lasts.'

She took off her hood and cloak. Unbeknown to her, Norbert who'd been looking past her at the scene when she removed her hood, turned away in embarrassment.

Caught by his sudden movement Zithia looked his way and beheld the forest. Vast tracts of ruby mixed with yellow, outlined by green firs. Was this, too, a vision? No. Fall, glorious autumn had begun.

The pony train descended through the veil of trees towering fourteen storeys high. A forest fire dripped, molten, from the branches, trying to set the ground alight. Scarlet birds exploded from a leaking canopy, to become visible against a pine.

Silvery aspens occasionally disrupted the blaze. Taking Kylyn's hands, Zithia spun them both in circles upon and within ruby confetti. Seth whistled his pausing, bemused hound on which were scattered tiny wrens, forking through the wine purple debris. Norbert picked hollow black trumpets of mushrooms.

During an afternoon break, Seth's dog suddenly caught a scent. First he stiffened to point out the prey, and then he was off like a runner in a race. They saw the tall dog's tail progress through grass and leaves. Halfway up a hill, he stopped and launched himself into digging beneath a tree. When he'd brought his black treasure to the surface, he bit into it then rubbed himself ecstatically in its pieces, rolling over and over again.

On the hound's return, everyone prepared to give him a wide birth. Then Zithia caught a whiff. Truffles. Black truffles. Soon she and Kylyn were digging wherever the hound pointed. No-one else seemed overly impressed. After persuading Seth to spend a couple of hours there, Zithia collected three small sacks of truffles. After, she tossed one truffle each to the hound and her two puppies; all of whom delighted in these treats-cum-toys.

In the evening, separate fires were set for men and women, as none of them was related. Likewise, they ate a little apart, with Kylyn crossing between. After finishing dinner, Zithia joined Seth briefly, holding a knobbly black truffle up, 'These would trade well on the coast.' Seth shrugged and lit his pipe. Zithia threw a truffle to Seth's dog and more to the puppies.

*

Reaching a lake, Kylyn dismounted a pony and played while the women gathered wide meadow mushrooms for dinner, plus shrimp mushrooms from the tree line. At a cranberry bog, Zithia inhaled vanilla perfume from a wand of tiny cream hooded orchids. Chewing on a stem, Seth declared a break for the night.

Before dusk, Norbert set an entire mushroom colony next to Kylyn's sleeping bag. Darkness fell, glueing the boy's attention to the luminous orange-yellow lanterns. Having set, watched and reset mushrooms smoking on sticks above the fire, as Norbert had shown her, Zithia attempted her first milking in the night's livestock barricade. The results were given to the guards, who'd be lookouts through the night. Finally Zithia lay down, she was so very tired these days. She'd not been long asleep when Kylyn brushed Zithia's face with a waxy flower, very much the shape of Matho's pipe.

Zithia's eyes were closed tight. 'What... is it Olondin?' He tickled her again. 'I'm tired darling, go back to sleep.' She rolled over, patted his arm, and cranked open one eye. 'My, your lanterns are very bright.' The eye rolled shut while her hand felt around for a jacket, and then threw it over the tableau. The lights still blazed. Opening both eyes, Zithia gasped.

A rose-yellow curtain flamed in the sky, with lower wings in blue. A hundred feet tall. Red shades banded the top, as the incandescent drapes folded and fluted to a rhythmic chorus of honeyed, whispering voices. Zithia hugged Kylyn. 'Olondin, it's angels... singing.'

Norbert commented, 'The lights are late this season. Early autumn is usually full of them.'

'They'll be with us for the rest of the journey.' Seth threw a stick for his dog; he'd been playing this game some time. 'Late winter displays are better. With the snow reflecting...'

The dog ran off once more, giving an occasional bark. From far afield the stick was thrown back. Out of the shadows and into a full moon's light stepped a nine-foot, hair-covered, being who waved at Seth. The dog cavorted back to his owner and the stick. Now three were in the game, with the hound alternately taking the stick to near the great being and waiting for him to throw it back in Seth's direction. Until a piercing series of hooting coughs announced goodnight from the big-foot.

Seth, 'We see him sometimes when we're in this region.'

*

A week further on, among a stand of huge, untidy white pines, nodding yellow-frilled orchids bunched next to cream cousins. With the Northern lights appearing through cracks in the foliage, the party slept. From deep unconsciousness Zithia sat bolt upright, peering into the dark. Someone was staring at her intently. A noise. Sheep and goats bleated disquiet, their three guards awoke.

Seth had been on his feet for several minutes. Cocking his head, he caught the stray sounds. A frog leapt, its squarish spots blazing alarm on golden skin. Lighting the always-ready extra fires, he passed Zithia. 'Wolves. Only two.'

Making her fire blaze up, Zithia stood astride Kylyn's sleeping form, dagger drawn. Then came the predators' calls.

Seth braced himself. 'Wolverines!' Zithia saw the guards fix arrows to stretched bows.

Chocolate fur, with lighter bands, emerged into sight on the opposite side of the campsite. Face taut, Seth hastily crossed to the quivering ponies and took out a haunch of dried venison. He threw the haunch far into moving ferns, and then fitted an arrow to his own bow.

Hackles rising, Zithia balanced the blunt side of a quarter-moon machete flush against her left arm, which protected her chest. Simultaneously, she raised her dagger hand, up and back. Her focus flicked between the two directions of attack.

Sniffing the tantalising goat scents, a male wolverine came into full view. He sat on his haunches. Seth and the mammal bared their teeth, while the wolverine counted the odds on his agile forefingers. Meanwhile, the female found the venison and called, stating the haunch's size. Her mate backed off.

When the night resumed its usual noises, Seth crossed to the women's fire. Both he and Zithia relaxed their holds on their weapons. The guards were already drinking.

Seth drank from his flask. 'Never cross wolverines. They mate for life. If you kill one, the partner tracks you down.' He handed his flask to Zithia. 'We'll all feel safer with more than the usual lookout tonight. Wake me for the pre-dawn watch.' Zithia took a gulp and sat, alert, next to her son.

She considered the wolverines. 'Soul mates.' She took another quick swig, thinking: *"This life I wanted my soul mate, children by my soul mate, and reading. Now I've only Kylyn."*

'Damn Galen!' But her heart reminded… *"Dazzling Galen… he used himself as bait to draw the barbarians away from us… he fought Eten for me."*
'Yet now he tracks us.' She couldn't make sense of him. Nor herself. Her heart mourned for the love still haunting her. She whispered, 'We've both made mistakes.' Tears started, Zithia tossed her hair. 'Next life, Galen can simply come to earth by himself!'

*

After breakfast the next day Zithia approached Norbert. 'Who should I see when I get to FallsFire?'

Norbert didn't look at her. Thinking *"He must be a little deaf,"* Zithia had noticed this before, she moved into his line of sight, repeating the question. His eyes sharply met the ground.

A lopsided grin formed on Seth's face. His eyes sparkled at Katerah. 'Your cousin wastes her time… while she speaks bareheaded. To Norbert, it's a great immodesty.'

Goggling, Katerah helped Zithia roll blankets. Zithia snorted abruptly, clapped on her hood and strode over to Norbert. 'Who do I see in FallsFire?'

'The patriarch and the priest. You'll...' Zithia withdrew her hood, brushing off a ruby leaf. Norbert's eyes inspected the tree. She slammed the hood on her head. '...speak to their wives first and they'll introduce you. That's the proper way.'

Sweetly, 'Thank you Norbert.'

Kicking a golden rod of blossoms, Zithia took the blankets to the ponies. Handing a roll to Seth, she whispered a Phoenician swear word Kylyn had been taught on the ship. It produced the first full-smile that Seth hadn't bestowed upon his hound.

Opening two packs, Zithia found the gauze mourning shawls she had bought and laughed. She threw the manta ray shape over her hair. Longer than it was deep, the tasseled edges hung down her back in three points. Seth said, 'It's worn further back on the head.'

'As if I'd trust your advice.'

'You can. And you'll like FallsFire; the winters aren't too long or deep to an unbearable degree. Plus they see the most northern lights of any district, so the name.'

Handing a veil to Katerah, Zithia shoved dry pine needles through gauze and hair. She did, however, push the whole thing back toward the top of her head, before doing so. Ranks of blonde waves now added charm to the lace edging.

*

Soon they were in a rolling landscape where the river wandered gently around shallow valleys and elk sauntered. Beside the road white berry-eyes, with black pupils, seemed to follow the party. Zithia picked an over-wide mushroom, on a sturdy long stem, and shaded herself from the sun.

The track thickened. From an adjoining lane, a wagon drawn approached. In the three-sided affair a man stood, controlling the four painted horses. Immediately Kylyn hid behind his mama. Despite herself, Zithia let out a short laugh at the gigantic child's toy, harnessed to monsters. Norbert waved, 'Jericho.'

The wagon stopped. 'How was the harbour trip?' Norbert patted the mares. Surprising Zithia and Kylyn, neither horse bit Norbert's arm through to the muscle.

'Good, God willing. This is the widow Melia and family.'

'Get aboard. I'll take you into the village.'

Norbert stood up next to Jericho, and Katerah stepped aboard.

Zithia cupped Kylyn's chin in her hand, 'Remember how we conquered the rapids?' Hesitantly he nodded. 'This is nothing!'

She stepped into the wagon and held out her hand for her son. He clambered aboard. Norbert's four ponies followed behind of their own accord. Seth, the guards and the other laden ponies also followed; the hound decided on a break and lay on the floor of the backless dray. Watching one of the huge solid wheels, Zithia and Kylyn's colour gradually returned.

Waist-high rice filled the slopes. Katerah murmured, 'But rice only grows in flooded flat land.'

'It's dry rice,' said Norbert. 'Our patriarchs discovered it while on roaming…' Jericho coughed, looking pointedly at him; Norbert went on hastily '…when roaming in the vast inland.'

A girl herded redheaded and ring-necked ducks. Painted horses and khaki sheep, with white rumps, grazed in paddocks. Fields still held the stubble of last year's crops, to keep the soil from blowing away in big winds and washing away in storms. Long-tethered goats nibbled unwanted berry brambles. The houses, so far screened from view, were set in clearings. Close to every dwelling was a thick patch of forest.

When passing the one such thicket of paperbark birch and fragrant firs, a man appeared holding large, soft leaves. These he briskly dropped. Ignoring the man, Jericho thumped a bag of tree resin. 'I'm going to the lacquer maker.'

Norbert looked straight ahead. The unknown man sidestepped into the shrubbery.

Zithia and Katerah raised their eyebrows at each other. A feud perhaps? Then, simultaneously, they understood the scene they'd witnessed and rocked with silent mirth. Zithia leaned over to Katerah. 'I was rather hoping for a toilet out of the rain.'

They both heard the unintentional tragedy in her tone, and tears welled-up in their smiling eyes.

*

Finally, from a hilltop, the party looked down upon the village dotted with trees a-shimmer in bright blue leaves. Log houses, mostly two storeyed, with glowing windows in the eastern walls, sat in an acre of grass. Mounted upon each sloping roof was a long bench made of rough-bent wood. These were reached by wide wooden circular stairways. Each low-backed pew faced the same direction. Similarly, in every crooked chimney's shadow a moss-padded miniature cabin was protected from the wind. Blue jays flashed into tiny doorways inspecting their multi-story winter quarters.

Zithia caught her breath. Above blue foliage, set on a peak at the village's end, was a shining gold building, with a gold steeple. 'Our prayer hall.' Said Norbert.

'But your village is wealthy.'

Norbert laughed, 'It's golden pine.'

Everywhere, a rainbow of patchwork quilts was draped for airing over lines, which were propped up by long V-ending kinked poles. Freshly washed blue or mauve sheets brightened the day. With white being the colour of mourning, even off-white was considered an unlucky shade. Bees buzzed between stout rectangular hives and fringed white orchids.

On a roof-bench, a child finished laying out frilly yellow mushrooms next to their purple brothers. 'Chanterelles.' Zithia thought, grinning. Ascending the traditionally circular stairway, rising up the outside of one end of the house, a young woman hung blue nappies over the sunny rails. The central core of the stairs was a smaller tree trunk; all the rails were warped.

Almost at the village centre, Jericho reined in the horses. Eager to be paid, the guards began unloading their ponies onto the baker's wide verandah, beginning with the light attached trolleys. Norbert called for the proprietor, Nathaniel. Soon a gaggle of brightly dressed children came from nowhere to pet Zithia's black-faced ewes and the merino ram with curling horns, while leading them to the fenced paddock out the back. The softness of the mohair goats' fleeces mesmerised them. The herd and the poultry were taken round the large quasi-oval village pond, right next to the bakery, to get there.

The water-wheel for the grinding mill turned in the current. It had dragons carved into the wheel. Widgeons and mute swans hunted a snack among pink flowers that resembled turtleheads. The bakery sat right alongside the pond. A latticework enclosure, on the side verandah, was completely shaded by an insect repellent tree. Another such tree sat at the back of the bakery.

As if by magic, the village green was suddenly awash with children who ignored the stone sundial, the green's usual drawcard, to watch the new animals. Eighteen sandy haired children retreated at a single shrill call home.

The baker's wife, Leah, heavily pregnant, came out with a toddler on her hip. Smiling serenely, she discussed the rent of two rooms with Zithia. Her husband, bringing out a baker's trolley, began transporting the packs into the rooms. These were newly strewn with aromatic sweetflag leaves, and a complicated wreath of pale blue blossoms hung in each. Raspberry tea and a punchy nutcase-coffee appeared, free of charge. Zithia bought a round of barley bread and goat brie cheese for all.

Never again would she find the proprietors as helpful as they were on that first day. Only Zithia managed to drop a package, fussing over it until she saw that the red marble pestle and the abacus were undamaged. Leah, having observed this incident, watched the transport of all the other packs with a very sharp eye for breakage. Her pale pink bodice was high necked and, like all apparel, covered her elbows. More interesting to Zithia, Leah wore a cap upon her light hair, not a veil; the cap delighted the eye with a treble layer of frills fringing it.

Soon Seth had his agreed price, weighed on his own scales, and everyone adjourned to the shop through an open triple door. A batch of rice cakes was coming out of the oven. In the room's centre was a stone hearth with a triangular chimney made of small river stones. Within its three round openings lay pink milkweed flowers. Light shone through two large windows, made of many very thick clear-quartz rocks split in half.

Sacks of grain stood aloof, as did bags of duck-down. Nuts encroached on flour in tiers of uneven shelves lining the rounded log walls. Various dried cherries filled sacks. A guard bought berry and may-apple preserves, ignoring the spiced honeycomb and honeys. Every cask of salt was snatched up by the trekkers, who then ambled over to the woodworker's shop where meads were brewed.

Except for one burly man, who dallied behind. He spoke in a whisper to Nathaniel, and then dithered around the shop while the baker removed a swan's down shawl from the wall. 'We've one in pink,' murmured Nathaniel. Staggering backwards, the guard's hands trembled. While he was still gulping hard, Nathaniel said quickly, 'No, no, obviously not.' Wrapping the cream shawl, Nathaniel reassured in an undertone, 'She'll love it.'

Leah asked Zithia, 'Pickled heart-of-fiddler-fern? It's a delicacy.'

Plaits of smoked or dried mushrooms hung from the wall; golden plugs, a stewing- steak fungus. Together with look-alike sections of stained glass windows, each made from the insect attractors of giant pitcher plants. The wide payment-counter was littered with a vase of unusual violets and a single snowball mushroom three feet in diameter. Strangely, pairs of fur slippers and sheepskin booties hung from a wall.

Beside a quartz side-window was a doorway from which wafted cold air. Walking through a waxed strip-curtain, Zithia stood in front of two cold-room counters. Sheep and goat cheeses abounded on one, camemberts, yogurt, fruit feta, ricotta, parmesan and even whey.

On the other counter were meats and fish. A turkey, a green winged duck and a dappled goose hung behind the counter, just in front of a rustic close-lattice-work wall of hammerwood. This room was on its own small verandah. Outside the hammerwood wall were two dripping hessian curtains a foot apart, water-fed by the mill's wheel. The air in the room was cooled by the evaporation of water off the wet curtains.

Coming into the frigid area, Nathaniel wiped his hands of flour saying, 'Fresh killed yesterday. Cravings! Right now, Leah must have turkey.' He looked fondly at his wife. 'And we can barely keep up with her need of rutabagas.'

'Just as well you got the prize, at this year's harvest festival, for growing the biggest, then.' Leah cooed with justifiable wifely pride.

Smoked caribou and salmon were also displayed. Nathaniel advised, 'In two days it's the holy day. Prized meat portions go early.' He then went back to the bakery and handed one of the village gossips a warm loaf of wheat bread.

That woman's eyes lingered on Zithia. 'Yeast, casserole bearberries and...' she winked prodigiously at Nathaniel, 'gooseberry tea leaves. Oh, I'm sure I've forgotten something.' She smiled brightly. 'Never mind, I can always come back.'

'No doubt about that.' Muttered a gaunt man biting into a raw burdock root. With a definite hmpf, the woman left.

Sharpening his knife on a hard razor-strop fungus, the man watched her speed up to another woman in the street. Bending closer together than usual, they nattered rapidly, flicking looks back at the bakery. The gaunt man called loudly, 'Nathaniel you'd better bake more bread. I predict an extraordinarily high demand today.'

Zithia handed over a little gold, which Leah weighed, for briny plover eggs and a cauliflower of a mushroom. While picking up her other foods from the counter, Leah's toddler reached for a white violet. Leah picked it from the vase 'Your last one today,' she stated, dipping it in honey, she popped it in the girl's mouth. Smiling, Leah gave one to Kylyn.

*

On the verandah Zithia, Katerah and Kylyn devoured fluffy bread and musk ox butter. Zithia eagerly awaited appointments with the patriarch and the priest. Sewing, following directions on her copy of the sample bag, she was watched by the single wide village street. Large numbers of ladies tramped the dust that afternoon, often pregnant.

In front of the shop, somewhat along and on the opposite side of the road, the woodworker sat on a walnut burl, talking to the guards over mugs of ale, while the guards tried on boots from a bentwood basket. Brush brooms slept against the wall. An adolescent hung a wind-whirler, which burred contentedly. A square bee hive, in dappled sun on the verandah, seemed to be trying to shrug off its top and its winter coat of carpet moss. After being thoroughly observed, Zithia's party was drawn to the honeyed scent from this shop.

There, in pride of place were small boxes of maple sugar. Standing beside an open trapdoor, Zithia picked up a little churn. A youth half-appeared from the cellar and grabbed a barrel of syrup from a stack. 'It's for creaming maple syrup.'

Picking out a small cask of maple mead, Zithia heard a cough, 'I think you meant to choose the cider, widow...'

'Melia.'

The woodworker's eldest son eyed her speculatively. Seth called from the doorway, 'The lady was getting that for me.' He'd stayed outside, at ease, with the woodworker.

'Oh, of course;' then calling back, 'Seth, don't you want the larger size?'

'I do indeed, boy.'

Zithia, demurely, 'And I'll have a small cider, plus some maple toffee. Which honey do you recommend?'

'Genko honey, from the miraculous pollen of a Dragon-Land tree growing on only one farm in FallsFire. We've the hiving rights, while it's vacant.'

Seth was beside her, 'Pity there isn't any left. I just bought the last tubs.'

'Salt and Genko honey. It must be good.' She turned to Seth, smiling. 'Seth, next time you're this way, drop in.' Then she lowered her voice so only he could hear, having just seen something. 'And, please, make sure, very sure, you're near a village in...' Zithia looked harder behind him, 'three month's time. ' He began to laugh. 'Don't, there's a dark shadow at your back;' Seth's lips lost the smile, 'it worries me.' It was in fact a cloud, and a death, if he were alone then.

Seth stopped laughing. He gave Zithia a look which was hard to read. Finally, with deepening gravity, 'I'll bring truffles for you next year.'

Smiling, immediately Zithia turned her attention to a shelf. Loudly, to the woodworker, 'Oh, all your beeswax candles. I'll have them.'

'We make tree-oil candles too, you'll never find animal fat used here,' the eldest son declared with some pride.

'Tree-oil candles? Ah, there they are.' A shelf, on the other side of the shop, held columns of many thicknesses. Some scented. 'Yes, I'll buy those too. I like a lot of light.' She paused, admiring. 'I didn't know there was a candle-tree.'

The woodworker, Finias, slapped Seth on the back in goodbye while saying, 'Another Dragon-Land tree on old Benjamin's property. He was a patriarch. One of my sons will deliver your goods to the bakery.' He knew his sons were dying to see Nathanial.

A younger son piped up, 'We could get some fresh bread.'

Almost directly opposite the wood-mead shop was a general store. An antler chandelier hung before one of two open terrace-windows. A fine glove was nailed to the shop-front. Inside, an elderly woman and her adult daughter were rummaging among central shelves of medicinal herbs. Perfectly tipped were their small noses, with matching pale pink lips. They hunted out spicebush for a child's fever. Seizing the mayapple rhizomes for warts, they cackled, while listing those in greatest need of the remedy.

A potter worked his wheel in the back corner, in front of a large clear-quartz window. A curtain, between himself and the shop, was half drawn back. His wife, Esalen, weighed minerals for a customer. 'With this you'll get a lot more colours from your mushrooms.'

The customer, 'To think I promised my eighth grandson sheets of two colours. The dyeing will take forever.'

'You spoil that child.' Esalen's pinched tone wasn't quite the commendation it might've been.

As Zithia's party wandered, all eyes were inexorably drawn to them. Katerah moved among sheets of silver, cloth and hessian. The guards, having chosen gloves, salt and sleeveless sheepskin jackets, now had the potter's attention. Gold was weighed and the scales watched most carefully by all the participants. The perfectly-nosed women hustled along to inspect a cap which was all lace, no cloth in it. Pulling their mouths into ugly shapes, they tutted over the showy use of that expensive stuff. 'And they call that modest!' added Lilac.

Her daughter, Briony, sniffed, attracting attention. 'It isn't as if it's even good lace.'

'Tawdry,' half-whispered Lilac.

Esalen's customer, instead of picking up her parcel, started examining semi- transparent hides, ready to be framed, for winter. She murmured, 'With a rose coloured wash it will be perfect for an inner window cover …'

Esalen, in a perfect frippery of a pale green cap, with triple lace dangling down over her shoulders, 'I prefer natural hide for both inner and outer covers. It allows more light to enter.'

Zithia and Katerah listened while inspecting the medicines; and the sour-lipped mother and daughter quietly moved toward the crockery, the better to observe. The potter, his watery eyes focusing on Zithia, approached. She frowned over wintergreen leaves. 'For brewing a painkilling tea, lady. And we've berry leaves for different ailments.' His fingertips brushed together. 'My name's Brice, a humble shopkeeper, trying to eke out a small livelihood here in FallsFire.'

Smiling. 'The widow Melia. Thank you, I've already bought sufficient berry leaves.'

Brice's eyebrows bobbed up and down. A hush had fallen. The potter gave a weak smile, 'You've… already? bought berry leaves?'

'Mmm. Teas. I love the taste of blueberry.'

The pallid freckled elder, Lilac smirked at her daughter, saying in a raised voice, 'Nathaniel put out some very fine teas today.'

Brice's colour changed. 'I assure you, widow Melia, that you'll always find the best leaves in my shop.' He washed his hands at her, his voice rising. 'The baker! He seeks to rob me of my modest profit. As I've told everyone, berry leaves are medicine! And so mine, alone, to sell.' This was an annual quarrel between the two proprietors starting afresh each leaf-picking time.

Lilac, 'I'll have some honey please, Brice.'

He turned a funny shade. 'Yes, it has wonderful antiseptic powers. A true medicine against burns scars and ulcerated wounds.'

Briony, who had true prettiness when not spoiled by her expression, added sarcastically, 'Plus a cure for skin infections,' then chuckling, 'young Jane should buy a lot more.' She smiled, 'Oh and, Brice, your salt's a great preservative.'

Another matron, dressed in mauve, entered the premises, oblivious to Zithia's presence. Observing, Brice pouted hastily back to his clay-covered wheel. 'I'll take the baker to a sitting of the patriarchs. See if I don't.' He snapped the curtain along its track, secluding him from the shop, then sat at the wheel with his back to them all.

Zithia picked up bundles of raspberry and strawberry leaves. Kylyn raked his hands through a box of black walnut husks, while looking at colour swatches at the fronts of different mushrooms and roots. A thick-sided pot standing on the highest shelf attracted Zithia. Made from pale clay, it was decorated with wavy green and blue vertical strokes.

The woman who had arrived last, Grace, collected all the writing paper and took it to the counter. The potter's wheel whirred with greater industry. Esalen named the price. Grace put a hand on her hip. 'That's much more than the price a month ago.'

'We're awaiting a new shipment.'

'And so the price goes up?'

Esalen's eyes turned glacial. 'We're expecting another shipment.'

Grace slammed half the paper on to the counter. Through the curtain, Brice saw Grace head towards the newly re-priced ink. The hum of the wheel ceased; an outer door was quietly closed.

Zithia made a pile of small sheets of silver, a lacy cap, plates and bowls. She picked up some lanolin soap. A small woman next to Zithia murmured, 'You can always trust Brice's jugs of lanolin my dear. Also his lanolin ointments.'

Zithia replaced the soap and ignored the face cream.

Esalen held up jasper firelighters, years old. 'It gets very damp here. These will be a great help during your first winter.' Esalen named the price that had so permanently put the locals off.

'I'll take them.' Zithia then pointed. 'Plus I'll have that chamber pot.'

Looking up fleetingly, from her delicious calculations, Esalen's words became clipped. 'That, widow Melia, is my husband's finest vase.'

Zithia smiled, very sweetly. 'Then I shall buy that fine vase.'

Scowling at the inks, a laugh escaped Grace's mouth before she gasped it into a coughing fit. Woodenly, Esalen glowered at Zithia. Yet, it was an expensive piece. Pride and profit fought across her face. More coughs burst forth.

'Certainly!' Esalen marked Zithia down for the first bad turn available, then had a fresh thought, and began that turn, 'Delivery is extra.'

*

Not two hours later, Zithia knocked on the priest's door. Kylyn was still complaining about the taste of the weekly dose of Dragon-Land herb, taken to thicken the blood so that the first winter would be much easier to bear. A fellow passenger on Matho's ship had told Zithia its use. As well, he'd described the uses of the other medicines in Zithia's kit from the dragon-Lands. Secretly, she'd written all down. 'Shh,' she rasped out one last time, roughly pulling Kylyn's shirt straight, before she knocked again demurely.

The priest's sister had presented the invitation, when they were outside the general store. Zithia's party entered a private garden dominated by vines, with brown curved pipes for flowers. Sitting beneath a black aspen tree, the priest's wife, Jessamy, spoke of quilting and assets. Taron, the priest, interjected occasionally with queries about faith and intentions. Finally Jessamy put out her hand. 'Your letter of widowhood?'

'On its way, my lady. Raiders burned my village, forcing me to leave before I received it.'

'Oh.' Jessamy's hand fluttered back into her lap.

'I'm hoping to take religious instruction immediately.'

'But the death certificate…'

'I wish my son to learn to read your holy language.'

'You think he has the ability?'

Bridling, Zithia hurriedly dropped her eyes. 'He reads the Phoenician alphabet.'

Taron, the priest, took a scroll from a table, giving it to Kylyn. Hearing Kylyn's letters, Taron asked in Phoenician, 'Have you any questions, Kylyn?

Kylyn, hesitantly, 'Are there brown bears as well as black bears in the valley?' Seth had been morbidly instructive about both kinds.

'Neither!' Taron settled himself. 'Now, about bears and history. The priest who started our community was a mystic. One day, in the Far World, he received a message from God. It was time to return to this land.'

'Return?' Zithia leaned forward.

'Yes, our distant ancestors came from this land. They called it, the First Land.'

Longing to ask questions, Zithia daren't. Jessamy proceeded to work a wool tapestry on a freestanding frame. She called 'Children, the legend.' A dozen children thronged around their papa, who recited:

"*Arriving on this coast the first settlers followed the river, not knowing where best to go. While the mystic dozed before the campfire, an angel appeared saying, 'There are brother bears in this area, twins. Beings with great heart. One, Han, has a sickness. Sheng suffers because he can't stop Han's pain.*

Go you to the brothers, they're goodly beings. Provide food and a daily soothing draft for Han. In exchange, Sheng will keep other bears out of these valleys. So long as kindness to animals remains your creed.'

"*Instantly the priest made the medicine according to the angel's instructions. At the same time others hunted deer. Arriving at nearby caves, the two bears waited for them. Without hesitation the priest approached. 'Han and Sheng, God has heard your prayers and sent me to help.'*

"*The others laid chunks of venison on the ground. The priest himself placed the bowl of potion before Han, who lapped it up. The priest told Sheng, 'I'll bring food and pain killers twice daily.'*

"*For three years, this was done until Han died. These years had been pain-free and contented. Sheng mourned for five days before he allowed the community to bury Han. The priest carried on daily visits to Sheng, walking for hours each day by his side. A year later, gentle Sheng went to God of a broken heart.*

"*Yet even in death the bears remembered their friends and continued to guard these valleys. They'd told the priest, after Han had died, that they'd do so as long as the village was kind to all animals it came into contact with.*

"*In the season when bears seek to claim new territory, the villagers watched the twins' transparent forms frighten off intruders. Wolves, bears, wolverines, big cats. Sometimes the priest checked the boundaries with them. To this day the brothers roam and the valley is free of predators.*"

Taron paused, looking at Kylyn. 'Widow Melia, your son has proved to me that he can learn. If the patriarchs authorise it, until your certificate of widowhood arrives, you're our welcome guests.' He tapped Kylyn under the chin. 'And this young man needs brothers. Soon you'll be free to marry again.'

Zithia looked at her feet. 'In my husband's world, a woman must mourn three years.'

'Here mourning finishes after one year. Remarriage occurs within the next.' He was solemn. 'My wife will instruct you and your cousin on our laws, twice weekly.'

chapter 23

The temples assigned their mystic priests to the battlefields. Galen rode a demon horse that, after capture, had been returned to its natural temperament. Cheering broke out when he rode by. Patting the horse's head, Galen dismounted and saw Eten exit her litter, at a distance.

Each moved among the broken warriors, fallen on the field. And among pieces of men. Looking for those still alive, whose temperature the magicians would drop with a touch. The coldness keeping many here, who would've expired before treatment was at hand.

Walking between little knots of people, Galen checked the pulse at a soldier's neck. Alive. So he rested two fingers in the hollow at the base of the man's throat, thinking with his mind and soul: *"Cool."* Staying still until he determined that the body was at the best survival temperature. The patient raised his own hand and tried to touch the silvering-gold envelope which was a foot larger, in every sense, than Galen's body, and thus eclipsed his physical form. Failing to make contact with a solid mass, the man passed his hand through this astral form, a groggily puzzled look upon his face. Smiling, Galen straightened up.

Immediately to the high priest's left, another fallen one lay, his hand almost touching Galen's patient's fingers. The second warrior rested on a bed of mauve flowers, with a fox sitting beside him. The fox laid his head upon this man's leg. Galen didn't stop.

Scanning further, Galen passed a lady fighter in her prime who leaned against a lush and beautifully gnarled juniper tree. Many patients later, a child ran across Galen's path and into the arms of another warrior, lying upon his side. Galen heard an astral melody, pulling at the strings of his soul; there for one fallen hero. That wonder of sound which created joy; Galen had to tear himself away, for fear of being lost, too great awhile, to the desire to be home.

A woman in floaty pink beckoned Galen to yet another man. When the magician priest approached, she said, 'Please, it really isn't the right time.'

Galen knelt, checked the pulse. It was thready, just there. He lowered the body temperature dramatically, while calling to a physician, 'This one; now!'

"A chunky fortyish warrior woman gave a death rattle, and seemingly breathed out a young imp of a wench. Barely materialised, wearing a soft skimpy dress, she flexed young-again fingers with pleasure. Tossing her glossy mane, the woman's light tread took her to her own tunnel of light.

Much, much later Galen paused to watch, a couple of dozen people round a grizzled soldier. Laughter, greetings and goodbyes filled the air. Eten, on the battlefield beyond the group, made to join Galen. 'Make way.' She demanded; striding out, and walking straight through any of the party in her path. 'Did everyone he's ever known have to come?' Eten muttered to herself. As her body passed through different spirits, one of them frowned at Eten's back, saying, 'Honestly.'

"When Eten was near, Galen spoke, 'Envy him, Eten'

Acidly, 'Never!'

She turned as a blue-white light tunneled from the sky to the grizzled soldier.

Galen took a deep breath, 'I do.'

A third of the happy crowd disappeared into the light with the man. The others simply faded away. The living had come, while half dozing, to farewell their friend.

Both high priests looked upon the battlefield, where tens of tunnels of light appeared and collected; where fragments of beloved scenes sprang up; as did loved ones plus friends, human and animal. Where dense patches of dark occurred, engulfing some of the newly dead. Mostly, it was barbarians who were dragged, thus, down through the earth.

Eten turned back to Galen, 'You've something for me.'

He handed her a letter from Franklin. It read:

"These are interesting times, high priestess Eten. Times when the brotherhood of priests must draw together. It's my wish that you and Lord Galen do more than simply ignore each other, for the common good. I expect you to act accordingly, else… may you always live in interesting times."

Folding the letter, Eten scowled.

'My reaction exactly.' Galen paused, then looked levelly at Eten. 'The enemy of my enemy… is my friend.'

'So we're commanded.' Eten bowed briefly. 'Till war's end!'

Slowly Galen also inclined his head, his eyes never leaving her face.

'Till war's end.'

Galen signalled for his horse, and remounted. 'Join me at the fighting, two days from here. Sharing our knowledge may double our strength against the warlock there.'

'Agreed,' she smiled. 'I have some understanding of warlocks.'

'I've never doubted it.' Galen spurred his horse on.

*

A day later, in her tent Eten bled herself in preparation for combat, before offering up the liquid to the dark side. On a high hill, lounging behind a stage, Eten waited for her entrance. The commander, Jiang Li, would signal when the high priestess's presence was required.

Supervising the conflict, the battle scar on General Jiang Li's cheekbone became more prominent. Vitality radiated from him.

Reading, Eten yawned yet again. They called for her. The high priestess stood and took up her staff. She nodded to Minuet, who threw four balls onto the stage. Purple smoke filled the air, to reveal Eten. Two jaguar-masked attendants displayed banners of power.

The high priestess surveyed the mayhem, which had paused. In a carrying voice Eten spoke a charm. Gesturing at a barbarian officer, she focused. About to loose an arrow, he did so. Into his commander's back. Eten turned to another officer, who fell on a friend's sword. With these deaths, the high priestess seemed to grow taller. Her eyes sought another victim; a captain spurred his horse in front of a battalion leader. The blood in the older barbarian's veins suddenly wanted to see the sun. All the surfaces of his body transformed into a bloody pulp. Bellowing in anger, the captain started a charge.

Eten was luminescent, her blood lust peaking. Seeing her thus, Jiang Li's expression was rapt. The high priestess heard the slightest whiz, and then was jerked by two punches. She looked down. A barbed arrow had pierced her breast, another her upper leg. Cloaked by the lead warlock, a single rider had circled the hill and shot while at full gallop, across his horse. In that moment he was visible. The barbarians cheered.

Eten took hold of the shaft fixed in her thigh. Clamping her teeth together, she pulled it free and brandished the arrow above her head. 'Your first missile lies in my heart, yet I live.' The missile had veered left.

In the masses, the warlock's eyes locked onto Eten's. He throat went

314

tight, when like met like. While a jagged smile developed, the warlock visualised the poison now eating at Eten, and she saw it.

Though the warlock had revealed himself, Galen remained under the awning of his tent. Waiting. Galen focused power and the bolt was thrown. Simultaneously, the darkness within Eten reached out.

Opening his distorting lips, the warlock exhaled a pall of smoke in a gush. The barbarians around him backed away. Galen and Eten increased their spell. Flames spouted from his nostrils igniting his moustache, above blackened lips. This was a first for the barbarians. They believed the warlocks were invincible, like their race.

With serpentine contortions, the warlock screamed chants for control. Falling to his knees, his hands clutched at roasting eyes. Then he sank back on his haunches, a charred skeleton within his robes.

Meantime, Jiang Li strode toward Eten's dais, wrath now in his smoky eyes. A charging horseman passed in front of the general, the rider already sliding down behind the horse's flank for an arrow shot. Mid-slide, Jiang Li had pulled the archer from his mount.

Without taking his eyes off Eten, the general placed one hand on the back of the rider's head and one on his chin. A single harsh snap and Jiang Li stepped over the body.

Eten automatically sucked in her stomach. 'My general.'

At the same instant, purple smoke filled the air and she fell backwards into the physician's arms. Jiang Li was by Eten's side. 'Save her.' He laid rough cotton over her. 'Carry the Lady Eten to my tent.'

He addressed a priestess with similar hair to Eten's. 'Dress as your mistress. Now.'

Soon the six foot tall general led the trembling woman to a picnic-table, which was arranged in full view of the enemy. Seating the impostor, he poured them both drinks from a golden jug and then watched the battle.

Meantime, Galen saw another leader. Concentrating on the invader's adam's apple, Galen pulled his thumb and forefinger together, until cartilage splintered. Galen felt for the next recipient of his attentions. A commander thrust the banner declaring his rank, out of his lieutenant's arms. But Galen had him and his movements became jerky. He raised his dagger, snagging it down his jugular vein. Now, no officer sat upon horse nor was seen on hill. The commander-of-region slipped into background trees.

315

Eten lay unmoving. A priest had already lowered her body temperate by two degrees. This trick, discovered in the Alps, increased coagulation of wounds and slowed the body's over-reacting defences. They cut away Eten's padded gown, then her silk underdress. The padding had slowed the arrows and the silk had wound around the arrowheads, preventing the spread of poison.

Blood-clotting tree fiber had been packed in the wounds. It should've sealed them, but blood saturated the packing. 'Sorcery,' pronounced the physician.

Galen entered, followed by Minuet. Spreading his hands over Eten's wounds, he intoned. The blood continued to flow. He tried other incantations, nothing. 'Probably the only one to know the antidote was the warlock.'

Because the poison had caused fever, Galen lowered Eten's temperature again. 'I can do nothing else. I must return to the other wounded.'

An hour later, unconscious, Eten began to writhe in pain. Rearranging the creases on his forehead, the physician looked into a reed box of painkillers. 'No, no, no! These won't cure a headache.' He shoved the container at his assistant. 'Get me a fresh frog, then release these.'

The youth returned with a single belligerent amphibian. The frog's irregular white stripes on a red background flashed. Carefully, the physician stroked the frog's back with a fluff-tipped stick. Putting this into water, he put a few drops between Eten's lips.

It was after dusk and the battle had been won when Jiang Li appeared. The wounds had bled her white. 'She looks to die.'

'There was an Atlantian way to help the Lady Eten. Except, a step has been lost in time.' He cleared his throat. 'I think I know the lost piece. At the least, it'll give her time.'

Jiang Li looked at him, considering hard. 'She was instrumental in killing a warlock today. Do it.'

Soon Eten's body icy lay on the ground, newly opened coconuts on the table above her. A healer inserted a mangrove-root straw in her vein. The other end of the straw was in the coconut. Eten's blood was gradually bulked up by coconut juice.

The high priestess awoke with a start and sprang up. The tent was dim. Irritated by a soft crooning, Eten peered to see who was there. An old woman, Koss, she'd known years before, with hands clasped. 'You're here then.'

Eten jeered. 'Obviously, you crone.'

Her pebble eyes looked into Eten's. 'I see your disposition hasn't improved since I died.'

Koss grimaced at the grass, her voice nasal. 'I don't know why I had to collect her.'

Eten screwed up her eyes, recognising the poisoner, who walked through the high priestess. 'Don't do that.'

But Koss leaned over a body, more a figurine than flesh.

The physician withdrew from bending over the body. Then Eten saw her own face, and stumbled away. Recovering, the high priestess was aware of a small drip, drip, drip and looked closer. 'I still bleed the living blood.'

Kos stooped for a better inspection. 'Don't worry.' She patted Eten's phantom arm comfortingly. 'That won't last long.'

The poisoner smirked. 'Much unfinished business?'

Eten didn't answer. The high priestess gasped, for her heart had stopped beating. The older woman shrugged, 'Better luck next time.'

'But I almost had it, the power! It was within my grasp.'

'Would've... could've...' Koss tutted. 'Nonsense!' She drawled. 'Without Zithia you had nothing.'

She stalked up to Koss. 'How dare you.'

'What're you going to do, kill me?'

With a clenched astral fist Eten thumped her own breast. Zithia!' She slammed her astral chest once more. 'Zithia.' Her emotions touched her heart like a lightning strike. Instantly, the body on the floor convulsed, and then a second time. Her physical heart jerked into beating and as it resumed its normal rhythm, Eten's body dragged her spirit back within it.

Moving rigid lips, Eten whispered the unspell of the black spell she'd seen in the warlock's mind. The blood stopped dripping.

Koss sulked at the slightly pinker body. 'Me and my big mouth.' Sinking back into the ground, she whined, 'Yes! But how was I to know?'

*

'The long dead hag was only being vindictive,' Eten told herself, time and again. She had been moved to the nearest temple. At the point when she could walk unaided, the high priestess went to a seer. Incognito.

Frankincense scented the air. The fortune-teller sat upon a vicuna pelt. His eyes followed Eten, even though the seer had been blind since birth. Eten looked at a jade bowl. It began to rotate. Min-Jho stopped it.

At her mystic level, few sooth-sayers could read the high priestess easily, therefore she opened wide her soul's lights, until her aura filled half the room. He began, 'Your mother had power... your sister, half sister, beauty... you miss her still.' His gaze darted around the colours. 'She's dead, no she's... you...?'

Undulating, Eten's aura halved its size, hues changing. Only her future was now open to the sight.

Min-Jho began his spiel, 'On earth, in sky and through all tomorrows, nothing is ever certain.'

Eten went white. 'You insult me with that peasant's warning.'

'I hold that only high priests need no such advice.' His eyes began flitting over Eten's aura. 'You're searching! It's the goal of your life to find this ancient... You almost found it before the invasion.' One eyebrow arched. 'Then again, perhaps not.'

Eten's throat felt sandy. 'When? When will I find it?'

Some vision flashed at him. 'Perhaps never; please breathe deeply.' The silence built.

'If she dies, your quest dies.' Eten goggled. 'There is no more.' He tossed a small pink glob on the incense burner. 'You already knew. May I ask how the knowledge came to you?'

Eten growled, 'In a dream.'

'My lady has true dreams.'

Eten stood, looking down her nose. 'No, my lady has nightmares!' She eyed the seer narrowly. 'What else did you see in my past?'

'Nothing, lady. It was too dark.' Eten examined Min-Jho's expressionless face minutely. Finally, she threw a purse on the floor.

*

On Eten's arrival at the next battlefield, she found her tent set up near Jiang Li's. The high priestess and Galen worked together, killing warlocks.

A happy time for Eten. Death all round her, and Jiang Li challenging those invading battalions with a warlock.

One drizzly day, Eten was writing to her old friend, high priest Augustus. 'You will like Jiang Li. He's extremely influential throughout the army. And he has such an exquisite sense of loyalty; he won't even divorce his wife. I'm sure he'll be a great asset to us in the future.'

Smiling, she put down a black ostrich feather pen, a gift from Jiang Li. Marching feet approached the tent. Jiang Li's captain, his brother-in-law, staggered in to Eten's presence. He whispered.

Through gritted teeth she said, 'He was where?'

'Jiang Li was on the next barricade, when he saw an opportunity.' The captain stood straighter. 'He shouted the battle cry "For duty and for family," and put his shoulder to the barricade making it a ram. In a pincer movement, we swept the barbarian officers over the cliff. Jiang Li died, with arrows pinning him to the ram.'

Applying a kerchief to the corner of one eye, Eten watched Jiang Li's body brought from the battlefield and carried into a stone hut.

His corpse was laid in state on two thin trestles. Beating her chest, Eten entered the hut with slowed steps and walked a full circle round the warm corpse. Ending a second circle, she stood looking at his face. Jiang Li had been dressed in his parade uniform, a long, ornate chain of office on his body.

Eten raised heavy, glistening eyes to those in attendance and motioned them away. The door shut. The high priestess leaned close to Jiang Li and ran her fingers down his neck. Without warning, she gripped the chain and pulled Jiang Li's head, then his shoulders, from their resting-place. The general's jaw dropped open in seeming surprise.

'For family and duty?' She barred her teeth, 'Traitor.'

A spasm passed through Eten and she flung the body away from her. Upsetting the trestles, the corpse landed sprawling on the floor. Eten took several hasty steps, throwing herself across Jiang Li's corpse barely before the crowd entered. They observed Eten's back jerk with emotion. When she looked up, there were real tears in her eyes. They weren't to know these were from anger. 'I desired one last embrace, and...' She spread her arms.

She stage-whispered, 'One last kiss my dear,' she brushed her lips across Jiang Li's cheek hissing, ever so softly, 'dead loss!'

*

The corpse slept in state through the night, before burial. In the shadows, a body was prone on the floor: Eten, lying facedown in prayer. Minuet arrived and deposited a basket in front of the high priestess. All of a sudden, the box collapsed and Eten's cane toad leapt to her, burring.

The high priestess raised her head, her chin upon her hand. 'Being prostrate with grief is very wearing.'

She put an arm around Venus, 'Have you a scroll?' Minuet nodded. 'Then write to Jiang Li's home village: *"Uncle, here are the daffodils I promised, from the Far World. The flowers will delight and one bulb, cut up as onion, when served to Jiang Li's widow will provide an interesting killing touch. Fried if you like. A sudden recovery would prove... an anticlimax at this point."* With brightening eyes she addressed Minuet. 'Oh, and send my condolences to the widow with a separate messenger.'

A fortnight after the general's funeral, Eten read:

"My dear niece, there's tragedy in the village. General Jiang Li's wife is now as light as a bird's feather. Burial is tomorrow."

chapter 24

While waiting the days for an appointment with the patriarchs, Zithia inspected properties, guided by the potter's wife. Her great grandfather had been a patriarch and so, apparently, it followed that Esalen should insist on being useful in this matter. Driving a woman's two-pony dray they inspected one farm each morning, and one in the afternoon. All three were adequate, yet Esalen simply didn't hear Zithia whenever she asked to be shown Benjamin's farm. Being delivered to a fourth property, the three ladies alighted and began exploration.

Katerah had been happy with every property and now climbed the wide circular stairs at one end of the farmhouse, glancing back at the others. Kylyn was looking upward, but not at Katerah.

Catching her son's panic, Zithia followed his gawp. A transparent man was descending at the top of the stairs, gazing at the toddler in his arms, not the steps. A third of the way down, he stumbled, over-balancing. Tumbling brokenly down, through Katerah, and down until almost the ground, with the child still in his arms for most of the way. The angles at which their bodies lay, across stairs and rail, were permanent.

Simultaneously Esalen called and beckoned, 'Come in,' having opened the farmhouse door.

Zithia, 'No! This house won't quite do.' Then to Kylyn, 'Darling, don't stare.'

'But it's a good farm.'

'However… it won't do.'

Kylyn still goggled at the spirits. A transparent memory of a tunnel of light pierced the sky nearby, as it had on the deathday, but was ignored by the father and child. 'Kylyn, it's rude to stare,' said Zithia and stood in front of his mesmerised, overwide eyes. Taking his arm, she began to walk back to the dray, blocking Kylyn's line of sight all the way.

'The owners will bring down the price.'

'I'm sure they would.' Zithia got into the dray, making a mental note to pay for a communal cleansing picnic to send the ghosts on their way, once she was settled.

'But you haven't seen...' Esalen came to Zithia, to bring her back.

'I assure you, I've seen enough!' When all were back in the dray, Zithia said, 'Now you'll show me Benjamin's farm.'

'There's no point, the patriarch won't sell to a relative, let alone a stranger.' Silent, they were soon back at the bakery. 'We'll do second viewings of what I've shown you, tomorrow.'

Zithia, 'I've an appointment with the patriarch's wife tomorrow noon.'

'Then that'll give you enough time to decide before you see her.'

Zithia gritted her teeth in a smile.

The next day, around ten, Esalen stormed out of the bakery, leaving Katerah on the verandah catching some sun with Kylyn and the puppies. Racing off, the ponies were happy to have their head, to Benjamin's property, yet startled at the sharp turn into its drive and the slewing stop. There, sitting on the roof bench, Zithia counted the quartz skylights. She'd already been non-plussed by the number and size of the farm's quartz windows. Now twice the number of skylights as well.

The single storeyed farmhouse faced the fast, straight river, from the top of a small, rounded elevation which ran the length of Benjamin's land. A widely spaced line of trees followed the length of the river, in front of the house. They were the back of the dragon, and instantly gave Zithia the same warm feeling that had caused the farm to be positioned just here.

On the right of the house, a very tall barn sat. A narrow island existed in the river, situated between house and barn. Once it had been bridged and Zithia planned to re-bridge. Somewhat after the barn, the river made a languorous curve before straightening on its way again, giving Benjamin an inordinate amount of river frontage. The forest on the other side of the river had already been fully inspected. Zithia had wet skirts from the fording of the river, downstream, to prove it.

Esalen's voice thundered. 'Widow Melia, you've no right to be up there.'

'But I can see it all from here, so clearly.'

'I told you. It's not for sale to you.'

'Did you not ask to buy this farm?'

She'd been guessing, but Esalen's mouth, opening and closing like a landed fish, supported Zithia's assumption.

'Many have asked to buy. It belonged to the patriarch's elder brother, who's been dead sixteen years. The patriarch took it very hard.' Brice had been prime among those wanting the land and had been so importunate, from so early in the patriarch's grief, that he'd only been silenced by a glare from the patriarch scarcely less potent than a punch.

Esalen added, 'There's a shortcut to the patriarch's house. Just go left from here, then the third right, then there's a pleasant ford in the river...' But Zithia had ceased listening, the baker had told her the way and it was all in the opposite direction. Esalen finished with, 'Take your time looking around, the patriarch's wife doesn't count the minutes.'

Watching Esalen drive off, Zithia said aloud, 'That's not what I heard.'

The patriarch's interview was conducted by an elderly wife, Hope, who transacted all family business in the patriarchs' absences. Given Hope's age, she was wife to the older of the two patriarchs. Currently, the patriarchs were... in the country. Looking out of an open window Zithia reflected: *"How much more 'in the country' could they be?"*

Huckleberry cordial sat in a jug on a low table, with mugs. Presenting a basket of plump oranges, plus another of dried segments and orange peel, Zithia began enthusing over Benjamin's forest. Hope's daughter waited for instruction to pour drinks. Zithia had recognised Dragon-Land crab apple trees, was in rapture over a king-steak fungus, and was surprised at the presence of one herb, which she only just stopped herself from naming as a potent aphrodisiac. And yes, it had had signs of being harvested over recent months; another piece of knowledge Zithia kept to herself. Could they discuss sale of the property?

'The patriarch does allow some of the rarer herbs to be harvested, when a villager is in need.'

Abruptly Zithia's eyes were trying to cross, while she thought: *"A need?"* She blinked hard: *"In this community?"* Where almost every house was built for thirty, just in case.

Hope was silent and stoically still. Yet the oranges had truly pleased her.

Frowning, Zithia pushed, 'I'm greatly interested in this farm, for its tea-roses and peonies alone... I've a wall hanging with such flowers on it, and I never hoped to see the real thing,' she added in thought: *"again."* 'Bought from a Dragon-Land trader.'

'And did you buy much from the trader?'

'This and that. I'm fond of Dragon-Land goods.'

'Who isn't?'

Zithia, her mind on the pretty farmhouse, 'I was fortunate; silk sheets, pasta, an acupuncture kit with bamboo needles; gold coated staples for closing wounds and the instrument for removing the staples, arrows that don't rust.'

Hope's daughter had, unbidden, started to lift the jug to fill the mugs. Hope put a restraining hand upon the woman's shoulder. 'I think tea would more refreshing. Green.'

The startled daughter dashed out, returning in record time with a lidded tea-cauldron, tea bowls plus a three legged mug for Hope.

Removing the lid from her own mug, Hope used a long bamboo ladle to pour tea from the cauldron for each lady. She said, 'Esalen will show you around the property, her husband has the fishing rights to the land until it's sold. Tomorrow afternoon I'll view your goods and discuss if the farm is for sale.' Seeing Zithia's total delight, Hope said again, 'If.'

Zithia had been rearranging goods, mainly Dragon-Land, for hours before Hope arrived next day. Without preamble, the patriarch's wife started inspecting, a daughter making a list. A calligraphy set, all that could be seen of the silks, two chromium plated daggers, teapots. The list just kept increasing. Every scroll, the ghost stories seemingly prized, the entire pantry. Bronze cauldrons, the treasured potted jade plant. On and on.

Desperately, Zithia said, 'The jackets are silk-padded, tripling their value. The quilts are the same, better even than eiderdown. The tea leaves are treble the cost of the tea bricks.'

Hope nodded her agreement.

Zithia began unconsciously tapping her foot, and glanced at the plate of gold she'd put out. 'Now gold... the quantity?'

'Coin won't secure this farm, Widow Melia.' Hope looked impassively at Zithia's shoe, Zithia ceased her tapping. 'The patriarch was very attached to his brother and to his work. Did you notice the visual balances Benjamin created, by his placing pairs or threes of trees... Elegance itself.'

'I wondered how they could be so arranged by nature.'

'Benjamin used his feng shui scrolls for all plantings. Have you found the orchid house? Made of quartz? Shaped as the upside-down hull of a boat, over the steep banks of a warm stream running off a hot spring.'

'All feng shui arranged?... orchid house? Hot spring?'

'Yes, yes and yes; and as the patriarch is partial to vanilla, all such pods would remain the patriarch's.'

'Certainly.'

'When the patriarch agreed to sell the farm, it was on condition that the purchase was sufficiently interesting.'

Hope signalled two grown granddaughters, who raised a cloth high. Both hanging onto a top corner, they unfurled an embroidered sheet showing the location of each tree and shrub, naming each. The second granddaughter then beckoned to Leah. While Zithia was still examining the twenty eight forest acres, another cloth unfurled showing herbs, mushrooms, flowers. Hope, 'I believe the patriarch doesn't think I can find a purchase of adequate import.'

Looking from one to the other, Zithia mulled. 'The last rug, circular with birds carved into it.' She unveiled two open boxes, crammed full. 'Fireworks!' Marvelous coloured explosions had been painted on the outside of the various packets.

Then, moving between the sheet-maps to inspect more closely, Zithia's foot crushed a small truffle the puppies had been playing with earlier.

Hope, 'Also, the truffles.'

Two sacks of truffles were set out; Zithia didn't mention the last, smaller bag. 'Truffles are worth their weight in gold, my lady.'

'Only in the Far World.' Then Hope gambled. 'I'd like the chess set, checkers board, the backgammon…' Zithia jerked in surprise. Hope, 'No Dragon-Land shop would be without its land's games. The patriarch adores board games.'

Zithia hadn't put any games out for the sale. Pulling the games from their place, Hope opened each up in turn.

'We're a very small household, my lady, and the nights are long.'

'The patriarch is devoted to backgammon.'

'I shall have a copy of each game made for him, in his favourite woods.'

'The patriarch has always wanted a chess set of this fineness. I'll have copies made for you.'

Very slowly, Zithia nodded.

Hope pointed to the second map-cloth. 'All his long life Benjamin was an avid collector. Orchids, mushrooms, roses,' smiling, 'and whereas other farms have five forest acres to one cleared acre, Benjamin had seven to one. Plus his river is one of the best fishing tracts in the valley.'

'And you won't take gold.' Zithia said to herself, biting her bottom lip. She went into the second room, returning, 'There are these,' She held a carved green lacquer box. Opening it, she revealed a red box within, then a yellow, then a black, then a box with all colours in it. Hope's face lit up. 'a sack of dried apricots… Far World fruits, incense, plus all the Dragon-Land seeds.' She'd hoped to keep the seeds. Absentmindedly, Zithia picked up a child's toy and put a finger into each end of a paper finger-trap.

She looked at Hope, who simply smiled encouragement. Pushing her trapped fingers towards each other, the paper un-stretched and Zithia flipped it off her fingers. Landing on a table, the trap rolled and dropped to the floor, inadvertently brushing a little bamboo box, which opened so instantly that a paper dragon popped out three feet, and bounced wildly hither and yon. Hope pointed to both and the daughter added them to the list. Zithia hardly noticed, as her face puckered at the dragon's swaying body. 'A moment please.'

She sank to her knees next to the bed and started pulling things out. Half disappearing beneath it, Zithia muttered sharply to herself, 'Goodness… will she leave me any Dragon-Land prize.' Bumping of things together could be heard. 'Any?' Then another bump, with 'Ouch!' Zithia emerged again, rubbing the back of her head with one hand, while pushing two cloth satchels to one side. Finally she held up a bamboo container, attempting a smile that was a little tight.

Hope looked into it, holding aloft the jumper. Hope touched it, then sank her fingers into it. 'Cashmere.'

'Wool of the Gods, from the Dragon-Land.' Zithia held up the long scarf, the extensive wrap.

'Where else?' She nodded, then read the characters on the two small bags. 'Widow Melia, the purchase becomes more noteworthy all the time. ….Catuaba and Turnerup; aphrodisiacs!'

'Oh,' Zithia blushed, 'bought with the Dragon-Land lot. When the trader's wife was loath to part with even these few, I felt they'd make noble trade goods one day.'

'Indeed.'

Reddening further, 'See… seeing that these herbal aphrodisiacs are almost legendary…their reputations vastly superior to other …enhancers in the Far World.'

'I'll have them.' Hope stood up, offering her hand; Zithia took it, 'The bargain is sealed.'

All was written up, signed and packed up. The deed was in Zithia's hand by sundown, with the baker and the carpenter as witnesses. The goods gone with Hope.

Before moving in, Zithia and a few women inspected the condition of the buildings. Esalen has insinuated herself into the group. Halfway across the living area were three steps, which led down into the large kitchen. A large rock hearth divided the rooms. Hollows within the main-room's clay floors spread warmth in winter, from the fire in the baked clay oven and stove.

Grace, 'A patriarch brought the design back from the Dragon-Land. In a blizzard, you'll all be sleeping right here.'

"Humming softly, Grace went from the kitchen to one of bedrooms, that stood on either side. All looked at a bed. Esalen volunteered, 'We sell mattresses.'

Grace scoffed, 'Carpet moss in a bag!'

'I fear, due to my limited funds, we shall have to make our own mattresses.' This statement, disbelieved by everyone present, was considered highly fitting by virtually all.

Outside, they came to the meat-smoker. Brown bootlaces of mushrooms had overtaken one side. Grace opened the lid. 'Disgusting!'

The word boomed unexpected from the cavern of a box. Her torso lurched back; children's laughter erupted until glared into silence.

The common grass way and a small stream divided the field from the forest acre known as the 'convenience', which was thirty feet behind the house. Lilies grew on the stream's muddy edges. Two very long planks crossed the narrow brook into the acre which abounded with highly scented trees and shrubs. Dragon-Land lilacs abounded there. After speaking quietly to her returning children, Grace said only, 'The three bee hives are doing well. The fisher-martin house is empty. Widow Melia, you must have these little mammals to keep down the snakes.' The potter's wife went to say something, but Grace continued, 'I know of a reliable pair.'

Beautifully placed trees became secret windows within thin woodland screening the river. Under one of several insect repellent trees dotted around the farm buildings, children were lowering a box that hung suspended there. When it reached head height a youth opened the door. His eyes popped. His expression hushed the others. The boy shut the door with a minimum of movement, frantically signalling for the box to be raised again. Even while the meat-keep was being tied off, a line of disgruntled bees zapped out and chased the children into the river.

Minutes later Esalen stood looking at the bees crawling all over the meat-keep. The priest's sister passed by on the way to the barn, saying in an aside, 'Luckily this isn't the potter's property, or the price would've included a hanging bee hive.' Esalen eyes became slits. Without smiling, Grace thought: *"Sometimes doing one's duty can be intensely satisfying."*

*

Within twenty four hours of opening the front door as her very own, Zithia withstood the welcome wagon of ladies. By tradition they streamed in for two days, with a cornucopia of homemade produce as gifts, all of which must be displayed and none of which may be eaten during the calling days.

Ezekiel and many of his twenty five daughters had been in a flurry of hammering, tidying or baking in preparation for the genteel flood. The carpenter and all his sons continued working on the two bridges joining Zithia's island to the river bank. Ezekiel had been the carver of Zithia's little chipmunk that had brought her to FallsFire. Leah, the baker's wife, had arranged an introduction to the family, after telling Zithia how Ezekiel had had two bad years, a broken arm one winter, pneumonia the next. As a result he couldn't keep his hunting licence, as it wasn't known if he could still kill with the first arrow shot. All that, on top of having only girl children. As both women agreed, the idea of the dowries was enough to make one quake.

The ladies, every lady in FallsFire, came, including one group of sisters only. Leah explained that the family was orphaned four years ago, a canoeing accident on the local lake, an unusually large family of thirty three. 'Nice children, sensible. The older six won't have the time to marry. The boys could help clear your forest clutter. If, um… '

'Perhaps they'll be interested in a trade. Ezekiel will be hunting again soon. I get a quarter of each kill for a year as I'm paying for the examination hunts and the licence.'

Zitha offered the welcomers baker-made treats and breads, fearing to cook for the village. Triple brie was a favoured indulgence. Introducing herself to each family, Zithia was relieved to find that every lady had attached her name to the home-warming gifts. Remembering peoples' names was going to be a lot easier than she'd thought. Still, she, Kylyn and Katerah practised fitting names to faces and farms every evening.

When the priest's sister, Grace, arrived, she brought fresh dried carpet moss.

Zithia, 'Such a welcome gift, as I need to insulate the entire barn and many of my rooms. Having grave doubts the potter has enough moss or animal feed to see me through the winter, I fear I'll have to trespass on the community's goodwill to assist me. There are truffles to barter.' The salmon and truffle open-sandwiches had been disappearing at fast rate. 'And sixteen quartz squares. I found them lying in the forest next to the orchid house.'

Choking on a truffle sandwich, Esalen fairly hissed, 'Widow Melia, I can't believe you're encouraging these good women to deal with you direct! The general store buys the village's excess.'

Zithia, in cool tones, 'Shall we leave it to the ladies, Esalen?' She paused. 'And I'll be buying from you.'

'All my goods cost gold.'

'Of course.'

Verity, who'd been eyeing Zithia's windows, 'We ladies have always had the right to barter our excess amongst ourselves, as you well know Eslaen. And as we do.'

'But,' Esalen spluttered, then rapidly, 'but… but widow Melia has far too much excess.' At once she drew her breath in sharply, at her own faux-pas.

Verity, an affluent far neighbour, spoke with a self-interested tact. 'Your windows, widow Melia, are twice the size of mine. Even this kitchen one.'

'Patriarch Benjamin had a cutting saw that halved all his quartz blocks. Finias possesses it now, in exchange for halving all the prayer hall's quartz windows.'

Esalen was forgotten in this most important of news, and a rush to examine the kitchen's quartz blocks which, had they been in a boat, would've capsized it. It was going to be an industrious time for the village men, enlarging all their wives' windows.

Verity, 'My husband will bring my trade for three quartz blocks.'

Jessamy, the priest's wife, 'It will be one per person.'

Verity, 'Then mine is the biggest block.'

'First come, first choice,' continued Jessamy. She turned to Zithia, 'I'm sure Ezekiel will conduct the trading for you, if you ask Charith.'

Charith graciously inclined her head to the lending of her husband. 'Tomorrow.'

On the morrow, even the squirrels were startled to see how early the women started arriving, with drays and husbands. Naturally, the men stayed outside, trading with Ezekiel while drinking berry cordials. Then they scarpered, after examining the bow Ezekiel was borrowing from Zithia. A Dragon-Land thing, seemingly made inside out, the shape pulling against the natural curve of the wood, so that the arrows went exceptional distances. This, and the fact that Ezekiel had laid out the two forest maps, cost the men an extra hour of the day.

When the eldest of the orphan family arrived, Ezekiel spoke quietly to him, pointing here and there on the map with the bow. A pleasant arrangement soon was reached with Anthony, and gold was the weekly wages. But Zithia had a further commission for Ezekiel, as she'd received the most magnificent floral arrangement as the welcoming gift from the orphaned family, all pansy orchids and fancy violets. Rosanthus, the eldest, when visiting mid-morning had spoken of their plethora of flower plants, so much so their farm was called by all Bloom Farm.

Zithia had found that she couldn't get the flowers out of her mind. They invaded her sleep, dancing before her. And Shiloh, Zithia's next door neighbor, had said that no pansy orchids grew outside Bloom Farm. She must have them. Truly, she must. And the violets. In the morning her need was a compulsion, a deep craving, driving her on. Ezekiel opened the discussion by asking Anthony, 'Which do you like best of venison, haunch or shoulder?' He left a silent moment. 'And if I remember rightly, your streams aren't well stocked with big fish.'

The patriarch's wife, Hope, arrived with her eldest girls and their girls. Quietly to Zitha, 'I hear you've ordered fifteen pairs of foresting gloves and milking stools.'

'Çharith has allowed her older daughters to come here daily to pick my forest produce and generally help with the animals. And a woman's hands must always be protected. Oh, I love the barn, with its walls and roof dotted with quartz windows.'

'Benjamin's animals were his friends. Thus the two mezzanine floors and the wide open stairs; so the stock can move to their favourite spots. Winter can be really boring for the animals. The fowls' nesting boxes, on the wall at the top mezzanine, are a particularly good design.'

After staying the half hour prescribed for a welcoming visit Hope, as all the ladies had assiduously done, left while having a word with Ezekiel as she retired. When the day was at last over, Zithia and Kylyn brought

Ezekiel a very special cooling drink. She'd scoured Benjamin's herbs, her temple memory of herbs and her own medicine boxes for the drink she gave him every day he worked here. She had high hopes that the concoction would bring on a boy at Charith's next birthing.

As Zithia saw him into his dray, Ezekiel said, 'The priest and the patriarch are arranging a communal half-day of work for you, to cut sixteen years growth off your fruit and nut trees. Three weeks from now. It'll be quite a day. So, you'll need lunch for... minimum...' he screwed up his eyes, 'a hundred and ten men.'

Zithia goggled. 'I really don't know what to say.'

'Don't worry, it's only the men.'

'Only!' she repeated, wide eyed, to his retreating back.

*

When the workers started arriving back at the farmhouse after the tree lopping, they were already licking their lips in contemplation of the meal. It had spread like wildfire that Esalen had had unnecessary words with Zithia, about losing Brice for an entire day, finishing with a muttered aside, '...and he's bound to come home still hungry.'

Breathless from this insult to her hospitality, Zithia had immediately gone to the baker and ordered a half a young sheep.

The weary men barely stopped to admire the new bentwood bridges, wide enough for their ponies and covered by thatch. No handrails, and each at the narrowest river flow between bank and island. They were met with a tot of honey or maple mead, once they'd washed in the river. Taron, with Kylyn assisting, dispensed the precise dram; after being assured that a wintering box had been placed on the leeside of each topped tree.

Collecting the plates and cutlery each man had brought to the day, it was on to breads fresh made by Ezekiel's daughters, along with various butters and nut spreads. In their new blouses, with a simple maiden's veil upon each head, the older girls were everywhere, modestly offering dishes they'd made themselves. Being especially attentive to the fathers of each family.

At first Zithia had been puzzled at the pleasure the girls were taking in the day, until Shiloh's soft comment, 'What father doesn't appreciate the joys of a potential daughter-in-law who really can cook. This is a rare opportunity for the girls.'

"This explained why every single FallsFire delicacy or favourite had been prepared; the forest scoured; why Zithia and Katerah had been sent to the bakery with list after list of ingredients; why foresting had been banned for days before the work-day, to ensure Ezekiel a good hunt. And today, why the home paddocks were scattered with fragrant herbs.

Tables groaned with the weight of the buffets, which were watched over by the youngest girls, while the roasting sheep, that expensive delight, was admired greatly. Almost as popular were the marinated venison steaks.

During the feast, no plate was left empty without a smiling young woman offering to fetch just a little more honeyed goose or turkey or pate or, perhaps, a set mushroom triple-omelette? Or was it a slither of pineapple cake, apricot pie or crepe that'd suffice? More berry and acorn coffee? Halfway through the feast, the patriarch's oldest son held a lottery. Kylyn pulled out wooden tabs with each name on it. Of the fifty trees topped, Zithia had promised the three golden pine logs to the prayer hall. And now she was raffling off thirty others. A charming surprise.

Zithia stood behind the cheeses, the only food the girls hadn't made. She found herself saying, 'Widow Shiloh has promised to teach Ezekiel's girls and my family how to make all her cheeses.' Shiloh was among the best cheese-makers in FallsFire. 'Even her medicine cheese.' She smiled, cutting slices of cheese with a special mould growing in ripples of breadcrumbs within the cheese. That'd cost Zithia's original sampler bag of stitches.

It was only as dusk was looming that the last morsel was fitted into already-stretched stomachs. One man announced that the feast had been as at a patriarch's wedding. And he a patriarch's nephew. Plus, who could've anticipated a second tot of mead? Taron so rarely made such a dispensation. Then, there were Ezekiel's soft spoken daughters, each grown into a peach. It had been a perfect day, on all sides.

*

The wet meadow near the bakery was painted now with drifts of tiny pink flowers. Every sunny area was. Sitting on the bench connected to her roof, Zithia watched the pink snow bob in the changing wind-tides. This fairy adornment would continue for a month. Black minks, twice the usual size, frolicked in the drifts.

Kylyn was putting a tiny bench on top of the blue jay's winter home. Finished, he collected a bundle of dried greenish mushrooms so like oysters. Zithia stood and pulled a weed from the verdant roof, and went back to the wheel-like water carrier. Made of two joined slabs of hollowed-out wood, Zithia rolled it the short distance to a corner of the roof's edge and emptied it into a low trough. This right-angled trough was filled twice a day. Hessian strips ran from the trough to two hessian curtains, keeping the cloth wet. At the bottom of the cloth the water drained into a barrel, ready to be transported to the top of the roof again. Thus the meat-keep was quite frigid. That corner of the verandah was towered over by an insect-repellent tree.

That done, Zithia rolled the chubby tube to the pulley and rope, then carefully lowered it to the ground where its detachable handle lay. Some of her new flock, the northern geese and ovenbirds, had spread themselves into her space on the bench. Shaking her head at them, she said, 'I was mad to leave the water till now.'

Everything was ready for the evening, when they'd again climb the interlaced logs to watch the Northern lights fluting beyond and over them. FallsFire seemed to draw the northern lights to it. Zithia left a silk cap, with cherry blossoms woven within the cloth, on the seat. If Kylyn fell asleep tonight while Zithia and Katerah lingered over the Northern lights, last night there'd been multiple dancing curtains, Kylyn would need the cap, to keep the full moon from his sleeping eyes. Time spent sleeping unprotected under the full moon wasn't recommended. Especially for children.

Putting a blackberry pie, made from dried berries, out to cool. Katerah faced the roof. 'Come down Kylyn, I've hardly enough time to bath you before dusk. Melia, you'll have to barn those birds now or we'll never be ready in time for the holyday.'

Kylyn raced down while Zithia herded the flock from the roof, geese honking.

Practically everyone attended the brief evening service. The women's pale dresses had a little pale embroidery on their modest necklines. Clothing was more severe on the holyday. Dark grey was the colour for men's breeches.

Walking the wide switch-back path up the steep pink-grassed hill, Zithia shaded her eyes against the looming golden glare that was the prayer hall. She wondered if she'd ever sit upon its roof-benches. When the Northern lights hovered above it, viewers could virtually touch the glowing symphony of waves. Sitting up there, the angels of the lights didn't just murmur, they whispered in your ear.

'God help me not to bump into a man, or I'll get a lecture on the laws of non-contact from every old aunt in sight.'

Entering the open doors, Zithia, Katerah and Kylyn were in a silvery oblong. The wall was lined with silver pine. Zithia's party made its way to a short backless bench halfway down the hall, far from either fireplace. Raised benches lined the walls, reserved for important families. The patriarch's wife was already seated, with her children. The village women were almost as tall as Zithia. But no one, neither man nor woman, had Zithia or Kylyn's large, vivid blue eyes. Except for some few of the patriarch's line.

Passing, Zithia nodded to the priest, who was talking to a narrow nosed woman. In her usual fashion, Lilac was gabbling on in a shrill flow, 'I'm sure the tithe of dough wasn't taken.'

Zithia kept walking, but her veil snagged on something. Tugging as she turned around, Zithia found Lilac clutching the veil roughly.

'Melia, sweetheart...' then she continued shrilly to the priest, '... people should be warned,' Taron glazed over, 'warned, I say, that bakery bread mustn't be eaten this holyday.'

Taron glowered, 'Absolute nonsense! I took the tithe myself, as usual,' and stomped to the front of the hall.

Simultaneously, children raced by, giggling. 'Have some respect!' Lilac hissed loudly. 'I blame the fathers, why don't they control their broods. Or can't they?' The service commenced.

Lilac still had Zithia's veil captive, and purred. 'Sit by me, my dear one; this side.' Then once they began to settle themselves, 'I'm so glad you're here; the next woman has a terrible cold,' Zithia was promptly and fluidly sneezed over; she raised her voice, 'Been coughing at me since I got here. I can't begin to describe it.'

The racers settled in front of one of three tall quartz windows, some trying to see through the distorting blocks. A clay Dragon-Land floor covered most of that side of the hall, and there, communal high-winter gatherings lighted everyone's days.

Wide aisles divided the wide rows of benches, and people moved into small huddles during the repetitions of the lesser prayers. Children came and went freely. Kylyn was easily seen as he was a head taller than the other boys of his age. Watching him, Zithia's heart swelled. She reflected: *"Pure Atlantis. From the set of his jaw, to his good cheekbones."*

Many people nodded, women almost smiled at Zithia and also at Katerah. Each holyday since Zithia had bought Benjamin's farm, the villagers were reminded anew of the advantages that the new ownership had brought. Previously, the baker had paid triple the current fishing fee to Brice, in gold. Now, not only had Nathaniel's cost decreased to one third, paid in trade, he'd passed much of this decrease on to the village buyers. And Zithia always had some needed thing to barter, if a lady called. Katerah tended to handle these transactions, with generosity. All looked forward to Zithia's excess next year, which would include the magic genko honey.

Noting the smiles, Lilac rasped out, 'I hear you're been wasting barter on bulbs now. Widow Melia, you seem insatiable where flowers are concerned. I gather you've enough irises to fill a field. And as for pansy orchids...' She raised her nose and her voice high. 'It's the talk of the village you know.'

Zithia's expression iced over, even further than it had already. She couldn't explain her craving for flowers, even to herself. 'Then please remember to spread that yesterday I obtained a dozen Dragon-Land joss flowers. It cost all my ginseng and garlic.'

Lilac rasped air inwards, loud and long, then emitted in guttural tones, 'Medicinal herbs.'

Zithia fell into silence, thinking with a sigh: *"And only my third prayer meeting."*

Throughout the service women played musical-seats, as was usual, conversing quietly with one another. As Zithia was unpractised at this game, Lilac managed to keep her hemmed in. Zithia was, after all, a drawcard. Thus she received advice from many quarters. On all matters, including how long her widow's veil must be to satisfy the righteous, plus the extra length required by the self-righteous. Women actually craned their necks like owls to be in on the giving of instruction.

Lusting after a frilly cap which sat, at one stage, almost in front of her, Zithia's mind strayed to laces on double ovals of cloth that were allowed to overlap each other down the wearer's back. Oh, not to be in mourning. She intended to wear a cap on the very first day she could be decently allowed to. No quips, about what a truly good woman would do, could change her mind.

Occasionally, throughout the service, the priest's eyes roamed the hall, shushing those who spoke too loudly. When the service finished, a bare hour later, he summed up the week's communal interests. 'We're all relieved that brother Ruben's prized, long-horn ram fully recovered from its illness.' There was a general murmuring of thanks. 'And finally sister Karody and brother Samuel have been blessed with twin sons.' The women gushed.

Zithia's mouthed to herself, 'Another set!?!'

*

A week later, Lilac greeted her visitors with a tightening of her cheek muscles. Her eyes lit with an inquisitive look. Zithia had been trying to be pleased to receive her very first invitation since their arrival in the village. An invitation which Lilac had made it clear that Zithia couldn't, in politeness, refuse.

'Welcome, welcome!' Lilac clapped her hands together. 'My dear widow Melia, what a short mourning veil.' Lilac's lips were truly smiling now. 'Who have you been listening to?' She became oddly pensive. 'I hope it wasn't Florence!' She shook her head, her face grave. 'The poor dear, I do believe she freezes her cider; all winter.'

"Lilac looked at Katerah. 'I'm sure your cousin wouldn't be interested in much of our conversation. Being widows' talk.' She looked at Katerah. 'Would you assist an old woman by dusting and slicing some mushrooms? And join us when you're finished.'

Katerah had been shoved into the kitchen, before either she or Zithia could object. Facing Katerah was a good two hours' work.

Lilac watched Zithia move toward a chair. 'No, not that one my dear. I like to sit there.' Lilac took her place. 'I've been so looking forward to getting to know you better. Feel free to ask me any questions.' She proffered them some holey sheep emmentaler cheese. 'And you came from the coast. What adventures you must've had. The guide, was he a very rough sort of man?' Frowning, Zithia shook her head. 'Were there always two separate fires at night?'

The front door opened. 'That'll be Briony, she often checks on her old widowed mama, in my own little dower cottage.'

Briony entered, handing Zithia a plate of barley cookies. 'Widow Melia!'

While Zithia swiveled to put the cookies on a table, Lilac gave a crooked smirk to her daughter. Briony instantly rose to her tiptoes, performing a mincing gallop to unite her mama. When Zithia turned back to them, Briony was still teetering mid-step, her cap jiggling. Almost nonchalantly, her heels descended to the ground.

Lilac mentally itemised Kylyn's features as Kylyn munched on little fruit leathers and dried berries. 'Charming child; might turn handsome.' She grimaced, 'Whose hair does he have? Is he much like his papa?'

'Yes, very like.' The two ladies waited, but nothing else was forthcoming.

Pouring a mug up of salmonberry tea, Lilac's eyes roved Zithia. 'You know, widow Melia, another woman in the settlement isn't as welcome as a man. Now you mustn't mind the ladies watching you like hawks.'

'No,' Briony contributed, 'they're simply frightened you'll steal a future husband already tagged by another.'

'Of course the men will be easier on you.' The men were still singing praises of the workday's feast. 'Proven child-bearing ability and so many possessions...' Zithia took another biscuit. 'Oh, and my dear, you must feel like a queen washing in the bath you had made,' a crumb caught in Zithia's throat, 'though I'm not quite sure what the laws of modesty say about a golden hipbath.'

Briony's several chins agreed. 'And almost five feet long. The extravagance!' Golden pine was expensive.

Zithia's hand flew halfway to her face, her eyes widening. All paused, mama and daughter seemed not even to breathe in their waiting for...

Then suddenly, Zithia gasped, 'Oh, I'm terribly sorry.' Zithia rose from her seat. 'I've just remembered that I didn't pen the goats before I left home. We shall have to go I'm afraid. Pray understand; I mean, forgive me.'

'Cousin.' She walked briskly into the kitchen and goggled at the mounds of saffron-ringed mushroom caps, bleeding yellow with each cut.

Caught out, Lilac's vaguely heightened, 'Oh dear, Katerah, you surely didn't think I meant you to do all those.' Then burbling on at Zithia, 'Undoubtably we forgive you my dear, but what a stupid thing to do,' Zithia grabbed their cloaks, 'and if the goats are damaged by your carelessness, well...'

Lilac opened the front door only a crack. 'Melia, I may call you Melia mayn't I? Dear one, when do you expect your husband's death certificate to arrive?'

Zithia's neck was rigid. 'Soon.'

Walking away from the cabin, Zithia attacked the foliage crossing the path with a stem of pink grass. Turning a corner on the path, a startled black-capped bird flew, calling 'chickadee, chickadee.' They watched the bird's progress, thus also seeing a movement from the roof of Lilac's house.

Lilac and Briony were standing there. Seeing Zithia looking, Briony quickly held a skein of gold wool up between her hands and Lilac began to wind the slack loop in her hand. Katerah followed Zithia's eyes and snorted.

Zithia glared at the harpies. 'I'm going into the forest when we get home. Care to join me?'

Katerah wrinkled her nose. 'That's the third time this week. No. I'll see the carpenter. He promised me a hardened fire poker, in exchange for razor-strop fungus he chops up for corks.'

Kylyn said to his mama, 'Can we take a pony?'

'Yes, Olondin.'

'Can I have a falcon?'

'When you're thirteen and become a man, dearest.'

*

Zithia arrived home from foresting loaded with pinecones and scented branches, to find Shiloh leading a shaggy, bearded creature that stood five feet high at the shoulder. A helmet of horn extended over its massive head, ending in short curled horns. Kylyn flew to the musk oxen, patting its muzzle.

Inside, labradour-coffee was already brewing. Kylyn's face lit up at a present of a hollow, bright blue egg. Then he went off to put it with his treasures in his room. Zithia smiled delight at the chicken-of-the-woods tree fungus freshly fired. Melting in the mouth, it tasted like real chicken. Katerah, seeing Zithia home, left off her dyeing of petticoat cloth using a pink mushroom which created a rare vivid blue.

Ezekiel's older girls were just leaving for the day, having stacked the green skinned rutabagers for winter feed, and the plump native parsnips. Katerah called out that they should take some eggs, the day's extras, now that their mama was pregnant again. Then the family ate some chicken-of-the-woods, Shiloh using the chopsticks Zithia kept for her use. All patriarchs used chopsticks, and Shiloh had picked up the knack when married.

After the break, Zithia brought out some long oblong nuts, with ridges, for Shiloh. Back in the kitchen, another cup of coffee was poured. Katerah showed the piece of golden beryl, native to the area, that had been traded that day for a silkey-chicken chick and some liquorice root. Quietly, Katerah settled before the living room fire. Admiring the stone, Zithia inhaled the aroma of the mushroom ketchup cooling on the large clay oven and range. She checked the apricot coloured mushrooms, each a frilly bunch, gently drying on racks above the stove. Shiloh was setting up backgammon; joining her, Zithia knew contentment.

*

Zithia and Katerah were in the woodworker's shop one morning, purchasing a new wooden kitchen sink, when Finias placed another of his Dragon-Land bows on the wall. Kylyn watched intently as Finias's third son created a small water-carrier. Zithia ordered one, for Kylyn's use. He was of the age to learn to roll water up a hill. The attachable handle was leather padded. Having spied Zithia one of the baker's boys came in, weighed down by a bag, plus a waterproof parcel.

'Widow Melia, this came for you from the coast, with supplies for the store.' He tripped over a pile of spruce bark waiting for a snowbound weaver. Dropping a dogwood hammer, Zithia snatched at the slipping bag. When a little flour escaped, the boy said, 'Wheat! Festival food.'

Grabbing the plant enzyme Finias sold for rennet in cheese, Zithia dashed off. At home, she unsealed the oilskin revealing the death certificate; also a letter of introduction singing the praises of Melia's husband and herself.

Shiloh and Kylyn were on the cabin's roof, planting a sculpted moss mountain next to the blue jays' house. Scattering village-bought, golden plovers and quail, Zithia fairly leapt up the corner ladder. Her head appeared. Shiloh had double-padded the miniature cabin with moss. 'Extra comfort for the blue jays. To bring you luck in winter.' Then, 'Has the baker made any mustard yet?'

'No. But he does have some fine vinegars.' Then Zithia waved her precious documents. 'They've come, I'm off to see the priest.'

That night, when the others slept, Zithia opened the bag of rolled papyrus. In the center was another letter. *"Melia, greetings. So you can read and write! Your request found me mid-trip, at the freshwater hole which surfaces in some unusual shallows in the Atlantic Ocean. I wrote to my wife and sent the letter on ahead with my nephew, Geirroor, who transferred to the Viking ship.*

"Four days from land, another water arrow met us, with these documents. My wife had been fascinated by Geirroor's descriptions of you and by anecdotes about our trip. It was her definite opinion that you must be given every assistance to settle in this FallsFire of yours. I'm sure the documents will more than serve your purpose. The emeralds were most welcome, Yours Matho."

*

Breathing out mist from an unusually early frozen front, they idled through a palace of trees each hung with elaborate icicle chandeliers. From every newly bare branch, a medley of glistening crystal stalactites belled slight tunes in zephyrs. Within this vision, Zithia searched for angel's-wings mushrooms. Ezekiel's daughters came only three days a week these days, so Zithia and Shiloh had the forest to themselves.

Lamenting the size of families in the valley to Shiloh, Zithia admitted, 'I'm nervous simply standing in the same room as such fertile men, and they expect me to marry one.'

'They're not all of them bonfire dangerous.' Shiloh cut a snowy bear paw mushroom.

'Remember our patriarchs.' Zithia nodded. 'Well, patriarchs produce but five children, at most. My own cousin, Elderic, has thrown back to the patriarch's legacy. Married seven years and only one child. Widowed now, yet no father allows his daughter's eyes to follow Elderic... despite his good looks.'

Zithia raised her eyebrows. 'And where is this poor marvel now?'

'In the Far World, trading.'

Kylyn reached for three shiny buttermilk flat caps. Zithia said, 'Not those darling, never touch, never eat. They're death caps.' Kylyn noted, then ignored the fungi.

Without a backward glance, 'Shiloh, I see the potter's devotion to his increasing family is showing once more. The cost of glazed kettles has doubled!'

Shiloh's glance was mischievous. 'When the potter spied the priest's wife yesterday he dashed to escape, running headlong into Grace. Knocked her clear off her feet. Well, obviously, he couldn't help Grace up and he didn't want to discuss paper. So he fled, with Grace ranting, "That man truly is the stuff of pearls! An irritating piece of grit!" ' They laughed until their ribs hurt.

Shortly after, Shiloh felled a wood duck by slingshot. The use of traps was forbidden. When Zithia's hand closed on the brown chest, the forest of crystals swirled around her. Zithia subsided to the ground. Seeing the dead bird's accusing stare, black spots and queasiness ensued.

Shiloh shrugged at Zithia's pallor. 'What do you expect, if you tramp the forest in your condition?'

Between deep breaths, while trying to get the myriad icicles to stand still, 'My condition?'

'Condition!' A hitherto unsuspected thought struck Shiloh. 'You do know you're pregnant?!' Zithia's stunned look gave rise to amazement in her friend. 'But the signs! I've recognised the signs; you're telling me you haven't.'

'But my cycle...' She paused, then shook her head, while her mind flashed through things unexplained. The bloated stomach, the extra weight she couldn't loose, the cravings. All those flowers! She forced a smile, '...it, uh, hasn't stopped.'

'Well, stopped or not, you're with child.'

At home, Zithia sat by the stream, emotions riven: *"Pregnant!"* She bit her bottom lip, thinking of Galen, 'I could've done without this complication.' Pregnant, without a husband, in a strange land. *"In the paradise of the Atlantians. First Atlantis, land of the ancestors,"* her mind corrected. 'Yet alone.'

Tears welled in Zithia's eyes. 'Galen, what you're missing! Another child, plus Greater Atlantis.' Abruptly anger rose: *"Why couldn't you be stronger?"* then lamented over fate; *"Or why couldn't I be weaker?"* She moaned. 'No, I could never have survived without the respect given by marriage.'

Abruptly Zithia was crying as though never to cease, at times finding breath hard to draw, due to the wordless sobs that rose and rose. Still keening after half an hour, semi-blinded by tears, Zithia walked shakily to milk the goats. One word kept pulling deep sobs from her, 'Galen'. Finally finished, Zithia entered the kitchen, still weeping hard. Washing her face, she gathered her strength so as to call to Katerah in a normal voice. 'Would you put some water in the bath for me, Katerah? I need… I want… I'll be outside.' Luckily it was bath night.

Zithia patted her belly. Her husband's second child. 'I declare this baby a blessing. Yes, a blessing.' She felt better. 'And the first of my family to be born in Greater Atlantis.' Zithia smiled proudly at the thought. 'So tonight while I sleep, we'll discuss Atlantian features, little one.' She was a heritage-caller after all.

*

Going to the priest's wife next day Zithia's voice was tremulous. 'My Lady Jessamy, I… I find myself five and a half months pregnant. My dead husband will have one more child.'

'Pregnant? Ah, yes, I can see it now. Our clothes can hide a pregnancy for months. Yet… find yourself with child?'

Zithia's face was puzzled consternation. 'My monthly cycle continues.'

'I see. Yes; a distant kin of mine has experienced such pregnancies. Rather an inconvenience, she always said. Don't worry, her cycle always stopped in the sixth month. And a flower craving, most unusual.' Jessamy thought back to Zithia's letter of introduction: *"Married to a fighting man… died with valor… woman of good character, from a family of standing all now dead."*

'With child,' Jessamy's voice was warm, 'delightful; let me say how pleased I'm for you.'

The priest was told. 'Blessings, widow Melia, it shall be announced this holyday. What a joy for your dead husband to have another child to carry on his heritage.'

Taron left. Jessamy patted Zithia's hand. 'We shall pray for a son, the better to keep his name alive.' Sliding to their knees, they prayed.

Standing again, Jessamy said, 'By tradition, Melia, you will come out of mourning until after the birth. For the baby's sake. No more wearing white. Your family still can't attend festivities, which is a shame because the patriarchs are back. With the newest patriarch. One month after the birth, mourning recommences and lasts for the remaining months of the year. How long… I mean… I don't wish to intrude upon your grief unnecessarily.'

'My husband died four months ago.'

'So, eight months of mourning left.' Jessamy paused, smiling, 'At least that gives us enough time to consult the scrolls on choosing the most auspicious name.'

*

Holyday yet again. That all important landmark. That day of enforced laziness, unless you happened to be a woman with people to feed. When alone, Zithia had quietly bled, salted and washed the goose Ezekiel had hunted yesterday. She often did this with the little meat she ate. How glad she was that salt was common here.

Half-skipping to the holyday eve service, Zithia twirled in a pale blue skirt. 'Ah, not to look like snowbird.' She twirled again, 'White doesn't even suit me.'

Katerah watched Zithia's ankles, 'Be careful Lilac doesn't see your emerald petticoat. Are you certain it's allowed?'

'Never ask a question, unless you're sure you want to obey the answer. I'll never be totally dowdy again. And you look wonderful in lavender.'

Before entering the prayer hall, Zithia received many congratulations, including from the patriarchs' kin. Jessamy was there, and Zithia peered around, eager to see the patriarchs. Shiloh said softly, 'Patriarchs are exempt from attending services.'

They moved inside. Standing in the doorway, Lilac was haranguing the father of a boy who'd outshone Lilac's grandson at reading. '...you must be very proud.'

Zithia and Katerah tried to edged past her, without success. 'My dear Melia, let me look at you.' Lilac immediately continued conversing with the man. 'Shame the boy can't repeat the basic blessings. Still, I'm sure you and your wife teach him what you can.'

Lilac moved inside. 'Dear one, a widow and yet pregnant! What a joy. Never mind that you don't glow.' Her voice became a stage whisper. 'I hate to have to mention this, my sweet, but I feel I must before someone else does. Your hair! That extraordinary blonde makes a plait the only decent way to wear it.'

Someone averted her eyes from Lilac and she was off.

Barely moving her lips, Zithia said to Katerah, 'Charming woman ... follows all the religious rules to the extreme and spreads nothing but misery.'

In the hall, Zithia was about to take her usual place when the priest's wife beckoned them. Seating them next to her, Jessamy invited Zithia's party to lunch on the morrow, the holyday day. This mark of favour caused frenetic conversations to break out around them.

Jessamy, 'Ezekiel's daughters look very fine in their new clothes; I hear they fish daily from your land.'

Zithia, 'And they always will.'

When Zithia was leaving the hall, the priest's sister, Grace, approached her. 'We hope to expect you at the cooking session in preparation for next holyday. It's at Esalen's house this week. I'm sure she'll be delighted when I tell her expect you in the group.'

Zithia only just controlled her facial muscles.

From then on, Zithia and Katerah regularly attended. They were also asked to attend the weekly sewing circle. Asked wasn't quite correct; they were directed to attend.

*

Wearing her flowing hair with one tiny plait encircling her crown outside a puffy cap of gauze, Zithia arrived at her first sewing morning. She settled at the kitchen table next to Shiloh, who was embroidering cloth made from her musk oxen wool. Dipping a miniature Dragon-Land stamp into dye, then onto her new cap, Hope's sister created a feather pattern. Zithia delighted in an Egyptian stitch. Quilting was a passion with most ladies. The hostess sat near a small fire, in a with a fur-covered footrest. Fur slippers peeped from beneath her quilt, of sunset colours.

Coming in, Lilac's top lip twisted at the sight of Zithia's plait. Approaching Zithia from the side, Lilac jabbed a finger into Zithia's belly. She jumped away, convinced she'd been clashed at by a wild animal. Smiling, Lilac criticised Zithia's stitchwork. Then, with hooded eyelids, 'Widow Melia, I'm told Charith's girls go foresting for you.'

Briony, in her high sharp voice, 'And with you.'

'Is that quite… genteel?' Lilac opened her eyes very wide.

'My sisters and I've often forested,' a patriarch's niece said, raising her chin, 'after all, what else do you call a "roaming"?'

Zithia opened her mouth to ask about roaming. Shiloh forestalled her. 'That does seem to make foresting ladies somewhat akin to patriarchs.'

Noses suddenly hitched high in the air, Lilac and Briony moved off, lips well puckered.

In the second hour, the younger women increasingly cast sidelong looks at their hostess. Eventually, she nodded at her eldest daughters, who led the others out to the garden. Humming began, then a multi-stringed instrument from the Dragon-Land sang, and the ladies were gliding, back and forth, past the open door. Dancing.

Zithia's head kept bobbing to the tune while she focused on her sewing. Finally, Jessamy laid down her quilt square. 'A little exercise would be refreshing. Let's all join the lines.'

Two sets later Zithia was still dancing. She executed a skipping turn, and Lilac detected Zithia's sky blue petticoat. Lilac gasped a deep breath inward. 'Has the woman no shame?' Instantly she crossed to the priest's wife.

Jessamy began, before Lilac could, 'Widow Melia wears fetching petticoats does she not?' She attended to her geometrically patterned quilt. 'My third daughter is making one in purple.'

Lilac's face puckered. With a friend, Briony joined her mama, and there were several minutes of hissing. The group moved toward a bench on the verandah, where lay this morning's mushrooms. Orange caps on pregnant stems.

Lilac squinted hard at Zithia. 'She's widowed four months.' She held up a very swollen mushroom. 'Five-and-a-half months pregnant?' Then she held up another mushroom, considerably less bulging. 'I'd say three months at most.'

By coincidence, or did she feel something in the air? Zithia happened to glance Lilac's way when she said this. Observing the titillated scene, the pupils within Zithia's suddenly unblinking eyes became tiny.

Before leaving that day, Zithia admired all the fur cloaks hanging in the entrance hall. For modesty, the furs were worn the leather-side out, yet they were always hung with the fur showing. Lilac's cloak was silver fox, and Zithia was in luck.

Late after the midnight hour, Zithia climbed a pine tree near Lilac's front door. When high enough, she took an old nest, surrounded by mistletoe, out of a bag. Seemingly the birds had woven a slice of quartz mirror on the outside. One of Lilac's hairs, with root, was strung across the mirror. And a very particular stone was next to the mirror; one known for its power to eat away the psychic shield which evil people built around them.

Zithia growled, 'Threaten my children,' and positioned the nest so that the mirror reflected the house and the pebble stared at it. 'Now, Lilac, careful what you say, careful what you do! For, whatever you send out... will come back to you.'

No spell was involved. It was simply a return of karma, with a hair as focus. The only Temple-sanctioned use of hair.

Three weeks later, Lilac lost her voice, and ever after she was reduced to painful whispering.

*

Steam rose from a rock pool that continually replenished itself. Ice reshaped the river and snowdrifts the wood. Mistletoe green and berries drooped from bare trees. Cabbage-like plants, with flowers, rose bravely through snow. Near a bonfire, Shiloh and Katerah sat on a log from which copper leaves sought the sky. Facing the river, Zithia's aches melted in the bubbles from the hot spring. She watched the frozen waterfall opposite. Every year the women set dripping dyes on top of it, the colours creating a fantasy.

Eating strawberry-flavored shaved ice, she floated in her undershifts. 'How on earth do you keep the men away?'

The midwife replied, 'It's called the birthing pool.'

Laughing, Zithia wrinkled her nose. 'That'd do it for me.' The woman continued to look at her and grin. All at once Zithia let out a deep breath, her eyes goggling. 'Ohh nnno!' Scrambling for the rock stairs.

Shiloh appeared at the pool edge. 'It's tradition.'

'No!' Zithia's cry sent a grouse fleeing away on tiny snowshoes, grown from its extended toenails.

'There'll be no more bathing in the kitchen.'

'Bathing I don't mind, birthing I do. '

Shiloh appeared at the pool's edge. 'This is a tradition which can't be flouted.'

'Then that's settled.' Said the midwife. Quietly Zithia sank back into the water.

*

Winter continued. It was a gossamer day. Ponies harnessed to sleighs nibbled the blackberry leaflets that attracted deer. Shiloh's musk oxen drew a sleigh to more yellow violets. Tiny white trailing arbutus flowers, plus dogtooth violets, were out. Snowflakes laced the wind, while prized gyrfalcons watched for invisible rabbits from their masters' arms.

The lake was solid ice. Children scampered across virgin snow, leaving little blue footprints in their wakes. A distant group of men fished in ice holes, with cut branches for windbreaks. At the lake's edge Nathaniel, the baker, balanced on dogwood skates. Leeward to the wind, he held up a framed silk sail and leaned into it. His tall ruby triangle, which was connected to thick leather straps with hooks attaching it to Nathaniel's belt, it caught the wind and the skater drifted off to the starting line. It was raced back, among other bright shields, with the men flipping the sails around their bodies to change direction.

Women applauded the competitors, from around bonfires, and kept an eye on skating children. Chestnuts and genko nuts were roasted. Hot drinks steamed in gloved hands. A boy appeared with a long rubbery oblong, glistening in peacock colours.

'The winter fungal leathers are far too prevalent this year.' There was a general chorus of mirth. Jessamy gave the boy two rough balls from the now half-full bags, one marked with a green flash and one purple. He sprinted off to swap a colour with a friend.

One woman huddled beneath her best patchwork quilt. 'Young Ruben put sheets of black jello in every boot in the house. Which,' she added, 'is quite an achievement in a house of twenty seven.'

A girl inspected her two spheres. 'Someone threw bubbly yellow gunk in my hair!'

Balls began whizzing high into snow-covered trees and landed on ice flags grown by the wind. Exploding, dyes painted the white. The girl was back, looking teary. She pointed to the lake where she'd dropped her spheres. The spongy dried calla lilies, which had been so cunningly folded when fresh to create a ball, lay exploded. The paint, sealed within each glued sphere only yesterday, had splattered everywhere. Turquoise and yellow blossomed.

Jessamy tutted. 'Such pretty splashes. Enjoy them, and next year be more careful.' But, coughing unnecessarily and loudly, she surreptitiously handed the child another ball.

The priest's wife continued handing out the communally-made spheres, exactly two dyes to each child. The rainbowing of the forest was already under way.

When the third lake race began, Zithia leaned over to add mushroom orange-peel to her bowl of gooseberry-flavored crushed ice. Her waters broke. *"Damn,"* she thought, *"I'm going to miss the day."*

Eventually the ladies reached the hot spring, the musk oxen making good time. Shiloh helped Zithia from the sled. Standing either side of Zithia, Shiloh and the midwife supported her into the sweet little hut. A fire already warmed the two rooms. Hours passed and the contractions grew. Freshly made chicken soup was simmering above the fire. Weeks ago the ladies had drawn up a roster for making Zithia chicken soup daily, for eight days after the birth. That most effective antibiotic food and a staple, by wise custom, of all new mothers.

Eased by a cup of pain-help tincture Zithia noticed, in highlight, the most mundane of things. She kept gazing at the best-quartz windows Their thick, angled-sills painted cream, inside the hut and out, drew in all the light. Every house had these glowing sills, yet today they were mesmerising.

Finally, the birthing party moved down to the spa where, submerged, Zithia concentrated on the pastel folds within the waterfall opposite. Throwing her head back during one violent set of pains, Zithia groaned open-eyed at the sky. Then, suddenly, every detail of the snow, descending like pepper from a shaker, fascinated her. As the pain ebbed, she smiled hazily. 'Ahhhhh!'

'That's quite enough for now.' Shiloh took the cup of soothing potion from Zithia's instantly stiffening grip.

Much, much later, will-of-the-wisps spun white clouds around Zithia while she gave birth. The healthy newborn drifted around the pool, beneath the surface, guided by the midwife to the air to take breath. Sparkling with joy, tears falling, Zithia drew her new darling into her outstretched arms. They touched noses.

chapter 25

A third of the invading forces trudged well inland, determined on treasure. There'd been virtually no booty these last months. It must be hidden somewhere. The promise of a city of gold was luring them further and further still. Llama trains had passed this way, heavily loaded. Scouts reported that a thousand defenders were somewhere ahead of them, in a valley off the main highway. The barbarians left the last paved roadway.

Galen spurred his horse on, scattering gold. His small mounted troop did the same. It was the defender's only horse contingent. One hundred volunteers had fast-marched through a pristine valley, lighting masses of fires and trampling scrub with logs dragged by horses. Way in the distance, the barbarians saw Galen and they let out a banshee cry. Their precious steeds. Galen's horse reared and from an open bag spilled a pile of golden vessels. The barbarian cavalry stormed after Galen.

The barbarians lost him. Horses walking on, the men looked for a fresh scent. They didn't notice the broken holes in the ground. Great gashes, where obsidian-edged sticks had hacked at long tunnels. In time, the invaders reached the wide, fast river. On the other side, jungle. Having been ferried across the river, Galen, the horses and the hundred were secure behind camouflage.

Corralling their herd at the water's edge, the barbarians stopped for the coming dusk. When the rest of the army jogged into view, the three thousand lit fires and put up tents. In camping tradition, all the dogs were set to guard the horses.

Only a sliver of moon lulled the invaders to sleep. There were no sounds in the night, for the jungle held its breath and fled. Yellow armor-plated chests caught the firelight, waiting above ground near their destroyed gateways. Finally the queen signalled 'March'. Another queen took up the call.

Near the river, a female on watch yelled at the thing that constantly scurried in the jungle dark. Unsheathing her sword, the blonde hurled herself at a bush. Going through the branches she found no animal. She had jumped upon thousands of tiny adversaries; their teeth ripped her to pieces.

Simultaneously, up the valley another sentry realised that the tree nearest him was solid ants. With a one-sided grin, the warrior put a lighted torch to the tree. Leaning back to watch the flames and ants climb, he became aware of a giant fist of ants swaying above his head. Slowly, they dropped.

The world turned crackling black and yellow. Pincers bit through tent fabric and poured, like molasses, onto a snoring man. Other invaders screamed, flailing, into wakefulness, their flesh disappearing down to the bone as they watched.

White with sweat, the horses whinnied. For a while now they had been stamping the ground hard, all round the corral's edge. The dogs were among the herd. With the first shrieks, the lead stallion reared and kicked the side of the coral down. Hurdling the wood and ants, they leapt straight into the water. The dogs were right behind them. All swam hard in fast currents till they reached the other side, far downstream.

In the camp itself, soldiers with feet being eaten from beneath them, over balanced and the dark cloud covered them.

Those near the main woodpile before the ants attacked, used it to create a firebreak. Two archers stood on top of the dwindling wood and put arrows through anyone who approached. Swarming, the ants devoured the growing circle of bodies, then chipped the bones to drink the marrow. Also swarming were the shadow patches; an army of darkness intent upon its mission, among and beneath the waves of ants. There was a thunder of phantasm screaming before the shadows were done that night.

A warlock chanted aside the swarm in front of him, and made for the river alone. Among the wriggling insects, a half-hand reached out to the sorcerer, who kicked it away.

'Warlock,' called an archer. A flaming arrow struck the sorcerer and he was down, spreading fire.

By morning the ants were gone and the valley was a desert, littered by three thousand jumbled skeletons and an occasional piece of gold.

*

Udo was meditating before a statue of the sacred horse, in front of which lay a silk banner. He'd lately returned from the day's judgments regarding the purity laws. The coven's examinations of the injured, as well as the captured; amputations and general infirmity had to be assessed.

Part of Udo's mind reflected: the months hadn't been good. Warlocks were dying and the defenders' use of guerilla tactics continued to be brilliant. There were fevers wherever they went and the battles turning.

Udo winced at a memory: the commander-in-chief bellowing, 'All warnings from warlocks about guerillas will be ignored.' The jungle fighters had planted staffs, drenched in magic. These staffs had soundlessly clamored 'ambush', while other areas were hit.

Also, the native flyers launched for mere seconds, baiting the coven. Hours of zipping from place to place left the warlocks exhausted before actual physical battle was joined. Then, there was the sorcerer who hadn't returned to his body.

'What has my coven done that the gods are stripping our power? Where've we failed you?' He raised manic-bright eyes to the silver horse. 'Give me a sign.'

A gale arose from nowhere, snuffing out the candles. The wind lifted the top of the banner high, till it became entangled on the statue's tail.

The commander in chief, Rhaim, stormed into the tent. 'A third of the army gone. I sent scouts to discover what was delaying them.' He pushed his shoulders forward and advanced towards Udo. 'They returned with this.' Rhaim emptied a bag of bones. 'And their booty has vanished.' His hand played with his sword hilt.

'I've had a sign!'

Ceremoniously, the warlock walked from the tent. Outside, soldiers crowded, and hardly moved back when the warlock advanced. Udo glared, but their eyes didn't flinch away from his. He reassured himself: *"All will be well again after tonight."*

'We, that race superior to all in the world, have been searching for our heritage for as long as we can remember. Many of you can trace your families back to the first days of settlement in our Fatherland. Before that, we've known nothing of our proud history.'

'Our enemies state they're descendants of Atlantis, that wondrous island of legend. I've discovered that Atlantis was our birthplace also. Indeed, we were princes of Atlantis. Princes exiled for demanding our right to rule. And Atlantis was destroyed because the other tribes wouldn't give us our due sovereignty. We, above all others, have kept our race pure. We remain princes of Atlantis.' Cheering clamoured.

From the altar, Udo's servant brought the banner. 'They call us the thirteenth tribe and dread our retribution for the wrongs done us.'

Abruptly, the cheering stopped as they watched the large silver 'thirteen' emblazoned on the purple silk. The temple people weren't the only ones superstitious of the number thirteen. Udos' audience silently peeled away.

Later, with his generals, the commander in chief walked among his sullen army. Soldiers muttered, their looks dark. 'So!' Rhaim spat, 'Here we are battling in the name of Atlantis, against fellow Atlantians.' He took a deep breath of air and didn't like the way it smelt.

A general, 'Supposedly, the last time we entered such a fight we lost our heritage... and our world.'

Rhaim spat more vigorously. 'Udo should've confided in me about this Atlantis nonsense, or at least about this announcement.' Rhaim grimaced at Udo's banner, now displayed in the main clearing. 'The thirteenth! If he'd only had the sense to lie about that.' He recalled the rhyme every grandmother recited when a child hurt itself: *"Fair are we; true to our line; forget thirteen; leave sorrow behind."*

The commander-in-chief slapped his second in charge on the back. 'Break out all the spirits. Tonight is a night to drink!' He headed off to the common soldiers' fire.

*

A captured banner, with its silver 'thirteenth', lay at an archpriest's feet. 'You sent every battalion one of these.' The man nodded. 'Then it's time.'

All over the continent the announcement was made, 'The thirteenth tribe is here again.'

Since learning the truth themselves, the archpriests had gradually strengthened the people's disgust in the thirteenth tribe. It hadn't been hard. The people had been afraid of the invaders as an unknown nation, but the thirteeenth tribe had been defeated before. And now a third of the barbarian army had been destroyed.

*

A battalion was marching on a lake city. An ebony staff was scored by seventeen lines, flyers who no longer flew. A black essence appeared before the warlock in his tent. Smiling, he held his staff high and followed the luminous dark. He walked past a sleeping guard into the pampas grass that was bunched like huge bouquets. Eyes on the translucent essence, the warlock spoke to the dark. Praised it. All his life he'd waited for this. In a clearing he met Galen and Eten. That left three warlocks.

Galen and Eten stalked all the warlocks in turn. The high priestess always wore a wide anklet these days.

*

A fleet of ships was coming to pick up treasure for home. The barbarians' numbers were reduced to fourteen hundred. It was then that Rhaim decided to cut his losses.

Word went out, all the battalions were to meet at Tancah in eight days. With malaria and dengue fever prevalent, the order meant a gruelling pace. Once the destination was known, each commander became a rigorous follower of the purity selections regarding illness. It sped up the journey, while decreasing the numbers with whom the treasure had to be shared.

*

In Tancah, Udo's tent occupied an auspicious place, much to his surprise. Black leaves drifted down on warm breezes. Rhaim had invited the warlock to a banquet. Walking there, Udo almost stepped on one dark leaf when it scuttled away. A heavily veiled and clothed concubine, crossing his path, backed away. He smiled.

Udo was relieved when Rhaim, smiling, indicated the seat immediately next to him, on his right. Throughout the courses, blue-eyed beauties danced among them. Rhaim personally filled everyone's goblets and, for once, Udo felt it politic to consume the alcohol.

A blonde, with a plunging neckline, now led the concubines. Polishing a red oval fruit on the curve of her breast, she offered half to Rhaim. She repeated this performance with his top staff. To rowdy approval, one commander took the fruit from between the woman's lips.

Picking up the last fruit, the dancer sidled over to Udo. The beauty blew gently on it; she bit half the fruit. Swallowing it, she pressed the other piece to his lips. Her perfume was dividing. The warlock munched.

While the dancing continued, Rhaim said, 'A toast.' Another drink was poured for everyone. 'We return to the Fatherland, to our new king and his advisers.'

Udo thought about his brother's elite position at court. 'To our...' Rhaim stopped. 'Wait. Brother Udo, let's swap chalices.' Udo accepted this pledge of alliance. 'To the king.'

The warlock took a drop of liquid into his mouth, habit really. It was ambrosia. Udo drank well, saying, 'And the sacred white horse.' They all drained their cups.

A cloud appeared on the warlock's horizon. He bit at the inside of his cheek, thinking: *"How am I going to face the sacred white horse."* Suddenly, that was no longer a concern. Udo slumped over the table before him, upsetting the gold cutlery. The cyanide in his wine should've been bitter, but was turned sweet by the peculiar fruit he'd eaten. Leaving the corpse where it lay, the commanders continued enjoying the night. Pulling its face up from his plate, Udo's ghost tried to throw power at the commanders and failed. He was still trying when the shadows pounced and he learned about true power. And justice.

Rhaim roared, 'Have the warlock's banners, anything with the new insignia, burned.'

*

An old man waited in the jungle, with his memories. Every crease on his weathered face pointed downwards; his dark eyes were finally at peace. He'd been away when Tancah had been murdered, and his children, all priests, with it. Pericles's hands shook: *"My line ends with me."*

An insect charmer, Pericles could ward off these pests. And he could call them. Even now he beaconed to a single species: *"Come to me; come!"* They'd begun arriving a day ago. As a new swarm of flat-bodied insects rode the air currents, Pericles stood and pointed to Tancah.

There the binchookas ignored the horses and dogs, their skins were just too thick, to crawl blissfully onto the humans. The bites stung, but nothing a warrior complained about. Where possible, the concubines didn't leave their sealed tents. And they took turns to stay awake, with a light burning, on guard in case one binchooka found a way through.

Uncommon creatures, binchookas carried insanity in their maws. This madness incubated silently, appearing after three months to two years.

The more the bites, the quicker and the worse the symptoms. While the barbarians could eventually overcome the shame of this campaign and begin to tell treasure stories, they'd die ranting. Their babblings not believed.

chapter 26

The people began to heal. Xalisco was Xalisco once more. Archpriest Franklin stood in his garden, addressing his upper priests. 'Now that we have peace, I long to spend my last few years in seclusion, where the monarch butterflies winter.'

In his mind's eye, Franklin saw the beauties asleep, covering a thousand trees, till the grey foliage changed to a living sunset.

'I retire in three months. Lord Augustus is one of the candidates for the archpriest position.' Amid congratulations, Franklin held up his hand. His first two fingers were nearly straight, the others curling.

'Lord Galen's heroics have been set to ballads. If he can resolve the issue of the bride-price, I'll put his name forward, also.'

Smiling, Galen advanced on Eten. 'Sister, it is war's end!'

'No more enemy of my enemy.'

'No longer friends.'

Her eyes came alight. 'But I hope, regarding one thing, we can stay friends.' Her voice deepened, 'I want Zithia.'

'Dead or alive?'

'Brother, your wife's blood is no longer of interest to me. Alive and here.'

Galen's eyes went to a tight knot of people. 'Have you discussed this with Augustus?'

One hand rested on her hip briefly. 'I can help.' His expression was haughty disdain.

'Galen, I'm not all patience. I want Zithia back. So get her and quickly!'

Thoughtfully Galen watched her join Augustus.

*

Galen tried many avenues for tracing Zithia, usual and rare. But she was adept at hiding. There was one other option. *"Do I dare?"* he thought, running his hands quickly through his hair. *"And what chance of co-operation, let alone success?"* Galen shook his head.

Another day went by. In the upper priests' hall, Augustus lunched with a group of influential deacons. Augustus's unforeseen acquisition of presence startled Galen. Observing Augustus's decisive expression, hearing his adroit conversation, Galen looked at his competition with new eyes.

That evening, Galen sent out a plea, asking to meet with an astral council, a meeting of advisors and guardians on one of the levels of the astral plane.

At first his request met solid nothing, then the word 'No' fanfared across his dreams. Having gone so far, the high priest continued asking. His tone, he convinced himself, always humble.

In the small hours of the eighth night Galen's eyes opened. A golden astral form stood beside his bed. The being said quietly, 'I've come to accompany you to the council.'

'I can find my own way.'

'Yes, but with so many doors open... may you not get lost?' At Galen's frown, 'It's entirely up to you. We don't have to go.'

The floor was dark, simply a shadow upon which to stand. There were no walls or ceiling to this endless place. He was aware of other people, one or two deep, around the edge of a pool of temperate light. Several golden individuals were seated in a loose semi-circle at one end of the lit space. Each sat at a distance from the other. They, also, were in the dimming of the light, and they literally grew in stature according to their thought or consideration.

Two men stood before the council, disputing points with passion. One began to shout at the other; the issue at stake was trust. One of the golden beings made a pronouncement and, beaming, the supplicant's witness faded from the astral plane. As did the two.

Galen waited. Twice more the council listened, questioned and made decisions. In time, Galen took his place, bowing his head low. 'Zithia isn't here yet?'

'She hasn't been summoned to this meeting.'

Galen's eyes were still downcast in his bow. 'Zithia's presence is imperative.'

'We've some doubts as to your motives.'

The leader added, 'Galen, will you never learn?'

'Learn? I assure the council, my progress this life has been substantial.'

One of the further councillors grew in size to ten feet tall and said, 'We're not talking about your status, your position, Galen.'

Frowning, Galen heard the leader's voice in his head: *"Nor your obsessions."* It was a little like being lightly punched on the temple. The leader smiled dryly, 'What're you here for, Galen?' The high priest blushed. 'Ah, an issue of right and wrong!' His clear eyes pierced Galen.

'It... it's more a problem between soul mates.'

'Go on,' dangerously polite. 'It's still possible to summon Zithia.'

'You know of the bride-price. I can't become archpriest without having the bride-price declared null and void.' There was total silence. 'I simply ask for a fraction of assistance.'

The council sat silent, conferring, their communications with each other totally private. Deceptively soft, came the decision. 'Galen, we will send no visions to the archpriests on your behalf.' The leader's moderate eyes glittered. 'And you're hereby banned from further councils during this lifetime. It's recorded.'

As the council chamber started to dissolve around him, Galen heard, 'Cousin, you have a decision to make. It's very simple! You either choose right or wrong.'

For the briefest of moments Galen was on the highest plane within the astral. A golden light filtered everywhere; beings sat in the love of that golden light and knew God. It was all a soul had ever wanted. Here, time was still and yet 'forever' was encompassed. In that single beat of the heart, Galen's soul overfilled with transfixing joy.

'You want to be in the light of God's love some millennia, don't you Galen?' A mist then enclosed the high priest. Leaving... was pain itself.

Then the high priest was in the Hall of Records. 'We give you this; for both of you.'

In a wide aisle, Galen and his guide walked along a tall library shelf. The golden being took a parchment from a shelf. He laid the Record of Life upon a slender stand that had appeared. Reading, the golden person moved a finger down thin columns of writing. Galen tried to read. All the words promptly went out of focus.

'Some futures.' The guide slowly touched a finger to one paragraph, then another some distance away. Then a third. Each sentence in turn became clear. 'You see, there's even the chance to have what you want and choose the right path.'

Galen knew what was written, and promptly lost the details. Nevertheless… he was left with hope.

Then he fell into a sweet, intoxicating sleep, where all his ambitions, desires and wants were fulfilled entire. He awoke smiling, but instantly became wistful, for he knew that that part of the night was only dream.

*

Masseuses had pummeled the tension from Galen and Xiao Chen's bodies. Presently they sat in the ancient steam bath.

Galen said, 'Kylyn is the key.'

'Then you need something with his imprint, to break through Zithia's cloaking.'

'Zithia gave all her possessions to the refugees. And Kylyn's.'

A memory came to Xiao Chen. 'I suggest we go to the storage vault.'

Once there, Xiao Chen tapped a low golden table. 'Look underneath. At the corners.'

Lying on his back, Galen searched. One corner was different. With a black cloth covering his hand, the high priest freed a triangular metal half box. Sliding out from under the table Galen looked. Looped within was an anklet Zithia had made for Kylyn, from the threads of a beloved shawl.

Xiao Chen said, 'I'd forgotten about the secret compartment Kylyn and I built.'

*

Galen stood on the roof of the hut, atop the pyramid where Zithia had often dried her hair. There, the memories of her were so strong that simply concentrating conjured an image of Zithia at his feet. He touched the anklet. And it was as though he'd awakened the very air. Connection!

Kylyn was running down a grassy slope to a clear brook. A voice called from the cottage, 'Be careful.'

Galen willed himself through the cottage wall. He felt his wife's influence everywhere. Katerah added raspberry juice to maple syrup. Humming a tune, she placed loops of spun-cotton, mauve and sand, in a basket. Finally, she gathered two large colourful wreaths of dried mushrooms. 'Olondin, wait for me.'

"Olondin." thought Galen, his eyes hard. She found the boy among milkweed plants, with a caterpillar on his hand. It crawled along his fingers, the yellow and white stripes bobbing on the black background. Replacing it on a red blossom, Kylyn and Katerah walked toward thin forest, inhaling the fragrance of double cabbage-roses. Forcefully, Galen thought to Katerah: *"It's lovely this village of ...?"* He let the thought trail off, hang there.

A minute later Katerah finished the sentence, 'FallsFire, a grand little village.' She was barely aware that she'd spoken aloud.

In the forest, Kylyn followed, distracted by gilt-shot butterflies. Mounting a rickety bridge to an island, Galen spied another bridge and instantly visualised himself on the other side of the river. To see how much his son had grown; to enjoy how well grown. Soon they were in a field, where a flock of swallows raced round and round the humans, almost touching them. Kylyn looked to his right. There was an empty space around which the flyers chirruped excitedly yet wouldn't enter. Jerking his body sideways away from the space, Kylyn continued to watch it. Then they were at a two-storey log house, on a rise overlooking a gentle valley.

It was the usual plain farmhouse, with benches and a multi-storeyed blue jays' cabin on the roof. Katerah entered via the half-buried, ground floor kitchen. Mounting narrow stairs to the dining room, she inspected an expansive table laden with luxuries. On three of Brice's festival plates stood carved animals, also in threes, representing the real thing. A basket piled high with black truffles was prominent. Zithia had traded with Seth for the black truffles. Placing the soy sauce next to herbs, Katerah eyed the display. 'Melia, I thought we were going to keep the Dragon-Land tumeric.'

A blonde woman, with her back to Galen, was adjusting sheaths of blue-tipped grass scattered throughout the rooms. Pale wavy hair swung in the breeze when she turned. The movement was familiar.

The woman said, 'Oh, that's part of my bulk buy from the coast, just unpacked. I knew you needed more to mix with milk for your aches.'

'From the coast! The potter, and his wife, will have apoplexies.'

But Galen wasn't listening. Galen, both astral and physical, was stunned. Transfixed. Which, in turn, astonished him. He simply stared. At his wife. Beyond thought, or movement until... Zithia slowly stretched to look behind Katerah.

Emotion, flashing, tore at him. Galen thudded hard back into his body with a splendid out-of-alignment headache. Concentrating, his spirit shifted marginally within his body. The pain ceased.

'Melia.' He drawled huskily. Looking at the view from the hut atop the pyramid, the whites beneath Galen's eyes were very obvious. He'd never considered it. 'A blonde.'

*

A week later, the Phoenician glassmaker Galen had hired, fashioned a glass mantle over a gilded wooden backing. Six feet by three. While it had been difficult following the ancient instructions, the large payment had guaranteed an eagerness to succeed. Now a dark mirror stood in the chapel near the archpriest's quarters.

This room had sizeable slit-openings in the ceiling and walls, letting moonlight enter at specified times. Usually a large stone turtle occupied the centre of the chapel's amphitheatre. Now the mirror stood there on its stand. Amethyst crystals had been placed around the arena.

When moonlight struck the mirror, Galen began to cast his spell, the one he'd found in an Egyptian papyrus. Circling the glass, he poured every ounce of energy he had into it.

At length, he sat on the top step, shivering. A zephyr brushed his cheek and Galen found his eyes had shut. Instantly awake. How long had passed? Minutes? Hours? Below him, a pearl grey luminescence was swirling in tiny whirlpools. These grew, frolicking around the shadow mirror, rising up the stone room.

When the tempests joined into one maelstrom... Lightning! Galen shielded his eyes. The pulse streamed out of every opening in the room, white searchlights scouring velvet sky. Darkness returned. Now the amethysts were seamed and cloudy.

*

Xalisco's room of mirrors was exactly as it had been before the war. Each golden plate had been reattached except for the ceiling. Two handpicked men waited there for Galen. Their eyes were pulled continually to a black marble pedestal; on it sparkled two thumb-sized emeralds.

Dressed in ceremonial regalia, Galen entered. 'I have a parcel for you to deliver.'

A tall, padded bundle was suddenly lit up. The mirror had been mummified. 'The fragility of your cargo worries me.'

'It shall be delivered intact, august lord. You've my oath on it.' The other courier made the same hasty promise.

'At each port after the New Nile, ask for the village of FallsFire. It's inland, several days journey.'

He unwrapped a note written in Phoenician. It simply announced, *"A gift."* 'Attach this to the parcel.'

They nodded, and Galen gestured toward the emeralds. The men clutched the beautiful gems.

Galen smiled. 'My friends, you're men without ties; well travelled. I admire men who dare to explore.'

Light flickered, revealing a closed chest on another pedestal. Opening the box, Galen dipped his hand in and brought out a dozen prize pearls. He let them fall back. 'In the Far World, pearls are almost emeralds.'

'My lord?'

'What you see before you is a king's treasure. A hundred times your agreed payment.' But the men looked worried. 'You doubt my word?'

'Never, mist maker.'

'Good! A man would be a fool to prefer a little gold over becoming a prince.' Galen smiled, 'I wonder if I'll ever see the Sphinx of our ancestors.'

Galen's knuckle briefly touched his lips. 'Now, a warning.' He paused. They all stood, paused, the hairs on the heads of the two messengers stood on end. 'The curse I put on the emeralds can only be broken if they're in your possession when my package is safely delivered. I assure you, on that day your normal lifespan will be restored to you.'

*

Galen couldn't resist seeing Zithia again. Having astralled to FallsFire, he found Zithia in the hillside garden. She was lovely in pale blue, with a blue cap on her hair. The house-field was filled with people, seeing a party off. Half the village's painted horses were saddled or well packed with goods. The morning was full of blushes and warmth.

All Zithia's attention was given to someone in a green-leafed maple tree. Zithia shaded her eyes to view the higher branches. Galen noted the sun reflecting off a silver ring on her little finger. In obviously new clothes, Kylyn leaned against his mama.

A man descended the tree. Tall, Atlantian tall, muscular, with light brown hair. He handed Kylyn a tame mink kitten. Zithia glowed into the man's lustrous grey eyes. 'Next time, wife, I'll leave the little menace...'

Zithia answered, 'With Shiloh, of course, you'd never leave...'

But Galen didn't hear the rest, for he was back in his study at the temple. There, promptly, every jar and bottle in the room exploded, the fragments flying away from Galen.

chapter 27

By the kitchen door, Zithia felt little puffs of breeze spurt up suddenly from all directions. A witching wind, tugging at her hair. She stood up and the maple-syrup cream she'd been churning fell to the ground. Clutching her skirts, Zithia ran, her petticoat flashing some of its bright colours. The zephyrs surrounded her, raced with her.

Dashing over the hill, and down, Zithia's eyes searched the dry-rice field. A man was leading a young musk ox in a circle, with Kylyn by his side. They waved at her. Slowing to a dawdle, she stopped to pet a foal painted in brown and beige splotches. Zithia waved back, remembering the first day she met Elderic.

The bluejays had long since returned and the river was full to overflowing. Zithia's island was covered with violets and pansy orchids. Hope, the patriarch's wife, had been right in that Zithia's waters were the best fishing grounds in FallsFire. Her particular stretch of river ran and wound through her forest acres, joining with good streams attached to a relatively nearby lake. From there, lake-locked salmon explored the river before generally returning home. They, and a rare genus of river salmon, added to the table for much of the year.

Two slim reed rods in hand, Zithia had tramped through soggy fields further down from the island. Jumping a brook that had appeared overnight, she skidded into a bush. Her head tipped into the masses of its white blooms before she recovered her balance. Soaked, Zithia laughed with the flowers, 'Now if you're out, there must be shad fish in the river.'

Shiloh had left a blanket on a picnic basket. They'd meet up later. Rolling up her sleeves, Zithia looked for signs of trout nosing the river bottom. Spying the wake of a fish, she cast and recast her trembling rod upstream. Landing a yellow perch, Zithia crouched to place it in a submerged fish basket.

'That's a nice size,' said a deep voice from the other side of the river.

Zithia's head snapped up. Lingering. A muscled chest and wide shoulders. As first impressions went, this man wasn't one you'd toss back. And his face! Carefully, Zithia placed the fish in the water, on the wrong side of the basket. It swam off.

'Pardon my intrusion.' He was crossing the river at its ford, ignoring the gnarled bridge further up. 'They said my cousin Shiloh was here.'

Zithia stammered, 'Shiloh's cousin?' She looked away from him, thinking: *"I've been too long without male conversation."* She looked back quickly.

'Yes, I've been in the Far World.'

Zithia picked up her slender reed rod and flicked it absently across water. 'Which cous…' The lure, a silk green fly, dipped. Her line started to stretch: *"Not now!"* She held the rod in stiff hands. Smiling, 'My name is Melia.'

He admired the smile and returned it warmly. 'I'm… ' His eyes drifted to the line's insistent motion. 'Do you want to get that?'

'Uh, yes.' She started to overplay the fish. The silver thread lifted, then grew taut with strain: *"The line must snap soon."*

'You're losing it.' His hands were on the rod and he turned large smoky eyes on her.

'I certainly am.' Their hands touched. Instinctively they both let go of the reed. He re-caught it, steadied it. 'Was. I certainly was.'

'Very fine rod.' He began to work the fish.

'Is it? I got it from Shiloh.' With concentration, Zithia stilled fidgeting hands: *"I traded a pony for that rod. Please don't break it."*

Grinning, Shiloh's cousin fought the trout, while Zithia watched him. Hesitantly, he cast a sidelong look at Zithia. His thick lashes framed gentle eyes. Zithia's fingers still sparked with his electricity.

'Steamy today, isn't it?' Zithia murmured, cutting a lacy fern and fanning herself. And then, realising how her fan-play looked, startled, she tossed it lightly over her shoulder.

When he reeled the fish in, Zithia simultaneously took in the eleven-pounder and her companion. 'I hadn't planned on anything so big.' Startled at her own words, she dropped her head forward to hide a blush. She hustled the fish into the basket. Feeling her cheeks cool, Zithia raised her face to his. Flipping a tendril of hair away from her eyes with the back of her hand, Zithia's inner wrist flashed soft white.

At that moment, several ducks rounded the bend in the river. These blue-grey birds were decorated with white dots, commas, and stripes.

With a last minute movement, the first ducks flew around the two people. Zithia stayed half-kneeling, the whoosh from a wing loud in her ears. Shiloh's cousin moved close to Zithia, shielding her.

Laughing, the stranger then raised his arm, as though to touch the following pair of ducks. The drake's wings flapped in time with the beat of Zithia's heart. Her half-opened mouth curved up.

More ducks flew by. 'Harlequins.' The man stated, 'Adventurers from the coast, looking for white water in which to raise their families.' As he talked, Zithia stood slowly up. 'Spirited pioneers.'

Her mind whispered: *"Like me."* Her heart adding, *"LIKE me."* She pinked again and looked away. Another gorgeous painted couple sped up the river. Zithia's smouldering eyes followed the pair until she met the stranger's eye. Harlequin ducks were now irrevocably linked in her mind with romance!

A cry ensued, 'Elderic!' Shiloh had returned. Elderic looked into Zithia's face a breathless moment longer, then went to Shiloh.

'Elderic,' repeated Zithia under her breath, then thought: *"So this is the man the village families forbade their daughters to court, the one who will have only five children at most."* Her eyebrows arched. *"Poor magnificent creature."*

Happening to catch Shiloh's eye, Zithia's expression melted into neutrality. Shiloh said, 'Melia, let me introduce my cousin Elderic, come home from over the ocean this very day.'

'I've been helping your friend land a fish.'

'Really?' Shiloh looked from one to the other.

Elderic faced Shiloh squarely. 'Melia was over-playing her line.'

Hidden from Elderic, Zithia frowned at her friend.

'Well, she gets so little practice.'

Yesterday they'd added a new shelf to Zithia's pantry, for the excess smoked fish. Elderic turned toward Zithia once more and her brow cleared. Her face seemed younger.

Sitting on a felt rug, Elderic half-reclined opposite Shiloh. While they exchanged family gossip, a last pair of harlequins flew by. Watching the ducks glide away, Shiloh wondered. It was spring after all. Courtship was everywhere. Zithia and Elderic weren't looking at each other, in a very calculated way.

Shiloh, 'What news bring you regarding my fiance in the Far World?' Zithia, who'd been leaning on one elbow, lost her balance.

'As if the token dowry you offered was intended to interest anyone.'

Shiloh offered Zithia an aniseed mushroom, 'The village was getting restless in its matchmaking. This stills their tongues.'

It was the community's custom to send men to the Far World every three years, carrying a list of eligible marriage partners. Obtaining a bride from the far world could be done in one trip. The matter of a groom required two journeys, plus the delivery of the dowry.

'It was a good trip. Remember I took dry-rice with me? When the plants were heavy with grain, I sold every pot. Those wonders fetched high prices.' Elderic added, 'I brought two strangers back. They've put up a tent in great great grandfather's field, awaiting his return from roaming.'

Zithia said, 'When are the two patriarchs expected?'

'It must be soon, father tells me they've been gone ten weeks.'

It was getting late. During the walk back, Zithia was alive to details. Warblers sang, vibrating yellow cheeks. Ashen tree-like mushrooms seemed to peer at the people, and their tobacco scent wafted to Zithia. Then they were at the flooded stream on the border of Zithia's property.

Elderic's eyes roamed the stream restlessly. 'Melia, do you attend the coming nuptials in Shiloh's party?'

Zithia caught her breath. 'I'll not be out of mourning for another three months.'

'Forgive me... widow Melia. I, I... didn't realise. I've been gone so long...'

Shiloh, 'You forgot that widows wear white here?' Then teasing, 'What's addled your mind, Elderic?'

Zithia smiled. And backed away, carefully... into the stream.

Sauntering alone, Zithia smiled at the clumps of orchids carpeting the forest around her pines. Countless white stars held pink clutch bags. A sun-shower fell, leaving myriad molten crystals clinging to the foliage. *"What am I doing? In FallsFire, to want a man is to marry him."* Zithia stopped abruptly. Could she so betray her soul mate?

'My husband.' She whispered and looked over her shoulders. 'Galen!' Her thoughts splintered, she pressed her hands against her temples. Unbidden she saw Galen's blue eyes. 'Nooo! We must be divorced.'

She nodded her head, thinking rapidly: *"He has his ambitions to consider... He betrayed me...us..."* His delectable mistress came to mind. *"In every way."*

Zithia whispered firmly, 'Certainly we're divorced.' She stood straight. 'I'll not think of it... and not of him.'

Part of her mind asked: *"Of whom, then, will you think?"* Zithia ran the rest of the way home.

*

A multiple wedding took place the day after the next holyday. Four couples, the brides all wearing red and, according to the newest FallsFire fashion, with coloured petticoats. The lowest section of each comprised of vertical panels, each a different shade. Zithia, the baby and another widow watched from a second story room at the bakery. Katerah, being but Zithia's cousin, didn't have to re-enter mourning after the baby's birth.

Having served the men, the women retired to their own tables. These were separated from the men's by hollow half-logs filled with tall bracken and yellow lilies. Family members talked across the barrier. At Shiloh's instigation, Kylyn ate with Elderic's son.

Like the rest of the village, the widows enjoyed caribou, wheat cakes and maple-sugar taffy. After everyone had eaten more than they ought, the music began. While the men and women went to separate dancing areas, Zithia's eyes lingered on Elderic.

Over the subsequent nights, each bride and groom was toasted at six large private dinners. Zithia heard all about the four that Katerah attended. Indeed, it was hard to enter a shop without getting an update on who said what. And what the retort was... or could've been.

*

Unexpectedly, Shiloh needed a lot of assistance around her farm and it was only natural that she should ask Elderic's family for help. As a point of duty, Elderic always volunteered. Thus, while Elderic tamed an unruly crab apple tree in full red bloom, Zithia was arranging white-pine cones, with tassels, by Shiloh's front door. Another time, Zithia learned to spin musk oxen semi-fleece, while watching Elderic mend the golden bench on Shiloh's roof. Et cetera.

Weeks were softly sliding by, when Shiloh decided on a lakeside picnic. Dawn at the nearby marshland. All the trees were lit on one side by glowing pink. Rosy hues streaked the sky, when a soft clapping began.

Thousands of mute swans stretched their necks as they flew in a V-flight formation. At staggered intervals came formations of black ducks and snow geese, succeeded by golden plovers. A lead goose trumpeted and the flock landed next to an acre of magenta orchids with yellow stamens. The beaver lake was an instant busy plaza.

After the massed landing, Zithia hugged Shiloh and went collecting lobster mushrooms, while ruffed grouse made drumming noises with their wings atop logs. Kylyn and Elderic's boy skittered around, gathering yellow cancan-skirted mushrooms. Having declared a pre-dawn walk a ludicrous waste of sleep, Katerah was still abed.

Zithia looked over her shoulder at Elderic, who was carefully shovelling a second clump of scarlet pixie-hat orchids onto a pony-drawn sled.

Shiloh said to Zithia, 'The taffy pulling afternoon at the carpenters isn't a festival, it's an occasion. So you'll be able to attend. The whole village comes and contributes in some way.'

Zithia smiled radiantly. Every event she could go to was cause for celebration. Walking slowly, with a small sway to her hips, Zithia went to a flood of magenta annuals. Even her hand movements had slowed, were delicate.

Elderic watched her go. Shiloh didn't look up from plants the on the sled. 'Melia's no village girl, Elderic.' Her cousin tripped over his feet. 'You've one child and she has two. I promise you, the idea of many more horrifies her.'

Looking pensive, Elderic excused himself and took the boys off to the beaver dam, disturbing a wild cat sunning its distinctive stripes. Watching iridescent loons run on the water, in courtship, he turned his head several times to look surreptitiously at Zithia.

*

It was the last day of mourning. Zithia sat on a low stool in her kitchen garden, eyes on her feet. Windblown, falling palest pink confetti of fringed flowers seemed to take on shapes from her past. She was barely visible in layers of white. Even her thick veil reached her waist. She'd not eat until sundown. The guests were received with a nod.

Every bachelor in the region had been tidied up and towed along by their female relatives. Zithia's own offspring were examined as keenly as her stock. The fields of rice seedlings and rye were promising. Massed pansy orchids flowered on the island in the river. Everywhere the female eye looked an orchid or a rose gladdened the eye.

Leaving the barn, someone commented, 'One of her ponies had twins.'

'Speaking of twins,' said his sister, 'Ezekiel's baby boys are bursting with health.'

Another woman, 'And Melia's naming gift is a length of red silk.' It had been Zithia's only remaining piece of silk, previously earmarked for Kylyn's thirteenth birthday.

Lilac shook with emotion at all she saw, and much of what she heard, yet had barely a whisper available for her carping. Briony was left to listen, then listen again to her mama before repeating, with painful hesitancy and often inaccurately, Lilac's venom. Briony had become but a squashy shadow.

During the afternoon Elderic's mother, Faith, arrived with the younger siblings. Faith was late because of Elderic. That very morning he'd asked her to make an offer of his assistance to Zithia. Faith's mouth had dropped open. 'But Elderic, the family honour... our reputation.'

All the way to the house, Elderic had pleaded with his mother. Her other ten sons, mostly married, added their voices to his, for it was Faith's right, and hers alone, to make an offer to Zithia. If she chose not to, no one else in the family could. On discovering this two months before, Zithia had become attentive to Faith's conversations whenever they met and had even demurely sought Faith's advice on various matters.

Unable to silence her sons, Faith had finally rasped out, 'Offer a woman of means damaged goods? I'll look a fool in front of all the women.'

'Whereas,' stated Elderic baldly, 'I look a fool every time a village girl reaches courting age.'

At sunset the priest prayed, 'We commend the soul of widow Melia's husband to God. May he find solace in that he lives on through his children. Now the widow Melia is part of the world.'

The men and children were ushered out, including Elderic, who gave his mother one last soulful look. When Zithia retired to her room, the ladies calculated assets at each other in the greatest hurry. When she returned wearing a most becoming pastel gold, two young ladies instantly thrust out their bottom lips.

Within the next few minutes mothers or aunts had offered to have their bachelor move bees, re-nest the roosting tree and more. To each offer, Zithia made the formal reply, 'Many thanks, but such a service isn't needed at present.'

The party was still going strong when Elderic's mother and sisters requested their capes. Mid-word, Zithia went after the departing women, picking up a hidden covered plate on the way. All the ladies unexpectedly found themselves out-of-breath. Shiloh appeared with capes and handed one to Faith.

Faith frowned, 'Shiloh, how could you mistake this for mine? I never wear green, even as lining.'

Zithia was then blocking Faith's way. 'Faith, please tell me you're not going.' Speedily she presented the plate, on which lay a very few maple candies topped with a miniature sugared violet. 'I particularly wanted your opinion... it took me hours to make these few.'

Faith let one melt on her tongue. 'And well worth it.'

'My thanks,' Zithia smiled tremulously. 'I've always considered that quality far outweighs quantity.'

Blinking, Faith searched Zithia's face. Slowly she took another candy, taking in all its aspects as a judge at a festival would. 'Shiloh tells me you admire my baked salmon.'

'Indeed!' Breathing shallowly, 'None better.'

'Then, someday, I'll show you how to prepare it.'

'Tomorrow?' Almost breathless, Zithia rushed her words, 'Here? That I might make it for the holyday.'

Faith straightened, projecting her words, 'Tomorrow then, Melia.'

The potter's wife appeared. She had a second cousin needing a wife with land. 'Here's your cloak Faith.' Her eyes bounced between Zithia and Elderic's mother. 'It was at the bottom of the... heap.'

This time Faith examined Zithia's face minutely. 'Then, of course, Melia, the recipe requires a large fire. My son Elderic could cut the extra wood we'll need.'

Zithia's smile was dazzling, 'Thank you, Faith I find myself quite desperate for firewood.'

This wasn't the required reply, but Faith's bosom expanded. Shiloh kicked Zithia's ankle and, remembering, she reddened. 'My thanks, mistress Faith; I'm most obliged for your son Elderic's assistance.'

Heads held with chins high, Elderic's womenfolk left. Going up the road they grinned on observing Zithia's fully stocked woodpile.

Almost as the door closed upon Faith, the other ladies were grabbing their cloaks. In noisy groups they all hooted over Zithia's woodpile. The potter's wife snorted, 'I've never seen anything so disgraceful; such forwardness.' She raced on, 'And I'm sure if Lilac still had her voice, she'd call it… more than that!'

Lilac's whispered ascent was cracked. She put her hand up to her throat, while digging Briony in the ribs. Squeaking, Briony peered at her mama, but couldn't quite figure out which nastiness Lilac wanted her to repeat at present.

One lady complained, 'Melia didn't even finish her conversation with me. She simply… ran off.'

It took a long time for them all to walk home that night, and the various dissections of events didn't finish even after the women parted.

Faith was halfway home when Elderic appeared from under a tree.

She looked grim. 'Mistress Melia has proclaimed herself desperate for firewood.' There was an electrified pause. 'You cut wood for her tomorrow.' She looked ten feet tall, 'And everyone heard Melia proclaim quality to be better than quantity.' Elderic whooped for joy.

*

The next morn was still blue-hazed when Zithia and Katerah heard a wagon approach. Peering out the windows they saw a dray, with what looked like an entire tree of logs overflowing the backless cart, drawn by six horses. Elderic, four sisters and three brothers walked beside it. Immediately, the men began unloading the dry logs, while the sisters stood around in their festival clothes.

Zithia and Katerah hurried into holyday attire. By the time Zithia opened the front door, the wood was piled high in plain view of the road. The brothers loaded themselves into the dray and went home. Thereafter, the rhythmic swing of Elderic's axe was heard constantly. Bringing out acorn coffee and the famous candies, Zithia greeted Elderic's sisters. Smothering laughter, the women all agreed the weather was very fine today.

Carrying the plate behind her back, Zithia took a mug to Elderic.

He mopped his brow with his sleeve. 'Good morning, mistress.'

Her pulse beat faster. 'Morning.' Putting the drink on a log, she brought out the candies. Elderic's eyes lit up. She couldn't hold his gaze and returned to his sisters. The ladies went inside and no one mentioned that finding a proper place for the wood was going to be difficult.

That afternoon, when Zithia tasted the baked salmon, she gave a little gasp. It was perfect. Contrary to local tradition, when passing on a prized recipe, Faith hadn't left out one ingredient or instruction.

*

A month later, the sun shone on the annual felt-making day. Wool was laid on sturdy covers, and then women created patterns by adding bright coloured strands. Men were rolling fibre into thick sausages. Painted horses already dragged similar bundles around a large field, gradually matting the contents into felt. The time needed to create rugs, in comparison to tent-felt, was passionately debated.

Dressed in pale green, with emerald flowers stamped onto the last inch of her mauve petticoat, Zithia accompanied Elderic across the field. Their first public appearance. He carried the wool Zithia had brought for her future parents-in-law's pile. Zithia herself toted rich golden loops and a basket of fine magenta strands.

Two tents flourished in the far field. The roaming patriarchs, great great grandfather Gabriel and great great uncle Adison, were back. Zithia observed the patriarch's wife, Hope, placing a white bison pelt beneath one awning. Attended by her middle-aged children and their adolescents, Hope organised everything. Since Gabriel had no wife, he was four times a widower, Hope directed his children and comforts also. Years ago Gabriel, and therefore Adison, had forsaken houses in favour of tents.

Brunch was being set up in the paddock below Gabriel's tent. Family picnic areas were scattered over two paddocks, being marked by blankets and bustling women setting up before the feast. A whole stag cooked on a spit, in celebration of the patriarchs' return. Zithia put succulent slabs of Benjamin's fillet-fungus, tender as marbled steak, plus a roast duck, on a communal table. All families contributed a good dish to the day. Everyone brought their own bread. Indeed there was a competition today for the best homemade bread. Knowing her limits, Zithia hadn't entered. Katerah had. Milling round with all the village women, they waited for the judging. Katerah received an honourable mention for a lemon peel loaf.

As the crowd dispersed, a man, a villager named Michael, saw something and walked to where another man stood. Ancient Jerabiah was cross.

'Where's my family? We always picnic here! Right here.'

'But Jerabiah, you all decided three years ago to set up for the feast under the crabapple tree in the next field, remember. So you'd be more comfortable in the shade.'

'But... our family picnicked right here for thirty years.'

'True, but the new family gathering place is...' Michael gave instructions. But, as Jerabiah's annoyance was visibly increasing, he added, 'I'll show you the way.'

'Thirty years.' repeated Jerabiah. Walking on along the clearest path, Jerabiah grew quiet. They passed smiling friends and relatives of an entire lifetime. Then, without looking at Michael, Jerabiah said softly, 'If I don't get a chance to talk to Magnolia, tell her... when my words aren't my own... when my mind isn't me... or I get angry... she mustn't worry. I'm not really there then, I'm halfway home.'

Finally in sight of his family, Jerabiah ambled off alone. Michael watched awhile, reflecting upon how Jerabiah was currently in his bed at home, slipping in and out of one of his comas. A recent complication. Sadly... Michael pondered that the end of life, with its mind illnesses, could be very cruel for all concerned.

A horseman rode by, playfully tipping off Michael's small-brimmed hat; delighted waves and some cheering hailed the rider's progress. Zithia and Elderic were crossing back to his family when the same horse trotted up beside them, too close to Elderic making them jump. The rider's face was swathed in a silk scarf and a deep-rimmed hat. Laughing heartily, he declared, 'You did well in the Far World, nephew.'

Then the horseman glanced a second time at Zithia, which glance lasted that much longer than expected. Kneeing his horse nearer to Zithia, the rider's eyes lasered her up and down and up again. 'I hear you're courting.' In silence, he stared a while more. 'Do you wish to ask for a blessing?'

'Ye... yes, great great uncle Adison.'

'Bring her to the tent.' He wheeled the horse around. 'The children, where are they?'

Elderic jerked his head towards the nursery paddock. Without another word Adison cantered off. He easily spotted Kylyn charging ram's-head orchids at another boy. Again, Adison watched the boy, then the baby in Katerah's arms. He looked most at hair, skin, chin. The baby's large, well set eyes were sparkling mauve. Elderic and Zithia were approaching the main tent's awning when Adison's stallion thundered up. The patriarch dismounted and went inside. Through the flap, Zithia spied her Dragon-Land mystic's window. A sheet of black wood covered by thirty layers of lacquer, the better for seeing.

Soon Gabriel came out, wearing cashmere, looking not a day over sixty. Zithia froze, Gabriel's features were pure seventh tribe, even in height. A strong chin, high cheekbones and skin that had once been pale. Such rare eyes. Blues, purples and mauves. The seventh was famous for its eyes. Gabriel's were shades of aquamarine and pale sapphire, shot through with gold. Twin kaleidoscopes, whose pupils weren't discs, but stars.

And while Zithia examined Gabriel, he examined her. Adison took off his hat and unravelled his scarf. Zithia blinked quickly several times; another from the seventh tribe. Again that tall stature.

Gabriel said to Adison, 'And the children?'

Adison smiled broadly, throwing his hat onto a falcon's perch. The bird, wearing a green gem with a mauve heart, eyed Adison. Raising his eyebrow feathers, slowly the falcon curled a powerful claw and flicked the offending article off his stand. Adison smiled, hurled himself into a chair and, picking up a piece of venison with chopsticks, tossed the morsel to the bird. Hope went and stood behind Adison's chair, draping her arms around Adison, after she handed him a bowl of orange flavoured tea. Adison turned his head to say cheerfully in her ear, 'You didn't mention this, sweetheart.'

She hugged him closer, purring, 'Surprise!'

Gabriel nodded to Elderic. 'Nephew.' His grin was lopsided Gabriel's eyes glittered at Zithia. 'Well then, where did you spring from?'

Her voice was softly demure, so that only four people heard. 'The same lines as you, by the look of us.' She tilted her head sideways. 'Why do you both look young? I was told you're elderly.' Adison and Hope laughed.

Gabriel asked him, 'Flattery or insult?'

'They came for a blessing, grandfather. Flattery and ignorance!'

Gabriel looked around at the crowd. His voice carried. 'Woman, my line, the founding line of this village, inherits the long lives that all Atlantians enjoyed. My brother Benjamin was two hundred and eleven when he died. I'm one hundred and seventy. Adison at one hundred and eight looks more his age, I think.'

There was general mirth. Adison looked forty, while his great grandfather appeared to be a handsome sixtyish.

'Now, mistress Melia, has Elderic told you that I can terminate your courtship?' Zithia goggled. 'Terminate or bless it. That's the law.' He rubbed his hands together. 'So, to the matter at hand.'

Elderic recited the usual refrain. 'Great great grandfather, we stand before you seeking your permission...'

Curtly Gabriel held his open palm. Elderic stiffened. Gabriel looked at the villagers. 'Mistress Melia and my great great grand-nephew... are betrothed.'

The colour drained from the faces of the happy couple. Elderic protested, 'Great great grandfather we've only begun courting.'

'What of that?' Gabriel slapped him on the shoulder. 'You came for my blessing and you have it.'

'Blessing to court, great great grandfather. Not marry!'

'Then you're in luck. You came for one blessing and I've given you two.'

Gabriel now turned his startling eyes on Zithia. 'Woman, I speak to you in lieu of male kin.' The village took in a sharp breath; in cases of this kind, a man was usually chosen from the community to speak on the woman's behalf. 'Will you have this man?'

Her eyes widened. 'P... patriarch, perhaps, Elderic can't marry...me!'

Gabriel scowled, 'Know you of an obstacle?'

The crowd was hushed in the silence of ages.

Zithia cleared her throat, 'I, I'm...' she closed her eyes briefly, 'I'll not bear more than seven children. And I already have two.' Gabriel raised his eyebrows. 'It's in my line.'

Some villagers shook their heads. Most waited. The patriarch only smiled. 'I expected as much.'

Elderic's voice rang out. 'Great great grandfather, I accept this woman in marriage.'

'Well, Mistress Melia, what say you?'

'Yes!'

Handing Zithia and Elderic each a cup, Gabriel toasted the union. 'Good. The wedding is in a month.' Elderic and Zithia spluttered violently. Adison thumped Elderic on the back. 'My nuptial gift is a honeymoon spent roaming. The bride's gift to me is for Elderic to escort a stranger to port and do a little trading.'

Adison sparkled at the gasping Zithia. 'Do you ride?'

'Ride?' Her eyes flew open wide and wider.

Gabriel beckoned to an adolescent in the crowd. 'And this will be Justden's first roaming. He has reached an age when he must take his place among the patriarchs, being the only long-lifer born to us since Adison. From now on Justden will need a champion. This day, I declare Elderic to be Justden's champion. This proclamation goes to our kinsmen in the Far World.'

*

A month later, velvety red rose petals topped the rippling spa. All the women had left Zithia alone. *"Two husbands."* She trembled with her thoughts. 'No,' she whispered desperately, 'that's dead.'

Then Zithia tossed her head, chin high. 'Elderic is a loving father… my children will have a half-brother, a large extended family… my darlings will be assured of their place here…'

In her mind's eye she again saw Elderic standing by the river, under a tall chinaberry tree and its purplish flowers, with the pairs of harlequin ducks flying by. Zithia flushed and immersed herself totally in the spa. Then Zithia arose and crossed her arms so that her hands touched her shoulders. She prayed: *"God of my heart, please understand. I'll make Elderic a good wife."*

Elderic's sisters returned, averting their eyes from Zithia when she left the ritual waters. Rose petals clinging to her, Zithia wrapped herself in the proffered towel. Soon, she was gowned in deepest red silk, the cloth bought at a quite outrageous price from the potter, embroidered by the village women with tiny dragons. Briony and Lilac's nasty tempered monsters had been quietly replaced. A loose netted veil covered Zithia's hair and matching ruby cap. Her slippers, peeping artfully from beneath the gown, were extraordinarily beautiful. Elderic's mama had had her own, fully embroidered and glass jeweled, wedding slippers altered for the occasion.

Finally Zithia entered the prayer hall late, by the prescribed amount, as was the custom, to remind a groom of the supreme importance of woman to family and the line. Keeping her eyes on the floor, Zithia was guided to her groom by Justden, upon whose high-held hand hers was laid with a red silk kerchief between them. The rafters were hung with orchids, red or dyed red, and velvety roses. Unseen by Zithia, Elderic had never looked more handsome. The groom had arrived back from the coast two days ago, while Zithia and Katerah were putting the finishing touches to their, absolutely necessary, six new dresses.

Elderic slipped a simple silver wedding ring on Zithia's little finger. At this, their first touch since carelessly grabbing the fishing rod at their first meeting, Zithia sighed lightly. The sigh was also custom. Putting one hand on the small of her back, Elderic slowly lowered his head to hers. She tipped her face up to him and, even at her height, Zithia needed to stand on her toes until their closed lips met. Time stopped awhile as they lingered there, wrapped in the moment.

*

At the wedding feast, the considerable dowry gifts were displayed. No gold, for gold wasn't considered a proper dowry good, having no soul. Many gifts were in groups of three, that luckiest of numbers, including jars of genko honey and golden truffles discovered by following little yellow flies attracted by the truffle scent. Plus the potter's heaviest-based ceramic frying pans; dearly wanted by most of the village women, Elderic's mama couldn't countenance the price. She wasn't alone. The bargaining, delicious to on-lookers, had been so sharp that Brice had brought the two flushing combatants a much needed cider midway.

When the dancing commenced, great great uncle Adison threw a scarf over the hedge dividing the men and women. Thus the bride and groom finished a line dance, on their own side of the paddock, each holding an end. At the witching hour, bride and groom disappeared quietly from the ongoing party.

The honeymoon tent was in a secluded meadow surrounded by tall clumps of large green orchids and early fragrant chocolate flowers. Elderic dismounted from the small two-pony cart, turned to his wife and, reaching down, swept her bodily from the dray; carrying Zithia into another life.

With dawn barely cracking, the day after the six wedding dinners, half the tent fell in upon the bride and groom. Blurry with sleep and fearing an attack, Elderic fought his way through the restricting felt, his knife unsheathed. Adison, with assorted men, sat on horseback laughing. 'The roaming begins. We ride in an hour.'

They cantered, single file, through a burn-hole in the centre of a living tree. The redwoods were a cathedral, each Atlantis-tree height. Katerah rode with the baby in a flexible bouncing basinet attached to a mama's saddle. Zithia and Gabriel were ahead of the others. 'Melia, I don't know your tribe.'

Never before had they spoken about their Atlantian features. 'While I was still dreaming in my mama's womb, a heritage-caller spoke to me, drawing out many an Atlantian feature of my ancestors for my own. Hence the mix you see.' She smiled wryly. 'I do think the ancestors might've allowed me more height.'

'Heritage-caller; interesting. And what about your children?'

'Before their births someone whispered to my children also.' Not mentioning that she could thus call.

'And yet, grand daughter, you didn't discover your pregnancy until you reached our village.'

Apparently attracted by a heady scent, Zithia suddenly dismounted and cut orchids with yellow balloons beneath thin red petals.

'Daughter of the house of Gabriel and of Adison,' he waited until Zithia met his gaze, 'Elderic's future children… will be pearls, will they not?'

'Very probably, patriarch.' She bit her bottom lip. 'The results are never guaranteed. Yet…'

'Given Elderic's lineage, we may even hope for another long-lifer born in the village.'

*

In the fifth week, Gabriel's inner circle dressed in holyday clothes and took extra horses loaded with maple sugar, flour and such. The others would continue along a sweet river, on the edge of a vast pastureland, while Gabriel's party crossed the lush prairie.

Elderic and the newest patriarch, Justden, carried two brace of grouse across their saddles. Adison brought an elk. A bison avalanche blackened the far distance. The grass went on forever, broken only by infrequent streams.

After a day of fast riding, changing horses every four hours, they came upon a small lake in the midst of the ongoing grassland. Dismounting at the middle, Zithia asked, 'Do you think it'd stain my feet?'

Elderic, still on horseback, 'We'll find out; only not here.'

"He gestured to the right. Seeing only endless grass, Zithia walked towards where Gabriel sat upon his mount, staring into the middle distance. The party had stopped at a horseshoe-shaped cliff. The lake poured two hundred feet into the River Royal.

Zithia's eyes glowed. In the semi-sunken valley was a mass of tents, with pennants flying high, each a beautifully painted harlequin-duck. These people claimed the harlequins as their own. Having descended a slender trail the patriarchs' party was on a pasture that went on for days. When at ground level, by a trick of the light, the tent–village seemed to be attended by a thousand hovering harlequins.

Crossing a ford, they avoided the huge thinly-woolly mammoths bathing in the blue waters. Going a particularly regal colour, the giant creatures trumpeted pleasure before shambling off to bamboo-columned mammoth marquees. Then the patriarch's party was in the midst of activity. Near one of two immense woodpiles, women prepared a bison they'd hunted. The ladies wore colourful suede or leather skirts and tops, which they'd dyed themselves.

Scattered tents soon mushroomed-up close together, as the party rode on. Clean-shaven men, with stiff brimmed hats, ambled along or sat whittling wood. Everyone had a knife and a dagger at their waists. Women went bareheaded. All the nomads were tall, with good jaw lines. Wiry, yet muscled. Constant exposure to the elements had bleached their hair, from brown to sandy colours.

People hailed the patriarchs when they passed by. And there were so many 'old' eyes, eyes aged beyond their years. Having a slow, considered look around, she thought: "*Every face is from Galen's tribes, the first tribe and the seventh.*" She couldn't credit it. The guardian tribes were still here, in First Atlantis.

Gabriel smiled, 'The guardians. Now nomads of the Greater Atlantis. Many are also patriarchs; it's always a relief to talk to people my own age. And now I bring them a heritage-caller.' Elderic beamed, he'd been told the night before.

With his usual boyishness, Adison whooped, then spurred his horses on, to arrive in front of a chosen tent with a flourish. There he leapt from his stallion and a woman, Zithia's age, threw herself into his arms. At the woman's waist was a familiar embroidered sash.

'Well!!' Righteous disapproval spread over Zithia's face.

Hand in hand, Adison and his woman came over. Guardians or not, Zithia's face froze. She respected Adison's wife, Hope. Elderic dismounted.

Adison announced, 'Virginia, may I present Justden, Melia and Elderic. Virginia, my wife.'

'Your wife!'

'My second wife, niece.'

Justden and Elderic went to Virginia, bowing their heads.

Zithia was still on her horse. 'Second wife?'

Virginia's smile became fixed. Elderic hurriedly offered to help Zithia dismount. Glaring at Zithia, Adison took Elderic's place. She returned his hard stare and swung her leg over the saddle. The patriarch clasped Zithia tight by the waist, lowering her. He said softly, 'Melia, you forget I'm your patriarch. Don't provoke me.'

Shutters seemed to draw down over Zithia's eyes. She went to Virginia. 'My lady.' Zithia kissed her cheek.

Virginia's lips barely moved. 'Much longer on your horse, kinswoman,' Virginia's eyes were icy amethysts, 'and we'd have matched daggers.'

Arms around each other's waists, Adison and his wife retired to her tent.

Elderic watched Zithia watch them. 'Hope is far past childbearing. She desired the patriarch to take a nomad wife. It's his duty to continue his line.'

'And exactly when were you going to tell me?'

'It wasn't my secret to give away.'

'We're husband and wife. We should have no secrets.' Her mind taunted: "*Really, two wives… two husbands.*" Instantly Zithia kissed Elderic before he could see her blush.

*

'It's called the Long Week and about a thousand of our nomad cousins have gathered. Here at the River Royal.' Gabriel had dropped into the tent Virginia had arranged for Zithia and Elderic. 'When I first came across the clans I took an oath that only I should know about them. I, and my small circle of companions. We all take the oath.'

Elderic took Kylyn with him for his first official introductions. Left to herself, Zithia watched a child's horse race, from under the tent awning.

Over the river, horse whisperers trained their children. In the sky above, the clan leaders' falcons dipped and soared, together with a dozen new silk kites. With the baby on her hip, Zithia wandered over to an archery competition. The competitors were dazed when Adison shot true at twice the distance of the others, with his Dragon-Land bow. Finias's four dozen bows, at Adison's feet, fetched extremely nice prices and much discussion.

Going into the tent-village, the lines of marquees looped around the valley like dozens of converging streams. Displayed under the awnings were salts, chicory hammers, silver goods and furs. Purchasing a river-tumbled star sapphire, Zithia had it enclosed within the silver claws of a pendant. Nearby hung a leather belt, with small jewels netted among its fringes.

Purveyors of rainbow sands took corner tents, displaying sand-pictures on stiff leather. Gabriel purchased bags of the full range of the Painted Desert's colours, for trading on the coast. Egypt and the south temples used the sands in mystic designs. Well attended stills processed white-lightning, through the fourth distillation, under the shade of awnings. People jostled each other to placarded postal tents, where men mixed dry ink on peacock-coloured ink-stones. Scrolls were posted or received; letters dictated and written. In Atlantian. Silk scrolls announced weddings and especially valued births.

Katerah left Zithia to trade for a squat column of clear mauve kunzite crystal, returning wearing moccasins, and minus her cap. On Zithia's admiring a scrimshawed horn knife-handle, the nomad woman pointed at a couple of inches of yellow cotton petticoat, peeping from beneath Zithia's skirt. Woven cloth was scarce. The lady stood in front of Zithia, who undid a drawstring and slipped out of the garment. In the process Zithia spied two pieces of amber, one containing a green-winged fly, the other a fern.

When Zithia removed her jacket for trading, the nomad glimpsed Zithia's delicately embroidered top. And noticed she had no dagger.

'Never go unarmed.' Declared the horrified the lady, who expertly attached a metal blade to Zithia's bone knife-handle. 'You live in the wide world; there are evil people out there.'

Zithia nodded slowly; hadn't she met her unfair share of barbarians.

'Carry it from today!' The trader put the sheathed knife on a leather belt, patting the dagger. 'Start as you mean to go on.'

Zithia's brow furrowed while she fastened her new belt. 'At the Long Week Festival?'

The trader drew herself up to her full height. 'We should never take our safety for granted.' She took Zithia's jacket. 'This is for the blade, a perfect size for self-defence. I'll exchange your top for the ambers.'

At a huge communal campfire, women were already busy de-quilling grouse with wooden tweezers. Elderic and Justden were there, presenting the elk.

They hailed Zithia, Elderic saying, 'We promised Virginia we'd collect something for her.'

The trader they met couldn't manage to pull her eyes from her new elaborate silk lantern, part of the bargain, as she pointed at a long-wool fleece. Two sons hefted it off its stand. The wool was clotted with gold granules. 'I laid it in a river for two years. Next year's fleece will have rubies clustered among the gold.'

Elderic and Justden carried the fleece on a pole between them. Forty pounds. Zithia was dazzled. Elderic, 'A gift for Hope...'

Zithia, 'Goodness, how do we to get it home.'

Elderic, '...from Virginia.'

Zithia's silence was audible. Observing the deep frown, Justden spoke. 'Kinswoman, Virginia is a patriarch, which was why Hope approved her over other proposed matches. Virginia had been widowed twenty years before this marriage. One spring, her husband and his hunting party were taken by a king tornado.' Justden became sombre. 'They found some of the bodies, each in several pools of blood. The tornado had sucked off much more than their clothes.'

'She mourned twenty years.' Zithia's eyes were moistening, 'I'll help deliver the fleece to Lady Virginia.'

The crowd at Virginia's tent was wholly female. Egyptian cosmetics, from Elderic's Far World visit, were rare joys and the selling brisk. Lavender scent, having originated in Atlantis, was snapped up. Virginia moved sideways to deliver the last vial, when a dagger flicked into the log beneath some kohl. Virginia, 'Have a care Magnolia. Your aim may've strayed and shattered the perfumes.'

'My aim's always true.' Magnolia sniffed indignantly; she'd been fearful of missing out. 'And I want an orange, plus a cherry perfume.'

'They're Dragon-Land scents.' Virginia warned.

Magnolia, 'I've plenty of dry lacquer for trading.'

A statuesque family, newly arrived at the festival, was rushing to the sale. One daughter, a few steps ahead of her mother, turned while racing. 'Mama, I can't see any perfume.' So distracted, the girl slipped and fell flat on the ground, winded.

Her mother stretched her next quick pace high, and stepped over the prone girl, saying, 'I see one.' She was at the tent, and bidding while the daughter was still elbowing through the crowd. 'I've giant redwood honey, the darkest ever harvested.'

Virginia paused, 'That honey is as magical as Genko honey.' She picked up the last scent vial, adding, 'And we could deal over the perfumes I've reserved for myself.'

Another woman, Clementine, asked, 'What about the aphrodisiacs?'

'We still have a little.'

'With the herbal aphrodisiacs that's all you'll need.' A grandmother declared, giving the crowd an eloquent smirk and a prodigious wink. Raucous laughter erupted.

'Good. I've an older brother who, mama insists, should give our family more children.' Everyone laughed. 'The trade: pink salt and the mineral to strengthen teeth.'

Virginia's oldest daughters took over, while Virginia approached Zithia. Virginia moved a little to one side. 'Kinswoman.' Her voice was flat.

'It's a noble gift, my lady.' Zithia gestured to the fleece.

'From one good wife to another.'

Directing where the fleece should be stored, Virginia waved the men away. They disappeared into the heaving melee.

Zithia, 'I saw Hope embroider your sash, speaking tender words of the recipient.'

Then, drawing out an oilskin pouch that hung between skirt and petticoat, Zithia unwrapped her poetry book. 'Yours during the Long Week.'

Opening the little book, Virginia beamed while Zithia recited the first words. Trading stopped mid-call. Virginia read aloud the rest of the poem. Only when she closed the volume, was the clamour renewed. 'Adison didn't mention you could read Atlantian.'

'He doesn't know. Where I came from, any reading was discouraged in women.'

'Elderic will be very pleased.'

Looking at her book, 'A copy could be made in this Long Week.'

The women went into another lull of trading. Virginia, 'Such a gift may only be received if you ask a favour of me during the Long Week, any favour within my gift. And I've a wide gift.'

*

At sundown, Zithia and Elderic joined the others for dinner. Zithia appeared garbed in leather and suede, ankles and elbows showing. Elderic had never seen his wife look lovelier; Zithia had borrowed Virginia's cosmetics.

Halfway through the meal, Gabriel beckoned Zithia to sit next to him on a silver fur rug. Looking at her face, at the expert application of colours, he declared, 'Word of your reading Atlantian spreads barely less swiftly than your being a heritage-caller. It appears I married my nephew to a greater mystery than I thought.'

'Great great grandfather, is that important?'

'I'm still considering.' He raised a single eyebrow, then, 'Teach your children Atlantian, in secret. The world of the Atlantian nomads stays on the roaming.'

'But is Olondin old enough to keep such a secret, grandfather Gabriel?'

Chuckling, Gabriel drawled, 'Go.'

A man rose to his feet and the legend telling began. In usual practice, the first tale was about Atlantis, in Atlantian. The rhythm of the Atlantian, combined with the meaning of the words, was intoxication in itself. Add a Dragon-Land poetry melody, and Zithia was taken to new heights.

"When the island of Atlantis fell, it fell through thirteenth tribe's treachery. The thirteenth decided they alone were fit to rule Atlantis and thus the world. Fighting for control of the technology that powered Atlantis, the thirteenth caused an explosion mighty enough to break the ground. Cracked to the heart, Atlantis heated the waters with her lifeblood, then lay cold beneath the waves. The survivors, including our tribes, dragged themselves to the closest shore. To the First Atlantis, greater Atlantis. Here the tribes exacted swift justice on the thirteenth tribe, depriving them of technology and damning them to isolation. They were exiled and their crimes remembered.

"Now, before Atlantis died, the thirteenth's overweening interest in gold had caused the elders of lesser Atlantis to transfer gold reserves to a secret vault. Mounds of gold ingots were deposited within the base of a mountain deep in the First Atlantis. Heritage jewelry was also hidden, with knowledge crystals and books.

"Five of those who knew the treasure's location were slain with beloved Atlantis. The remaining two flew an airship to the mountain, bringing back the books and knowledge crystals. They were transporting the first gold shipment and jewelry.

"When the shuttle went down off the coast, in shallow water, it had entered the area presently called the bad sea. In the crash, a palate of gold smashed the map crystal showing the treasure's location. Worse, the two pilots were drowned. The remaining wealth was lost."

Applause showered the speaker. Tomorrow would see the tale continue.

*

Heads of clans, sitting with emperors' dogs at their feet, had already bartered for much of Gabriel's goods. They'd go home with loads of salt, a musk ox, horses, and furs; silver lanterns, fine blue sapphires. Adison wanted a mammoth… more white-lightning was poured for nomads and patriarchs.

Carrying rye flour to the kitchen, Zithia saw Elderic being introduced to more clan leaders. Adison sat on sacks of newly acquired dry lacquer. Elderic's eyes followed his wife, though he continued to face the elders. One man leaned over to Gabriel with questions.

At the campfire, Zithia savoured feverwort coffee and found Virginia among the bread makers. The sourdough had already risen in clay bells; each family carried a bell. Similar containers soaked up the heat over a fire. Virginia manoeuvered the upside-down bells, filled with dough, into holes dug in the embers. Young women helped positioned the hot tops like caps over the dough-filled ones.

While the bread cooked, the daily wood-chopping competition rang out its refrain. The prize for this Long Week was a full bag of dried Dragon-Land mushrooms. The chopping melded with tunes played on three-string violins carved from resonant spruce, peculiarly nomad, plus Dragon-Land moon and balloon guitars and bronze bells. Some melodies were pure nomad, some Atlantian.

Clothes were being de-wrinkled in the sun, using copper water-thieves to sprinkle water over the cloth. Older children were relegated to this task, raising water-filled silver balls from leather buckets. Taking their thumbs off the end of the long silver tube which served as a handle, water thus fell from the many tiny holes in the bottom of the ball. Once the clothes were

386

done, a fine water fight always ensued.

Every night there was more of the nomad's Atlantis legend, played to gentle Dragon-Land tunes.

"The loss of the treasure ship galvanised the Atlantians into leaving for the Far World, while their crafts were still sound. Until then, they were reticent to leave. Our ancestors wept afresh. To leave the First Atlantis was to truly lose Atlantis. Beloved ancient Atlantis, larger Atlantis, whose eastern coast and fabled cities had fallen into the sea. Whose one remaining city had become the sanctuary of civilization: the island Atlantis.

"For the first time they regretted not allowing the Egyptians and similar petitioners to settle this vast land.

"They left, scattered by the winds of opportunity and preference to different lands all over the world. Some of their destinations were: Jerusalem, the Nile, Stonehenge, the Yellow River." Shrill whistling stopped the recitation. An error had occurred and no inaccuracies were tolerated. A new teller was chosen.

"their destinations: the Yellow River, Jerusalem, Stonehenge, the Nile. A multi-tribe group chose to live in the lands far south of here. Some few couldn't tear themselves away from this land, beloved of all, and settled in the New Nile's basin. The first and the seventh tribes remained totally true to the land and wouldn't leave First Atlantis. They chose to remain and were named, by all the tribes, Guardians of First Atlantis. In so remaining they earned the esteem, the love, of the other tribes. For none wished to think of First Atlantis unpopulated for thousands of years. Only a few of the first and the seventh, chosen by lot, went to the Far World so that their tribes wouldn't become isolated."

"Living in the Far World, the wild world, life changed for the Atlantians. Their energy sources were limited and their technology power hungry. The Atlantians themselves were altered. Many married into the local nobility. Their flattered egos grew beyond expectation, on the reputation of their knowledge and longevity. Watching successive generations around them be born and die, some Atlantians even came to think they were Gods. Gods who needed gold. So after a time, when they trekked to the First Atlantis they thought not to recapture memories. Their minds were set on the mountain whose honeycombed base was littered with gold bars, stacked man-high. The guardians were glad the flying ships were already scarce, then finally gone."

"We, the first and the seventh tribes, remain in the land entrusted to us. Entrusted thus, when the island Atlantis was newborn." There was a roar of applause.

"Yet one day we too must leave. And join our Far World kinsmen, who pilgrimage here even now. For a prophet has seen that the ocean's currents will change and change again, until voyages between the Far World and First Atlantis is beyond us. Then we must leave our charge to silence. But we will pine for this greatest of lands until, once more, travel between the worlds is possible. Then we will return to reclaim what is ours, the continent that First Atlantis plus the ruins of the island Atlantis."

*

On the third afternoon, Gabriel's party stood, with the rest of the Long Week gathering, in a huge circle. Gabriel leaned on a new chicory walking stick, made knobbly by a herd of bison running its length. The crowd looked upon a clear empty space. A horn was blown once and then you could hear the crickets sing. They seemed to be electricity building in the air, and Zithia awaited a brilliant rendition of history. Sixteen people, evenly spaced around the ring, stepped forward two paces into the empty area.

Seconds passed. Suddenly, the ball of space within the field, twenty feet high and twenty feet wide, quivered, distorted. People held their breaths as a hologram materialised before them. The atmosphere within the sphere darkened till they saw a midnight void. Holding Kylyn, Elderic took Zithia by the hand, leading her out onto a pale grey powdery ground. When the vision rippled, Zithia and other walkers jumped.

Someone pointed up, and Zithia's eyes followed. In the night scene, the stars were a close and blazing multitude. Yet it was the blue-green disc, with white wisps drifting across it, which stunned her into unthinking awe. This luminous ball filled one-quarter of the vision area. Spellbound, Zithia walked towards it. Announcers called, 'We're on yonder moon, seeing our homeland in its splendour.'

Zithia looked out of the vision to the white moon in the sunlit sky. Could it be true? Yet she knew it was, because the very air felt different here, within the vision. It felt less, much less dense, sparser than on the plain; and noises seemed muffled. The reason for either she didn't know. Feeling the great distances involved in this scene, Zithia gripped her husband's hand tighter. 'It's magic.' He nodded and looked up at the earth floating above.

Zithia turned to watch the visioners, standing there in long leather coats. Without decades of rigorous temple training, these people had produced an evolution in astral travel, eclipsing anything attained by the priests. A solid image into which others could enter and journey.

The scene began to fade. 'The great canyon paintings. Plus the cliff village.'

People sped into the circle's centre. Then a portion of a sheer rock face snapped into being. Some youths stayed within the materialising rock, on teenage dares. They ran out, gasping for breath and stumbling over sky blue ground. Successive parades of oversized rock paintings appeared. Big horned sheep, stick people and swirling zigzags were all examined. Then the visioners sped them all to the middle of the canyon; grand, wide and deep.

Moving on again, portions of a canyon reeled by until the eagle's eyrie of a village was gained. People stood on thin air, with the stone-carved village before them. The holograph-makers moved down the village's tiers to the main level. People walked through balconies to see into rooms, to walk down empty corridors. Outside the village, while standing on nothing, it was easy to think that you'd stepped out of your body, such a peculiar sensation it was to hang mid-space looking down the five hundred feet to the desert floor.

Once the visioning was finished for the day, Zithia feverishly sought Virginia out. With bated breath she spoke, 'You spoke of favours.' Virginia smiled and nodded. 'I pray the favour I request is within your gift, good kinswoman. If it isn't, well... be assured I'll find another to ask.' She paused, biting part of her bottom lip. Then it came out in a rush. 'I long to see a place I can never visit. This circle of phantom travel, this visioning, could provide my only opportunity.' Virginia tilted her head to one side, her smile softer.

'You want a visioning?'

'Rarely have I wanted anything so much.'

Virginia's eyes seemed to be regarding the sky, speeding from right to left and right again. Finally she looked at Zithia, 'It can be done.'

*

Before the dance being held on the last night of the Long Week, Gabriel's party had missed the first night dance, the vision makers again gathered. A finale.

'The jade serpent of the middlelands.'

The setting changed to an aerial view above a gigantic grassy mound in the shape of a curling serpent. Zithia's stomach lurched. The vision gradually went down to ground level. Children reached to touch the grass.

'From the hot plains.'

They were above a pebbly desert, and backing up higher. The outline of a man on a darker background became clearer, followed by geoglyphs of lizards, mountain lions, and birds. The drawings were the same as those in Zithia's homeland.

'The Painted Desert.'

They stood upon a large coloured geometric pattern, repetitiously laid out in vibrant sands. Outside this, the desert flowed in rainbow splashes of colour to the horizon.

Without warning, a temple flyer appeared high above everyone. Zithia took her son from Elderic. Bedraggled and desperate, the flyer had bounced into the real desert. Wildly she scanned the sky. Next instant, a black hound leapt into sight. For a second he was aware only of his prey and dashed to her. The audience fled, gaining both astral travellers' attention. Two seated men left their bodies and immediately hovered in front of the temple flyer. The wolf's maw opened wide.

A clan leader declared, in physical words and in mental ones, 'Your kind was warned. Not in our land.'

The wolf skidded to a sliding halt, eyes growing wide. Changing to human, the warlock turned, fleeing the desert and the circle. It was a race to the coast. Three nomads astralled after the demon, gaining quickly on the dark one. The hologram moved with the fight. Snarling into a wolf once more, it pounced and missed a man. Raising its claws, the warlock lunged at another nomad who was in front of it. The man drew a thought-dagger and threw the blade into the inky heart. Howling ripped across the vision while the warlock disintegrated. Cheering went up from the gathering.

The temple flyer smiled and pirouetted in a circle. She glided in a dance, graceful as only an astral dance can be, bowing her head to the assembly. The word *"Thank you"* melted over them all and all understood, without a common language. For when one speaks in the astral, or astral flight, each person hears that which he can understand. Zithia had recognised the flyer on her appearance. The woman was an acquaintance, with whom Zithia had studied self-defence. When the girl's eyes neared Zithia's part of the audience, Zithia dropped the golden harlequin-duck pin Elderic had given her. She bent over to retrieve it, staying there a little longer than necessary. On straightening up, the grateful flyer was looking elsewhere. Then the girl disappeared, followed by the entire hologram.

The leader of the Long Week boomed. 'The war in the distant Southland persists. Last month our brother died when aiding a southern flyer. He's avenged! So will perish any who bring terror to our land.'

Musicians began to play at fever pitch. Silver-discs attached to clattering sticks, drums, a nomad harp plus violins played in harmony with men who could whistle up notes sweet enough to take your heart away.

Couples took the ground. Recognising the routine the others danced, Zithia's hand trembled in Elderic's. 'Don't be frightened.' He rubbed her fingers, 'The warlocks fear crossing our borders.'

During the first reel, Virginia was positioned close enough to speak to Zithia. 'The interruption to the visioning hasn't delayed your favour. It's planned for midnight.

Under the jewel-spangled sky, the party would carry on until dawn. People lit their way with gold and silver lanterns, shining richly in candle light, plus the bonfires. Soon many women melted off, to add finery and to gather spectacular furs against the evening chill. Virginia and Zithia were among them.

The patriarch's wife glowed, and applied a smoky shadow to eyelids at a silver mirror. Twin candles, in a delicately wrought golden holder, lit Zithia's face.

While she added eyeliner, an unbidden thought flashed: *"Galen is fighting those demons."* A black line jagged down onto her cheekbone. Hand still upraised, Zithia merely looked at the line: *"How many years will he lose this time?"*

Using the mirror next to Zithia, Virginia brushed on lip powder. After a frozen moment, Zithia touched her little finger to her tongue and removed the black jag. Flushed, the patriarch's wife slid a spotted fur coat over her shoulders, blew out her own two candles, then winked at Zithia. Through her emotional distraction, Zithia's annoyance was about to be given voice, when the candles re-lit themselves. They both giggled.

'From the Dragon-Land.' Virginia smiled mischievously. 'You didn't think I'd leave you in the shadows, did you? Join us at the dance, after you secure flame-snuffers on each candle.'

Alone, Zithia smiled a little more at the candles, before her breathing became ragged. Unmoving, she gazing at herself. Scenes of death haunted her. Dark rings appeared under her eyes. 'My children are safe.' She raised her chin. 'And I'm happy.' Zithia camouflaged the dark circles.

*

Once Zithia returned to the party, Elderic raised his hand formally to lead her into a sedate dance. 'It's Atlantian, let me show you.'

She knew the exact stance, on a different man. Zithia's eyes, slowly followed by her head, slid away from him. 'My lord husband.' His hand covered hers.

Hesitantly, Zithia followed the choreography. Virginia's sons next asked for Zithia's hand and, soon, her performance improved to near perfection. Finishing a set, Zithia curtsied low, one arm stretched gracefully sideways. She was rising, when Adison curled his fingers into hers and twirled her into the next brisk dance.

After a few awkward steps, Zithia stopped abruptly. 'Patriarch, I fear I can't keep up.'

'You know that from experience?' His smile was sardonic. 'Melia, your Atlantian dancing is poetry!'

At this most 'temple' of compliments, she swallowed hard. 'And your poetry book is pure Atlantian. Virginia only thought to show it to me today.' Adison put his hand on the small of her back and began the measure once more. 'Where exactly are you from Melia?'

Zithia gave him an arch smile. 'Great great uncle, I'll gladly answer that question when the first patriarch Gabriel asks it.'

Adison's grip on Zithia's back and hand tightened, 'Gabriel is asking.'

'Patriarch... is this quite the right time for such a question?' Adison glared. 'South. Far south.'

'The land of magicians.'

'Yes,' then hurried on, 'but I was born a peasant.'

Adison spoke Atlantian. 'I'll warrant your children weren't.' Zithia feigned not to understand him. His tone deep and harsh, Adison ground out, 'Where did you study?'

'Xalisco,' she whispered.

They passed Elderic, who looked puzzled. 'Smile, we're enjoying ourselves, kinswoman. Xalisco.' He rolled the word around. 'I visited Xalisco once.' Zithia's eyes were now saucers. 'In fact, I spent a year there when I was fifty.' He felt her relax. 'So you were with a priest… married?'

Her back stiffened, while she snapped, 'Certainly!'

'A deacon perhaps, then… died in this war of yours?'

'So I brought my child here for safety.'

'Your husband's tribe?'

'The first and seventh tribes.'

He twirled her round, eyes gleaming. 'Any other surprises?' His face became set, his eyebrows lowering. 'The truth now.'

'I know that very spot on the shore where our ancestors rested after the island Atlantis died.' She continued breathlessly, 'I've been there and brought away a piece of Atlantis marble washed up there.' She'd been dying to tell someone, ever since that wonderful day.

Adison stopped dancing, 'Where is this treasure?'

'In Maples, in your cousin's bronze puzzle strong-box.'

'Safe then, thanks to the ancestors. Come.'

He took Zithia straight to Gabriel, who sat with a clan leader. Adison motioned for Adison to speak in front of Methuselah. 'Where is this place?' was the only question, and by Methuselah.

'I could give the general location… if I had a map.'

Methuselah, 'We've maps.' And quietly conversed with one of his clan.

'I approached it by boat. Without a boat, I think it's lost.'

'We have skin boats.'

Two people returned, one with a bundle of maps, the other a visioner. Methuselah, 'Show them.'

The map holder asked questions, and then unrolled two maps. Soon the general location was established. Then the visioner clasped Zithia's forearms and she his. 'Think only of the place,' he instructed, which was all she had any intention of thinking about while a visioner had her in his grasp.

Instantly, she was back in the flamingo cove. The visioner stood a little back and to one side of her. Then he was high above her, then… on the Phoenician ship looking at the shoreline. Then he zoomed inland, memorising landmarks, committing all to memory. He said, 'Think of the day when you first knew where the dead island of Atlantis lay.'

They seemed to stand together over the Phoenician map. Immediately, Zithia was at that time when she was overwhelmed by the vision of the tide's flow from the submerged island Atlantis to where it met the shoreline of First Atlantis.

'I can find it.' He dashed away with the map holder, putting pen to paper as he went. 'We'll vision again, mistress Melia, to be sure.'

Adison, 'Melia, how will you like roaming every year?'

She caught her breath. 'It'll be my delight.' With a single movement, Adison spun her back the short distance to the dance. 'I might even find spouses for my two children here.'

'Gabriel has already had inquiries, and will now have more,' stepping, in good time, into the current dance.

Zithia lowered her chin. 'I prefer my children to marry for love.'

'Why not?' And swung them in a fast circle, wilder than the dance required.

After midnight, the dancing halted awhile and everyone caught their breath. 'The last vision,' called the clan leader.

A day, becoming dusk, materialised in the eagerly cleared circle. A river wended through a plain, from which individual rocky peaks rose almost vertically, covered by trees and shrubs. From one summit there floated huge birds. When the visioners rushed up and close to these, the birds were men. Men ajoy with flight, each floating under a single fixed, silk and bamboo, wing. Gasping, the watching nomad and Fallsfire audience followed the gliders gently through the air to the ground. There, a herd of massive cattle grazed, standing six-foot tall at the shoulder, the cattleman moving the aurocks along home.

The visioners then zipped to a large nearby village, where gas lamps on all the streets were being lit. Focusing, the vision makers kept the main square of streets alone. The crowd stood now on the hard-earth streets, eager to explore. They scattered. Zithia, and many, walked close to the men lighting the lamps, careful not to walk through the villagers, as this was the height of bad manners.

A very long, gas-heated brick wall stood down the street. It was covered, on both sides, with sheets of drying paper. The gas powered bathhouse was already steaming. A group of nomad adolescents tried to enter, only to be forcefully thrown backwards by the visioner-imposed bar. At once, a clan head pointed the way out of the entire vision, giving him a boot to his rear when he went sluggishly.

Many visitors were attracted to the wonder of a ceramics production line. There, one man etched patterns, another painted red designs, another yellow; a further man arranged green to flow molten down a line of jugs' sides. Nomads peeped over Dragon-Land shoulders, watching as though their lives depended on it.

Elsewhere, workers carefully placed rice paper over wooden stella, and then applied ink from extra wide ink collectors. The instant page of written text caused a buzz throughout the watchers. These copies, this time of a myth, were dried briefly on a line with fifty other copies. The same was seen achieved with silk and with lines of moveable wooden characters set between bamboo strips.

Elegant silks hung, after laundering, in gentle steam. On a porch, a woman stood with a wooden handled, small hollow bronze container, filled with hot charcoal, and ironed the last wrinkles from a festival silk. The energy of the visioners diminished well before the audience ceased its marveling.

Piece by piece the village dimmed. A large fossil slab, of a small leather winged reptile, seemed highlighted until almost the end.

The noodle shop was the last to go, with a wide, simmering cauldron that sat on three gas flames. The shop's wooden, hand-turned, machines produced spaghettis and angel's hair noodles until the last moment. A man standing in the fading shop, said to his friend, 'Next Long Week I'm going to request visioning to the Dragon-Land's grand canals. Including the underground one through the desert.'

*

The roaming had finished. Elderic and Zithia had been home for a week. Zithia still admired her silver cutlery, possessing settings for six, while Katerah's hammered gold back scratcher lay safe under her pillow. Returning from the foresting around mid-morning, Zithia announced, 'Look at these blueberries.'

But Elderic merely waved at several large parcels cluttering up the main room. 'Wedding presents, from the Far World. They arrived this morning.'

He cut the ties on a package. 'When I took the stranger to the coast before our wedding, he had a letter from great great grandfather.' The sacking revealed a crate, quickly opened. 'It announced our wedding, while informing the clans that I'm champion to the young patriarch.'

Zithia delved in the box of wheat flour. Two elaborate china-plates, orange blossom scent and a jug. Elderic moved on to the next bundle: a waist-high jar with its pointed bottom nestled in a timber frame. 'Olive oil for lamps.' He smiled, 'I told great great grandfather how you hate the winter's dull sunlight.'

She kissed him. Exhuming linen from an oblong box, Zithia cooed over camelhair cloth. With a flourish, Elderic unrolled a woven rug. Turning the empty crate upside down, he gently levered off the outer veneers to expose a table with a carved top. 'The other box will also be a table.'

Unwinding linen from the largest package, Elderic negotiated skeins of snowy camelhair. A double veil of silk fell. Elderic whistled. Zithia looked up from a cloth sash, bedecked with tassels. 'Ohhhh!'

The black mirror gave a perfect reflection. 'Are you sure they don't think you're the newest patriarch?'

'It must be a mistake!' He found the note, *"A gift."* His face cleared, 'I know, it's a communal gift from the Far World cousins to our village. Because it came to us, it's our privilege to decide where it goes.' He blew dust off the mirror's surface. 'Tomorrow we'll take it to the entrance hall in the baker's building.'

Zithia grinned. 'Such bravery, Elderic. The potter will complain to the priest, about encouraging vanity, before you can say berry-teas.' She piled her hair up high.

'Let's keep it for a week,' both hands arranged the sash artistically around her tresses, 'until we can seek the priest's wisdom on its proper place in the village.'

chapter 28

Galen's mirror developed a blue sparkle. The second mirror had been unwrapped. In the witching hours, the high priest lit copal incense around the stand. Retreating ten feet, he gave a command.

The room in FallsFire appeared, littered by unpacking and toys. Several times over the next days, he visited. One afternoon, he found Zithia alone sitting on the floor with her back to the mirror. She was intent on oiling a table. Kylyn could be heard playing outside the window.

A hand brushed her hair. With a scream, Zithia jumped. Elderic laughed, so she tossed a cushion at him. Then he was tickling her, while she wriggled away from him. White-faced, Galen closed the portal.

Later that afternoon the high priest returned. Kylyn played under the table. Galen intoned, 'Let these mirrors be, in truth, gateways through which man may move.'

Even now he daren't go through to FallsFire himself. Zithia would feel him at once. Galen blew softly on a little bird-shaped whistle. Kylyn appeared from under the table. Swirling smoke formed itself into a tapir family. Galen walked toward the mirror, speaking Phoenician. 'Hello Kylyn.'

The boy looked at his father, then down at a smoke jaguar, a frown appearing. The high priest let the illusion wisp away. 'Kylyn, darling.' He was unable to keep the yearning from his voice.

'I'm not talking to you.' Pouting, Kylyn came close to the glass. 'You died!'

Galen replied, under his breath. 'No, mama lied.' The boy looked startled. 'No, the man who told mama I died, lied.'

'You're...alive?' Kylyn's lips drew into a tremulous smile.

'Yes! I'm at home. Kylyn, do you remember home?'

Kylyn looked as though Galen were a simpleton. 'Yes.' He fiddled with his shirt. 'Can we play?'

'Yes, darling.' His gaze was sublimely intense. 'Simply walk to me, and we'll play.' He went down on one knee and opened his arms to Kylyn.

Kylyn put his hand slowly through the mirror. The high priest's fingers began folding around Kylyn's hand, while the boy balanced over the threshold. Suddenly Kylyn pulled his hand away. Hardly breathing, Galen watched Kylyn rush a few paces to snatch up a piece of amber. He retraced his steps.

As the boy walked, he looked to one side and grinned. Then Kylyn stepped through the mirror, to his father. The high priest clasped his son in his arms.

Zithia had been coming to investigate what kept Kylyn so quiet. She observed him pick up his amber. They smiled at each other. Then he was disappearing into the looking glass.

The marrow in Zithia's bones froze. Running to the mirror, she gasped. Kylyn stood beside Galen, holding his father's hand. In his other hand Kylyn clutched a six sided gourd. Galen didn't smile. 'Finally, I found you.'

'Galen,' she growled. Kylyn jerked and Zithia softened her tone. 'Dearest!'

Galen stroked his son's hair. Behind Zithia, the baby started howling. Zithia bent to the floor where the baby had been sleeping. Galen's top lip drew back; emotion dulled his senses. He spoke Atlantian, 'Leave your bastard behind.'

Zithia turned white, ignored him, and entered the portal. In Xalisco, she went to her son. The mirror hardened behind her. 'Galen, beloved, a wanderer from a temple told me you were dead.'

His expression was contemptuous. 'But tell me his name, that I might have him properly punished.'

'And here you are... alive! I give praise to the one God.'

FallsFire faded from the mirror. 'I've looked for you everywhere.'

Zithia brushed cheeks with Galen; her voice was monotone. 'And you never gave up. Only you know how that touches me.' Zithia put a hand on her heart. 'Husband, I'm speechless... with happiness.'

Wearing a prince's headdress, Xiao Chen came from the hall beyond. 'Kylyn!'

Galen gestured to the toddler. Xiao Chen's smile only temporarily deserted him. 'Kylyn, come and meet my son.' He took the baby from Zithia's arms, without deigning to look at either.

They'd just gone into the hall when a loud slap resounded. Kylyn peered around the corner, to see Zithia's hand still on Galen's cheek. Xiao Chen suggested, 'I expect there was a bug, Zithia.'

Zithia threw her head back. 'A slug, actually, deacon prince.'

Xiao Chen led Kylyn off. 'Mosquitoes, often a problem, Kylyn. Tell me, do you still like rainbow frogs? I'll have the chamberlain fetch one.' Their footsteps echoed down the hallway.

'I'd almost forgotten what a joy you can be.' Galen's eyes glinted. 'Welcome home.'

'This isn't my home.'

'It will be, again.' Galen went to the door. 'I'll join you in our apartment.' He paused. 'Right now, I wish to see my son. I promised him I'd play a game.'

'That's all you ever do Galen. Play games!'

'Speaking of which…' He tossed a metal object lightly to her. 'You'll need this.'

She caught a wedding ring.

Zithia walked alone down the familiar corridors. At the nearest T-junction she observed Minuet, Eten's assistant, dawdling there. Without slowing her pace, Zithia drawled, 'When you see Eten, remember to mention my hair.'

*

Galen's apartment was arranged the way it had been before the war, with the golden furniture standing in positions Zithia had chosen. On the desk were Galen's wheels of time; the wall hangings were virtually identical to the ones she had bought. At the sameness of the place, Zithia gave a brittle laugh.

Stumbling, she crossed her husband's threshold and went to the nursery where two priestesses bustled around the children. Handing Kylyn some popcorn from a bright pile, Zithia spied a clutch of cherries in a golden bin. Previously, her favourite. Wandering into the bedroom, she found dresses ready for her. She knew each piece.

Zithia fled onto the balcony. A large ornate golden urn, overflowing with fragrant lavender orchids, dominated the base of a tree. At the far end of the communal terrace, Zithia came to rest. Here the war-tattered city was on view, blossoming in vivid, busy hues. Colours filled holes in the grandeur and the walls. Newly adorned, buildings fought with each other for Zithia's attention. Ornamentation surviving the invasion was picked out in blazing paint. Young trees lined the streets.

'Elderic!' she groaned. A loving father, a gentle man, who always put her needs before his own. 'He…' Zithia declared aloud, 'can be compared to a soul mate,' she gave a long deep sigh, 'and win my heart.'

She smiled at how much Elderic and Kylyn adored each other. 'If only I were pregnant.' Longing to give him a child, she'd acted accordingly. *"I'd have born you a patriarch someday."* Already Elderic's mama was showing off an Atlantian grandson by her daughter, through Zithia's heritage-caller skills.

'I'll never see Elderic again.' In physical pain, her sobs were ragged.

Moments later, Xiao Chen was next to her. Sniffing, she controlled herself. 'I thought you'd be a high priest by now.'

'I inherited a title and decided, instead, to take a wife.'

Zithia flinched. 'A princess of your tribe? Thus enabling you to reclaim the title you gave up when entering the temple?' She raised her eyebrows. 'How opportunely your heart is called.'

'Let's go back to your apartment.' As they walked he added, conversationally, 'Please tell me that Kylyn can read.'

'What kind of mother do you take me for?'

Po faced, he simply looked at her. '… and as for a wife.'

In the apartment, a nurse came in with the children. Madison, the chamberlain, was absent; Galen didn't want too many witnesses to Zithia's first day back. Xiao Chen took the baby, holding the elfin child at arm's length. 'How old did you say this child is?'

'I didn't, deacon prince.'

'I've a toddler myself. A son.' He said to the nurse, 'Take the children across to my wife.' Xiao Chen looked at Zithia, 'The princess Liang.'

'No! Let them play in the nursery.'

The woman awaited Xiao Chen's instructions. 'The nursery.' He watched Zithia from narrowed eyes.

When they were alone, Zithia went to the door of a small bedroom. 'Goodnight, deacon prince. Pray tell Lord Galen he must wait till tomorrow to enjoy his victory.'

But Galen had walked silently through the door. He saw her puffy eyes. 'Tears? Really?'

Galen turned to his friend. 'Xiao Chen, let us drink. Franklin announced his abdication. He goes to the mountains tomorrow afternoon.' Galen's eyes lit up. 'And I have his support for the archpriest election in seven days.'

Xiao Chen rang a gong, and a priest appeared with a kettle of boiling water. Zithia's eyes wandered around the room while she dabbed them with her sleeve. Observing this, Xiao Chen averted his eyes.

Galen filled three cups with high tequila. 'Why are you still in those rags? I ordered your usual size.' Then his gaze flew critically down Zithia's body. 'Oh, did I underestimate?'

Zithia shot him a hot look, tracing a jade symbol on a ceramic lock-top box. Chocolate. 'Impressive. When did you develop a taste for decadence?'

'A gift in appreciation of my war efforts.'

'She must've been very grateful.'

'She was. We never use it.'

They heard Xiao Chen break the seals on the box. 'It's a rare occasion,' he said and spooned cacao into a glazed green and blue bowl, handing it to Galen. The high priest mixed the cacao to a paste before adding Dragon-Land rice syrup as a subtle sweetener. Soon four petite gold mugs of chocolate were ready.

Giving Zithia a mug, Galen noted the wedding ring on the table. Calmly he took out six of the feathered-serpent bracelets which Zithia had used to escape Kylyn's nurse so long ago. He fanned them out around the ring.

Xiao Chen picked up two mugs. 'I see you two have a lot to catch up on.' He retired to his own apartment, across the hall.

Zithia raised her mug in a toast. 'To drinking money!'

His eyes drifted to the bracelets. 'To stealing it!' They sipped deeply.

She smiled, and let a third long swig of chocolate float silkily down her throat. Her senses responded to its light euphoria-inducing magic. Rosiness flooded through her. The room glowed.

'How many emeralds did you take?'

With the chocolate, Zithia's emotions had softened and become playful. Her eyes did something sparkly. 'Only husbands remind women about their errors, with so little chivalry.'

'How appropriate that you use the plural of the word husband. Considering you've more than one.' She looked winded; the impish smile evaporated. 'You seem to have a penchant for marrying regardless of cost. Or was this, third time lucky?'

Carefully, Zithia put her mug down. 'It appears I've lost my appetite.'

Galen turned his face away from her, stating, 'Perhaps if I looked like this,... Melia.' Turning back, he was taller and his face had changed to Elderic's features.

'A peasant. His mind was beneath you. Obviously his body wasn't.'

Zithia shuddered, her mouth agape: "*I was watched...*" Shallow breaths came quickly. "*We were watched.*"

He read her mind. 'Don't disgust me. I didn't demean myself by voyeurism.'

She growled, 'Take it off!' But Galen only smiled through Elderic's visage.

Then, straightening, Zithia called lightly, 'Kylyn, come and see the face your papa's making.'

Galen dropped Elderic's features and picked up a ceremonial mask lying on a shelf. It was a jaguar mask in a jade mosaic, and Galen held it before his face. Kylyn beamed.

'Take it, darling' the words were hypnotic, 'and go to sleep.' Kylyn become visibly drowsy.

Galen led the child back to the nurse. 'Put him to bed and take the other away for an hour. We're not to be disturbed.'

Pivoting, Galen's anger swept over Zithia in a tidal wave. It sucked the breath from her. 'You married him.' She heard him shout within her head. In the room itself, the statement was merely a whisper.

'I had to.'

Galen thought about the toddler. Zithia found herself hurled against the wall, pinned there five feet above ground. 'Don't be insulting! He has morals.'

The pressure released fractionally. 'And where were your morals?'

She spat out, 'I gave them to a high priest. Now put me down.'

The mind-wind vanished and Zithia dropped heavily to the floor. Neither spoke. While she rubbed her ankle, Galen saw the ring on Zithia's little finger.

'You dare wear that here?'

She closed her hand into a fist and stood up. Inexorably, Zithia's fingers uncurled. Then the ring was in Galen's hand. Physical contact brought with it images of love. Galen threw the ring high, where it exploded into silver flecks. Zithia dashed to catch the dust but Galen scattered it, in a breeze, over the balcony.

Then ghostly hands were around her throat, strangling her. Their unwavering eyes locked.

'I gave up a great deal to marry you.'

She gasped for breath. 'I thought I was the one with the temper'.

He released his hold, sending her staggering. Galen sounded aloof. 'We will live as man and wife, for my son's sake. For the same reason, your bigamy will be a secret.'

'Don't you mean, for your ambition's sake?'

Coming close to Zithia, Galen stroked her cheek with the back of his fingers. 'So that we understand each other; say goodbye to your peasant forever.' He took on Elderic's features once more, kissing her violently. When she tried to pull away, Zithia felt his hand tighten around her throat. On their lips parting, Galen wore his own face. He traced the bruises on her neck. 'I believe you're right, I really will have to watch my temper.'

*

At the baths, water sprays pummelled Zithia's body. She could still feel Galen's hands on her. Touching her throat, Zithia found she wore a platinum band. It prevented conscious astral travel. Crying hard, Zithia scrubbed every inch of her skin.

Back in the room she'd claimed for her own, she ignored the glistening gown on the bed, and put on a simple shift. Into the bodice Zithia tucked an oilskin pouch. Then, taking a scroll and candle into the children's room, Zithia sat on the sofa. She read until she slept.

Galen entered the nursery later that night. A paperbark concertina, about Atlantis, lay over Zithia's knees. Passing a hand over her flat belly, the high priest discerned no new life within. For a few minutes, Galen watched the heave of Zithia's breasts. Then, holding his fingers above her hair, Galen's hand slowly moved down the tresses.

Soon Galen went to his sleeping son, silently intoning, *"Forget the life since you left here; t'was a dream; now faded to nothing."*

Zithia's bastard was staring at him. Galen looked at eyes that mirrored his own. 'Your turn.'

Into this quiet moment, knowledge flooded. Galen's face glowed. Cradling the toddler in his arms, he whispered, 'I name you Manaca.' Gently, he rocked his daughter to sleep.

*

403

Sunlight warmed Zithia's face. Her eyes peeped from beneath heavy lids. On moving, burgundy curls fell over her face. An attendant came in. 'My lady, the masseuse and hairdresser are here.'

Dressed in an elegant gown, Zithia was fastening a pectoral. Entering, Galen drawled, 'That's better.' She crinkled her hair and smiled a thank you. Deliberately pacing his words, 'Well, I could hardly have you,' Galen strafed Zithia's body, 'looking like a barbarian.'

The high priest walked through to the nursery. Shortly, Zithia went after him.

'Yes my lord, I'll burn them.' The nursery assistant came out, loaded down with Zithia's and the children's village clothes.

Galen was tidying Kylyn's outfit, speaking in a low voice. Kylyn's hair had been cut short, temple style, plus he wore the rough kilt and loose shirt of a priest's student. All at once, realising what was taking place, Zithia backed to the wall.

Galen said quietly, in Atlantian, 'The bride-price must still be paid.'

He changed languages. 'I've been telling Kylyn about the journey he'll go on, in a week. How he'll represent us in another temple,' Galen smoothed Kylyn's hair, 'and how proud we're of him.'

'A week.' Zithia echoed, forcing a smile. 'Yes, darling very proud.'

'When will I come home?'

Blinking back tears, Zithia retreated.

*

Near Torim's garden, Zithia didn't see the blue columns on the building enclosing it. The vaulted ceiling of the hall leading to the inner sanctum was now sun-yellow. Within the hallway, Zithia heard leaves swishing in the breeze. Looking at the archway, she was relieved that the shining concave eye remained intact. Vanilla scent wafted from the orchids clinging to the stone arch. She hurried through the opening and... the first mahogany was gone. Nearby trees and vines had burned. Another mahogany was now one-armed.

Wandering in distraction, Zithia winced at the scorch marks on the walls and crumbling brown vines. Only rain had saved the garden. Gathering herbs, Zithia looked at the stairs. Rope and a horse had pulled the elaborate archway down. Large stones lay on the balcony and the ground.

Climbing a tree to a thin foothold in the wall, Zithia perched there. She pulled a stone plug from a fissure and a rock pivoted out. The delectable perfume from manaca flowers took her back years. After adding her herbs, Zithia took the pouch from her bodice. Kissing it, she placed the purse of Atlantian earth on the leaves.

Standing by one of the ponds, it hit her. 'Galen still controls my destiny.' Zithia touched her bruised throat. 'And he's jealous, even now.'

With this, her thoughts flew to FallsFire. "*A place to bring up a son… contentment … in a land that tempted angels from heaven… love, gentle and rare… then roaming… wild Atlantians calling me sister.*"
Zithia whispered, trembling, 'It was all mine for a time.'

Zithia felt a presence behind her. 'Don't say a word! Let's savour the sweet recollection of eighteen months' separation.'

A butterfly in metallic blues dithered around saplings and orchid slips.

'Why didn't you tell me I had a daughter?' Taking aquinoa seeds from a tray, Galen scattered them in front of the stairway.

'You didn't ask.'

He closed the distance between them. Zithia didn't move. Galen slowly brought his face down to hers, touching his brow to Zithia's. The contact was almost unbearable. 'It's good to see you again.'

Galen drew back, sighing. 'The council wants you tomorrow morning.'

She blanched. 'You've lost me my son.'

'Galen, remember the fabled last Atlantis tree; I could lead you there tomorrow.' Galen winced. Her stare was dagger sharp. 'And I've…'

'…astralled to the ruins of Atlantis, yes, I know.' His bitter mouth transformed into a smile. 'Didn't you feel me, seeing it through your eyes?'

Her skin crawled. 'But you don't know where it is.' Zithia turned her head away, 'Leave me, I'm in mourning.'

He grabbed Zithia by the arms. 'I've wiped some trivia from our children's memories. Perhaps it'd be better to do the same for you.'

'Try it!' She sneered, baring her teeth.

Galen looked grim, and let her go.

*

Two massive stone heads, with the features of the fifth tribe, decorated the wide pedestrian way that led from Torim's garden. Eten slid from behind the first statue. 'A lover's tryst with your wife?' Her smile was crooked. 'Is she still so fascinating to you Galen?'

Galen's pupils grew small and hard. 'Brother, I'll be candid.' The high priestess touched the statue's earlobe. 'Once, hovering between life and death, I had a most unfortunate vision. Only Zithia can help me achieve the goal of my life.'

Galen moved off. Eten trailed him, her eyes hot, brittle. 'When the council meets, an advocate could be invaluable to your wife. To you!' She stopped. 'I'll support the lightest judgment possible in return for Zithia's assistance.'

Galen faced her. 'This goal of yours must be immensely powerful.'

'An Atlantian artifact.'

Galen didn't reply for a little. 'Sacrilege.'

'Then again, I could be a hindrance in the council.' Galen said nothing. 'And Augustus will follow my lead.'

Galen scrutinised Eten's face for those minute muscle twitches that give away a lie. He found none. 'We'll start looking after the council meeting.'

'No, tonight.'

'After!' He paused. 'Now let's discuss Zithia's banishment.'

*

In her own apartment, Eten sent a message to Augustus. Arriving, Augustus was focused and his carriage commanding. He smiled, and presented to small bag. Upon untying the ribbon at its neck, several oversized flies buzzed out. 'How thoughtful.' Eten cooed. 'Venus, Augustus has brought you a gift.'

Instantly the cane toad jumped between Eten and Augustus, gobbling a fly midair. They watched the chase for a minute. 'They'll keep him amused for ages.'

She guided Augustus to a seat on the balcony. 'I've a proposition, my dear.' In the background Venus could be seen leaping off furniture to catch his treats. 'It will appear to be against all we've wanted, but when you hear me out I know you'll approve.'

Soon the high priest was leaning back in his chair, hands clasped behind his head. The laugh, when it came, was vindictive. They were rising to leave, when there was a tinkling of glass. Luminous shards bounced into view. Augustus grimaced, 'That sounded expensive.'

'It was never a favourite piece.' Indulgently she pursed her lips, burring at the toad as he did himself. And then, 'Did darling Venus get a fright?'

*

The next morning, the council chamber was austere. The high priests sat on thrones, three steep steps above the arena. Archpriest Franklin was seated in the middle.

These high priests were quite a different group from those at the beginning of the war. There had been deaths, retirements, plus one transfer. They were a harder group. For two hours Eten and Augustus worked the room, before summoning Zithia. Galen entered with her, there as husband only.

Zithia wore a simple silk gown. Her make-up showed off her Atlantian features.

'Lady Zithia, you've been called here to answer for your crimes,' announced Franklin.

A chairman took over, Petronius. 'Lady, you deserted your husband, and stole the bride-price promised when your wedding was arranged.' She clenched her hand, hidden by overlong V-shaped sleeves. 'Do you have anything to say to these charges?'

Zithia had been instructed by Galen to keep silent, for the sake of the children.

A stone table stood beside Petronius. He banged a judgement jade three times. 'Then it's the decision of this council that you'll be confined on a reed island on Puma Lake, to float there for seven years.'

Zithia turned grey. In a barely audible whisper, 'With my daughter?'

'The Lord Galen has requested the care of his daughter.' Zithia glowered at him. 'Therefore the child won't be fostered.' His expression softened.

'Lady Zithia, your sentence will be carried out once the bride-price leaves Xalisco. Prepare yourself.' Petronius banged the heavy jade a final time.

'Lord Galen, we assume you'll now wish to sever ties with this unworthy woman.'

Galen watched a vein throb at Zithia's temple, in suddenly translucent skin. He was about to be free, without a mark on his reputation. Inconvenient memories spun by. The high priest opened his lips, when his throat went dry: *"On my death day, what will I regret?"*

Silence. 'Most noble councillors, this woman and I are soul mates, therefore my decision doesn't come easily.' He smiled wryly. 'Having accepted the care of our daughter I can't, in moral duty, abandon her mama.'

On the murmurs dying down, 'Further, I claim a husband's right to visit my wife in her exile. Annually.'

Over the ensuing babble, Zithia looked at Galen with shining eyes.

After some minutes, the chairman said, 'In deference to you alone, Lord Galen, to your valor throughout the war, we consent. This visiting right doesn't extend to your daughter.'

'I'm overwhelmed by the council's generosity.'

*

Zithia was escorted from the chamber, while Galen remained to see the judgement signed. Once high priestess Rachael had scrawled her name, Eten was the last to append her signature. She inked the quill.

Augustus was a little behind Galen. 'When I'm archpriest, Galen, you'll regret not putting Zithia aside.' Galen continued to watch the proceedings. 'To lose the archpriesthood for love. I could almost laugh.' Galen looked round into Augustus's deadly eyes.

At that moment Eten smiled at the witness. Simultaneously crushing a seaweed pod, between her teeth, Eten expelled the vaporous contents into his nostrils. He stood transfixed, whereupon the high priestess murmured, 'She writes her name.' The words echoed in his ears. Eten's hand scratched her scrawl. 'How fluid is her pen, how firm her signature.'

The witness saw the words on the paperbark, even though Eten held the pen above the scroll. He blotted the non-existent signature. Eten handed him the quill and the witness appended his own name after the rest.

Galen's attention returned to the table as the paperbark was folded and sealed. Eten made sure not even to think a smirk.

*

Zithia sipped hot chocolate, and watched her children playing with Xiao Chen's son.

'It's over.' Xiao Chen produced a shot-cup of high tequila.

They both thought of the Puma Lake, the highest lake on the continent. A man's lungs labored in the thin air, yeast didn't rise properly, and water boiled when lukewarm. At night the world froze, and people aged four years for every one.

'At least I can fish,' she was blank-faced. 'And swim. I'm told the water isn't chilly.'

'My cousin is a prince of Puma region. You'll not be friendless.' He retrieved his son. 'Liang will be waiting for us.'

Galen came in, holding the door open for Xiao Chen.

Tiny wrinkles appeared across Zithia's forehead. 'Why only five years?' He concentrated on his drink. 'Galen, you haven't...' Zithia bit her bottom lip.

'I'd never turn to darkness.' He paused. 'We're simply going to help Eten look for an Atlantian relic.'

Her brow cleared. 'An act punishable by death.'

'In return for a light sentence.'

With a puzzled look, Zithia approached him tentatively. 'Why not... divorce?'

'My dear, I'm a traditionalist, I fear that death is the only way to dissolve our marriage.'

Zithia laid her head on his chest, shutting her eyes. 'Oh, Galen...'

'Seven years is a long time to be alone, wife.' He nuzzled her ear. 'We can always have more children.'

Mind whirling, Zithia looked up at him. Her husband kissed her, and she kissed him back.

*

Minuet guarded the entrance to the room of mirrors. Her squinting eyes moved continuously, as did her feet. Within, Eten used a stingray to open a vein near her ankle. Venus watched, reflected a hundred-fold by the mirrors over which dark gauze fluttered. When the blood cup was a third full, Eten sealed her vein.

She stood up, her right hand behind her back. In a singsong tone, 'Venus. Venus, darling.'

The cane toad Venus leapt to Eten's open arm. In a lightning fast movement Eten's right arm appeared, skewering Venus mid-leap on the stingray spine. A single tear rolled from Eten's eye. 'A martyr to my cause.'

She tipped Venus's warm body, pouring his lifeblood into the cup. Flicking the stingray spine, the carcass dropped onto the floor. She laid down her weapon. The blood burst into a blue flame and Eten completed the ritual, bringing more power to her night's tasks.

Stunned, Venus's shade had fallen near Eten's foot. *"But you said you'd never hurt me,"* the darkness, the shadows were coming for him, *"let alone kill me."* Eten didn't even hear him.

chapter 29

In the oldest mushroom caves, natural light streamed down through sealed skylights. Luminous rose parasol mushrooms added to the light from rocky outcrops. Branches hung like rafters on the ceiling, growing a vineyard of fungal grapes. Self-sewn giant puffballs grew from this vantage point. Blonde string mushrooms liked the ceiling, mature bundles two-feet-long waving in the eddies.

Used for gumdrops, a mattress-sized gelatinous sheet covered a log. Coconut and cinnamon scents perfumed the air. Fruity, cherry-red coral fungi grew in crevasses. A square tray of glazed buns looked like they'd come fresh from the bakery ovens. On the walls, myriad brown ears listened.

Galen and Zithia wore flowing brown capes of fasting priests. After midnight, they walked up to a colony of bright cups, which exploded with tiny popping hisses, of spores. This terrified a big bullet-capped mushroom, which promptly liquefied into ink. Zithia's head wrenched back.

Eten, dressed in ceremonial garb beneath a cloak, stood at the back of the cave. Approaching the high priestess, Zithia launched a dagger. It went straight through Eten's palm and pain flashed on her face. Snarling she moved her hands in a spell, the knife glittering in its flesh scabbard. Zithia's upper lip curled. 'You need me.'

Breathing hard, Eten stopped mid-spell. Looking at the obsidian visible on both sides of her hand. 'Is this little outburst for your son, or a few grey hairs?

Zithia entered the high priestess's space. 'Oh, I've cut your lifeline.' She grabbed the handle. 'Mine I think,' and pulled it out, smiling when Eten winced.

'It's easily mended, unlike yours!'

Zithia's hair fell back and Galen observed the additional lines at his wife's temple. Eten smirked at Galen. 'Ten years.'

'I should've stopped your heart that night.'

Eten's fingers ran over her two wounds, and they were gone.

Galen said, dryly, 'Can we get on?'

The area behind Eten was thick with stalactites and stalagmites. One group gave the impression of teeth, not quite meeting in a huge half-grin. Hollow black trumpets carpeted the ground. Eten handed Galen a scroll, copied from papyrus that had crumbled as the scribe memorised each page. Carved on the edge of a mushroom drawing was: *"Somewhere within, old dreams begin."*

Eten said, 'There were three jack-o-lantern colonies here when this cave was discovered.'

These fungi were luminous, and thus couldn't be disturbed. Taking a trowel from a flat mushroom cap, as big as a cushion, Galen went to examine the colony on the floor.

Eten snorted and the jack-o-lanterns evaporated. A crystal knob was revealed. It moved with a click, nothing happened. The high priestess raised her hand against the lanterns on the roof and a sloping ledge. Simultaneously, each switch moved.

Stone bars grumbled out from a wall, slotting into the stalagmite teeth. An unnatural stairway had been formed.

Arms akimbo, Galen leapt onto the first bar, which was at waist height, then up the next two. A heavy mist rained over the stairway. Galen pivoted around. 'It's steady enough.'

Zithia cried out wordlessly. There was blood streaming down his face and arms. Galen inspected a bloody arm, and then looked up at the red liquid dripping from a thin ruptured sheet on the ceiling overhead.

'Bleeding leather. Eten, we have a rain of blood and...' he pointed at the mushrooms crowded beneath the stairs. 'trumpets of death.'

Zithia said, 'Two warnings, before we even begin?'

Eten rasped out, 'Two warnings aren't three.'

Three signs meant the message was carved in stone.

Zithia took Galen's hand and he pulled her onto the steps. Going further up, the staircase curved dramatically, changing direction. When Galen stood on the last bar, a rock door slid sideways into the wall, shearing off a black mushroom nest. The stairs now faced west.

'West, for death,' frowned Zithia.

'Ever the peasant,' Eten sneered.

'Three warnings.'

'Superstition!'

Galen was po-faced. 'Last time I checked, Eten, we were in the business of superstition.'

'We have a deal.'

'So we do.'

Waving his hand, Galen lit a torch and stepped into darkness. The door slid back into place. Immediately, Zithia was on the last step, banging on the wall. Registering her weight, the portal opened. Eten clambered in after them, to find them close to the entrance, in a never-ending horizontal slit.

Galen traced a hexagon imprint beside the hatch. 'The trap door doesn't open from this side without a key.'

Lighting her torch, Eten illuminated the crouch space they occupied. 'There'll be another way out.'

They skidded downhill over pebbly debris. After humidity and much sweat, the ceiling lowered to six inches, except for one place. They wriggled into the bulge in the stone.

"The world might sneeze." Zithia thought, shivering. She counted slowly to a thousand before the pressing rock raised itself and they were in a tall, slim corridor.

Tripping over some loose stones, Eten collided with Zithia. They each recoiled as though scalded. The high priestess picked up the offending rock to cast it away. Within the limited light they saw it gleam. Zithia's gasp was wonder. Instantly, Eten began to loosen her grip on the glassy rock, but Galen caught her hand in his. His palm against the back of Eten's hand, his fingers over hers, Galen was turning the object into sight; Eten resisted and clenched her jaw. Then she winced, grinding her teeth, but it was revealed.

She held a thick emerald slab, fist-sized, complete with feather, or garden, within its depths.

Galen's torch flamed high, illuminating the floor. The ground was littered with fiery grass-green hexagons. An emperor's ransom, to go no further.

Galen put one last pressure on Eten's hand and let go, leaving painfully raised blisters where he'd touched her. He said softly, 'What've you gotten us into, Eten?'

'If they're this serious about bribes,' Zithia weighed, and then wielded a gem column as a cosh, 'what of their warnings?'

'We have a deal!'

Galen looked into Eten's eyes. 'Your call, Zithia.'

Eten growled softly.

'Well, we know where they keep the keys to the front door. So, we go on.' Surreptitiously Zithia stowed a gem stick in her bag.

*

An hour later, they traversed a sandy area, setting off an ancient mechanism. In the distance, a light gradually appeared. They doused their torches in the sand.

Water could be heard, and then seen, falling into a clear pool, which was lit from within. Tasting the water, they all drank and filled their canteens. Feeling clammy, Zithia dropped her outer clothes to slip into the cool blue.

Eten scanned the immediate area. 'You should be searching.'

'For what, Eten?' Galen dove in.

Zithia wafted toward the waterfall descending from a gap in the ceiling, off-centre of the sapphire pool. Eten ground her teeth. 'I'd better need that witch.'

Her dark thoughts rattled past Galen and Zithia's minds. Simultaneously, both turned to look at the high priestess. Eten's mouth twisted. She prowled off to explore a dripping tunnel.

Igniting her torch once more, she stalked the hard-earth burrow. Powdery, light sky-blue stones became visible, sticking out of the lower wall. She thought: *More gems to sidetrack us.* Waving the light, the darkly veined gems came to life. 'Turquoise.'

She reached for one pretty piece, scowling when it moved only a few inches. Bending closer, a smile wreathed Eten's face. In her clasp she held a skeletal hand with a turquoise ring. The skeleton had been there so long that the moist wall had part-flowed over its spine, suspending it where it had leaned.

Seizing the ring firmly, the high priestess yanked on it. But it was stuck fast. 'No, not stuck.'

The knuckle of the index finger was turquoise. She looked anew at the other flashing gems. Here a rib, there a toe, occasional teeth, a piece of skull had been replaced by turquoise. Eten snapped off the index finger. 'Bone turquoise, unlucky for some.'

Before leaving the graveyard, she tied her find to a hidden lock of hair.

All this time, Galen and Zithia were idling at the pool. Watching Galen swim, Zithia thought: *"He wants babies; a son to rear."* She softened toward him, then quickly admonished herself: *"Simply because a man doesn't divorce you... Is prepared to commit blasphemy for you..."* She glowed, and then peeped in the direction of the tunnel.

Watching the straight lines of Galen's back while he swam, Zithia swayed slightly: *"Don't be so romantic, remember everything he's done,"* Galen swam underwater to her, 'and everything he should've done.'

He surfaced in front of her. 'Galen, kindness becomes you. Still, no more pleasant surprises, husband, my heart isn't yet healed from the last time we lived together.'

His gaze smouldered. 'Why should your heart be intact, when mine is not?'

Zithia moved her hands slowly through the water, knowing the liquid caressed him. As it did her. She wrapped her arms around his waist. 'Let me share with you willingly.'

Zithia flashed a memory of the ruins of Atlantis to Galen. His gaze was everywhere. Three seconds, not just the flash he'd caught on the day she'd visioned there. then it dissolved. He was breathing fast, madly trying to trace the vision. In vain.

Liquid moved along his washboard stomach. She slipped into Atlantian, 'I've missed you, beloved. And now... to see you but once a year...'

'Each visit could be a honeymoon.' He put his palm to hers; their fingers opened and meshed together. 'And each honeymoon... productive, if you so desire.'

The Atlantis tree appeared to Galen. Another two untraceable seconds. She'd grown to be a true adept at hiding things in her mind. 'I could take us to the Atlantis tree.' She fleetingly revealed the library at the tree, 'Knowledge as old as time.'

His pupils dilated. 'Where?'

'Where we could live happily the rest of our lives.'

Galen focused on her. 'What're you saying?'

Throwing yet another patch of memory at Galen, her unexpectedly plump lips tasted his. Nectar. One leg twined around him. Yet his eyes remained open, growing colder. Zithia was a little dizzy. 'The Atlantis tree. We wouldn't need status or money there.' Galen threw her off. She pleaded, 'I don't want to lose my son.'

'What about losing me?'

'I don't have to lose you.' Her lower lip trembled. 'Galen, choose me!'

His arm muscles bulged. They drifted apart, near the waterfall.

'Galen!'

His face was expressionless. 'You should've offered yourself, before you spoke. You'd have had the advantage of surprise.'

Her face flushed. Her tone became determined. 'Then I'll trade. Your treasures for my son. Simple say the word.'

He raised a hand, palm flat, then his hand slowly descended.

Zithia began to sink. Floating several inches below the surface, she kicked her legs wildly. When in the waterfall, one of her hands broke the surface. Her lungs were bursting when she drifted to the other side of the liquid curtain. Without warning, Galen's pressure evaporated, letting her head pop above the surface. She spluttered frantically.

'Is that enough of an answer for you?'

Zithia swivelled round and gaped at the waterfall. An Atlantian symbol was carved there. Still coughing up water, Zithia floated through the curtain and reached the edge of the pool.

Eten arrived back when Zithia sprayed out the last mouthful of liquid. 'Galen, nice to see your dark side, but you might've drowned her. Then where'd I be?'

'Did you find anything?'

'Merely dead... ends!'

*

Zithia stretched on the edge of the pool. Observing Eten's sharp strides around the cave, Zithia smiled. Galen knew that look. 'Tell us.'

'The sign is on the other side of the waterfall.'

Eten marched rather too close to Zithia. The high priestess's foot itched. 'Keep no more secrets Zithia!'

Zithia shrugged a shoulder. 'Oh, I'd have told you, when I ceased to be amused by your efforts.'

'We go up,' she snarled, waving at her hands across the ceiling.

A rock lever clicked and the opening in the roof widened, releasing a torrent, which rapidly dwindled. They took out ropes, and then looked up the water. The symbol had changed. A tree of life.

Dressing, Zithia pushed her cape back. 'Look for paintings on the rock. Lichen, anything.'

A flick of Eten's hand cleared the sand, piling it up thirty feet away. Shortly after, Eten found a smooth oval. There, camouflaged by speckles, they deciphered words:

"Transform a thing set in time. Make it live, while all who search read this line."

Eten reached her right arm out beyond the oval, to a fossilised armored beetle. Cupping a hand over it, Eten felt change. Her eyes opened wider. The armor flexed outward, re-positioning itself into a faceted crystal heart. Veins lit the interior, with one terminally dark patch. Zithia had left the others while this transformation occurred.

Eten touched the heart, reading the phrase. Nothing happened. 'Zithia, recite the rhyme with us.' They all repeated it. Still nothing.

'It literally wants us to read the riddle together!'

Zithia stood next to Galen. The words were read while Eten once more touched the heart, leaning her shoulder over the edge of the oval.

A heart's drumming echoed through the cavern. The ground vibrated, and then moved upwards at speed. All eyes on the descending ceiling, Eten forgot her hand. At the last minute she snatched it back into safety. Ashen, the high priestess was instantly examining her fingernails and fingers, shakily stroked her right hand. And then cradling it tenderly; fearful, at first, of taking her eyes from it.

'That was a close,' smiled Zithia, with a momentary flash of her eyebrows upwards, 'almost!' Knowing the reasons for Eten's fright.

With its extremes and savagery, the dark path easily upset the minds of its followers.

Eten's brother had lost his dominant hand, his powers and his sanity. Thus it was, for all who loved darkness. Such a disability had no effect on a priest on the light path.

The platform kept increasing velocity. Then their stomachs flipped over as the elevator abruptly stopped. They were totally enclosed by rock. Galen and Zithia searched for a trigger in the thinning air.

Zithia slumped down beside Eten. 'I'd always hoped to see your tomb, only not from the inside.'

'We all have dreams. My fantasies include holding your beating heart in my hands!'

Under their feet Galen uncovered a hexagonal outline. 'Had we been mere looters we'd now be in a position to live.'

Zithia cleared her throat. 'I dislike the word looter.' And she produced the gem she'd pocketed earlier; raising her chin high, 'I simply can't abide waste.' Zithia fitted the emerald into the floor. They speed upwards once more.

*

It was a palace hall. Stalactites and stalagmites had met, producing columns worthy of Atlantis. Myriad icicles winked from the roof. Eten was fast advancing on a crystal prison that stood at the heart of this temple. Four lines of thin stalactites formed the cage. The light from Eten's touch increased threefold. Her hot, feverish gaze could hardly penetrate the murk within.

Galen and Zithia made for a shaft of sunlight drifting at an angle onto the floor. Weaving her fingers through the dust particles hung suspended in liquid air, Zithia stepped fully into the dazzle. Galen examined the tunnel itself. The angle and rough wall encouraged ascent.

Zithia's eyes danced past Eten to a treasure box, sitting some distance in front of the crystal vault. Gem necklaces curtained the sides of the open lid. Eten paced around the cage, dislodging jewels. A huge pearl tumbled after a faceted ruby, in a game of marbles, until swallowed up by the dark. At the box, Zithia fastened twin sapphire ropes around her waist; and couldn't resist the diamond rope, its faceted gems seven carats apiece. They were a treasure unknown to her. She dropped jade pectorals of emperor's quality and emeralds into her emptied satchel.

'Eten, obviously we've arrived, so you'll excuse us if we don't hang around.' Galen's words barely registered.

He observed his wife add a rope of clear stones, with rainbows in their hearts. 'Are you coming, Zithia?'

'Yes…yes…', topping the bag with loose gems. She ran lightly to him as he began to climb the tunnel.

'Would you help me with my satchel?' Jumping down into the light, he raised his eyebrows.

Galen pulled at the belt ties like someone cinching in a corset that was too small. Grimacing, Zithia rubbed a lower rib and said, 'Imprisonment is easier to survive with money, than without.'

'In that case, when we get out of here I'll keep the bag safe for you.' He knotted the ties.

'No need to trouble yourself.'

'My pleasure.' He had steely eyes. The satchel now hung from the small of Zithia's back to her buttocks. A jewel encrusted headdress stuck out to one side.

Eten yowled in pain; her hand had brushed a glassy bar. Red dripped from several gashes. Despite a healing spell, the dry cuts gaped. 'More Atlantian craft. The bars are lined with razor and magic.'

Curious, Galen walked back into the main cave. Following him, Zithia had barely left the golden circle when the first rocks tumbled. Stones colliding together displaced others, then raced each other to the ground. Muted thunder accompanied the spillage, driving Galen and Zithia further into the main cave. The sunshine was snuffed out, and a dozen icicles fell in the cave. Galen said, 'It appears we had a choice!'

Unconcerned, her mind on the cage, Eten eyed the bars.

Zithia marched up to Eten and struck her on the shoulder with ball of her hand. 'Trapped, because of you.'

The high priestess turned to her, her face contemptuous. 'It's always because of me.'

Zithia slammed the high priestess's shoulder blade again. 'You know, Eten, once you're dead I'm sure we'll get along much better.'

Eten's tone was light. 'I don't need you any more, Zithia.' She growled. 'Let's play.'

Galen instructed, 'No powers.'

The high priestess lifted the jewel box, pitching the contents at Zithia with force. Bruised by a hard fortune, Zithia circled Eten. Giving each other more room, they stalked. Zithia was in front of the glassy vault. Near them, Galen noted a rock shattered by a thin stalactite.

One-handed, Eten threw the box at Zithia, who ducked. Cape flying, Galen launched himself and caught it mid-air. He and the chest landed mere inches from the cage. Both women glowered at him.

Galen pointed at the embedded stalactite in the rock, 'Look up.' The ceiling sparkled with jingling stilettos. 'Break the cage this way and the noise will bring death down.'

Forgetting Zithia totally, Eten reassessed the cage. 'We'll have to pulverise the bars using magic.'

'What we? Our bargain has finished.'

Eten's face was sullen. 'Well?'

'I want your oath never to harm Zithia or my children again.'

The high priestess barely hesitated. Afterwards, 'Satisfied?'

'I'll be, when you cancel any arrangements already made regarding my family. In writing.'

Eten's eyes reptilian. 'No!'

'Come Zithia, we have a key. We'll find our way to the front door eventually.'

Zithia's smile was infuriating. 'So very close.'

Eten hissed, pulling out paper. Galen dictated, adding, 'Seeing you're fond of blood, sign it in yours.'

Eten promptly sliced her open wound with a long fingernail, dipped it in blood and appended her name.

*

The two high priests focused their power while Zithia directed, with eyes glued on the vibrating icicles. In the cavern, the power was a palpable undercurrent. All at once the bars turned milky, before crumbling into sharp dust.

Light flooded a stalagmite pedestal beyond the dust. On it sat an exquisite jade skull. Advancing to it, Eten fell to her knees while her hands caressed the pedestal. With one quick movement the high priestess flipped the skull from the stalagmite.

Pouring water onto the stand, she used her cape to wipe off centuries of grim. Nestled within the glass, another skull, its outlines alone discernable.

Galen didn't breath. 'The thirteenth skull! Have you lost your mind?' Zithia looked a question. 'Legend proclaims the thirteenth skull holds vast Atlantian power; left for the next period of enlightenment. Its very name is a warning.' Shaking his head. 'I'd not dare touch it.'

'You always were weak. Still I thank you for your assistance.' Eten gave Galen a low bow. 'With the thirteenth skull, I'll be supreme.'

Galen raised his spread arms high, palms upward. 'I speak to the power that's here. Know you that we're not part of this.'

The high priestess read aloud from the top of the pedestal. *"Know the motive of your quest, then accept its total consequence."*

Zithia took a few steps backwards. 'Sounds ominous.' But Galen's brow cleared.

The high priestess laid her hands on the flat surface. 'To hold this land in my power, I accept all and any consequence.'

The stalagmite glowed purple and was candle wax melting. Freed, the thirteenth skull sat there like the last remains of an angel. Eten's lips soundlessly rehearsed the lines of possession; her hands reached for the perfect crystal.

Galen taunted. 'I might've expected you to hide in a hole to perform your blasphemy.'

Eten's lips curled, then she straightened. 'You're right. The occasion does demand an audience,' from her pouch she took some black silk, 'witnesses, who will tell their children and their children's children what was seen today.' Draping the cloth over the skull, Eten lifted her prize from its bed.

The cavern knew its loss, and a small part of the wall began to shiver in grief. An aperture opened up. Astonished cries grew louder. Simultaneously, the daggers above chimed together. The cavern hailed sharp icicles. Striding toward Zithia, Galen raised his hand, creating a bluish shield of light over himself. He yanked Zithia beneath it, and to an overhanging ledge at one side of the widening gap. They pulled their hoods over their heads.

Eten walked at a stately pace to where the wall was disappearing outwards. Out of deference to the thirteenth skull, the daggers didn't fall until it passed.

*

Outside, the wall was reforming into a gracious curved stairway leading into a busy plaza. Heralding the thirteenth skull, gold dust gusted out as each stair-tread slotted into place.

Obnil, the herb-seller, was to the side of the emerging doorway, his hand raised, for he was smoking a cigar. Here, against design, the dust sprayed fivefold what it should've.

When the cascade stopped, Obnil opened his eyes. Grinning, he held out his shirt and ashed his cigar. The gold that was piled on his arm fell into the cloth. Tipping his head forward, another metal avalanche descended from his thick, wavy hair. Carefully Obnil let his short cape slip to the ground, shook each of his feet over it, and then bent to cup up piles of gold which had gathered on and around his two baskets of wares. He winked at the world in general, 'I believe I need a bath,' and walked off, rounding a corner.

A minute later, a gale burst forth from the cavern. Those who were fixedly scraping up gold, clung desperately to it while the dust was torn away. When the blow ceased, it had gilded two square miles.

Eten threw off her cape, arranged her clothes and stood framed by the doorway at the head of the stairway glazed with lapis lazuli powder. Holding the skull at heart level Eten descended the tongue of shimmering, deep-heaven's blue.

Inside the cave, intermittent icicles still fell when Galen and Zithia heard another sound, a heavy stone moving. The light changed. Galen tore one of the ties on Zithia's satchel, pulling an emerald pectoral from near the top. Whirling it at the floor, the high priest cleared a path of crystal arrows embedded there.

On reaching the doorway, they watched a massive boulder sliding sideways to entomb them. Zithia gasped at the sight. Then gasped again, when Galen dropped the pectoral in a nest of razors. She started to bend for the gems but Galen, watching the doorway, put a restraining hand upon her shoulder. 'Not yet, the crowd will see us.'

At the bottom of the steps Eten raised the hand on which she held the covered skull. 'Behold, a great gift.'

The doorway diminished. Satisfied that every eye was on her, Eten swaggered into the masses.

At the same time, Galen entered the gap in the wall. The moving boulder was six feet thick. While walking through, Galen beckoned Zithia but she was tentatively retrieving her emeralds. Then she strode after him. Galen was in the sunlight when the stone picked up speed.

Closing rock caught each end of the tall ruby headdress in Zithia's backpack, holding her fast. Her hands scrambled nervelessly at the ties round her waist, as she tugged hard against the increasing grip of the rocks.

Having heard the rumble of stone changing gear, Galen swiveled to Zithia. Instantly, his knife was out. He cut the straps securing her pack, hauling her free by the jewel rope at her waist. Peering back, Zithia saw the headdress break, throwing the satchel toward her. It was a bare six inches within the cavity. Before Galen could prevent her, Zithia had thrust a hand back between the rocks. She wrenched the bag out, spilling gems.

'Idiot.' Galen towed her down two steps and spun her round. The opening snapped shut and the high priest gestured to where the doorway had been. Dozens of heads turned, momentarily, in that direction.

Throwing her voice far, Eten said, 'I, the mystic high priestess, Eten,' all the faces swung hastily back to her, 'bring you a gift from Atlantis.' She lifted her hand higher. 'The thirteenth skull.'

Like a conjurer she tore the cover off without disturbing the crystal. Her fingers curled up to touch the skull.

'I, Eten, master of the dark path, claim possession of the thirteenth skull.' She lowered the skull to eye level. 'Let me know your power.'

The crystal eyes sprang into life. People began to sweat. A green energy beam leapt forth to kiss her eyes. There was a cry of raw pleasure. Atlantian words, formulae, scenes filled Eten's soul and mind.

Pastel pink overtook the green light from the thirteeth's eyes. In mindless euphoria, Eten levitated from the ground. Past, present, future meshed together for her; each piece reachable. Significances were understood. *"I'm a God,"* she thought, her laughter, malicious, brimming over the plaza and pervading the entire populace. Skin crawled everywhere.

'Enough!' was the disembodied command that then entered everyone's mind in the city. The power within that single word turned its hearers' ashen.

The energy beams were instantly orange. Eten flinched as the cool flame hit her eyes. Her face contorting, the high priestess willed her hand to let go of the skull. Eten touched ground. The building opposite shuddered, cracks appeared in the plaza. A scream was heard, jarring the bones. People scattered, pouring over each other to get away, Galen and Zithia among them. Paralysed by the fear in the shrieking wail, a few stayed.

Eten's body was withering before their eyes. Drying, burned up by energy, the skin darkened, her skeleton pressing hard against its confines. After an eternity, Eten seemed to catch her breath and all was quiet. She fell. Rolling from her lifeless claws, the skull was inanimate once more.

*

An old blind man, Min-Jo, crouched at the top of the blue stairs. It was the seer that Eten had visited after her near-death experience. The high priestess had had him dismissed from the seer's guild, for seeing too much. He'd been wandering with his apprentice ever since. Min-Jo observed Eten's soul separate from her mortal husk.

Eten surveyed her body, and she screamed anew. At that moment the old poisoner, Koss, shimmered in. She pulled a face. 'You made a prettier corpse last time.'

From a distance, a dense shadow-mass thundered towards Eten's shade. 'Seeing how we've done this dance before, I thought the histrionic would make a nice change.'

The dark cloud broke into two giant patches, and then engulfed Eten. Before she was dragged into the dark below, her life flashed before her, slowing down at times. To the high priestess's horror, she saw and felt through her victim's bodies during these scenes. Eten silently shrieked her pains.

'An appetiser only.' The poisoner's head lowered to the cringing Eten's. 'True judgement is yet to come.'

'Noooo!'

The two spirits disappeared.

Min-Jo had foreseen this possible future months ago, and had come to Xalisco for this performance. Putting his hand out for his cane, the seer touched a scattering of large gems, jewels that had escaped Zithia's bag.

*

It was three hours later. A row of temple guards surrounded the corpse, facing outwards. The whole city looked abandoned. Witnesses to Eten's death had shakily repeated the story before locking themselves in their houses. Having heard Eten's dark laughter, plus that one word, 'Enough', the rest of the city lit incense in doorways and followed suit. Fervent prayers rose, with the copal smoke, against the anticipated retribution for the high priestess's blasphemy.

Eten's corpse lay where it had fallen. Xalisco's remaining high priests, plus five prominent deacons, arrived in silence. Most went to the thirteenth skull. 'The archpriest's council will decide where to hide it,' said one.

'Until then' suggested Rachael, 'the Truth-sayers could protect it.'

Xiao Chen, the master witness, conferred with the leader of the archpriest's guard.

While everyone was so absorbed, Augustus went on one knee and touched Eten's hand. He jumped when one of Eten's talons peeled off in his grasp. Breathing hard, Augustus tottered backwards, but continued to view Eten's clawless finger. When the others joined him, Augustus averted his gaze, only to be mesmerised by split teeth between lips stretched open by drying.

Ten temple guards manoeuvered long poles under the cadaver, and then lifted it. More guards pulled a net under the suspended corpse. On this lay a thick bed of bitter wood. Once Eten was lowered onto the pyre, fine granules were scattered, to a background of protective chanting. The wood burst into blue-white flame.

The rock beneath the fire started to melt. Struggling with himself, Augustus was outwardly neutral. 'Once the good citizens get over their shock, they'll want blood,' burning bones popped, 'which they can't have.'

'I still find it hard to believe,' frowned high priest Petronius. 'Eten, a warlock, bent on personal power.'

'I had my suspicions,' said Galen. 'Never any real proof.'

A shiver ran up Augustus's back at the sound of Galen's voice.

Augustus clenched Eten's long curling fingernail. 'I, too, had suspicions, but I thought it a mere flirtation,' for a millisecond, the muscles at his eyes contracted, 'a faltering step along the way.'

'To go after the thirteenth skull...' said Rachael. 'She'd have ruled us all.'

More powder was fed to the fire, so that it ate itself. On a third scattering, the ash was consumed and the stone beneath it. Throughout that day, priests added a top layer of stone to the plaza, all the while uttering protection prayers.

chapter 30

Augustus stood in his elegant apartment and put down the written judgment, condemning Eten. He had volunteered to oversee the scroll's placement in the archives.

Eten's missive had awaited him. He read and re-read it, tracing the bloody signature. Tipping his head back, the high priest narrowed heavy lidded eyes at the note. Augustus used it to light a cigar.

*

With a deacon in tow, Augustus stood in the chamber of Judgments. He placed the scroll regarding Eten in its rightful place. Then, walking about the chamber, Augustus's eyes skimmed over the scrolls on a shelf he knew. Placing a hand on the deacon's arm, the high priest pointed. An official Witness's seal was missing from one manuscript. Opening the suspect document, they had found that not all the council members deciding the case had signed. Eten's signature was lacking.

Immediately, the high priests had been gathered. Excluding Galen.

Augustus addressed those in the quiet room. 'Brothers, sisters, we've been given an opportunity to show the people how we act against those who break the laws.'

The high priest let his body slump. 'I have a confession. Eten pressured me for a light penalty in Zithia's case.'

There was a general cry of, 'Why.'

'I wasn't allowed to know. Perhaps Galen ...' Augustus let the words trail off. 'He and Eten did work closely together during the war.'

*

The prime council-room was used for receiving archpriests and royalty. Its walls were faced with chalky marble. Seven high priests sat on tall gilded chairs, behind a marble table. In front of the chairman, who sat in the center of the group, was a hand sized jade turtle nestled on a jade platter.

Galen and Zithia walked down the hallway.

Before they'd left their apartment, Galen had fastened an ancient necklace round her throat, covering the platinum band. 'Your great, great, grandmother's.' Zithia patted it, trembling.

'If they thought we helped Eten, we'd be surrounded by guards.'

They crossed the council-room threshold.

Petronius, the chairman, banged the jade gavel. 'High priest Galen, Lady Zithia. You've been summoned here because the blasphemer Eten didn't sign the Lady Zithia's judgement. Therefore, the case may be retried.'

Breath left Zithia's body. Galen's face remained blank. 'In general, we're satisfied with the last judgement. It's only the punishment that we question. We consider the sentence was over lenient.' Silence reigned for a full minute. 'Let us begin.'

Slowly, Augustus stood. 'Today a high priestess's crime has rocked the people's faith in the priesthood. Now we consider another case involving a high priest.' He paused. 'Brothers, sisters, the city needs to know that the clergy and their families are accountable to the same laws that apply to the ordinary citizen.' The high priests banged their staffs gently on the floor. 'Indeed, the upper clergy should be held to harsher standards,' One side of Augustus's mouth tweaked into a tiny smile. 'to set the example.'

Augustus pointed at Zithia. 'This traitor bewitched a high priest into marriage,' Galen's eyebrows thundered down, 'then stole the agreed bride-price.' The whites around Zithia's eyes became visible. By calling her a traitor, Augustus had changed everything. Any softness on treachery had ended when the war started.

Another high priest nodded. 'A traitor, yes.' The council had been discussing interpretations of this law for an hour. There was general assent.

The chairman said, 'There is only one punishment for treachery.' He looked at the high priests. 'We must vote.'

Francios waited an almost decent interval before standing. 'Death.'

Zithia dragged in a sharp breath; the back of her spread fingers pressed against her mouth.

One by one, the others rose. 'Death.' All except Rachael.

'Under the circumstances, we don't need a unanimous decision.' Petronius stated. 'Sentence is passed.'

Galen glared. 'This isn't justice, it's expediency.'

'Lord Galen, prepare you wife for execution. Noon, two days hence.'

'Murder isn't the way to redeem the high priesthood's reputation.'

Raising an eyebrow, Augustus drawled. 'My lord, you forget your place. You're not here to speak.'

In an aside, the chairman said to the scribe, 'Declare a public holiday, the whole city must see justice done.' He raised the jade turtle to close the meeting.

Instantly Petronius felt the gem jerked from his grasp. It shattered against the wall.

'This council isn't concluded,' Galen ground out. 'Will you betray our Atlantian heritage, after all we've been through in the war?'

Petronius grabbed the platter and banged it hard. 'The council has spoken.' Galen stepped close. 'Lord Galen, you're excused!'

Guards had rushed in. 'Accompany the Lady Zithia to her apartment.' He added softly to Galen, 'Unless you feel that Zithia should be placed in custody.'

*

Barely had the door closed on Galen and Zithia, than Petronius hissed, 'He accused us, us...of expediency...' His eyes became slits, 'We need to look into his connection with the blasphemer Eten.'

Rachael said, 'None of us here seriously believes Galen has anything to do with darkness.' She looked around steadily.

Amok-Zerxe's spoke,. 'Yet, it appears he has been more contaminated by Zithia than was thought.'

One high priest picked bits of jade from his hair, 'Violence in this chamber.'

'Using magic!' snarled Petronius.

Augustus said casually, 'Was it the first judgment gavel?' Everyone knew it was. 'A future archpriest, yet he puts his wife equal with duty.'

One man was already thinking about potential future patronage. 'With Zithia's death, Galen will come to his senses.'

'But unpunished.' Pouted the man who was still removing jade shards.

'He has to pay the bride-price,' stated Rachael.

The pursed lips continued, 'He has always agreed to that. The bride-price is no punishment to him.'

'As it stands.' Augustus's lashes touched his cheeks, and then rose up slowly, 'there are older bride-prices.'

The chairman took up his pen. Writing heavily, he added a line to Zithia's judgement, then signed it. Petronius handed the paper. 'The marriage is an abomination. Zithia's bloodline has no place in any temple.'

The paperbark was passed around. It came to Augustus. *"Death for the son as bride-price, foreign slavery for the daughter."*

It was offered to Rachael, who wouldn't touch it. 'I've already told you, I'll not sign.'

'Your signature isn't a necessity in law.' The chairman said. 'A second execution will make a magnificent surprise.'

Augustus looked at Rachael. 'Obviously, for now, this judgement must stay within this chamber. To maximize the surprise… for the city.'

*

It was mid-evening when Jacov, a white-haired ancient, pottered into the library's inner sanctum. Xiao Chen sat at a bench reading a four foot wide book. A watchful under-librarian read at the next bench. Near Xiao Chen, Jacov dropped the scrolls he carried. The deacon prince bent to help him, and saw an open miniature scroll. A private scroll, with one line upon it. In Atlantian it read: *"To save a single life, is to save the universe."*

Jacov threw up his hands. 'The head librarian will cut off my borrowing privileges, if she sees this.' He looked myopically at the under-librarian. 'Would you check to see if she's heard?'

Grinning, the younger man glided into the main library, examining the shadows for the formidable lady. Jacov muttered, 'My hands, you know… My dear niece Rachael insists I send a servant on these little errands.' Then, suddenly, still muttering, 'His son follows his wife, his daughter goes to slavery.' Fleetingly Jacov met Xiao Chen's eyes, while the ancient accepted the rescued scrolls. And then, Jacov's voice resumed a more normal volume, 'But I like my independence. You understand, don't you Prince Xiao Chen.'

The under-librarian was back, winking. 'Only don't drop a book, or you'll never see the inner sanctum again.'

'As if I'd drop a book! As if… ' Jacov's voice trailed off lamely as he tottered away.

Thirty minutes later Xiao Chen thanked his watcher, closed his volume and left.

*

Xiao Chen immediately went to Galen's study, dismissing Madison. Galen was staring into the fire and didn't look round. 'They're going to kill her.'

The truth-sayer stood ramrod straight. He didn't know how to tell Galen. The high priest looked up and heard the words Xiao Chen couldn't say.

Galen's face hardened to stone. Xiao Chen went to speak. Galen's eyes stopped him. Finally the deacon prince said, 'You may ask anything, brother.'

It was past the witching hour when Galen walked through his balcony doors. He saw Kylyn's amber at the base of a lush palm tree. Holding onto the tree trunk, the high priest's knuckles whitened beneath taut skin. He picked up the amber and then, with one savage movement, Galen pulled the palm from its pot, removing Zithia's treasure from beneath the root ball.

*

The sun shafted through the deaconess's waist high windows. Galen's cape was pushed back over his shoulders, revealing the blue jade rope around his neck. Since Galen had arrived the deaconess's eyes continuously flicked to the carved beads. They had been talking about the weather for five minutes now.

Deaconess Jillian licked her lips, 'A remarkable antique, Lord Galen.'

'An heirloom.' Jillian's eyes lusted. 'To me it's but a bauble, in comparison with the archpriest's office, ' Galen sighed, 'my goal since I was first initiated.'

Jillian thought: *"Don't we all know it."* 'With the Lady Zithia's journey up the Pyramid of the Sun, I'm certain your dream will soon be fulfilled.'

'If only I could be so sure.' Galen stroked his chin once. 'It'd look better to the people if I were able to deliver my wife to her justice personally.'

Jillian's gold earplugs bobbed. 'The people would be reassured by your... piety! Has it not been arranged?'

He took the rope off and draped it on the table between them. 'There are those who don't wish the people to love me.'

'I, my lord, am not among them. Knowing how you've suffered at your wife's hand, I feel you must be allowed the opportunity to accompany Lady Zithia to her destiny.'

'Perhaps with the children, up to the second level. We, alone, on the pyramid steps.'

'It'd increase the drama.' Jillian smiled: *"And maintain focus on you."*

'The perfect spectacle.'

When Galen had gone, Jillian's eyes glittered happily, for the august high priest had forgotten to take the jade rope with him.

The next interview was in the same apartment building. Surrounded by lists, Deacon Richard let pieces of confetti drop. 'How do they expect me to arrange the entire occasion in time.' From the corners of his eyes, Richard followed Galen's figure from head to foot. 'Should we have confetti...' Richard gave a tiny meow of a grimace, 'under the circumstances?'

Galen sat down. 'I'm arranging the confetti myself.'

'Really Lord Galen?'

'Since I'm to attend the Lady Zithia to her fate, I thought my involvement with the fanfare appropriate.'

'Ohhh, yes.' Richard's chins wobbled. 'A sad occasion, very sad, but by seeing your wife off well you'll be a shining example to us all.'

He fluttered a hand. 'It's the alcoves, to be erected on the pyramid, which are a positive nightmare to me, Lord Galen. Three!'

'Deacon Richard, call me Galen.'

'Galen,' Richard put spread fingers theatrically to his chest, 'Richard.'

'Richard, I understand your concern. After all, the entire city will be there... ready to criticise.'

'And the cost! Really, the temple has given me nowhere near enough.'

'Considering the delicacy of the event,' Galen placed a bag into Richard's hands, 'I feel duty bound to help with the expenses. To ensure the... festival will make worthy remembering.'

The deacon extracted an emerald necklace, running the large facets very slowly through sunlight. He hid some emotion.

Galen added conversationally, 'I'll inform the other high priests about my contribution, tonight.'

A hiccup sounded. 'But Galen... you know that anonymous donations find the greatest favour with the heavens.'

Galen's response was sardonic. 'With the election so near, Richard, I fear anonymity may be a little too expensive for me.'

'The archpriest's election... yessss.' He held the necklace close to his chest. 'But Galen, your name is already going to be praised in every way at the ceremony. The people will be well aware of your glory.'

'How reassuring. Then consider my contribution anonymous.'

Richard sighed with satisfaction. The emeralds were magnificent.

Galen's gaze became a laser. 'Now, about those alcoves, Richard. Allow me the privilege of preparing those. And let that, also, be between us.'

Richard worked hard at stopping a frown. *"The alcoves?"* he thought pensively.

Galen, 'Children are such a comfort at these times. Have you not heard so?'

Richard swallowed with difficulty. Galen had once saved the deacon from a terrifying situation. Fingers shaking, Richard remembered that dreadful girl who'd sworn that he, he, Richard, was the father of her... newborn. Within the day, Galen had discreetly uncovered the truth.

'Yes, yes, children...' He shuddered. 'Of course, the alcoves, Galen.' He hurried on, 'And now, please, what ballads do you want sung?'

*

The high priest's pool was an oasis, shaped like a dog's leg to fit into the terrace. Zithia was tapping her foot outside the main entrance, while a guard quieted the pool attendant. A blustering consort sniffed audibly as he was hustled through the exit.

Ignoring the expansive rural panorama, Kylyn jumped into the pool. With Manaca in her arms, Zithia floated around the overfull oasis. Thus looking into the distance, the blue of the water met the blue of the sky. Manaca wore the Atlantian rainbow jewels, which remained dry despite the water.

When they tired of swimming, hitting a gong brought men through the far exit. Under Madison's supervision, they poured several large buckets into the water. Two dozen bright fish swam free. Floating water hyacinths and drifts of tiny single-leafed weed abounded. Zithia and Kylyn cast their lines until an hour to sunset.

The boy was walking passed the pool's highborn attendant when she noticed the fish. 'Child,' she shrilled, 'where did you get that?'

Kylyn lost his smile, 'Fr, from the pool.'

'Is there a problem?' Zithia was in the room. The woman's mouth worked noiselessly. 'Ah, the fish.' Zithia drawled, 'Don't worry, there's plenty left for you.'

The attendant skittered off.

*

The sounds of story telling drifted from Galen's balcony. Half-reclining on a sofa, Zithia held her children spellbound with a fairytale from Atlantis. Manaca's eyes kept falling, as did the sun. The fiery reds reflected off Zithia's double-looped necklace. Drinking chocolate, Kylyn smiled at his fish, which was cooking on lattice over a fire in a pottery bowl. He had a golden feeling of deja vu.

Entering, Galen finished the story and strolled over to Kylyn. 'What a handsome fish, darling.' He laughed, 'The first one ever caught in the high priests' pool.'

They went back to Zithia. The gems flooding over her breasts luminesced with their own inner light. Galen touched the necklace. 'They've taken on your radiance.' The diamonds had absorbed the fire from the dying sun. Kylyn went back to the barbecue.

'I'll think of you when I'm home.' Her Atlantian words were tearful.

Galen traced Zithia's chin with his fingers. 'I'd never have brought you back if…' a silvery gleam of moisture lined his lower lids.

'I know.' She managed a small smile.

Then words failed them and, tenderly, they kissed.

Later, Galen told her about the ceremony. By the time he'd finished, the scent from the white moonflowers was suffocating them both.

'Such a grand occasion.' Her lips smiled shakily. 'I fear I've nothing to wear.'

Galen clapped his hands. A priestess appeared carrying a cape, with a train, plus a matching headdress. Each black net of the cape was edged in gold. There were thick white lines and the patches of sunset colour were gilded. Pearls dotted the black. Zithia's eyes shone. 'A monarch butterfly.'

Eten had desired it; the temple had paid for it. Galen thought: *"Let Augustus savour his triumph."*

chapter 31

It wasn't quite mid-morning when Augustus's servant bowed insufficiently to Galen. 'My lord high priest,' the man looked down his nose, 'my august Lord Augustus summons you to the archpriest's private garden in forty-five minutes.'

Though making a detour, Galen arrived well before Augustus expected him. Cape gracefully hanging, Galen stopped in the shade of a tropical cherry tree, twenty feet from the sheer drop, overlooking the distant farmland. Coconut perfume wafted from orchids.

Augustus was pacing in front of the garden's freestanding archway. Franklin had completed the coloured mural on the archway.

Jaw clenched, Augustus strode toward Galen. 'You're early!'

'The invitation implied some urgency.' Galen flashed his eyebrows at Augustus. 'I hope this won't take long, this is rather a big day for me.'

Augustus showed his teeth. 'I've come straight from my final check of the pyramid.'

'Straight from checking?' Galen asked casually. He knew Augustus did his rounds alone.

'Yes and I found the mirror. Once the guards arrive I'll have it taken back to where it belongs.' His smirked, 'When I'm archpriest I'll keep it as a reminder...'

Galen interrupted. 'A reminder of what? You're disregarding Eten's last wish.'

'What do you know of her wishes?'

'I know a blood oath when it's signed in my presence.'

Augustus pushed his shoulders forward. 'It wasn't Eten's wish for you to transport your bitch, and her litter, away from their fates.'

'But what do my children have to do with anything?' Augustus only glowered. 'And Augustus, that bitch is my wife.'

Galen's left hand, hidden until then in the folds of his cape, appeared bringing forth a black cloth-swaddled ball. Fixing Augustus with his eyes,

Galen spoke in slow measured tones. 'Augustus, it seems I can't live this life with Zithia.' Galen peeled the thick covering off the object he held, to reveal a thinner silk cover. 'But I can't see her murdered, either.'

Staying in the shade, Galen let the black silk fall in petals over his hand. Augustus stopped in his tracks. 'The thirteenth skull. Impossible!'

'Xiao Chen is a very old friend.' Galen gave an icy smile.

The skull's eyes blazed green. 'Did you think I'd let anyone touch my family?'

In a voice in full power, Galen commanded, 'Augustus, high priest of Xalisco, look into the depths of the thirteenth skull and find your fate.'

'Why aren't you...?' Every hair on Augustus's body stood on end.

'A grizzled carcass like Eten? The trick is to operate the skull without touching it.' Galen shook his head sorrowfully. 'If only Eten had known.'

"If only," Augustus thought, the phrase recurring in his mind until his eyes rolled back into his head. The crystal's eyes blazed pink.

'How to die is such a personal question.' Augustus's pupils scrolled back, glued now to the skull. Suddenly the crystal eyes blazed orange and grew in size.

Simultaneously, a dozen voices gibbered in Augustus's mind. Ever since Eten's talon had come off in his hand, Augustus he had heard these voices. At first comforting, after he'd publicly reviled Eten, the voices had become increasingly discordant. Blaming.

Galen heard the whispers. 'Perhaps your voices will become violent.' Augustus lurched, his hands raised defensively in front of him.

'Yes,' Galen started to intone in Atlantian, 'power of the thirteenth skull, I, Galen of mist-night, call on you to destroy Augustus of Xalisco. Let his voices madden him unto death. Let it be slow.'

Galen intoned a second time, his voice penetrating the recesses of Augustus's mind. The personalities within Augustus shrieked while he backed away, hands hard over his ears. When Galen recited the final time, the crescendo of mastery in his voice set the core of Augustus's body quivering uncontrollably. A few frothy specks appeared on Augustus's lips. He felt the parapet's edge under his heels. And simply, stepped back.

The voices ranted down with him, down the hundred-foot drop. They only stopped their banshee wails when a blood vessel in Augustus's brain exploded.

Galen put the skull down at the cherry tree's base. There was the sound of movement to his left. Armed men. Instantly, there was a catch in Galen's voice, 'Brother don't jump, a physician can help you.'

Hearing this, the soldiers rushed the stairs, where they mentally measured the distance between Galen and the parapet. Twenty feet. Augustus's assistant priest, plus a truth-sayer, followed.

'You're too late,' his face fell, 'to restrain Augustus from harming himself. He has jumped.'

Stalking over to Augustus's assistant, lightning filled Galen's eyes. 'Your slow pace has cost your master his life. Where is the physician?'

Galen glanced at the two soldiers. 'Arrest this man for negligence of his duties.'

The guards clapped their hands on the young priest. In a frenzy he sobbed, 'My august lord, I,' he paused, 'couldn't find Lord Augustus's physician. So I brought guards to restrain him.'

'You had time to find a witness, yet not a physician.'

'I merely happened upon the truth-sayer.' This was true. He wrung his hands. 'Forgive me, my august lord, forgive me.'

Galen replied very deliberately, 'What could you possibly say that'd merit clemency?'

'But my lord,' sweat dripped from the priest's brow, 'when Lord Augustus requested your assistance… ' Luckily the priest hadn't told the guards who had summoned them, or why. 'I never dreamed,' his eyes darted around, 'that Lord Augustus would carry out his joke of yesterday,' the priest trailed off, 'about jumping!'
The priest's eyes pleaded with them all. 'Lord Augustus hasn't been quite right since the blasphemer died.'

Galen offered, 'He spoke of voices.'

'Yes, yes!'

Galen rocked his clenched fist, and then opened it. 'You should've warned me.'

He addressed the guards, 'Stand down.' They took two paces back.

The high priest stood next to a crystal bowl. It was two-thirds full of scented liquid, and on the surface twin lit candles floated. It was an unusual shape, reminiscent of a skull. Galen gestured to the crystal, 'A gift I didn't get the chance to present.'

*

In an enclosed pavilion facing the Avenue of the Dead, a mare pranced. Having knelt, Zithia was sitting on her heels, praying. Arising, she was composed. The golden headdress was arranged on Zithia's head, and then she mounted the horse. A priestess spread the train of the starlit cape for fifteen feet behind the mare. Meanwhile, Zithia was handed a shot cup of tequila. She gulped it down; there was an unusual aftertaste.

Beneath the cape Zithia wore a modest silk gown, topped by the rope of diamonds.

Waiting for her cue to leave, Zithia tossed her head, saying to herself, 'Before they murder me, I'll make them love me.'

After using the siren's spell to its full extent, her image took on a mysterious lustre. Her beauty, her sensuality evolved, ripened, to become magnetic. With no tomorrows she'd not pay the spell's huge cost in pain.

*

Outside, a moving rainbow of feathers covered every building, pyramid and plaza. There was gold, too, yet not the amount of previous years. Those crowds fortunate enough to be on steps, sat while waiting. Men balanced feather shields on their staffs, to shade their ladies.

The entire city's whisperers had been working since last night. Over and over they had repeated the word 'Enough,' that one word heard magically throughout Xalisco at Eten's death. With goose-pimpled arms, the hearers had made the sign of protection against evil so often their hands ached.

It felt like a festival. 'But,' reminded the whisperers in the crowd 'it's an execution. On the sacred Pyramid of the Sun. A sacrifice, such as was banned by our ancestors.' Others made a background, barely audible, 'Enough!'

Groups of musicians were sprinkled among the masses. Pan pipes, shamisens and other stringed instruments and bells rang out a mist-night ballad, then a guerilla fighting song. Minstrels sang the lyrics, which most people knew. An expensive day. Zithia's illicit treasure was gone and, even at that moment, a merchant was removing the furniture from Galen's apartment.

When Zithia's horse finally trotted out into the light, she found Galen riding to join her from a pavilion opposite. Husband and wife proceeded side-by-side up the Avenue of the Dead. A gasp went through the immediate thousands. Few men rode the demons, never a woman. The war flooded back; scars itched. At the sound of the hooves striking the pavement, children hid their faces.

Today Galen was a warrior first, high priest second. He took Zithia's breath away in his short kilt, cape and pectoral. A fitted gold wreath adorned Galen's brow. Quexatl feathers hung down his back in a V. The pectoral and headdress had been gifts from the people. A jaguar pelt shield was lashed to his saddle, a symbol of being a jaguar knight. Over the muscles of his right bicep was painted a monarch butterfly, and in his hand Galen carried his ceremonial staff.

At intervals along the Avenue of the Dead, jaguar knights and monarch guerillas stood at ease. Immediately after Galen and Zithia passed each section, retainers announced, 'For the citizens of Xalisco from their humble son, Galen of Xalisco.'

Abundant gold leaf and cocoa beans arced wide. After scrambling for their share, the masses shouted the high priest's praises. A thunder began, of feet and staffs hitting the ground.

Jagged lines in the hollow beside Galen's right eye were highlighted in black and gold. Legacy from mist-night, the loss of ten years of life was obvious to all those on the high priest's right. Similarly Zithia's mist-night sacrifice was highlighted, on her left temple.

The high priest's wife was bathed in a pearly incandescence. Within this radiance, a battened down sensuality echoed. Many still remembered Zithia's beauty those years ago, when she'd danced for them in the square and her chi blast had dazzled the city. Some who caught her eye looked hastily away. A whisper undulated through the crowds, 'Are we really going to kill this butterfly?'

Suddenly the mental block Zithia had put up, about what was to happen today, dissolved. The purpose of this journey flooded her: "It's real. It's now." She expelled a sharp breath. 'Beloved God, help me through my journey home.'

With great difficulty, Zithia pushed her coming death into the background. As far as she could. Breathing fast and shallow. Then, glorious comfort ebbed through her veins and her mind. She was warm, where before she'd been chilled. Soon after, feeling somewhat disconnected from the scene, Zithia rode with a fluid grace.

Finally, the couple neared the end of the grand promenade, and the tallest pyramid on the continent loomed above them. Watching the

Pyramid of the Sun grow, Zithia remembered Galen's words. 'A small incision will be made on each side of your neck.' Zithia's shaky thumb and forefinger touched the veins just below her jaw.

'I'll hardly feel it.' She clutched at the pommel. It wouldn't do to fall off now.

Zithia looked up into the jaws of the first alcove, erected a third of the way up the pyramid steps. The facade was an open-mouthed jaguar's head. A drum started at heartbeat rate, beginning the refrain from Galen's post-war triumphal procession. Both horses reared. Once they'd reined in their steeds, Galen and Zithia cantered to the base of the pyramid.

Zithia took Kylyn and Manaca from Xiao Chen's princess. Galen barely stopped, forcing Zithia to follow her husband. When they went into the first alcove, Zithia observed Galen in a stance used solely for gathering power. His lips moved momentarily, and then he stood straight again.

'Galen,' she called, but too late. He was already outside the alcove, and continuing up the stairway. Carrying Manaca, Zithia led Kylyn up the pyramid.

They were midway between the first and second alcove when Zithia heard screams from the crowd. Scanning the surrounding temples and pyramids, Zithia found all pointed up past her. Then Zithia saw it. Two endless streams of blood ran down the steps to her. The thick liquid flooded from the corners of the second alcove. Kylyn's fingers dug into hers, Manaca tensed in her arms. But the stench of blood failed to surround them with the liquid. 'It's only paint, my darlings. It can't hurt us.' Yet her pulse raced when the edges of her cloak were soaked.

The whispers went round, 'Blood, staining the Pyramid of the Sun. Desecration. Not since the war...'

Hemmed in between two bright rivers, Zithia concentrated on each step immediately before her, avoiding the ruby colour. Her throat was parched.

They were very near the second alcove when Zithia saw Galen's gold scandals on red-washed stone. Facing her.

His orator's voice boomed, 'Descendants of Atlantis.' Galen's arms spread wide, 'People of Atlantis...' He surveyed the masses. 'I deny paternity of this woman's children.'

Zithia rocked on the heels of her feet.

Xiao Chen and another witness stepped from behind the jaguar head. 'Bear witness.'

Tilting his head back, Galen glared down at Zithia. 'Lady, I divorce you.'

Zithia felt winded, as though he'd punched her.

Galen watched her with disinterest. 'I divorce you.'

Clumsily Zithia drew off her wedding ring and threw it in Galen's face. 'I see ambition won over love, after all.'

He said, for her ears only, 'My dear, if I play the game well today, I'll probably be archpriest by nightfall.' She drew in a deep breath, but Galen held his hand up to silence her.

For the third and final time he declared, 'I divorce you.'

The masses didn't dare blink. One of their favorite sons had publicly admitted his mistake in marrying.

'For the people.' He raised his hand. 'My people,' once more, gold flew until the air was awash with tinsel, 'for whom I've given everything. People of Atlantis!' Galen entered the alcove; the confetti increased.

Claws out, Zithia came after him, gathering speed to throw herself at Galen. 'So, you disown your own children.'

Inside, the high priest stood quietly near a corner. 'They plan to kill Kylyn, after you, and enslave our daughter,' he said in Atlantian. Zithia stopped dead.

Galen carefully drew a shadowy veil from the dark mirror.

'Kylyn is no longer the bride-price. Their plans are now illegal, as well as immoral.' He placed his hand on the dark solid glass. He intoned a phrase. The mirror shivered into a vertical pond. It rippled.

She stood watching, slowly comprehending. Galen loved them. He loved her. Zithia's faith flowed back like a blessing. Her smile lit up eternity. 'How long have you planned this?'

'Since the hour you were sentenced to death.'

Galen bent to his children and passed a hand before their eyes. They became still.

'Let these days in Xalisco be the faded dream, and FallsFire your reality.'

'Why tell them that?'

Galen turned Kylyn toward the mirror. 'Go!' And the boy walked through the gateway, then over to the table where his toys lay strewn.

Elderic hadn't been able to bring himself to do more than enter the room since his wife had disappeared.

What colour she had in her face, drained away. 'You're not coming with us?'

Smiling, Galen put Manaca into Zithia's arms. 'You have to smash your mirror, for our children to be safe. I'll destroy this portal from here.'

Thinking furiously, Zithia deposited Manaca in Fallsfire, where the toddler wandered off to her favourite blanket.

Then she whispered, breathlessly, 'But you'll be killed!'

'You underestimate me, dearest. I'll horrify the masses with the blasphemy planned by my honourable, oh so honourable, colleagues. Human sacrifice of a child, in front an unsuspecting populace! I'll be a hero.'

Zithia hadn't yet moved; her look was wild. 'Galen...' He put a finger on her lips.

'Beloved, by the time I'm finished, the city will be clamouring to take the moral high ground. It'll be my honourable brothers and sisters who need to worry, not me.'

Galen took her hand as if he were leading her onto a dance floor. While they walked the two steps, he promised huskily, 'If I ever feel you in widow's grief, I'll come to you. Else... see you on the other side.'

Love, unconditional and breathless, surged between them. Zithia's eyes holding his seemingly forever, she found she was over the threshold. Very gradually Galen was letting go of her hand. Her fingers. Then Zithia curled her fingers over his and his curled also. Only for an instant, in which she visualised the Atlantis earth in Torim's garden. Another scene rapidly succeeded this. For traceable seconds Galen was looking up at the map in the library at the Atlantis tree. A beatific smile wreathed Galen's face. Their hands parted.

His smile faded. 'Gateway, begone.'

Zithia laid her palm flat on the solid window. Galen's hand covered hers, for a heartbeat. Then he struck the mirror with his staff and his image fragmented. Was gone. Letting out a single low moan, she took up a wooden vase and hit her mirror.

On the verandah, Elderic had been reflecting on Adison's earlier words. 'Magic has taken Melia against her wishes.' At the time, Elderic had been rubbing the harlequin duck brooch he'd given Zithia. 'Don't despair, your wife is a harlequin. If she can return, she will.'

Hearing sundering glass, Elderic walked into the room. Zithia, sobbing violently, was smashing the looking glass again and again and again. Oblivious of Elderic's presence, suddenly Zithia reeled away from the shattered mirror, pivoting into Elderic's welcoming arms.

In another world, Galen, Zithia's cape in his hand, made his way to the top of the pyramid. Eager for the limelight, all the high priests were there, except Rachael. Galen's eyes sizzled with force. The others moved, pell-mell, away from him. A fact the audience, grabbing the last of the golden tickertape, noted.

Galen flung the jewelled cape, its design facing down. A monarch butterfly reared towards the high priests. The multitude cheered anew at this gossamer emblem of Atlantis. It reared once more before swooping low, and then completely surrounded the high priests in a close circle. Moving both his hands in command, Galen brought the monarch fluttering to him. For a moment the vision undulated peacefully above him. Then Galen gestured it to waft down the pyramid, a few feet above the steps. When at the lowest alcove, the glorious butterfly began to cavort along the Avenue, bound for the distant sacred mountain.

Galen opened his arms, embracing the people. 'The Lady Zithia,' his voice, brimming with power and magnetism, was audible to all gathered, 'a hero of mist-night, isn't my wife. Her children are not... my children. There's no bride-price to pay.

Yet these honourable high priests demand her heart's blood. Indeed, they demand her son's murder.

Galen indicated the butterfly. 'People of Atlantis, there we see freedom. The monarchs live uncaged, live the life of their choice. Without fear.

Brothers and sisters in Atlantis, we can follow the glory of our ancestors. Or we can stand idly by while butterflies are ripped from the sky.'

*

In FallsFire some long minutes later, tears coursing down her face, Zithia smiled. For she could hear a ghostly echo of a city's tumultuous applause.